A TIDE of BLACK STEEL

AGE OF WRATH: BOOK ONE

ANTHONY RYAN

orbit

orbitbooks.net

Copyright © 2024 by Anthony Ryan Media Ltd.
Excerpt from *The Pariah* copyright © 2021 by Anthony Ryan
Excerpt from *The Sword Defiant* copyright © 2023 by Gareth Ryder-Hanrahan

Cover design by Ben Prior | LBBG
Map by Anthony Ryan
Author photograph by Ellie Grace Photography

Orbit
Hachette Book Group
1290 Avenue of the Americas
New York, NY 10104
orbitbooks.net

First Edition: September 2024
Simultaneously published in Great Britain by Orbit

Orbit is an imprint of Hachette Book Group.
The Orbit name and logo are registered trademarks of
Little, Brown Book Group Limited.

The publisher is not responsible for websites (or their content)
that are not owned by the publisher.

The Hachette Speakers Bureau provides a wide range of authors for speaking events. To find out more, go to hachettespeakersbureau.com or email HachetteSpeakers@hbgusa.com.

Orbit books may be purchased in bulk for business, educational, or promotional use. For information, please contact your local bookseller or the Hachette Book Group Special Markets Department at special.markets@hbgusa.com.

Library of Congress Control Number: 2024939119

ISBNs: 9780316574587 (trade paperback), 9780316574594 (ebook)

Printed in the United States of America

LSC-C

Printing 1, 2024

For Frank Frazetta – the sunburst of fantasy art

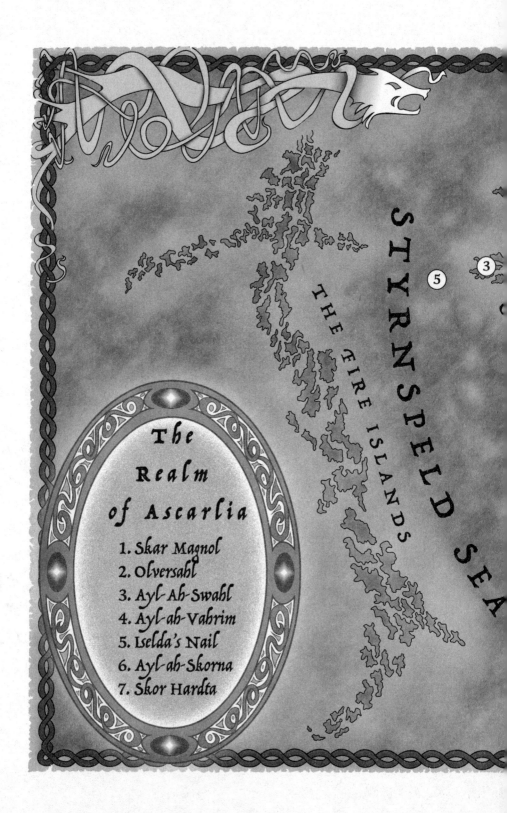

STYRNSPELD SEA

THE FIRE ISLANDS

5

3

The
Realm
of Ascarlia

1. Skar Magnol
2. Olversahl
3. Ayl-Ah-Swahl
4. Ayl-ah-Vahrim
5. Iselda's Nail
6. Ayl-ah-Skorna
7. Skor Hardta

Dramatis Personae

Margnus Gruinskard Tielwald – Principal Advisor to the Sister Queens

Felnir Skyrnak Seafarer, warrior and spy in service to the Tielwald, captain of the longship *Sea Hawk*, great-grandson to Margnus Gruinskard, brother to Thera

Thera Speldrenda Vellihr of Justice to the Sister Queens, captain of the longship *Great Wolf*, great-granddaughter to Margnus Gruinskard, sister to Felnir and Guthnyr

Lynnea Trahleyl Daughter to the slain Veilwald of the Skor Geld, Thera's ward

Coelnyr Principal servant and spymaster to Margnus Gruinskard

Sister Lore Co-monarch of Ascarlia, Mistress of Word and Legend

Sister Silver Co-monarch of Ascarlia, Mistress of Wealth and Trade

Sister Iron Co-monarch of Ascarlia, Mistress of Sword and Ship

Ruhlin ehs Kestryg Fisherman of the Outer Isles

Berrine Jurest Renowned scholar and Skierwald at the Archive of the Sister Queens in Olversahl

Elvine Jurest Dockmaster's Excise Agent at Olversahl and daughter to Berrine

Uhttar Apprentice shipwright in Olversahl, friend to Elvine

Bahn Wool merchant in Olversahl, uncle to Uhttar, leader of the city's clandestine Covenant community

Guthnyr Warrior aboard the longship *Sea Hawk*, brother to Thera and Felnir

Sygna Healer and archer aboard the longship *Sea Hawk*, lover and trusted counsel to Felnir

Wohtin Freed prisoner of an Albermaine dungeon, apparently mad

Colvyn Freed Albermaine-ish prisoner of unclear origins, speaker of numerous tongues, friend to Wohtin

Gelmyr Johtenvek Sailing master and navigator aboard the *Great Wolf*, warrior in Thera's *menda*

Eshilde Warrior in Thera's *menda*

Ragnalt Warrior in Thera's *menda*

Kodryn Estrynlud Former mercenary captain, friend and lieutenant to Felnir aboard the *Sea Hawk*

Behsla Sailing master aboard the *Sea Hawk*, warrior in Felnir's *menda*

Hemund The Chief Dockmaster of Olversahl, friend and employer to Elvine

Mohlnir Ship's cat aboard the *Great Wolf*

Eldryk Slave owner and pure blood member of the Nihlvarian nobility

Aleida Daughter to Eldryk

Achela Morvek in service to Eldryk

Angomar Slave catcher and pure blood Nihlvarian noble, sister to Eldryk

Mehlga Outer islander, captive of the Nihlvarians

Radylf Morvek whip-man and overseer of Eldryk's slaves

Ilvar Kastrahk Vellihr of Lore to the Sister Queens

Hakkyn Rohnlank Veilwald of the Aiken Geld

Tuhlan Caerith prisoner of the Nihlvarians, friend to Ruhlin

Julette Ahlpert Former Albermaine-ish pirate and prisoner of the Nihlvarians

Sygurn Nihlvarian slave

Iyaka Morvek slave

Gynheld Volksora Vellihr of the Sword, captain of the longship *Swift Spear*

Alvyr Kahlsten Vellihr of the Sword, captain of the longship *Wind Sword*

Feydrik Member of the Nihlvarian tuhlvyr caste, governor of the Vyrnkral Veld

Deyna Member of the Nihlvarian tuhlvyr caste

Ossgrym Styrntorc Veilwald of the Kast Geld

Aldeyn Nephew to Ossgrym

Kahlvik Vahrimdorr Uhlwald of the Northern Shore of Ayl-ah-Vahrim. Renowned explorer and seafarer. Cousin to Ossgrym

A Tide of Black Steel

PART I

"Let every hand know the sword, for the Ascarls shall
be warriors all. And battle shall be our glory."

Ulthnir Horuhnklehr – the Worldsmith

– from the Altvar Rendi

CHAPTER ONE

Ruhlin

The morning mist hadn't yet begun to thin when he saw the red sail. At first, it was just a vague interruption in the lingering, pale grey haze, a patch of dark that took on a bloody hue after a few seconds of squinting. As Ruhlin stared at it, captured by the novelty, he realised the sail bore a design of sorts. It wavered and swelled in the stiff breeze coming off the rarely calm waters of the Stern Speld Sea, requiring yet more squinting before he recognised the crossed hammer and sword sigil of Ulthnir, first among the gods. However, this arrangement differed from those he had seen carved into many a lintel, or the motif adorning the aged statue atop Aslyn's Hill. The overlapping weapons were arranged to point down rather than up. The inverted hilt and haft created a cradle for another emblem Ruhlin didn't recognise. It resembled a thicket, irregular, jagged spines set along a smooth, curved line.

"What do you make of that?" he said, turning to Irhkyn.

At first, the *mahkla* didn't look up from his work, spade shovelling damp sand from the base of the hole they had dug. The old, rusted chain about his neck rattled in concert with his labour. Unlike many who wore the chain of an indentured servant, Irhkyn was no shirker when it came to work. Sour of mood and harsh of tongue, but never lazy, and Ruhlin knew the reason why: every day of toil performed to the satisfaction of Ruhlin's grandmother meant one less day of servitude.

Ruhlin had awoken early that morning, an inescapable feature of living under his grandmother's roof. "Up and out!" Bredda commanded, her old oakwood stick thumping the shore-scavenged timbers of his bed. "Work awaits idle hands, boy!"

His first awakening in this house, a scant five years ago now, had left Ruhlin painfully aware that his grandmother was not averse to redirecting her stick from the bed to its occupant should he prove a laggard. Still, on this particular day he found himself unwisely tempted to suffer a few blows if it meant just another few moments abed. The night before had been given over to his cousin Mirhnglad's trothing celebrations, a raucous gathering which had seen ale and mead flow freely. Everyone had been there, all those who made their home in Buhl Hardta, and more besides from the surrounding skyrns. Once the ceremony was done and the strikers struck to send sparks into the great bonfire constructed in the centre of the village, songs were sung, fish and meat roasted, barrels tapped and bottles un-corked. Ruhlin wasn't particularly seasoned when it came to liquor. Bredda wouldn't have it in the house, proclaiming it the ruin of his father, that and dice.

"Hands that never reached for an oar nor a shovel were always keen to reach for a drinking horn or a wager," she told Ruhlin more than once, sometimes jabbing her stick at his legs or belly for emphasis. Ruhlin often pondered the notion that his poor, drowned father might have been less fond of the distractions of drink and gambling if his mother's hearth had been more welcoming.

It was an unworthy thought, however. She had taken him in when his father's boat foundered in the great storm, her door open when so many others had been shut. Life in the Outer Isles was ever harsh, and another mouth to feed rarely welcome. He sometimes wondered if the villagers of Buhl Hardta would have let him starve that winter, even though he shared blood with at least half their number. Still, he found he couldn't hate them for it. The darker sentiments had always been difficult for Ruhlin to muster, along with the anger and profanity that came with them. So, as he grew, they had taken to calling him Ruhlin ehs Kestryg: Ruhlin the Quiet.

"How the shit should I know?" Irhkyn said, his standard response to most questions, even those addressed to him by the likes of Ruhlin's uncle Dagvyn, Mirhnglad's father and Uhlwald of the village. Such truculence from a *mahkla* would usually earn a whipping. However, Irhkyn's stature and violent reputation tended to discourage such chastisement. Before his slide into debt and shame, he had sailed far, raided distant lands, and fought battles. He rarely consented to share tales of these adventures with Ruhlin, preferring the misery of silent brooding.

Ruhlin watched Irhkyn scoop more sand from the hole, grunting in satisfaction at the worms he saw wriggling amongst the clumped grains. "Decent harvest for once. Might even have a few salmon weighing the bait lines tomorrow."

"There," Ruhlin persisted, nudging Irhkyn's shoulder and pointing into the mist. "A sail, isn't it?"

The *mahkla* snorted in annoyance and finally consented to raise his head. "Tides too low. And who berths a ship on sand when there's a perfectly good harbour a stone's throw away . . . ?"

Irhkyn's words faded as his sight lingered on the shape in the mist, his heavy, blue-inked brows tightening into a frown. Straightening, he shifted his grip on the shovel, Ruhlin seeing his knuckles whiten. He also saw how the *mahkla*'s stance had altered, a hunch to his shoulders, knees slightly bent, and both feet placed for balance. Ruhlin had seen Dagvyn and some of the other adults of the village adopt such bearing when they taught use of sword or spear to their children. Ruhlin's own father had never done so, even though, like Irhkyn, he had sailed far and known battle in his youth.

"You know that sign?" Ruhlin asked him, a small knot of worry forming in his chest as Irhkyn continued to regard the sail.

"No," he murmured. Ruhlin discerned an additional weight to Irhkyn's tone as he spoke on, imbuing it with a disconcerting significance. "Never seen it before in my life."

"A sail that size means a big boat, doesn't it? Too big for the wharf, perhaps. That's why they berthed here."

"Not a boat," Irhkyn corrected. "A longship. And yes, it's a big bugger."

He paused, narrowed eyes flicking to either side of the red sail. "And didn't come alone."

The *mahkla*'s sight proved keen, for Ruhlin quickly saw two more sails resolve out of the mist to the right of the first. Each bore the same crossed hammer and sword emblem with the spiky thing on top. "Is it a thorn bush?" he wondered, then hefted his own shovel and started forward. "I suppose we can ask them . . ."

"No." Irhkyn's large hand fell heavily onto Ruhlin's shoulder, holding him in place. "Ships that beach close to a port don't do so with trade in mind, lad. Come." He turned, tugging Ruhlin along as he spurred to a run. "We've a warning to deliv—"

Irhkyn's hand hadn't yet fallen from Ruhlin's shoulder, so he felt it clench in pain and shock before it slipped away, the *mahkla* tumbling onto his face with a groan that was as much angry as it was despairing.

"Irhkyn?" Ruhlin stumbled to a halt, a wholly unfamiliar and uncomfortable chill coursing through him from head to toe as he watched Irhkyn convulse, then cough a red spatter onto the sand. Ruhlin dithered for another few beats of his labouring heart, fascinated by the deep hue of Irhkyn's blood, then by the long, gull-fletched arrow that jutted from his back. He might have dithered longer if the *mahkla* hadn't reached out to snare his ankle in a large hand and drag him down. A rush of displaced air and a flicker of movement, then Ruhlin found himself staring at a second arrow embedded in the beach less than a yard away, shaft still shuddering.

"Go!" Fresh blood erupted from Irhkyn's mouth as he gasped out the command, Ruhlin looking into fierce, implacable blue-grey eyes. "Warn them . . ." The dying *mahkla* jerked, his grip loosening on Ruhlin's ankle and his head slowly subsiding into the damp grains. "Go . . ."

Ruhlin's chest heaved as he drew in rapid, panicked breaths, continuing to regard his friend's unmoving body, watching the sea breeze twitch the feathers of the arrow's fletching. He had known Irhkin from boyhood. They worked side by side on Ruhlin's father's boat in the days before one wager too many had made a renowned warrior into a *mahkla*, a chained man condemned to work off his debts or suffer the dread fate of exile. Now he was gone, his life snuffed in an instant. An impossible, horrible truth.

It was the hard, short thrum from the direction of the red sails that banished Ruhlin's indecision. He knew the sound of a bowstring well enough. Shouting in fright, he twisted, rolling across the sand, the arrow arcing down amidst the scrape left in his wake. Sobbing, he scrambled upright and pelted away. More bowstrings thrummed behind him, but Ruhlin, although far from being the strongest lad in Buhl Hardta, had at least always been amongst the most fleet of foot. Hearing the thud of falling arrows, he dragged more air into his lungs and ran faster, soon losing himself amongst the grassy dunes beyond the beach. In the months to come, he would have occasion to reflect on whether he would have been better if one of those deadly darts had found a target.

He smelled the smoke before he crested the bluffs south of Buhl Hardta, an acrid sting to the nostrils that grew with every breathless, clawing step up the rise. *Dagvyn!* The name had become a mantra of sorts during his flight from the beach. *Find Dagvyn!* As Uhlwald of the port, and therefore holder of the Sister Queens' authority on this island, Dagvyn would know what to do. He would call the village to arms. He would herd the old folk and children into the Uhlwald's hall. A battle would surely be fought against these unseen interlopers and their red-sailed longships, but it would be short, for this was Buhl Hardta, the furthermost port of the Sister Queens' domain. Here dwelt the hardiest folk in all their broad realm. Here there were warriors who had voyaged almost as far as Irhkyn, some who could even match his renown. Dagvyn himself had won fame when the Fjord Geld was reclaimed from the hated thief-king of Albermaine . . .

All such thoughts dwindled into shocked despair when, chest heaving and limbs shaking with the onset of exhaustion, he crawled to the top of the bluffs, there to see the Uhlwald's hall aflame. The blaze appeared to have started on the roof, thrown torches or fire arrows setting light to ancient reed thatching, birthing an inferno that soon engulfed the building from end to end. The smoke settled in a thick blanket over the whole of Buhl Hardta, though not so thick as to conceal the sight of other buildings burning. Gethora's gutting shed, Loffar's smithy, his grandmother's storehouse where she stored stockfish for the yearly tithe, all blazing bright through the drifting pall.

Ruhlin's horror deepened at the sounds rising from the smoke. Whilst his eyes could detect only fleeting shadows, his ears collected the screams with terrible clarity. Some were brief, terrorised cries, quickly cut off. Others were more prolonged, screeching shrieks of distress that put him in mind of pigs in the slaughter pen. A tumult to his left swung his gaze to the harbour where the smoke was thinner and he saw a cluster of dim shapes on the wharf. Shouts rose in anger and distress and he fancied he heard the clang of clashing metal. *A battle after all then*, he decided, his blossoming hope fading when a gust thinned the smoke to reveal a broad red sail bearing the hammer, sword and thicket sigil.

With the tide so low, the longship's rail sat below the edge of the wharf. It was a far larger vessel than Ruhlin had seen before. The wide, overlapping planks of its hull were of familiar construction, but the spiked iron ram jutting from its prow was beyond his experience. Ladders had been raised from its deck to allow the ship's occupants to gain the wharf, finding themselves contested, but not so fiercely as to prevent many investing the village with arson and murder in mind.

Indecision gripped him as he knelt amidst the grass. Join the battle or find Bredda? Taking shameful fortitude from his dearth of arms, his shovel abandoned on the beach and only the scaling knife on his belt, Ruhlin staggered upright and set off towards the further reaches of the village. His grandmother needed him. He would see her safe, then arm himself with the wood axe and join the fight. Yet, as he straggled down the slope, ears filled with the screams of his dying kin, a small, viciously honest voice hissed in his mind: *You won't be fighting anyone today. You'll be hiding, you worthless craven dog.*

Ruhlin grunted angry, wordless defiance at the whispering truth, pressing his sleeve against his nose and mouth before forging on through the haze. The pall had grown thicker in just a few moments, stinging his eyes and sending tears down his cheeks. He caught brief glimpses of people, faces lost to the gloom. He heard some babbling in fear or confusion, knotting together in confused terror, soon to be assailed by others moving with swift purpose. Ruhlin made out the shape of an unfamiliar helm on one. A flare of blossoming flame from the Uhlwald's hall painted a gleam on the conical form, marking it as a thing of iron rather than the hardened leather favoured by those who kept arms in this village. The fire also drew a thin shine from the sword in the helmed figure's hand and the boss on the round shield it bore.

Ruhlin deafened himself to the screams, hunching smaller and hurrying on. He collided with an upended cart a few steps on, rebounding from it only to lose his footing, his shoes slipping on wet cobbles. Landing hard on his arse, Ruhlin raised a hand from the damp stone to find it red. His eyes quickly fixed upon the unseeing visage of Selvy, daughter of Loffar the smith. A hearty soul several years his senior, and possessed of enticing curves his youthful gaze couldn't help but admire, Selvy was now transformed from person to thing. Her round, apple-cheeked face was still, mouth gaping open and lips loosened in a way that revealed her bottom teeth, tongue lolling from the corner of her mouth. The blood he had slipped in flowed from a recent wound in her belly, pale, snake-like innards strewn amongst the crimson slick. Ruhlin found himself once again fascinated by a novel but dreadful detail, this time in the form of the steam rising from Selvy's wound, the warmth remaining in her corpse seeping away to merge with the swirling smoke.

Cover yourself in her blood and lie still, the irksomely honest whisperer advised. *The guts too. Make it look real.*

Snarling defiance at his cowardice, Ruhlin crawled clear of Selvy's blood and regained his feet. The house was close now, just a short run through the gap between Othyr's pig pen and the woodshed. The dwelling he shared with Bredda sat atop a rise near the eastern edge of the village and, he saw with a welling of relief, appeared untouched by flame. He had often griped about the steep climb to his own door, to which Irhkyn replied that his grandmother chose to build her home on this spot so she could have a clear view of everyone else's business. Scaling the slope in a rapid frenzy, he barrelled into the sturdy door, finding it unlatched. Inside, he looked upon a roundhouse dwelling as neat and orderly as ever. The floor swept, seasoned firewood stacked. Pots, pans and knife were all arrayed in the proper place along the counter where Bredda fashioned inarguably excellent meals she assured him his idle carcass didn't deserve. Everything was how it should be, except for his grandmother's absence.

The snap of wind-tossed laundry drew him to the dwelling's rear door, heart flaring in hope as he shoved it aside. And that was where he found her. Not, as he dared wish, engaged in pegging a shawl to the rope whilst offering waspish commentary on this bothersome smoke. No. Bredda, daughter of Ilthura, mother of Kultrun, grand-mother of Ruhlin, who, by the grace of the Altvar, had drawn breath upon this earth for more than seven decades, lay dead in her own herb garden. She had been killed by a single stroke to the throat, recently judging by the blood still gushing from it. Her features were slack, much like Selvy's, although Ruhlin detected an expression in it. A slight drawing of the brows and pursing of the lips betraying something he had never seen on this woman's face in life: surprise. It captured him more completely than any other dire novelty this day, so much in fact that he barely noticed the man crouched at his grand-mother's side with a bloody knife in hand.

Turning to Ruhlin, the man grunted and rose to his full height. He stood an inch or two taller than Ruhlin, his iron helm and armour of broad ringed chain mail and leather concocting an impres-sion of some unassailable monster. Angling his head, eyes narrowed on either side of the brass nose guard, the man took a moment to study the blank-faced youth staring at the murdered old woman. Grunting again, this time in apparent derision, the man said some-thing in a harsh, rasping tongue. The words, if words they were, meant nothing to Ruhlin. He shrugged, faintly annoyed by the distraction from his fascination with Bredda's absurd expression. *She would have said something, at least*, he decided. *She would never have died wordless.*

The man sighed, weary and workmanlike. Ruhlin swayed as a hand descended onto his shoulder, holding him in place, the bloodied knife coming up, angled for a lateral stroke across his throat. Ruhlin barely noticed, eyes finally shifting from Bredda's face to track over her form. Never fond of finery, her dress was the same plain, scrupulously clean garment of homespun wool she always wore, although today he noticed a stain. There, on the sleeve near her wrist, dark and wet. He also noticed the red spatter discolouring her hand and the blade lying close by, the small sickle she used to harvest herbs.

Ruhlin shuddered then, feeling a grinding lurch deep in his guts. The movement drew him back from the iron-helmed man, causing him to mutter something in his gibberish tongue, tightening his grip on his victim's shoulder. Ruhlin stared at the face of the man about to kill him, not in fear but scrutiny, searching across the bearded, part-obscured features, set in a grimace of anticipated slaughter. It was under his left eye, a cut, still bleeding. Small, but deep enough to require stitching in time.

Ruhlin's gaze returned to his grandmother's face, words coming unbidden to his lips. "So, she had something to say after all."

The lurch in his guts grew in violence when his neck felt the edge of the helmed man's blade, pressing hard, then stopping. Ruhlin saw the man frown, eyes narrowing then widening as he looked upon Ruhlin's face. Features suddenly pale, the man stepped back. The hand on Ruhlin's shoulder slackened and fell away, much as Irhkyn's had done. Ruhlin felt a small pulse of puzzlement at the man's fear, but it was soon smothered by the sensation building within. He shuddered again as the grinding pain flared, transformed in an instant into a raging, burning flame in the centre of his being. When the flame settled, and the shuddering abated, Ruhlin thought it strange that the helmed man, who had seemed so tall seconds before, now seemed so small, and so fragile.

Although hate was a rare visitor, Ruhlin was not immune to anger. Sometimes it was slow to arrive, but, even as a child, when it came, it could be a frightening thing, something his father would shame him for on many an occasion. Now, Ruhlin felt no shame at his burgeoning rage. In truth, he welcomed it, and in so doing, stoked the fire raging inside into an inferno. It blazed through him, clouding his sight with a red fog and drawing a roar from his gaping mouth, a mouth that now felt impossibly wide.

He heard screams, joined by the squeal of crushed metal and the crack of bone which ended them. The fog receded a little, revealing the mangled mess of iron and pulped skull between his hands, hands that were clearly far too large to be his own. A small corner of Ruhlin's mind wondered if he had gone mad at the point of death, if his gift from the Altvar upon entering the Halls of Aevnir would be this gruesome vision of vengeance. If so, he was allowed no time to ponder the curious nature of such a reward.

A hungry, feral snarl filled his ears as his overlarge hands, now affixed to arms of equally monstrous proportions, cast aside the life-less carcass and the red fog descended once more. Ruhlin would always recall much of what followed as a vague, unwelcome nightmare, though some brief moments lived on his mind with terrible clarity for the rest of his days. Another man in an iron helm swinging an axe at his head, Ruhlin catching the descending blade with bare hands that suffered no injury. Fortunately, the memory faded at the moment he began to force the haft of the axe down its owner's throat. Another man he caught near the Uhlwald's hall, this one lacking a helm which revealed his red tattooed features in full, along with the gibbering, spit-flecked terror that doused his legs in piss before Ruhlin bore him down. He remembered delighting in the tattooed man's screams, laughing as his impossible hands snapped legs and arms like twigs before tossing the wailing figure into the blazing ruin of the hall. But mostly, the rampage of Ruhlin ehs Kestryg through what remained of Buhl Hardta village would be a tale told by others, for he knew little of it.

It was only when he neared the wharf that clarity began to return. He ascribed it to the sight of so many of his kinfolk lying dead in a heap, faces and bodies bearing the signs of battle. Plainly, they had fought well, their many wounds a testament to the ferocity of their resistance. But they had died for it. He recalled rising from the still twitching corpse of a man who had broken his spearpoint attempting to jab it into Ruhlin's throat. His sight was once again captured by horror, this time in the form of the two corpses lying atop the pile. Dagvyn lay partly across Mirhnglad, as if he had been trying to shield her from a final blow. If so, he had failed, and both father and daughter lay entwined in death.

A sob built in Ruhlin's chest as he staggered towards them, sorrow momentarily overcoming rage. It still burned bright, and he would soon return to his slaughter of these red-faced strangers, but in this moment, his grief forced a pause. He couldn't claim to have harboured great affection for his uncle. He had offered food and a shed to sleep in when Ruhlin's father passed, but no place by his hearth. But he had been a good Uhlwald, fair in his judgements and scrupulous in administering the laws of the Sister Queens. Ruhlin hadn't loved him, but he was blood kin and would be missed. But Mirhnglad . . . Sweet, soft spoken Mirhnglad, who had cried with him the night his father failed to return from the sea. His kind, golden-haired cousin who sang at every celebration with a voice that was surely a gift from the Altvar. Her gold hair was matted with blood now, her hands stained red from finger to wrist. He hoped it was the blood of their foes, of which he would spill all before he was done.

The rage surged again, the red fog along with it, and Ruhlin accepted both with gratitude. Another inhuman snarl scattered drool from his mouth as he scanned the wharf for victims, finding only one. A slender figure with long dark hair. Like the others he had slain, her face bore designs in red ink, though they seemed more elaborate and artfully crafted. Unlike the others, she wore no armour, clad instead in a cloak of fox fur and hardy leather gear, lacking any weapon he could see. What distinguished her most from her compatriots, however, was her complete absence of fear at the sight of what she beheld. Her eyes were wide in wonder rather than terror.

Advancing towards her, the red fog obscuring much of his vision, Ruhlin had occasion to note the woman's evident beauty, but neither that nor her fearlessness would save her. He closed the distance to his prey quickly, gore-covered hands rising. When he drew within a dozen feet of her, the woman raised a small metal tube to her lips and Ruhlin felt a sharp, searing pain in his tongue. The flare of agony was so intense it brought him to a halt, instinct bringing his fingers to his mouth to pluck forth a long metal dart. Looking again at the woman, Ruhlin saw her slotting another such projectile into the tube. Lurching forward, he found his legs no longer consented to obey him and he stumbled onto all fours. The pain left by the dart had shifted into a chilling numbness, spreading from his tongue to his throat before making icy, inexorable progress through his whole being.

Trying to rise, he gaped at the sight of his hand upon the granite surface of the wharf, watching it twitch and reduce in size. Dark, knotted veins paled and bulging tendons pulsed, then thinned until, once again, he beheld his own hand. It was the last thing he saw before darkness claimed him, although his ears did detect a voice, presumably that of the tattooed woman. Unlike the other, she spoke words he recognised as old Ascarlian. Although the meaning behind them escaped him then, he would learn it in time and come to detest their every utterance: "*Vyrn Skyra*" – Fire Blood.

Chapter Two

Thera

"Don't!"

The warrior's sword halted its progress from its scabbard, his arm frozen by the curt snap of Thera's voice. He was young, a few years shy of her own age. Had he been older, and therefore more attuned to the shift in fortunes her presence signified, he might have saved himself. A veteran would most likely have taken one look at the Vellihr's brooch on her leather breastplate, slid his sword back into its sheath and disappeared into the night. But the young are ever keen to prove themselves, especially when given the honour of guarding their Veilwald's hall. So, despite the authority in her tone, and her brooch, the youthful warrior chose duty to clan, and a chance at glory, over wisdom.

Thera struck before he managed to draw the sword another inch, reading his intent in the sudden narrowing of the eyes and hardening of the mouth. Her spearpoint, black except for the silver gleam of its edge, took him under the chin, thrusting up through the lesser bones of the skull to skewer his brain. A swift and, she decided as she drew it free, more merciful death than that deserved by one who defied a servant of the Sister Queens. She caught the body before it fell, wary of the thud and clatter drawing unwanted attention. However, the raucous sounds leaching from the narrow windows above would most likely have smothered the commotion.

Propping the corpse against the weathered stones of the hall's east-facing wall, she moved towards the front of the building. The unwise young man was but one guard Kolsyg had set this night. Others were scattered about the village and would at this moment be making their own choices between duty and wisdom. The warriors of her *menda* were skilled in such things and she detected only a few muffled shouts and scuffles as she rounded the corner to stand before the ornately inscribed doors of Kolsyg's hall. The two warriors stationed there, a man and a woman with the blue-inked features and scars of veterans, stood warming their hands next to a coal-filled brazier. Both displayed a good deal more judgement than their youthful kinsman when Thera stepped into the light cast by the glowing coals, neither reaching for their weapons nor attempting to bar her path.

"We had no part in it," the woman said, eyes flicking between Thera's brooch and her spear. Thera couldn't recall a previous encounter with her, but the tale of the Vellihr who bore a black spear was well known. "Counselled against it, in fact. Didn't we, Gryn?" The woman darted a glance at her companion, a large man, bald of pate but with a copious red beard. In contrast to the woman's contrite submission, his features were set in grim acceptance.

"Weren't there, either of us," he grunted. "That's the truth of it." He hesitated, then stood straighter. "But I'll not pretend I've ever gone against my Veilwald's word, and will pay for it if that's the law."

Prideful, Thera concluded, turning away from the pair without a word. *But not so much as to bare steel or stand in my way.* She took comfort from the notion such attitudes were likely to be common amongst Kolsyg's kin. It would make the night's work easier.

As Thera reached for the great iron ring on the door, Eshilde and Ragnalt appeared from the shadows beneath the low edge of the hall's tiled roof. Not for the first time, Thera reflected on how, when silhouetted in the gloom, the pair resembled a cat and a bear; shaven-headed Eshilde, all lithe lethality, and shaggy-haired, black-bearded Ragnalt, the embodiment of Ascarlian strength. She watched Eshilde wipe a rag over the blade of her dagger and took note of Ragnalt's untarnished axe.

"One fought, one didn't," he explained before inclining his head at the door. "Will you need us?"

Thera shook her head, lifting the ring and pushing hard to lever the great door open. After the smoke-laced chill covering the port of Skor Hardta, the warmth of its Veilwald's hall was so fierce as to be uncomfortable. Nevertheless, Thera kept her sable-furred cloak about her shoulders. At first, the general din of merriment continued unabated, but gradually diminished at the sight of the tall, spear-bearing woman maintaining a purposeful stride towards the Veilwald's chair. Soon, the only sound in the hall came from the fall of her boots and the steady thud of her spear's brass butt on the flagstones.

The gathered folk of the port parted before her, the young amongst them either curious or defiant, the older souls displaying much the same air of sour acceptance as prideful Gryn outside. Although she didn't allow her gaze to linger, her experienced eye picked out those who bore arms this night. These were mainly the better dressed, for what well set up Ascarlian would attend a Veilwald's celebration without a prized sword at their belt to proclaim their status? Most, however, bore nothing more than a knife with which to carve meat from the huge boar spitted above the firepit.

Kolsyg Ehflud, named the Saltskin for his many seagoing exploits, Veilwald of the Skor Geld, however, wore no sword. Instead, he sat in his tall-backed chair with one hand resting atop the haft of a double-bladed battle axe. The weapon commanded more of Thera's attention than its owner, for it was such a fine thing. Both its blades, curiously free of rust or the pitting of age, were shaped to resemble butterfly wings. The edges shone bright, but the inner portion was black and engraved in ancient runic, the characters flowing across the dark metal in elegant silver arcs. Although Thera's knowledge of letters was meagre, she knew enough of the old script to make out the name etched into the steel amongst the many others that listed his deeds. The fact that it was not the name Kolsyg Ehflud, but instead a far older and more celebrated title, said much for the Veilwald's guilt and his shameless willingness to flaunt it.

"So," he said in apparently affable welcome, "you've come at last, oh faithful dog of the vile sisters." As he spoke, he reclined into his chair, an impressively crafted thing carved all over with the sigils of the Altvar. Kolsyg grinned, keeping one hand on his stolen axe whilst using the other to raise a drinking horn to his lips.

Thera said nothing, instead coming to halt beside the firepit. Resting her spear upon her shoulder, she extended both hands to the fierce warmth of its flaming logs. She scented apple wood on the smoke flavouring the boar's meat as it ascended to the open slats in the roof. Looking up, the sight of the stars brought a smile to her lips.

"Do you come to offer only insult, woman?" Kolsyg demanded, his good humour having faded with as much alacrity as the rising smoke. "Will you not at least state your mistresses' terms so that I may be fulsome in my rejection?"

Again, Thera said nothing, but she did consent to turn and afford the Veilwald's axe a moment's additional scrutiny before surveying the rest of the hoard piled to the side of Kolsyg's chair. Seeing it all gathered together, she felt it to be a paltry collection of loot considering its famed origin. Old, rusted swords and daggers lay piled together alongside bow staves that had withered and cracked with age. Still, there were undoubted riches amongst it. An open chest brimmed with silver, both coins and strips. Fine bejewelled cups and bracelets. But the axe, of course, remained the real prize: the battle instrument of Gythrum Fihrskard, the Dreadaxe, most celebrated Ascarlian warrior of his, and any other, age.

A slight shift in the shadows reflected on the axe's edge drew Thera's gaze to the other side of Kolsyg's chair, finding a sight yet more captivating than even his stolen treasure. The maiden leaned against the Veilwald's seat, hands clutching the armrest, her oval features part veiled by long, jet-black hair, a rarity in Ascarlia. She wore a simple dress of cotton, marking her status despite the lack of finery: only the Veilwald's daughter would clothe herself in such expensive foreign fabric. Despite its plainness, Thera felt it enhanced her slender form far more than any elaborate concoction of lace and silk could ever do. The beauty of Kolsyg's only child was an oft-told tale, but the sight of it in the flesh was . . . distracting. The maiden blinked large, sapphire-hued eyes at Thera, her expression lacking both the defiance of her father and the submission of his kin. Instead, she just seemed sad.

"Keep your sight from my daughter!" Kolsyg's facade of civility disappeared completely as he shot to his feet, hefting the axe in both hands. "Is it not enough that you insult my hall with your mere presence? Must you inflict your lascivious gaze upon a Veilwald's own blood . . ."

"No terms." Thera's words, although softly spoken, cut through the Veilwald's burgeoning rant with the ease of a blade parting rotted timber. "And, by the word of the Sister Queens, you are Veilwald of the Skor Geld no longer."

She heard the nervous mutter and shift of the assembly, detecting a few discontented murmurings, but mostly it was just the muted alarm of those forced to witness an event soon to escalate into bloodshed. She also found it notable that Kolsyg's attention didn't waver from her. He cast no entreating glances at the dozens of kinfolk filling this hall, or at the armed members of his *menda* seated to the left of the Veilwald's chair. Seasoned warriors all, they either averted their gaze or stared at the unfolding drama in wary anticipation. One or two even appeared to view what was about to unfold with a marked eagerness. Plainly, Kolsyg Ehflud was not well loved, even in his own hall.

"How many of my kin did you kill to get in here?" Kolsyg demanded, jerking his chin at the Thera's wet spearpoint.

"Just enough," Thera replied. "Most were content to let us pass. It asks much to expect a decent soul to die for a murderer and desecrator of graves."

"Desecrator, you call me!" Kolsyg barked a harsh laugh. "What does that make you, bitch servant to bitch queens? They who have trampled upon everything that makes us Ascarls. You infect us all with your weakness. This—" he brandished the axe "—is mine by right. For the blood of Gythrum runs in my veins and puts fire in my soul . . ."

"By virtue of a great-grandmother who was grandniece to his cousin, I believe." Once again, Thera's soft spoken interjection staunched Kolsyg's invective with ease. "The blood of the Dreadaxe must be potent indeed to run so thick."

Kolsyg gave no immediate retort, instead lowering his head and fixing her with a glower. As his gaze lingered on her face, hate burning bright, she saw something surprising and significant: the unblinking yet twitching gaze of one unmoored from reason. She also noted the matted, grease-laden state of his beard, and the grime covering the skin around his eyes. Basic ablutions were apparently beneath his notice now.

"I had thought you just made foolish by avarice," Thera grunted in sombre realisation. "Stealing heirlooms from a most sacred barrow to enrich yourself and buttress your claim to other lands. Now, I see otherwise." She shook her head in apology and stamped the butt of her spear to the flagstones once more. "But there is no dispensation for the mad in the Sister Queens' law."

"There is no madness in me, weak-blood." Kolsyg hunched lower, hands tightening on the axe as he took a step forward. "Only truth. The truth of the Uhltvar . . ."

Her spear hadn't been fashioned as a throwing weapon, but she had perfected the skill after long months of practice. Ending a fight with a surprising tactic was always preferable to the chance-ridden game of combat at close quarters. The spearpoint punched into Kolsyg's unarmoured chest as he began to take his second step, piercing him from front to back and pinning his body to the chair.

Uhltvar? Thera repeated inwardly as she rose from the throw. An old word from old tales. Not one she expected to hear from a man about to die. Ignoring the chorus of shock and dismay echoing in the hall, she rushed towards the chair, leaning forward to hear any final words from the lips of the dying former Veilwald. But all he could offer her was a sputter of dark blood, a parting glare of hatred and, strangest of all, a knowing smile that quickly broadened into a rictus of bared teeth as a spasm of pain shot through him. Kolsyg Ehflud jerked several more times and coughed out a good deal of gore before eventually slumping lifeless in his chair, the fine carvings stained and the air made rank with the effluent of his passing.

Thera gave a sigh of muted frustration, then straightened, turning to address the hall. "Justice has been done in the Sister Queens' name. Any who wish to contest the rightness of it, speak now and bare your steel."

She cast a pointed and lingering glance at the still seated warriors of Kolsyg's *menda*, finding none willing to meet her eye. She stilled her face against the contemptuous sneer provoked by their cowed quiescence. Mad, greedy, or just foolish in the extreme, Kolsyg had been their Veilwald, the receiver of their blood oaths of service unto death. Thera contented herself with a disgusted snort before turning to the Kolsyg's daughter. Surely she would have something to say about her slain father. However, instead of the spitting defiance or wailing grief, the maid paid her no heed whatsoever. She had risen to play a hand over her father's sagging features, the sadness Thera had noted in her more evident now. Yet no tears fell from her eyes as she extended two fingers to close Kolsyg's half-open lids over dull, unseeing orbs. Finding the sight strangely uncomfortable, Thera shifted her attention to the occupants of the hall, surveying an assemblage of tense, wary faces.

"Rolnar Tarhrimvest," she said, voice echoing loud in the thickened silence. "Known as the Goldhair. Step forward."

There followed a brief interval of nervous shuffling before a stocky man emerged from the throng. He was of middling years and well dressed with a sword at his side, the belt part concealed by an overhanging belly. The presumably glorious mane that had gifted him his name was mostly grey and not particularly tidy, strands coming loose from his braids as he halted and bobbed his head to Thera.

"I am Rolnar, Vellihr Blackspear."

Thera quelled a spasm of anger at being addressed by that name, for she had never liked it. Still, custom dictated that no Ascarlian could choose the name they earned in life. Like it or no, she would always be Thera of the Blackspear, called Speldrenda in the old speech.

"You were Ledgerman to the Veilwald?" Thera asked him.

Rolnar swallowed before replying, but Thera was impressed by the absence of a quaver in his reply. "I am . . . was, yes."

"By the Sister Queens' word, you will assume the duties of Veilwald of the Skor Geld until the succession is decided. I am given to understand that Kolsyg had no other issue besides his daughter." She glanced over her shoulder at Kolsyg's heir, frowning in bemusement at the sight of her resuming her seat. As she did so, a grey-pelted cat slinked from under a nearby table to climb into her lap where it purred and arched its back in delight as the maid traced a hand over its fur.

"Correct, Vellihr," Rolnar said. "Lynnea is his only child. There was a brother, born a few years ago to the Veilwald's third wife, but neither child nor mother survived the birthing. It was after that sad event that Kolsyg's judgement began to veer in unfortunate directions."

"Can you attest that his daughter had no part in his crime?"

"I can." Rolnar impressed her yet again by moving around her, going to Lynnea's side and placing a protective hand on her shoulder. "Most firmly. She does not possess the means to do harm. Nor should she be judged for her father's deeds. That is the law, I believe."

"It is. But matters of inheritance must be decided." Thera inclined her head at Kolsyg's corpse. "Judged as an outlaw or not, he died a man of many lands and holdings. And his child retains the right to petition the Queens to keep it, and press her claim to the Veilwald's chair. That is also the law."

Rolnar's grip on Lynnea's shoulder tightened, a measure of defiance creeping into his gaze. Thera further noted a burgeoning tension amongst the hall's occupants, including the *menda*. Heads previously lowered in submission were now raised, faces hardening. *Wouldn't fight for Kolsyg, but they would for her*, Thera mused, looking again at the Veilwald's daughter, once more blinking those sapphire eyes behind a veil of black tresses. It would be wise to leave her here, regardless of Sister Iron's instruction. *Bring me the child, Thera*, she had said, voice firm and clipped, as was typical, though the lack of an explanation as to why she put so much value in this young woman was not. Still, as Vellihr of Justice to the Sister Queens, Thera had leeway to use her best judgement. Antagonising these people further could be dangerous. Their fear of her was stark, but she had learned that even the most cowed could be pushed only so far.

"Can she not speak for herself?" she asked, raising an eyebrow at Lynnea. "How about it, girl? Care for a trip to the famed majesty of Skar Magnol? There to entreat with the Sister Queens in person. It'll be something to boast of in years to come, at least."

"Lynnea does not, in truth, speak, Vellihr," Rolnar said. "For herself or anyone else." He lowered his gaze to Lynnea, smiling fondly. "She never has. Trahleyl we call her, the Silentsong. Therefore—" he straightened, meeting Thera's eye "—I am bound to speak for her. I will pen a petition on her behalf that you will carry to the Sister Queens . . ."

He faltered to silence when Lynnea, still cradling the grey cat, got to her feet and moved to stand at Thera's side. She offered Thera scant greeting, save a short, expectant glance, before holding the animal closer and rubbing her face to its fur.

"It seems the Silentsong has sung," Thera said. "I depart on the next tide. I leave the choice of rites for Kolsyg Ehflud in your hands, though his barrow is to be afforded no marker." Thera strode towards Kolsyg's corpse, bracing a boot against his chest and grunting with the effort of drawing the spear free.

"You lot," she said, pointing the dripping spearpoint at the *menda* before flicking it at the pile of stolen treasure beside the Veilwald's chair. "Gather that up and bring it to my ship. Rest assured, I have a very precise accounting of all that was robbed from the Dreadaxe's barrow and any more thievery by the denizens of this geld will be punished in like manner."

Pausing, she stooped to retrieve the axe of Gythrum Fihrskard from beneath Kolsyg's limp feet. Raising it so that the light from the firepit played over the silver lettering. The elegant lines of intersecting curves were very different from the hard angles of modern runic, an echo of a time when poetry was prized as highly as sword skill, at least according to Sister Lore. She couldn't read any of it, but knew enough of Gythrum's tale to be sure that one word was almost certain to repeat amongst it.

"Uhltvar," she murmured, lowering the axe. As she did so she noticed a change in Lynnea's demeanour. It was just for an instant, a tightening to the shoulders as she continued to snuggle her cat, but also a guarded flicker in her gaze as she spared a short glance at the axe in Thera's hand.

"You know this word?" Thera asked, moving closer. Lynnea avoided her eye, however, turning away and drawing a mewl from the cat as she hugged it. "No matter," Thera said, keeping her voice low. "Sister Iron will get it out of you, mute or no. Come on, then." She waved the spear, still wet with the blood of the maid's father, and strode towards the doors. "And bid goodbye to that beast. I've already got a mouser aboard the *Great Wolf* and he's like to kill any rivals."

CHAPTER THREE

Felnir

He had always detested the sea off the southern coast of Albermaine. To the subjects of that realm it was usually named simply "the Southern Sea", or more poetically, "the Azure Tides". But to Felnir, and many an Ascarl forced to bring their longships to these waters, it was the *Lygnar Helv*, the Liar Sea. Becalmed and dappled by a golden sun one second, it could in mere moments transform itself into a capricious, deck-swamping monster of white waves and driving rain. This night had proven to be no exception.

Near twilight, Felnir had ordered the *Sea Hawk* to anchor three miles off the southern shore of the Albermaine duchy of Dulsian. For near an hour the longship bobbed in a gentle swell, her rigging painted pleasing hues by the dipping sun. However, barely moments after he, Sygna and Guthnyr climbed into the rowboat and begun to make for the rocky coast, the Liar Sea decided to earn its name afresh. Rain fell in ever thickening sheets and placid waters swelled into fractious choppiness.

"Give me the Styrnspeld any day," Guthnyr griped as he and Felnir hauled on the oars and Sygna worked the tiller, striving to keep the boat's prow pointed at their destination. "She'll freeze your balls and cast bergs at you all year long, but at least you know where you are with that bitch."

Felnir grunted agreement but didn't echo his brother's complaints. Guthnyr could moan, Felnir couldn't. It was one of many prices he paid to remain captain of the *Sea Hawk*, for a crew such as his would never follow a leader given to endless whining.

Fortunately, despite the turn in the weather, Sygna displayed her ever skilful hand on the tiller. Whilst he and Guthnyr laboured to power them through the swell, she guided the small craft to the large, flat rock protruding from the base of a tall cliff. With a deft, final heave on the tiller, she nudged the boat's prow onto the rock's edge, Guthnyr and Felnir quickly leaping clear with the ropes. They secured the lines around a fortuitously placed mound of stone, allowing Sygna to join them, crouching with her bow in hand and a shaft already resting against the stave.

Felnir possessed a decent pair of night eyes, but Sygna's ability to pierce the shadows rivalled a cat. He watched her survey the cliff from top to bottom, he and his brother also crouched low. As Sygna continued her inspection, Felnir noticed Guthnyr reaching for the handle of his sword. They both had their weapons strapped to their backs, which made it easier to clamber from boat to shore, and had left their shields aboard the *Sea Hawk*. Hissing a wordless warning, Felnir touched a hand to his brother's arm, shaking his head. The gleam of a revealed blade in this moment could pose as much a danger as a blazing torch.

Guthnyr frowned but consented to lower his hand. *A year and a half since I allowed him to follow me into this cursed life*, Felnir sighed inwardly, *and still every lesson must be learned at least twice.*

Your brother is not you. Oft spoken words echoed in his mind, as they usually did whenever his judgement of his brother proved poor. *Nor is he your father. Remember that and guard him well, for I see great value in him.*

Felnir's brows twitched in irritation at the implied critique in his great-grandfather's injunction. *I see value in him too*, he had insisted, as much to himself as to the ancient, grave-faced man before him. *So much that I believe him worthy of more than this.*

The memory slipped away at the sight of Sygna's sudden tension. She crouched lower, bow creaking as she drew the string taut, although Felnir could see nothing of note in the gloom. Through the shifting curtains of rain, the craggy edifice appeared to him as just a jumble of abstract shadows that grew in size as they descended its span. He knew there was a cave mouth at the base of the cliff, one leading to a cramped tunnel winding through the mass of rock to the top. This was an old smugglers' route, one Felnir had used before, though never in such parlous conditions.

He shuffled to Sygna's side, blinking away the constant patter of droplets but still seeing only shadows. "What?" he asked her, the wind and the unceasing torrent forcing him to speak louder than he would have liked.

"Sound not sight," she replied. "Fall of stones. Echo of laboured breath. A scared man in a hurry."

Felnir didn't question her judgement, her hearing being as keen as her vision. The man they had come to meet would have only one reason to be scared. "Now's the time to bare your steel, brother," he said, glancing over his shoulder. Guthnyr's grin showed white teeth through the rain, his sword, longer and broader than most, coming free of the scabbard in a swift, metallic flicker. Felnir put a hand to his own weapon, edging away from Sygna before drawing it, eyes straining for the first glimpse of friend or foe.

Like Sygna, he heard the man before he saw him, the rapid, high-pitched breaths putting Felnir in mind of a yelping terrier. Consequently, when he finally came into view, the sight of him proved a surprise. He was tall, and broad with it, almost matching Felnir's stature. Also, he was armed with one of the long swords the Albermaine-ish cherished so much. Felnir made out the dull gleam of wet mail as the man came closer, his heavy cloak flapping in the deluge, features obscured by a hood. Felnir waited until he came within a dozen paces, an easy mark for Sygna's arrow, then stood. The hooded man came to an abrupt halt, his yelping breaths ending in a shocked gasp. He stared at Felnir for the space of three full heartbeats before gulping air and speaking in heavily accented Ascarlian.

"I am ..." the man staggered a little and was obliged to gulp more air before continuing, "... but a simple trader come to buy your wares."

"What wares?" Felnir asked, aggravated by the fact that he couldn't see the man's features. The face of a stranger always revealed more than mere words.

"Sleep weed," the man replied promptly before casting a nervous glance back at the cliff. "And spices from Ishtakar. Cinnamon . . ." He paused, the hood scattering water as the man shook his head, apparently striving to remember the additional required detail. Felnir's eyes narrowed. The face could tell a lot, but so could a gesture. "And black saffron," the man finished, a sigh of relief colouring his voice. "If you have it."

A faint echo of raised voices shifted Felnir's attention to the unseen cave. "You brought friends?" he asked the stranger.

"They are uninvited, I assure you," he replied, forcing a thin note of humour as he added, "and certainly not friends."

Felnir jerked his head at the boat. "Get in."

Sygna leaped onto the craft first, moving to take up the tiller once more. Felnir took hold of the prow to keep the boat in place whilst their foreign guest clambered aboard with markedly less expertise.

"Only sounds like a handful, brother."

Felnir turned to find Guthnyr gazing towards the cliff, a keen glint in his eye, sword scattering arcs of water as he twirled it. The shouts of their uninvited guests grew louder, Felnir glimpsing a dim, growing shape through the rain that soon resolved into a dense cluster of running figures.

"Get in the fucking boat, Guth!" he snapped, voice hard enough to command his brother's notice. He met Guthnyr's gaze, watching good sense vie with frustration and resentment.

"I was promised glory and renown," Guthnyr muttered, sliding his sword into the scabbard on his back before putting both hands on the boat's rail to swing his large frame into the craft. "Instead, all I get is pissing rain and a chilled arse."

"I don't recall promising you anything better," Felnir returned, pushing the boat clear of the rock then leaping on board.

"Not you." Guthnyr offered him a bland smile as they sat side by side to take up the oars. "Great-grandfather. 'All you wish for shall be yours, my young bear.' That's what he told me."

The flat rock soon faded into the rain as they drew away from the shore, the gaggle of pursuers lost to sight. It didn't prevent one launching a crossbow bolt, the shaft raising a white spout from the waves ten yards short. A hopeless attempt Felnir might have ascribed to the rage of hunters denied their prey. But he doubted it.

"Then the old sod lied," he told his brother, both grunting in unison as they worked the oars. "You'll find he does that a lot."

"Sir Aurent Vellinde." The foreigner accompanied his introduction with a bow, his hand making a curious, flowery gesture and his head tilted at an angle Felnir suspected might be insulting. Like most Ascarls, he found Albermaine-ish customs irksome in both their frippery and obscurity. "At your service," Vellinde added, straightening. Shorn of his hood, the foreigner's features were revealed to possess a strong-jawed handsomeness, mostly clean-shaven save for the spearpoint moustache and beard. Still, creases about the mouth and eyes dimmed any impression of youthful vitality and Felnir found it odd that the face of a veteran knight would be so free of scars. Also, his mail bore patches of rust and his leather sword belt was cracked and frayed. *Noble of birth, all right*, Felnir concluded. *Although, not fat of purse.* But then, he had never yet encountered a wealthy spy.

Felnir gave no introduction of his own, merely pointing the foreigner to the hollow below the midship deck boards. "Sit there," he said. "Don't talk to my crew."

"As you wish, good captain." Vellinde inclined his head, once again adopting the same potentially insulting angle. "Though I had hoped to prevail upon your generosity for a cup or two of wine. It has been a somewhat trying night . . ."

"Sit," Felnir instructed. "Don't talk."

He stared hard at the foreigner until, smiling without obvious offence, he made his way to the hollow and sat. Felnir spared a short, meaningful glance at Druba. The thick-armed Sylmarian nodded, hefting his club and moving to stand closer to Vellinde. Whenever they had strangers or captives aboard, they were put in Druba's charge since mere proximity to his silent, perpetually expressionless bulk worked better than chains to ensure compliant quietude.

"Fair wind is Ulfmaer's blessing to atone for foul weather," Behsla quipped, coiling rope as Felnir moved to her side. Her long, salt-scraped face formed a squint as she cast her expert eye over the sea. "Though it'll be a bastard to keep course in this."

Behsla was his *Johten Apt*, the windmaster given charge of the *Sea Hawk*'s only sail and he doubted there was another soul with sounder judgement of the elements. As was customary amongst those of her craft, she was assiduous in her obeisance to Ulfmaer, god of sea and wind, most capricious of all the Altvar. The rain had abated by the time he had returned with the foreigner, ordering the anchor and sail raised with all swiftness, but the wind was undiminished. However, as befitted the Liar Sea, the gale shifted direction with annoying frequency.

"Just put as much distance betwixt us and the shore as you can," Felnir told her. "We'll set the heading when we get some calm."

He left her to her business and went aft. Sygna had resumed her customary place at the tiller whilst Guthnyr perched on the stern rail alongside Kodryn, the longest serving and most trusted warrior in Felnir's *menda*.

"Anything?" Felnir asked, the question addressed to Kodryn, but it was his brother who answered.

"Not a sail to be had." Guthnyr laughed and stood upon the rail to shout into the darkened sea. "Where are you? At least have the balls to chase us a while, you craven fuckers!"

Felnir ignored his brother's antics and raised an eyebrow at Kodryn. They had known each other since their days as mercenaries in the court of the Saluhtan of Ishtakar, and there were few Felnir trusted more. Kodryn peered into the gloom a while longer, fingers stroking the silver-laced braids of his beard, the lines around his pale green eyes deepening.

"He's right," he said in his whispery rasp, the legacy of a scimitar to the throat years before. "No one's hunting us this night."

"Then he can't be that important." Guthnyr climbed down from the rail, nodding at the foreigner now hunched amidst the lower deck cargo. "Whoever he is."

"Whoever he is doesn't concern you," Felnir told him. He jerked a thumb over his shoulder. "Go help Behsla with the lines."

His brother's response to commands could be as unpredictable as this deceitful stretch of ocean. But tonight Guthnyr exhibited no urge towards truculence, or snarling defiance verging on violence, simply shrugging before making his way to Behsla's side.

"It's still a fair point," Sygna said. "The foreigner had plainly been unmasked, else why would they have come for him? Yet they won't risk a ship to hunt him down."

"The weather is foul and they're not the sailors we are," Felnir countered, without much conviction. The events on shore played out in his mind, suspicion peaking at certain points. *Black saffron. That crossbow bolt.* He turned to Kodryn, lowering his voice. "Would you forget words that your life depended on? Would you not, as a seasoned spy, commit them to memory over and over so there was no chance of forgetting?"

"That I would," the veteran conceded, beard bunching with a rare grin. "But then, I've never been a spy, unlike you, old friend."

Felnir frowned at this, for it pertained to a time best forgotten, although he never could. Amongst his *menda*, only Kodryn enjoyed the leeway to say such things, and even he was wise enough to raise it only rarely. Felnir found it significant that he did so now.

"We keep a full watch until dawn," he said, starting back towards the mid-deck. "In the meantime, fetch wine. Alundian red. I think this one will appreciate a taste of home."

In Felnir's experience there were two types of drunkard. Some would quickly lose themselves in the oblivion of liquor, thereby spilling all manner of useful information from their slobbering lips. Others, like Sir Aurent Vellinde, were of a far more frustrating stripe. Whilst plainly being addicted to the milk of the grape, this latter sort retained most if not all of their faculties despite copious drinking. The foreigner attempted to play it otherwise, slurring his words with a consistent precision that told of practice, the performance enhanced by a lolling head and dolorous blinks of the eyes. This didn't necessarily stoke Felnir's suspicion further, since gulling an inquisitive companion was a creditable habit for a spy. But nor did it enhance his trust.

"Shcars?" he slurred in response to Felnir's observation regarding his mostly unmarked face. "Put no stock in such things, sir." He waved his quarter-empty wine bottle at Felnir. "As my father, may the Martyrs pish upon his pestilent soul, used to say, the dangerous man is not the one with the scars, but the one who gave them to him." Laughing at his own wit, he drank some more.

"Then your father had plainly never been in battle," Felnir said. "For even the bravest and most skilful can still earn a cut in the press of blades and spears. As you would know yourself, had you ever tasted it."

"Battle, ish it?" A twitch of offence passed over Vellinde's features, one Felnir was sure had nothing to do with artifice. Watching his creases deepen, Felnir decided he had underestimated the man's age, now putting him closer to fifty than forty. "Rest assured, oh warrior of the north," Vellinde said, momentarily forgetting to slur, "I've tasted battle. Swallowed it whole, then sicked it back up again. I was there when the Scribe bested the Pretender at the Vale, and . . ." He paused, gulping more wine, the lines of his face made yet more stark by the frown of a man experiencing unwelcome remembrance. "And I rode against the blackhearted Martyr Queen herself at the Battle of the Crest."

"Meaning you were on the losing side," Felnir said. "And, I note, talk of battles fought over two decades gone."

"Albermaine has been a peaceful kingdom under good King Arthin, thanks mostly, it must be said, to his mother's guidance."

"That I won't argue. The Dowager Princess is famed for her statecraft." Felnir watched closely for the knight's reaction to his next words. "And her spies. It's said there's more snoopers, thieves, and rogues in her employ than ever ran in all the outlaw bands of Albermaine combined."

"And you think me one of them?" Vellinde laughed, raising the wine bottle in salute. "Which, of course, I am. Or rather, was. Such is the fate of those who play the game of shadows. Loyalty is a luxury we can never afford, especially to a mistress who would happily see us dead."

"So, you were in her pay, but now you're not. That's the tale you intend to spin when I take you to the Tielwald?"

"Simple, unvarnished honesty, sir. I find it surprisingly effective, on occasion."

"And what led to this change of fortunes? Betrayal? Thievery? Murder, perhaps?"

"Lies." Vellinde took on a sombre aspect again, lips pursed and brows arched in regret. "A concoction of old, perfidious slander against my honour, one I thought laid to rest, but no. There's always another churl crawling from the gutter to besmirch the reputation of his betters." He raised the bottle to his lips, draining the last dregs. Wincing at the empty vessel, he brightened when Felnir relieved him of it and handed over another.

"I must say," Vellinde said, uncorking the fresh bottle to sniff the contents, "for a northern barbarian, you keep an excellent cellar, sir. It's been many a month since I partook of so fine a vintage. Pillaged on the high seas, I assume."

"Purchased from a trusted wine dealer in Assyrna who knows well my preferences. You were saying, about the concoction of slanders against you?"

"Indeed." Felnir sensed a genuine pitch to the knight's drunkenness now, his slur less mannered and a slight loss of focus to the eyes he widened in affronted pride. Even the most hardened drinkers couldn't stave off the effects of liquor indefinitely.

"And all I did, all I had ever done," the knight continued, "was my duty as ordained by King Tomas. It was my reward after the Vale, you see. 'The Pit Mines are yours, Sir Aurent,' he told me. 'Keep the ore flowing and all shall be well.' And I did." Vellinde's nostrils flared then, his mouth forming the defiant grimace of a man clinging to a long held grievance. "Oh, the ore flowed under my stewardship, I can tell you. Far more was dug out of that hole in one year under me than that oafish fool Gulatte managed in a decade. And what was my reward, may I ask?" The grimace became a sneer. "Ignominy. Disgrace. Vile accusation after vile accusation. Torturer, they called me. Ravager of women, too. As if I'd ever have soiled myself with one of those poxed bitches. The Martyr Queen put a price on my head and I spent months dodging the noose, scurrying from one piss-hole to the next like a hovel-born churl, condemned by a woman who slaughtered thousands. Thankfully, when the monstress fell, the Dowager Princess was more forgiving and appreciative of my talents, for my time as a fugitive had provided me with certain contacts in corners of the realm no royal foot could tread. Once again, I was useful."

"But, I would guess," Felnir ventured, "no longer received at court?"

Another twitch of the knight's features, genuine resentment dulling his already wavering gaze. "No. No place at court for me. Too much mud upon my banner, the Dowager's spymaster told me, for I never did meet her in person again, regardless of all the messages carried, bribes paid, and secrets unearthed on her behalf."

"Such poor treatment will wear on a man's soul. Perhaps turn his heart to treachery."

An angry flash lit Vellinde's eyes. "Not treachery. Survival. Months ago a beggared churl, an aged, back-bent miscreant who had somehow crawled from the Pit Mines, managed to gain an audience with the king himself. Prostrate before the throne, he pleaded for recompense and justice for long forgotten crimes that either never happened, or were at best gross exaggerations. King Arthin is not famed for his soft heart, but his queen is. After the complainant bared his much scarred back, twisted from the countless hours of labour I supposedly whipped him to, it was Queen Ducinda who prevailed upon her husband to issue a proscription against me. And so, this most valuable servant of the realm once again found himself dodging nooses."

"Until you acquired something worth selling to the Tielwald in return for safe harbour."

"Well . . ." A smile ghosted across the knight's lips. "Yes. I suppose so."

"What is it?"

Vellinde paused in the act of raising the wine bottle once more. "I crave pardon?"

"What you intend to sell to my great-grandfather. I require you to tell me what it is."

"That would be between myself and him . . ."

"Not on my ship. This ship upon which you sit your foreign arse after my kin and I risked our necks to rescue it. This ship sailing broad, very deep seas with a crew that owes fealty to me alone." Felnir leaned forward, staring into Vellinde's eyes to ensure, drunk or not, he couldn't mistake the intent he saw there. "Whilst you are aboard this ship, you will do as I say. Now, spill your guts or find them filled with seawater. The choice is yours."

Despite his inebriation, Vellinde's features retained a creditable measure of composure, though he was unable to quell the urge to cast a wary glance at Druba. The Sylmarian had drawn closer during their conversation and begun toying with the iron-studded club chained to his belt. Subtlety had its uses, but not for one such as Vellinde.

"It's a thing of material nature, in point of fact," he said, gathering up his cloak. Felnir made out a small object sewn into the hem, too light to be a weapon, although Druba took the precaution of half raising his club as the knight went about tearing the stitching to reveal the hidden item. "Here," he said, handing it to Felnir, "and please don't expect me to explain it. I've no knowledge of what it means, just its value."

At first glance, Felnir could discern no worth in this thing at all. It was a small piece of scrolled vellum tied in coarse twine. Pulling the twine free, Felnir unfurled the scroll to find a complex sigil of some kind. It resembled no emblem or clan icon he could recall, though the flowing, intersecting curves that comprised the design put him in mind of ancient runic. Below the sigil, a far more familiar set of characters had been inscribed in modern Alberic, their meaning gibberish to Felnir's eyes. It was assuredly one of his great-grandfather's cyphers. Felnir had memorised many such codes, both with and without the Tielwald's knowledge, but this one was beyond his ken.

"Where did you get this?" he asked Vellinde, once more staring hard to allow for no obfuscation.

Again, the knight didn't quail under the scrutiny, but Felnir did see the bob of his throat as he swallowed from a presumably dry mouth. Another characteristic of a drunk of his type was the ability to sober up with remarkable alacrity. "From a man now dead," Vellinde said.

"By your hand, I'd guess."

"The value of a secret diminishes with every eye that glimpses it. A truism you would well know, Felnir Redtooth. Yes." He smiled as Felnir's eyes narrowed. "I know your name and your story. The lesser brother to a renowned sister. Condemned for transgressing the rules of a just challenge. Thereafter, you were spared exile but compelled to your great-grandfather's service. It's his word that commands the tiller of this ship, not yours." Vellinde extended his hand. "Might I trouble you for the return of my property, good sir? It being for the Tielwald's sight, not yours."

Felnir might have done just that, if not for the mention of his sister.

Smiling, he rolled the vellum sheet into a scroll and pushed it into his belt. "If you had truly heard my story," he said, reaching for the empty wine bottle, "you plainly weren't paying close enough attention."

Moving too swiftly for the knight to counter, Felnir smashed the bottle into the side of his head. Spittle flew from Felnir's clenched teeth as he closed on Vellinde, clamping one hand to his throat and using the other to drag the knight's longsword free of its scabbard. Tossing the weapon away, Felnir drove a salvo of punches into Vellinde's already bloodied face. Hauling the foreigner onto the upper deck, Felnir dragged him to the starboard rail.

"Just so you know," he said, pausing to regard the knight, his face streaked in red, eyes wide in shock and terror. "It was the pause before you said black saffron. A trifle too much mummery. And the crossbow bolt. Too badly aimed to be convincing. I'd offer my regards to the Dowager Princess, but you won't be in a position to deliver them."

Vellinde struggled in his grip, swinging a punch at Felnir's face. He angled his head to let it land on the crown of his skull, then replied with a knee to the knight's midriff, doubling him over. "Mayhap your

Martyrs will look kindly on such a worthless soul," Felnir said, stooping to take hold of Vellinde's legs then pitching him over the side. "But I doubt it. I've heard many a tale of the Pit Mines."

The knight's tumbling form scraped over the *Sea Hawk*'s hull before splashing into the sea. He flailed and attempted to grab the planking as the ship swept on, soon leaving him in its wake. Felnir watched him thrash until the weight of his mail bore him down into the depths.

Spying the fallen longsword on the deck, Felnir retrieved it, striding to the port rail where Guthnyr regarded him with an expression mostly composed of puzzlement. However, Felnir saw something else in it, a tightening of the lips that told of disapproval, even disgust. This more than anything convinced Felnir that his brother was not suited to this life, regardless of their great-grandfather's judgement. Guthnyr was a fighter, and a fine one. But murder was not in his heart.

"You spoke of a reward, brother," Felnir said, handing him the longsword. "Here it is."

Turning away, he spent a moment gauging the pitch of the sail and the temper of the weather. "Behsla, time to turn west. I reckon Ulfmaer's seen fit to shift the wind in our favour. He always does appreciate a sacrifice."

CHAPTER FOUR

Elvine

H er mother always began the day with a written task. Before breakfast, and all her other chores, Elvine was required to sit at her desk and inscribe letters. This she would do until the last gloom of dawn had faded and the city outside their door fully roused. She didn't mind. In fact, this was often the high point of her day, for words and the characters that formed them had been her delight since childhood.

Today's task, however, proved more onerous than most, for it was a triple translation. It wasn't the mental contortions required to shift meaning from one form of writing to another that aggravated her so, but rather the choice of script. Elvine had no objection to the script her mother had used to set down the original passage, having always enjoyed the flowing curves and eloquence of ancient Ascarlian runic. Nor did she object to transcribing this version into contemporary Alberic, a less elegant but beautifully economic form of lettering, the one Elvine chose for her own writings in truth. No, it was the third script she objected to, not without a pang of guilt, for it was the language of her people. But, however much she tried, she could never summon any fondness for the hard-edged characters and limited grammar that formed modern Ascarlian. Translating poetry into such drab form felt like taking a sweetly singing bird and stuffing it in a cage.

"The bird will still sing sweet enough, child," her mother told her when Elvine, not for the first time, gave voice to this complaint. "It all depends on how well you craft the cage."

Rising from her own desk, she looked over Elvine's shoulder to appraise her work. "Finely formed as ever." As Skierwald at the Archive of the Sister Queens, she often came home with ample supplies of discarded writing materials. Elvine rarely wrote upon pages lacking a ragged edge or scribbling. As yet, however, she hadn't seen a hand that could match her own for clarity or finesse.

"But, the phrasing is less so," her mother went on, picking up the parchment to hold it closer to her squinting eyes. Years spent in her chosen occupation had left Berrine Jurest with worsening vision, although she continued to refuse the frame and lens contraptions beloved of many scholars and scribes. "'Thus did Nerlfeya ascend on wings of flame to light all the world in the Altvar's glory.' Yet, in your modern Ascarlian, it becomes: 'Nerlfeya flew, and her fire wings lit the world. Glory to the Altvar.'" She sighed, setting the parchment down and pressing a kiss to Elvine's cheek as she whispered, "I can't help but think it's lost something, my clever, darling child."

"All translations lose something of the original," Elvine countered. "It's inevitable, surely."

"But it is the burden of the translator to ensure such loss is minimal. It behoves you, Elvine Jurest, finest scribe in all Ascarlia, to do justice to the labours of our ancestral scholars. Thus do we honour the Altvar, and ourselves." Berrine moved away to brew the tea she would take with her to the Archival Hall.

Elvine concealed her frown by turning to the tall bookcase positioned to the side of her desk. Her eyes traced over cracked leather bindings and faded lettering, stained with years old soot, survivors of the inferno that had claimed their prior home. The great Library of King Aeric had fallen to flames kindled by the hated Albermaine occupiers the night they finally fled Olversahl. Elvine knew her mother had risked her life to rescue these aged tomes, but sometimes wished she had chosen a more eclectic range of titles. Save for a few bestiaries and guides to foreign tongues, this collection was almost entirely devoted to the sagas and legends of the Altvar and their myriad semi-mortal children.

Elvine had read every word on every page, firstly, at her mother's insistence, but later with more diligence and scrutiny as her thirst for knowledge and insight grew. What she discovered scared her, for the paths opened by study are often dangerous, albeit irresistible.

A familiar, tentative knocking at the door had Elvine reaching for her shawl and satchel. "It's Uhttar," she said, hurrying to peck a kiss to Berrine's cheek. "I promised I'd help with his letter."

"You haven't had breakfast," her mother protested as Elvine rose to answer the knock. "Can't you write it here?"

"It's a private missive. You know how shy he is." Hauling the door open, she found Uhttar's tall, skinny personage standing well clear of the opening. He also kept his eyes averted from the interior of her house, as if wary of waking the monster within. Although he was older than Elvine by a year, not for the first time, she felt the sense of having surpassed him in age. However, his child-like fear of her mother was not completely without foundation.

"Tell that walking bundle of sticks to pay you for your time," Berrine called before Elvine swung the door closed, her mother's next words muted but still clearly audible. "And make sure he knows that time is the only thing of yours he's getting."

Uhttar's beardless, hollow-cheeked face betrayed both bafflement and hurt as Elvine took his arm and led him along the street. "Pay you?" he asked. "For what?"

"I told her I'm helping you write a letter to the Veilwald about your inheritance." Elvine spoke softly, so as not to attract the ear of the folk they passed. "I needed a reason why we're in each other's company so much. It'll also be my excuse for leaving the house tonight."

"She's suspicious then?" Uhttar cast a glance over his shoulder, Elvine feeling him tense in her grip.

"She's mother to an unmarried maid of nigh twenty summers. A maid whose only apparent friend is an equally unmarried lad of scant prospects. Of course she's suspicious." She tugged his arm until he consented to face her. "Did you speak to the others?"

"Dehny and Harryk. They said they'd spread the word as usual."

"What about Senhild?"

"Couldn't get to see her. She's sick, according to her father. Although, he hates me almost as much as your ma does, so he could've been lying."

Elvine grimaced. Senhild was ever sickly, but her varied bouts of illness tended to coincide with the more important events in their shared but secret endeavour. *Fear is an illness, of sorts*, Elvine chided herself against the rise of judgemental thoughts. She couldn't begrudge Senhild her fear, given the risks they were running, especially tonight.

"And our . . . visitor?" she asked, voice lowered to little more than a murmur.

"Safe and well. Uncle's Bahn's shearing shed is comfortable enough."

Elvine nodded in satisfaction. Uhttar's uncle was as solid and trust-worthy a soul as they could hope for to oversee this hazardous enterprise. He also had taken no part in the scurrilous scheme that saw Uhttar deprived of his rightful inheritance upon his father's death five years ago.

"Here," she said, reaching into her satchel and extracting a folded letter. "It covers all the particulars. Just add your mark and take it to the Veilwald's hall next hearings day."

"You actually wrote it?" A surprised smile lit Uhttar's face as he unfolded the missive. His reading skills were meagre, and he could barely scratch out his own name despite the many hours she expended in trying to teach him. He had responded to her frustrated criticism with an affable shrug, holding up his calloused apprentice's hands and saying, "These were only ever meant for the boatyard, Elvie."

"Of course I wrote it," Elvine said. "Mother is bound to ask ques-tions if she doesn't hear of it being presented to the Veilwald. Is Bahn still willing to stand witness to your claims?"

"He is. I reckon he'd do it just to put a flame up the arse of his brothers. He'd long thought them a worthless bunch even before they forced me to put my mark on that false will they cobbled together. Though I'd best drop him a silver clip or two by way of appreciation when it's all settled."

"Better if you don't tell the Veilwald that."

He smiled again and consigned the letter to the inside of his jerkin.

"It could be," he said as they resumed their progress towards the harbour, "that you'll be walking arm in arm with a man of property before long." There was a forced lightness to his tone that warned her he was about to stray into territory she had cautioned against before. Several times, in fact. This morning, however, she found she hadn't the patience to dance around the issue.

"In Olversahl, men of property don't marry bastards, Uhttar," she said. "You know that. Bahn is kind to me, which I appreciate, but I can almost hear his thoughts when he sees us together. It wouldn't surprise me if he's already made a list of marriageable merchants' daughters, all of whom can put a name to their fathers."

"Old customs," Uhttar said. "Remnants of a banished age. If the Ascarls gave us one thing, it was the sweeping away of all that nonsense. The Sister Queens' law doesn't even recognise the word 'bastard.'" He came to a halt at the junction of the Slipways and Harbour Row, turning to face her. His expression was tense, but not so much as the last time he broached this subject. "And I don't recognise it either," he told her. "So what if your father was an Albermaine-ish sea captain? So what if he sailed off when the city fell and never came back? I know who you are." His hand covered hers, warm despite the chilly, fish-scented air sweeping off the docks. "And it's more than enough."

Perhaps, Elvine wondered, looking up into his earnest but steady eyes, *a man stands before me, after all.* But, love him as she surely did, it was not the love of a woman for the man she would wed. Patting his hand gently, she disentangled it and stepped back.

She expected hurt, perhaps anger, but Uhttar offered only a rueful smile and a few parting words. "I won't give up," he told her. "You know that. Not until you tell me to."

"Tonight," Elvine said. "You'll be there?"

"I always am." With a short bow, he turned to make his way down the Slipways. Elvine watched him for a short time before proceeding along Harbour Row, pushing away all the distracting thoughts to gird herself for the trials ahead.

* * *

"Why, if it isn't the sweetest, most flaxen-haired maid in all the Fjord Geld. Verily, 'tis as if one of the Seraphile had made themselves flesh just to greet me."

Captain Olfren took Elvine's hand and attempted to press a kiss to it, a task he quickly abandoned at a warning growl from Hemund. The chief dockmaster of Olversahl was rarely verbose. But then, standing several inches taller and wider than most men, with a craggy, expressive face and no gift for artifice, he hardly needed to be. On the infrequent occasions when visiting sailors failed to divine his starkly obvious meaning, the lead-weighted cosh and manacles dangling from his belt provided ample clarification.

"How nice to see you again, Captain." Elvine greeted Olfren with a brisk tone and a smile that possessed a measure of genuine warmth. For all his excessive flattery and patent lust, this one never exceeded his bounds. He also made some effort towards honest dealings whenever his merchantman hove into port, albeit meagre. "Your manifest, if you please?" she added, holding out her hand.

Olfren inclined his head and handed over the required document. "Gladly given, as always."

Another reason she appreciated Olfren's visits was the neatness of his accounting. The varied cargo had been listed on the manifest in precise columns in well-rendered Alberic, albeit with a few dots of spattered ink and an occasional crossing out or two.

"Ten casks of rum taken on board in Yarnsahl," Elvine observed. "Since changed to only eight, I see."

"Took on a new hand in the southern seas," Olfren said. "A man of extensive experience and a fine way with knots. Also, it transpired, the worst drunkard I've ever encountered. Emptied two full casks before we noticed the theft. Flogged the villain myself and booted him off in Highsahl."

Elvine felt it more likely that the two casks had been distilled into bottles and secreted about the vessel in various cunningly constructed hiding places. Once the formalities had been agreed and she and Hemund went on their way, said bottles would be spirited ashore, free of the required duties, for supply to various taverns. Glancing at the dockmaster, she divined he had come to much the same conclusion. But searching so substantial a vessel would be a protracted business, expensive too, since Hemund would have to hire in a few extra hands. All this was known to Captain Olfren, of course. He had also surely been aware that Elvine's scrupulous eye would spot the reduced number of casks. Undoubtedly, there was more contraband aboard. Sleep weed, stolen jewels and sundry ornaments fenced from bandits across the southern seas, but all too well concealed to be worth Hemund's time to dig out, especially when a more economical solution was at hand.

"Submission of an incorrect manifest demands a fine," Hemund stated in his perennial growl. "Ten clips of silver or equivalent in coin."

Olfren's bright, amiable countenance dimmed considerably. The scale of the fine was exorbitant, extortionate in truth, but he knew this port and its dockmaster well enough to confine his protest to a frowning mutter. "Wasn't like this when the Algathinets still held the Fjord Geld."

"No," Hemund said, the shift of his beard indicating the smile beneath. "But they got their foreign arses kicked out, didn't they? Now pay up or we can settle matters by act of law." He jangled the manacles on his belt for emphasis. "Sister Queens' law, that is."

Olfren paid, as Elvine knew he would, and she spent the next hour tallying the cargo as it was ported from ship to shore. At their first meeting the previous summer, the captain had been one of many to make allusions to the value of a less than keen eye when it came to the performance of her duties. She responded to all such attempts at bribery with the simple expedient of forcing the captain, and his entire crew, to turn out their pockets and purses for inspection. Whatever her feelings regarding Ascarlian rule of this port, she performed her role as the dockmaster's excise agent with diligence and honesty. Such dedication wasn't entirely due to the sense of civic obligation her mother had instilled in Elvine from an early age. An excise agent was a servant of the Sister Queens, and as such, enjoyed a useful degree of trust and protection in a city where loyalty remained an unresolved question for many.

The day proceeded along its routine course until the evening tide brought a novel sight. Having overseen the unloading of four merchant vessels, and recorded payment of duties and inevitable fines, Elvine retired to her customary perch atop the stout beacon tower at the end of the harbour mole. Few ships arrived when the sky began to darken, preferring to anchor offshore rather than risk the shifting currents of the fjord. It was her habit to sit here once the beacon had been lit and transcribe the day's dealings into Hemund's principal ledger. The dockmaster had an official residence but Elvine disliked the cramped mustiness of the vaults where the voluminous documents of her trade were stored. Besides, she always took pleasure in watching Olversahl's transition from day to night. There was a simple aesthetic satisfaction in the way the glow of candle and lamp crept from window to window and the stevedores on the wharf lit the long line of oil-doused torches. Reflected by the churning fjord waters, the city's lights became an abstract but fascinating melange, a spectacle that would become something magical in later months when Nerlfeya's Lantern blazed emerald glory across the sky.

She was wistfully contemplating the darkened cloudscape above the mountains, imagining the celestial illuminations to come, when the corner of her eye caught the arrival of another sail amongst the dozen or so anchored to await the morn. It was the size of it that captured her attention, bigger than a typical merchantman, but also flying from a single mast. Looking closer, she saw the unmistakable lines of a longship, but not one of the twenty-foot trading craft from the Skar Geld that were such a common sight in Olversahl. This was the far larger, more high-sided silhouette of a warship.

Elvine stood, a hard knot forming in her stomach. This ship could be from anywhere in Ascarlia, drawn here by all manner of business. Many a warship also worked the trade routes. Why assume this one was here for another purpose? But still, its appearance now, tonight of all nights, was inarguably troubling.

Quickly gathering her things into her satchel, Elvine set off along the mole, forcing herself to walk rather than run.

* * *

"Waste of good food is an insult to the Altvar," her mother reminded her over supper as Elvine sat contemplating a mostly untouched plate of fish stew. "Eat up or there'll be no sweet dumpling for you." Berrine smiled as she said this, a regular warning throughout Elvine's childhood that had become a joke in later years.

"Nyhlssa baked cakes for the midday meal," she said, referring to Hemund's wife. "Insisted I have more than my share. She always says I'm too thin."

"Tell her it's a family trait. Your grandmother wore the same dress to her funeral that she wore to her wedding." Another old joke and Elvine forced a smile through the haze of preoccupation. *Just another ship*, she told herself, the large sail looming in her mind. If only she could have made out the sigil.

"We have two choices tonight," Berrine said when the accoutrements of supper had been cleared from the table. "An all new Alberic translation of 'The Saga of Gythrum Fihrskard'. Or . . ." She placed a freshly bound book on the table before, smiling in anticipation, producing a thick bundle of documents from behind her back. "Some recently arrived letters from the Pretender's War and the Martyr Queen's Reign. There's one in here that actually purports to bear her signature."

It was their nightly habit to either read to each other in Alberic, often taking delighted amusement in the mistranslations and clumsy phrasing of Berrine's fellow scholars at the Archive, or set about cataloguing some of the documents sold to her by foreign traders. The latter were always Elvine's favourites, having long nurtured a fascination with the history of Ascarlia's southern neighbour, especially the notoriously chaotic period that had come to a bloody finale with the death of the dread Martyr Queen Evadyn Speldkrayl, the Blackheart. The supposedly insane, and also supposedly divine, self-proclaimed queen of Albermaine was a particularly keen subject of study for Elvine. Although, her interest didn't arise entirely from scholarly curiosity.

"I can't tonight," she told Berrine, wincing in apology. "Uhttar's letter still isn't done."

"That boy . . ." Her mother's hands formed fists on the table, a familiar scowl drawing her features tight. When they were children, and Uhttar a more welcome presence in this house, the scowl had betrayed more irritation than anger. These days, however, it was usually far richer in the latter than the former.

"It's important, Mother," Elvine said. "He was cruelly cheated. You know that . . ."

"Yes, I do know that. I also know that of all the clever and educated young men in this city, you choose to expend your time on a barely literate apprentice boat scraper, from a family of old loyalist Covenanters no less."

"His Uncle Bahn is the only true family he has now, which you also know. And when he has his rightful due, he may have enough to start his own yard one day . . ."

"Oh, prospects, is it?" Berrine's scowl shifted into narrow calculation. "I trust you haven't encouraged any foolish hopes on his part, daughter of mine?"

"Of course not!" Elvine instantly regretted the retort upon seeing how it stung Berrine. Their life together was not free of argument, but harshly spoken words and outright anger were a rarity. Still, she wasn't so sorry as to prevent her wordlessly reaching for her heavy woollen jacket. Talk of Uhttar's intentions, frustrated though they were, chafed on already raw nerves. Her glimpse of the warship waiting offshore had made her ponder the wisdom of attending tonight's event, but now she pushed such doubts aside.

"Be back before the midnight bell!" Berrine called after her as Elvine departed the house, forcing herself not to slam the door.

Bahn greeted her at the entrance to his shearing shed. Sag-roofed and long out of use, it was one of their less regularly used meeting places and therefore a sound choice for tonight's occasion.

"You're almost late," Bahn said, pushing the doors aside a fraction to allow her to enter. "Not like you, Elvie. My nephew was getting a little fretful at your absence."

Elvine hesitated before entering the dimly lit interior, glancing over her shoulder as she had done many times during her journey tonight. Once again she saw nothing of concern, just the wide streets, barns and fenced yards of Olversahl's northern district where rearing and butchery of livestock formed the principal trade.

"Something wrong?" Bahn enquired. He was a large man, not so large as Hemund, but still an imposing figure. The patch over his right eye and the mostly missing left ear, legacies of the night Olversahl fell to the Sister Queens, gave his appearance a threatening edge, even though he had never been a warrior.

"I saw a warship at the docks," she said, keeping her voice low. On the way here she had debated whether to tell him, ultimately deciding prudence demanded honesty.

"Vellihr's sigil on the sail?" Bahn asked. Like her, his gaze switched to the nearby streets, hand straying to the knife at his belt.

"I didn't see," she said. "And it was anchored in the fjord, waiting for the morning tide. Could be nothing."

"And probably is." Bahn's beard parted in a smile. "Still, better that you told me. If they're still at anchor, whoever they are, they'll be no threat tonight. Our visitor will be well on his way before dawn's first glimmer. Come on." He opened the doors wider still. "We're about to start."

Inside, she exchanged nods with the others, seeing many of the usual faces. However, the size of the congregation was twice that of the previous week. Evidently, those usually too fearful or far removed from Olversahl for regular attendance felt an obligation to be here tonight.

"You all right?" Uhttar asked in a whisper as she made her way to occupy the empty portion of bench at his side.

Still taut with nerves and the lingering stain of cross words with her mother, she confined her response to a half-smile. Harryk, seated to Uhttar's right, leaned forward to offer Elvine one of his signature gurning faces, cheeks drawn in, eyes crossed and lips pouting. Usually, his antics provoked her to laughter, but tonight all she could do was broaden her smile a little. Dehny's greeting consisted of a short, distracted raise of her hand before she returned her attention to the alcove at the rear of the shed. Always prim and straight-backed at these meetings, tonight Dehny's willowy form was especially stiff, although her features were lit with a serene expectation. The most devout of this group, clearly eager for the sermon their visitor would offer this night.

Leaning across Uhttar, Elvine whispered to Dehny. "Senhild's sick? Did you see her?"

Dehny maintained the same poise, her eyes flicking to the boys. "Silfaer's curse," she said shortly.

"Again?" Elvine gave a disparaging huff. Most women could expect the cramp-inducing touch of Silfaer's unseen hand but once a month. Senhild, however, was unique in suffering the goddess's attentions weeks in a row, typically when presented with something she didn't want to do.

"She's delicate," Dehny replied with a defensive sniff. "As you'd know if you ever spared time for a visit more than once a month." Senhild and Dehny had been neighbours from birth and their closeness was more like sisters than friends. "Shush now," she said as Bahn made his way to the rear of the shed. "It's starting."

A hush settled over the assembly when Bahn stood before the table that had been placed in the alcove, two candles flickering atop it. "How gratifying it is to see you all here for Supplications, my friends," he said. "Though it would have been nice if so many had also turned up last week." He paused to allow the ripple of laughter to run through the congregation. There was no real chastisement in his words. He, more than any of them, understood the risks inherent in this gathering.

"I know you are all keen to express your appreciation for our visitor's presence," Bahn went on, "but would ask that you refrain from applause or acclaim, for very obvious reasons." Smiling, Bahn turned and raised a hand to the shadows beyond the candlelit table. "Supplicant, we await your word."

The man who stepped from the gloom was of slight build, his face hidden within the confines of a hooded cloak. Upon drawing it back, Elvine was struck by the ordinariness of his features. It was the countenance of a man of middle years, notable mainly for the absence of a beard and the prominent cheekbones and weathering of one who spent his life travelling. At first, she found his expression stern, even judgemental in the way he surveyed his audience, but the impression faded at the smile that spread across his lips. Elvine had an uncanny facility for spotting artifice and saw none in that smile, only welcome and compassion. Her fears dimmed at the sight, then fled completely when the Supplicant began to speak.

"I shall address you, friends, in my own tongue," he said in Alberic. "For, whilst I can converse in Ascarlian, I would not wish to offend your ears with my accent, which, I'm assured, rather resembles a strangled seal."

A thrum of surprised mirth greeted this; they hadn't expected humour from this man, only the faithful invective they hungered for.

"I am also bound by the danger we share not to impart my true name," the Supplicant went on, his smile shifting into a regretful frown. "So I shall introduce myself by the name given unto me by the Luminants Council when they sent me forth as missionary of the Covenant of Martyrs. I will therefore be known to you as Supplicant Truth, for that is the Covenant's gift to you. It was Martyr Sihlda Doisselle herself who said this of truth: 'It is as malleable as clay for the faithless, but hard and unyielding as stone for the faithful.' And it will be my honour on this day of Supplication to impart to you a sermon drawn from that most holy source."

As he spoke on, Elvine recognised his sermon as the third chapter of the Testament of Martyr Sihlda, the most recent Martyr Scroll in the Covenant's canon of scripture. She had heard how missionary Supplicants were capable of remarkable feats of memory, it being far too dangerous for them to travel in possession of books. However, the unerringly precise rendition provided by Supplicant Truth told of a facility for recall that might even put her mother to shame. Nor was this just a rote recitation, for the Supplicant spoke with passion.

"'Look not outward for validation of your faith,'" he said, his gaze seeming to capture them all at once, his tone beseeching rather than hectoring. "'Instead look inwards. Into your heart, into your soul. Search the long winding road of your life not just for joy or triumph, but also failure and shame. For it is in these hidden corners of ourselves that we find truth, that most precious gift of the Seraphile and their Martyred servants upon earth.'"

Although Elvine had been a regular attendee at these hidden services since her fourteenth birthday, it was rare for her to be swept along by the rhetoric of the speaker. This was due to the fact that most sermons were delivered by members of the congregation or, on occasion, a visitor from another hidden gathering in the Fjord Geld. Ardently faithful to a soul, they were also invariably lacking in inspirational oratory. Her connection to the Covenant had been born from the written word rather than the spoken, her faith arising from guilty study of texts her mother provided as evidence of the foreign faith's idiocy. Berrine had ever been steadfast in her devotion to the Altvar, and Elvine sensed her mother's disappointment that her daughter's faith burned less brightly. However, she couldn't deny the lure of the Covenant and its many Martyrs. It all just made so much more sense than interminable quests and wars of gods and semi-gods, surely mere legend elevated by the passage of time to an absurd level of reverence. Or perhaps it arose from the blood of her vanished father, but Elvine doubted it. It seemed unlikely that a man who would abandon his pregnant lover during a dire crisis would have harboured much faith of any kind.

Tonight, however, Elvine found herself swept up in the words spoken by Supplicant Truth, her heart swelling and tears brimming her eyes. Murmured agreements to his statements came to her lips, as they did to the lips of her fellow congregants. She was unaware of the increasing and unwise volume of their acclaim, but fear was a faraway thing now. Now, there was only the word of Supplicant Truth, it filled her, made her weep and laugh with joy.

"I'm sure the fate of Martyr Sihlda Doisselle is known to all here," the missionary said, a tone of finality colouring his voice as he raised his hands to calm their joyous outpouring. "It was not glorious. It was ugly, for death is always ugly. For years, her body lay under earth and stones until the Covenant was finally able to claim it. Her bones now adorn shrines the length and breadth of Albermaine, and beyond. Some will bow to these relics and beseech her for healing, or fortune, as is their wont, which I will not decry. But, whenever I kneel before the bones of Martyr Sihlda, I offer only thanks. For she gave us so much to be thankful f—"

The whoosh of something heavy parting the air caused Elvine to duck, feeling her hair flicked by whatever passed within an inch of her scalp. Instinctively, her eyes tracked the swift, whirling object as it struck Supplicant Truth full in the chest. He staggered back, gaping at the axe buried in his flesh. Frozen in shock, Elvine noted how the mortally stricken cleric exhibited no serene acceptance or defiant resolution. His face was simply the bleached, terrified visage of a man facing gruesome death. As there had been no glory in Martyr Sihlda's end, nor was there any in his.

Screams erupted as the Supplicant collapsed, overturning the table and candles to scatter chaotic shadows about the interior of the shed. The congregants rose into panicked flight, surging towards the doors only to halt at what they saw framed in the opening.

A tall man clad in a long sharkskin coat, worn over ringed mail, straightened from throwing the axe to regard them with small, dark eyes set in a narrow, cadaverous face. His beardless features were mostly expressionless, save for a disgusted curl to his thin lips. Behind him stood a group of warriors, swords bared and faces grim. However, Elvine found herself unable to look away from one detail. Gleaming bright on the dark grey of the narrow-faced man's coat, the brooch of a Vellihr of the Sister Queens.

As her gaze shifted back to his face, she realised he was returning her scrutiny in equal measure, his small eyes widening fractionally in recognition. "That one," he rasped in a voice that sounded like gravel scraping on a shovel blade, raising his hand to point a long finger directly at Elvine. "Spare her. Should the rest of this Altvar-hating filth resist, kill them all."

CHAPTER FIVE

Ruhlin

He knew he was dreaming, but the knowledge didn't wake him, for which he was grateful. The sky was an unnatural shade of red and he felt no chill despite the wind stirring the reeds. He stood on the bank of the river mouth north of Buhl Hardta, playing the coiled bait lines through his hands whilst Irhkyn worked his way along the boards they placed on the wet sands at low tide. The *mahkla* moved with deft, economic swiftness as he fixed the lines to the poles where they would await the influx of salmon come the sea's rise.

"Why won't you teach me?" Ruhlin asked, a peevish note to his voice that stirred the knowledge that this dream was crafted from memory.

"You know why," Irhkyn grunted back. "Your father said fighting was not for you. And swords are for fighting."

"Yet he wielded one. In battles far and wide, you said. Why deny me what brought him glory?"

A very rare laugh escaped Irhkyn's lips in a harsh bark. "Glory, eh? You ever wonder why it was me that told you stories about his battles, boy? Why he never spoke a word of it, to you or anyone else?"

"He was quiet by nature, like me."

"No. He was clever by nature, and quiet because he knew the world tends to detest the clever. Whereas you . . ." he paused to jerk the line harder, scraping it through Ruhlin's fingers ". . . are quiet because your cleverness makes you think too much. Something else Ausluf was guilty of, though not so much as you." His brow creased in a frown, a distance creeping into his gaze. "No, he said nothing of his battles because he didn't relish the memories. Some men just take no joy in fighting, even when they're good at it, as he surely was. The blood we spilled, the lives we took, it all played on his mind."

"That's why you won't teach me the sword? You fear battle will disturb my mind like it did his?"

"No. I won't teach you because I swore to him that, should he depart for the Halls of Aevnir before his time, I would follow his example in rearing his cub. Battle is not for you, Ruhlin."

"Why? Am I not an Ascarl? Are we not warriors all, as decreed by Ulthnir?"

Irhkyn fell silent then, a certain puzzlement colouring the gaze he settled upon Ruhlin's face. "You really don't remember, do you?"

"Remember what?"

"That day your mother passed. The day with the dog."

"Dog? What dog?"

A sudden darkness overtook the sky then, thick enough to cover the sun completely and shroud Irhkyn's features in darkness. The wind grew harsher, churning the shallows around them, raising them up.

"What dog?" Ruhlin persisted, but Irhkyn gave no response, continuing to stand in shadowed stillness. A fearsome gust raised a whirling spout of water, the twisting column of spume hurtling towards Ruhlin as he continued to demand an answer. He gasped in shock as it reached him, the icy chill on his skin and the brine invading his mouth and nostrils, sending a sharp ache through his head. When it faded, Irhkyn, the river, the sky, were all gone, and he beheld dark timbers, wet with the moisture dripping from his soaked hair.

"*Vayk ip, ir doc!*" a grating, angry voice barked. Ruhlin shrank from it, trying to raise his hands to cover his head in anticipation of a blow, but finding them constrained. Blinking the water away, he saw that both his wrists were encased in thick iron manacles, each affixed to sturdy brackets bolted into the wooden floor. The chains were short, preventing him from standing, so he was forced to kneel, raising his head when the grating voice yapped out more unknowable babble.

His eyes tracked across the dark metal bars of a cage until they focused on the red-tattooed face beyond. A single glance was enough for Ruhlin to judge it as the sharp-featured, pinched visage of a man for whom cruelty and anger were constant companions. From the way his lips twisted around the words he spoke, Ruhlin concluded he was being subjected to an insult of some sort. The thought of spitting back his own diatribe of defiant profanity flitted through his mind, but the urge slipped away quickly. With the shock of his awakening subsiding, a terrible weariness seeped into Ruhlin, from his aching head to the protesting muscles of his back and legs. His body felt stretched and strained in ways it never had before, leaving little energy for more than a groan when he sagged, falling onto his forearms, the manacles digging into his skin.

The sharp-faced man grunted, either in satisfaction or disgust, and Ruhlin heard the clatter of wood on wood. "*Eht!*" the voice barked. "*Eht liek de doc irh arr!*" This was followed by a short laugh and the stomp of boots on the decking. Nostrils twitched by the scent of food, Ruhlin looked up to see a bowl of what appeared to be stew resting a few inches from his face. The sluggish slosh of the bowl's contents, and the incremental sway of the boards he crouched on, brought the realisation that he was aboard a ship at sea. Craning his neck, he beheld only a depthless shadow beyond the bars. However, from the absence of sound, he concluded that the man with the red tattoos had gone.

Returning his attention to the bowl, the roil in Ruhlin's belly revealed a painful hunger. He reached for the bowl, only to be stopped short by the chains. After several attempts to bring the bowl closer, Ruhlin realised his only option was to lean forward and dip his face into it. The stew was a cold melange of bony fish and greasy water, all of which Ruhlin gobbled down with wolfish enthusiasm.

Not a wolf, he thought as his tongue scraped the last dregs from the bowl. *A dog.* The notion brought two thoughts to mind with near simultaneous urgency. The first was his parting question in the dream, the question Irhkyn wouldn't answer: *What dog?* The second was the fact that he had partially understood the sharp-faced man's insult. What had been gibberish to his ear, he now discerned as a heavily accented form of Ascarlian: *Eht liek de doc irh arr!*

"Eat, like the dog you are," he muttered aloud. Were his captors not then foreigners? But how could they be anything else?

"You noticed too, then?"

Ruhlin jerked at the sound of a fresh voice, one lacking the near-unintelligible coarseness of the sharp-faced man and the warriors he had encountered at Buhl Hardta. Ugly recollection crowded in then, making him clamp his eyes shut against the tide of horror. *Irhkyn coughing blood on the sands. Bredda lying dead in her garden. The iron helm crushed between hands that were his but not his, along with the skull beneath . . .*

"You must be very dangerous," the voice interrupted his slide into dark remembrance, snapping his gaze to the source. At first he saw a pair of eyes glinting between the bars to his right, green eyes, the whites tinged with red. They blinked, and a face resolved out of the gloom. A girl about his own age. Her small, freckled faced was marred with bruises and he realised the redness of her eyes to be the result of weeping. However, her expression was strange in its calmness as she angled her head to study him. "They didn't bother chaining me," she added, raising her unfettered hands to clasp the bars that separated them.

For an instant, Ruhlin could only gape at her. Then, feeling grease dribble down his chin, experienced a welling of shame at his bestial appearance and the manner of his feeding. He wanted very badly to wipe his face, but the chains wouldn't allow it. Instead, he contented himself with looking away from her, licking the worst of it from around his mouth before rubbing his face on his shoulder.

"Where're you from?" the girl asked as he went about his clumsy ablutions.

"Buhl Hardta," Ruhlin replied. "It's the largest village on Ayl-Ah-Lyhsswahl—"

"I know where it is," she cut in. "My father and mother went there many times, though I never did. Cold and barren, they said it was. And misnamed too, for they never saw a white whale when they visited."

"Then they were mostly right." Ruhlin drew his legs beneath him and sat back, finding it the most comfortable position permitted by his confinement, at least for now. "Though it could be warm, in places. As for the white whales, you see them when the seasons are right, and then only from a distance. It's not wise to get too close."

He turned to the girl, his eyes having accustomed sufficiently to the gloom to allow him a better view of her. Unlike him, she had been granted clothing, a deerskin shift too large for her slender form. He decided his first guess at her age had been off; she was at least two years his junior.

"Ruhlin," he said by way of introduction.

"Mehlga," she replied. "From Ayl-Ah-Rahk."

The Crow Isle. A place he had never been, but Irhkyn had, so Ruhlin knew it to be larger and more populous than his own. "Your home was attacked too?" he asked, quickly recognising it as a superfluous question, since how else would she come to be here?

"Yes," Mehlga replied in a curiously matter-of-fact tone. "They killed everyone but me. I'm still not sure why. Do you know why you were spared?"

The woman at the harbour. The sharp pain of the dart in his mouth . . .

Steeling himself against the flood of unwanted images, Ruhlin shook his head, grating out, "No."

Mehlga frowned, tilting her head again as she looked closer at his manacles. "They chained you, but not me. Why would they do that?"

The warrior's gibbering terror as Ruhlin snapped the bones of his limbs. The screams when the fire claimed him . . .

"I don't know." Closing his eyes, Ruhlin let out a weary sigh. "I don't know anything."

"You knew enough to make out their speech," Mehlga pointed out. "As did I. It's our tongue, but not. Mangled, you might say. Listen close enough and you can understand it well enough. It only took me a day to realise, but I've always been clever. Mama said so. It seems you are too, Ruhlin of Ayl-Ah-Lyhsswahl. Perhaps that's why we were spared."

"Perhaps," he said, although he doubted her reasoning. He recalled the woman from the harbour again, the word she had spoken as she watched him slip into unconsciousness. "Have you ever heard of the *Uhltvar*?" he asked Mehlga.

The question brought a frown to her small brow, and a narrowing of her green eyes. "Tales told on feast nights," she said. "Old tales of the Age of Kings. The war against the murderous cult of the Volkrath, those who imagined themselves the Uhltvar reborn."

Ruhlin grimaced, trying to fight through the lingering ache in his head to rummage through his memory. "The word goes back further than that. All the way to the forging of the earth. The Uhltvar were the first race of men, sired by the Worldsmith himself. Builders of the Vaults of the Altvar."

"Just more old legends." A scornful note crept into Mehlga's voice, though when he opened his eyes to regard her once more, she had rested her head against the bars, a faint smile playing on her lips. "Ascarls have sought the Vaults for centuries, never finding them. My father said those who went off in search of the Vaults and their fabled hoard of treasure were lost to the fool's quest . . ."

Her words were swallowed by the sound of feet descending steps somewhere in the gloom beyond their cages. There came a short silence, broken by the striking of a flint before a lantern flared into life and the tread of boots resumed. Ruhlin's aching head pulsed with renewed anger as the light approached, though he forced himself to blink through the glare. Looking up at the face of the tall figure who halted outside his cage, he shuddered through a spasm of fear and mounting fury as he recognised the woman from the harbour.

"*Vehl*," she said, smiling with a warmth that Ruhlin found both disturbing and aggravating, "*theh's eh ferss glaar.*"

Well, Ruhlin translated silently. *There's a fierce glare.*

The woman crouched, holding the lantern closer to play the light over him, eyes tracking over his chest, arms and legs in a manner that reminded him of his nakedness. "*Neht eh scritsch*," she murmured. *Not a scratch.* "*Yu truhly eir eh prayz.*" *You truly are a prize.* She said something more, spoken too rapidly and her accent too thick for him to decipher. However, his momentary frown of concentration evidently caught her notice.

"*Eiy zee yu*," she grunted, shifting closer. *I see you.* Ruhlin was annoyed by his own fascination with her features, the way the crimson spirals of her tattoos arced over the smooth planes of her face, accentuating rather than marring the undeniable beauty. "*Ent yu hier meh, eh?*" she asked with a broadening grin that revealed very white teeth. *And you hear me, eh?*

He said nothing, averting his eyes from the lure of her face. "Hah!" she laughed, a short bark of satisfaction. When she spoke again, however, the humour had faded, and he found he could discern her meaning with ease: "You will speak to me, boy, or I'll take a whip to that little bitch in the next cage. Perhaps you would like that? Does the prospect of seeing blood upon her flesh stir your true spirit to life?"

Ruhlin's chains drew tight as he lunged at the bars, a wordless snarl of frustrated rage sending spit onto this woman's irksomely pleasing countenance.

"Not that then," she said, a rueful arch to her brows as she wiped the speckled moisture away. "What will do it, I wonder?" This was asked in a reflective murmur, her gaze tracking over him once again with an air of critical study. *Like a butcher with a fresh carcass*, Ruhlin decided, still straining against his chains. The links ground and squealed, but neither they nor the brackets they were affixed to showed any signs of giving. Frustration fed his anger, lighting a fire in his chest. His pulse began to pound, and a haze darkened the edges of his vision. The sensation was sickening in its familiarity, summoning yet more memories of his rampage through the village. *The sound the axe stave made when he forced down the warrior's throat . . .*

His anger shrank, withering inside him amidst a welter of fear. The chains slackened as he subsided into slumped kneeling. His breaths came in ragged draws as a slick of sweat bathed his naked form from head to toe.

"It's in you, boy," the woman told him. "It always has been."

Raising his head, Ruhlin saw her face had taken on a grave aspect, her gaze serious and lacking any artifice or taunting glimmer.

"Who are you?" he asked with a tired groan. "Why have you done this?"

"You think me a captor?" The woman gave a marginal shake of her head. "No, I am your liberator. Hers too." She jerked her chin at Mehlga's cage, Ruhlin glancing over to see the girl had shrunk into the shadows. "But liberation requires a price, boy. One I hope you can pay. Otherwise ..." She rose, looking down at him with a surprising cast to her features. It wasn't so much apologetic as resigned. "This enterprise will have been a very expensive waste of my time."

She turned and strode away, the lantern's glow receding, then snuffing out, leaving him in shadow.

"You heard all that?" he asked Mehlga, but the glimmer of her eyes was gone now, nor did she consent to reply. Instead, the only answer was a soft, piteous weeping that would follow him into the dark when sleep finally claimed him.

She had stopped crying by the time he woke. This time, his slumber had been the absolute void born of exhaustion that kept all dreams at bay. As he lay with his face pressed against the deck, the lack of any lingering nightmares brought to mind his dream from the day before, and the unanswered question: *What dog?*

Another bowl of cold stew sat near his head, raw hunger drawing him to it with irresistible force. As he ate, the question continued to plague him. Quite why he couldn't yet fathom, but his preoccupation was buttressed by the return of the treacherous, whispering truth-speaker that had taunted him for his cowardice in Buhl Hardta. *You don't want to know*, it hissed. *Bury it deep. Cover it over. Forget it. Knowing will only bring pain ...*

"What dog?" His defiant grunt scattered a portion of the thin stew from the bowl. "We never had a dog."

It was unusual for the denizens of the outer isles to keep pets. Crofters on the larger islands kept sheepdogs, but providing home, hearth and food to an animal merely for the sake of companionship was an amusement indulged by only the few who could claim to be wealthy. Dagvyn had a cat, a vicious beast that hunted out the mice from under his sheds, but they too were a rare sight upon White Whale Island.

The day of your mother's passing, Irhkyn had said. *You really don't remember, do you?*

Knowing will only bring pain, the whispering traitor chimed in again and this time Ruhlin heard a shrill note in its warning. It appeared some part of him, the craven seed lurking in the shadowed corners of his soul, feared what might be uncovered if he continued to probe this mystery. Ignoring it, he cast his mind back to the day his mother died.

It remained dim, a jumble of vague images captured by his seven-year-old eyes. What he recalled of his mother focused mainly on the kindness of her smile, the feel of her fingers stroking through his hair, the softness of her voice singing him to sleep. Such thoughts darkened as her illness grew, turning her bright, cheerful face into a gaunt, hollow mask, one rarely glimpsed because his father began to keep him from her. Strangely, he had no memory of his father telling him of her death, but he did remember the day they placed her body in the barrow. Guilt coloured the image of the wool-wrapped bundle being carried to the shallow scrape in the dark, peaty earth, because he remembered being more bored than sad. He wanted to cry but couldn't. Instead, he shuffled and squirmed in his grandmother's grip whilst the adults spoke the rites demanded by the Altvar to see a soul safely to the Halls of Aevnir. When it was finally done and they retired to the Veilwald's hall to drink and feast as custom required, he was glad to be released, scampering off to seek amusement on the shore.

There was a narrow inlet a half-mile north of the harbour, visited by the adults only a few times a year to cut the jet they crafted into beads and brooches. However, it held other treasures too. Nestled amongst the stratified rock and kelp-covered boulders, there were strange spiral stones that proved a potent lure to Ruhlin's curious nature. Some were small enough to sit in the palm of his hand, others too large to carry home to join his growing collection. "The frozen worms," his father called them, although their resemblance to any worm Ruhlin had seen was superficial. That they had once been creatures of some kind was obvious to him, frozen in death like his father said, and transformed into stone by means unknown. Others claimed they were the remnants of Ulthnir's initial attempts to forge the world, discarded forms of life judged unworthy of inclusion in the Worldsmith's glorious creation. Even as a boy, it had been Ruhlin's delight to ponder such things as he peered closely at his gathered spirals, fingers exploring every ridge and bump as he imagined what they must have looked like when unfurled and wriggling.

The pickings were poor that day, at least at first. The shore had been subjected to a fierce storm only days before, and the inlet was altered by its pounding. The nooks and alcoves where he usually found the spirals were bare. However, as he clambered down into a newly carved fissure in the rocks, he saw something altogether new. Eyes less attuned to the search for unusual shapes might have missed it, but not Ruhlin's. It sat between two of the lower layers of compressed stone, a long triangular form marked out as a skull by the teeth. And it was big, bigger than him, in fact. This, he discovered as he discerned the curve of a jaw and vacant sockets where ball-sized eyes once rested, had been no worm.

This was all Ruhlin could remember of that day, although he found it puzzling now that he hadn't made any effort to dislodge the skull. Nor had he told his father or any adult of his discovery. He also couldn't recall coming back to the inlet after this. His collection of spiral stones was long forgotten, discarded, he assumed, by his grandmother during one of her visits, when no loose object was safe from her busy hands. But why hadn't he at least tried to take one of the teeth from this wonderfully enticing skull?

The memory grew dim as he attempted to focus on the dark, ancient bone, imagining himself reaching out to dislodge the treasure. But had he done that? Yes. Yes, he must have. Concentrating, Ruhlin forced his imagined younger self to reach for a tooth, the largest one in fact, a curved dagger of a thing requiring both hands to work it free. It was then that he heard the growl . . .

The sudden heave of the deck dragged him from the haze of memory. The ship shifted with such violence it upended his bowl, scattering the half-eaten contents across the floor of his cage. Timbers groaned and nails squealed as the vessel rose then fell, Ruhlin hearing the distant boom of the hull striking water. Above it all, the wavering howl of an angry gale.

"They've sailed into a storm." Mehlga's face appeared between the bars separating their cages, once again composed and lacking the distress so evident in her weeping. "A bad one," she added, eyes rolling to the deck above, where raised voices could be heard.

Ruhlin couldn't fault her judgement. He knew storms, both on shore and at sea. From the pitch of the wind and the increasingly energetic movements of the ship, this was the kind of tempest that would have any sensible fisherman turning for home.

"Perhaps we'll sink," he said, surprised by the fear the notion brought forth. *Would it be so bad?* he wondered. Whatever that woman had in store for him, he doubted he would enjoy it. He had not been spared out of kindness. Drowning was at least an honourable fate.

"No," Mehlga sighed, voice soft with regret. "We won't."

For a time, it appeared her prediction would be proven false. Ruhlin's chains were drawn taut a dozen or more times as the ship ploughed its way through steep seas. He found himself flailing amidst water gushing into the hold from some unseen gap in the upper deck. The torrent waxed and waned with the fury of the storm, never ceasing. Within a few hours, a pool of chilly brine sloshed from one end of the hold to the other. It had the benefit of washing away the spilled stew, but also left him shivering. Throughout it all, Mehlga's face remained a constant, unconcerned presence at the bars. Her words were often drowned by the wind, but he caught snatches now and then.

"Not yet," he heard her say, voice sad and reflective. "We haven't smelled the sulphur yet . . ."

Incredibly, at some point in the midst of the maelstrom, Ruhlin succumbed to sleep, or at least exhaustion. When he woke, it was to the surprising sight of his undone manacles sliding across damp timbers. The voice of the sharp-faced man gabbled something it took Ruhlin's befuddled mind a moment to decipher.

"*Zhee sez uhr nuh drett.*" *She says you're no threat.* Something glimmered through the fog clouding Ruhlin's eyes and the stench of unwashed skin filled his nostrils. Blinking, he beheld the gaoler's visage looming close, and the long knife in his hand. "I'm not so sure," he said, playing the blade's tip over Ruhlin's nose. "So know this, dog, one look from you I don't like and I'll be seeing your guts. And fuck her if she don't like it." This last was delivered in a hushed, furtive whisper that told Ruhlin most of the preceding threat had been empty. This man's fear of the woman was of an even greater pitch than his own.

"Get up," the sharp-faced man growled before moving to unlock Mehlga's cage. "You too, weeper. She wants you both on deck."

After so many hours of forced crouching and kneeling, it took Ruhlin several attempts to stand and several more to walk. His slowness earned some harsh words from his impatient gaoler, but no blows from the whip on his belt. His mistress, apparently, wanted no harm done to her human cargo.

"Here." The sharp-faced man tossed Ruhlin a jerkin and trews, both fashioned from deerskin. He noticed old stains on the garb as he donned it, but at least it held no particular odour beyond a sour mustiness. "Up!" The gaoler jerked his head at the stairs ascending to an open hatchway. Moving to the first step, he saw Mehlga hesitate, her calm demeanour now replaced by the fearful gaze she fixed upon the rectangle of daylight above.

"It's all right," Ruhlin said, taking her hand and leading her forward. "Just a stroll to stretch our legs."

It seemed she hardly heard him, her expression betraying only a twitch in response to the offered comfort. However, she did permit herself to be led up the steps. The perennial ache in Ruhlin's head deepened into outright pain at the chill air and harsh sunlight. After the gloom of the hold, the glare was initially blinding. Eventually, it resolved into the sight of a ship's deck, far broader than he had seen before. Large vessels were not unheard of in the waters around the Outer Isles, but usually amounted only to two or three a year. They were typically the wider beamed longships favoured by traders from the Skar Geld, or sometimes a warship sent north on an errand of the Sister Queens. Ruhlin had once seen a merchantman that had sailed all the way from the southern seas, a three-masted, oarless giant. But even she would seem small next to this. The tallest of its four masts rose above them to a height of fifty feet or more, Ruhlin gazing up the length of the wind swollen sail to make out the sigil he recalled from that morning on the beach. His eyes tracked over the crossed hammer and sword to the curious thorny thicket above, the meaning of which he still couldn't decipher.

"It's a crown," Mehlga said. Turning to her, he found that once again the serenity had returned, and she met his puzzled frown with a smile. "A crown of blades," she added before the gaoler gave an impatient grunt, pointing them towards the tall figure at the ship's prow.

As they approached, the woman turned to cast an appraising look over each of them in turn. "Too thin," she said, glancing at the gaoler. "Double the rations, Uhtgyr. Since we know they're not going to do themselves in." She paused to favour them with a brisk smile. "Else they'd have done it by now, eh?"

Ruhlin heard a taunt in her voice, as if she found their failure to find some means of ending their lives a sign of weakness. His anger flared again, but it was a small thing, a faint, diminished growl compared to the roar it had been in Buhl Hardta. It was also accompanied by a surge of the ache in his head, the pain enough to make him stagger and push a groan from his lips.

"It seems we had the correct dose, at least," the woman observed. Noting the confusion on Ruhlin's face, she laughed. "A little something to flavour your meals," she explained. "Helps to keep that precious blood of yours from boiling. You don't imagine I'd have removed your chains if there was any chance of your true self emerging again, do you?"

"My true self?" Ruhlin asked. His words provoked a narrowing of the woman's eyes that made him realise she had more difficulty parsing his accent than he did hers.

"How can you not know?" she wondered aloud, having discerned his question. "How ignorant your people have become."

Shaking her head, she gestured to the empty sea beyond the prow. "Tell me," she said, this time addressing her words to Mehlga, "what do you see, little one?"

Mehlga's calm remained undisturbed as she cast an incurious glance at the choppy water stretching off to the horizon, silent and serene.

"Nothing of interest?" the woman persisted, stepping closer to Mehlga. "Another storm, perhaps? A marauding pack of white whales keen to rend our hull to splinters?"

Puzzled by her enquiry, Ruhlin looked again at the sea, but could find nothing of note. He had hoped to glimpse a landmass, possibly the familiar outline of an island that would enable him to fix their position. Instead, it was just the dark grey of the middle Sternspeld in late summer.

When Mehlga continued to offer no response, the woman moved closer still, red-spiralled visage darkening as she loomed over the girl. "Speak, little one. Or would you rather Uhtgyr whipped it from you?"

The gaoler unfurled his whip then, the long leather snake sliding over the deck with unmistakable meaning.

"He won't," Mehlga said with a shrug. "And I have no warnings for you, in any case."

The woman's voice became a dangerous hiss. "Then what use are you?"

To Ruhlin's profound surprise, Mehlga laughed, turning to meet her tormentor's eye. Her mirth sounded genuine rather than a calculated insult. It proved disconcerting enough to cause the woman to retreat a step, face twitching.

"To you," Mehlga said when her laughter faded, "I'm of no use at all." Turning to Ruhlin, her humour faded into a grim smile. "But I think I might be to him very soon. As for what I see." Her face remained composed and lacking emotion, although Ruhlin discerned a certain anticipatory glimmer as her eyes slid back to the woman. "I doubt you want to know."

"Guard your tongue!" Uhtgyr snarled, stepping towards Mehlga with his whip handle raised. "You will address Aerling Angomar with due respect . . ."

"No!" the woman, Angomar, snapped, halting the gaoler. Taking a breath, she once again moved closer to Mehlga, though not so close as before. "Make clear your meaning," she demanded, and Ruhlin saw genuine fear in the tension of her jaw and thinned lips.

Mehlga afforded her no reply save a faint curling of her lips before returning her attention to Ruhlin. "Can you smell it yet?" she asked, nodding to the horizon.

At first, he just frowned at her in bafflement, but then it reached him: a faint but undeniable acrid tinge to the air. Looking again to the horizon, he made out a dim, wavering glow through the haze. His guts plummeted as their position upon the Styrnspeld Sea became dreadfully clear.

"The Fire Isles," he said, looking to Angomar in the hope she might contradict him. "We are sailing directly towards the Fire Isles."

Her fearful ire dissipated in the face of his alarm, and she laughed. "Of course we are. How else would we get home?"

CHAPTER SIX

Thera

Eshilde groaned in protest as Thera gently shifted to disentangle their entwined thighs. On the other side of the bed, Ragnalt's reaction was confined to a short interruption in his soft but steady snoring. Before rising, Thera paused to allow Eshilde to slip fully back into slumber, watching the slow sway of shadows play over her body as the *Great Wolf* rolled in the swell. The sight stirred a familiar lust but also a tinge of guilt, for it summoned memories of a different form, no less athletic and finely shaped, but always more compelling. She knew this to be misplaced, for she owed Eshilde no more than she gave her, or Ragnalt for that matter. But still, she felt cheapened by the knowledge that, in a heartbeat, she would cast them both from her bed for another, even though that particular possibility remained as remote as the moon.

"Such is the nature of longing," Thera quoted in a bitter sigh, reaching for her clothes. "It doesn't have to make sense to plague you all your days." One of her great-grandfather's sayings, which, like many of his pronouncements, she found held ever more wisdom with each passing year.

Pulling on her trews and blouse, she donned boots and a cloak before drawing aside the waxed leather covering to step from her shelter onto the deck. The sky was dark blue, fading into gold towards the eastern horizon. It was her habit to wake before the rest of the crew, save those who had the last watch. Taking over the tiller and sending them off for a few hours' sleep was her favoured way to greet the dawn, for she found she relished the interval of solitude.

She found Gelmyr at the tiller, his grey beard tousled by the rising wind and shrewd eyes crinkled as they switched continually between waves, sky and sail. His earned name of Johtenvek, the Windcaller, was the product of more years at sea than Thera had drawn breath. She valued the wisdom of a man who had served two Vellihrs in his time, more than any in her *menda*, and not just in matters of sailing. This morning she saw that his attention was not solely on the pitch of the great canvas square billowing from the mast, but on the slender figure standing at the ship's prow.

"She's been there for hours," the *Johten Apt* advised Thera. "Told her to go back to her berth, but she just smiled and kept looking out to sea." She detected something beneath his words besides the usual gruff disdain for anyone lacking his span of years. It was there in the way his gaze darted continually to the maiden and away again, as if fearful of what he might see.

"Has she done anything?" Thera asked.

"No." A defensive curtness coloured the reply, Gelmyr now averting his eyes from the slain Veilwald's daughter.

"But?" Thera prompted.

"Just. . ." The *Johten Apt* grimaced in suppressed chagrin. "Got a feeling, is all. Some folk are not supposed to be carried aboard a ship."

"She's a Vagryd, you mean?" Thera allowed a little mirth into her voice. Despite a lifetime engaged in the most superstitious of trades, Gelmyr remained the most imperturbable sailor she had ever encountered. Allusions to a Vagryd, those named for the luckless hero of an old fable who cursed every ship he sailed on, were not for this man. The *Great Wolf*'s sailing master put his trust in what he could see, smell, and hear, as well he might, for his finely honed senses had saved both their lives more than once. The presence of Lynnea Trahleyl, however, was enough to discomfort even him.

"Didn't say that," he muttered. Sensing unsaid words, Thera lingered in expectation until he consented to speak on. "Orca pack passed by shortly before dawn. Usually, in calmer waters, they might circle a ship for a bit, but on the open sea they'll give us a wide berth. Not this lot. They stayed for near an hour, keeping near the prow. Near *her*."

He jerked his head at Lynnea. "Chirping and clicking away, too. And she wasn't the least bit afeared, I can tell you. They swam off when the Inner Isles hove into view, and she waved as if bidding farewell to old friends." He paused, avoiding Thera's gaze, no doubt in fear of mockery, before repeating, "Some folk are not supposed to be carried aboard a ship."

Rather than indulging in a taunt, Thera merely nodded. She had reasons of her own for finding the girl's presence disquieting, necessity though it was. *Bring me the girl*, Sister Iron had said. Thera had not yet failed the Sister Queen, nor would she now.

"Abide at the tiller a while longer, if you would," she said. Making her way forward, she exchanged nods with the others on deck, noting their evident wariness. Clearly, the orcas' visit had made an impression on the entire watch.

"You should be abed," she said, coming to the maiden's side. Lynnea turned to greet her with a wide smile, revealing the bundle of ragged fur in her arms. In accordance with Thera's injunction, she had left the grey-pelted cat at home only to find a willing replacement in Mohlnir. Typically a sack of mouse-hungry viciousness with a distinct aversion to petting, the beast had sprung into Lynnea's arms the moment she stepped on board the *Great Wolf*. There he had remained ever since, displaying no desire to return to his predatory duties. Seeing Thera, Mohlnir bared his fangs and narrowed his eyes in warning. She hissed in response, causing the cat to burrow deeper into Lynnea's embrace.

"If you'd care to throw that useless little shit in the sea," Thera said, "I shan't complain."

A small scowl of reproach creased Lynnea's forehead as she pressed a kiss to the cat's brow, hands stroking his patchy fur in reassurance.

"First cats—" Thera rested her arms on the rails, watching the young woman's face closely for a reaction "—and now orcas. Is there a beast you can't make friends with?"

Lynnea laughed a little at this, before responding with a shrug. She wore only a light shift and shawl, but didn't appear to feel the cut of the wind. Her hair, unbound save for a poorly tended braid, fluttered in the breeze like a pennant of black silk. Thera found the

sight sufficiently distracting to force her gaze towards the dim silhouette of the island approaching off the starboard bow.

"Ayl-Ah-Kahl," she said. "Home to the barrow of the most famed
Gythrum Fihrskard, and the site of your father's crime."

The maiden's brow furrowed as she set Mohlnir down on the rail,
the cat emitting a mewl of protest. Turning to Thera, Lynnea then
used her hands to describe a triangular shape, forehead creased in a
question. What little communication they had exchanged so far
consisted of such combinations of gesture and expression. Lynnea's
meaning wasn't always clear, so Thera had offered a slate and chalk,
but it appeared Kolsyg Ehflud hadn't troubled himself to teach the
runes to his daughter.

"No, Skar Magnol is still days away," Thera replied. "First, we must
call in here to return what your father stole. I can't compel you to it,
but it would reflect well upon your petition to the Sister Queens if
you were to make atonement for his misdeeds."

The arch of Lynnea's brow increased and, strangely, Thera understood without need of additional gestures, almost as if the maiden
had spoken it aloud: *How?*

"How else?" Thera laughed. "With blood, girl."

Gythrum Fihrskard had been laid to rest upon the deck of a ship set
into the earth atop the highest point on the west-facing coast of
Ayl-Ah-Kahl, the Silver Isle. This inner craggy spine of this narrow
island was home to several mines where a goodly weight of precious
ore was still dug out even now, though less with each year. In ages
past, it was the silver that made Gythrum wealthy, and his domain
the target of numerous raids and potential conquerors. So feud and
battle had been his lot, yet the tale spinners oft spoke of a quiet soul
who preferred a warm hearth and company of family to red slaughter.
As Thera's eyes tracked over the carved granite posterns set around
the long hump of the barrow, one for every chieftain or renowned
warrior claimed by Gythrum's axe, she found reason to doubt the
legends. A man who slew so many, by fair means or foul, could not
have been immune to the lure of combat.

The fabled axe wielder's descendants, over a hundred in number, stood in silent vigil as Lynnea knelt beside the barrow, head lowered. Thurveld, Uhlwald of Ayl-Ah-Kahl and most prominent bearer of Gythrum's blood line, exchanged a brief glance with Thera, standing at the kneeling maiden's side. A tall, quietly spoken man of usually kind aspect, Thurveld made a creditable effort to compose his features into a stern mask of righteous ire as he addressed Lynnea in strident tones: "Who is it who comes seeking our forgiveness in sight of this sacred barrow?"

"Lynnea Trahleyl," Thera said. "Known as the Silentsong, for the Altvar saw fit to take her voice at the moment of birth. So I, Thera Speldrenda, Vellihr of the Sister Queens, will be her voice this day. Although she had no part in her sire's crime, as daughter of the thief, Kolsyg Ehflud, she comes in her family's name to beseech the good folk of this island for forgiveness. Know that she has made no defence of Kolsyg's actions, nor sought to hinder the administering of justice. Even though, as you see—" Thera gestured to the canvas sacks containing the loot stolen from the barrow "—all that was stolen has been returned. The Silentsong still wishes to atone. Will you, as Uhlwald and kin to the Dreadaxe himself, accept her honourable submission to your judgement?"

Although almost all present would know that the outcome of this performance had been pre-agreed, Thurveld still felt obligated to provide a show of grave contemplation. "Kolsyg's crime was great," he mused, stroking his chin, brows creased. "And he spilled blood in its commission. As you know best of all, Vellihr, a blood crime demands a blood price."

"And Lynnea Trahleyl will pay it," Thera confirmed. Drawing a knife from her belt, she took hold of Lynnea's dark mane, now neatly braided and laced with ribbons thanks to an hour of toil by Eshilde. "Her blood she offers, without fear or complaint," Thera went on, drawing Lynnea's head back and setting her knife blade to the pale skin of her throat. From the tension on the girl's face, Thera divined she might not be as fearless as claimed. Not that it mattered.

"Hold your blade, Vellihr!" Thurveld implored, stepping towards her with hand extended. "I beg you. A blood price need not be mortal."

It was Thera's turn to look thoughtful, a task performed with considerably more conviction than Thurveld. Years as a Vellihr had taught her that the role required as much mummery as it did ruthlessness, so she was well practised in performative ritual.

"You are certain in this?" she asked the Uhlwald. "You will forsake your claim on this maiden's life?"

"We of Ayl-Ah-Kahl are not needlessly cruel, that we leave to the likes of Kolsyg Ehflud. And ever do the Altvar look ill upon the killing of the blameless."

"Very well. By your word shall she be spared. However . . ." moving with swift efficiency, Thera snared one of Lynnea's wrists in her free hand and stroked the tip of the knife across her palm ". . . a price in blood must still be paid this day."

The cut was just deep enough to draw blood, and a suitably shocked gasp of pain from Lynnea. Thera had warned her it was coming, but not the exact moment. To her credit, the maiden allowed only a brief spasm of reproach to colour her features before composing her expression into dignified acceptance. After getting to her feet, she moved towards the grass-covered mound of the barrow and raised her bloodied hand to allow red droplets to fall upon the earth.

"Blood has been taken and blood has been given," Thurveld intoned in sombre respect. He and the assembly of Dreadaxe kin all closed their eyes and lowered their heads, maintaining the moment of silent reverence until the Uhlwald straightened, clasping his hands and rubbing them briskly. "Well," he said, "that's enough of that. Let's get this hoard in the earth and have us a feast, shall we?"

As most of the audience drifted away, Thera lingered to oversee the return of the stolen treasure to the barrow, a task performed by her own *menda* rather than left to the locals. Although she didn't doubt their reverence for the grave of their renowned ancestor, the value of this collection would tempt even the most honourable hands.

"I may have exaggerated somewhat," she confided to Thurveld as they watched Eshilde and Ragnalt unfurl the canvas sack containing the stolen coinage and silver. "I can't be certain to have recovered every bit of it. Some of Kolsyg's kin likely kept hold of a coin or an old blade."

"Then," the Uhlwald replied with a shrug, "I pity those thieves the curse that will surely arise from keeping them."

"Curse?" Thera asked. Looting a barrow was a serious crime in the domain of the Sister Queens, one that carried a lasting stigma for only the most vile would deprive a departed soul of the items they needed to navigate their way to the Halls of Aevnir. However, she had rarely heard of those who committed such transgressions earning a curse for their labour.

"It's another old tale about the Dreadaxe," Thurveld said. Thera noted the cautious gaze he afforded the barrow, and the way he shied away from the dark rent in its flank dug by Kolsyg and his *menda* the night of their thievery. "The last tale, in truth. You've heard he was slain by treachery, I assume?"

"So the tale spinners would have it. 'Since no warrior possessed the skill to defeat him, only by betrayal and deceit could he fall.' Or some such."

"Quite so. Some tales have it that it was his brother, Tyhlsic, who poisoned Gythrum's mead out of jealousy for his wealth and renown. Others say it was his wife, Pehlsa, in punishment for the one time he slapped her face years before. But amongst my kin, there is another, darker tale, one rarely told." Thurveld paused, raising a hand to halt Eshilde and Ragnalt as they began to haul another sack to the barrow, this one bulging with the telltale shape of Gythrum's axe. "Hold a moment, if you would."

Stooping to extract the weapon, the Uhlwald held it up so the sunlight caught the runes etched into the metal. "There are none alive today who know the true count of souls fallen to this axe," he said. "Some say dozens, others hundreds. Only Gythrum himself knew the true number, and the tale told by my kin makes plain that it tormented him. He was north of his fiftieth year upon this earth when he died, a veteran of more skirmishes and battles than any warrior who ever lived. His renown was such that none would come against him, even in a land where glory garnered in battle is prized above all else. Such a reputation breeds fear, and fear breeds solitude.

"More and more Gythrum's days were spent alone in his hall,

surrounded by the many treasures and trophies, the tokens of enemies slain. He brooded upon them, reflected on the swords and axes of those fallen to his blade, striving to recall their names and finding he no longer could. And always the number sang in his head, for he had never lost count, or forgotten a face, even though the names often eluded him. In time, solitary brooding inevitably drew him into madness. Gythrum came to believe the weapons of his foes were speaking to him. The souls of their long dead owners trapped in the steel, denied the Halls of Aevnir. Endlessly, they begged their killer for release. 'Only blood can unlock these iron cages,' they implored. 'Free us, oh Dreadaxe. Grant us the Mercy you denied us in life.'

"Long into the lonely, sleepless nights of Gythrum Dreadaxe, they pleaded, stripping away a vestige of his reason with every whispered entreaty. 'Free us. Free us.' Until one night Gythrum's cracked mind could tolerate no more. Taking each sword in turn, he stabbed them into his body, over and over again, staining the steel with the blood they begged for. Then he took up the axes and hacked at his own limbs. When, come the morn, his kin came to his hall, they found him barely living, gasping out a question with his final breath: 'Is it enough? Did I spill enough?'

"And so, if it was treachery that slew the Dreadaxe, it was the treachery of his own madness. Or it was the spirits of those trapped in the steel, for his kin claimed to still hear those voices when they consigned his body and hoard to the barrow. In time, the folk of this isle came to look upon it as cursed, for some were said to have lingered here too long and suffered Gythrum's fate. These days, we come here only when custom demands, and we rarely linger, lest we hear those pleading voices."

Thurveld fell silent, lowering the axe to regard the elegant arc of runes upon its blade. "This, however, was never stained by Gythrum's blood, and so remains un-cursed. Perhaps that's why it's never rusted. Though I prefer to think it was waiting for another worthy hand to wield it." Grasping the axe's haft in both hands, the Uhlwald held it out to Thera. "A gift, willingly offered to the Vellihr of Justice by the grateful kin of Gythrum Fihrskard."

Thera wasn't accustomed to the sensation of shocked surprise, so expended several seconds gaping at the proffered axe before shifting her widened eyes to Thurveld's grave, insistent face. "This . . ." she faltered. "This is too great a gift for any hand, Uhlwald." She shook her head, gently pushing the axe away. "I can't . . ."

She fell silent when another hand reached for hers. Lynnea had tied a bandage around the wound in her palm, though it still leaked a trickle of blood as she gripped Thera's hand and placed it upon the haft of the axe. Meeting her gaze, Thera found the girl's features transformed. The open, perennially cheerful countenance of a curious and kindly soul was gone now, replaced by a hard, serious mask. Once again, Thera discerned her meaning as clear as if she had spoken: *Take it.*

Thera's initial urge was to shove Lynnea away, perhaps with a curt reminder of their respective status. But she didn't. The abrupt change in the maiden's demeanour, and the depth of insistence on her face, made Thera pause. *Take it.* The unheard voice repeated, this time joined by another statement as Lynnea's expression softened. *You will have need of it. Trust me.*

For the first time, Thera gained an insight into why Sister Iron wanted this girl so badly. *There is more here than just an uncanny way with beasts.* "But," Thera went on, turning back to Thurveld, "I cannot insult you or your kin by refusing."

Taking the weapon from his hands, she found it weighed less than when she had held it in Kolsyg's hall. Although she had always preferred lighter weapons, such as her cherished black-headed spear, the axe sat well in her grip and she even began to relish the hours of practice it would take to master it.

"My hall stands ready to welcome you," Thurveld said, casting his arm towards the settlement at the base of the hill. "My wife has even promised to sing, though I trust you won't hold that against us."

Thera gave a dutiful laugh and watched the Uhlwald lead his kin away whilst she lingered to see to the final sealing of Gythrum's barrow. *At least until another mad braggart chooses to raid it*, she thought, recalling the deranged gaze of Kolsyg Ehflud.

"Your father said something," she said to Lynnea. "A word that made me curious. 'Uhltvar'. You know this word?"

The maiden shrugged and moved away towards the edge of the steep drop beyond the barrow. Following her, Thera couldn't help but conclude she knew what a captivating sight she made standing there with the wind pressing her gown to her body, dark hair trailing.

"Sister Iron will be more insistent in her questioning," Thera warned her. "I suggest you find a way to impart what you know."

Lynnea merely smiled, her thoughts again made plain to Thera as she gazed out to sea. *Beautiful.*

"Yes," Thera agreed, her eyes tracking over the gulls wheeling about the rocks closer to shore, then across the crashing waves and out to the sun-kissed waters. "Just so you know, don't expect beauty to be your shield against Sister Iron. She cares nothing for it. Come on." She took hold of Lynnea's hand and led her from the hilltop. "Let's find out if the Uhlwald's wife has improved her singing. When last I visited, she put me in mind of a goose being strangled by a rabid goat."

CHAPTER SEVEN

Felnir

In all Felnir's years, the immense, steep-sided peak of Skar Magnol had always made an early appearance once his ship began to plough the dark currents of the Linsker Fjord. Regardless of season or weather, the great mountain would rise through fog and cloud, as vast and permanent a feature of Ascarlia as the Altvar themselves.

"Hungry to climb the old bitch again, my love?" Sygna asked, joining him at the prow. He would normally have preferred she stay at the tiller when approaching port, but the fjord's currents were kinder than most and young Jolnyr needed the practice.

"Not for all the jewels in the Saluhtan's summer palace," Felnir replied in simple honesty. Climbing Skar Magnol's treacherous slopes alone had been a feat embarked upon in an effort to wipe away the disgrace that would see him exiled. It had failed in that regard, though he had made ample use of the renown it brought since. Over the years, the scale of his achievement had been enhanced by the failure of many to emulate it, often with fatal results. Despite the countless times he had been asked to relate the story of his epic victory over the mountain, Felnir never did, for the memory was dark and best undisturbed. *You weren't really alone up there, were you?* his great-grandfather had enquired once, his voice rich in that infuriating tone, bespeaking a question asked although he already knew the answer.

"Guthnyr wants to try it," Sygna said. "Says he might as well since we're here."

Felnir glanced over his shoulder at his brother, finding Guthnyr engaged in assailing Jolnyr with a barrage of good-natured taunts. To his credit, the youngster afforded Guthnyr little more than an irritated shrug as he concentrated on steering the *Sea Hawk* towards the base of the mountain. "Then be sure to get him drunker than usual tonight," Felnir told her. "Tie him up if you have to. He's just about mad enough to attempt it even when hungover."

"He wants to be like his elder brother," Sygna stated, eyes narrowed in reproach. "Is that so bad?"

"He wants to exceed his elder brother," Felnir corrected. "And one day is like to get himself killed trying to do so."

He settled his gaze on the misted waters shrouding the fjord's narrow terminus, making out the jumbled rooftops and smoking chimneys of the port that took its name from the mountain looming above. Skar Magnol was the only Ascarlian settlement that could match the size and squalor of an Albermaine-ish city. Consequently, Felnir had always hated the place, despite being so frequent a visitor. Although he was aware that there was another reason for his dislike beyond the oppressively odorous cramped maze of street and alley, rarely lit by sun or moon.

"What will you tell him?" Sygna ventured. "About our missing cargo?"

The object of her question didn't need to be named. Even though Skar Magnol was home to the court of the Sister Queens, there was only one soul here that truly mattered to Felnir and the crew of this ship. "This," he said, tapping a finger to the canvas-wrapped sheet of parchment tucked into his belt, "is what matters. The spy was incidental."

"And yet, our instructions were clear: bring him back alive."

Felnir said nothing and Sygna moved closer, her hand clasping his, voice lowered. "Do you seek to test him, my love? I know you had crossed words regarding your brother joining your *menda*, but jabbing at the Tielwald's patience is never wise, regardless of shared blood."

Felnir bit down on an angry snap, annoyed by her inarguably sage insight. Had he killed the knight just to irk his great-grandfather?

He hadn't thought so in the moment. The man was a liar sent by the Dowager Princess to spy upon the Sister Queens. He had probably murdered, or overseen, the murder of the Tielwald's true agent. But was that why Felnir killed him? Or had it been his talk of the Pit Mines? Having been a prisoner once, Felnir knew well the lash, and the hated shame of labour performed under its sting. Despite his protestations of innocence, he knew Vellinde's sort, knew with near certainty that all the allegations against him were true. Not killing such a man would have been more of a trial.

"Trim sail!" Behsla's voice, sharp and clear, calling out the customary commands upon nearing port. "See to your oars, and let's be quick about it."

There was no natural harbour at Skar Magnol. Instead the moorings consisted of a series of jetties poking out from the broad curve of the town's western shoreline like the spokes of a half-wheel. It was ever a busy port, but with the grand annual celebration of the Veltgruhn at hand, most moorages were already crowded with ships large and small. Consequently, the *Sea Hawk*'s crew were obliged to row for the farthest spoke in the wheel. Still, the waters were cramped, and they bumped oars with smaller vessels, entailing the usual exchange of mutual insult and obscene gestures. It was as the crew raised their oars and young Jolnyr hauled the tiller to angle the ship's drift to the jetty, that Sygna nudged Felnir's arm. She said nothing, nodding to the neighbouring pier where a ship even larger than the *Sea Hawk* was busy tying up.

Felnir had no need of the arcane runes carved into her prow to recognise the other vessel. The *Great Wolf* was a legend amongst Ascarlian warships. Her timbers had been hewn from ancient oak decades before and the most skilled wrights had laboured for four seasons to shape her into not only the swiftest of craft but also the strongest, capable of withstanding the worst storms even in deep winter. A ship worthy of the Sister Queens, for only Vellihr were permitted to captain her, an honour these days held by the tall, auburn-haired woman who stood watching the *Sea Hawk* from the bows.

Thera Speldrenda wore a sable-trimmed cloak this day, and the *Sea Hawk* had drawn close enough for Felnir to make out the small twinkle of the Vellihr's brooch glittering amidst the fur. Felnir's jaw ached as he fought to contain the flare of resentment and envy provoked by the sight of that trinket. He took some solace from the certain knowledge that his sister was experiencing a similar welling of emotion due to Sygna's presence at his side. They exchanged no greeting, save for a wordless meeting of eyes, the angular planes of Thera's face betraying no emotion. This was how it was between them, an unseen yet undeniable wall that had existed for so long now Felnir could barely recall a time when things were different, when they were truly brother and sister. For Guthnyr, however, that time persisted.

"Still not dead, then?" he called out, leaping onto the starboard rail with a wave. Whereas Thera had no greeting for Felnir, she had warmth aplenty in the smile she afforded their brother as, without waiting for a reply, Guthnyr dived into the water. He covered the distance to the *Great Wolf* in a few strokes and hauled himself up, the ropes dangling from her stern to come to his sister's side. Felnir turned away from the sight of their laughing embrace.

"If she's here, it means something," Sygna said. "You should be on your guard."

Felnir resisted the urge to pull her close, perhaps press a kiss to her lips. Thera would be sure to see, and he didn't doubt the sight would put a swift end to her laughter. But it would also cheapen him, and Sygna. Their love, despite his sister's claims, was a true and honest thing and he had no desire to besmirch it with petty theatrics. So, he merely nodded and went to oversee the unloading of the wine casks. Besides the canvas-wrapped parchment tucked into his belt, wine was his most precious cargo.

Approaching the end of the jetty, Felnir was dispirited but not surprised to find Coelnyr waiting. A slender, clean-shaven man somewhere north of his thirtieth year, he could easily have passed for a southerner if not for the near-white shade of the hair swept back from his narrow features. His clothing was also more Albermaine-ish than

Ascarlian, a neatly tailored if unadorned doublet and trews fashioned from expensive pale grey cotton. Any impression of wealth his garb might have conveyed was diminished by the thick chain about his neck bearing a medallion crudely stamped with the runes of an indentured servant. By way of greeting, his great-grandfather's *mahkla* afforded Felnir one of his tight, patently insincere smiles.

What did surprise Felnir was the even less welcome sight of Thera standing nearby in evident impatience. Felnir found it noteworthy that she bore a fine, double-bladed battle axe instead of her famed black-headed spear. Also, besides Guthnyr, she had acquired a new companion, one that appeared to have captured most of his brother's interest and Felnir could see why. Black hair and blue eyes were an unusual combination amongst Ascarls. Added to conspicuous come-liness, this made her an irresistible target for Guthnyr's attentions. Not that she appeared to care one whit, ignoring his lingering stare to track her curious gaze over Felnir. He felt a disconcerting weight to that gaze, a knowledge that it drank in every detail of his person.

Another spy? he wondered, but doubted it. His sister had no truck with their great-grandfather's shadowy games, one aspect of her char-acter that garnered his grudging admiration, albeit whilst providing an additional source of envy. She, after all, had the standing to refuse him. He did not.

"You are alone," Coelnyr observed, casting a pointed glance at the empty jetty to Felnir's rear. "Your cargo is still aboard?"

"The Liar's Sea is treacherous," Felnir said, not without a certain relish. Irritating this man was one of his favourite diversions. "The clumsy bastard fell overboard. But the voyage was still a success, as I'll tell my great-grandfather when I see him."

He started forward, intending to make his way into the docks and find a suitable merchant for his wine, then halted when Coelnyr stepped into his path. "The Tielwald will see you now," he said, turning and gesturing to Thera. "Both of you, in fact."

This managed to rouse Guthnyr from his preoccupation with the black-haired maiden, an aggrieved scowl marring his face. "All three of us, I trust you mean," he said in a low mutter.

Guthnyr's anger was famed and rightly feared, but not by Coelnyr. "No," he stated simply, meeting Guthnyr's eye with a cold steadiness. "*You* are not required."

"Guth," Felnir said, halting his brother's forward step. "Kodryn needs help unloading the wine."

Guthnyr's darkened visage swung to Felnir, twitched a little, then reformed into a smile. "I hope," he said, inclining his head at the dark-haired beauty, "to see you at the festivities. Do you dance at all?"

Felnir saw a patient indulgence in the smiling nod the girl provided in response, also a certain sympathy that bordered on pity. His brother had always enjoyed considerable success with women, but her expression told Felnir that this one was so far beyond the reach of Guthnyr's charm she may as well reside amongst the stars. Not that Guthnyr noticed, of course.

"Then I shall greet the dawn with gratitude for the Altvar's favour," he said. Sparing Coelnyr a glance full of dire promise, he strode off along the jetty towards the *Sea Hawk*'s berth.

Where many a man might have quailed at the prospect of Guthnyr's ire, Coelnyr exhibited no concern at all, instead shifting his focus to the blue-eyed maiden. "The Tielwald requested only you and your brother, Vellihr."

"This is Lynnea Trahleyl," Thera replied, the hardness of her tone making it plain that she was no more appreciative of Coelnyr's company than Felnir. "Daughter of Kolsyg Ehflud, justly executed Veilwald of the Skor Geld. She will remain in my care until I deliver her to the presence of Sister Iron. If that is unacceptable, please tell my great-grandfather to stick his request all the way up his ancient arse."

Felnir watched Coelnyr's eyes flick between his sister and her charge, face as inexpressive as ever, although there was surely a good deal of calculation behind it. Guthnyr might not arouse his concern, but Thera was another matter.

Wordlessly, Coelnyr turned away and walked towards the labyrinthine mass of house and alley beyond the docks. Clearly, he expected them to follow. Felnir ventured a raised eyebrow in his sister's direction but, receiving only a glacial blink of her dark eyes in return, sighed and started in the *mahkla*'s wake. Thera and the maiden fell in along-side a few paces on.

For a time they walked in silence, wending their way through the dockside markets. The melange of fish, spices and dung put a sting in Felnir's nose and, although he strove to ignore it, he couldn't help but notice the disparate reactions of the townsfolk they passed. His sister received nods of grave respect from stallholders and customers who hastily cleared her path. Even without her signature weapon, she still enjoyed instant recognition here. But then, so did he, although these folk had no such deference for Felnir Skyrnak, the Redtooth. Instead, all he saw was the fear and suppressed sneers of those too cowardly to voice an insult.

As they reached the quieter, and marginally more fragrant streets beyond the docks, he felt the weight of the maiden's stare once again. Turning, he found her regarding him with head tilted, her unusual eyes narrowed in a manner more disconcerting than it was insulting.

"Commiserations," he said, feeling the need to offer some form of greeting. "For your father. I met him only once, and I was just a boy then. 'Twas the night Olversahl fell to our Queens' glory. They say he fought with great fury."

He heard Thera emit a muted snort at this and knew she had decided not to bother giving voice to her regular taunt on this subject: *Whereas you didn't fight at all.* From his sister, even an unspoken jibe was enough to set Felnir's heart pumping, but he refused to rise to it.

"He was a fine sailor too, by all accounts," he went on, addressing his words to the maiden. "Navigated the farthest passage into the northern ice floes than any other, so they say. A feat equal to the voyages of Kahlvik Grey-eye. A man doesn't earn the name Saltskin without reason." He paused, awaiting some form of polite acknow-ledgement, but Lynnea's response was confined to a cautious curve of her lips whilst the depth of her scrutiny undiminished.

"She doesn't speak," Thera told him, voice flat. "Hence the name."

Silentsong, Felnir thought, offering Lynnea a rueful grin before turning to his sister. "Very nice," he said, gesturing to the axe she carried. "Is it loot or did you actually open your purse for once?"

"This is the weapon of Gythrum Fihrskard," she replied, her tone as uninflected as before. "A gift from his grateful kin. Loot is your province, brother, not mine."

Brother. It had been years since she called him that, but then, it had been years since she called him anything at all. However, any crumb of sentiment he might have drawn from the gesture was smothered by his renewed interest in the weapon she bore. *The dreadaxe itself.* Felnir eyed the engraved double blades with a mingling of greed and shame at his weakness. Like a child, he wanted it because his sister had it. His certainty that this mightiest of gifts had been thrust upon her, rather than requested or demanded, made it all worse. *Always she rouses me to envy without even trying.*

Their great-grandfather's house sat squarely upon the border between the cramped streets of lower Skar Magnol and the wider thoroughfares of the town's upper reaches. Here the homes of merchants and court luminaries rose in tall, rectangular stacks of sloping roofs and narrow chimneys, gaining in height as they ascended the slope to the walls of the Verungyr, the Queens' Holdfast. It appeared a modest castle compared to many fortifications Felnir had seen in Albermaine and the far-flung domains of the Saluhtan of Ishtakar. However, the vast stone face carved into the base of the mountain looming above the stunted towers provided all the majesty demanded of the home of the rulers of Ascarlia.

The grave, bearded visage of Ulthnir the Worldsmith rose to a height of near two hundred feet, gazing down upon the heart of his creation with what Felnir always felt to be an expression of stern disapproval. Those more attuned to worship of the Altvar insisted the army of masons that carved the great edifice had been guided to render the face of the highest of gods as a warning against those who transgressed his laws. Whatever the truth of it, the Worldsmith's inescapable frown of judgement was another good reason to spend no more time in this port than necessary.

The house of Margnus Gruinskard, Tielwald to the Sister Queens, stood three storeys tall, making it tower over the surrounding dwellings. Any sense of noble importance conveyed by such grand proportions was diminished by the structure's decidedly ramshackle appearance. From the sagging, part-rotted shutters on every window to the damp streaks and flaking mortar of the walls, an uneducated eye might take this place for the run-down domicile of a rich man lost to the neglectful indolence of old age. But, as with much that pertained to Felnir's great-grandfather, the overall impression of unkempt decay was a mask, and what lay behind it still far too potent and dangerous to be underestimated.

There were no guards posted here: only a fool would approach the place uninvited. Coelnyr led them to the large oaken door, long since stripped of varnish by the elements, pushing it open and leading them inside without the need to consult a functionary or servant. The interior of the ground floor was a musty, untidy match for the building's exterior, all piled logs and cobwebbed shelves where mostly cracked pots and crockery had sat unused for decades.

"The Tielwald awaits you," Coelnyr said, gesturing to the stairwell at the rear of the room. "She, however," he added, flicking a hand to Lynnea, "must stay here."

"I'm not leaving her with you . . ." Thera began, falling silent when Lynnea touched her arm. Felnir saw something pass between them, a sharing of expressions, the maiden's reassuring but Thera's doubtful. Whatever it meant, it was over in an instant, after which his sister failed to repeat her objections. Smiling, Lynnea turned away and moved to a corner of the room where she crouched, cupping both hands and extending them to the shadows beneath a jumble of broken furniture. A second or two later a small mouse hopped into view, whiskers twitching as it nudged the girl's fingers before jumping nimbly into her palms. Rising, Lynnea afforded the room's human occupants no further heed, her focus entirely on her furry companion. Letting out a grunt of apparent satisfaction, Thera spared Coelnyr a final glare of warning and mounted the stairs.

"If she wasn't clear," Felnir said, pausing at the *mahkla*'s side. "I know your habits. I hear the slightest scuff, I'll be back here in a trice. My sister will beat you half to death, but you know I'll do far worse."

Coelnyr's reaction consisted of a twitch to both eyes and lips, which

Felnir knew amounted to as close an expression of fear as he was ever going to get. This man's mind was ordered differently to most, making him of great use to the Tielwald, but also a considerable danger to others, especially when young and pretty. His excesses were kept in check by two things: a blind and unquestioning obedience to the word of Margnus Gruinskard, and a certainty that any transgression would be severely punished. One of the few amusements Felnir had found in his great-grandfather's service was the opportunity to remind Coelnyr of this fact. Leaving him to his twitching, Felnir followed Thera up the stairs.

The transition from unclean, chilled squalor to elegant warmth and comfort was always jarring, no matter how many times Felnir came here. His great-grandfather's principal living space was a chamber rich in bookshelves, tapestries and paintings, few of which originated in the realm he had sworn to protect. There were some ornamental concessions to Ascarlian culture in the Altvar sigils carved into the beams and, of course, the huge stone-bladed axe that hung over the fireplace mantle. Otherwise, this could well have been the room of an Albermaine-ish scholar.

The Tielwald sat close to the fire in a large chair padded with furs. Myhsta, his oversized, shaggy-haired deerhound, lay at his feet busily chewing a boar bone. During Felnir's boyhood, Margnus Gruinskard had been accompanied everywhere by two wolves, one white, one black. Huge beasts of vicious temperament, some said they must have shared blood with the great wolves of Ascarlia's fabled past. Both had been slain in the Tielwald's famed confrontation with the dread Evadyn Blackheart during the re-conquest of Olversahl, a clash that had also cost him an eye. Roused from apparent torpor by the sound of their boots upon the steps, Margnus blinked his one working orb at them both. Curiously, Felnir always found it easier to read his great-grandfather's moods by focusing on the puckered flesh of his empty eye socket, the movements of which the old man seemed to have no control. Whether Margnus knew of this, Felnir had never asked.

The single eye, dark like those of the siblings it scrutinised, lingered first on Thera before tracking to Felnir. The temper of their relationship was made plain by the fact that none in the room felt obliged to offer a greeting. For the second time today, Felnir felt himself to be studied. But where Lynnea's gaze had been irksome, his great-grandfather's always cut like a knife. It scoured his face before moving to the canvas bundle in his belt. The old man's beard, more white than grey these days, bunched in a manner that Felnir knew betrayed the disapproving curl of the lips beneath. However, when he spoke, it was to Thera rather than Felnir.

"Is that what I think it is?" he enquired, extending a finger to the axe she bore. His voice resembled the wind finding passage through the beams of an aged barn. It was, Felnir fully understood, but a feeble echo of a once mighty roar.

"I assume so." Thera's voice was curt with a refusal to elaborate, as had been her habit when addressing this man for years now.

Margnus let out a short grunt, his finger falling. "And that girl downstairs? Another trophy, or something of greater import?" How he knew of Lynnea's presence was a mystery, but not one either Thera or Felnir would trouble themselves to probe. The old man was a living tangle of secrets and attempting to unravel even a portion of the knot was a fruitless exercise.

"I make no trophies of people." A flush appeared in Thera's face, her curtness now bordering on outright anger. "She is my charge, as ordained by Sister Iron. As I have stated before, Tielwald, if you have questions regarding my duties as a Vellihr, you must ask the Sister Queens, not me. *I* am not beholden to you."

She didn't look at Felnir as she said this, but the pointed barb found its mark, nonetheless. Felnir's jaw clenched with the effort of caging his retort. Rising to her bait always left him pained by the fragility of his pride. Furthermore, he saw the expectation in his great-grandfather's eye, and took a mote of comfort from disappointing him.

"I assume you have a reason for calling us both here," Felnir said.

"Should not a man pay heed to his great-grandchildren? I have so few remaining." He spoke in a sombre, reflective tone that didn't match the annoyed squint to his empty socket.

"If you had drawn less of your kin into your schemes," Thera returned, "perhaps more would be alive to stand before you today."

It was an old grievance, one Thera rarely missed an opportunity to raise despite its failure to rouse Margnus to more than vague annoyance. "Your parents knew the stakes of this game," he said, waving a hand in weary irritation. "As their parents had before them. They also knew I would endeavour to do right by you both. And I have, to the best of my meagre ability. Have I not?"

Felnir knew well the folly of expressing an honest opinion to this man, but not due to any danger it might entail. Rather, it was the pointlessness of seeking to arouse guilt or regret in a soul that lacked the capacity for either. Today, however, the Tielwald's words proved one provocation too many. "You do right by us both?" Felnir asked. "I am condemned to ignoble skulking at your whim whilst my sister steals all glory."

"I steal nothing," Thera said, still addressing her words to their great-grandfather. "That, I leave to my brother." Another barb, this one spoken with a passion that made her subject obvious.

Sygna, he thought with weary annoyance. *With her, it always comes back to Sygna.* "My sister is surely wise enough to know," he said, "that a heart cannot be stolen, only given—"

"Enough bickering!" Margnus cut in, all vestige of an aged quaver stripped from his voice. "I've had my ears filled with it ever since your parents died and I find I've reached my limit. Felnir, if you so passionately dislike the role I arranged for you, at no small effort I would add, you have my leave to forsake it and return to the life of an exiled trader or mercenary, as it suits you. Thera, in one respect at least, your brother speaks true. Mooning over a lost love ill becomes one of such renown. Put it aside and set your eyes upon your duty."

Felnir clenched his jaw with renewed energy whilst Thera stiffened further. "I echo my brother's question," she said in icy flatness. "Why have you called us here?"

"Why—" the frailty returned to Margnus's voice as he leaned forward and began to rise "—merely because it is the advent of the Veltgruhn, a time of gift giving between kin." After a moment's toil, he managed to stand, his grunts and groans drawing an inquisitive whine from the hound at his feet, who was concerned enough to forsake her bone. Margnus rummaged amongst the various trinkets atop the fireplace mantle, then reached for the stone-bladed axe on the wall. For a dubious second, Felnir thought he might be about to gift the weapon to one of them, but instead the old man used it as a walking stick. "Here," he huffed, dragging himself towards them, free hand extended. "These belonged to your parents, who wore them with pride, I might add."

Driven more by curiosity than sentiment, Felnir raised his hand to accept the proffered item. When Margnus dropped it into his open palm, he beheld a teardrop-sized nugget of silver shaped to resemble a knotted rope. A small thing indeed, but with some value, and the craftsmanship was undoubtedly impressive. He saw Thera hesitate before consenting to take her own gift, which appeared to be identical to his.

"This has some meaning?" Felnir asked, rolling the silver knot between his forefinger and thumb. "An Altvar sigil?"

"No." The Tielwald stood back, resting both hands on the axe head and regarding his great-grandchildren with a thoughtful crease to his brow. Even stooped and shrunken by age, he still towered over both of them, and neither could be called short. "But yes, they have meaning for those of our bloodline. Guard them well and wear them close to your skin."

"Why?" Thera enquired, regarding her own trinket with mild curiosity.

"Because your great-grandfather asked you to!" The quaver vanished again as Margnus growled, though he swayed a little, large, gnarled hands gripping the axe head tight. "Is that not enough?"

Thera glared back at him, making Felnir wonder if she would throw the gift in his face and storm from the room. However, she did some jaw clenching of her own and spoke on after a calming breath. "This was my mother's?"

"Yes." The fierceness faded from the Tielwald's eye. "As the years pass, you look so much like her, it's somewhat . . . disturbing. She would have been a Vellihr too, had her heart not led her along a different course." He blinked and the dark eye swung to Felnir. Margnus said nothing, but Felnir felt he could hear the unspoken judgement, nonetheless. It was true that they were both the image of their parents, and not far off the age they had been when they died, cut down storming the flame-lashed streets of Olversahl. But whilst Margnus Gruinskard still mourned the loss of his grand-daughter, Felnir had never heard him utter anything other than disdain for her husband.

"No matter," the old man grunted, the haft of his axe thumping the floorboards as he made his way back to his chair. "Keep them or leave them here." Groaning, he sank into the furs, Myhsta's whining increasing in pitch as she lay her head upon his lap, tongue lapping at his hand. "My thanks for your visit, Thera," Margnus said. "Would that it was a more frequent occurrence. I won't keep you from your business at the Verungyr, and I have a matter to discuss with your brother."

Thera looked again at the silver knot before consigning it to her purse. She afforded the Tielwald a formal nod, Felnir a brief, expressionless glance, then started for the stairs.

"Remember," Margnus said, making her pause. "Wear it next to the skin."

Thera merely nodded again and descended from view at an unhurried pace. From the absence of a violent tumult when she reached the lower floor, Felnir divined that Coelnyr had heeded their warnings.

"You killed him then?" his great-grandfather asked after they heard the opening and closing of the door downstairs. "That man I expressly instructed you to bring to me alive."

"That man was an imposter," Felnir replied. "Sent by the Dowager Princess in place of your agent, who I assume is either dead or nursing the wounds of his torture in a dungeon somewhere."

"I do not employ you for your insight, Felnir. Such judgements lie outside your province. In any case, I doubt you killed him because you marked him a liar. He angered you in some way, did he not?

Pricked that troublesome pride of yours, the same pride that saw you exiled."

The Tielwald's good eye narrowed in disapproval whilst Felnir saw his empty socket barely register an emotion. The old man, it appeared, regarded Felnir's infraction with indifference.

"I suspect," he said, "it was not the messenger that mattered in any case." He plucked the canvas bundle from his belt, holding it up. "But the message. Am I wrong?"

Margnus said nothing, merely gesturing at Felnir to deliver his prize. "I would guess," he said, unfurling the canvas to reveal the parchment within, "you've spent a goodly portion of time attempting to decipher this, without success. No one amongst that motley band of yours was equal to the task either, eh?"

Felnir didn't bother with a denial. During the voyage north, he and Tuahla, his translator and scribe, had spent many hours poring over the sigil and the cypher beneath, to no avail. "Since you've kept me here," Felnir said, "I assume you're going to tell me."

Margnus gave no immediate reply, instead setting the parchment on his knee and studying it in silence whilst Myhsta nuzzled his fingers. When he spoke, it was not to provide an explanation, but to ask a soft, weary question, "Do you know how old I am, Felnir?"

The answer to this was a mystery Felnir had pondered all his life. He had never known this man as anything but an aged soul, one Felnir's mother called grandfather. It was true Felnir's boyhood recollections regarding Margnus Gruinskard were of a far more hale and robust figure, frighteningly so when he had a mind to make use of the stone axe that earned him his name. But even then his beard had been grey and his face etched in creases. Also, the tales his parents told of the Tielwald went back many a year, alluding to battles and events that no other soul now living had seen, but Margnus had.

"No, Great-grandfather," Felnir said. "In truth, I do not."

"No, neither do I." The old man splayed his fingers, allowing the hound to lick them in turn. "Stopped counting a while back. It seemed a pointless exercise, and I already have so much to remember.

Suffice to say, however, that I have lived long enough to know the scent of change on the wind when I catch it. And catch it I do."

"Change?"

"Oh yes. That most feared of things. For it has long been my charge to keep change at bay. That is how I serve the Sister Queens and the people of this vast collection of fjord and isle. But ever have I known it a fool's task, for in the end, change is as certain as winter frost or summer sun. It cannot be stopped, but if we make the most of our gifts—" he smoothed the parchment out on his lap "—we can at least hope to survive it."

"Is it war?" Felnir asked, wishing he could read the cyphered letters. "The southerners intend to reclaim the Fjord Geld?"

"I imagine they do, but not quite yet. The legacy of the Blackheart's reign was far more damaging than I imagined. She cost them much, and not just in treasure and blood. She opened a rent in the fabric of that pestilent Covenant faith of theirs. Princess Leannor guides her idiot son well, and does her best to heal her kingdom's wounds, but still they bleed. We need not fear Albermaine, at least not while the Dowager Princess holds sway over their court. No, I sense change approaches from another, far more perilous direction."

Margnus looked up at Felnir, his good eye steady whilst the empty socket twitched. "The Veltgruhn is upon us, and yet for the first time I can remember in all my uncountable years, the tribute of stockfish from the far north of the Outer Isles has failed to arrive."

"An absence of stockfish." Felnir sighed a laugh. "That is your terrible portent?"

"Yes." The socket's twitching became more pronounced as a note of irritation crept into the Tielwald's voice. Apparently, his great-grandson was failing another test. The knowledge put a glower on Felnir's brow, but also spurred an inner caution. *That troublesome pride of yours . . .*

"You suspect some manner of trouble in the Outer Isles," he said, voice clipped with forced patience. "And wish me to take the *Sea Hawk* to investigate."

"No. The Sister Queens are aware of the issue and will take the necessary steps in that regard. For you—" he returned his attention to the parchment "—I have a different task. Tell me, how well do you know the waters off the coast of the upper Cordwain?"

"Sailed through there, but not often. Behsla, my *Johten Apt*, did some smuggling there in her youth. She'll see us right if needs be."

"Good. This—" Margnus traced a finger along the cyphered characters below the sigil "—is the name of a castle on the coast where the Duke of Cordwain keeps his more valuable prisoners. There you will find a man with this—" he tapped a digit to the sigil "—tattooed upon his skin. Go there, free him, and bring him to me." He folded the parchment and held it out to Felnir, the empty eye socket narrowing in dire warning. "And this time, great-grandson of mine, he better fucking well be alive when you come back."

CHAPTER EIGHT

Elvine

It always shamed her that she didn't fight, or offer any real struggle against the hands that gripped her beyond a panicked jostle of her arms. The sight of Supplicant Truth gaping in terror at the axe embedded in his chest clamped a numbing hand upon Elvine's mind, allowing scant freedom to notice the scene unfolding around her. She was aware of congregants screaming in panic, others bowing their heads in cowed acceptance. Some, Dehny amongst them, almost immediately started to beg for forgiveness, sinking to their knees and babbling out denunciations of a faith that had been so ardent mere seconds before.

She saw Bahn reach for the knife on his belt as the warriors invaded the shed, but fortunately he thought better of it. Instead, he composed himself into a stiff, stern-faced pose that lasted until one of the warriors drove a hard punch into his midriff. The sight of violence done to his uncle stirred Uhttar into unwise action, starting forward with a shout of protest, then halting in mid-stride, turning back to Elvine, torn in indecision. The internal debate over whether to go to Bahn's aid or stay at her side was rendered moot by the club that cracked against the base of his skull, leaving him senseless on the floor at Elvine's feet. She was staring at Uhttar's slack features, the eyes half lidded and blood pooling under his head, when large, strong hands closed on her and the sight was replaced by the coarse weave of a sack.

Fear finally descended when they dragged her from the shed, the chill of outside air and lack of vision combining to shatter the icy grip on her mind. "Uhttar!" she cried out, attempting to turn, but finding it a hopeless task. The hands that held her were so strong she felt like a bird struggling in a cat's claws.

"Shut your yap, you Covenant bitch!" a voice growled, the accent that of upper Ascarlia rather than the more lilting tones of the Fjord Geld. *The warship*, Elvine thought, a sob of realisation escaping her. *They didn't wait for the tide.*

Her captors halted and pushed her arms behind her back, swiftly binding her wrists in cord before lifting her off her feet. She felt the hardness of timber beneath her and heard the squeal and clop of cartwheels and dray hooves. Elvine rolled about as the cart carried her along the rough track leading away from Bahn's shed. In a short while, the violence of the passage abated as cartwheels met the more forgiving cobbles of the city proper. With the return of her senses came the overwhelming understanding of her predicament: she had been captured by a Vellihr of the Sister Queens in the midst of a Covenant rite, a practice not tolerated in Ascarlia for decades. A practice usually punished by exile, but not always. Sometimes, the reward for rejection of the Altvar was a very ugly and public death.

Elvine convulsed as a wave of terror swept through her, threatening to spill her supper into the sack. Fortunately, she managed to swallow it down, but not the sobs that followed. Nonsense words streamed from her lips amidst a welter of tears and snot whilst her mind raced with all manner of chaotic thoughts. Fantasies of escape warred with notions of abject surrender. She would work her wrists free of these bonds and slip unseen from the cart. She would kneel before her captors at the first opportunity and give them the name of every congregant in the Fjord Geld.

The whirlwind of self-recrimination and defiance came to an abrupt end when the cart stopped. The same numbness that had gripped her before returned, although this time it permitted her a single thought, one that escaped her lips in a tearful whisper: "Mother."

* * *

She realised later she must have fainted before they dragged her from the cart, for she awoke to find the sack had been removed from her head. Also, the cord was gone from her wrists, though they were raw and aching from the binding. Elvine blinked at a faint yellow glow playing over a rough surface, ears detecting dim and distant echoes. Trying to discern the source, she cast a bleary eye at her surroundings. What she saw brought an instant and sickening realisation. The cell she lay in was in truth a cave, its walls damp, irregular rock, the floor an uneven product of inexpert chiselling. The only salient features were a bucket, revealed as empty when she peered closer, and a heavy door set into the wall opposite. One look was enough to convince her the door was an unassailable barrier of bolted iron and thick timber, featuring a small, barred window near the top through which the dull light of a lantern flickered.

"The Rent," Elvine murmured, her tongue working around a foul-tasting mouth. "They took me to the Rent."

The Rent was perhaps the most notable yet least talked about feature in Olversahl. Created via the cunning stratagem of the Tielwald Margnus Gruinskard when he retook the city for the Sister Queens, it had persisted ever since as a stark reminder of the destruction wrought that night. Given that the Tielwald's stratagem had resulted in such severe vandalism to one of the most magnificent monuments to the Altvar, Elvine had always thought it odd that no attempt had been made to repair it in the years since. Instead, the huge, jagged crack in the stone face of Ulthnir the Worldsmith, through which the thousands of warriors comprising the great *menda* had streamed, remained, but not without modification. The tunnel within had been expanded, new passages and cells carved out of the mountain. Before the Sister Queens reasserted their sovereignty, Olversahl had little need of a prison beyond a cage in the harbour master's cellar reserved for drunken sailors. Not so now. Those who disappeared into the Rent, mostly a collection of folk clinging to old Albermaine-ish loyalties or, like her, heretical Covenant belief, never came out again except to provide the spectacle of their execution.

She tried to stand but found the manoeuvre required several attempts before she achieved success. Tottering on bare feet and unsteady legs to the door, she stood on tiptoe to peer through the barred window. A few seconds gazing at a shadowy passage lit by a lantern hanging from the ceiling provided little in the way of enlightenment. The echoes that had roused her persisted, however, though were too far off for her to make out any actual words. Were these the voices of guards or prisoners? The notion summoned a cry to her lips before she could ponder the wisdom of voicing it.

"Uhttar!" Her voice reverberated down the passage, smothering the echoes. "Uhttar, are you here? It's Elvine!" She fell silent, waiting for a response, hearing nothing. "Bahn!" she called out, desperate for some response. "Bahn! Can you hear me!"

"QUIET!" A hard, annoyed shout came back at her from the gloomy recess of the passage, followed by a low growl of grim promise. "Any more prattle and I'll take away your bucket."

Stifling a sob, Elvine rested her forehead against the unyielding mass of the door. *The warship*, she thought, a fresh jolt of guilt sending a roil through her already churning gut. Why hadn't she told Bahn to cancel the Supplications? Why hadn't she just stayed home?

Sorrow claimed her then, robbing her legs of strength so that she slid down the door, eyes blinded by tears, her body convulsing with the agony of utter despair. Eventually, her weeping subsided in the face of exhaustion and sleep took her again. When she woke hours later, it was to the hard clatter of the door's lock.

Gasping in panic, Elvine scrambled away, feet scraping the rough floor until her back connected with the wall. She fought the urge to close her eyes against whatever the door might reveal, forcing herself to watch it grind open on aged hinges. The sight of the figure outlined in the lantern light was both terrifying and unsurprising. His features were lost to shadow, but the glitter of his sharkskin coat and narrowness of face were horribly familiar. Elvine bit down on the plea that came to her lips when he stepped into the cell, trying and mostly failing to quell the tremble of her limbs. Her eyes flicked to his hands, expecting to find a weapon. Perhaps a whip or a knife. But they were empty. It appeared he intended to question her without resorting to torment, at least at first.

But he asked no questions, nor spoke at all. Instead, he paused to regard her for a moment of scrutiny, his expression concealed by the shadow, before stepping aside to reveal the figure standing to his rear.

"Mother!"

Berrine hesitated for a second in the doorway, her face like the Vellihr's, lost to shadow, then came to her daughter in a rush, pulling her close. Elvine rejoiced at the smell and feel of her mother, finding they had the near magical power to banish fear. It was impossible to contain the sobbing, incoherent torrent of apology, and Berrine held her until it finally dwindled into weeping. Easing her back, Berrine teased the damp strands of hair from Elvine's face. Blinking the wetness from her eyes, Elvine beheld an expression that was mostly relief mixed with regret and found her fear returning as she pondered what it might mean.

"Are you hurt?" Berrine asked, eyes roving Elvine's form, then fixating on the red marks banding her wrists. "What is this?" she demanded, turning to the Vellihr. Her tone struck Elvine as decidedly out of place. The curt lack of respect seemed dangerous, almost absurd. She could see the tall man's cadaverous visage now, outlined in the light from the passageway. Curiously, the expected harsh reminder of his authority failed to come. Nor did his expression alter beyond a slight hardening of the mouth.

"A necessary precaution," he said, his gravelly voice flat. "For her own protection."

Elvine saw her mother's jaw clench before she jerked her head at the open doorway. "I would talk with my daughter alone."

"As you wish. However, I was told to give you this." He held something out to Berrine, a small silver trinket of some kind. "A gift from an old friend."

Berrine stared at the trinket, her expression hard but otherwise unreadable. "A gift can be refused," she said in a bitter mutter, reaching to close her fist around the proffered item.

The tall man gave a small grunt of satisfaction and shifted his gaze to Elvine. Whereas he had been careful not to show any emotion to her mother, for Elvine, he offered a lip-curling sneer of utter contempt. "You," he said in a grating hiss, "shame your mother . . ."

"Just get out!" Berrine snapped.

Once again, Elvine was struck by the failure of a person who enforced the law of the Sister Queens themselves to respond to such disrespect with anything beyond a marginal crease to his brow. Berrine waited until he had departed the cell and his footfalls faded before turning back to Elvine.

"Well, daughter of mine," she said, grimacing as she tried to work her fingers through Elvine's matted hair, "quite a knot you've woven for me."

"Mother . . ." Elvine sagged against her, fighting down another bout of sobs. "I . . . I'm sorry . . ."

"Are you?"

Pulling back, Elvine saw a weary inquisition on Berrine's face. Her question lacked anger, but there was an edge to it, nonetheless. "Or," Berrine went on, "are you sorry you got caught?"

She sighed and returned to the task of working the tangle from Elvine's tresses. "The Covenant, Elvine? Of all the trouble you choose to bring to our door, you settle upon the one thing the law cannot forgive. Kill someone and a blood tithe will set you free. Steal something and they'll let you go less a finger or two. But you choose to spit in the faces of the Altvar themselves."

Despite everything, her mother's tired judgement managed to stir a small measure of defiance in Elvine's breast. "My faith is no less true than yours," she said. "You bow to stone faces and ancient runes. I dedicate my soul to something real and true . . ."

"Real and true?" For the first time, an angry line appeared in Berrine's brow, her hand momentarily tightening in Elvine's hair. Sighing again, Berrine released her, her features slipping into sorrowful purpose. "This is not the time for a debate. I have to tell you some things. They will be hard to hear."

Elvine's gaze slipped to the empty doorway and the passage beyond. She could see the lantern light catching the edges of the doors to other cells, but heard no voices. Nor had any answered when she called out after her first waking in this place. "Uhttar . . ." she said, faltering to a choked silence when she saw the sorrow deepen on Berrine's face.

"An accident, or so Vellihr Ilvar claims. One of his men was too free with his club. I'm sorry, Elvine."

Uhttar . . . She recalled his indecision, that instant of confusion as he looked from her to his uncle, just long enough for a warrior to read it as defiance. His half-open eyes as he lay at her feet, the blood pooling beneath his head . . .

Although it burdened her with yet another bundle of shame, she found she had no more tears in that moment. Perhaps she had wept herself dry, or the magnitude of Uhttar's death was too great, a loss that dwarfed the trivia of mere weeping.

"The others?" she asked, voice hoarse.

"Most have already recanted their Altvar-hate, though they can expect to lose their property and positions by way of additional punishment. A few refused and now await the judgement of the Sister Queens, Bahn amongst them."

"Harryk? Dehny?"

"Both recanted. Dehny was particularly passionate about it all. Claiming she had been swayed by some vile Covenant magics, which would indicate to me that her understanding of your cherished faith was minimal at best. Your friend Senhild was there too, not so passionate, but unwavering in her denunciations."

"Denunciations?"

The line appeared on Berrine's forehead once more, this time more critical than angry. "Did you imagine the Vellihr of Lore sailed here by mere happenstance, Elvine? It was Senhild. Apparently, her father discovered some Covenant scripture in her room and forced her to go to the Veilwald. They knew all about the Supplicant's arrival weeks ago. You walked into a well-prepared snare."

Senhild? Who had been taken by Silfaer's curse, again. Elvine closed her eyes with a groan. She wanted to feel anger, betrayal, hate even. But instead, there was just the sickening knowledge of her own foolishness.

"What . . ." Elvine began, pausing to swallow in order to get the words out. "What will happen to me?"

"Nothing, as long as you remain under my authority. For—" Berrine got to her feet, holding her hand out to Elvine, "—I am elevated by the grace of Sister Lore to a new role, and you will be my assistant."

"Role?" Taking her hand, Elvine hauled herself upright, wincing at the competing plethora of aches from her back to her ankles. She had committed perhaps the worst transgression in Ascarlia, except for child murder, and yet one of the Sister Queens had seen fit to reward her mother. "What role?"

"One I refused many times, but now have no choice but to accept . . ." Berrine trailed off but Elvine could guess the conclusion to her statement: *or watch them kill my daughter.*

"The voyage ahead will be unpleasant," Berrine went on, voice brisk as she led Elvine from the cell. "And it would be best if you said as little as possible until we reach our destination."

"Where?" Elvine struggled to match her mother's pace along the passage, her unclad feet finding a painful patch of stone with every step. "Where are we going?"

Berrine made a short, harsh sound that might have been a laugh but for the bleak resignation it held. "Skar Magnol, daughter of mine. Where else would you find the new Vellihr of Archives to the Sister Queens? But," she added with a grim sigh, "those bitches are the least of our worries."

CHAPTER NINE

Ruhlin

The sulphurous stench of the Fire Islands grew to a gut-churning thickness the day after their visit to the ship's deck. Repeated coughing fits brought Ruhlin to the point of retching several times, though on each occasion he managed to contain his gorge, which was fortunate. He was sure Uhtgyr would be happy to let him wallow in a cage besmirched by his own vomit. Mehlga coughed too, but not with the same violence, nor did she return to weeping. With each passing hour, she appeared to grow more composed. But, she spoke less now.

"The Fire Islands," Ruhlin breathed after another round of coughing. He peered up at the dim light filtering through the boards above his head. Although he reckoned the hour was well short of dusk, the few glimmers of daylight he could see were growing fainter. "How can they hope to navigate through them? It's suicide."

He didn't expect Mehlga to have an answer, the girl having remained silent since Uhtgyr returned them to their cages. But she spoke now, her voice once again absurd in its calmness. "Not for them." A pause before she added in a quieter tone, "At least not yet."

"That woman said they have to sail through the Fire Isles to get home," Ruhlin went on. "But there's nothing on the other side. Just vast empty ocean. Everyone knows that."

"How could they? Since no one has ever returned from the Fire Isles to tell the tale."

After pondering this, Ruhlin was forced to admit she had a point.

A long chain of mountainous islands belching gas and lava was a place to be avoided at all costs. Even those portions of it that appeared relatively lacking in billowing smoke or glowing rivulets needed to be shunned. The channels between the isles were rich in poisonous humours and boiling currents. Yet, for all the dire stories, Ruhlin had never met a sailor or fisherman who had ventured closer than a few miles to this most dread archipelago.

For the rest of the day and into the night, he strained for to hear some significant sound from beyond the hull whilst also trying to discern any appreciable shift in the pitch of the deck. Apart from distant thunder, presumably the rumble of a volcano disgorging fumes or molten rock, and an occasional tremble to the boards, he sensed nothing especially alarming.

"You should sleep," Mehlga told him when the last speck of light had vanished from the timbers overhead. "Nothing will happen until tomorrow."

She spoke with soft assurance, but this time he detected a grave undertone. Ruhlin thought back to their visit to the upper deck, the way the woman, Angomar, had questioned Mehlga. *What do you see, little one?* The question had possessed a definite weight Ruhlin hadn't understood at the time. Now, the first inkling of comprehension began to form. But it was still vague, a conclusion beyond his reach.

"Why did she keep asking you what you saw?" Ruhlin enquired, moving to the bars separating their cages. Uhtgyr hadn't bothered shackling him when they were returned to their prison, so he was able to put his face close to the barrier. Mehlga had retreated to the far side of her cage, a small, huddled shadow. When she gave no reply, he leaned closer, pressing his face to the metal. "You were spared for a reason too, weren't you? What is it? What do you see?"

Still no reply, but he saw her curl into a ball, her back to him.

"Please, Mehlga?" he said. "What do you know? Please ..." His entreaty faded when he heard her weeping once again. Sighing, he sat back, a surge of guilt pushing a whisper from his lips. "I'm sorry." Turning away, he lay down and attempted, mostly without success, to sleep.

* * *

The next day brought a lessening to the stench, but also a more pronounced movement to the ship. The thunderous outbursts had grown more frequent, their varied volume indicating some eruptions were close whilst others were distant. Despite the relative freshness of the air, Ruhlin was forced to conclude that they were now sailing through the heart of the Fire Isles.

"Time for your scraps, dog!" Uhtgyr's rasp banished the fog of Ruhlin's half-sleep, the gaoler's grinning visage appearing beyond the bars as he shoved a stew bowl into Ruhlin's cage. "Don't worry," Uhtgyr added with an unpleasant wink, "only pissed in it a little today."

Moving to Mehlga's cell, he crouched to deliver her meal, then jerked in surprise when she rose to her feet, addressing him directly. "I have something to say to your mistress," she said. When Uhtgyr continued to glare in suspicion, she spoke on, inflecting her words with his own accent to ensure he understood. "Aerling Angomar asked questions. Now I have answers."

The gaoler departed the hold for several minutes before returning, moving hastily to unlock Mehlga's cell. Sliding the barred door aside, he gestured impatiently for her to come out. "Him too," she said, nodding to Ruhlin. "He will be needed."

Uhtgyr's sharp features formed an exasperated snarl. Ruhlin assumed he was under orders to hurry, so instead of seeking further instruction, the gaoler also slid his key into the second cage's lock. He muttered as he went about the task, his accent too harsh to make out more than a few words, but Ruhlin divined his complaints as pertaining to the relative worth of this voyage compared to the annoyance of his allotted role.

"Same warning, dog," he advised Ruhlin upon sliding the bars open, one hand on his long-bladed knife. "Let's go!" he snapped, jerking his head when his prisoner failed to move immediately. Beset by an inexplicable but potent sense of foreboding, Ruhlin glanced at Mehlga, now standing outside her cage. Her serenity had returned, though the weariness of a night spent in forlorn sorrow showed on her face. Still, she managed to craft a smile, which provided sufficient encouragement for him to vacate his cell.

Upon ascending to the deck, Ruhlin expected to behold a spectacular and ominous view of towering, fire-belching mountains crowned by vast columns of black smoke. Instead, the ship appeared to be sailing through a dense fog. It shifted in swirling clouds on all sides, an impenetrable miasma tinged in yellow. Still, there was no mistaking their position. Flares of reddish orange lit the depths of the haze, followed soon after by a deep rumble and tremor to the boards beneath his feet.

Angomar stood at the prow of the ship, accompanied by a member of the crew Ruhlin hadn't seen before. He was a crooked-backed old man with a face dominated by a large beak-shaped nose. The dark cloak about his shoulders and tasselled cap on his head made it appear as if Angomar conversed with a giant, malformed crow. The old man held a curved stick that resembled a shepherd's crook, but with some manner of device affixed to its hooked end. A brass and iron box about the size of a fist residing within a mesh of tightly woven twine. Ever curious, Ruhlin attempted to move closer for a better look, only for Uhtgyr to halt him with a hard shove to the chest from his whip handle. Ruhlin watched the old man squint at the box for a time before he said something to Angomar, his accent so impenetrable and voice so ragged Ruhlin wondered if he truly might be some bizarre mix of bird and human.

"You're sure?" Angomar asked. In comparison to the old man, her voice resembled the smooth flowing tones of a practised story spinner. Her question earned a withering glance, the aged's spindly form stiffening in offence. Accepting the rebuke without notable rancour, Angomar turned and cupped her mouth to cast a shout towards the helmsman. "Four points to port!"

After an answering call of confirmation came from the stern, the angle of the deck altered a little as the huge ship responded to the helmsman's touch on the wheel. Apparently satisfied, the crow-shaped figure made a ticking sound and stalked off to the starboard rail. As he did so, Ruhlin's curious eye tracked the box affixed to his stick, noting that it was in fact some form of metal sphere within a box, one that revolved as the old man moved.

"So, little one," Angomar said, snapping his attention to shift back to her. "You have something to tell me after all, I hear?" She stood with her back against the tall wooden figurehead rising from the ship's prow. Ruhlin could only make out a portion of the carving's form, but gained an impression of a helmed warrior of stern aspect.

Looking to Mehlga, Ruhlin saw neither the serene calm and or pitiful sorrow that characterised the girl's moods since he had awakened beside her. Now she was tense, her reddened eyes unblinking and face set in a purposeful mask. Her demeanour put him in mind of Irhkyn on those nights in the mead hall when he allowed an unwise taunt to stir him to violence. He would sit and drink for an hour or more, anger simmering, his shoulders hunching lower and gaze becoming ever more steady despite the liquor. It never ended well and Ruhlin had learned young to depart the hall before the inevitable fracas.

"I do, Aerling," Mehlga said, once again altering her own accent to ensure she was understood. As the deck settled afresh, she shifted her sight from Angomar, looking at the foggy void to the right of the figurehead. Following her gaze, Ruhlin at first saw nothing of interest but then made out another reddish-yellow bloom through the swirling clouds. This one was far closer than the others, nearer the sea, too. His ears detected the hiss and roil of molten rock meeting water, and within seconds, the fog was tinged by paler billows of steam.

"So?" Angomar prompted. "What is it?"

Mehlga darted a look at Uhtgyr before replying. "It concerns your family, the circumstances regarding your father's legacy. This was once his ship, was it not? Her name is the *Sea Sword*, I believe. But she bore another name when your father captained her, before his debts . . ."

"Enough!" Angomar's command was like a slap, Ruhlin seeing a sudden paleness to her tattooed features. Her jaw clenched as she stared at Mehlga, a murderous glint in her eye. She was quick to master herself, however, taking a breath and fixing Mehlga with a cold glare. "I care nothing for the past, girl," she said. "Your value lies in what you can tell me of the future."

"I can tell you many things, Aerling," Mehlga assured her, once again flicking her eyes to Uhtgyr. "But how much do you wish known to other ears?"

Angomar's nostrils flared and her hands closed into fists before she once again bottled the evident rage building within. "Come then," she said, beckoning Mehlga to her. "And speak soft."

Mehlga nodded, but paused before obeying the order. Turning to Ruhlin, she offered him a wavering smile before voicing a short and utterly baffling statement: "You can trust the Aerling's daughter." With that, she strode to Angomar's side, leaning close to murmur something in the taller woman's ear.

Ruhlin would never know what words Mehlga spoke to Aerling Angomar that day, nor would any but the two of them. Whatever they were, they sufficed to bring about a shockingly abrupt change in the Aerling's expression. The grimace of contained anger shifted instantly to gape-mouthed fright. The woman's eyes widened, and it seemed to Ruhlin that she shrank as Mehlga spoke on. Angomar drew back a little but also appeared to be snared by the girl's speech, unable to look away from her face even as she began to tremble.

"Aerling?" Uhtgyr said, stepping forward, his hands clutching both knife and whip.

Angomar paid him no need, staggering against the prow, apparently borne down by Mehlga's torrent of words. A sob escaped the Aerling, and she cowered lower, her hand going to her mouth.

"That's enough!" Uhtgyr barked, advancing on the pair, whip raised. "Move away, girl."

Before he could land a blow, Mehlga ceased her diatribe. She paused to glance at Ruhlin, the smile firm now, as if she had been shorn of all fear in this moment. Then she turned and threw herself against Angomar. Had the taller woman been in a less distressed state, she might have saved herself. But what Mehlga lacked in size, she made up for in determination, clamping her arms around Angomar's neck and launching herself over the rail before the Aerling could react. By the time she raised a hand to claw at the arm enclosing her throat, they were already halfway over the side. Uhtgyr rushed forward to save his mistress, but a final heave from Mehlga saw both women disappear from view.

The sound of the splash and instant chorus of screams sufficed to shock Ruhlin from immobility. Charging towards the prow, he looked down at the misted waters, seeing two figures flailing in a welter of steam and bubbles. The passage of the ship swept them both towards the starboard beam where, after a final bout of thrashing and a small howl of despairing agony, they slipped under the hull.

A harsh bark came from Uhtgyr, something probably profane but too mangled by his accent to make out, then Ruhlin felt the gaoler's whip coil itself around his neck. A hard jerk and he was dragged onto the deck, the whip tightening to close his throat. A kick slammed into his gut, followed by two more. Ruhlin's ears filled with Uhtgyr's torrent of enraged abuse, but it was soon smothered by the pounding of his own heart, his vision turning a dark crimson hue as the whip continued to starve his lungs of air. Another kick sent a jolt of pain through him, a flare of agony so acute it cut through the barrier of Angomar's drugs to stir the nascent fire in Ruhlin's core.

The breath-stealing coil around his neck abruptly slackened, his dimming sight shifting into a lighter, but angrier shade of red. Ruhlin's choking gasps became a low growl, his hand lashing out to snare Uhtgyr's ankle as the gaoler attempted to drive another kick into his prisoner's midriff. A tightening of Ruhlin's grip and Uhtgyr lay on the deck, shrieking and clutching the foot dangling from a crushed ankle.

A deeper growl emerged from Ruhlin's lips as he reached to tear the whip from his neck, rending it to pieces and casting the leather scraps away. Rising to his feet, his red-tinged vision surveyed a circle of crewmen closing around him, all gripping weapons and exchanging panicked glances. Strangely, although Ruhlin knew he wanted to kill them all, he found he lacked the impulse to do so. The ship swayed around him with too much violence to be the product of the sea. *The drugs*, a dim vestige of his own awareness told him. *Fight it. Kill them!*

Balling fists, he raised them before his eyes, looking upon veined, enlarged parodies of his hands. However, they weren't as large or deformed as they had been during his rampage through Buhl Hardta. Also, they appeared to be rapidly diminishing. "Fight!" Ruhlin grunted through spittle, lurching towards the nearest sailor, attempting to summon rage. Yet all he felt was a terrible, growing weariness. The sailor he lunged at stepped back a pace, eyes widened in terror. But, as Ruhlin staggered, his massive fists flailing without finding a target, the sailor's courage stiffened. Yelling something, he drew back the pike he held for a thrust, then froze as a new voice filled the air.

"*Leevim bae!*" The words were a screech rather than a yell, making it easy for Ruhlin to identify the source. "*Nigh proffet eyena courpss!*" This time the old, crook-backed man spoke with enough vehement authority to make his meaning clear. *Leave him be! No profit in a corpse!*

The circle of sailors widened as the old man stalked towards Ruhlin, his curious staff thumping on the boards. He exhibited no fear as he drew closer, and Ruhlin found he lacked the strength to summon further rage in any case. A shudder ran through him, a strange, uncomfortable vibration seizing his limbs. When he raised his hands again, he saw they were back to their former size. Sagging, he sank to his knees, borne down by an irresistible need for sleep.

"Heh." The old man grunted in satisfaction, prodding Ruhlin's chest with his stick, squinting pea-sized eyes in careful scrutiny. When he spoke again it was with a leer Ruhlin only vaguely recognised as a grin, and this time he had no trouble deciphering the words: "Our Aerling won't get any less dead. And I doubt she'd want her loyal crew to lose out. This one—" he prodded Ruhlin's chest again "—is worth a lot more than we thought."

"To who?" one of the sailors asked, having to shout to be heard over Uhtgyr's unabated chorus of agony. "The Aerling knew all that stuff. And she kept it in her head."

The old man gave an irritable wave of his stick. "Doesn't matter. There's only one fucker we can sell him to, anyhow."

Finally overcome with fatigue, Ruhlin fell face first to the deck. He heard voices raised in argument, then more of the old man's squawking, after which there was only Uhtgyr's cries, abruptly ended in a distant splash. Before Ruhlin slipped into oblivion, he felt the familiar scrape and pressure of iron manacles being fastened to his wrists.

He woke to air that stank of human effluent, but at least lacked the sulphurous sting of the Fire Isles. The bars of the cage separating him from Mehlga resolved into view as he blinked grit from his eyes. Ruhlin groaned as the memory of her death pierced his confusion, the shrieking agony of it knotting his stomach. Chains rattled as he fought the urge to cry out, making him realise that his captors had opted to take no more chances with their prisoner. Thick manacles enclosed both his wrists and ankles, with another coil of chain around his knees and hips. Yet more chains secured each set of restraints to brackets in different corners of the room, allowing him bare inches of movement. Once again, he was naked, his flesh stained with his own waste. From the state of the filth, and the stench, he divined he must have been caged like this for days. His jaw ached worse than the other pains that beset him, the absence of hunger and thirst making plain that the crew had found some means of feeding him.

"No profit in a corpse," Ruhlin muttered. His head ached with only marginally less fierceness than his jaw, which meant the food they had forced down his gullet had assuredly been well laced with Angomar's concoction. For want of anything else to do, he tested his iron bonds. After several minutes of attempting to flex his limbs, he gave up and slumped into miserable contemplation. Chief amongst his thoughts were Mehlga's smile just before her act of suicidal defiance, and her baffling final statement: *You can trust the Aerling's daughter.* But she had killed the Aerling. Did Angomar have a daughter then? It occurred to him that "Aerling" might well be a title shared by many, not just the slain mistress of this ship. If Mehlga's gift for divining the future could be trusted, then at some point, he would be meeting another.

He strove to remember all that Mehlga had said during their shared confinement, all her allusions to events yet to come. *We haven't smelled the sulphur yet . . . She knew.* She had known where they were going, which also raised the terrible notion that she had also foreseen her own death. *No wonder she wept.* This all raised yet another question, just as unanswerable as all the others: *If she knew it was coming, why didn't she avoid it?*

His pondering was cut short by a new sound from beyond the wooden walls of the hull, distant but instantly recognisable to a youth who had spent his life as a fisherman: the keening of gulls. From the increasing din, a great multitude of the seabirds thronged the sky not far off, the kind of scavenging mob that only forms around a port. Ruhlin greeted the realisation that this vessel would soon reach its destination with as much excitement as he did trepidation. He had no inkling where this anchorage might lie, suspecting even one as widely travelled as Irhkyn would never have glimpsed or heard of it. Wherever this benighted ship called home, Ruhlin knew it be a place few if any of his own kind had ever seen. These folk might speak a mangled, bastardised version of Ascarlian, but they were not his people and he had never heard even the vaguest tale of their existence. His innate inquisitiveness drove him to know more, but also feared that same knowledge. This lot saw value in him, or rather, the monster that lurked within. That folk such as this would see value in so terrible a thing made an ill omen of his continued survival.

Hours passed, punctuated by raised voices aloft, also the footfalls and squeal of ropes through blocks that told of furled sails. By the time he heard the double splash of two anchors dropping into harbour waters, Ruhlin found his head lolling once again into sleep. His fear kept it at bay for a time, but mounting fatigue caused by the manner of his confinement eventually exerted an inexorable grip. His slumber after Mehlga's demise had been a sojourn into blank unconsciousness. This time, however, he dreamed once more. He dreamed of the dog . . .

His fingers jerked back from the ancient stone tooth when he heard the growl, eyes snapping to the source in panicked fright. It stood on the ledge above him, no more than a yard distant. Viewing it through adult eyes, Ruhlin felt that to call this creature a mere dog was an absurdity. He had never beheld one of such size, twice the height at the shoulder of any sheepdog. The overlapping slabs of muscle encasing its neck put Ruhlin in mind of a bull seal, but it was the drooling, many toothed maw that captured most of his attention. Also, the unblinking, baleful stare of its eyes. Where the beast came from was a mystery to Ruhlin now, as it had been to his younger self. He assumed it must have come from a passing ship, probably a foreign vessel. Perhaps it was a survivor of a wreck, or had been cast overboard by an owner who tired of its viciousness. The only certainty was its presence here at this secluded inlet where its snarls, and the cries of its intended victim, would not be heard.

Ruhlin's boyhood self did none of the things his adult mind expected. He didn't run, which would have been perilous but also the inarguably correct course of action. Nor did he try to scare the beast away with shouts or thrown stones. He also made no effort to endear himself to the creature with a placating word or gesture. No, Ruhlin the Quiet lived up to the name he would earn in later years, by saying and doing precisely nothing. He stood transfixed as the dog dripped drool onto his face, crouched and lunged, jaws widening to clamp those many teeth on a spindly, easily snapped neck.

But that hadn't happened.

The dream became a vague, confused melange of sight and sound as the dog's jaw loomed closer. The snarl ended in a yelp of sudden, plaintive fright. The gaping maw and its rows of teeth shifted into a red and white splash, rather like the spilling of a butcher's bucket. His vision turned black for a time, then it seemed as if he viewed the world through a pink fog. Ruhlin had a sense that his arms were moving, but it was a faraway thing. He felt wetness on his skin, but it was no more than a light drizzle on a sunlit day. Then, without warning, a great weariness seized him. Blinking drooping eyes, he saw that the dog had gone, though the lingering redness in his gaze allowed for only a dim awareness of detail. And so, he sat down and rested his head against a rock, needing to sleep more than he ever had before . . .

* * *

"Have a care!" a tense voice snarled close by, Ruhlin's ear easily deciphering the accent now. "This fucker's waking up."

He jerked as returning consciousness earned a jolt of pain, his roused body instinctively struggling against its iron bonds. The tread of many boots upon boards and the rhythmic ache to his head and neck made him realise he was being carried across the ship's upper deck. The stink of the cage was gone, and he breathed air laced with fish and brine. Blinking, he looked upon a wharf. A line of longships of varying dimensions passed before his eyes, the steep slope beyond covered by a dense mass of buildings. They were strange, constructed on unfamiliar lines, all hard angles and jutting chimneys. A sprawl of close packed wood and tile, they leaned into each other, sagging roofs and dark unpainted walls creating an impression of a place worn down but still heavily populated.

"Let's just get this done," another voice said, speaking with a careful lack of volume. "Then he won't be our burden any longer." Recognising the croaking quality of the voice, Ruhlin craned his neck to see the aged, crow-shaped figure plodding alongside the half-dozen sailors porting their captive's bound form. The beady eyes weren't focused on Ruhlin, but on something towards the prow of the ship, something that made him poke out a small, narrow tongue to lick at dry lips. "None of you shit-swabbers say a word," he added in a whispering rasp, casting a baleful glare at the crew.

A few more steps and Ruhlin felt himself lowered to the deck, far more gently than expected. For a second, the sky above remained a grey emptiness, then a face came into view. Although inverted, Ruhlin made out the features of a handsome man of middling years, his chin covered by a neatly trimmed black beard. Rings gleamed in both ears and a medallion dangled from his neck, all fashioned from gold. The face was expressionless apart from a small narrowing of the eyes as they tracked over Ruhlin's form from head to toe and back again.

"I assure you he is intact, Aerling Eldryk," the old crow said, voice lathered in obsequious solicitation. "Barely a scratch and just a few bruises, and those due to his own brutish struggles."

The neatly groomed man's face continued to exhibit no emotion, eyes blinking once before he consented to speak. "He's awake. You assured me he was drugged."

"He is, Aerling." The crow paused and Ruhlin heard a poorly suppressed gulp. "But we had to give him so much it seems he's starting to resist the compound. It's the way with such things. Your esteemed sister could have . . ." The old man choked into silence as the face finally betrayed some emotion.

"Could have what?" the man with the gold adornments enquired, shifting his gaze from Ruhlin, voice hardening a fraction and brows arching. Ruhlin had seen Dagvyn adopt a similar expression from time to time, usually when about to chastise a truculent youth or lazy kinsman, but taking a moment to savour the fearful preamble.

"I meant . . ." A pause, another more noticeable gulp. "I merely meant that cherished Aerling Angomar was so skilled in mixing of the required ingredients. Had we been blessed by her presence for the succeeding part of our voyage, she could surely have arrived at a more potent recipe."

"But she wasn't?" the handsome man asked. "Was she? For my sister now rests beneath the waves as a boiled corpse, failed by her own servants."

"Failed by that wretch Uhtgyr, in truth, Aerling." Ruhlin saw the hooked nose bob into view as the old man crouched lower. "His sloth and indolence were as much to blame for Aerling Angomar's death as that Teilvik wench, for which we punished him, didn't we, lads?" Ruhlin heard a loud chorus of agreement from the sailors before the crow ploughed on. "Tossed him in right after, we did. Just execution."

"For which you are to be commended, if true," the Aerling said, lowering his eyes to their captive once more. "You were there, weren't you, boy?" he asked, going to his haunches so that his face hovered only an inch or two above Ruhlin's. As he spoke on, Ruhlin found he could understand the words with ease and realised this man had altered his accent to be understood. "You were there when one of yours killed my sister. Is what the Wayfinder says true? Did Aerling Angomar die due to a whip-man's laziness?"

Ruhlin considered ignoring him. He had no stake in this matter and it seemed unlikely the outcome would have much bearing on his fate. But then he recalled Mehlga's last smile and wondered at the courage it must have taken to do what she did. Such courage deserved some kind of testament, even if he might die for voicing it.

"No," he said. "Your sister died by my countrywoman's hand alone. There was nothing Uhtgyr could have done to save her. This lot—" he jerked his head at the surrounding sailors "—threw him over the side after I crushed his leg when he began to beat me."

The handsome face regarded him in bland silence for a moment longer, then, to Ruhlin's utter surprise, creased into a laugh. "It seems you've brought me a prize after all," the Aerling told the crow, slipping back into his own accent. "For which you will be rewarded with forgiveness for your deceit. Under crown law, all that was my sister's is now mine, including this ship and its cargo. So, get your bent-backed carcass off my property and take the rest of these scum-lickers with you."

There was some argument, carefully phrased by the crow but less so by the crew. However, the tramp of considerably more boots upon the deck and the sound of blows being struck indicated the man with the gold adornments hadn't come alone, nor was he in a mood to negotiate.

"Something curious about the character of the Wayfinder caste," he said, his face looming into view once more. "Never met a one of them more trustworthy than a starving rat. He was right about one thing, though." He reached down to grasp Ruhlin's jaw, pressing hard. He tried to resist, but the Aerling was a strong man and quickly succeeded in prising Ruhlin's mouth open. "A more potent dose is required for one such as you." He kept Ruhlin's jaws apart whilst he raised a small bottle in his free hand, thumbing away the stopper. "I apologise in advance for the nightmares. I hear they're quite terrible." With that, he upended the bottle, pouring something thick and foul-smelling down Ruhlin's throat. One swallow and the world disappeared into a swirling fog. As the Aerling promised, the nightmares followed soon after.

CHAPTER TEN

Thera

Thera's darkened mood persisted long after she departed her great-grandfather's house, a typical reaction to being in his presence. However, she felt it might have lifted sooner if she had also been spared her brother's company. *My sister is surely wise enough to know that a heart cannot be stolen, only given.*

Her jaw ached with the effort of clenching teeth against the muttered riposte which, as was the way of such things, had only occurred to her when the Tielwald's domicile was well to her rear. *Even the truest heart can be swayed by cunning deceit.* A sharp enough barb, albeit blunted by the rarely acknowledged truth lurking in Thera's breast: her brother had never made any pretence to Sygna. She saw all his flaws, and his crimes, and loved him anyway.

For once she found herself grateful for the long, winding path to the Verungyr's gate, so steep it had to be interrupted by several flights of stone-cut steps. The Grind, as the people of Skar Magnol called it, at least provided a lengthy interval with which to calm her temper. It would be foolish to present herself, and her charge, to Sister Iron with a less than focused mind.

For her part, Lynnea betrayed no apprehension towards the impending meeting, even appearing to enjoy the walk. The paved track was bordered by overgrown tangles of bush and stunted trees for much of its length, affording the maiden fruitful opportunities to smile at the many darting birds. She also seemed unaffected by having had to endure Coelnyr's presence, a trial for any woman, especially when possessed of youth and beauty. Although, when Thera had descended the stairs to the dusty room, she found the *mahkla* hunched in a corner, his eyes downcast, almost as if he feared looking in Lynnea's direction. Thera knew instinctively that something had passed between them, but saw no disarray that might indicate a struggle. Lynnea appeared unmolested, paying the lascivious wretch no heed as she continued to fuss over the mouse perched in her cupped hands.

"Did you do something to him?" she asked Lynnea now as they climbed the last set of steps before the blessedly flat stretch of pathway leading to the gate. "That man back there," she elaborated when her question earned only a baffled furrow of Lynnea's brows. "I know fear when I see it. And he was fit to dirty those expensive trews of his."

Lynnea gave a shift to her shoulders and a small quirk of her mouth, a combination of gestures Thera had come to interpret as the closest thing her charge came to outright deception.

"Don't want to talk about it, eh?" Thera paused at the top of the steps, gesturing with the dreadaxe at the gate ahead. "Mark you this, girl. In there, you will be given no such largesse." When Lynnea replied only with a guileless blink, Thera sighed and stepped closer. "I mean to say, in there I can offer you no protection. You understand?"

The maiden's expression took on a rare seriousness then, leavened by a small curve to her lips. Once again, Thera's uncanny facility for reading words in Lynnea's bearing made itself known. *Do not worry over me.* She reached for Thera's hand, squeezing it briefly. A twitch of sympathy before she turned away revealed her next thought clearly. *Save your worries for yourself.*

Thera had expected her audience to be with Sister Iron alone. Yet, upon being granted access to the famed Hall of Nerlfeya, she found herself going to one knee before all three of the Sister Queens. The hall was a cavernous space in the deepest bowels of the holdfast, carved from the very fabric of Skar Magnol itself. A forest of pillars taller than any tree ascended to a vaulted ceiling beyond the reach of the glow from the fire that burned in the pit at its centre. The smoke birthed by the blaze ascended into blackness, but never lingered to choke the throats of the chamber's occupants. Legend held that Nerlfeya herself, the goddess in whose honour the hall had been built, had blessed the hall during its construction. Ulthnir's most exalted daughter, accorded dominion over fire by her father, had woven the blessings of the Altvar into the stones of the chamber in such a way as to banish the smoke. Thera, who had never harboured particularly deep convictions regarding the gods, thought it more likely that the acrid vapours escaped into the hollows of the mountain via an unseen fissure in the ceiling.

As custom dictated, it was before the fire that the Sister Queens stood when holding court. They never sat here; Nerlfeya's Hall was shorn of such frippery as comfort. The vast space lacked the smallest scrap of furnishings or ornamentation, for it was said that the goddess despised such things. For her, the only beauty lay in the abstract dance of flames.

The first words came from Sister Silver, another ancient custom, since she was the longest serving queen of the trio and therefore held the honour of speaking first. "Vellihr Thera Speldrenda," she said, voice as clipped and curt as Thera recalled from their first audience years before. Sister Silver was over seventy years of age, with the wrinkles and poor eyesight to prove it, yet stood with a straight-backed vitality. She did bear a staff these days, mostly to prevent her bumping into things. She blinked cloudy eyes at Thera, then squinted as her attention shifted to Lynnea. "I may be blind as a piss-drunk bat," she said, flicking her staff at the maiden. "But I can tell this one has forgotten to kneel."

Glancing back, Thera swallowed a grunt of annoyance at finding Lynnea still standing. This despite the stern instructions Thera had imparted on their journey through labyrinthine corridors and tunnels from the gate to this hall: "Do as I do." She gestured for the girl to kneel, but received only an incurious glance in return.

"I apologise, my queen," Thera said, turning back to Sister Silver. "My companion is unschooled in many things. Also, she lacks the power of speech—"

"We know well who your companion is, Vellihr," Sister Iron cut in. "And I doubt her failure to kneel has anything to do with a lack of schooling and certainly nothing to do with her absence of voice."

Sister Iron had always struck Thera as the personification of intimidation. A blunt-faced, stocky woman of middling years, she wore her usual garb of a warrior's leather armour and a sword at her belt. She gripped the weapon's hilt as she stepped forward, striding past Thera's kneeling form to approach Lynnea. Coming to a halt, she leaned close to the maiden, peering hard into her face.

"None should kneel to another, right, girl?" Sister Iron said. "That's what your father and his pestilent ilk believed, isn't it? The creed of the Volkrath in their deluded conception of the Uhltvar."

Uhltvar. That word again, bringing the twitching, maddened gaze of Kolsyg to mind. Yet it was the other word spoken by Sister Iron that stirred Thera's memory. It was an old tale recalled from girlhood. In the days before her great-grandfather's self-imposed seclusion, he had dwelt in a large, fortified house beyond the walls of Skar Magnol. There he welcomed many visitors, and few were more heartily greeted than the travelling story spinners. Come the night's feast, all voices would quiet as the spinner began to earn his supper. The tales she heard in those days were many, too many to remember easily. But the tale of the Volkrath had lingered, at least for a time. *The most vile of cults,* the story spinner had named them. *Twisters of the Altvar's wisdom. Murderers and oath breakers too . . .*

A small noise from Lynnea snapped Thera back to the present, finding the maiden regarding the growling face poised an inch from her own with lips thinned in the manner of one containing a laugh. Thera's alarm rose at the sight and she began to voice another excuse for her charge's behaviour. Fortunately, Lynnea forestalled further confrontation by raising her hands in a gesture of submission and going to one knee, her head bowed low.

Thera hadn't seen Sister Iron dither before, the woman being as decisive as she was imposing. Yet now she hesitated, regarding the kneeling maiden with a frown of both annoyance and confusion. Thera saw more than a desire for punishment in the queen's expression, reading in her face a fervent but frustrated need. For all Lynnea's obvious charms, Thera knew Sister Iron's interest had nothing to do with lust. She desired knowledge, but for some reason chose not to demand it in front of her fellow queens.

The moment stretched until Sister Lore's soft, precise tones broke the silence. "I think formality has been served, sister," she said. The youngest of the three, Sister Lore was also the tallest. As Sister Iron embodied the aggression inherent in her role, so Sister Lore conveyed the elegant serenity expected of hers. Many thought her the epitome of Ascarlian womanhood, with her flaxen hair and finely sculpted features. The words "beauty" and "radiant" were often ascribed to her, regardless of her perennially simple garb of plain woollen dress and shawl. Her only concession to ornamentation was the medallion bearing the moon and stars sigil of the goddess Trieya that dangled from a chain about her neck.

"And our faithful Vellihr has knelt long enough," she added, gesturing for Thera to rise.

Thera waited until Sister Iron had resumed her place alongside her fellow queens before consenting to stand. Lynnea followed suit, a small, poorly concealed giggle escaping her lips as she did so.

"You appear to be bearing treasure," Sister Lore said, inclining her head at the axe in Thera's hand. "That is the fabled weapon of Gythrum Dreadaxe, is it not?"

"It is, my queen. Gifted to me by the Dreadaxe's kin when I returned the treasures stolen from his barrow." Thera hefted the axe, holding it out. "Of course, my hands are not worthy of such a thing and I hereby offer this treasure to the Sister Queens. Long may it rest in your care."

Thera's offer was another custom, since all riches accrued to a Vellihr in the course of their duties were considered the property of the Sister Queens. She also felt scant hesitation in surrendering the axe. Her brother's envious desire for the weapon during their journey through the town was obvious, but Felnir had ever been a greedy soul, especially for renowned instruments of death. Thera's attitude to such things had always been practical: weapons were tools. She valued her spear, but, come the inevitable day when it broke or dulled beyond use, she would bid it a fond farewell and cast it into the sea. Having practised with the axe aboard the *Great Wolf*, she found it sat well in her hand and cut the air with satisfying efficiency. But there was nothing remarkable about it save it a deceptive lightness, and, of course, the craftsmanship of the engraved blade. Also, although she didn't like to admit it, the thought that it bore some stain of the curse of Gythrum's barrow muted any possessiveness.

From the way Sister Lore's features tightened as she looked upon the proffered axe, Thera wondered if Uhlwald Thurveld's tale might have some credence to it. Sister Lore's place amongst this triumvirate had not been earned by virtue of her beauty. There were few who possessed a more fulsome knowledge of Ascarlian history and she undoubtedly knew well the tale of the Dreadaxe's fate.

"A gift too great even for us, Vellihr," Sister Lore said, expression softening as she turned to her fellow queens. "Do you not agree, sisters?"

Sister Iron replied with an indifferent shrug whilst Sister Silver's squint narrowed in a manner that Thera was sure indicated a calculation of the axe's monetary value. The aged queen had also earned her allotted role for sound reasons, for there was nothing within the grasp of the queens' rule that this woman's still sharp mind couldn't reckon into a stack of coin. In the end, it appeared she decided Thera's reward was worth the cost to the treasury.

"Very well," Sister Silver said, stamping her staff upon the stones. "Can we proceed to business? My knees are fucking killing me."

"Yes, to business," Sister Iron said. She addressed her next words to Thera, but kept her eyes upon Lynnea. "Vellihr Thera, you were dispatched to the Skor Geld to punish the criminal Kolsyg Ehflud for his desecration and looting of the barrow of Gythrum Fihrskard. May we assume this mission is complete?"

Thera bowed her head. "It is, my queen. Kolsyg has been justly executed, the stolen treasure returned to the barrow, and—" she glanced at Lynnea's bandaged hand "—a blood price paid by Kolsyg's only child, Lynnea Trahleyl, to the satisfaction of the Dreadaxe's kin. She comes before you now to plead her case for inheritance of lands and goods held by Kolsyg in life. She swears before the sight of the Altvar to use such wealth in a manner that will wipe her family's disgrace from their ken and win their favour for her geld. As Vellihr of Justice, I vouch for her honesty and sound character. I also testify to the high esteem in which she is held by the people of the Skor Geld."

"Esteemed or not," Sister Iron replied, "she's still little more than a child. Placing so important a geld into the hands of one so untried would be foolish." Her eyes slid towards Sister Silver. "Do you not agree, sister?"

"Youth and foolishness are often bedfellows, it is true," the aged queen replied. "But her claim cannot be so easily dismissed, especially when vouched for by our most trusted servant. The law holds that the child of a deceased Veilwald may petition this court for the right of inheritance. It also holds that proper consideration be given before judgement." She turned her squint upon Sister Lore. "Does it not, sister?"

"It does indeed." Sister Lore's lips were usually formed in a partial smile, but Thera saw how that slipped away as the youngest queen's gaze lingered on Lynnea. Reading the faces of Sisters Iron and Silver had always been an easy matter for Thera. Not so Sister Lore. Thera didn't doubt the woman's basic goodness of heart, it being so evident in her every word and deed. However, serenity could also be a very useful mask and Thera often found Lore as inscrutable as any seasoned card player.

"However," Sister Lore continued, "although I don't doubt our Vellihr's word on this matter, I should like confirmation from the claimant herself before proceeding further. Tell me, child." The smile returned to her lips, widening to favour Lynnea with radiant regard. "Do you wish to inherit your father's lands and wealth? Do you wish to become Veilwald of the Skor Geld? A simple nod will suffice."

A small crease appeared in Lynnea's smooth brow as she returned the queen's scrutiny, but not her smile. The uncanny way she had of communicating her thoughts, at least to Thera, was absent now. Instead, Thera felt there to be as much calculation behind the maiden's eyes as there had been behind Sister Silver's when she contemplated the axe. Then Lynnea blinked, and the crease was gone. Stepping forward, she failed to provide the expected nod and instead placed her hand on Thera's before pointing the other at the Vellihr's brooch on her cloak.

"What's she doing?" Sister Silver asked, cloudy eyes slitted as they strained to discern meaning.

"It seems she wants to be a Vellihr," Sister Iron said. She let out a soft grunt of amusement, the closest she ever came to laughter, and added in a faint mutter, "Altvar save her."

"Is this true, child?" Sister Lore asked Lynnea. "You wish to become a most trusted servant to the Sister Queens?"

Lynnea nodded this time, her hand shifting to entwine her fingers with Thera's.

"You realise, girl," Sister Iron said, "that those who submit themselves to our service give up all claims to wealth and land? Also, you know that, although many start upon this path, few reach its end?"

Another nod, Lynnea's fingers tightening in Thera's grasp.

"I am bound to ask, Vellihr Thera," Sister Lore began, "if this fervent ambition is the product of your encouragement?"

"It is most definitely not, my queen," Thera stated. "In truth, I knew nothing of it until this moment."

"But do you know of any impediment or flaw in character that might bar this woman from our service?"

"Isn't that obvious?" Sister Silver cut in. "She can't fucking speak."

"Nor would she be the first Vellihr so afflicted," Sister Lore replied. "Vellihr Cartyg lost his tongue to torture early in his career and stands as one of the most honoured servants ever to bear our brooch. Then there was Vellihr Mostvig the legless, not to mention Vellihr Hesfa, who, I believe . . ." the queen paused in apparent recollection ". . . was quite blind."

Sister Silver's lips curled as she prepared a snarling response to the barb, but Sister Iron forestalled her with another enquiry. "It is not merely a matter of choice, or ambition," she said, now staring hard at Lynnea, "but talent. Vellihr Thera, to your knowledge, does this girl possess any particular abilities that would make her especially suited to follow you into this life?"

The cats. The orcas. That pervert Coelnyr huddling shit scared in a corner. Although speaking of it might invite scorn from these most pragmatic women, her duty to honesty in their presence was clear. Yet, as she began to voice her reply, she saw Sister Iron's eyes widen into a glare of warning, her broad head moving in a barely perceptible shake. *Why ask the question if she cautions me against an honest answer?* The prospect of lying to the other queens sat ill with Thera, but as Vellihr of Justice, her primary allegiance lay with Sister Iron, whose judgement she had learned to trust. In the end, she chose omission over voicing an outright lie.

"She's clever, my queen," Thera said. Looking at Lynnea, she saw her lower her head, a faint flush on her cheeks. "Also brave," Thera added, thumb tracing over the bandage on the maiden's hand as it clasped hers.

"So, you vouch for her?" Sister Iron continued. "As you vouched for her inheritance?"

"I do, my queen."

"Then—" Sister Iron turned to address her fellow queens "—I submit Lynnea Trahleyl be placed in the custody of Vellihr Thera, so as to prepare her for her chosen path. In time, she will return here to advise us on the girl's suitability to begin formal training."

"What about the Skor Geld?" Sister Silver said. "Still needs a Veilwald, doesn't it?"

"Rolnar Tarhrimvest struck me as a capable man, my queen," Thera said. "I submit the Skor Geld be left in his charge for the space of four seasons. If he governs to your satisfaction, he may be confirmed as Veilwald."

"Then it's done," Sister Silver said, sighing in relief as she turned and began to walk stiffly away from the fire.

"We have other business, sister," Iron said, but the old woman waved her stick in dismissal.

"My knees, sister." Her thin form disappeared into the gloom, voice echoing as she added, "And, Vellihr, tell those laggards in the Outer Isles they had better have a decent excuse."

"I too am content to leave the subsequent matter in your hands, sister," Lore said. She bade farewell to Thera and Lynnea with another smile of appropriate radiance, then strode off in the opposite direction to Sister Silver. Each of the queens came to this hall via different channels hewn into the mountain ages past. In between such meetings, they kept to their towers positioned at each corner of the Verungyr.

When Lore's footfalls had faded to silence, Thera turned expectantly to Sister Iron, finding the queen still engaged in stern contemplation of Lynnea. Clearly, the outcome of this audience hadn't assuaged her interest in the maiden, or was it suspicion?

"The Outer Isles, my queen?" Thera prompted when the silence grew long.

"Mmm?" Iron's gaze shifted to Thera. "Yes, that. Come." She started away from the fire, heading for the pathway to her own tower. "And I suppose you'd best bring your apprentice."

In some ways, the decor of Sister Iron's chambers at the top of the Iron Tower reminded Thera of her great-grandfather's room, but without the foreign influence. Instead of Albermaine-ish tapestries, the walls were adorned with Ascarlian shields bearing designs from all corners of the realm, along with an appropriately parochial collection of swords and axes. Whilst, like the Tielwald, she had an impressive library, much of the space in each room was taken up with maps. They were all neatly arranged and catalogued, furled into leather tubes and stacked on shelves. Yet, whilst the trappings of the queen's domicile were firmly Ascarlian, the contents of the maps were not.

It was one of the paradoxical aspects of Ascarlia that few could claim the title of cartographer. Despite owing near everything they possessed to their seafaring prowess, the Ascarls hadn't felt the need to chart their dominion until learning of the practice from their southern neighbours. Traditionally, sailors relied on the tales of their forebears for navigation, together with various runic inscriptions relating to tides and stars. This combination of ancient sagas and scratched bones had enabled a people once reduced to grubbing on the banks of fjords to conquer a vast panoply of mountain, island and shore. The old ways were still venerated and clung to by many, some even espousing a suspicious detestation of such foreign notions as maps. Sister Iron, however, for all her attachment to the accoutrements of Ascarlian warrior-dom, knew the value of an accurate chart over a tale your grandmother memorised as a girl.

"You've sailed the Outer Isles before, I believe?" the queen asked.

"Four years gone, my queen," Thera said, keeping the tired grimace from her face. The protracted climb here from the Hall of Nerlfeya wasn't as onerous as the Grind, but it still put an ache in both legs and back. "That business with the stolen brides, if you recall."

"Vaguely." Sister Iron went to the tall stack of shelves beside the narrow south-facing window, eyes busily searching the various tubes. "One of the few you resolved without bloodshed, I seem to remember."

"Yes, my queen. The brides hadn't actually been stolen, you see . . ."

"No matter." Iron plucked a tube from the shelves and moved to the large map table in the centre of the room. "Here," she said, removing the cap from the tube to extract the chart within. Unfurling it, Thera was struck by its size, a yard or so square. Also, as she scanned the clean lines on the unblemished vellum, it was newly drawn.

"Paid a chart-maker to come all the way from Ishtakar to make this," Iron explained. "Took him three summers and his labour didn't come cheap. But this—" she cast her hand over the map "—is surely the most accurate rendering of the Outer Isles ever set down."

Thera had some understanding of charts, and certainly no traditionalist objections against using them. But, since her duties rarely took her from well-travelled waters, she relied on the combination of her own experience and Gelmyr's wisdom to sail a true course. Looking at this one, she was intrigued by the way in which the sprawl of islands differed from her mental picture of the region. It was plain that there were far more landmasses making up the archipelago at the edge of the Sister Queens' realm than she had imagined. Her previous voyages to the Outer Isles had been to the larger ports, easily found anchorages with towns of a decent size, where the miscreants that attracted her notice were likely to congregate. But seeing the chain in its entirety put her in mind of an unnavigable maze.

Any hope that Sister Iron would send her on a straightforward mission to one of the southern harbours was quickly dashed when she tapped a broad finger at the north-western portion of the map. "The Kast Geld," she said. "Land of Storms, and fittingly named it is. Ever sail there?"

Once again, Thera was obliged to control her features, this time to quell a frown of reluctance. The Kast Geld lay on the eastern edge of the Styrnspeld Sea. Renowned for its inclement temperament, not to mention packs of the notoriously hostile white whales, it was not fondly regarded by any Ascarlian seafarer with a modicum of sense. "No, my queen," she said in as neutral a tone as she could manage.

"Well, tomorrow that's where you're going. The other gelds in the Outer Isles have all delivered their required tally of stockfish in advance of the Veltgruhn. Not so the Kast Geld. Nor is there any record of a ship from there arriving in Skar Magnol in recent months. Something is plainly amiss and you, my most faithful Vellihr, will find out what it is and put it right."

"You suspect rebellion?"

"It's been a long time since any portion of this realm rose to challenge the Sister Queens, but that provides no guarantee it won't happen again." Sister Iron cast a pointed glance at Lynnea. The maiden appeared to be paying their conversation little heed, instead occupying herself by wandering the room to peer at the various shields and weapons on the walls. "And the old tales relate that it was in the Outer Isles that the Volkrath first arose."

Once again, mention of an ancient menace, one the queen clearly felt to be connected to her new apprentice.

"Forgive me, my queen," Thera said. "I know the story, as do most who ever sat by the fire to lend an ear to the story spinner. But, by all accounts, the Volkrath were wiped out some five centuries ago."

"Not wiped out," Iron replied. "Cast out, albeit in greatly reduced numbers. And it was six centuries ago, not five, in the days following the self-imposed exile of King Velgard, greatest monarch of the Age of Kings. Riven by guilt for the slaying of his brother, he sailed away to the west, never to be seen again. In his wake arose 'The Age of Discord', as Sister Lore calls it, but the 'Age of Slaughter and Chaos' would fit better. For generations, kin fought kin for the right to claim overlordship of this realm, few achieving victory for more than a season before war descended yet again. And in the shadowed, neglected corners of Ascarlia, something vile began to take root amongst the destitution and lawlessness. The cult of the Volkrath was like a diseased tree, feeding off blood-soaked soil to grow into something monstrous. You know their creed?"

"They believed themselves inheritors of the blood of the Uhltvar, the first race of men set upon the earth by the Worldsmith. Those of lesser blood they considered impure and worthy of only servitude."

"It went deeper than that. The Volkrath massacred entire settlements they judged as 'weak of blood'. They would also kidnap children from families they believed to possess the purest bloodlines so that they might breed a race as blessed as the Uhltvar of old. All this, of course, earned them many enemies, but still their numbers grew as the Age of Discord persisted. Finally, an alliance of clans from the Fjord Lands and Inner Isles defeated them in a great sea battle off Ayl-Ah-Rohn. Hundreds, perhaps thousands, were slain, and the shattered remnant of their fleet sailed away, some say to perish in the Fire Isles. All we know is they never returned to plague us, but the taint of their creed lingers on, sometimes threatening to blossom into another pestilence."

The queen paused, eyes hardening as she continued to stare at Lynnea. "As it did in your father, girl," she said, voice pitched to a commanding note. "Stop pretending you're not listening to every word we say and get over here. If you're going to be a Vellihr, at least pay proper attention."

Lynnea gave a small, sheepish smile and dutifully came to the table. She returned Sister Iron's intense, searching stare with raised eyebrows, but no sign of alarm.

"Your father," Iron said. "You knew of his . . . interests, did you not?"

A shadow clouded Lynnea's eyes as she nodded.

"Did you share his beliefs?"

A shake of the head, the maiden's brow creasing in firm denial.

"Do you know how he learned of the Uhltvar and the Volkrath? What led him to such folly?"

Forming both hands into a fist, Lynnea raised them to her chest, placing them over her heart before pulling them apart. After this, she shrugged.

Sister Iron grunted in annoyance and looked about the room. "I have quill and parchment. She can write her answers . . ."

"She doesn't know runes, my queen," Thera said. "However, I believe she means that her father's heart was broken, I assume following the death of his second wife. Grief apparently led him into unwise choices. As for how he came by his knowledge, she doesn't know."

Iron's features shifted into a sceptical squint. However, she allowed a long pause before speaking again. "Do you remember your mother, girl?" she asked. "I believe you were very young when she passed into the Halls."

This time, Lynnea's expression became much more guarded. Lowering her gaze, she responded with a slight nod.

"I too remember her," Iron said. "Very well, in truth, for we were friends. Back in the days when I was Vellihr of Justice, like Thera. Your mother was very skilled in healing, especially the mixing of curatives and ointments. Given the nature of my work, I had cause to call on her often. So we have met before, Lynnea Trahleyl, when you were just a tottering infant, but even then you had such a curious way of looking at the world. Your mother told me much about you, how proud she was, but also how troubled. And it wasn't your lack of speech that troubled her. Nor your uncanny way with beasts, although she marked it as surely a blessing from the Altvar. 'She sees so much,' your mother told me. 'More than she should. And I hear her tell of it, but not with her voice.'" Iron tapped her head. "This was where she heard your words. And though she rejoiced that the Altvar would allow her such a gift, also it frightened her, as well it might. So—" the queen leaned closer, voice lowered but no less lacking in command "—can you explain how, when you see so much, you failed to see your father's descent into a mad and murderous creed?"

Lynnea kept her head lowered, allowing her hair to veil her features. However, through the dark, silken barrier, her eyes flashed at the queen, bright with defiance and the first glimmer of anger Thera had seen from her. Although the maiden's hands formed no further gesture, Thera found she could read the meaning clearly.

"He was her father, my queen," she said. "A daughter should not speak ill of her sire."

Sister Iron's attention moved from Lynnea to Thera, her squint narrowing. "Such perception, Thera," she observed, reaching out to tap a finger to Thera's temple. "Or do you too, perhaps, hear something in there?"

As Thera fumbled for an answer, the queen decided to spare her. "A matter best not poked at too much," she said. "As is the way with the Altvar's more enigmatic blessings. But it seems the girl is well placed in your charge. Have the highest care for her, for I cherished her mother and made an oath regarding the well-being of her child."

"I shall, my queen." Thera hesitated, uncertain as to the wisdom of voicing the question she wanted to ask, but Sister Iron was nothing if not perceptive.

"Out with it," she said.

"In the hall," Thera said, "I divined a certain reluctance on your part to discuss my apprentice's . . . blessings in front of Sisters Lore and Silver. Could I ask why?"

"Because they have their responsibilities and I have mine. Sister Silver keeps us fed and free of penury. Sister Lore preserves our history and oversees our laws. And I, for my part, am charged with preventing the Ascarls from once again falling to ruin, either through foreign agency or their own folly. Therefore, the Altvar's gifts, given their import, fall within my province."

Thera discerned an additional firmness in Iron's tone, as if she might be warding off argument. "But," Thera ventured, "Sister Lore might disagree?"

Iron said nothing, but did consent to shift her head in a fractional nod before asking, "But do you disagree, Vellihr of mine?"

Of mine. An incontestable description. Although Thera had sworn loyalty to all three monarchs, the responsibilities of the Vellihr of Justice had always sat within the gift of Sister Iron. Furthermore, when Thera eschewed her great-grandfather's service and presented herself to the Sister Queens, this woman had been her mentor, only new crowned after many years occupying the role Thera now held. She trusted no one more completely.

"I do not, my queen," Thera said with grave assurance.

"Well and good, then." Sister Iron returned her focus to the map, tapping a finger to the southern reaches of the Outer Isles. "Although you are to investigate the Kast Geld, best if you start your enquiries in the Aiken Geld. Veilwald Hakkyn's loyalty has never been doubted. Find out what he knows about his northern neighbours. You can take this with you." She gestured to the map. "I have copies. You'll also have the Swift Spear and the Wind Sword to aid you. You've worked with both Vellihrs before, as I recall."

"Alvyr and Gynheld, yes. Both excellent Vellihrs of the Sword who shall do fine service. My thanks, my queen."

"Save your thanks, Thera." Iron turned to her, features set in grim regret. "Putting down a rebellion is a task you have not yet undertaken. It's an unpleasant business, for you must be as harsh as you are kind. If they have grievances, listen to them, make what restitutions you can, and promise to bring all other matters to the Sister Queens' attention. But you must allow no further breach of their obligations. If every geld in the realm takes it upon themselves to stop sending stockfish, the Fjord Lands will starve come winter. Draw steel only if you must. But if you must, don't spare."

Seeing Lynnea's features betray a mingling of disgust and disapproval, Thera responded quickly, "As you command, so it shall be, my queen." She garnished the statement by sinking to one knee, holding Iron's notice whilst Lynnea continued to scowl at her back.

"Hmm," Sister Iron grumbled, awkwardly patting a hand to Thera's bowed head. "Right," she said, stepping back. "Off you trot, then. Best take that axe along too. I've a sense you'll need it."

CHAPTER ELEVEN

Felnir

"An inch to port," Behsla whispered, hands busily hauling the lead weight up from the dark water below the *Sea Hawk*'s prow.

"Inch to port," Felnir repeated to Kodryn, matching his whisper. The veteran nodded and hurried to the stern, where he leaned close to Sygna to pass on the instruction. Her deft touch on the tiller steered them closer to the centre of the reed-banked channel. The clouded sky and quarter moon this night concealed their progress along this waterway, but also made for hazardous navigation.

"Best slow the oars," Behsla advised. She lowered the weight again, but her attention was now fixed upon the gloomy stretch of river ahead. "We're getting close."

Instead of calling out a command, Felnir crept from one rower to another, softly repeating the order until the faint splash of oar blades had dimmed. Each oar had been liberally smeared in pitch the day before and the row-ports further buttressed against noise by a wrapping of sheepskins. Still, Felnir heard every creaking board and swaying rope as a shout. The task ahead required a stealthy approach lest they find themselves slain come the dawn. *Or worse*, he added inwardly. *Captured.*

Moving back to Behsla's side, he peered into the dark, straining his eyes until, finally, he saw it: a faint scattering of flickering lights. "There," he said, pointing.

"I see it." Behsla had returned her attention to the weighted rope, brow furrowed in consideration as three knots slipped through her grasp.

"Do we anchor here?" Felnir asked, receiving a head shake in response.

"Not unless you want to wade through bog all the way. Reckon it'd take two days at least to get there from here."

He swallowed an impatient sigh and concentrated on the lights ahead. There were more of them now, the cluster growing and widening to describe a definite shape. Felnir judged the castle's dimensions to be that of a minor holdfast, but with annoyingly high walls. As they drew nearer, the light of the many torches adorning the stronghold revealed a three-tiered structure. Two fortified enclosures formed the base topped by a tall, rectangular tower. The darkness concealed the pennant flying from the tower's summit, but he knew it to be the standard of House Lambertain, the family that had held the dukedom of the Cordwain for generations.

"Two inches to starboard," Behsla said, hauling the weight up once more.

This time the altered course brought them into a yet narrower channel, so narrow in fact that the oars rustled the reed-covered banks. Felnir quelled the impulse to question his *Johten Apt*'s judgement. She had assured him she could navigate a passage to Castle Granoire, one that concealed them from the eyes of its defenders, and had never let him down. Finally, when the reeds had grown so thick the oars could barely be worked, Behsla signalled for the *Sea Hawk* to halt and drop anchor.

"Grass grows so thick here the mast will be easily missed," she said. "The channel ahead winds a bit, but a boat can make it through to the road in short order. From there, it's a quarter-mile walk to the castle gate."

"Nicely done, as always," Felnir complimented her, which earned only the barest nod in response. Behsla was not a soul that responded to praise. Nor, in truth, did she appear inspired by riches, not that sailing with Felnir brought much of those in any case. After years at sea together, Felnir had come to the conclusion that the only reward this woman regarded as worthwhile lay in the satisfaction of a difficult job well done.

"Those are some high walls," Kodryn said, peering through the encroaching vegetation at the torchlit holdfast. "Not a climb I'd relish. The dark might protect us, but also makes it more likely you lose your grip."

"We wait for dawn then," Guthnyr said. "The light will be better, but not enough to reveal us." When his suggestion received only a short, disparaging glance from Felnir, he went on. "I'll do it if the rest of you are too craven."

Felnir knew his brother's ardent lust to garner renown from this enterprise arose, at least in part, from being denied the chance to climb Skar Magnol. He was also plainly still irked over the fact that the *Sea Hawk* had sailed from port before the annual bout of cele-bratory excess that was the Veltgruhn. Their mission required urgency and Felnir had no desire to encounter his sister again, regardless of his brother's need for regular bouts of drunkenness and brawling.

"One man alone inside a castle?" Felnir asked. "How exactly do you intend to free our quarry from what will surely be a very securely locked dungeon, and get him out again?"

"Mere details, brother." Guthnyr laughed. "A sword and a strong rope is all I require."

"One they'll hang you with before the setting of the midday sun." Felnir turned away and moved to the mid-deck. "Falk," he said, resting a hand on the broad shoulder of the man seated to starboard. "Time for you to betray your countrymen again. What can you tell me about stealing from a castle?"

Felnir had discovered Falk chained to a grindstone in Assyrna, punish-ment for knifing a man in a dispute over a card game. As part of a highly unofficial arrangement with the local guard captain, Felnir paid for prisoners who might make a useful addition to his *menda*. At first glance, he found Falk a doubtful prospect. Although of impres-sive stature, an inch less than Felnir in height but a few inches broader, the dullness in the man's eyes showed a lack of the required cunning. Also, he spoke barely any Ascarlian and could converse only in his native Alberic. Questioning revealed he had no memory of the fracas that earned his chains, and only the vaguest recollection of the course of his life before that. Felnir ascribed the man's dulled wits to the old scar on his forehead, mottled flesh surrounding a patch of depressed skull. Although he saw little use in this man, his plight stirred Felnir's occasionally troublesome sympathy and he paid the guard captain the usual fee. At least he could work an oar. It was only weeks later, after further careful interrogation, that Falk's true value became known. Although the last dozen or so years of his life were a mystery, to him and others, large portions of his prior life were not, and a very interesting life it had been.

"Castle Granoire is known as the tightest gaol in all Albermaine, m'lord," he told Felnir, speaking in his native tongue. His fluency with Ascarlian had improved over the years, but he stumbled over details and nuance, both of which were required now.

"Not a lord," Felnir sighed. He had told Falk this more times than he could remember, but it never stuck.

"Sorry, m'lord." Falk bobbed his head. For a man who had spent his life an outlaw, Felnir thought Falk's attachment to subservient formality just one of many strange things about him.

"Then, no one has ever escaped it?" Felnir asked, jerking his thumb over his shoulder at the hazy outline of the castle. Dawn had come and gone an hour before, leaving the surrounding marsh wreathed in a low-lying mist. It provided an additional measure of welcome concealment but also a good deal of damp, cough-provoking botheration.

Falk's scarred forehead creased, the dullness gone from his gaze as his mind churned. This man possessed only a dim recollection of spending nigh a year chained to a grindstone, and, in truth, had confessed more than once that he wasn't even sure Falk was his given name. Yet, when it came to the subject of outlawry in his homeland, he could spout a wealth of detailed lore that would shame the most learned scholar.

"Heard tell of a fellow who got himself out through bribery," Falk said. "Some lordling who fell foul of the Cordwain duke. Had the coin to buy his way clear, but no means of escaping the marshes. Hounds tore him apart within sight of the walls. The duke decreed one in five of the guards hanged as punishment. All this would be more'n fifty years gone, m'lord. Since then, any poor sod who got sent to Granoire never came out again."

"No hidden tunnels?" Sygna asked in Alberic, near as smooth as Felnir's. As it should be, for he had taught her. "A drain perhaps?"

As Falk had trouble comprehending the fact that Felnir wasn't noble, he had similar difficulty with Sygna. "None, m'lady," he said, head bobbing in apology. "The whole place is built on the largest chunk of rock in all the Cordwain marshes. So there's no sewers as such, just slots halfway up the walls through which they chuck all their filth."

"No way in or out." Sygna grimaced at Felnir, slipping into Ascarlian. "Except by storm, and we've neither the numbers nor the rams and ladders for it. The old man's set us an impossible task, my love." Her voice took on a bite as she said this. Sygna had known Felnir's great-grandfather near as long as he had, but her view of the Tielwald had ever been sour, sometimes bordering on hatred.

"Beg pardon, m'lord," Falk said, bobbing his head again. "But there's more'n one way into a castle that don't involve grubbing through tunnels or climbing walls whilst waiting for an arrow in the neck."

Felnir noted that there wasn't even a vestige of confusion in the outlaw's gaze now. In fact, he appeared more enlivened and focused than Felnir could remember. "And what are those?" he asked.

"No holdfast can be built without gates," Falk said, nodding towards Castle Granoire. "And, though this one's a prison, it's still the same, sitting all the way out here with no drinkable water or crops for miles. Victuals and folk have to get in somehow. Means there must be carts come trundling along the road at least twice a month, maybe more. Also, given the purpose of it, stands to reason they'd likely be bringing prisoners too. Had a captain once told me the key to a prison is . . . what y'call it?" Falk paused, his scar puckering as he delved deeper into the vault of his memories. "Routine. Show a guard what he expects to see and he'll undo all the locks for you. Or something like that." Falk shook his head, muttering, "Do wish I could remember that captain's name."

"You're right," Felnir said, raising an eyebrow at Sygna. "We don't have the numbers to take a castle. But I think we've enough to seize a cart or two."

Three days later, they spied a trio of carts making their way along the road cutting through the marsh. Felnir had filled both the *Sea Hawk*'s boats with his most reliable hands, save Behsla, who had to be left behind to take charge of the ship. The nights encamped alongside the road had been a miserable trial, for he dare not risk a fire even this far from the castle. The dank, bug-infested annoyance of it all led to some muted complaints, mainly from Guthnyr, but for the most part, his *menda* bore it well. Like Falk, the majority of his crew had chosen life aboard the *Sea Hawk* as a preferred option to something far worse. All were, therefore, accustomed to discomfort.

"Four guards," Kodryn reported. They lay amidst the shorter grass fringing the road, Kodryn training his spyglass on the approaching caravan. "Mounted and armoured," the veteran went on. "Two in front. Two in back. The drovers don't seem to be armed." His weathered skin wrinkled around the eyepiece. "No cage wagons. Must be just a supply run."

Felnir cast a glance at the dim smudge of Castle Granoire. The lingering mist ensured that any disturbance on this road would be concealed from a lookout on the walls, but sound carried far in the marshes. So, a bloodless ambush was not an option. He turned to Sygna, lying alongside with a six-strong party of archers to her rear. "All the guards," he told her. "The drovers too, if it looks like they're going to cry out."

She passed whispered instructions to the others before they rose into a crouch and spread themselves along the roadside. Three of the archers bore windlass crossbows capable of piercing armour at close range. Sygna and the others carried the ash hunting bows common in Ascarlia. Felnir had absolute faith in their ability to find a gap in the guards' plate.

Turning, he met Guthnyr's eye and gestured for him to crawl closer. "Reckon they'll have ale in those barrels, brother?" he asked with a grin. "Brandy too, I'd wager."

Felnir didn't return the grin, instead fixing his brother with a cold stare. "This has to be done quietly," Felnir stated, voice pitched to an intent murmur as he held Guthnyr's gaze. "No challenges. No battle cries. No laughter. You understand?"

The grin faded quickly from Guthnyr's lips, familiar resentment tightening his face. "I'm not a fool, brother."

"Then here's your chance to prove it. Keep your sword sheathed until the first arrow flies."

Felnir raised a fist just above the level of the grass, the signal for the rest of the party to make ready. He then lay on his front, both hands pressed to moist soil, poised to spring upright when the moment came. Although he had lost count of the times he had lain in wait for victims or enemies, this tense interval never failed to stretch his nerves and add a beat to his heart. Inevitably, the memory of his first ambush rose to mind as the clop and trundle of the caravan drew nearer. Back then, it had been the sun and sand of a baked desert that brought misery to him and his comrades, and their foe that day had been far more formidable. A thirty-strong contingent of rebel cavalry from the Saluhtan's southern provinces, grim-faced men hardened by years of rebellion in which massacre and battle were bedfellows. Having been their captive, Felnir had very much wanted to kill them all. His ambition hadn't been disappointed.

The thrum of Sygna's bowstring banished memories of screaming men and blood spilled upon the dunes. Instead, he heard the surprised grunts and thud of arrow and bolt striking home. The leading guards were nearly level with his position when Sygna's party loosed. Felnir watched the two armoured riders tumble from the saddle, then surged to his feet, drawing his sword and charging for the carts. A glance towards the rear of the caravan revealed a pair of riderless horses already being calmed by Kodryn and Druba. Tuahla and Falk took command of the other two whilst the rest of the party descended on the carts.

The drover seated on the leading cart was clearly no fool. A heavily bearded man of middling years, he dropped his reins and raised his hands as Felnir approached. The fellow on the cart behind him proved to be of a less perceptive disposition. Standing with his face twitching in panic, he cast a terrified eye over the warriors thronging the road before fixing his gaze on the distant castle, drawing breath for a shout. Felnir expected one of Sygna's arrows to skewer the drover's throat, but Guthnyr got to him first, vaulting onto the toe board to deliver a punch that left the fellow senseless on the road.

The third drover was also foolish, but inclined towards flight rather than clamour. Wiry and quick, he sprang from his cart and pelted into the long grass, successfully dodging the hands and blades that sought to bring him down. He managed a dozen sloshing paces into the marsh before Sygna's arrow took him between the shoulders.

Felnir issued instructions to strip the slain guards of armour before turning his attention to the drover on the leading cart. The bearded fellow hadn't changed his position, but the alarm on his face had now shifted into wary calculation. "You strike me as a man of uncommon good sense," Felnir said, resting a hand on the cart's brake lever. "Am I wrong?"

The drover's eyes narrowed at Felnir's accent, a measure of fear creeping back as recognition dawned. The beard bunched in a manner that told of a swallowed insult. "*Ascarlian dog*", or maybe "*filth*"? Felnir didn't care either way. "You've made this trip before," he said, twirling his sword for emphasis. "Otherwise you wouldn't be in front."

The eyes narrowed further as the drover responded with a cautious nod.

"Good. I'll need the name of whatever lord has charge of this shit-pile and the name of the sergeant on the gate. Also—" he beckoned for Tuahla to come over "—you're going to describe the layout of Castle Granoire in detail and my talented friend here is going to draw a map. To ensure your honesty, I'll be leaving you here with her when I pay a visit to the castle. Should I fail to return, she will assume you lied and do many interesting things to you before you die. Tell the truth and you'll be free to trot off back up this road as soon as our business is concluded. How's that sound?"

The drover's narrow gaze twitched as it tracked over Tuahla. Like Falk, she had led an eventful life before finding herself exiled from her homeland and in need of employment. So, whilst Felnir knew the inked scars that marked her face to be a sign of high status, and signifiers of considerable learning, this bearded cart-man looked upon her and saw only the personification of a foreign menace. Once again, he nodded before swallowing and speaking for the first time.

"It's Lord Elbyrn Dumalle has charge of the castle," he said, banishing the croak in his voice with a cough. "Right cruel bastard he is too. And a miser. So if your business involves his end, I doubt the Martyrs will curse me for not standing in your way."

"Good man." Felnir clapped him on the shoulder and moved away, unhitching a length of rope from his belt. "Guth, come here a moment, would you?"

"I wouldn't get too close," Falk warned the guard sergeant on the gate as he leaned towards Guthnyr's bound form in the bed of the cart. "All Ascarlians are beasts, to be sure. But this one's the worst I've yet clapped eyes on."

Felnir felt that it was Guthnyr's glower that made him such a convincing prisoner. His eyes blazed at his brother in baleful intensity as he wriggled in his bonds, insults caged by the wooden peg gagging his mouth. He thrashed at the sergeant with a rage Felnir knew to be only partially faked, causing the stocky, hard-faced soldier to draw back in instinctive alarm.

"What'd he do?" he asked Falk. The outlaw wore the armour of the slain corporal who had been leading the caravan. As the only one amongst them fully fluent in Alberic, and capable of mimicking a Cordwain accent into the bargain, it was best if any questions were addressed to him. Felnir harboured only minimal concerns that Falk's incomplete memory would fail them now. Another curious aspect of his malady was its tendency to disappear when fighting or thievery were called for. Falk's mind, it seemed, was only complete when his criminal tendencies were wholly engaged.

"Got drunk at the harvest festival in Leavinsahl," Falk said. "Smashed up a tavern and then, if that weren't bad enough, went out into the street and blundered straight into the ducal procession. Thereupon, he outraged the person of the duchess herself."

At this, the hardness of the sergeant's brutish features became a snarl of genuine rage. "Filthy cur!" he spat, hefting his halberd to jab the butt of the pole into Guthnyr's gut. "I fought alongside duke and duchess both in the Martyr's War. To have her besmirched by the likes of you . . ." The sergeant's diatribe sputtered into incoherence as he repeated the jab, then reversed his grip on the halberd, aiming the spiked tip at the prisoner's throat. Felnir knew of the widespread affection for their duchess amongst the folk of the Cordwain, hence his reasoning behind the story of Guthnyr's imprisonment. Only those who did injury to the ducal household, either through fraud or violence, were consigned to Castle Granoire. However, it was clear he had underestimated the reverence enjoyed by the duchess, for he saw true murderous intent on the sergeant's face.

Fortunately, Falk's wits remained true, and he spoke up before the halberd drew more than a bead of blood. "It's thanks to the duchess that he's still got his head," he said. "Duke Gilferd wanted him hanged then and there, but his wife's kind heart is famed, as you know. So, this bugger's got five years in Castle Granoire's deepest dungeon to look forward to instead."

The sergeant paused, lips twitching, before he huffed and withdrew his weapon. "Kind heart, aye," he said. "That she has to be sure. See this?" He drew the collar of his mail shirt down, revealing an old jagged scar tracing from his ear to the hollow of his neck. "Rhianvelan peasant's billhook at the Battle of the Bluffs. Stitched closed by the hands of the duchess herself, it was." He turned an expression of dire promise on Guthnyr. "Was gonna take my pension at winter's end. Now, I reckon I'll stay on a bit longer. Make sure this fellow has all the comforts he needs."

Guthnyr, as was his wont, returned the sergeant's glare with one of equal ferocity, which at least prompted the soldier to grunt out a laugh. "You've papers?" he asked, turning to extend a hand to Falk.

"Signed and sealed by the duke's chamberlain," Falk said, handing over a folded parchment bearing the appropriate drip of embossed wax. As the sergeant went about scrutinising the document, Felnir remained seated atop the cart, features composed into the boredom of routine. Tuahla had laboured over the papers during the voyage south, drawing from correspondence supplied by his great-grandfather to create a convincing simulacrum of the chamberlain's hand and phrasing. Still, although Guthnyr's appalling crime had done much to distract the sergeant, he struck Felnir as irksomely diligent, a man who might well possess the wit to spot a forgery.

"Why no cage wagon for this shit?" he grunted, jerking his head at Guthnyr.

"Busted axle," Falk said. "Wasn't worth the delay waiting for it to get fixed, since there's only him to deliver. Drovers refused to take him, on account of his viciousness. It's why there's just us two."

The sergeant shrugged, lowering the papers to cast an eye over the supplies piled on the cart. "Hope you remembered his lordship's pickled trotters, otherwise you'll be heading back to Leavinsahl with a sternly worded letter for your captain."

"All requested goods are present and correct." Falk gave a good-natured laugh. "So I'm told, least ways."

"Save a brandy cask that fell off on the way, eh? Usually does." The sergeant grinned and returned the document to Falk, waving a hand at the guards standing at the gate. "All right. Let 'em in."

Passing beneath the stone archway and into the lower keep, Felnir found the beat of his heart transformed into a rapid thud. Although this place differed in both smell and appearance to his desert prison, proximity to such places never failed to put him on edge. The hour had grown late and the dimming light crafted deep shadows from the innards of Castle Granoire. Memories of long months spent locked away from the sight of sky and sun, of torment and toil under the lash, dampened his brow and set his guts to roil. One misstep now and he might well find himself consigned to another prison, a fate he found less preferable than death.

He took solace from the relatively few guards he saw on the walls above, barely half a dozen and only one holding a crossbow. His questioning of the sensible drover had revealed Castle Granoire to be poorly garrisoned, since its purpose was to keep folk in rather than out. The plethora of doors, each one thick and bearing a heavy lock, was less encouraging, but locks presented no barrier to those with keys. They jangled in a complex bundle upon the belt of the man who awaited them in the courtyard beyond the gate. Judging by his fine velvet doublet, Felnir deduced that Lord Elbyrn Dumalle himself had come to meet his new prisoner.

He offered no greeting to Falk as he strode to the cart, casting a shrewd eye over its occupant. "Is this one of a violent or cunning temperament?" he asked, voice cultured but clipped, his gaze lingering upon Guthnyr with a depth of scrutiny Felnir didn't like.

"Truth be told, I couldn't say much beyond the violence, m'lord," Falk said, proffering the document once more. "A drunken Ascarlian who outraged the duchess . . ."

"The details of his crime do not concern me," the gaoler cut in. "As Lord Warden of this castle, I am charged by Duke Gilferd to keep his guests alive and contained, and have been mostly successful in both regards. Prior experience has led me to the conclusion that those of a violent disposition are, in the long run of things, less troublesome than those gifted with a cunning mind. A few strokes of the lash is enough to quiet the former, whilst the latter will scheme and wriggle for months or years until they find a way to worm free of my grasp, not that any have ever succeeded."

Felnir's jaw clenched, heart thumping yet harder at mention of the lash. Through his mounting rage, it occurred to him that he may well have blundered in putting himself at the centre of this mission. A prison overseen by a man such as this presented a dangerously tempting combination. His great-grandfather had, of course, been correct in guessing his true reason for tossing the spy into the Liar's Sea.

"To your great credit, I'm sure, my lord," Falk said, still holding the document out for inspection.

"Leave that with the gatehouse guard," Lord Elbyrn replied. Waving a hand in dismissal, he shifted his attention to the rest of the cart's contents, presumably in search of his cherished pickled trotters. "Get this unloaded and be off with you. I've no stores to spare of your supper."

"Beg pardon, m'lord," Falk said. "But if you were to cast your eye over this, you'd see we have orders regarding this prisoner's situation here."

"What?" His lordship snatched the document from Falk, brows knitting as he scanned the neatly inscribed script. "'Upon your honour, you are directed to provide the bearer of this missive proof that the prisoner is afforded all due comforts and assurances of no ill treatment.'" He gave a disgusted snort before turning his glare upon Falk. "She is aware that this is a fucking prison, I assume?"

"Any questions for the duchess are far above my station, m'lord," Falk said. "And best asked by your honoured self. If you'd care to pen a reply, I'll be glad to bear it to her with all dispatch."

Lord Elbyrn's face darkened at this, but he raised no further argument. The Duchess of the Cordwain's kindness was famed, but so were the consequences of arousing her ire. "Get him up, then," he snapped, flicking a hand at Guthnyr, the many keys upon the warden's belt jangling as he made for the largest door in sight. "And I'll find him a cell with the least number of rat droppings."

Cutting away the rope binding Guthnyr's legs, Felnir and Falk dragged him from the cart. His stumbles were convincing, for a man will lose the sensation in his limbs when bound for a long time, as was the spittle rich if muffled profanity he grunted around his gag.

"A shouter, is he?" Lord Elbyrn said as he worked the last of three keys to unseal the huge door. "No great matter. They always quiet down in the end. Had a fellow some years back screamed his innocence for the length of a full year." The door squealed open to reveal a steeply descending stairwell dimly lit by the wavering glow of torchlight below. Elbyrn continued his anecdote as he started down the stone steps. "Then one day, midwinter I think it was, he just stopped. The guards found him the next morning with his head bashed in. He'd run at the wall, you see? Must've taken him a dozen or so attempts until he managed to end himself. Curious thing was, less than a month later, a missive arrived from the duke ordering his release on the basis of newly discovered exonerating evidence." He gave a wry chuckle. "Then there was that pirate woman, didn't speak a single word her whole time with us . . ."

His tales continued as he led them ever deeper into the castle's bowels, Felnir keeping a careful count of the doors they passed through and the various turns of the passages they navigated. He noted that Elbyrn never failed to find the right key for each lock, his hands moving with unconscious precision to pluck the required implement from amongst the extensive collection. The three guards they encountered during the journey were also smartly turned out and showed no sign of fatigue, meaning his lordship had the good sense to ensure their shifts weren't overly long. Whilst Felnir's heart would never find room to admire a man such as this, he could at least recognise a soul well suited to his allotted task.

". . . flogged her until she breathed no more, of course," Elbyrn said as they came to another door. "No choice in the matter. Once they do violence to my soldiers, a painful death is the only appropriate response. Now then." The door featured four separate locks, Felnir intuiting that what lay beyond it was of some importance and therefore this trek was finally at an end. "Let us find a suitable abode for our most honoured guest."

With the locks unsealed, he heaved the door open and stepped inside, gesturing for them to follow him into the corridor beyond. Glancing left and right, Felnir saw no further guards, but a long row of yet more doors, candlelight glimmering at the edges. A soft voice echoed from the shadowed recess of the passageway, raised in plaintive song.

"I usually order them two to a cell," Elbyrn said. "Unless they're particularly mad or dangerous. A lone captive rarely lasts long. I've often found the mere threat of locking them up all alone suffices to keep them quiet. For the moment, however, I think our new arrival would benefit from some solitude, until we can gauge his temper . . ."

The warden's words came to an abrupt end when the point of Felnir's dagger jabbed into his chin. Elbyrn's eyes widened in both anger and terror as Felnir increased the pressure of the blade, forcing the noble against the wall. "There is a man in this castle with this inked upon his skin," Felnir said, holding the unfolded parchment bearing the archaic design in front of Elbyrn's face. "You will open his cell. If you do not, my lord, I assure you I shall take the greatest pleasure in depriving you of various bodily accoutrements until you do, starting with your ever so busy tongue. Please," he hissed, a hungry quaver in his voice as he leaned closer, staring into the warden's eyes, "do me the favour of saying no."

CHAPTER TWELVE

Elvine

Vellihr Ilvar said almost nothing to Elvine for the entirety of their voyage to Skar Magnol, for which she was grateful. Much less gratifying was the copious attention he afforded her mother. Throughout the years Elvine had been witness to plentiful male interest in Berrine Jurest, all of it met with polite discouragement or, when it became unduly persistent, firm and far less polite rejection. In the case of Ilvar Kastrahk, the Stormcrow, however, Elvine's mother proved surprisingly willing to endure his constant inquisitiveness regarding Ascarlian history and legend. Curiously, unlike the suitors in Olversahl, Elvine saw no obvious lustful intent on the Vellihr's part. If anything, his demeanour towards Berrine was courteous to the point of reverence.

"But," Ilvar said, frowning as he sat with Berrine in the hold, "was not Velgard's slaying of his brother the fair outcome of battle? And was not Einlaf deserving of such an end? He had murdered their father, had he not?"

"So all the sagas agree," Berrine said. "But, as dreadful a man as Einlaf surely was, he had always been the kindest and most diligent protector to his younger brother. Love is not an easy thing to set aside, even in the face of duty to a father treacherously slain by poison."

Elvine watched them from her corner of the hold, a position she was allowed to stray from only in her mother's company. She felt little resentment at her constrained circumstance, given that Ilvar's *menda* were as intent on ignoring her as their leader, and she had at least been spared chains. Her daily forays to the deck of this warship, insisted on by Berrine, who avowed a desire for regular intake of fresh air, were an uncomfortable trial. Elvine couldn't help but stare at the face of each crew member and wonder which of them had struck the blow that robbed Uhttar of life. For their part, this collection of weathered and scarred warriors returned her scrutiny with either scowling judgement or subdued hostility. She supposed it made sense that the Vellihr charged with rooting out Altvar-hate would choose to recruit those who shared his sentiments.

She found little distraction in the view beyond the confines of the ship, apart from grey waves and a continually overcast sky. A tree-covered shoreline occasionally resolved out of the mist, but soon faded. Consequently, she had no notion of where this vessel sat within the realm of Ascarlia. Berrine assured her that Skar Magnol was only a few days away now, but Elvine couldn't shake the sense of journeying through a void that might never end. Although, given her uncertainty regarding what lay at the conclusion of this voyage, that could be no bad thing. She was also forced to confront the notion that, given how badly she had failed her fellow congregants, interminable anxiety was the least of her due. Thoughts of Uhttar rose with gut-clenching regularity, as did dark imaginings over the fate of Bahn and the others who had refused to recant their Covenant faith. She had asked Berrine if her newly elevated status might offer some avenue to arranging their release, only to receive a stern rejoinder: "I expended all the influence remaining to me in securing your life. Ask me this no more."

"But to forsake his kingdom out of guilt," Ilvar continued. "When he stood acclaimed as the greatest of kings, does that not indicate . . ." The Vellihr paused, his long face taking on the cautious frown of a devout man straying into potentially blasphemous waters. "Perhaps a slide into madness?" he finished in a near whisper.

"Following Einlaf's defeat, Velgard ruled for over two decades before decreeing his own exile," Berrine pointed out. "And the Ascarls flourished under his wise but firm guidance. That's hardly the tale of a madman. But, by all accounts, his guilt preyed upon him more with each passing year until he felt himself judged by the Altvar, with but one way to atone for his crime."

"To seek out the fabled Vaults of the Altvar." The troubled crease to Ilvar's brow faded as his features took on a familiar cast; the unblinking stare of an earnest believer. "The realm of stone constructed in their honour by the first men to tread the earth. Do you think he did it? Is such a thing even possible?"

Elvine saw her mother suppress a shrug. Ilvar was the kind who harboured little appreciation for such annoyances as nuance or uncertainty. Elvine had come to understand that his constant badgering of so celebrated a scholar as Berrine was in fact a quest to banish doubt. She wondered if it ever occurred to him that allowing himself even the smallest portion of uncertainty rendered his faith in the Altvar an incomplete thing and, therefore, he was as much a heretic as those he persecuted.

"There are tales," Berrine said, "or rather, fragments of tales that allude to Velgard's success. And many others that speak of his abject failure. All are fanciful, however. Some relate how the exiled king sailed with a fleet of the most pious souls into the heart of the Fire Isles and there did he make his grand discovery. Others say he found naught but empty ruins, or that he and his followers perished of starvation in the maze of tombs and galleries. Yet more tell of a great second kingdom of the Ascarls built amidst the Vaults of the Altvar where myriad treasures were unearthed, artefacts blessed by the gods themselves to grant wisdom and long life. But—" this time Berrine allowed herself a shrug "—these are the scribblings of lesser scholars or those given to absurd imaginings, their names often lost to history. In truth, no source agrees on the fate of Velgard ehs Trehka, the Exiled King."

Ilvar sat back, eyes distant with thought. Had they still been at home and this man just another suitor, or one of her mother's more attentive students, Elvine could have banished him with a pointed clearing of the throat or a reference to the lateness of the hour. But he was the Vellihr of Lore and, whilst he continued to afford Berrine a strange level of deference, she had made it clear that they were obliged to stomach his presence for as long as he willed it.

Fortunately, any further questions were forestalled by a shout from the deck above. It was too muffled and filled with sailors' jargon for Elvine to divine its meaning, but was apparently important enough for Ilvar to make his apologies and ascend the steps, leaving them in peace at last.

"You didn't tell him all of it," Elvine said. Rising, she moved to sit opposite her mother, hands extended to the warmth offered by her small oil lantern. "All the tales about Velgard's fate, I mean. Why not?"

"I doubt he would have appreciated further vagary." Berrine tossed her a fox fur blanket, one of several provided by Ilvar. "Put this on."

"How about the one relating how his Tielwald went mad and tried to murder him?" Elvine said, pulling the covering about her shoulders. "I always appreciated the drama of it. In fact, didn't some Albermaine-ish mummer write a play about it?"

"She did. 'The Ice Bound Treachery' by Jeanivere D'Ambrille. It's terrible." Berrine paused, lips forming a half-grin and eyebrow arched. "And the name of the traitorous Tielwald was . . . ?"

Elvine's lips bowed into a grin of her own, her first since the seconds before she watched an axe crunch into the chest of Supplicant Truth. The familiarity of having her memory put to the test kindled a welcome spark of comfort. "Angmund Sictalvyr, the Diretongue," Elvine replied with prompt smugness. "For his crime, he was cursed with endless life by the Altvar and exiled to wander the earth in eternal contemplation of his guilt."

"Very good, daughter of mine." Berrine's grin faded as a shadow crept across her face. Reaching into her blouse, she retrieved the trinket Ilvar had given her in Elvine's cell. It was attached to a thin leather cord now, Berrine's voice lowering to a grim murmur as her fingers turned the small silver knot so that it caught a tiny gleam from the lantern's glow. "And, as our destination draws near, we must talk of another Tielwald. One who is, sadly, very much alive and we are like to meet soon."

"I thought we were being taken to Sister Lore," Elvine said. "You are entering her service, are you not? And Ilvar answers to her."

"Apparently. But appearances grow ever more deceptive the closer you get to those who hold power. This—" she held the silver knot up "—is the Tielwald's gift to his servants. A little thing of scant notice, you might think. But, in truth, it weighs as heavy as a *mahkla's* chain."

Elvine could think of only one way her mother could know such a thing, though she hesitated before voicing it. This was something Berrine had never spoken of before and the notion that she would withhold secrets stirred a morsel of hurt in Elvine's breast. "You?" she said. "You were once his servant?"

"I was." Berrine closed her eyes, breathing out a long breath. "Before you were born, in the days when the Fjord Geld was the possession of the Albermaine crown. There were those of us who longed for a return to the Sister Queens' rule, and bright did our passion burn. Bright enough for us to take ship and sail off to take part in the Pretender's War. He had promised freedom for the Geld, you see? If we could but make him king of Albermaine." She opened her eyes, regarding Elvine with a grimace of sardonic regret. "I'm afraid I didn't make much of a warrior, but I did meet some interesting people. And you know what became of the Pretender."

"Tormented to death for the pleasure of the Dowager Princess," Elvine said.

"Quite so. For all his folly, I think he deserved a less agonised end, for at heart he was a good man. And he would have made a half-decent king if given the chance. But, it all came to nothing and back to the Fjord Geld we went, shamed, defeated, and grieving the friends we lost. The Tielwald's agent found me within a few days of my return. 'There is more than one way to slip a cage,' he said, and gave me this." She dangled the trinket on its cord, then returned it to her blouse. "Told me to keep it next to my skin. I didn't understand why for a very long time." Berrine paused, settling a steady gaze upon her daughter. "What do you know of the Tielwald?"

"His name is Margnus Gruinskard, a warrior of famed repute and principal counsellor to the Sister Queens, said to bear the blessing of the Altvar from which he derives his wisdom."

"And the title? Tielwald. What does it mean?"

"It pertains to counsel, 'insight' in the ancient tongue. 'Leader in thought' would be the closest modern translation."

"It would. But there is another, older meaning. Did you know that before Margnus Gruinskard assumed the title of Tielwald, there hadn't been one so named since the Age of Kings? And in those days a Tielwald's role was often shrouded in mystery, for it's said those who held such rank possessed skills of an arcane nature. In the most ancient sagas, the words 'magician' and 'Tielwald' are interchangeable. But then, it is also often equated to 'spymaster' too, which is more fitting of the current holder."

"You spied for him. Before Olversahl fell, you helped him." Elvine felt her stomach tighten as understanding dawned. "The city's fall to the Sister Queens . . ." Her voice caught around her next words, but she forced them out in a hoarse rush. "The library. King Aeric's Library. It burned . . ."

"Elvine . . ."

"All those books. The wisdom of centuries . . ."

"I didn't know it would happen." Berrine's voice held a forceful note but also a tinge of weariness, as if this was an often repeated statement, albeit one spoken to herself. "There was so much chaos that terrible night, so much fear, death and flame. To this day, I don't know if the library's destruction had been the Tielwald's plan all along. He denied it, of course, for such a crime could never be forgiven by the Sister Queens. But I had also heard him speak about how the library had been tainted by foreign lore. 'An ancient Ascarlian treasure sullied to the point where it had lost all meaning,' he said. Either way, it burned. And yes, I had a hand in it because it was I who found the path through the mountain. It was thanks to me that the mountain was rent open and the great *menda* flooded in to take the city. It was the worst of my crimes."

Recent events had provided Elvine with a great deal of novel experiences, but finding herself with nothing to say was particularly jarring. Looking at Berrine sitting with her head lowered in shame, Elvine felt the world tilt at the notion that her own mother was, in truth, something of a stranger.

"Why have you never told me this?" she managed when the silence had grown to an uncomfortable length. A redundant and foolish question, since the answer was so patently clear.

"Why didn't you tell me about your dalliance with the Covenant of Martyrs?" There was no criticism in Berrine's voice, just sombre acceptance. When Elvine didn't answer, Berrine raised her head, her lips forming a grim smile. "So, there we have it, daughter of mine. All souls harbour secrets, and often for very good reason."

She straightened, letting out a brisk sigh as she reached to clasp Elvine's hands, her eyes hardening. "Listen to me and heed my words, for I do not exaggerate when I say your life depends on it. The Tielwald wants something from me. What it is, I don't yet know. I do know he will assuredly use you to force it from me. Trust nothing he says. Agree to nothing he suggests. Whatever questions he asks you, offer no more than you must, but remain truthful. And—" Berrine's grip tightened, hard enough to make Elvine gasp "—accept no gifts."

In light of Berrine's dire predictions regarding their reception in Skar Magnol, Elvine expected to be immediately conveyed to the Tielwald's presence. Instead, Ilvar and two of his warriors escorted them from the docks, through dense, ill-favoured streets that made Olversahl appear a picture of orderly construction, and up a steep, leg-straining path to the Verungyr itself. After a brief exchange of formalities at the gate, Ilvar led them through a dizzying succession of halls, corridors and stairwells.

Elvine had always pictured the Verungyr as a grim, if magnificent, fortress of monolithic proportions yet, whilst the exterior had partially matched her expectations, the interior certainly didn't. They passed walls of bare stone or unclad brick and walked upon uneven flagstones. Doorways were often narrow and so short even she had to stoop to enter. Also, she found it stark in its lack of finery or basic decoration. The descriptions she had read of foreign castles spoke of corridors adorned with paintings and tapestries and corners occupied by ancient suits of armour. Here there was only the occasional runic etching or Altvar sigils carved into stone so long ago the edges had softened.

Eventually, they emerged from a narrow doorway into a small courtyard at the base of a tower. Elvine knew that, when not attending joint council, the Sister Queens each occupied one of the three towers adorning the Verungyr. Judging by the scroll motif to the goddess Vysestra carved into the lintel above the door, she deduced that this one must be occupied by Sister Lore.

"Vellihr Berrine," Ilvar said, "you and I are instructed to wait here. Your daughter will proceed alone." He offered Elvine a curt nod and gestured to the door. "Sister Lore awaits you."

"My daughter," Berrine stated with icy precision, "will not be going anywhere without me."

"My instructions are clear." Elvine could see no vestige of Ilvar's prior consideration in his uncompromising stare. His interest in ancient tales had no bearing on his duty. Here, he was the Vellihr of Lore and nothing else. "I was also instructed to inform you," he went on, "that any refusal of a lawful command will result in the dissolution of your agreement. You will find the cells of the Verungyr even less appealing than those of the Rent, I'm sure." He completed his unsubtle threat with a pointed glance at the two warriors standing to either side of Elvine and her mother.

Berrine fixed him with a flinty stare, her face flushing. "If she wants my skills—"

"Mother," Elvine cut in, grasping Berrine's arm and shaking her head. "We've no choice," she added in a soft murmur. "You know that."

Berrine's jaw clenched, body stiffening with the effort of controlling both anger and fear. "What I told you about the Tielwald," she said, clutching Elvine's shoulders and staring into her eyes. "It applies also to the queens."

Elvine nodded, forcing a smile. "I understand."

"Sister Lore awaits you," Ilvar repeated, drawing a venomous glare from Berrine. She might well have uttered some choice but incautious insults if Elvine hadn't pulled her into an embrace.

"Worry not," she whispered into Berrine's ear. "I doubt they brought me all this way for an execution."

* * *

The tower's spiralling steps were many and Elvine's breaths echoed loud by the time she reached the door at the top. Unsure whether to simply open it or knock, she dithered for a time until a female voice from within called out: "Just come in, dear child."

Still Elvine hesitated, her abundant fear now laced with puzzlement, for she was sure she heard a note of amusement in that voice. Had she been summoned merely to be taunted by this queen? Taking a breath, Elvine stiffened her back and pushed the door open, entering the chamber beyond with all the poise she could muster.

"So, here she is at last," the woman before her said, coming forward to clasp Elvine's hands. Her poise faltered in the face of the woman's unexpected warmth, and her beauty. She stood several inches taller than Elvine, a veritable picture of the Ascarlian female ideal. The tale of her origins was universally known to all Ascarls, an orphan girl no more than twelve found alone aboard a drifting longship. The vessel appeared to have suffered an attack by white whales, though how every soul aboard save her had been claimed by the sea beasts remained a mystery and the terror of the experience had robbed the girl of memory. The story spread quickly, some seeing the hand of the Altvar in her miraculous deliverance. Such notoriety brought her into the care of the previous Sister Lore, who set her upon the Vellihr's path and a seemingly inevitable rise to queendom. To many she was not just one of the Sister Queens but "Ulfmaer's Gift". Such a combination of beauty, compassion, and intellect must be a blessing bestowed by the gods.

"Elvine, is it not?" the woman asked as Elvine continued to stare. She saw no artifice in her countenance, only welcome touched with sympathy.

Realising her mouth was open, Elvine closed it with a gulp, swallowed, and forced out a response. "It is, my queen."

"And I am Sister Lore. So now, we are well met." The queen's grip momentarily tightened on Elvine's hands before she turned, gesturing to the room's other occupant. "All three of us. Allow me to introduce Margnus Gruinskard, Tielwald to the Sister Queens."

Given the size of the figure silhouetted in the stained glass window occupying much of the far wall, Elvine failed to understand how he hadn't been the first thing she had noticed. Much of his form was concealed in shadow, but Elvine could discern the shape of the huge axe he rested his hands upon. A portion of his aged, grey-bearded face caught a multi-hued shaft of light from the window, so she was able to make out the deep scrutiny in his eyes as he afforded her a short nod by way of greeting.

"You are younger than I expected," Sister Lore went on, looping her arm through Elvine's and leading her deeper into the chamber. "For I was assured your depth of learning exceeds even that of your mother."

"It does not, my queen." Elvine was proud of the fact that she kept a quaver from her voice, although the contents of this chamber provided a useful distraction from her fears. Berrine maintained a decent-sized library at home, her collection limited by space and want of funds. Sister Lore clearly felt no such constraints, for books were everywhere. Most sat neatly in tall cases lining the curved walls, each one equipped with a ladder to reach the highest shelves. Others rested in less orderly stacks, the scrap paper jutting from between their pages indicating them as the most actively read. Clearly, this library was not for show.

"I doubt there are many who could make such a claim," Elvine said, wresting her focus back to the queen.

"Assuredly," Sister Lore said with a small chuckle. She led Elvine to a couch alongside a large blazing fireplace, gesturing for her to sit. "But your mother's knowledge, vast as it is, remains largely concentrated on Ascarlian scholarship. Whilst you, I am told, have far broader interests."

The queen perched herself at Elvine's side, her smile still in place, but one eyebrow raised in expectation. Apparently, this was a question that couldn't be ducked. Elvine considered resorting to obfuscation, stuttering out a vague allusion to a liking for foreign tales, but knew it wouldn't wash with this woman. Her gaze was warm, to be sure, but there was unmistakable intelligence to it, not to mention regal authority.

"I assume my queen refers to my . . ." Elvine swallowed again. "Covenant beliefs."

A sound came from the Tielwald then, the first he had made. He made no obvious movement and spoke no words, but Elvine heard the grind of his axe stave upon the flagstones.

"I do," Sister Lore said. "And have no fear, dear child, for your crimes stand pardoned and I am keen to converse with an adherent of the foreign faith. I find it all quite fascinating, truly. A form of belief that eschews worship of gods in favour of, forgive me, what I can only term as an ill-defined assembly of otherworldly beings residing in an insubstantial and unseen realm that plays host to human souls after death. Or do I misunderstand?"

Another grind of wood on stone from the direction of the Tielwald whilst Elvine strove to formulate an inoffensive yet accurate response. "My queen's description is . . . correct in basic terms. However, it is also incomplete."

"In what way?"

"The Martyrs, my queen. The true name of the faith commonly referred to simply as 'The Covenant' is, in fact, 'The Covenant of Martyrs'. It is a divine compact between humanity and the Seraphile, guardians of the Eternal Realm, a compact that has been sealed in the blood of the Martyrs for generations. The Seraphile provided us with their divine guidance, but it was the Martyrs who gave us the example of how best we may live our lives in honour of that guidance."

"Martyrs, yes." Elvine saw a mischievous glint in Sister Lore's eye as she turned her attention to the Tielwald. "And how fortunate we are that there is one here who has actually met a living Martyr. Come, Margnus, tell us all about your meeting with Evadyn Blackheart. Did she strike you as a personage of exemplary divine attributes?"

For a second, Elvine wasn't sure the Tielwald would respond to the queen's question. She heard his axe haft grind once more, the old man so still that when he actually took a forward step, Elvine was unable to contain a start of surprise. "Evadyn Blackheart was a deranged fanatic," he said, supporting himself with his axe as he approached. His voice put Elvine in mind of an aged, wheezing ox, albeit one that retained a good deal of strength. When he came to a halt a few yards from the fireplace, Elvine risked a glance at his face, now fully revealed by the glowing coals. Her gaze was instantly captured by the dark void of his empty eye socket as he continued his description of the woman who had crafted that wound: "A deluded fraud who would have greatly benefited her people by consenting to die the night of Olversahl's liberation. If she was the best of the Covenant, I'd judge them all to be worthy of naught but eradication."

"Harsh judgement indeed," Sister Lore said. "Though, given the Blackheart's infamy, one that history would seem to agree with. But it is your judgement I crave this day, dear Elvine. What say you of the dread Martyr queen?"

Elvine forced her attention away from the Tielwald's vacant eye and back to Sister Lore, attempting to modulate her tone into something resembling her mother's when she imparted a nuanced lesson. "Evadyn Blackheart," she began, surprised by how well the words flowed from her lips, "is the Ascarlian name for a woman who, through violence and perfidy, briefly rose to hold sway over the kingdom of Albermaine. Her true name was Evadine Courlain, daughter to a distinguished noble family and, by all objective accounts, a brave warrior, a skilful commander of troops, and possessed of a remarkable gift for oratory. However, her virtues will be forever eclipsed by the inarguable facts of her cruelty, tyranny and insanity. She was not a true Martyr but one who perverted the tenets of the Covenant to serve her own vile ambitions. Such is the doctrine of the Luminants Council, and I find no credible argument against it. Evadine Courlain represents a perversion of my faith, and she was never truly a Martyr."

She wasn't sure what form of response she expected, but the amused and faintly triumphant grin Sister Lore turned on the Tielwald was unexpected. "Dearest Elvine sounds like . . ." The queen frowned in apparent consternation. "What's that Alberic word, Margnus? The one for those who make a living by enmeshing folk in the vast, contradictory web of their customs?"

"I believe the term is 'lawyer', my queen," the Tielwald supplied. Once again, Elvine found her gaze drawn to his face, although this time to his good eye, finding it narrowed in careful appraisal. Also, his shaggy head was now tilted in a manner that bespoke recognition.

She assumed he was looking upon her and seeing a vestige of the woman who had once spied in his service.

"Yes. Such a strange people our southern neighbours are." Sister Lore gestured to one of her taller bookcases. "I possess many a history of Albermaine, but as yet, they remain an enigma. So many contradictions. Their kings pay obeisance to the Covenant, yet their actions are no different from any dynasty that seeks only to cling to power. And I find it odd that an entire realm given over to a creed that supposedly promotes love and harmony should so persistently mire itself in strife."

"Such is the way with false beliefs, my queen," the Tielwald said. His scrutiny of Elvine remained undimmed, and she found herself squirming under the weight of his stare. "The Altvar were wiser than the ancient liars who concocted the Covenant. For they knew that strife would always be with us."

Sister Lore lapsed into contemplation, allowing a lengthy to silence to descend whilst Elvine debated the wisdom of looking away from Gruinskard's eye. She felt a rising urge to speak of her mother, remind this man of their former association so as to gauge his reaction. However, it struck her that revealing such information to the queen might prove unwise, if she, in fact, knew nothing of it, which seemed unlikely. Elvine's head began to ache with the accelerating swirl of doubt and calculation. Being in the presence of people who could order her immediate execution was exhausting.

"Still," Sister Lore said, interrupting Elvine's racing thoughts, "matters I shall enjoy discussing with you at length. For now, the Tielwald would like your learned opinion on another matter." She angled her head at Gruinskard, brows raised.

Elvine noted the length of the pause before the huge old man consented to extract something from the inner pocket of his faded leather jerkin. "What do you make of this?" he said, holding out a piece of parchment to Elvine. She saw how his good eye betrayed no emotion whilst the puckered flesh of his empty socket narrowed considerably.

Taking it, she found the parchment to be freshly pressed, lacking the stains and ragged edges of age. Unfolding it, she beheld a sigil of unfamiliar design ringed by runic inscriptions in ancient Ascarlian. It was evidently a recent copy, legible if inexpertly rendered with several smudges and inelegantly formed characters.

"I don't recognise the sigil," she said. "But this form of runic dates back to the Age of Kings. It's one of the rarer variations of the script, in fact, most commonly found in the upper Skor Geld."

"Can you read it?" Gruinskard asked.

"The phrasing is difficult, as ancient runic was a reflection of a time when different dialects of Ascarlian were far more common." In fact, Elvine's translation of the inscribed words had been near instantaneous. This variety of runic was one of her favourites and, although challenging to many scholars, presented little difficulty for her. However, her mother's warnings rang loud as she pondered the reasons why two of the most exalted figures in all the realm would seek her opinion on this thing. *Whatever questions he asks you, offer no more than you have to, but remain truthful.*

"Well?" the Tielwald prompted as Elvine's eyes lingered on the parchment.

He already knows what it says, she realised. *Or at least a portion of it. This is a test, of honesty if nothing else.* So she couldn't lie, but she knew Berrine wouldn't want her to reveal the full scale of her skills to this man. Possibly not to the queen, either.

"It alludes to a common legend," she said, frowning as she read from the script, taking care to labour over the translation. "'From the . . . Altvar's Vaults . . . shall all blessings flow.' A phrase that crops up repeatedly in relation to the fabled Vaults. There are many legends about them, as I'm sure you know, my queen."

"I do." A knowing but amused frown creased Sister Lore's brow as she added, "And the rest?"

"'In time of . . . shadow shall he rise . . . The Age of Wrath will . . . craft a . . .'" Elvine hesitated, unsure of the queen's reaction to the final word. However, her certainty that Sister Lore and the Tielwald most assuredly already knew every word inscribed on this parchment made concealment a redundant exercise. "'A king,'" she finished in as neutral a tone as possible.

"A prophecy then, wouldn't you say?" Sister Lore asked.

"Possibly, my queen. The Age of Kings was a fractious time, and those who claimed arcane insight made frequent claims regarding the hoped-for ascendancy of a figure who could wring order from the chaos. Prophecies borne out by the reign of King Velgard, some say. Though the peace he brought proved short-lived and it may well be that this was set down after his sojourn into exile."

Sister Lore nodded in approval, reaching out to briefly clasp Elvine's hand before taking the parchment from her. "The last scholar we showed this to required ten days to make sense of even a portion of it. And he translated 'Age of Wrath' as 'season of disgruntlement.'" She looked up at the Tielwald. "It seems, Margnus, we have a more than worthy replacement for that old drunk you dug out of the archives."

"Yes, my queen." Gruinskard's empty eye socket twitched and once again Elvine's sense of being recognised welled, but now it was tinged with a palpable mistrust. Had the Tielwald suspected her mother in some way? Or was it that he harboured resentment for her abandonment of his cause?

"Excellent." Sister Lore rose to her feet. "Then please have all the relevant materials brought here so that dearest Elvine can make haste with her work. My thanks, as always, Tielwald, for your peerless service."

The creased edifice of Margnus Gruinskard's face remained impassive as he gave a formal nod, though the scarred hole of his missing eye continued to twitch. Before he turned to make a slow but steady progress to the door, Elvine discerned a frustration in that involuntary shifting of flesh as he afforded her a brief parting glance. The queen might be satisfied with her answers, but he assuredly was not.

"Come now," Sister Lore said, taking hold of Elvine's hand once more and tugging her to her feet. "Let me show you your rooms."

"Rooms, my queen?"

"Of course." The queen led her towards a gap between two bookcases, which revealed itself as a stairwell. Elvine was pulled inside and found herself struggling to match the taller woman's pace as she ascended the steps. "You shall reside here with me now. I have, hence-forth, appointed you to the position of . . ." She came to a halt, brow furrowed. "Personal Scholar and Scribe to Sister Lore. I think that suits, don't you?"

"But . . ." Elvine took a breath to prevent herself stuttering. "My mother . . ."

"Has already been conveyed to her own quarters. As a Vellihr of Lore, she will be very busy. Don't fret over it. You'll see her soon." Sister Lore's laugh echoed loud as she resumed her rapid ascent. "In the meantime, I have so much to show you. Such fine times we'll have together."

Chapter Thirteen

Ruhlin

The nightmares were strangely cunning in their torments. Sometimes they assailed him with all manner of screaming horror, such as the gibbering, part-rotted faces of those slain at Buhl Hardta. Dead but yet somehow alive, the empty-eyed corpses of those he had known since boyhood would surround his flailing form, bone fingers clawing at his flesh. They tore at him with desperate cruelty, some portion of his terrorised mind recognising in their savagery a desire to make him one of them. Other horrors were more inventive, less frenzied, but always painful like the white whale that dashed his fishing boat to pieces and swallowed him whole to be slowly digested in its vast, acid-filled gut. But, occasionally, he was granted a small interval of calm, gulling him into the delusion that his torture might finally be over.

"Why are you asking me about that?" his grandmother demanded from her chair by the fire. "That was years ago."

Ruhlin, who had just emerged from a distorted remembrance of Mehlga's fate in which the sailors had pitched him over the side to join her in death, gaped at the old woman in bafflement. "Asking you about what?" he said.

"That perishing dog," she snapped. One of the curious aspects of his grandmother's unquiet tongue was that she never resorted to any form of profanity, even though such restraint did nothing to dull its edge. The women of Ayl-Ah-Lyhsswahl were famed for their ability to turn the air black with the foulness of their language, but not so Bredda Knifetongue. She barely glanced up from her work as she spoke on, continuing to thread the long needle through the sail she was mending. "It tried to bite you. Your father killed it. What else is there?"

"No." Ruhlin shook his head, unsteady gaze roving the interior of his grandmother's cottage. It was mostly familiar, but laced with jarring differences. The few adornments to the walls had consisted of dried flowers and herbs to ward off the foul humours that obsessed this dwelling's principal occupant. Now they were transformed into bones. They stained the stonework red with gore, gristle and tendon sticking to their joints as if freshly rent from a carcass.

"No," he repeated, forcing his wavering sight to focus on the woman in the chair. "No, that's not what happened. I killed it. I killed the dog."

"Hah!" She barked a laugh, something she never did, even as a taunt. "As if you've killed a perishing thing in your life. 'Cept the few fish you and that wastrel manage to drag from the sea, and them's all maggots by the time they meet my table. Useless bleeders, the pair of you."

"I killed it," Ruhlin persisted. "Tore it apart with my hands alone."

Bredda made a harsh clacking sound with her teeth. Unlike the laugh, this had been a frequently employed weapon in her verbal armoury, one brought into play when she wished to bring the latest argument to a close. "Salted guts, but you never did, boy. Y'father killed the beast and well done it was. They still talk of it in the mead hall."

"I killed it!" For reasons he couldn't fathom, the old woman's irate stubbornness angered him far more in this dream than it had when she still drew breath. "Something happened . . ." he insisted, advancing towards her. "Something happened to me. I . . . changed. My hands . . ."

He held them up, but they were small now. Neither the hands of a youthful fisherman nor those of a monster. These were child's hands, lacking calluses or deformity.

"Spared proper punishment," his grandmother said in a tone she had never used in life. This was the steady calmness of a soul that knew only cruelty. He had heard it before amidst this welter of nightmares, placed into the mouths of dead kin, but not hers, at least until now. "That was always your flaw, Ruhlin," she went on, rising from her chair. Gaping up at her, he realised his child's hands matched the rest of his form, whilst Bredda stood taller than a merchantman's mast.

She leaned down until her face was level with his, still speaking in that alien voice. "Your father's mistake. One I'll not repeat." The needle flashed in her hand, stabbing towards his eye. This then was the moment the trap was sprung, when pain arrived and the nightmare scored its next triumph. Yet, it didn't.

Ruhlin's small hand blurred, rising with unnatural swiftness to intercept the needle before it could skewer its target. He felt the point of the six-inch length of steel meet his flesh and braced for the agony, but it didn't come. Instead of his own scream, he heard the metallic ping of a broken needle hitting the floor. Looking again at his hand, he found it returned to monstrous proportions, and also, apparently, rendered invulnerable.

Blinking, Ruhlin shifted his gaze from his hand to his grandmother and realised she was now the one shrunken into childlike size. She stared up at him with dark, accusing eyes, her cracked lips curled in disgust. "*Sictskyra*," she said, the cruelty replaced by a tone of grim recognition.

"I don't know this word," Ruhlin said.

Bredda smiled and a veil of darkness surrounded them both, swallowing the cottage and creeping over her face until only the lips remained. They formed a smile and spoke. "You heard it before, Ruhlin. And will again." With that, they vanished and for one brief, blessed moment, he knew the bliss that came from the sudden removal of all pain.

Ruhlin woke to the sound of distant hammering, a rhythmic ring of metal on metal too remote to be truly irksome, but too close to ignore. To his surprise, he raised an unshackled hand to rub at his gritted eyes and felt the softness of a mattress beneath his back. Sitting up, he saw that all his limbs were free of bonds and his unclothed body mostly lacking the bruising or scars he expected. However, a glance at his immediate surroundings quickly dispelled any notion that he may have been granted some form of liberty. Thick bars rose on all sides, rising to over twelve feet high, where they bent inwards to meet a grindstone-sized bracket of solid iron. Ruhlin realised he was enclosed in a greatly enlarged cage of the type he had seen foreign sailors use to keep birds. Torchlight glimmered beyond the bars, but his sight was still too blurred to focus on details.

"Tehrweir, dein lihl?"

Jerking to his feet, Ruhlin sank into an instinctive crouch as he sought out the source of the voice. He had to spend a long interval blinking until his vision cleared, revealing another cage alongside his own. It was of identical construction, illuminated by a torch resting upon a stanchion in between. Moving closer to the bars, Ruhlin saw a man in the other cage. A tall figure with skin a shade darker than his, the man's naked body was sculpted in lean muscle. Looking at his face, Ruhlin's first impression was of features distorted by the flickering torchlight. Peering closer, he saw that the face of his fellow prisoner featured numerous marks. They clustered around his brows and swept back over his shaved head in a mottled sweep. Ruhlin wondered if they were the result of torture, or perhaps burning. But, as he squinted, he realised they were natural discolourations to the skin. The realisation stirred a dim memory, something Irhkyn had told him during one of those nights when the mead made him nostalgic for his sojourning days.

"Isktao-at lihl wahrveil bihen," the man in the other cage said. The words were completely meaningless to his ear and possessed no vestige of the accent or phrasing his captors aboard the ship had used. This was not a mangled form of Ascarlian but a true language, one he had never heard before.

"I'm sorry," he said, shrugging in apology. His head still throbbed with lingering confusion and a plethora of ugliness garnered from his epic nightmare. Slumping onto his bed, he rubbed at his brows. "I . . . can't understand."

Hearing a grunt of frustration, he looked up to find the other man had cocked his head, frowning in a manner that made it clear his comprehension of Ruhlin's words was equally lacking. Watching the marks on the man's hairless scalp shift with his expression, the kernel of relevant memory fought its way through Ruhlin's confusion. *Far to the south they live,* Irhkyn had said that distant night, the drink beading his beard catching a gleam from the fireplace. His moods would vary when he talked of his travels, darkening to an ominous glower when he spoke of battles or raids, but growing wistful when the subject turned to women or spectacle. Ruhlin recalled that, on this occasion, Irhkyn's face had been a curious mix of wonder and regret.

In a land cleaner and less spoiled by the hand of man than any I saw, he went on. *They don't wall off their fields like us or the southern wretches. Let their beasts roam free for the most part. Nor do they have any use for silver, except as jewellery. Not one looks the same as the other, though they tend to be darker than us, and they're all marked in some way from birth. The fools amongst us thought it a curse or some such. But I think it's just how they're made. And they're fierce, lad. Not folk to cross lightly, as the Blackheart found to her cost. That old bastard who had charge of our* menda *called them the Vaerling, an old word that means "strange ones". But the southerners have another name for them.*

"Caerith," Ruhlin said. "You are Caerith."

The man stiffened at this, then, after a pause for contemplation, responded with a cautious nod.

"I am Ascarlian," Ruhlin continued, returning to his feet. He patted his chest as he approached the bars. "Ascarlian."

The man nodded and patted his own chest. "Tuhlan."

Not his people, Ruhlin realised. *His name.* He patted his chest again, saying, "Ruhlin," which seemed to confuse the Caerith until he let out a small laugh of realisation and nodded.

"Ruhlin," he repeated, extending a hand through the bars, palm upraised and fingers spread. The cages were separated by an eight-foot gap, so clasping the proffered hand was impossible. However, Ruhlin still felt obligated to return the gesture.

"Tuhlan," he said, extending his own arm and attempting to mirror the position of the Caerith's fingers. From his satisfied grunt before he withdrew his arm, Ruhlin concluded they had completed a formal greeting. He wanted to ask how long Tuhlan had been here, but could think of no form of gesture that would convey his meaning. Instead, he gripped the bars of his cage and flexed his fingers, eyebrows raised in an unspoken question. The bars failed to move under the pressure and he knew Tuhlan's answer before he voiced it.

"*Ihsa*," he said, shaking his head with a grimace. *No.* These cages were too sturdy to be breached.

"Where are we?" Ruhlin said, turning to scan the shadowed space beyond the bars. The question was rhetorical for, even if he knew, Tuhlan couldn't tell him the answer. Off to his right, he saw a bright stream of daylight bathing a flat surface at the centre of a circular depression of some kind. Straining to make out some detail, he saw that the circle was surrounded by a series of broad, shallow steps. Seeing no features of note, Ruhlin shifted his gaze to the surrounding shadows, where more torches flickered. Their meagre glow caught on the bars of other cages, arranged in a great circle around the central pool of light. The closest was on the opposite side to Tuhlan's but positioned at twice the distance. Ruhlin could see a figure lying on the bed within, but this cage's occupant was either asleep or indifferent to a newly arrived neighbour.

"Hello?" Ruhlin ventured, voice modulated to little more than a whisper. When the figure failed to move in response, Ruhlin tried again, pitching his call at a near shout. "Hello!" It echoed for a long time, failing to raise any answer from the cage's occupant, but at least giving Ruhlin some notion of the size of this space.

"Must be vast," he muttered, looking up at the featureless void beyond the bars above his head. He saw no stars or moonlit clouds, meaning they were either underground or contained within a building of unfeasible proportions.

"Oh, it is."

Ruhlin's fright at the unexpected comment was compounded by two things. First, the voice was female. Second, he was abruptly aware of his nakedness. He made out only a dim outline at first, a slender form standing at the edge of the torchlight. Then she came closer, head angled in curiosity as her unabashed gaze roved over Ruhlin's unclad form. Hurrying to the bed, he removed the blanket and pulled it around his waist, something his new visitor found greatly amusing judging by the length of her laugh.

"Nothing I haven't seen before, I assure you," she told him when her mirth faded. Moving closer, he saw that she wore some manner of warrior's garb, a skilfully made assemblage of leather armour that enhanced rather than concealed her charms. Afforded an unobstructed view of her face, the word that sprang first to Ruhlin's mind was "cat".

"You Teilvik are always strangely bashful," she went on, large eyes blinking as she studied him further. From the unlined flawlessness of her skin and litheness of her form, he guessed her age at close to his own. But the predatory cast to her expression made her appear considerably older. It put him in mind of Angomar, and he discerned a definite echo of the dead Aerling's features in this girl's face. But, unlike Angomar, she spoke to him in a cleaner, less accented version of Ascarlian, sounding much like the well-groomed man who had forced the nightmare-inducing drugs down Ruhlin's throat.

"Except for him," she added, inclining her head at Tuhlan's cage. "Couldn't care less if I see his cock. Happy to shit in front of me, too. Aren't you, you filthy beast?"

Tuhlan gave no response, although the intensity of the gaze he directed at their visitor was starkly obvious. Ruhlin saw hatred in it, but also a hunger that had nothing to do with lust. The Caerith's eyes swept over the girl, keen for every detail. This Ruhlin recognised as a hunter's scrutiny. Tuhlan was in search of a weakness to exploit, something that seeded both admiration and hope in Ruhlin's breast. Here at least was a companion who pined for escape and, if they had experienced a similar route to this cage, revenge.

"Such a fierce look," the girl said, turning back to Ruhlin. "Since he speaks only gibberish, I can never tell if he wants to kill me or fuck me. Which do you think?"

"The first," Ruhlin said. He kept his voice flat and eyes steady upon hers. She betrayed no offence, however, merely laughing and sauntering closer to the cage, casting a pointed glance at his concealed groin.

"And what about you?" She laughed again when he gave no reply, resting herself against the bars and redirecting her attention to his face. "Father says you're Vyrn Skyra, a fire blood," she mused, studying him. "'Perhaps the most dangerous specimen yet found', he said." She leaned closer, dropping her voice to a conspiratorial whisper. "I'm supposed to stay very far away from you."

"Father?" Ruhlin asked, but another voice forestalled the girl's answer.

"Aleida!" Ruhlin felt little surprise, but also an upsurge in tension at the sight of the well-groomed man striding from the shadows. *Eldryk*, Ruhlin recalled. *The old crow called him Aerling Eldryk.*

The girl's face tensed in both resentment and fear before she hastily removed herself from the bars. She lowered her head in apparent contrition, which did nothing to lighten Eldryk's darkened visage. "I believe I told you to seek amusement elsewhere," he growled, advancing upon her.

The girl lowered her head further, and Ruhlin saw how she was fighting an impulse to flee. Eldryk's wrath was apparently something to be properly feared. He carried no weapon that Ruhlin could see, but was followed close behind by a very large man carrying a heavy, iron-studded staff and a whip on his belt. Pale as a fish's belly, hairless of head, and as broad of shoulder as he was of stomach, this one's role here was obvious from his accoutrements and the cruelty that seemed to be etched into every line of his craggy face. From the anticipation evident in his narrowed, dark blue eyes, Ruhlin divined that it would be Eldryk's whip-man who meted out any required punishment here.

"I . . . crave pardon . . . Father," the girl faltered. Ruhlin found it strange that she would risk speaking to him with such nonchalant ease and cower in the face of the consequences bare seconds later. Yet he was sure there was no artifice in her bearing, or in the fearful glances she shot at the pale giant's whip. "I . . ." She swallowed and choked around the next words. "I . . . was just . . ."

Whilst Aleida stuttered on, Ruhlin found his mind filled with Mehlga's face, that instant before her fateful act, the smile wavering on her lips. *You can trust the Aerling's daughter.*

"I called out to her," he said, rising to approach the bars. He spoke with all the forceful disrespect he could muster, casting the blanket aside in the hope his nakedness would enhance the sense of insult. "I'm thirsty and there's no water. Or do you want me to expire for want of sustenance? It seems a waste after all your trouble." He had been about to add "and your dead sister", but the glowering rage on the Aerling's face made it plain he had aroused his ire to a sufficiently distracting degree.

Eldryk gave no command, but the hulking whip-man knew his master's moods well. He unhitched and unfurled the whip with the swiftness born of lifelong practice. The ear-paining crack came next followed by searing jolt above Ruhlin's left eye. He jerked back from the bars, grunting in pain, his hand coming up to explore the cut. It was deep but not long, the kind that bleeds a good deal but shouldn't need stitching. The fact that the whip-man had delivered it through the bars was a testament to a remarkable level of skill.

"There." Ruhlin thumbed a trickle of blood from his eye to see Eldryk pointing to two iron-covered drains in the floor. "You draw water from one and piss and shit in the other," the Aerling said. "Do not talk to my daughter again or I'll have Radylf whip your hide down to the bone, regardless of how precious it might be."

Glancing at the whip-man, Ruhlin was bemused to see him inclining his head in a greeting that appeared disconcertingly genuine, the smile on his lips lacking the expected sadistic leer. Whatever he was, this one was no Uhtgyr.

"Away with you!" Eldryk barked, flicking a hand at Aleida, who promptly vanished into the shadows. Ruhlin watched the Aerling stare in her wake for a moment before drawing in a calming breath. When he returned his notice to Ruhlin, his features were free of rage, even bordering on affability. However, Ruhlin could see the falsity.

"Indulge a child and regret for a lifetime," Eldryk said with rueful resignation. "All her siblings I drove out and disinherited for unworthiness, but her I kept and I'm still not sure why. I suppose you're too young to know the trials of parenthood?"

Ruhlin pondered the wisdom of ignoring him, but the cut still leaking blood above his eye served as a potent warning. "I have no children," he said.

"Aerling," Radylf said, his whip drawing a hiss from stone as he swished it back and forth. He spoke in a high-pitched voice, the words heavily accented but comprehensible. Another aspect of his character that jarred with his appearance. "'I have no children, Aerling.'"

Jaw clenched to swallow a retort, Ruhlin afforded Eldryk a short nod before dutifully repeating, "I have no children, Aerling."

"I've found it a best avoided chore, but one I'm bound to by duty. And it is to the subject of duty that we must now turn."

Eldryk moved closer to the cage. In contrast to his daughter, he wore a long dark robe instead of armour, the collar and cuffs embroidered in complex swirls of gold thread. Although no giant like his whip-man, the Aerling was both tall and well built, his jawline absent of excess chins. As he clasped his hands together to concoct a pose of calm reflection, Ruhlin saw the thickness of his wrists and knuckles, and the scars that marred his skin. He might not dress as a warrior, but Ruhlin was sure Eldryk had known battle, most likely more than one.

"You may be labouring under the delusion that you are my slave," the Aerling went on, jerking his head at Tuhlan's cage. "Like him. But he is just another Teilvik, a savage valued only for whatever entertainment can be wrung from him before the Meidvang claims his otherwise worthless life. But you, my scion of the Vyrn Skyra, are no slave. You are my charge. A sacred responsibility that I will not shirk lest the Altvar curse me."

"Altvar?" Ruhlin repeated, surprise overcoming his caution. He flinched when Radylf gave another swish of his whip. "Aerling," he added quickly. "You worship our gods?"

"*Our* gods?" Amused disapproval showed in Eldryk's features, also a modicum of anger that made Ruhlin fear he might be about to earn another cut to the face. However, the Aerling merely grunted a disparaging laugh. "You truly have no notion at all of where you are, do you?" He shook his head in apparent bafflement. "How can this be? Still—" Eldryk sniffed and turned away "—a knot to be unravelled in due course, for we have time aplenty to explore our respective mysteries."

He addressed his next words to the whip-man, speaking so fast in his own dialect that Ruhlin could comprehend only a portion of his words. However, those he caught were concerning: "fierce but untrained" and "won't flinch from the killing strike". Eldryk paused, his gaze shifting back to Tuhlan. "This one, perhaps?"

"Too trained, Aerling," the whip-man replied. "He was deadly long before he got here. However, I have another who should serve very well indeed."

"See to it." Eldryk waved in dismissal, Radylf nodding before striding away into the gloom. The Aerling's face took on a sombre cast as he turned back to Ruhlin. This time, he saw no pretence in the expression. "Know this and mark it well," he said. "I was once as you are. Now, see the glory of my standing. It can be yours also, if you would just reach for it."

Somewhere off in the dark there came the echoing rattle of a lock and the squeal of iron hinges followed soon after by an outburst of growls and screams. At first, Ruhlin assumed the noises rose from an alarmed and enraged beast. When Radylf's whip cracked and the animalistic chorus choked off into fearful sobs, he realised this was the product of a human throat.

"As I said," Eldryk went on, now offering Ruhlin a smile of grim apology, "our association will be a quest to fulfil my duty, the first step being that I must try to kill you. For the value of your most precious blood lies in the spilling of it."

PART II

"Curse ye not troubled waters, for the sea's tribulations
shall shape the Ascarls as a sword is shaped by the forge."
Ulthnir Horuhnklehr – the Worldsmith –
from the Altvar Rendi

CHAPTER FOURTEEN

Thera

As the smallest vessel in their three-strong fleet, the aptly named *Swift Spear* proved the most adept at catching the wind and would often take the lead during the day's sailing. Thera felt no pique at this since Gynheld, the Vellihr in command of the *Swift Spear*, was an old friend and had earned the name Volksora – Waverider – for good reason. Gelmyr, however, viewed the smaller vessel's position at the head of their formation as an insult, both to the *Great Wolf* and his own esteem as the Johtenvek. Consequently, he spent much of the westward voyage hounding the crew to squeeze every last ounce of speed from their sails. Every rope was tightened and every yard of canvas angled to the perfect pitch. So far, they had succeeded in matching the *Swift Spear*'s pace only twice, and then barely for an hour before she inevitably drew ahead once more.

"'Tis unseemly," Gelmyr complained at the dawn of their second week out from Skar Magnol. He was fresh from sending Eshilde up the mast to untangle a knotted rope that marginally impeded the shifting of the mainsail. "You are Vellihr of Justice and her merely a Vellihr of the Sword," he went on. "She exceeds her authority. At least the Silverlock knows his place."

Thera glanced southwards, watching the aged bulk of the *Wind Sword* rise and fall upon the swell beyond the stern. Alvyr Kahlsten, named the Silverlock on account of the white streak in his otherwise black hair, was of a more sedate character than Gynheld, at least until battle was joined. In combat, he became a frenzied bear of a man with no regard for his own safety. Alvyr's fury and Gynheld's cunning made them an effective partnership where fighting was required. However, as the days passed, and the sea grew more fractious, Thera continued to nurture the hope that this mission could be resolved without recourse to steel.

"The *Wolf* was built for war, not races," she told Gelmyr. "As long as she stays within sight of the *Swift Spear*, I'll consider her well handled, old friend."

Gelmyr replied only with a peeved grunt before striding off to take over the tiller from Ragnalt. The young warrior was a fair hand at steering but better at swordplay, and there were few with a keener feel for the sea than Gelmyr Johtenvek. Thera remained at the prow, gaze drifting from the ship ahead to the horizon, part concealed by intermittent cascades of rain. The weather was typically miserable for this region and likely to grow worse the further west they travelled. They hadn't yet reached the Styrnspeld proper and when they did, their progress would slow. Thera intended to hug the coast rather than risk the open waters of the Iron Dark Sea. The course would also enable a reconnaissance of the islands they passed. If trouble brewed in one region of the Outer Isles, the odds were it festered elsewhere too.

"Keep that beast clear of me, witch!"

The harshness of Eshilde's shout drew Thera's attention to the mid-deck, where she saw Mohlnir flee the warrior's kick. The cat leaped into Lynnea's arms before turning to cast a reproachful hiss at Eshilde. Face darkening, she took a purposeful step towards maiden and cat but stopped when she noted Thera's interest in the confrontation. Scowling, Eshilde turned away and resumed the task of untangling the rope she had retrieved from the mast top.

Once again, Thera could easily divine Lynnea's thoughts as she came to join her at the stern, Mohlnir now purring contentedly in her arms. The apprentice's brow bore a rare crease and her lips formed a disapproving pout: *She's mean.*

No, Thera thought with an inward sigh, glancing at Eshilde, who was now fastidiously avoiding her gaze. *She's jealous.*

It had begun the night of the Veltgruhn. Thera had returned from her audience with the Sister Queens in a sombre mood that left her uninterested in the annual celebration. In previous years, she had been happy to lose herself amidst the raucous, drink-soaked revelry. As the celebration wore on and the streets ran with spilled mead and ale, things would inevitably turn both violent and carnal. This time, however, she confined herself to the *Great Wolf* and watched the unfolding bacchanal from a distance.

She had been entertaining a guilty temptation to engage in some unabashed revels with both Eshilde and Ragnalt on the stern deck, given that it was in full view of the *Sea Hawk*'s anchorage. Whether such a deliberately provocative escapade would have aroused the smallest crumb of envy in Sygna was doubtful, but still the urge lingered. In the event, her brother evidently had no more interest in the night's festivities than she had, for he sailed his ship, and Sygna, from the harbour before the first chorus of discordant song rose from the town. Thera hadn't even been afforded the chance to say farewell to Guthnyr. She worried over him a great deal since his decision to throw in his lot with Margnus and Felnir. Guthnyr was fierce, to be sure, but he remained a boy in so many ways.

She had been pondering a means of persuading Guthnyr to give up his foolish choice when she felt Eshilde's lips press against her neck. Her breath was hot and richly laced with the foreign brandy she liked so much. "Why, most honoured Vellihr," she whispered, tongue tickling at the silver ring in Thera's ear, "do you not bless us with your presence this night? Have we offended you so?"

"No offence, Esh," Thera assured her, gently easing free of the smaller woman's embrace. When the mood was upon her, she was usually happy to surrender to its whims. But, with no Sygna to witness her indulgence, she found desire had fled. "Go," she told Eshilde, inclining her head at the brightly lit town and its many enticements. "Fill your cup and seek your joy, as the Altvar will it."

Eshilde was not yet fully drunk, so the gaze she cast in Lynnea's direction was steady in its baleful recognition. The maiden sat near the mast, labouring over a vellum sheet of runes Thera had set her to learn. She had also been given a staff to practise basic weapon craft, but it sat ignored at her side. Lynnea had consented to copy the moves Thera showed her, and done so with easy precision, but also the perfunctory resignation of one undertaking an unavoidable chore. The runes, at least, seemed to garner some genuine interest in the maiden's breast.

"Is it her?" Eshilde asked, allowing a poorly suppressed note of demand into her tone. "Does she command *all* your notice now?"

Thera chose not to rise to the implication, replying simply, "She is my apprentice."

"Apprentice, yes." Eshilde's gaze darkened further. "As I have remained for years now."

"I told you in the spring, if I consider you suited, I will submit your name for the Vellihr's path before the next Veltgruhn."

"You were two years younger than me when you began the path."

"It winds differently for us all." She reached out, gently taking Eshilde's chin between her fingers and turning her face to hers. "When you're ready, Esh. Not before."

She watched Eshilde swallow unwise words before stepping clear of her touch and striding off towards the gangway. She returned come the dawn with a face marred by several bruises and her knuckles scraped red. Thera hadn't shared a night with her since and felt a growing certainty that she never would again.

A touch to her hand recaptured her attention, and she found Lynnea nodding at the horizon, brows raised in a question: *Land?*

"Yes," Thera said. Her student might lack a voice, but she had excellent eyes. The dark smudge was barely visible through the distant curtain of rain. "Ayl-Ah-Rohn. Our first port of call and the place where this mission truly begins. We'll be meeting with the Veilwald here and, hopefully, he'll be surprised to see us. It's always easier to discern the truth in an unready soul. I'll be watching him closely, but you will be watching elsewhere. Take a tour of the town, listen to what folk are saying. Ill rumours or talk against the queens, especially."

Lynnea's frown shifted into puzzlement, lips forming a doubtful grimace: *Why would they talk to me?*

"For a start, they won't fear you repeating their words when they realise you don't talk. Secondly—" Thera shrugged "—you're beautiful. Beauty breeds envy, but it also breeds trust, or at least an urge towards conversation, even when it shouldn't."

Hakkyn Rohnlank, Veilwald of the Aiken Geld, southernmost region of the Outer Isles, received Thera in his mead hall overlooking the port of Skyrn Hardta. It was a small structure in comparison to its equivalents in the Inner Isles or the Fjord Lands where timber was more plentiful. Like many islands in this chain, Ayl-Ah-Rohn was mostly bare of trees. Unlike the other isles, however, it was rich in crops. Hakkyn had earned his name, the Greenhand, by transforming the limited farming of the local crofters into a profitable agriculture. The island's wealth had increased considerably in the three decades of his tenure, all derived from the export of root vegetables. Some even referred to him as the Turnip King, though not to his face. The Greenhand was a farmer, it was true, but in his youth he had been a warrior of impressive reputation and age hadn't much withered his strength and stature.

"So, Vellihr," he said after formal greetings had been exchanged. "You've come at last. I was wondering if my missive to the queens had fallen into the sea."

They sat alone, a clay jug of mead and two tankards on the table between them. The Veilwald had a large chair positioned atop a wooden platform at the far end of the hall, but felt no need to stand on ceremony today, for which Thera was grateful. The chair was unusual in its colouring, a pale yellow that Thera took a moment to recognise as whale bone. It was carved all over in runes, a discordant mix of ancient and modern Ascarlian she hoped to inspect should time allow.

"Missive?" Thera asked. "I was not told of any such communication, Veilwald. My mission derives from the failure of the Kast Geld to deliver their quota of stockfish."

"I sent a messenger with fulsome tidings over six weeks ago," Hakkyn said, the wrinkles of his brow forming a deeper matrix. "And the contents were of far more import than stockfish, I assure you." He leaned forward, voice lowered a pitch despite there being no one present to overhear. "Four ships. That's how many have sailed north and failed to return since the advent of summer. Two were foreigners that stopped in for supplies. Two were mine, sent to trade coal for copper and iron that some in the northern islands still dig from the earth. Nor have any vessels from the Kast Geld called here in nigh four months. It's not unusual for there to be lapses in trade when the weather's bad, but not in summer."

"Have there been no rumours from other ships?" Thera asked. "Whispers of discord, or piracy perhaps?"

Hakkyn shook his head. From the rapid blink of his eye and the tightness of the grip on his tankard, Thera didn't doubt this was a troubled man. "Veilwald Ossgrym of the Kast Geld is an old friend and regular correspondent," he said. "And before the ships stopped coming, there was nothing in his letters to indicate trouble." A faint smile twitched the lips beneath his whiskers and he took a gulp of mead. "Beyond the ordinary, that is. Those northern folk are ever fond of grumbling. A consequence of living on the edge of the Styrnspeld, I suppose."

"And your own geld, Veilwald? Can I tell the Sister Queens that peace reigns here?"

"Had to take the beating stick to a bunch of crofters on my north shore I caught smuggling foreign goods a few weeks ago. They took it well enough. Beyond that, the Aiken Geld is as quiet as it's ever like to get. My people grow anxious, however. They can count ships as well as I and have a keen sense for when things are amiss."

Thera paused to take a gulp of appropriate size from her tankard. She didn't usually drink the stuff, except for celebrations like the Veltgruhn, but it wouldn't do to leave it untouched. The folk of the Outer Isles put a great deal of stock in observance of custom, especially when it came to sharing food or drink with a guest.

"There is another matter," she said, keeping her tone one of routine annoyance, as if compelled to a minor but unavoidable task. "As Vellihr of Justice, I am often required to chase after fanciful tales, most of which turn out to be nonsense, of course. Recently, I keep hearing mention of the Uhltvar, and the Volkrath that once wrought havoc in their name. Have such tales reached your ears, perchance?"

"The Volkrath?" Hakkyn's creased brow took on a puzzled arch. "As a child, my grandmother delighted in scaring us with stories of their misdeeds, stories she had heard at her own grandmother's knee." His eyes narrowed as he delved deeper into his memory. "There was Draglyn, of course. But he's been dead these fifteen years."

"Draglyn?"

"A young man I led to war when the Tielwald mustered the great *menda* to retake Olversahl. Draglyn was brave enough but not greatly skilled. Came back with a dent in his skull and no memory of his own wife's face. He took to raving after a time, calling himself the first of the Volkrath reborn. Got bad enough the folk of his village had to drive him out and he took himself off to do his ranting in a cave on the east shore. Dropped off a cliff a few years later, either by mischance or madness. Can't say the name Volkrath's been heard much since in this geld, and then only from the story spinners' lips."

She spent another hour with Hakkyn, listening to his complaints regarding Sister Silver's recent increase in excise rates, about which she could do nothing. With the mead drunk, she thanked him for his counsel, politely refused to accept the offer of one of his own ships to join their mission north, and agreed to attend the feast he would convene in her honour the coming night. She would have preferred to slip away with the morning tide, but this was another aspect of propriety she couldn't avoid. Besides, the three crews under her command would surely appreciate a last bout of revels before sailing into the chilly embrace of the Styrnspeld.

They feasted beneath the stars that night, for the sky was clear and the wind kind. Tables were set up in Skyrn Hardta's marketplace, the centre of which was occupied by a large firepit where hogs roasted on spits and fish sizzled on grates. The crews of the *Great Wolf*, *Wind Sword*, and *Swift Spear* had mostly met before and took the opportunity to renew acquaintances via the customary bouts of competitive drinking and boasting. Watching them jibe and jostle each other, Thera knew the evening was unlikely to pass without a scuffle or two, but such things were inevitable when warriors met and liquor flowed free.

She hadn't managed to converse at length with Gynheld or Alvyr before departing Skar Magnol, so made a point to spend most of the night in their company. Alvyr was his usual mostly silent, good-natured self whilst Gynheld, always the more verbose of the two, was particularly opinionated.

"The Styrnspeld," she grimaced, eyes rolling and cheek bulking from a nugget of half-chewed pork. "I'd rather lay my nethers open to a starved weasel than sail that bitch again."

"We go where the Sister Queens will it," Thera reminded her, keeping her tone mild, for she had always found it best to let this woman vent her frustrations. Complain Gynheld did, and often, but neither did she shirk.

"And all for the sake of fucking stockfish, by Trieya's divine tits." Gynheld chewed some more and swallowed, chasing the meat down with a hefty gulp of mixed brandy and ale. It was her third tankard full, but she was a woman of impressive stature and it would take a good deal more before true drunkenness took hold.

"There's more at stake than stockfish." Thera clapped a hand to her friend's leather-armoured shoulder, leaning closer. "As I think you know." She grinned at Gynheld's scowl and stepped back, turning to Alvyr. "And you, my friend? Any misgivings to share? Do your crew stand upon the brink of rebellion and yearn to seek a pirate's life?"

This was an old joke between them. Only a mad or suicidal member of Alvyr's *menda* would ever dare question his command, any more than he would question an order from the Queens.

"Always," he said with a half-smile, raising a tankard in salute. Unlike Gynheld, it was his first, for he was not a man given to drink. "I can barely keep them in order. It's near certain they'll hang me from my own mast rather than sail a single day upon the Iron Dark Sea." He and Thera shared a short laugh whilst Gynheld consented to issue a grunt of amusement.

"Best be about it, then," Thera said, reaching for the bronze striker on her belt. Like most captains who sailed Ascarlian waters, she had a collection of such implements, each one fashioned into a sigil corresponding to the gods of the Altvar. The one she carried this night was crudely made, a bequest from Sister Iron who had in turn inherited from her predecessor as Vellihr of Justice. Thera had no true idea of just how old the striker was, and wondered if its inexpert shaping into a semblance of the goddess Trieya's moon and stars indicated truly ancient origin. Raising it above her head, she strode towards the firepit. The merriment died away as the assembly of warriors and locals recognised the onset of a ritual.

"Bring forth fuel for the Altvar's blessing," she called out. Ragnalt, who had been allotted the task earlier in the evening, emerged from the crowd bearing an iron basket filled with coal and wood shavings liberally soaked in oil. It was important the flames caught quickly else Thera suffer the embarrassment, and ill omen, of a blaze that refused to catch at the first spark.

"To Trieya Vorlspeld, daughter to Ulthnir and Aerldun," Thera began, lowering the striker to the basket. "Mistress of the stars, she who holds dominion over travellers and sees the destiny of all. May she bestow her favour upon our course and keep our purpose true."

Alvyr came next, striding forth with his own striker in hand, a far more elegantly fashioned representation of a boar spear. "To Karnic ehs Lyndir," he intoned, bronze sigil poised over the basket. "Son to Ulthnir and Nerlfeya, master of hunt and quest. May he look well upon our hunt and ensure our spear finds its mark."

"To Ulfmaer Kastwald," Gynheld said, raising high the god's bronze lighting bolt before lowering it to the basket. "First-born son to Ulthnir and Aerldun, master of sea, wind, and storm. May he spare us his anger and grant us his strength for what lies ahead."

As one, the three of them took hold of the iron rods dangling from each striker and scraped them across the bronze. The shower of sparks was fulsome and the resulting fire gratifyingly instant. The crowd cheered and chanted the names of the three gods whilst Thera clasped hands with her fellow Vellihrs. As the chorus dwindled into an exuberant din, she went to look for Lynnea, having noted the maiden's absence during the feast.

Her search took her beyond the market and into the town where, to scant surprise, she discovered Lynnea had made a new friend. The dog was massive by any standard, bigger than many a wolf but more resembling a bear with its broad snout and pelt of shaggy brown fur. It perched its paws atop the stone wall that separated it from Lynnea, huge head angled as it panted in delight whilst she scratched behind its ears.

"You're supposed to be ingratiating yourself with the folk of this town," Thera said, coming to her side. "Not their beasts."

Her apprentice responded with a sheepish grin, the dog voicing a huff of consternation as her hand ceased its scratching. Noticing Thera for the first time, the animal turned its block-sized head to lick her fingers. Unable to contain a laugh, she raised her palm as the slathering tongue continued its explorations. "I trust you at least made some attempt to scour up some rumours for me," she said.

Lynnea's expression conveyed a hint of apology. *Nothing.* She gave a helpless shrug and gestured towards the market, loud with the raucous song of folk at feast. *They're all just happy.* Her face altered a little to convey a modicum of qualification. *Scared, too. A little. But mostly happy.*

"No grumblers?" Thera asked. "Malcontents spinning lies about our queens? Or any making mention of the Volkrath?"

Lynnea shook her head and returned her attentions to the dog, her face clouding. *He's miserable in this pen.*

"Then I'm sorry." Thera ran her fingers through the beast's thick fur. "But he'll just have to remain so. He's not ours to take."

If the dog's panting hadn't abruptly become an ominous growl, the muscle beneath the fur tensing under Thera's fingers, she would have missed it. Just a small creak of wood and strained twine, easily lost amidst the echoing tumult of the feast. She had no time to shout a warning, but the hard shove she delivered to Lynnea's chest saved her from the arrow. It buzzed the air between them. The dog's growl transformed into a whining yelp as the projectile scored a bloody furrow across its brow. The beast's alarm was brief, however, a sound that mingled a bark with a roar emerging from its throat as it launched itself over the wall. Battered aside by its passage, Thera spun to the ground, glancing up to see the dog transform a fence between two houses into a cloud of splinters. It rounded a corner whereupon the air became filled with ravening growls and screams of pain. Human screams.

"Are you hurt?" she said, scrambling to her feet and rushing to Lynnea.

She appeared more aggrieved than pained, a stern, accusatory frown on her brow. *You pushed me.*

"Get up." Thera took Lynnea's hand, dragging her to her feet and rushing in pursuit of the dog. "You'll need to calm your friend."

They rounded the corner between the houses to discover the dog busily worrying at the legs of its prey, the sound of snapping bones audible through the chorus of hungry grunts. Through the gloom, Thera made out the flailing form of the beast's victim: a trim man in sailor's garb. Lying nearby was an ash hunting bow and a scattering of arrows. The sailor's screams had dwindled into gasps now, the raw, desperate grating of the mortally stricken.

"I need him alive," Thera told Lynnea, gesturing to the dog. The maiden expended a few seconds staring at the ugly spectacle, eyes wide and face, for once, blank, then mastered herself and clapped her hands. The dog's response was jarringly immediate. Leaving off its gorging, it raised its eyes to Lynnea, then, keeping its bulky body close to the ground, slunk back from the dying man.

Thera already had her dagger in hand as she placed a boot on the sailor's bloodied chest, lowering herself to tap the point of the blade between his eyes. "Not a good thing to enter the Halls of Aevnir as a blind man," she said. Through the welter of pain that dominated his flickering gaze, she discerned a crumb of understanding. He knew Ascarlian. Also, the blue ink tattooed into his brow marked him as a countryman.

"Who set you to this?" she demanded, dagger poised over his left eye. "Speak or know eternity in darkness." His only answer came in the form of a cough that spattered gore across her face. His eyes twitched once, then stilled, and she knew she looked into the face of a corpse.

CHAPTER FIFTEEN

Felnir

L ord Elbyrn's hands shook so much he would have dropped the key had it not been attached to the ring on his belt. "Faster, if you would, my lord," Felnir whispered into the noble's ear, dagger point tickling his lobe for emphasis. "Faster . . ."

The key rattled in the hole before finding purchase on the mechanism, letting out a loud clatter as Elbyrn turned it. He had remained silent until now, but, hesitating before pushing the heavy door open, he swallowed and managed a hoarsely spoken comment, "Don't know why you would want him. He's quite mad, you kn—" His words ended in a pained hiss as Felnir sliced a shallow cut into his ear.

"Why is of no concern to you," Felnir said. "And I find your excess of curiosity worrying."

Elbyrn's already pallid face paled further and a loud squeal arose from his stomach. Bobbing his head, he pushed the door open to reveal the cell beyond.

The first thing to occupy Felnir's notice was the absence of stink. His ample experience with places of confinement had instilled a sense that cells invariably acquired an odious stench. It was a unique mingling of effluent with unwashed flesh undercut by the lingering acrid redolence that came only from death. This cell, however, whilst hardly fragrant, lacked the signature aroma. Adding to his surprise, was its stark division into two dissimilar spaces, albeit unmarked by any physical boundary. The left side was much as he would expect a prison cell to look, dark walls and floor of bare stone, a single bed upon which sat a young man. Brows arched to a curious angle, his eyes flicked from Lord Elbyrn's patently terrified person to the guard at his side holding a bloody dagger, whereupon they registered more amused understanding than alarm.

The cell's opposite half provided a striking contrast. Every inch of wall and floor had been scrawled on in white and black. Diagrams and lettering that bore some semblance to ancient Ascarlian runic, others Alberic or varied forms of eastern script, all mangled together to create a bizarre decoration. A wooden bowl filled with fragments of chalk and stubs of charcoal sat close to a bed occupied by a man at least twice the age of his cellmate. He appeared to have been roused from sleep by Felnir's arrival, sitting up to part the lank, greying hair with twitching fingers. The revealed features were both craggy and angular, a face that had known considerable hardship, the eyes darting about with feverish excitement.

"Him?" Felnir said, prodding Elbyrn forward and pointing to the older man. Receiving a nod from the noble, he approached the prisoner's bed. In response, the fellow huddled against the wall, busy eyes freezing in terror. His bare feet scrabbled on his threadbare blankets and he hugged himself tight, a whispered torrent of meaningless words emerging from his lips.

Ignoring the man's babble, Felnir held the parchment bearing the sigil in front of his eyes. "You know this?" he demanded. Just for a second, the prisoner abandoned his sibilant diatribe to stare up at Felnir. He saw a measure of comprehension return to those eyes, the twitchiness replaced by a sudden hard focus which bordered on recognition. Did he know this man? Had they met in some distant port to the east? But it was gone as quickly as it appeared. The prisoner blinked and shrank back further, letting out a moan which soon degenerated into a pitiful series of sobs. Closing his eyes, he slumped onto his side, tears leaking from tightly closed lids.

"You're scaring him."

Felnir turned to find the cell's other occupant had gotten to his feet.

"Mind your business," Guthnyr growled. Stepping from the doorway, he levelled the longsword he had taken from Elbyrn at the young man. Freed of his bonds, Guthnyr's anger at recently endured indignity was evidently in need of a target. It also made him forget Felnir's injunction against speaking Ascarlian.

"Ah," the prisoner said, inclining his head at Guthnyr, although his next words, spoken in a fluent and barely accented version of their tongue, were addressed to Felnir. "I offer greetings to our friends from the north. May the Altvar bless your endeavour, whatever it might be."

"I said," Guthnyr grated, moving closer to press the longsword's point into the hollow of the young man's throat, "mind your own."

The prisoner leaned back, but failed to stop his flow of uninflected Ascarlian. "You won't get anything out of him when he's scared," he told Felnir. "Why not let me calm him a little? I've learned how these past few months. Better that than listening to him scream his way through another nightmare—"

"Enough," Felnir cut in. Catching Guthnyr's eye, he shook his head and motioned for him to step back. Rising from the older man's bed, Felnir fixed a demanding glare on Lord Elbyrn, nodding at the youngster and demanding in Alberic, "Who is he?"

The noble managed to rasp out a reply after a bout of nervous coughing. "A thief and a fraud. Inveigled his way into the duke's good graces, then attempted to pilfer from his library."

"Purest calumny, I assure you," the young man scoffed, still in Ascarlian. "I found honest employment with Duke Gilferd, it is true. But my unjust incarceration results from a perfidious web of lies spun against me. The vile work of servants envious of my standing—"

"Shut up," Felnir instructed. Moving closer to him, he found this one was only an inch or two shorter than him, his frame lean with well-honed muscle. His features possessed a blockish handsomeness beneath a half-grown beard, complexion plainly that of one who hailed from northern climes but also tinged with bronze. *This one's no stranger to the eastern sun*, Felnir surmised. Grabbing the prisoner's wrists, Felnir inspected his palms. They were callused, but not

192 • ANTHONY RYAN

excessively so, with the coarsest patches near the thumb and forefinger. It was the kind of wear that typically came from frequent handling of weapons.

"You're a librarian, are you?" he asked.

"But one of many skills." The youth smiled. "Principally, however, I ply my trade as a linguist. In point of fact, Duke Gilferd had employed me to translate several volumes from Ishtan into Alberic—"

Felnir interrupted his flow again, this time switching to his coarse but serviceable Ishtan: "You think I don't know a lying son of a whore when I see one, boy?"

The youngster's smile became strained, but Felnir saw scant fear in his eyes. His reply was delivered in Ishtan, so smooth and cultured it might have come from the lips of a courtier in the Saluhtan's palace. "I know nothing of my mother's occupation, esteemed sir. Nor did I ever even hear her name. I'll not insult your intellect by claiming never to have uttered an untruth. But, as I can tell, you are a man with a keen ear and eye for such things. So, I assure you I speak now with only the utmost honesty."

Felnir felt his lips twitch in amusement, but quelled it. Guthnyr's slip meant he would most likely have to leave this cell occupied by two corpses. "What's your name, boy?" he asked, switching back to Alberic.

"Colvyn." The youngster gave a half-bow. "And I assure you, I am very much at your service."

Felnir grunted and held up the parchment, inclining his head at the cringing man. "Does he have this inked onto his skin?"

Colvyn squinted briefly at the sigil and nodded. "On his back, if I recall correctly, amongst a great deal more. He's a veritable walking book of pictographic nonsense."

"His name?"

"If he has one, I've never learned it. As you can tell, the words he speaks are mostly gibberish, though there are occasional exceptions."

As if to illustrate the point, his fellow prisoner let loose a sudden outburst, the words mangled and heavily accented, but Felnir still recognised it as a strange form of Alberic. "Thou art Malecite made flesh!" he gasped, pointing a wavering finger at the interlopers invading his domain. "Vileness hast thou visited upon the earth . . ." His eyes dimmed then and his finger dropped, speech subsiding into meaningless mutters.

"What was that?" Felnir asked Colvyn.

"Archaic Alberic," he said. "I doubt it's his native tongue, however. I think he only speaks it because he knows I understand it, and then only when his nerves have grown taut. I call him Wohtin for want of a real name. The principal author of the Altvar Rendi," he added in response to Felnir's puzzled squint. "It seemed most appropriate since when he's not spouting Covenant scripture, he's rambling in poetic Ascarlian. If I may?"

The youth raised an eyebrow at Felnir, gesturing to his cellmate who now huddled in his blankets, beset by fearful whimpering. Felnir stood aside, allowing Colvyn to approach the other bunk where he knelt to grasp the other man's hand. He began to speak in a soft voice, also in the same aged version of Alberic, though Felnir recognised the words as scripture from the Covenant Faith: "Look ye not to any soul but thine own for truth, but stand ye wary of thine own deceits . . ." As the murmured recitation continued, the older man's breathing slowed, the feverish panic receding from his eyes.

Felnir turned back to Lord Elbyrn, who had sidled his way into a corner, one hand clutching at his bleeding ear. "How long has the madman been here?" Felnir demanded. "What was his crime?"

The noble gave a small shake of his head. "I have no knowledge of either. He was here when the duke gave me charge of this castle. None of the guards could tell me when he arrived. I found only one reference to him in an old ledger, and that from fifteen years ago. It lists him only as 'Prisoner Four' with no mention of his offence. There was a note that said simply: 'Not to be released by order of the duke.'"

Looking again at the two inmates, Felnir saw that Prisoner Four, Wohtin according to Colvyn, now appeared to have adopted a trance-like state. He regarded the murmuring youth with half-closed eyes, their hands still entwined. "Can you keep him calm like this when we take him out of here?" Felnir asked the youth.

Colvyn ceased his recitation and glanced back at Felnir, eyes lingering on his dagger. "I'll certainly do my best if the reward is passage out of this dung-hole."

"Then get him up." Felnir jerked his head at the door. "We've tarried long enough."

As Colvyn gently coaxed his friend to his feet and guided him through the door, Felnir saw the suppressed shame in Guthnyr's gaze as he nodded at Lord Elbyrn, features drawn in grim necessity. "The task falls to me, eh, brother?" It was a noteworthy aspect of Guthnyr's character that he saw a cold-blooded killing as a punishment, and yet another confirmation that their great-grandfather had erred in drawing him into this life.

"No," Felnir said, flicking his dagger at the door. "Falk will check the passage. You stay with the lad and the madman."

Left alone with Lord Elbyrn, Felnir found himself disgusted by the man's cravenness. He continued to press himself into the corner. No longer attempting to staunch the blood leaking from his wounded ear, trembling hands clasped together, eyes wide with stark entreaty.

"Always the same with your kind," Felnir said. He spoke in Ascarlian for he didn't care if this man understood him or not. "Full of swagger and cruelty when it's you holding the knife or the whip. The moment they're taken away, what are you?"

He stepped closer to Elbyrn, the noble letting out a whimper as he closed his leaking eyes and turned his head, pressing it into the wall as if trying to fade into the stone. Watching him weep and hearing the rush of piss escaping his trews to stain the floor, Felnir saw Aurent Vellinde's flailing hand disappear under the waves. Also, the shattered skull of the rebel overseer he had bludgeoned to death during his escape from that desert pit. Drawing back the dagger, Felnir thought it strange that no matter how many of these wretches he killed, his anger only ever seemed to burn all the brighter.

As Felnir wielded the dagger, Lord Elbyrn Dumalle convulsed and unleashed a thick torrent of vomit. Felnir stepped back to allow him to collapse to all fours and disgorge himself. After a prolonged bout of heaving, the noble looked up, face blank in shocked surprise as Felnir hefted the severed belt holding his copious chain of keys.

"I think you would benefit from some time in your own care," Felnir said in Alberic. Exiting the door, he slammed it shut. Finding the right key was quickly done, for he had made careful note of the required implements during their journey through the castle. "Mayhap," he called out whilst working the lock, "your guards will let you out soon enough. Or not. They didn't strike me as being overly fond of you." He pounded a fist to the door before turning and hurrying along the passage. "Enjoy your rest, my lord."

They had to knock the first guard unconscious, Falk delivering the blow to the back of his head with his sword pommel when the fellow grew suspicious over the absence of Lord Elbyrn and the presence of the two prisoners. The next one was of a far wiser character, quickly surmising the change in circumstances when Guthnyr pressed the edge of his sword against his neck. Raising his hands, the guard assiduously followed the murmured instructions to keep quiet and allow himself to be disarmed, bound, and gagged. Their luck ran out at the final door, where the guard proved both wise and dutiful. Comprehending the situation with a single glance, instead of reaching for his halberd he promptly turned and disappeared into the passage at the run, loudly proclaiming the presence of outlaws in the keep. From the echoing tumult of shouts and rattling weapons and armour, he had been quick to attract a response.

"Fight our way to the gate?" Guthnyr asked, twirling his stolen longsword.

"Too many." Felnir nodded to a stairwell to the right, the steps winding upwards. Tuahla's map, based on the sensible drover's recollections, had been incomplete, for the cart man hadn't been permitted to venture much beyond the courtyard when calling at Castle Granoire. However, there had been one location Lord Elbyrn graciously allowed the drovers to visit.

They pounded up the stairs in a rush, emerging onto a narrow battlement overlooking the gatehouse. The smart but cowardly guard's warning had clearly spread quickly, as demonstrated by the cross-bowman atop the outer battlement. His bolt was well aimed, forcing Felnir to duck before careening off the wall behind.

"Stay low," he grunted at the others, adopting a crouching run and following the line of the battlement to the castle's south-facing flank. As they ran, the mad prisoner once again began holding forth in his archaic Alberic, a breathless diatribe inflected with a terrorised quaver: "Lo, dost thou see their perfidy? Cry ye all alarums and light all beacons, for the Scourge is upon the faithful . . ."

"Can't you shut him up?" Guthnyr said in annoyance.

"Not when the mood takes him like this," Colvyn replied. "You should count yourselves lucky he's not screaming. Did that for a full day when I first got pushed into his cell."

Another bolt arced down as they rounded the next corner, taking a chunk of stone from the edge of a crenellation and sending a stinging flurry of grit into Felnir's eyes. Wiping away the resultant tears, he saw no guards ahead, but the sound of a dozen or more boots pounding to their rear allowed for no pause. Spying his goal some twenty yards on, he rose and sprinted towards it, barking at the others to follow.

"Do we have to?" Guthnyr's face wrinkled in disgust at the smell and sight before them. The Privy Ledge, as the drover called it, consisted of a long wooden bench suspended over a gap in the battlement floor. The slanted stretch of castle wall below was stained brown and green all the way to the marsh water below.

"No," Felnir replied, tossing his helm aside before cutting away the straps on his breastplate. "You are free to stay here and die." He glanced back at Colvyn and Wohtin, finding the latter now thankfully quiescent and apparently free of fear. "He'll have to swim," Felnir told the youth. "Is he up to it?"

"I have no notion at all," Colvyn said with an honest shrug. "I imagine we'll find out in short order."

"That we will." Felnir sat on the bench, using his dagger to slice away the straps of his boots, then kicking them off. Before launching himself clear, he tossed Lord Elbyrn's keychain into the water below, taking satisfaction from the tallness of the splash. At least he wouldn't break his legs on reaching the bottom. Hearing the uproar of enraged shouts from the fast-approaching guards, he launched himself from the bench without further delay.

His foul-smelling skid down the shit-stained angle was mercifully short, followed by a brief sensation of weightlessness as he was propelled from the wall to plummet the last few yards. The marsh water enveloped him in a chilly embrace, his body descending until he felt the hardness of bare rock beneath his feet. Pushing against it, he broke the surface, gulping air and uncaring of the stench. Guthnyr came next, raising a tall spout of brownish green water a yard away. Colvyn, the madman and Falk all arrived simultaneously an instant later.

"Stay close to me," Felnir sputtered, striving to keep his mouth clear of the water. The prospect of swallowing even a droplet of this stuff was far from appealing. He swam directly away from the castle, kicking for the safety of the reeds he saw through the low-lying mist some twenty yards off. The marsh fog seemed thin to his eyes, but must have appeared thicker to their pursuers above. The industrious cross-bowman managed to let fly with two bolts by the time they reached the bank, both falling wide by a considerable margin.

Heaving himself onto a patch of sodden, moss-covered earth, Felnir sucked in a few breaths before helping Colvyn drag Wohtin from the water. Upon achieving comparative safety, the newly liberated prisoner immediately lay down and huddled himself into a ball. Once again, a stream of whispered gibberish came from his lips, but at least he had forsaken scripture for the moment.

"This one's quite a prize," Guthnyr observed. "Hope he's worth it."

Felnir saw that, whilst his brother had divested himself of armour and other soldierly accoutrements, he had managed to keep hold of Lord Elbyrn's longsword. Guthnyr grinned, hefting the weapon. "That's two now. Reckon I'll have a fine collection before long."

Felnir expected a hunting party complete with hounds to issue forth from the castle gate before nightfall. But, as the sky darkened and a shivering chill settled over the marsh, their tortuous escape remained bare of both dogs and soldiers. He ascribed the absence of pursuit to Lord Elbyrn's continued incarceration. Lacking orders, his soldiers had dithered and Felnir took no small pleasure imagining them scouring Castle Granoire for the key needed to free the enraged warden. At least his fear-born piss would have dried out by then, though he would face the unpleasant duty of explaining his embarrassment to the Duke of the Cordwain. Felnir reflected that killing the bastard might have been more a mercy than a punishment.

Successfully navigating a course back to the *Sea Hawk* through marshland on foot was a hopeless prospect. Consequently, Felnir kept the road in sight on his left as he led their bedraggled and increasingly chilled party away from Castle Granoire. With night coming on, every moment they spent labouring through reed banks increased the chance of Elbyrn's release. Felnir's hopes lay in rejoining Sygna and the others on the roadside and making a swift escape via boat. Luckily, Sygna had decided not to wait.

He spied the signal after an hour or so, a bright ball of flame waving back and forth above the reeds fifty yards ahead. With no more need for stealth, Felnir cupped his hands around his mouth and called out Sygna's name. The reeds soon parted before the prow of the boat, Kodryn perched on it with torch in hand.

"You smell like an outhouse," the veteran said, grinning as he tossed Felnir a rope.

The journey back to the *Sea Hawk* was more protracted than Felnir would have liked, but once again torches came to their aid, for Behsla had lit many along the ship's rails to guide their passage. Once aboard, he ordered all hands to the oars. The prospect of Elbyrn getting a message to the nearest port was remote, but Felnir had learned that lingering in the vicinity of a recent crime was the rankest folly. The *Sea Hawk* could outrun any Albermaine-ish vessel, but only in open waters. Therefore, he allowed no rest until the ship's prow cut through sea-born waves and the dark silhouettes of the Cordwain coast had faded beyond the stern.

"Swiftest course home," he told Behsla. "Rouse me if needed."

Rising from his oar, he made his way to the canvas-covered shelter on the mid-deck, fully ready to sleep for as long as providence allowed. Yet, as he settled into his furs, Sygna slumping down to nestle into his arms, he found slumber elusive. The madman had begun speaking again. He and Colvyn had been placed nearby in the hollow beneath the deck boards. Wohtin's voice, quieted now to nearly a whisper, still contriving to reach Felnir's ears. The stridently fearful Covenant rhetoric had been replaced with something more quietly spoken and mostly incomprehensible, but Felnir was sure at least a portion was uttered in Ascarlian. Before fatigue bore him down into welcome oblivion, he caught two words he could make sense of: "Vaults" and "Uhltvar".

He awoke to the sound of voices raised in discord, which was not especially unusual amongst a crew mostly scoured from gaols or other criminal misfortune. Arguments were common, although not in Felnir's presence, but fights were rare and then typically quelled with painful efficiency by Kodryn or Druba. This particular disagreement, therefore, was notable for its increasing volume and, as Felnir realised with a groan of annoyance, one of the shouters was his brother.

Pulling aside his furs, he muttered an apology in response to Sygna's peeved sigh, pulled on his spare pair of boots and left the shelter. He was unsurprised to find Guthnyr being restrained by Druba and Falk. More unexpected was the sight of blood staining his brother's dark blond beard. Wordless snarls came from Guthnyr's mouth as he strove to loose the arms enclosing his own, livid gaze fixed upon the far more composed figure on the opposite side of the deck. Colvyn regarded the raging warrior with a stern frown and no sign of injury. Felnir did note the red smear on the edge of the youth's right hand, but could tell the blood was not his own.

Strike a man with a closed fist and you'll break something, Felnir mused, recalling an old lesson from the days when his great-grandfather troubled himself to impart more than criticism. *Mostly likely your own hand.* He also saw how Colvyn stood, feet a measured distance apart to ensure his balance upon an uncertain surface, shoulders slightly hunched.

"Fucker!" Guthnyr writhed in Druba and Falk's grip, crimson spittle flying from his lips. "You're dead! Y'hear?" He lunged forward, failing to break free, his rage-fuelled strength bearing all three of them to the deck. "Dead!"

"It's too fucking early for this," Felnir grated. He spoke without much volume, but the sound of his voice sufficed to bring an abrupt end to Guthnyr's struggles. He stared up at Felnir, eyes blazing, grunting under the weight of his two captors.

"I demand right of combat!" Guthnyr grunted. "For insult and injury. My right under the Queens' law, brother."

"Accepted," Colvyn said. He pointed to where the two recently acquired longswords jutted from Guthnyr's bundled gear. "Very fine. Give me one and I'll happily afford you a lesson in how to use it."

"You heard!" Guthnyr spat. "Accepted. A fair fight under law. Now get the fuck off me!" He jerked, trying to dislodge the two hefty men on his back. Receiving a nod from Felnir, they both released their grip and stood clear whilst Guthnyr raised himself into a predatory crouch, chest heaving. "Fetch the swords," he panted, holding out an expectant hand.

Kodryn raised an eyebrow at Felnir, staying put when answered with a shake of the head.

"What's the cause of this?" Felnir said. He addressed his question to Guthnyr, but it was Colvyn who answered.

"I told him to leave Wohtin alone," he said. "And I believe I was fairly polite about it."

Glancing at him, Felnir saw the madman huddled in the youth's shadow, soaked to the skin. An upturned bucket lay on the boards nearby.

"He stinks," Guthnyr said. "I was sick of it. Mad sod needed a wash, is all." Guthnyr turned to Felnir with a laugh colouring his voice, one that died at the sight of his brother's steady, unblinking gaze. "Right of combat," Guthnyr continued, looking away. "My right—"

"My ship," Felnir cut in. "My judgement. You dealt out an insult and received one in return. The matter is settled. Go back to your oar."

Watching Guthnyr tense and shudder, jaw clamping tight, Felnir knew he had just dealt him a far more painful blow than that delivered by Colvyn. It was an ugly sight, in truth, but not one Felnir would shirk, for he had no doubts regarding the outcome had he allowed a duel between the two.

"Back to work!" Felnir called out, casting his gaze around the deck to force the roused crew to leave off their gawping. It was a mark of how well they read his moods that none proved foolish enough to voice a taunt or even let out as much as a snicker before resuming their tasks. Such consideration, of course, did nothing to lessen Guthnyr's pain. He continued to stand, hunched and shuddering, until he forced himself to turn about and walk stiffly to his nook.

Turning to Colvyn, Felnir saw how he kept his face impassive. He betrayed not even a flicker of fear or defiance as Felnir approached, standing close enough to ensure his meaning could not be misconstrued. "If you have an issue with my brother," Felnir said, voice low but intent, "bring it to me. Lay a hand on him again, and there *will* be a combat upon this ship. And mark this well, boy, he may not know how to use a longsword, but I do."

Colvyn's expression barely altered, save for a marginal raise to his brows that Felnir chose not to interpret as defiance. "I most humbly seek pardon for any insult or disturbance, most esteemed sir," Colvyn said in his flawless Ishtan, completing the ritual of subservience with a bow of appropriate depth.

Felnir swallowed a laugh into a grunt, irked by this one's ability to rouse his humour. "Before we get where we're going, I'll have the story of how you learned courtly Ishtan."

"Happy to oblige, though it's a long tale."

"We have time." Felnir jerked his chin at the youth's soaked companion. "Ask Druba for dry clothes. I've gone to too much trouble over him to have him freeze before he's been made use of." This was a verbal trap, intended to lure Colvyn into enquiring what that use might be, thereby earning a harsh reminder of his status as the most expendable life aboard this ship. The youth saw it, however, replying only with a subdued grin before turning to coax the madman to his feet and usher him towards a waiting Druba.

202 • ANTHONY RYAN

Spying his brother standing at the prow, Felnir resisted the urge to leave him be. Guthnyr's temper could usually be counted on to fade as quickly as it rose, but not when it was directed at his elder brother. Felnir said nothing when he came to Guthnyr's side, merely resting his arms upon the rail, knowing it wouldn't be long before his brother spoke. Next to fighting, talk was his principal passion in life. However, on this occasion, he proved unusually taciturn.

"Why?" Guthnyr didn't look at him, keeping his dark, glowering gaze on the horizon. The sea was calm today and only a soft spray of white water rose from the *Sea Hawk*'s prow as she cut the waves.

Because he would have killed you. Knowing Guthnyr would take this as yet another challenge, Felnir left the truth unsaid. "The lad is useful, for now. And our great-grandfather recently enlightened me as to the consequences of killing those of use."

"And when he's no longer of use?"

"We both know you'll have forgotten this by then. It's not in you to bear a grudge, Guth."

"But it is in you, eh, Redtooth?" Guthnyr turned to face him, tense with a refusal to regret his words. Of all those who had ever cast this earned but unwanted name at Felnir, he had never before heard it from his brother. "Is that not why we're on this ship?"

Had he been just another warrior in this strange *menda*, Felnir would have beaten him bloody, perhaps even tossed him over the side. Instead, he felt an urge to simply walk away and leave Guthnyr to fester, one he suppressed with difficulty. "I told you not to accept the old man's offer," he said, voice clipped so as not to growl. "I told you to beseech our sister for a place in her *menda*, which would have been gladly given, I'm sure. You chose this, Guth. Not I."

"Where else could I be? Thera would've taken me, it's true, but only out of pity, a despised disgrace to be looked down upon by her warriors, as all had done in the years of your exile, brother. The shame covers both of us, don't forget. Our sister won glory that night. What did we win?"

Our lives. Another thought best unspoken. The night Guthnyr spoke of was not the scene of the crime that had earned Felnir the name Redtooth. No, this stain upon their character arose from an older and, in his brother's mind, more grievous offence of cowardice. Margnus Gruinskard's grand scheme to retake Olversahl for the Sister Queens was widely acclaimed as a masterstroke of cunning and courage, but victory had exacted a high price. Whilst work parties laboured under the mountain overlooking the town to undermine the great statue of Ulthnir, the Tielwald ordered the entire Ascarlian war fleet into Aeric's Fjord. Shorn of warriors and bearing only old men and youngsters, the multitude of ships had succeeded in drawing the Blackheart's troops to the harbour, leaving the town itself mostly undefended when the statue fell and the great *menda* issued forth from the rent in the mountain. What the Tielwald hadn't foreseen, however, was that the Blackheart would send a portion of her cut-throat soldiers to attack the fleet that very night. The first ship they boarded had been crewed by Felnir, Guthnyr, and a doughty but forgetful old soak named Halfor.

What nagged at Guthnyr most was that Felnir had at least tried to fight, making a mad rush at one of the southern scum with his dagger, only to be swiftly disarmed. His brother, ten years old and yet to acquire the courage that so marked him in manhood, had stood in frozen weeping. More troops would come later, seizing many ships which would be put to use carrying the Blackheart's host to safety, save for one warship which had been crewed by none other than their sister. Aided by an aged giant named Kaeric, Thera had fended off the southerners long enough to douse the vessel in oil and set it ablaze. Kaeric died in the conflagration, but Thera dived clear and swam to shore. It was an impressive, if pointless, exploit, for the Blackheart's scum had subsequently burned all the ships they couldn't steal. Yet Thera's achievement was still celebrated, winning her sufficient renown to gain the notice of the Sister Queens. Not so her brothers.

There had been many others who failed to die that night, boys and girls overwhelmed by fear or numbers, but they hadn't been the first to falter. Nor did they have to suffer the stark contrast of their sister's example. So, as the tale of the brothers' cowardice grew, it became a convenient excuse for the loss of almost the entirety of the Sister Queens' fleet. As Olversahl had set Thera on the path to the Vellihr's mantle, so it began Felnir's long trudge towards infamy and exile as the Redtooth.

"What did she call herself?" Guthnyr asked, breaking through Felnir's reverie. He saw that his brother had calmed a good deal, as was his habit. Guthnyr peered at the horizon with sombre reflection, mind no doubt filled with best forgotten memories. "That woman who was kind to us. I didn't know their language then, but I'm sure she told us her name."

Felnir well remembered the slender Albermaine-ish girl who had smiled at them as they huddled together in fear, for she seemed so out of place amongst such company. Also, she had been very pretty. "Ayin," he said. "Her name was Ayin."

"Yes." Guthnyr voice an ironic laugh. "Same as the Duchess of the Cordwain, if I'm not mistaken."

"Live long enough, brother, and you'll find the world is just one large collection of bizarre coincidence. Come—" he jostled Guthnyr's arm and moved back from the prow "—let's take a look at these swords of yours. Might be a sensible idea if you actually knew how best to hold them."

CHAPTER SIXTEEN

Elvine

"Ouch!" Elvine put her finger to her mouth, tasting blood and mangling her subsequent outburst. "You vicious little swine!"

Strike, the well-named, piebald cat that had just inflicted her injury, spared her a disdainful hiss before leaping onto the shelves beside her desk. Turning his rump towards Elvine, he trotted away to resume his unending task of scouring Sister Lore's library clean of vermin. The beast had seemed fairly placid in the queen's presence, happily accepting her petting hand with an arched back and appreciative mewl. Apparently, he saw no reason to extend such consideration to a mere servant.

Clutching her finger so as not to besmirch her work, Elvine stood and retreated from the desk, huffing in annoyance when she dislodged a sheaf of documents from one of the piles crowding this chamber. Sister Lore had kept her busy in the days since their meeting. The stacks of scrolls and books requiring translation grew by the day, regardless of her diligent application to the task. Curiously, Elvine felt no resentment at the scale of her toil, for there were nuggets of fascination amongst the often mundane materials ported to her room by a succession of servants. They consisted of correspondence between the Sister Queens and a wide variety of foreign monarchs and bankers. The latter were located mostly in the ports across the southern seas and utilised a modified form of Ishtan as the principal language of commerce. Nearly all were concerned with some manner of loan, of which Sister Silver appeared to have obtained a great many over the years at escalating rates of interest. More interesting, both in terms of the content and the quality of the phrasing, were the letters from the court of the Saluhtan of Ishtakar. Some had even been signed by the Great Eminence himself.

So far, her role had been simple: render each document into modern Ascarlian. A more complex task than might be assumed. Her native tongue, at least in its written form, often lacked the vocabulary required to capture the nuance of the original. Elvine's labours would have been eased considerably if she were permitted to translate the letters into ancient Ascarlian, but Sister Lore's instruction had been clear: "Modern script only, dear one. I am determined to build an archive that all in this realm can read." In Elvine's experience, barely one Ascarlian in ten could read at all. Yet this didn't appear to concern the queen in the slightest. Elvine also felt it strange that she had not been presented with any more ancient runes to translate. The Tielwald had kept the parchment bearing the ancient sigil and hadn't returned during the successive weeks Elvine continued to abide in Sister Lore's tower.

As she moved back from the desk, sucking blood from her scratched finger, Elvine dislodged a portion of letters from one of the taller stacks. Muttering another curse at Strike, Elvine crouched to retrieve them, pausing as she spied the contents of one particular missive. The wax seal had been broken when the letter had been opened, some time ago judging by the yellow hue of the parchment, the design too damaged to make out. However, the revealed letters were rendered in a smooth, flowing version of Alberic.

Picking it up with her unscathed hand, she unfolded it, smiling at the quality of the penmanship on display. It was both precise and artful, compelling by dint of its elegance more than its meaning, which consisted of a formal greeting, albeit more poetically composed than most. Elvine's personal fondness for Alberic had instilled a certain amount of skill in setting it down. This, however, put her to shame. Remarkable as the calligraphy was, the most intriguing aspect of this letter was the signature it bore. It had been set down in a far less accomplished hand, the letters slashed rather than inscribed. Nevertheless, Elvine had no troubling discerning the name: *Evadine Courlain, Ascendant Queen of All Albermaine.*

"The Blackheart herself," Elvine whispered. Her hands took on a tremble as she espied three more missives with the same broken seal scattered across the floor. Unwilling to stain such treasure, Elvine took the time to bind her injured finger with a strip of cotton before gathering up each document and returning to her desk.

She sorted them by date, identifying the first three as diplomatic overtures of a kind that a recently ascended monarch would make to a neighbouring power. All were the product of the same highly accomplished hand that Elvine felt sure hadn't just inscribed the words, but also composed them. The characters and the content complemented one another too well. The fourth letter was a stark contrast. Gone was the flowing script and carefully phrased combination of flattery and pragmatic solicitation. This brief, jagged confluence of threat and extreme Covenant dogma could never be the work of the Blackheart's skilled scribe but instead her very own hand: *Your savage misrule is founded upon naught but the empty legends you term gods and sustained through base oppression. Liars, I call you. Thieves, I call you. Murderers, I call you.*

Reading the missive through in its entirety, Elvine found ample confirmation that Evadine Courlain had, by this stage in her life, slipped into outright madness. She also felt a pang of humour in the realisation that translating a madwoman's rantings into modern Ascarlian would be far easier compared to the finely worded letters penned by her scribe. Elvine recalled that many of the tales regarding the Blackheart's brief but bloody career made mention of a scribe, a faithful former cut-throat who remained at her side for much of it. Some painted him as an untrustworthy intriguer given to vile habits who schemed endlessly in his dark queen's service. But she vaguely remembered another story relating how he came to accept the love of the true Covenant and turned against the Blackheart. His name escaped her at present, but she felt sure her mother would know.

Perhaps she might be able to point her towards some more products of his wonderful hand.

Elvine picked up her quill and began to copy the first letter, attempting to mimic the flow of the characters. She had barely managed a decent facsimile of the opening line when a strident call echoed up the stairwell to her chambers: "Elvine! Dear one! Attend me, if you would!"

She found Sister Lore waiting in her library, and she wasn't alone. Ilvar Kastrahk's face was customarily absent of expression as he nodded and offered a softly spoken greeting, employing Elvine's newly acquired title: "Scholar Elvine". She returned his nod, resisting the obligation to address him by name. Such an implied insult was potentially dangerous, but she had spent long enough in Sister Lore's company now to recognise herself something of a favourite. Other servants came and went from the tower, but none lived here alongside a queen. They ate their meals together and, when the day's work was done, devoted long hours to discussing volumes selected at random from the library. Elvine tried to suppress the notion that she might actually have found true friendship with a queen. Besides the absurdity of it, she knew it to be risky for her mother's warning hadn't faded from her mind: *What I told you about the Tielwald, it applies also to the queens.*

"Best take this, my dear," Sister Lore said, handing Elvine a thick wooden shawl. "We're going out."

"Out, my queen?" True to her word, the queen had permitted Elvine a few visits to her mother's quarters in a secluded wing of the Verungyr. Here Berrine worked to catalogue those books allotted to what would one day become the Great Ascarlian Library, Sister Lore's grand design to one day match or even eclipse the lost majesty of King Aeric's archive in Olversahl. In truth, this veritable mountain of books consisted of those not deemed worthy of inclusion in the queen's personal collection. Organising it all was a tedious task well below Berrine's skill set, but Elvine knew neither of them had the standing to complain. Apart from these brief sojourns, she hadn't ventured from the tower since her arrival.

"Quite so." Sister Lore wrapped her own shawl about her, a plain garment of undyed wool that acquired an air of finely cut elegance as she arranged it around her head and shoulders. She glanced at Elvine's feet and tutted in disapproval at her sandals. "Too flimsy. You'll find something more sturdy in my chambers. I think they'll fit you. Hurry now, and bring along parchment, quill, and ink. I'll need a record of today's business."

Elvine's hope that she might get to walk the streets of Skar Magnol again was quickly dashed when the queen led her into the bowels of the Verungyr. Her first impression of the town had hardly been edifying, but it at least offered the prospect of a market where she could purchase a small treat for her mother, if not herself. Two weeks ago a servant with the lock and key sigil of Sister Silver stitched onto her dress had appeared in Elvine's chambers. A thin, stiff-backed woman of middling years, she curtly requested Elvine's signature on a receipt. "Payment for your service," the woman stated, handing over a purse before smartly walking out. Upon examination, Elvine found the purse to contain three silver coins, each one precisely stamped with the three-headed symbol of the Sister Queens on one side and the crossed hammer and sword sigil of the Worldsmith on the other. Coins were rarely used for day-to-day commerce, and Hemund had always paid her in hack silver. She estimated each of these coins was worth the equivalent of three months her previous wage. Whilst Elvine had never been overly interested in money, having been presented with such wealth, it would have been nice to actually spend some of it.

The lower reaches of the Verungyr were even less appealing than the upper levels. Sister Lore followed a seemingly chaotic course down a succession of stairwells and along numerous corridors, all of unclad stone and mortar, coming to a particularly constricted spiral of descending steps. Elvine found it noteworthy that Ilvar took the lead here, lit torch in hand, and that Sister Lore didn't follow until receiving an echoing shout from below. However, the queen's cheerful demeanour remained unchained as she started down, beckoning Elvine to follow with a reassuring chuckle.

"Don't worry, dear one. Even the rats don't come down here."

The spiral went deep, requiring several minutes of uncomfortable, shoulder-scraping labour to reach the bottom. Stepping clear of the stairwell, Elvine gazed around at a circular chamber of rough-hewn stone, the surface interrupted by six tunnels spaced at regular intervals.

"Our first sisters were wise when they constructed the Verungyr," Sister Lore explained, smiling at Elvine's puzzled frown. "A holdfast with but one gate can become a trap if those inside have no hidden means of escape." She nodded to Ilvar, who promptly started down the tunnel opposite the stairwell entrance. "But," the queen went on, taking Elvine's hand and leading her in the Vellihr's wake, "these tunnels have more uses than just deliverance in times of crisis. Can you guess our direction, dear?"

Elvine replayed their journey from the tower, tracking through many turns until she arrived at an answer. "West?" she ventured without any measure of confidence.

"Very good." Sister Lore squeezed her hand. Elvine couldn't suppress a shudder as the tunnel walls closed in, leaving them in a world of shadows cast by the yellow flicker of Ilvar's torch. She had never liked small spaces and the thought of all the many tons of rock above their heads put a nauseous clutch in her belly.

"A queen should walk amongst her people regularly," Sister Lore continued. "The better to gauge their moods and know their troubles. But not when she wishes her business to remain private."

Elvine cast her gaze at the uneven ceiling. "We're under the town?"

"Not yet, but we will be." Another squeeze to her hand. "It's quite a long walk, I'm afraid. Why don't we pass the time discussing your recent endeavours. Anything of interest lately?"

"Oh yes, my queen. At least to me." She went on to describe what she chose to call "The Blackheart Letters", and the curious shift in the quality of their penmanship.

"Ah, yes, her infamous scribe," Sister Lore said. "An interesting character, though not one you'd want to meet on a dark night, by all accounts. He was at Olversahl, you know? Apparently, it was due to his intervention that the Blackheart survived her encounter with our Tielwald."

"So, the scribe was a warrior, too?"

"As fair a hand with a sword as he was with a pen, so the tale is told."

"And his name, my queen? Do you know it? I find I'm keen to seek out more of his work."

"Actually, I don't think I do. The Tielwald might, since he actually spoke with him once. You can ask him when we get where we're going."

This news served to quiet Elvine as the knot in her stomach tightened, save for providing answers to the questions Sister Lore peppered into her otherwise unbroken monologue. "That last letter from the Blackheart caused quite a ruckus, as I recall. Of course, I wasn't queen then, just another Vellihr of Lore slaving away in the archives. I do remember a lot of talk about mustering another great *menda* to deal with this newly ascended mad queen, but Sister Silver forbade it. 'Why fight a war when we can pay her own to bring her down?' she said. As always, her wisdom proved the truest arrow in the end. Do you know how many years Sister Silver has reigned, dear one?"

"Forty-two, my queen?"

"Very good. Yes, four decades of sage queenship is a most remarkable achievement. I recall the day I first met her. I was a few years shy of your age then, and terribly nervous . . ."

Fond as she was of Sister Lore, Elvine was grateful when the journey finally came to an end, despite the fear-provoking sight of Margnus Gruinskard waiting to greet them upon emerging from the tunnel. The Tielwald stood alongside two other men on a stretch of otherwise empty wharf. Beyond them, a longship sat at anchor with ropes securing her to the quay. She was a large vessel, but sleeker than Ilvar's warship. A carved hawk figurehead jutted from her prow, its vicious beak widened in a silent screech. Looking around, Elvine saw that the tunnel exit stood at the base of a high cliff that shielded this stretch of dock from the eyes of the town.

Upon their arrival, the Tielwald and one of his companions both knelt, bowing their heads. The third, a tall, thin man with long scraggly hair and a beard to match, remained standing. He was clad in a woollen cloak, but Elvine saw how he shivered. From the way his eyes, wide with near feverish alarm, darted about, Elvine decided his shuddering arose from fear rather than cold. Also, although she afforded him a short glance of shrewd appraisal, Sister Lore appeared to take no offence at his failure to kneel.

"Rise, my good friends," the queen said, advancing across the wharf, arms extended to the man at the Tielwald's side. "Felnir!" She clasped the younger man's hands and pressed a kiss to his cheek. "It's been too long. How well you look."

Elvine quickly marked this one as a warrior, not just because of his impressive frame and the sword at his belt. His dark blond hair was braided so that it wouldn't impede his sight and his stance and movements were much like Ilvar's. She noted how his sea-grey eyes flicked to the Vellihr even as he afforded Sister Lore a smile. "My thanks, my queen."

His tone held a forced note of warmth, making Elvine wonder if this Felnir might actually possess some immunity to the queen's charm. Studying his face, Elvine found the name chiming in her memory. *Felnir . . . The Redtooth?* This, then, was the famed exile, most vicious of men? The story was often told, garnished with varying degrees of lurid detail depending on the teller. Yet Elvine found it hard to reconcile such a gory event with this handsome and assured fellow. The contradiction summoned one of her favourite quotations from *The Aphorismus*, a centuries old collection of Ishtan wit and wisdom she had memorised as a child: *All beauty is an illusion and all charm a lie. Those who may not appear monstrous can yet remain monsters.*

"And how may I address this good fellow?" Sister Lore asked, turning to the nervous man with the scraggly hair.

"As yet, we know not his true name, my queen," Felnir said. "His gaoler called him naught but Prisoner Number Four, and his cellmate refers to him as Wohtin." The warrior paused to offer a grimace of apology. "I regret to report that either the trials of imprisonment or some unknown vexation appear to have robbed him of reason."

"We don't need his reason," the Tielwald said in his grating wheeze. "Just his skin."

The nervous man's shudders increased as Sister Lore stepped closer to him. "Fear me not," she said, extending a hand to caress his bearded chin. "You find yourself amongst friends . . ."

"Malecite!" The word erupted from the man's lips in a cloud of spittle as he reeled back from the queen, stumbling in fright and falling to the cobbled wharf, where he continued to rant in archaic Alberic, eyes blazing at Sister Lore. "Lay not thine vile hands upon my flesh! I who hath been purified in the blood of Martyrs!"

Ilvar's sword scraped free of its scabbard as he advanced towards the flailing mad man, face hardening with imminent violence. "Hold!" Felnir said, raising a hand and stepping between Ilvar and his target. "He raves, but does no hurt, my queen. Nor do I think he even knows where he is."

Ilvar came to a halt and, receiving a nod from Sister Lore, sheathed his sword. "It appears, dearest one," the queen said, beckoning to Elvine, "we have another Covenanter in our midst. Perhaps he'll respond more favourably to one of his own."

Elvine found that her borrowed shoes had abruptly become a good deal heavier. Looking at the madman now cowering in Felnir's shadow, she felt a keen desire to remain at a decent remove from his presence. But, friend or not, a queen's command was not to be denied. Swallowing despite a suddenly dry mouth, she shifted her satchel to her front and clutched it tight, managing an unfaltering approach. Coming to a halt, she saw the whimpering fear of this deranged soul had abated. Where he had looked upon Sister Lore with terror, he regarded Elvine with cautious relief.

"Thine art come," he said, raising a trembling hand towards her. "The Seraphile's messenger, come unto me as she came unto he who awaited the pyre . . ."

Elvine was quick to recognise the allusion as originating from the Scroll of Martyr Lemeshill, one of the first souls to sacrifice himself in service to the Covenant. It was rarely referenced in modern sermons and the concept of the Seraphile having any messengers

214 • ANTHONY RYAN

beyond the Martyrs themselves had long fallen out of favour with the orthodox faith.

"I am no messenger . . . brother," she told him in Alberic. "Merely another student of the Martyrs' example."

"Messenger thine art," the man insisted, baring yellow teeth in a smile. "Come now at the hour of mine trial . . ."

He plainly had more to say but was cut short by a hard, insistent grunt from the Tielwald: "His skin."

"Quite," Sister Lore said. She favoured Elvine with an apologetic wince. "We need to see his back, dear one."

"His back, my queen?"

"I'm afraid so. I hate to ask this of you, but it's so terribly important, you see. And—" the queen stepped closer, inclining her head at Ilvar "—if you can't coax him to it, less kindly hands may be required."

Fearing further delay, Elvine took a breath and knelt at the madman's side, frowning as she sought to concoct an appropriately phrased request. "Wouldst thou consent, brother, to disrobe?" Receiving only a baffled squint in response, she tried again. "Didst not Martyr Stevanos willingly bare his flesh to the false priests, fearing not their lashes but only the Seraphile's disfavour?"

This appeared to gain purchase on his mind, for he asked a tremulous question: "Is it thine command, oh messenger?"

I'm not a messenger. Elvine wasn't sure why the need for dishonesty grated on her so, as she doubted this one was even capable of recognising deceit. But, despite everything, she still held to the Covenant and pretending some form of divine authority to a deluded soul could only be termed as blasphemy. *Then why not refuse and suffer the consequences as a Martyr would?* she asked herself. However, a glance at the Tielwald, features set in a glower of dire promise, left her in no doubt that the consequences would be severe indeed, for her and her mother.

"Dost thou not crave the Martyrs' example as the parched crave water or the starved crave meat?" she asked, turning back to the madman. "Wouldst thou earn the Seraphile's disfavour?"

Eyes widening further, he began to divest himself of his cloak with feverish energy, rising to his knees to tear the garment away before ripping off the shirt beneath. When, gasping in panic, he began to unfasten his trews, Elvine reached out a hand to stop him. "Enough, brother." She exerted a gentle pressure on his shoulder to turn him about, stifling a gasp of her own at what she saw.

The tattoos began at the base of his neck, a dense collage of inked skin continuing to the small of his back. Unlike the uniform shade of blue favoured by Ascarlians, the designs here were rendered in different colours. At first, the varied hues of red, green and blue created the impression of a chaotic, near abstract swirl that defied interpretation. But, as Elvine peered closer, she recognised the confluence of shapes in the centre of it all.

"It's the same, my queen," she said, turning to Sister Lore.

"It does appear so," the queen agreed, stooping to inspect the circular motif. Although mostly of red ink, the design was unmistakably identical to the inexpertly drawn version on the Tielwald's parchment. Straightening, Sister Lore afforded the old man a smile of appreciation. "I must admit, old friend, when you came to me with this, I thought it fanciful at best, but at least worthy of investigation. I am glad to find my judgement vindicated."

Gruinskard acknowledged the praise with a nod, though his attention remained mostly on the madman's back. "And the rest, girl," he grunted. "What does it say?"

"A great many things I imagine." Elvine scanned the sprawl of inscribed flesh, seeing a plethora of ancient Ascarlian runes amongst the intertwined lines and vaguely animalistic forms. Some words were obvious, such as "Altvar", albeit set down in a barely legible version of Ancient Ascarlian. Others were completely unfamiliar, though their shape echoed the flowing runic of the Age of Kings. "To translate all this would be the work of months," she added. "And I couldn't promise to parse every word into modern Ascarlian. Not all the old forms are known to us."

"Months," the Tielwald repeated with gruff emphasis, his eyes sliding to Sister Lore. From her frown of restrained consternation, Elvine concluded she had been expecting more from her new favourite.

"It might help," Elvine went on, "if I knew where he came from. This style of decoration is unlike any I've seen before—"

"He came from a prison in the Cordwain Duchy," the Tielwald cut in. "Beyond that, we know nothing. As for a full translation, it's not required. Confine your efforts to but one phrase: 'the Vaults of the Altvar.'" He jerked his chin at the madman. "And best be quick about it, girl."

Resisting a foolish urge to argue, Elvine sighed and returned her gaze to the tattoos. They had taken on a shudder now as the man who bore them began to feel the chill breeze coming off the fjord. She wanted to put his cloak about his shoulders and deliver a stern lecture on the folly attempting to rush proper scholarship, but she didn't. This unfortunate was not the only prisoner here, regardless of how well she liked her cage.

Leaning forward, she rested a hand on his bared arm and whispered into his ear, "Forgive me, brother." As he turned his head to her, she saw a new clarity in his gaze. Gone was the widened stare of a deluded mind, replaced by a sharp, knowing focus. He spoke then, a weak mutter from barely parted lips, and no longer in old Alberic, but in a lilting form of Ascarlian she hadn't heard before: "The isle of the Exiled King. Start there."

Then it was gone. His eyes dimmed into fearful misery and he began to whisper to himself, yet more Covenant scripture delivered in a soft diatribe. Elvine stared at him in mystification until a pointed thud of the Tielwald's axe stave on the cobbles stirred her to resume her examination of the tattoos. *The isle of the Exiled King . . . Velgard.*

Thus armed, she found it quickly. The letters were only just comprehensible, the curve of each character less acute than she was accustomed to, but the meaning as clear as day once she adjusted her perception. The title was inscribed above a shape she had assumed to be another motif, a jagged triangle she now recognised as a mountain.

"It's a map," she said in realisation, drawing back to afford herself a view of the whole thing.

"Of what?" Gruinskard demanded.

"Ascarlia." Elvine's mind raced as her eyes drank in word after word, revealing many names she knew, but even more she didn't. "At least in part. The way the symbols are arranged seems haphazard. This—" she pointed to the pictogram of a river at the base of the design "—is the Fjord Geld. Yet this—" her finger moved to a neighbouring patch of disturbed waves "—is the Iron Dark Sea, even though they're separated by many miles."

"The Vaults, dear one," Sister Lore said. "Where are they?"

Additional inspection revealed no complete mention of the required phrase, with but one occurrence of the word "Vaults", and its location was no surprise. "Here," she said, pointing to the mountain symbol. "I believe this represents Ayl-Ah-Skorna."

Sister Lore let out a faintly exasperated laugh. "If the Vaults were located there, dear, I think we would have noticed by now."

"Not the Vaults, my queen, for if they are on this map, I can't see it. But look here." She traced a finger along a line of runes curved around the upper portion of the mountain. "Unless I mistranslate, I believe this to state: 'Seek ye the Vaults at the grave of the Exiled King.'"

"Velgard." Sister Lore pursed her lips in thought before shaking her head. "But he has no grave. In fact, we have no record of his final resting place."

"No grave, my queen," Evline agreed. "But the word is interchangeable with 'monument' in ancient runic, and Velgard does have one, a great statue upon the western shore of Ayl-Ah-Skorna. Beset by many woes, his subjects raised it as a plea to the Altvar to bring about his return, so the tale is told. If these words can be credited, the statue may provide some insight into the location of the Vaults."

"I've seen that thing," Gruinskard rumbled. "It's a ruin now, just fallen stone about a cracked base overgrown with weeds."

"Ruins have been known to harbour treasure, my friend," Sister Lore said. Crouching, she gathered up the madman's cloak and set it upon his shoulders, murmuring, "My thanks, good man."

Rising, she afforded them all a brisk smile before speaking on, voice strident yet still imbued with a kindly note. "A prize long sought but never found now hovers within our reach: The Vaults of the Altvar.

218 • Anthony Ryan

I need not elaborate on the value of finding this most fabled place. Treasures there will be, if the tales are true, but more than that, the Vaults made real will form the heart of our people. This most sacred of sites, where those with blood of the Altvar once trod, cannot be left to dust and shadow. Felnir." She turned to the warrior. "Will you do this thing for your queens? Will you sail to Ayl-Ah-Skorna and discover the path to the Vaults of the Altvar, and from there follow it to wherever it shall lead?"

"I shall do all I am commanded to, my queen," he said, lowering his head with grave assurance.

"I had no doubt of it. Find us the Vaults and all honour shall be restored, and the Vellihr's brooch will be yours to wear with pride. And fear no failure." Sister Lore paused, her smile broadening into prideful affection as she extended a hand to Elvine. "For I send my most accomplished scholar with you."

CHAPTER SEVENTEEN

Ruhlin

Before unlocking his cage, Radylf called six more guards from the shadows. They were large men clad in similar garb to the whip-man, though none came close to matching his stature. Also, they lacked the same paleness of skin. Four bore long spears and the other two carried rods with looped ropes dangling from one end. The spear men levelled their points at Ruhlin as Radylf swung the cage door open, the rope bearers standing a pace or two further back. All were tensed with narrow, careful eyes flicking across Ruhlin's form. Evidently, they had been fully apprised of the danger he posed. Radylf, however, was a marked exception.

"Out you get," he instructed in his curiously affable, high-pitched voice, gesturing for Ruhlin to depart the cage. Whilst the other guards all retreated a step when he complied, Radylf apparently felt no compulsion to follow suit. Eldryk appeared to have withdrawn to the shadows. Nor, Ruhlin saw with an odd pang of regret, was Aleida anywhere to be seen. Still, despite her father's dire injunction, Ruhlin harboured a strong suspicion that she lingered in some hidden corner of this place, keen to witness what came next.

"Follow me," Radylf instructed. "Say nothing and keep your movements small, lest my dogs decide to bite."

Tuhlan called out as Ruhlin was led away. Glancing back, he saw the Caerith once again extending his arm through the bars, fingers splayed. His words were unknowable but Ruhlin could discern the meaning in the man's grim but encouraging expression: *Good luck, my friend.*

Twenty yards from the cage, they emerged into the circle of daylight at the centre of this vast structure. Radylf led him down the shallow steps to the flat space in the centre, the guards keeping pace all the while, spearpoints never wavering. Stepping from the lowest tier, Ruhlin found that the circle's surface was composed of fine, powdery sand warmed by the sun. Shielding his eyes, he looked up, a smile coming unbidden to his lips at the sight of blue sky and clouds. He made out the edge of a massive roof, which appeared to have been constructed from rock, but couldn't fathom how any combination of hand and chisel could work it into such a shape.

"Stand there, laddie," Radylf said, Ruhlin lowering his gaze to find the giant pointing to a spot a dozen paces from the circle's edge. When Ruhlin did as he was bid, the whip-man crouched nearby, spade-sized hands digging into the sand. "Doubt even you could break this," he said, raising an arc of powder as he hauled a thick chain clear of its covering. He grinned as he took hold of the iron cuff affixed to one end and knelt to fasten it about Ruhlin's ankle. "But, we'll soon find out, eh?" Rising, he looked down at Ruhlin with features composed into something that formed a curious match to Tuhlan's a moment before. "You've got twelve feet to play with," the whip-man said, nudging a boot to the chain. "Make good use of it."

He strode away and the guards retreated to the edge of the surrounding shadow. Before long, another sound echoed from the gloom, a fresh upsurge of the growls and snarls Ruhlin had heard before Radylf opened his cage. A second contingent of guards came into view, four of them wielding the rope and pole devices. The loops encircled the neck, chest, and arms of the figure struggling at the centre of the party. Ruhlin was unable to make out more than fleeting details of the captive, for their ceaseless thrashing compelled the guards to shift constantly, creating the impression of a clumsy dance that might have been amusing but for the sounds emanating from their prisoner. Ruhlin caught flashes of pale skin and a whirl of dark curls as the cluster reached the sands. The captive's struggles increased upon setting foot on the circle, powder rising in busy gouts while the guards grunted curses in their accented Ascarlian and forced the screeching soul to a spot twenty paces from Ruhlin.

Coming to a halt, they closed in about the captive, Ruhlin hearing a howl, louder than the cries that preceded it, followed by the rattle of a chain and snick of a manacle. The guards retreated quickly, loosing their ropes and vacating the circle at a run. At their departure, the soul now crouched opposite Ruhlin fell into a silence so sudden it felt jarring.

Having no doubt as to the nature of this impending trial, seeing his intended opponent fully revealed, Ruhlin wondered if Eldryk had orchestrated some manner of joke at his expense. The figure facing him was barely two-thirds Ruhlin's size. His frame was thinned to such a state the grate of his ribs stood in stark relief. Like Ruhlin, he was naked, his skin the same pale hue as Radylf's but even more scarred. Stripes of damaged flesh criss-crossed his limbs in a pattern that was too chaotic to be anything other than the result of violence rather than deliberate decoration. His face and upper torso were concealed by a dense, matted tumble of dark curly hair, though Ruhlin discerned the glimmer of two unblinking eyes behind the greasy veil. The sense of outmatching his adversary faded under the steady, appraising glare of those eyes. Like Tuhlan's, this was a hunter's gaze.

"No rules." Radylf's cheerful voice broke the moment of mutual scrutiny. Striding into the centre of the circle, he drew a knife from his belt and twirled it, affording Ruhlin a comradely grin. "One lives. One dies. That is all." With that, he tossed the knife onto the sand directly in front of the crouching, scarred wretch and strode from the circle.

Ruhlin barely had time to register the not insignificant fact that he hadn't been given a weapon before the creature opposite let out a snarl, snatched the knife from the sand and came at him in a rush. Ruhlin caught a glimpse of a small, sharp-featured face amid the flailing dark hair, baring teeth that had been filed to points. What captured his notice most of all, however, was the gleam of the knife blade aimed at his throat.

He twisted as the ravening wretch closed, the knife slashing within a whisker of Ruhlin's cheek. His opponent spun about with feral speed and attacked again, knife clasped in two bony fists raised above his head. His swiftness bore fruit this time, the blade scoring a cut on Ruhlin's thigh as he attempted to sidestep. Pain blossomed in a fiery shudder, sending a jolt into the core of Ruhlin's being and birthing a now familiar response.

A low growl escaped his lips, rapidly expanding muscles causing him to drop to all fours. Looking at his fingers half buried in the sand, he felt the sensation of the grains upon his skin begin to fade, the veins on his forearm taking on a visible throb. A sound snapped his reddening gaze to the adversary, a strange forlorn whine. The pale figure was crouched barely four feet away, bloodied knife in hand, but made no move to renew his attack. Ruhlin could see most of his face now, but instead of the snarling, animal rage of seconds before, he beheld the features of a soul comprehending his own death. A great weariness showed in his eyes, along with a grim resignation. *This is no beast*, Ruhlin knew. *This is just a man, as much a victim as I.* How long had this poor soul been held here? How much had he suffered to twist him into this, only for his captors to toss his life away in this grotesque trial?

The grinding stretch of his muscles abruptly ceased, and he saw the vessels throbbing in his forearm sublime back into the flesh, feeling the soft caress of sand upon his fingers once more. The man facing him let out a grunt, scarred brow creasing and eyes narrowed in bafflement. He bared his filed teeth, emitting a harsh snarl of challenge, punctuated by a short lunge. Ruhlin stood, shaking his head, both hands raised as he backed away.

"I will not do this!" Ruhlin called into the shadows, knowing his words would reach the unseen Aerling. "I will not kill for you!"

No answer came from the gloom, and his focus was instantly recaptured by the pale little man. Letting out an enraged yowl, he launched himself at Ruhlin, knife slashing in a frenzy. He suffered more cuts on his upraised arms as he backed away, retreating until the chain about his ankle grew taut. Forced to duck another assault, he hissed in pain as the knife left a long slice down his back. His assailant landed nimbly and hunched low for a lunge.

"Please," Ruhlin said, his voice choked by the resurgence of the change once again knotting his muscles. He stared into the pale man's eyes, imploring. "Please don't!"

Mystification returned to his adversary's brow as he remained crouched, chest heaving. It was the fearful flicker of his gaze towards the shadows that buttressed Ruhlin's recognition of his humanity. *There is no hate here*, Ruhlin decided. *Just fear. He wants only to live. But do I?*

The smaller man began to circle him, keeping low and moving with predatory grace. A mingling of puzzlement and fear showed on his sharp features, also a recurrent wince of reluctance. Ruhlin extended his hand, fingers splayed to mimic Tuhlan's gesture from the cages in the hope this man might recognise it. At first Ruhlin thought he had unwittingly enraged the pale man, for he snarled and lunged again. But, from the way he compelled his body to a halt, Ruhlin discerned the movements of a soul quelling long instilled instinct. He grunted out another series of snarls, each one less fierce than the last, his gaze unwavering throughout. Finally, he quieted, Ruhlin seeing once more the same weariness creep over his expression before the pale man's eyes flicked to the bloodied knife in his hand. Then, with a disgusted twist of his lips, he dropped it and backed away.

A loud, ear-paining crack sounded from the shadows before Radylf strode into the light, his whip trailing over the sand. No vestige of his prior equanimity showed on his features, now set in the dour mask of professional brutality. He directed a glare at Ruhlin, but his anger was principally focused on the smaller man. Flicking the whip, he caused it to twist, snake-like, until its tip lay across the fallen knife, whereupon he grunted a short instruction: "*Tu-ak ch-taw.*"

The words were as undecipherable as Tuhlan's, but Ruhlin detected no similarity in the sound. This was yet another language new to his ear. However, from the pale man's involuntary shudder, Ruhlin could tell he understood it fully. *Same skin, same language*, Ruhlin thought.

Same people? And yet one brutalises the other for a master who speaks a mangled form of Ascarlian.

Despite his obvious fear, the pale man refused to obey. Nor did he deign to look at Radylf. Ruhlin wondered if it was this rather than the failure to comply that brought an abrupt quiver of rage to the giant's face. "*Tu-ak ch-taw!*" he shouted, sand flying as the whip coiled and struck, leaving a red slash across the smaller man's shoulder. He shrank from the strike, clenching his teeth against the pain, but otherwise refused to move or afford any notice to his tormentor.

Growling, Radylf struck again, raising the whip high before bringing it down so the tip slashed the length of the pale man's forearm. The sight of white bone amongst the sundered flesh brought a resurgence of Ruhlin's anger, the pulsing throb returning to his muscles. A barely coherent sputter emerged from his lips as he sprang from the sand, launching himself at Radylf, fast-growing hands extended. "Leave him be!"

For one so large, the whip-man possessed an impressive turn of speed. Dodging under Ruhlin's arms, he turned and pelted clear of his reach. The crimson cloud edging his vision, Ruhlin pursued Radylf, happy to surrender to the frenzied desire for carnage. The hard clank of the chain about his ankle reaching its limit forced a pause. Ruhlin crouched to snap the links with a single jerk of his overlarge hands. Roaring, he resumed his pursuit only for a flurry of darts to streak out of the shadows and strike him in the face. Most rebounded from his unnaturally thickened skin without piercing flesh, but two succeeded in finding their intended mark. Ruhlin staggered as the needle points sank into his mouth, one embedding itself in his tongue, the other his cheek.

The collapse was quick, though not so rapid as when Angomar had darted him in Buhl Hardta. Falling to his knees, Ruhlin plucked the barbs from his mouth, casting them away before regaining his feet. He managed only two paces before tumbling face first into the sand. The expected nightmare-filled slumber failed to arrive immediately, the red fog receding to allow him a clear view of Radylf's approach.

He furled his whip as he stood over Ruhlin, a measure of affability returning to his face as he offered a regretful shake of his head.

"I can tell," he said, flexing his whip in preparation, "you and I have many hours of education to look forward to . . ."

His words ended in a shout of surprise and pain when the pale man landed on his back, knife stabbing at his throat. Radylf managed to intercept the blade before it could inflict a fatal wound, stopping the knife's descent with his hand. Eight inches of steel pierced his palm, stabbing through to score the skin of his throat. Screeching something in the same unfamiliar tongue, the smaller man dragged the blade from Radylf's flesh and tried again, this time delivering a flurry of strikes at the giant's eyes. Blood sprayed as Radylf fended him off, though not without suffering a slice to the ear which left a portion of it dangling. The pair reeled briefly from Ruhlin's sight, lurching back into view a moment later by which time Radylf had succeeded in bracing both his arms against the pale man's chest, bloodied face grimacing as he tried to throw his ravening assailant off.

The pale man's efforts came to an end when one of the spear-bearing guards charged out of the gloom to lance him through the back. The spearpoint emerged from his belly as he was dragged clear of the whip-man, falling to the sand to writhe and twitch as his blood stained the powder. Incredibly, he still possessed the strength to direct a final glare at Radylf. The giant stood a short way off, shredded ear hanging and red gore streaking his face which appeared curiously free of anger, but did twitch a little when the small man gasped out what would surely be his last ever words: "*Rulchakin . . . t-chen!*"

Before a dark curtain descended on Ruhlin's vision, he watched the man who had tried to kill him, only to save him, lay his head upon the wet sand. Their dimming eyes met and Ruhlin experienced a flutter of amazement before sliding into the terror-laced dark, for, as he died, the small man's lips had twisted into the smile of a contented soul.

* * *

For no reason he could fathom, this time, the pain and fear inflicted by the nightmares felt lessened. The sight of the entirety of Buhl Hardta's population lined up on the dock, every one sedately drawing a knife across their own throats, certainly hurt, but not so much as before. He watched Irhkyn hack his way through some foreign settlement, bloodied face lit with manic glee, and felt more pity than disgust, for he knew how this deed, if it had ever happened, would torment his friend in later life. Eventually, the inevitable deceiving moment of calm descended and Ruhlin found himself on the slipway, boyish hands working caulk into the seams of his father's boat. All the youngsters gathered at the harbour to do this every few weeks, a semi-ritualised chore rich in mingled merriment and bickering. The fishermen would share the toil of overturning the beached boats, whereupon their children set about the less strenuous but more tedious task of sealing the planking.

He remembered this occasion well, for it was the day Tenryk earned a black eye from his father. Strong of body but dull of mind, Tenryk had grown big earlier than the other children and wasn't shy about asserting his role as their self-appointed leader. He lacked the wit and, Ruhlin had to concede, the innate sadism of the true bully. So instead of cruel jibes and taunts punctuated by violent reminders of status, he expressed his dominance through hard shoves to the ground and the occasional kick. Perhaps because Ruhlin only tended to mix with other children on days like this, spending most of his time on his father's boat or seeing to the endless chores his grandmother set for him, he had largely been spared Tenryk's attention. Today, however, he succeeded in attracting the dullard's notice. He realised later Tenryk's ire had been piqued by the smile Ruhlin shared with Lystra, the boatbuilder's daughter, who carried the buckets of caulk to the labouring children. She and Tenryk would marry some years later, and a happy couple they made until, ever prone to bad judgement, he sailed forth in foul weather and failed to return. Ruhlin had mourned him then, for manhood had shaped an ineffective bully into an amiable soul, albeit with a mind none would call quick. But when the shove to his back propelled Ruhlin into hard contact with the hull of his father's boat and left him reeling on the ground, he had gazed up at Tenryk's glaring face with baffled resentment and a heart-pounding desire for retribution.

"Eyes on your work, *sictskyra!*" Tenryk spat.

At the time, Ruhlin assumed the unfamiliar word to be an overheard adult obscenity. Tenryk was fond of adopting such terms into his armoury of insults, even though he displayed scant understanding of their meaning. Ruhlin began to rise, lips forming a more common rejoinder. But before he could voice the retort, a large shadow fell upon them both. Hilfar, Tenryk's father, was one of the largest men in the village, and well liked for his generous spirit and placid temper, but neither were on display that day. The backhanded blow he delivered spun his son to the ground, provoking a shocked silence amongst the onlooking children. This was not the disciplining cuff of an annoyed parent, but a true act of violence intended to cause hurt. Ruhlin saw no guilt or regret on Hilfar's face as he stooped to clamp a hand to Tenryk's neck, hauling him to his feet and dragging him away. Before the pair disappeared into the gap between upturned hulls, Ruhlin heard Hilfar's snarling rebuke: "Arse-brained little bugger! I told you to steer clear . . ."

Instead of the usual shift into impossible and ghastly terror, this time the nightmare simply slipped into a grey haze. Ruhlin's boyhood remembrance of the boats and staring children dissolved, then, upon blinking, became the bars of his cage. As he began to rise, he felt a jolt of pain from something hard resting on his upper chest. His fingers pressed against unyielding metal, exploring the thing until he recognised it as an iron ring set deep into his flesh, so deep in fact that it encircled his collarbone. There was no blood where it pierced his skin. Though healed, it still ached with a persistent throb.

A glance at his naked thigh revealed the livid scar left by the pale man's knife, but not so ugly as he might have expected. The ache in his back told the same tale of the other wound. He couldn't see any sign that the cut on his leg had been stitched, yet the flesh had knitted together well and lacked the dark hue of corruption. The sight made him wonder how long he had slept this time. A day? A month?

Rising to his feet, he turned to Tuhlan's cage, finding it empty. However, the clack and clatter of wood on wood from the direction of the sunlit circle provided a swift explanation for the Caerith's absence. He and a dozen or so others were at practice in the circle, assailing each other with staves. Yet this wasn't the chaos of true combat. Radylf paced the lowest tier at the circle's edge, calling out instructions: "Right strike. Left strike. Central thrust. Feint left . . ."

In time with the whip-man's calls, half the figures in the circle swung or jabbed their staves at opponents who parried each blow. In Buhl Hardta, Ruhlin had seen fathers tutor their children in use of sword or axe in a similar manner, but the movements were never so precise. His own father had never seen fit to teach him. Neither had Irhkyn, but Ruhlin hadn't minded all that much. Most other boys hung on their elders' tales of distant wars and raids, eager for the day they might have their own chance at renown, perhaps even the honour of an earned name. Ruhlin, though interested in the stories and keen to one day see other lands with his own eyes, felt no great urge towards the warrior's mantle. Now, it appeared, he had no choice. But, if it was Aerling Eldryk's desire to see him fight, why had he inflicted this burdensome collar upon a captive he supposedly prized above all others?

"Best if you don't touch it," a voice advised in a soft but audible murmur as his fingers explored the ring once more. "Don't look at me," Aleida added when he turned in her direction, catching a glimpse of her slender form crouched in the shadows at the rear of his cage. "Not supposed to be here, remember?"

"And yet you are." Ruhlin sat on his bunk, resisting the urge to cover himself with a blanket. She might see it as another opportunity to poke fun and he had need of a real conversation. "What is this?" he asked, tapping a finger to the ring.

"Why should I tell you?"

"Why should you not? And did I not suffer the whip on your behalf recently?"

A pause before she muttered a sullen reply, "I didn't ask you to."

"No, you didn't. But where I come from, a debt is still a debt, even if you didn't invite it."

"You come from the Teilvik lands, a realm of savages who, in your weakness, have lost the Altvar's favour." Ruhlin heard little conviction in this statement, her voice flat with the rote utterance of dogma. After another, shorter pause, she said, "It's called a *stagna*. Only the most dangerous slaves get them. I assume my father considers darting you too risky a tactic now, since you're probably already developing a resistance to the drugs."

Two darts to bring me down instead of one, he thought, feeling the double pang in his mouth. *And the nightmares were less potent.*

"A mere piece of metal won't be enough," he said. "Not when . . ." He trailed off, realising he didn't have the words to describe his peculiar affliction.

"When the Vyrn Skyra boils," Aleida said, Ruhlin hearing a certain relish in her voice.

"Vyrn Skyra," he repeated. He had a sense that the words might be old Ascarlian, but her accent made them unfamiliar.

"Fire Blood," she said. "In the old tongue. The name for those like you."

"There are others like me?"

She shrugged. "Some. Never seen one quite like you, though. How does it feel? Father says it would be like hearing the voices of the Altvar themselves."

"Then he's wrong." Keen to sidestep this topic, he spoke on before she could advance her curiosity further. "*Rulchakin t-chen.* Do you know what that means?"

"Noticed that, did you?" He didn't like the amusement colouring her tone. It bespoke a young soul far too inured to the sight of death. Still, he resisted the impulse to turn and display his disgust. With Eldryk as a father, how could she not be twisted?

"It's a Morvek insult," she went on. "Means 'Outlander's dog'."

"Morvek?"

She let out a faint laugh. "You truly know nothing of where you are, do you? The Biter was Morvek, as is Radylf, if you hadn't guessed. But *he* knows his place."

Watching Radylf stride along the circle's edge, Ruhlin saw new meaning in the paleness of his skin. "Radylf and the man I fought are of the same people," he realised aloud. He knew the names of all the lands and folk Irhkyn had encountered in his travels, but had never heard him mention the word Morvek. "Where do they hail from?"

"Here, where else?" Aleida said. "The Morvek were ancient in these lands long before we came here. A gift from the Altvar, so the old ones say, for they were so easily bent to our will. Strong of body, but weak of blood. It is right that they serve us." More rote dogma, but this time laced with a bitter edge. Ruhlin decided to risk a glance in her direction, finding all but her face concealed in shadow, feline features cast in soft yellow by the torch's glow. However, the dimmer light catching a portion of her neck enabled him to discern its true colour. Not pale like Radylf's, or the man with the filed teeth, but still a shade lighter than his own skin, and her father's.

"You're Morvek, too," he said. "Aren't you?"

She stared at him, face mostly blank save for a twitch to her eyes. "I said don't look at me," she hissed, adding with a cruel twist to her lips, "Savage!" before disappearing into the gloom.

CHAPTER EIGHTEEN

Thera

"I know not this man, Vellihr."

Hakkyn looked upon the body laid out on the slab with a mix of shame and outrage, Thera seeing no sign of a lie in the Veilwald's bearing or expression. They had taken the corpse to one of the gutting sheds alongside the harbour, the Veilwald swiftly banishing the folk at work there whilst Thera's *menda* guarded the exterior. A search of the sailor's clothing produced a purse with but a single strip of hacksilver and a few copper coins from the southern seas. The tattoos adorning his face and upper chest bore no runes that would indicate a name.

"Nor do the captains of any ships in the harbour tell of a missing hand," Hakkyn went on. "And I assure you, my harbour master has been stern in her enquiries. Ships come and go here all the time, as you know. It's likely the vessel that brought him here sailed off days ago."

"Leaving him to lie in wait," Thera mused, peering closer at the dead man's brow. "Ragnalt." She glanced up at the warrior and pointed to a design inked into the corpse's right temple. "What do you make of that?"

"Fox," Ragnalt confirmed after inspecting the tattoo. He was the most skilled and knowledgeable amongst her *menda* when it came to such things and there were few aboard the *Great Wolf* who didn't sport at least one product of his needle upon their skin. "Poorly done," he added with a judgemental sniff. "It's a common hunter's motif in the upper Fjord Lands. Boys earn them when they make their first kill. This one." He tapped a finger to another more elegantly rendered design on the body's impressively thick bicep: a barbed arrow ringed with oak leaves. "Sign of a master archer."

"He couldn't have been that good," Eshilde put in. She shrugged in response to Thera's glance. "He missed, I mean."

"So." Thera stood back, crossing her arms and surveying the corpse from its relatively intact head and torso to its dog-ravaged lower portions. "A hunter from the upper Fjord Lands. Arrived here in advance of us with the purpose of killing me." *Or Lynnea*, she added inwardly, deciding it would be best not to bring any more attention to her apprentice than she had to.

"Then he must have had notice we were coming here," Ragnalt said.

"Unless he's just some wayward madman," Eshilde suggested. "The kind who gets his prick stiffened by killing women. Plenty of those about."

"We sailed here swiftly," Thera said, ignoring her. A tendency towards flippant and asinine conjecture was another reason why Eshilde wasn't yet ready for the Vellihr's path. "Less than a day after receiving orders from Sister Iron. No ship could have put forth at the same time and got ahead of us. This one was set in our way before I even met with the queens."

"But why, Vellihr?" Hakkyn asked, his aged brow laced with worried mystification. "And who?"

The question brought a soft laugh to Thera's lips. The list of those with scores to settle against the Vellihr of Justice was long. It could be this slain archer was kin to some justly executed soul. Having missed his ship's departure due to mischance or drunkenness, he saw his chance for vengeance when the *Great Wolf* sailed into port. It was plausible, but she didn't believe it. The more she contemplated the events of the previous night, the more she became convinced the arrow hadn't been aimed at her. If Lynnea was the true target, someone had anticipated that she would become Thera's apprentice and accompany her on a mission to the Outer Isles. *If the dog hadn't growled . . .*

"We've learned all we can here," she said, turning to Hakkyn. "I'll leave this one to be disposed of as you see fit, Veilwald. And please accept my regrets at bringing trouble to your door."

"Your trouble is mine to share, Vellihr," he assured her with a tight smile before nodding at the corpse. "As for that, I'll not till good earth to cover his worthless carcass nor waste timber on a pyre. There's a tide pool north of the harbour where we dump our miscreants. The crabs always appreciate a meal."

The three ships sailed from Skyrn Hardta at the turn of the tide, with the *Great Wolf*'s crew enlarged by a count of one, somewhat to Gelmyr's dismay. "I'm not sure we have the stocks to feed the brute," the *Johten Apt* said, casting an uneasy eye over the massive dog. Thera suspected his attitude arose from concern that the beast's additional weight would negate his attempts to match the *Swift Spear*'s pace.

"I bought a barrel of salted seal blubber before we left," Thera said. "Apparently it's his favourite." As with Mohlnir, the hulking beast hadn't strayed from Lynnea's side since Thera allowed him on board. Her decision was ostensibly born of pity, for the animal's owner had avowed an intention to put him down.

"Tasted human meat, he has," the fellow said. One of the few dog breeders in the Outer Isles, he was patently unsentimental about his trade. "Means he won't hesitate should the chance arise in future. Can't have it, Vellihr. But, if you're fool enough to risk him, I'll not stand in your way. No offence meant. His name's Snaryk, by the way. Thought it was ironic when I gave it to him, since he's so sweet natured and all. Now, I'm not so sure." Snaryk was an infamously cruel raider during the Age of Kings. Over time, the name had come to be applied to anyone with an appetite for wanton destruction.

In truth, whilst Thera had no desire to see a beast that had saved her apprentice slain, her reason for taking him along was more practical. Lynnea's combat practice remained perfunctory if efficient, and it would be a long while before she could be trusted to defend herself. With Snaryk at her side, Thera would worry less about any more arrows that might be aimed in the maiden's direction.

She held to her plan upon clearing the western coast of Ayl-Ah-Rohn, tacking northward in sight of shore and keeping to the channels between islands. Constricted waters made for hard sailing that limited even the *Swift Spear*'s speed, but Thera felt it preferable to the uncertain whims of the Styrnspeld. For days they spied no other craft save a few fishing boats, the settlements they saw diminishing in scale and number the further north they sailed. Two weeks after leaving port, the weather worsened. Gelmyr judged the increasing rain and stiffening wind to portend a storm sweeping in from the west. Thera followed his advice in signalling the other ships to follow the *Great Wolf* turning east to gain shelter from the more mountainous islands in the heart of the chain. Although the manoeuvre spared them the worst of the storm, it still proved a wearisome trial. Three pairs of hands were required to keep the tiller true, and the crew worked ceaselessly to prevent the gale tearing sails from the masts.

The tempest abated after two full days of fury, Thera looking out on becalmed waters with only the *Wind Sword* in sight. It was common for ships to become separated during a storm, and she expected the *Swift Spear* to hove into view before the day was out. However, when the midday sun passed its zenith with no sign of the smaller vessel, she began to fear the worst.

"Gynheld's too good a skipper to let a storm take her down," Gelmyr assured her. "She'll be along soon enough."

His judgement proved sound by the onset of evening, but it was not due to the sighting of a sail on the northern horizon but a rising column of smoke from an island to the north-west. "Signal fire," Thera decided, perched on the prow and squinting into the wind as she made out the small but bright blaze atop the headland jutting from the island's shore. As the *Great Wolf* drew closer, she saw a figure standing alongside the fire, waving a blazing torch. Rounding the headland, they found the *Swift Spear* at anchor in a shallow bay with her boats beached. The reason for the signal fire became grimly apparent at the sight of the small settlement perched atop the slope beyond the bay. Every building, from cottage to shed, stood blackened and roofless, with no sign of life.

* * *

Sister Iron's map named this island as Ayl-Ah-Veyn, the Granite Isle. Just a small and unremarkable speck upon the chart, situated on the western edge of this lower portion of the Kast Geld. It was a place that had existed in much the same state of contented unimportance for centuries, but had now earned the most dire form of notoriety.

"The bodies are back there." Gynheld's heavy features were grim as she jerked her head at the ruined shearing shed, which had been the largest structure in this wasted village. "Fire scorched, so it's hard to say how many. Best reckoning is about two dozen in all." She paused, jaw muscles working as she swallowed. "Children too."

Thera forced herself to look at the bodies, surveying twisted limbs arising from a messy bed of ash like an obscene parody of a recently planted orchard. "Get to work on a barrow," she told Ragnalt. "We'll not leave them like this."

A tour of the other dwellings revealed little since the contents had been consumed by flames, however, the detritus littering the paddocks and sheds told at least part of the story. "This was well made," Alvyr mused, crouching outside a cottage door to pick up a shard of pottery. Sniffing it, he raised his eyebrows in appreciation. "Wine not mead. From Alundia, if I'm not mistaken. Curious."

Seeing the puzzlement on Lynnea's brow, Thera explained, "Raiders don't break things of value. An amphora filled with Alundian wine is worth something. Those who did this weren't interested in plunder." She glanced back at the shearing shed. "Only slaughter."

"Arrow here," Alvyr went on, plucking a broken shaft from a nearby bush. "Bone," he added, displaying the arrowhead to Thera. "This is locally crafted. Flecks of dried blood on it, too. Seems someone put up a fight."

"And maybe even had the good sense to run." Thera cast her gaze to the steep incline above the village. It ascended to a rocky crest, which seemed the most likely point of refuge in an otherwise feature-less landscape. "Take your *menda* and scout this isle from end to end," she told Alvyr. "Starting up there."

Unlike Gynheld, Alvyr displayed no outward fury, but Thera could see the dark simmer behind his eyes. All three of them had seen plentiful bloodshed in their time, but such merciless carnage was rare. Touching the broken arrow to his forehead in acquiescence, Alvyr strode off, calling to his warriors.

Hearing a whine, Thera turned to see Snaryk crouched in Lynnea's shadow. His brows crinkled in distressed confusion and his fist-sized nose wrinkled at the melange of corruption and damp ash. *He doesn't understand.* Lynnea frowned as she ran a comforting hand through Snaryk's fur before looking up to meet Thera's eye. *Neither do I.*

"It's the lot of a Vellihr of Justice to look upon what others won't," Thera told her. "And rummage through the leavings of those who do evil. For that is how we find them."

Thorough investigation of the village revealed only more evidence of murder and destruction, with no clear sign of who had committed so foul a deed. "The storm would've washed away any blood trails," Gynheld surmised. She and her *menda* had checked the livestock pens and sheds along the shoreline north of the settlement. "Found plenty of dead sheep they didn't bother to burn. From the state of rot, I'd say at least ten days ago. Could be longer."

Alvyr returned when night had fully fallen, having ordered his warriors to light torches and complete the search in darkness. "Not a living soul," he reported with a grimace of apology. "He's all we found." He nodded to a small bundle cradled in the arms of Imhar, the largest warrior in his crew. Never one to shield his feelings from the world, the big man made no effort to hide the tears beading his copious red beard. Moving closer, Thera saw that he held the body of a boy no more than eight years old, the splintered shaft of an arrow jutting from his back.

"He must've walked for a mile or more with that in him, Vellihr," Imhar said, voice hoarse. "Then lay down to sleep." He pulled the boy closer, fresh tears welling. "Brave little man . . ."

"Put him with his kin," Thera said, pointing to the spot near the beach where Ragnalt had dug the long ditch of the barrow. "We'll find who did this. You have my promise."

With all the bodies interned, Thera struck sparks from a striker shaped into the eye of the goddess Aerldun. "May the ever watchful guardian of the dark paths see these people to the Halls of Aevnir," she intoned as the blaze caught kindling and spread to the coals. After receiving the sombre murmuring of agreement from the assembled warriors, she sent them to their rest with a warning that the following day would require all their fortitude. "No longer can we abide the safer course. Those who did this came from the west, else we would have seen more of their crimes before now. Clearly there is evil abroad in these waters and the sooner we find it, the better. Tomorrow we sail the Styrnspeld proper, and may Ulfmaer grant us his mercy."

Before departing Ayl-Ah-Veyn, Thera gave Gynheld a stern enjoinder to remain in close order with the *Great Wolf* and the *Wind Sword*. "I smell battle on the wind," she told both Vellihrs on the beach that morning. "Best if we meet it together."

"And when we do?" Alvyr asked. "My lot are in no mood for granting quarter."

"Nor mine," Gynheld grunted.

"Justice will be served on all we find," Thera assured them. "But I need answers, so spare any who look to be in charge. I would know the names of those who roused so fierce a rebellion that the islanders would turn on their own with such viciousness."

"If rebels they are." Alvyr spared a glance at the ruined village on the slope. "When little more than a lad, I fought for pay in wars the length of the southern seas and never saw the like of this."

"Who else?" Gynheld said. "All our foreign enemies are far to the south, and I doubt they would sail so many miles just to wreak profitless bloodshed."

"We'll know when we find them," Thera said. "And daylight's wasting, so let's be at it."

Fortunately, for the next few days, the Styrnspeld proved fractious but not treacherous. At Thera's instruction, Gelmyr set a course following a broad arc out into the sea before angling back towards the upper reaches of the Kast Geld. She ordered a double watch upon all approaches and commanded the crew to keep their weapons close. Yet, after a week of sailing into worsening weather, the horizon remained stubbornly free of sails and their hunt found no prey.

When they made the turn back towards the isles, Thera called upon Gelmyr's judgement as to their first port of call. "Ayl-Ah-Vahrim is home to the Veilwald of the Kast Geld," the *Johten Apt* said, pointing out a large island near the upper limit of the Outer Isles. "But getting there is another week's sailing, at least. Be wiser to call in here first." He tapped a smaller landmass to the west.

"Ayl-Ah-Lyhsswahl," Thera said, reading the neat runes below the island with a dubious arch to her brows. "The Isle of Whales?" The prospect of encountering even one of the notoriously hostile white giants that prowled the northern stretches of the Styrnspeld was not something to relish. She had once caught a distant glimpse of such a beast years before and that, together with the myriad tales of their aggressive dislike of ships, had been enough to dissuade her from seeking a closer look.

"In truth, they're not all that common in these waters," Gelmyr said. "Though their seasonal migration takes them within a few miles of the isle come winter, hence the name. Buhl Hardta is the only decent-sized settlement on the island. I wouldn't call the folk there friendly, but they're usually happy to trade with passing ships. Take a dim view of being cheated though, at least they did twelve years back when I last called there. A Cordwainer pushed his luck palming cards and paid for it with his fingers. The Uhlwald was a fair man, though, and didn't take them all."

"Did he strike you as the rebellious type, this Uhlwald?"

Gelmyr shook his head. "That's the curious thing about all this, none of them did. The folk of the Kast Geld have more to worry over just keeping themselves fed through the year. Can't see them embarking on wholesale slaughter just 'cause they're annoyed at the Sister Queens' taxes."

"It's not always money that rouses people to revolt." Thera looked again at the map. Heading for the Veilwald's home island made sense, but her small fleet had endured many days at sea and their stocks could do with replenishment. "Buhl Hardta it is," she said. "And best tell our lot to forgo games of chance when we get there."

One look at the small port made it clear that there would be no games here, nor anyone to punish those caught cheating. Unlike the settlement on Ayl-Ah-Veyn, the houses of Buhl Hardta were a mix of stone and wood, meaning many had survived destruction, though Thera saw none with an intact roof. The few dozen fishing skiffs in the harbour appeared mostly undamaged, but, as the *Great Wolf* approached the wharf, she made out the unmoving bodies littering the slipway. Despite the eerie quiet and absence of life, she opted for a cautious approach. The *Swift Spear* and *Wind Sword* were dispatched to the broad beach further along the shore with orders to scout the land beyond the port whilst she made for the town. She instructed all her warriors to don armour and bear shields before leading them onto the short quay and into the settlement. Thereafter, they divided into groups of five and spread out, checking each building.

"Didn't bother burning them this time," Eshilde noted when they discovered a pile of bodies near the slipway. Corruption and the detrimental touch of the elements had degraded the corpses, but enough flesh remained on their bones to show that all had died by violence. Although the ground was bare of weapons, Thera also saw that many bore cuts on their arms and hands.

"At least they died fighting," she muttered, her focus snared by the sight of a large man entwined with what she assumed to have been a young woman. His daughter, perhaps? Had he been slain trying to shield her?

"The Uhlwald," Gelmyr said, crouching to peer at the desiccated flesh of the large man's face. "I remember his ink." Rising, he let out a sigh. "Wish I could remember his name."

Their inspection of the settlement revealed a similarly grim tale to Ayl-Ah-Veyn; wrecked houses, many still containing valuables, and slain people. Some, like those at the slipway, had plainly fought whilst others, mostly children and old folk, had been cut down without mercy.

Thera ordered all storehouses and gardens checked for concealed holes where folk might have taken refuge. It was a common custom in the Inner Isles and the Fjord Lands for homesteaders to dig a hiding place, an unfaded legacy of the endless raids during the Age of Kings. However, after a thorough search, she had to conclude that such a practice was not followed here.

"Full count comes to two hundred and twenty-three," Ragnalt reported when the *menda* had completed their task. "All local, so far as we can tell."

"If it was other islanders who did this, how would we know?" Eshilde wondered. "The murderers could be lying there amongst their victims."

Thera's gaze was drawn by a loud growl from the direction of the well at the centre of the settlement's market. Snaryk had perched his spade-sized paws on the well's rim and lowered his head to peer into the depths. Drool dripped from his quivering lips as he maintained his growl, soon blossoming into an angry bark. Moving closer, Thera saw the beast's hackles rise despite the calming hand Lynnea stroked across his back.

"What is it?" Thera asked her.

Lynnea's wrinkled nose and grimace were ample answer. *More death.* Her eyes narrowed as she peered into the well. *But I think he scents something different about this one.*

"Fetch grapples," Thera told Eshilde. "And let's see what we can catch."

The corpse was heavy, its armour and flesh bloated by long immersion in water. It required the strength of Ragnalt, Eshilde and Gelmyr combined to haul it clear of the well. As it tumbled, stiff and wet, onto the cobbles, Snaryk let out another bark, though the stink arising from the body was enough to prevent him coming closer.

"Warrior, whoever he was," Gelmyr said, features bunched as he endured the stench to crouch for a closer look. The corpse's belt held an empty scabbard and two daggers. His armour was decorated in unfamiliar sigils and a form of runic Thera didn't recognise. But the principal focus of interest was the angle of his neck.

"Looks like his head's on backwards," Eshilde said with an amused huff.

"Could be he broke it when he fell," Ragnalt suggested.

"No." Gelmyr pointed to the body's mangled spine and jaw. "Three separate breaks, I reckon. Something twisted his head near off then stuffed him down the well."

"Never heard of a beast that could do such a thing." Ragnalt shook his head in wonder, then frowned and nodded at the corpse's swollen face. "Nor seen ink like that."

Stepping closer, Thera saw that the tattoos on the man's brow, though faded and distorted by his bleached, waterlogged flesh, were rendered in red rather than the customary blue. "Can you read any of this?" she asked Ragnalt.

"All nonsense to me," he said, shaking his head. "Some of it looks a bit like ancient script, but I can't read that either."

Ancient script. The kind used in the days of the Volkrath. Had the cult been reborn and resumed its old ways? But how could it gather the numbers required to wreak such havoc in secret? "Search him thoroughly," Thera said. "Strip him bare. I want every trinket you can find."

"Such glorious feats we garner at your side, Vellihr," Eshilde commented with a roll of her eyes. Although she set herself to the task without hesitation or further complaint, Thera resolved to speak to her later about her tendency to gripe. It was another bar to the Vellihr's path.

They inspected all the other wells in the settlement, without finding any more mangled bodies, and completed a search of the outlying crofts before nightfall. Thera oversaw the burial, taking her turn in carrying the corpses to the barrow they dug atop the bluffs to the west. Gynheld returned at dusk from scouting the northern shore of the island, reporting only ruined dwellings and murdered people. "Spared most of the sheep this time," she said, gesturing to the small bleating flock her *menda* herded into the village. "Thought we could do with some more meat."

Alvyr's band arrived an hour later. Once again, their hunt had discovered a body in the wilds, but this time he was still breathing. "We found him shivering in a cave on the western cliffs," Alvyr said. "Haven't been able to get a great deal out of him, as yet. Just his name."

"Annuk," the thin, dirt-covered man at Alvyr's side said, bobbing his head at Thera then repeating the gesture to all in sight. He was clad in a sheepskin and threadbare trews, rags bound about his feet. "Annuk," he repeated as Thera moved closer. Looking into his eyes, she saw how their focus wavered, his brow creasing intermittently in concert with the pitch of his confusion.

"You hail from this island, Annuk?" she asked, keeping her tone gentle.

His head bobbed again, a smile curving his lips, then fading quickly. "All my years . . . Seihlva too."

"Seihlva?"

"My wife. She's at home, waiting . . ." His face spasmed in alarm and he turned about. "I should go. She's waiting . . ."

"Linger here a while with us," Alvyr said, clamping a friendly arm about the thin man's shoulders. "We've a feast ready and you strike me as a man in need of a meal."

They sat him by the large fire they had built in the market to roast two of the sheep from Gynheld's purloined flock. With his hunger sated, Annuk appeared to recover a modicum of reason, though he tried several more times to get up and return to his wife's side. From the sob that coloured his voice whenever he spoke of her, Thera didn't doubt that, should they let him go, he would be returning to a ruined cottage occupied by a dead woman.

"Came from the north, they did," Annuk said once Alvyr had finally coaxed him into telling the tale of the calamity to befall his island. "Not long after dawn. Me and Seihlva was out gathering kelp on the shore when we saw the sails. Three ships, there was, sails flying the sigil of Ossgrym Styrntorc. It was strange to see three ships of his, since he sends but one a year and usually later in the season. Still, we thought little of it until we saw the smoke rise from Buhl Hardta."

"The Veilwald of the Kast Geld?" Thera asked. "You're saying he did this?"

"Aye, his own *menda* sent to do murder upon his own people." Annuk's features tensed into a grimace of frustrated grief. "Seihlva said we should run for the cave in the cliff, but I said I had to fight. Told her to go without me, took up my sword and shield and made haste for the town. Such things I saw when I got here . . ." He trailed off, eyes tightening in an effort to stave off tears. "I ran, Vellihr. To my shame that I'll carry to the Halls of Aevnir, I ran to the cave, but Seihlva wasn't there. I searched . . ." His sobs burst forth then, Alvyr running a hand across the islander's neck as he convulsed in grief whilst an angry silence settled over the assembled warriors.

"Ossgrym Styrntorc," Thera murmured. "The Ironbones."

"Not a well-liked man, to be sure," Gelmyr said. "But not one I'd ever judge a rebel."

"Some might have said the same of Kolsyg Ehflud." The memory of the slain Veilwald's face just before her spear ended him, full of hateful invective, drew her gaze to his daughter, whereupon Thera stiffened at the maiden's expression. Her uncanny ability to read Lynnea's thoughts in her face had never been more clear, even though her features remained as still as any statue. The blue eyes fixed on Thera, unblinking in their certainty: *He's lying.*

As if in confirmation, Snaryk shifted at Lynnea's side, a low, ominous rumble emerging from his throat.

Looking again at Annuk's shuddering form, Thera saw no artifice in such abject sorrow. Her years as Vellihr of Justice had taught her how to spot many a lie, but she wasn't so prideful as to imagine herself infallible. Once Annuk had calmed a little, she ventured another question. "Did you hear any words from those who did this? Any reason for their crime?"

Annuk wiped his face, drawing in a ragged breath before answering. "All I know is this: from atop the hill, I saw Veilwald Ossgrym himself. He stood with bloodied axe in hand, surrounded by those he had slain, calling out words I can't understand."

Thera shuffled closer. "What words?"

Annuk closed his eyes, teeth clenched as he summoned an unwelcome

memory. "'So do the weak of blood perish! So do the Uhltvar rise!'
Those were his words, Vellihr. I swear it."

Thera sat back, brows furrowed in contemplation, before she
nodded to the corpse propped against the well. "That man. Was he
amongst the Veilwald's *menda*?"

Annuk's face betrayed only miserable disgust as he regarded the
body. "I assume so, Vellihr. His armour marks him as a warrior, and
none of our people were girded for battle." Once again, Thera saw no
glimmer of artifice. This man, if he was lying, was by far the most
accomplished deceiver she had yet encountered.

"His skin is inked in red," she persisted. "Were they all marked in
such a way?"

"As I recall it now, some were, but not all. It's strange, I suppose."

"Any notion of how he came to find himself cast into a well with
his neck snapped?" Gelmyr asked, receiving only a baffled shake of
the head in response.

Thera studied the islander's sagging features, seeing only more tired
misery. *Just as I would expect from so wounded a soul.* But another
glance at Lynnea confirmed the same stark warning in her eyes: *He
is lying!*

"My thanks, good man," Thera said, favouring Annuk with a brief
clasp to the forearm. "And have no shame, for the knowledge you
give will aid us. On the morrow, we sail to Ayl-Ah-Vahrim, where
Veilwald Ossgrym will be compelled to answer for his crimes. Will
you sail with us so that his people might hear the truth of your words?"

"I will, Vellihr, and gladly."

Thera settled herself back onto the stool she had found unbroken
in one of the houses near the slipway, reaching for her drinking horn
and holding it out to Ragnalt. As he brought the mead cask over to
fill her vessel, she met his eyes and tapped a finger to her dagger. He
blinked to acknowledge the order and moved along, filling more horns
as went, but not straying far.

"Just one other thing, good man," Thera said to Annuk who had
slipped back into morose contemplation.

"Yes, Vellihr?"

"We found a body that bears the marks of an Uhlwald, but none amongst us knows his name. I shall need to record it for my report to the Sister Queens. Can you oblige?"

"Of course, Vellihr. His name—" The attack came mid-sentence, Annuk springing at Thera with no sudden tension to betray his intent, nor any hesitancy in drawing the small knife hidden in his sheepskin. Thera was saved by well-honed instinct, reeling back to tumble from her stool, the knifepoint stabbing the air inches from her throat. Annuk scrambled after her, his face now set with the predatory focus of one accustomed to killing. Before he could attempt another strike, Ragnalt landed on his back.

"Alive!" Thera shouted as the warrior bore Annuk to the ground, dagger poised at the base of his neck. The would-be assassin thrashed, displaying more strength than seemed possible for his frame. He almost succeeded in throwing Ragnalt off before Eshilde and Gelmyr closed in to snare his arms whilst more warriors pinioned the islander's legs.

"I couldn't remember the Uhlwald's name either, you fuck!" Gelmyr grunted, slamming Annuk's hand to the cobbled ground to dislodge the knife.

"Get him up," Thera said, rising to her feet. Ragnalt dragged the captive to his knees, thick arm braced around his throat, Eshilde and Gelmyr keeping a tight hold of his arms. "Anything to say?" Thera asked, stooping to peer into Annuk's glaring eyes and seeing only defiance. "It would save us both a lot of time, and you a lot of pain."

His only answer was a brief shower of spittle upon her face, choked off when Ragnalt tightened his grip. "As you will it," Thera sighed, wiping the spit away. "But I can assure you, before the sun sets tomorrow, you and I will have had ourselves a *very* interesting talk."

Chapter Nineteen

Felnir

Colvyn contemplated the coins in his palm with scant sign of greed or gratitude. They were a mix of copper and silver from Albermaine and the southern seas ports, enough to keep him fed for a few months or buy passage on a ship.

"For your trouble," Felnir said. "And the story. It was quite entertaining."

As promised, during the voyage to Skar Magnol, the youth had related the tale of how he came to know courtly Ishtan. It was the saga of a lad escaping the hovels of some southern Albermaine port to seek his fortune in the east. After many adventures, Colvyn fetched up in Ishtakar where he found work as a bookkeeper for a wealthy merchant. "A fine man and a kindly employer with a daughter he wished to see presented at the Saluhtan's court one day. To this end, he had hired a number of tutors to coach her in courtly manners and etiquette. She found it all tremendously boring, but was happy to share her lessons with a foreign bookkeeper of whom she had grown unwisely fond."

Colvyn had gone on to describe the inevitable moment when the forbidden tryst had been discovered whereupon he made his escape, bare arsed naked, via the rooftops with the merchant's curses ringing in his ears. A ribald and amusing tale, and Felnir didn't believe a word of it. Still, it wasn't his business, and the lad had done his job. Felnir had chosen not to enlighten his great-grandfather as to Colvyn's presence aboard the *Sea Hawk*, anticipating the consequences. This one saw and understood a great deal more than was healthy, yet Felnir's facility for murder only extended so far.

"So you feel you have no more need of my skills, esteemed sir," Colvyn said, directing a glance at his former cellmate. Wohtin sat in a nook between deck boards, his back bared to Sister Lore's scholar as she went about the task of reproducing his many tattoos. She had already filled several sheets of parchment with meticulously executed facsimiles of the intricate designs. Whereas Felnir would have found such toil tedious in the extreme, this bright-eyed young woman set to it with fascinated zeal. Furthermore, the object of her study was even more quiescent in her company than he had been in Colvyn's.

"My ship feels overfull at present," Felnir said.

"I would wonder if you shared your people's famed intolerance of foreigners," Colvyn replied with a grin, "if there weren't so many in your crew. Most of them rescued from circumstances not dissimilar to my own. Why not make room for one more? A man as shrewd and well travelled as you can surely see my value."

As he spoke, Felnir saw how the youth's gaze continually strayed to the scholar. When she came aboard, Guthnyr had been quick to afford her his usual round of hopeful attention, receiving polite but firm disinterest in response. Perhaps Colvyn felt he would have better luck, though Felnir doubted he would willingly place himself in such uncertain company merely to pursue a woman.

"Running from something, eh?" Felnir asked. "Something that might catch you if you venture south again? And I'm guessing it's not an aggrieved father."

Colvyn shrugged. "Does it matter? I'd wager I'm not the only soul aboard this ship with scant options for refuge."

"Refuge?" Felnir snorted a laugh. "That's something I can't offer, lad. Stay with me and all I have for you is hard, perilous voyaging and the prospect of blood to break the monotony every now and then."

"Sold." Colvyn returned the coins to the purse and held it out to Felnir. "In truth, it's the best offer I've had in a long while."

Felnir began to reply that he hadn't made an offer, then realised Colvyn had, in the space of a few sentences, manoeuvred him into doing just that. *Too wily*, he thought, contemplating the purse. *Sees far too much. Kick him down the plank and let's be off.*

"Keep it," he said. "But don't expect any more until our current task is done. You'll have charge of them." He nodded to the scholar and the madman. "No harm comes to either, on your life. You'll also take your turn hauling rope and working oars without griping and keep your nook clean and tidy. Last man who shit on my deck had to swim home."

Colvyn pulled the purse strings tight before affording Felnir a deep bow. "I've always been careful where I shit, esteemed sir."

"That merchant in Ishtakar would probably disagree." Felnir jerked his head. "See Druba. He's got blades for you. And lad," he added as Colvyn made to leave, "forget any notions you have about the girl. Those that pay us made it clear that hers is the only life aboard this ship they truly care about. Be nice, but don't be charming."

The youth's eyes flicked towards the scholar again, just for a second, before he looked away. Felnir knew this one had a considerable facility for deceit, but felt it curious he should fail to conceal his interest now. His parting honorific was also surprisingly muted, confined to another bow, and a murmured, "As you will it, esteemed sir."

"Kept him then?" Sygna asked, coming to his side as Colvyn proceeded aft. "Thought you might. Always the way with you, my love. Even as a boy, there wasn't a stray dog you wouldn't drag home. Annoyed the old man mightily, as I recall."

"A tendency we share," Felnir returned, pulling her close. "Else, why would you be with me?" He pressed a kiss to her forehead and strode to the mid-deck, voice raised to a commanding pitch: "Get all loose gear stowed and ready your oars! Sygna to the tiller and Behsla to the sails! Quick about it, you mob of bastards! Don't you know we've treasure to find?"

"Treasure? That's what you told them?"

Felnir turned from surveying the twilight speckled horizon to find the scholar standing nearby. She was well wrapped against the cold with the fox fur cloak he had seen Sister Lore gift her on the quay. There had been another woman there to see her off, one that stirred Felnir's memory. She was a little taller than the scholar, and her hair a shade lighter, but there was no mistaking the similarity of features. For an instant the sight of the older woman's tear-streaked face transported Felnir back to Olversahl, that terrible morning after the battle when he and Guthnyr had wandered black-ened, smoke-drifted streets to find their parents. Instead, after a great deal of searching, they found their great-grandfather. The Tielwald sat amid the rubble that had been King Aeric's library, a bloodied bandage covering one eye, his face as stony as the axe resting at his side. Nearby this very same woman, features ravaged by grief, blurted a string of barely coherent curses that Margnus Gruinskard endured without word or movement.

When she had exhausted her diatribe, the woman took hold of a trinket on a cord about her neck, snapping it free and tossing it at the old man's feet. "Never . . ." Felnir heard her grate as she stalked away into the grey haze. "Never again . . ."

"Who was that, great-grandfather?" Felnir had asked, leading his brother closer.

The old man blinked his one eye at them both. In later years he would master the art of concealing emotion in this orb, but then Felnir had seen a mix of grief, weariness and irritation: a man being presented with an inescapable chore. "Just a scribbler who no longer has a job," the Tielwald grunted, getting to his feet. "Your mother and father are fallen in glorious battle. Best if you come along with me."

The librarian's daughter, Felnir thought, studying what he could see of the scholar's face through the enclosing furs. *How much does she know?* His great-grandfather hadn't been there to witness the *Sea Hawk*'s departure that morning, which wasn't unusual since the old bastard could hardly be termed sentimental. Now Felnir wondered if the Tielwald might have been avoiding the woman who once cursed him for his crime.

"Is not knowledge also treasure?" Felnir asked the scholar. "And that is what we are sent to find."

"The Vaults of the Altvar," she replied. "Home to all manner of treasures, so the tale is told. Yet you haven't told your crew our true goal. They seem to think we go in search of the lost hoard of Teygnar Vyrnaptir, the Fireraiser. A notorious, but most probably fictional, pirate from the Age of Discord." Her eyes were steady, but he gained a sense of a timid soul forcing herself to courage. *Fearful of the Redtooth's wrath*, Felnir thought, smothering a sour laugh.

"Nor will they know the truth," he said. "Until the time is right. And I'll thank you, Scholar Elvine, not to enlighten them."

"Do you fear their greed so? The Vaults, if they can be found, are a far greater prize than any pile of pirate's loot, real or not."

"I fear distraction, and the peril of imparting knowledge to those from whom it could be forced later. The lure of treasure is a potent thing. Useful, in fact, for it will compel my crew to greater efforts. But the prospect of treasure forged by the gods will compel others to the direst acts. Should it become known that Sister Lore has uncovered a true path to the Vaults, there are countless villains who will spill an ocean of blood to claim them."

He saw her hesitate then, a question rising to her lips only to be caged. However, he had little difficulty in discerning its object. "You wonder if it would also compel me so," he said, allowing himself a smile at her small shudder of discomfort. "For the cruelty and avarice of the Redtooth is famed, is it not?"

She gave a small cough, quelling another shudder, and said, "Only the cruelty, so far as I know."

Despite her meaning, the scholar's words stirred a kernel of fondness in him. Summoning the fortitude to speak her mind to one of such dread reputation was admirable. But he would have to warn her to caution her tongue when they encountered less forgiving souls, an outcome that seemed inevitable given the nature of their mission.

"That was your mother back on the dockside, was it not?" he said. "I recall her from Olversahl. A librarian named . . ."

"Berrine Jurest," she said, voice flat and eyes narrowing.

"Yes, that was it. I note she wears a Vellihr's brooch these days."

"Sister Lore is gifted in seeking out those with skills that can best serve the realm."

"Like yourself."

The eyes narrowed further. "Yes. Like myself."

"And yet your mother, a celebrated scholar in her own right, remains in Skar Magnol whilst you sail away on this curious mission."

"It is not for me to question Sister Lore's commands." She left the second part unsaid, but he read it easily in her scowl: *Nor for you.*

Feeling he had poked this sore spot enough, Felnir changed tack, adopting a more complimentary tone. "Your knowledge is certainly impressive. Don't think I've ever encountered an Ascarlian who can spout Covenant bilge so well, in old Alberic no less. I'd heard there's some addled folk in the Fjord Geld who still cling to it. You hail from there, do you not?"

"I do." She drew her cloak more firmly about her shoulders and turned to go. "I've troubled you enough. My thanks for your candour."

"That foreigner isn't causing you too much bother, I hope?" Felnir asked, compelling her to pause. "I've asked him to have a care for your person, and the loon. But I can set him to other tasks if you find his manners irksome."

"No, his manners are . . . acceptable. It's not often I meet someone who can speak and write more languages than I." A faint smile curved her lips. "He's been helping me improve my Ishtan. It transpires there were many nuances to the spoken form I had missed."

"That there are," Felnir agreed, slipping into his own version of Ishtan. Having learned it from an assortment of outlaws and outcasts, he knew it to be far more harshly spoken than Colvyn's finely crafted phrases. "Very easy to cause insult, even when it's not intended. As for Colvyn, which I doubt is his true name, I've been in the company of enough villains to know one when I see one. Best exercise caution over everything he tells you."

Her scowl deepened, but she confined herself to a nod before turning to go then huffing in frustration when he spoke on, in Ascarlian this time to ensure no misunderstanding. "Tell me, Scholar Elvine, do you really think we'll find them? The Vaults, I mean to say.

Or are we chasing shadows at the whim of a conniving old man and a deluded queen?"

Dangerous words, intended to provoke offence or outrage in a loyal soul. The scholar, however, betrayed no sign of either when she responded. "I've no idea. I am compelled to obey the queen wherever it may lead me."

Or your mother suffers for it, Felnir concluded. *Such are the perils of losing a daughter to the cult of the Covenant.* Thinking it prudent not to say any of this, Felnir offered her a smile of grim understanding and turned back to the horizon. "Sleep well, Scholar."

He sensed her dithering but didn't turn, letting the moment stretch until she said, "I would prefer simply 'Elvine', if you don't mind. I have little liking for titles."

"As it please you."

Another pause and Felnir knew she was engaged in some rapid calculation regarding his trustworthiness. "As for the Vaults," she said, moving closer, voice lowered. "I've always thought them just a legend. At best an allegory, at worst a fable that grew with the passage of time. But now . . ."

Turning, Felnir saw her directing a glance at the nook she shared with the madman. "What is etched onto that poor soul's skin is unlike anything I've seen before. This may sound strange, but I feel almost as if it speaks to me, and its voice is very old. What it all means, I don't yet know. But I've a sense that if the Vaults can be found, this is the only map anyone is ever likely to find."

The Vaults made real, he thought. Upon being commanded to this mission, he had seen only the chance to finally expunge his disgrace. The promise of a Vellihr's brooch was a valued augment to an already rich prize. But if the Vaults could actually be found, such a discovery would render all other reward small indeed.

"Now it is I who must thank you for candour," he said. "And know this, Elvine: as long as you sail on my ship, speak only truth, raise no hand against me or mine, in word or deed, you are of my *menda* and I will allow no harm to you." He took the striker from his belt, a finely crafted bronze of Aerldun's eye. Given his course in life, he had long thought it fitting to favour the goddess of dark places and hidden paths.

"Will you swear so, in her sight?" he asked, offering the striker to Elvine. Seeing how she stared at the object, face rigid, he added, "For my benefit, not yours. For it's Aerldun who'll judge the truth of your words, whether you believe her real or not."

She stared at the striker a moment longer, then took it, holding it over the rail and taking hold of the iron rod. "I swear to do no harm to this ship or its crew," she said. "And to speak only truth to its captain." With that, she struck a brief flurry of sparks into the sea.

Shrewdly phrased, Felnir thought as she handed the bronze eye back to him. She had sworn to voice no lie to him, but not the rest of the crew. "We'll drop anchor off Ayl-Ah-Skorna in seven days," he told her. "Will your studies of our strange friend be done by then?"

"The transcription, yes. The translation, no. That would require the work of months. But I feel I shall have enough to at least enable a careful study of the Exiled King's statue."

"Then I regret that I must enjoin you to work faster. My great-grand-father is jealous of his secrets, but one so valuable as this can only be guarded for so long."

"You fear betrayal?"

Felnir grunted, shifting his eyes to the waves beyond the *Sea Hawk*'s stern. "Worse than that, I fear competition."

The statue raised in honour of King Velgard ehs Trehka must have been an impressive sight in its day. Situated atop the tallest cliff over-looking the southward approaches to Ayl-Ah-Skorna, and standing near thirty feet high according to Elvine, it would have commanded the notice of any ship making its way to the natural harbour a mile to the east. Now all that remained was a cracked and weathered base. A substantial chunk of red and black marble the size of a house, it was overgrown with moss and weeds, requiring a good deal of hacking and scraping to reveal the runes beneath.

As Elvine went about her work, she complained of the shadows cast by the encroaching trees. Contemporary accounts of the statue's creation made no mention of a forest covering the slopes of the island's hills, but one had evidently grown during the intervening centuries. Her task was also complicated by the growing lateness of the hour. The *Sea Hawk* had encountered a patch of poor weather shortly after dawn, entailing a delay before reaching the island. Felnir eschewed mooring up in the harbour, knowing it would draw too many inquisitive eyes. Instead, he had Behsla drop anchor off a narrow inlet beyond the western headland, waiting for the evening tide before leading two boats to shore.

Felnir set out a loose cordon amongst the trees, instructing the warriors to remain in sight of each other. With night coming on, and Elvine's labours incomplete, he was forced to order torches lit so she could continue. For hours, he quelled his tongue and watched the young scholar circle the fallen monument with parchment in hand. Elvine showed no awareness of the passage of time, her attention fully occupied by the runes and various less easily recognised designs etched into the stone. Sometimes she muttered to herself as she compared her drawings to the markings, tutting in restrained consternation.

"Worthwhile scholarship cannot be hurried, esteemed sir."

Felnir glanced at Colvyn, perched nearby on a fallen tree trunk with Wohtin at his side. Felnir had wanted to leave him on the ship, but Elvine insisted he be brought along. Why remained a mystery, for the fellow reacted to the statue's base with blank-eyed indifference, maintaining a huddled silence throughout her inspection. Fortunately, he had at least left off his Covenant ramblings.

"A quote from some Ishtan luminary, I suppose?" Felnir asked Colvyn. "Yamoril, Sage of Wine and Song, perhaps?"

"No." Colvyn's face clouded and he returned to sliding a whetstone along the stout blade of the falchion Druba had given him. "Just something someone told me once."

Felnir noted the guarded glances Colvyn directed at Elvine as she worked, bespeaking an undimmed interest, but one he was wise enough to make some effort to conceal. Still, Felnir made a point of stepping into his eye line. "No gripes about your weapon?" Felnir asked in Alberic, jutting his chin at the falchion. "Carrying a peasant's arm isn't too humbling for you, I trust?"

"Humility is the finest virtue," Colvyn replied in Ishtan. "And yet the hardest to learn." He gave Felnir a bland smile. "That one is from Yamoril, by the way."

"I once knew a man who was also fond of the Sage," Felnir said. "A gaoler, as it happens. He would quote him at length during the distribution of the water ration, roaming about on the walkway above the pit with his cock out, pausing occasionally to piss in the water casks. A highly educated fellow and distant cousin of the Saluhtan himself, as he never tired of telling us. I deeply regret not having the opportunity to make him recite some more poetry before I killed him. It would have been amusing to watch him try with that cock stuffed in his mouth."

He saw a small tic in Colvyn's otherwise placid features. A betrayal of inward disgust, perhaps? Or a realisation regarding the character of the man he had chosen as captain? Wisely, the lad said nothing and resumed his task, though this time he made a point not to look too much in Elvine's direction.

By the time she spoke a word more audible than a mutter, the darkened sky was lit by a fully risen moon. "Trieya's Quill," she said, voice coloured by a rueful laugh. Looking up from the fire he shared with Sygna, Felnir saw the scholar on her hands and knees. Rising, he moved closer to find she had scraped some earth from the lower part of the base to reveal a particularly small collection of runes.

"Might you have found something?" Felnir asked, attempting without success to keep the impatience from his tone. Elvine didn't seem to notice, letting out another laugh as she used a twig to scrape away yet more earth.

"Of all the inscriptions on this stone," she said as she worked, "this is the only one surrounded by a constellation of stars. Trieya's Quill, in point of fact."

"This is significant . . . ?" Felnir's question was cut short by a soft but commanding grunt from his brother.

"Fel!"

Turning, Felnir found Guthnyr on his feet, scabbarded sword hefted, brow furrowed as he cocked an ear to the forest. Going to his side, Felnir motioned all others to silence. A highly sensitive ear was one of his sibling's undoubted gifts. He watched Guthnyr close his eyes, better to discern whatever had caught his interest. Felnir could hear nothing but kept questions from his tongue.

"There," Guthnyr said, opening his eyes and drawing his sword. "Quite a lot coming, brother. Best shorten the line."

"A lot of what?" Felnir asked, but then he heard it too, distant but coming closer, the signature hungry baying of hounds.

"Who hunts at night?" Sygna wondered, joining them with bow in hand.

"No one," Felnir said. Cupping his hands around his mouth, he called out to the warriors in the forest. "Rally to me! Draw your steel and guard the scholar!"

"What's happening?" Elvine said. A shrill note of barely contained panic put a catch in her throat. She stared wide-eyed at the warriors running from the forest to form a tight circle around her.

"The competition we spoke of, I assume," Felnir grunted, settling his shield onto his left arm. After tightening the straps, he drew his sword and began to snap a command at Colvyn to take charge of the scholar. But the youth had already grasped her arm, guiding her and the madman to the lee of the statue's base. The three of them crouched together in the shadow, Colvyn's falchion blade catching a sliver of moonlight through the trees. Sygna, who always eschewed the encumbrance of a shield, hopped onto the great granite stump and set an arrow to her bowstring.

Felnir settled a steady gaze on the forest. He couldn't yet see the hounds in the gloom, but the growing chorus of yapping aggression made it plain they were approaching fast. "It'll be dogs first to sunder our line, then blades after," he told his *menda*. "Hold fast. No one breaks, even if one of these fuckers bites your leg off."

In response, each warrior began thumping sword pommels or axe staves to their shields, raising a loud continuous clatter. Save for Colvyn, there wasn't a warrior here Felnir hadn't fought alongside before.

He harboured no doubt as to their steadfast willingness to die rather than break a shield wall.

Sygna's bow thrummed before Felnir even caught sight of a hound, the arrow whipping into the trees as their hungry tumult grew to deafening proportions. He glimpsed a tumbling form in the shadows before the entire pack burst from the forest. Felnir had time to recognise the breed, Fjord Land bear dogs, bred for both size and viciousness. Each one was five feet long from nose to tail, broad-snouted with a mane of shaggy fur and small, pointed ears. They came on without pause, yapping maws trailing drool and long legs covering the distance in an instant. Sygna brought down one more before they closed, the beast cartwheeling into a whining halt just short of the shield wall. The howling mass of dog flesh impacted the line a heartbeat later.

Felnir braced his feet upon the earth to fend off the hound that thrashed against his shield. Its teeth scraped the edge of the oakwood barrier, glaring eyes showing above the rim, jaws snapping and long-nailed paws swiping. Felnir crouched whilst simultaneously raising his shield, forcing the beast's forelegs up and allowing him to slash at its belly. It yowled as the blade bit, a flood of entrails spilling forth. Felnir put his shoulder to his shield and pushed the hound off, its snarls fading into pitiable whimpers as it slumped to the ground.

An upsurge of growls to his left drew his gaze to the sight of a yet more massive dog forcing Druba back. Seemingly heedless of the wounds the Sylmarian's axe left in its face and neck, the hound came close to wedging itself between his shield and Felnir's. Another thrum sounded from behind, one of Sygna's arrows skewering the beast through the mouth.

"Fought a hyena once," Druba grunted, heaving the slain beast aside. "It was easier than this."

Calm descended with jarring instancy, the guttural yelp of the last hound cut short by the sword blade cleaving its skull.

"It's not over!" Felnir shouted as the first murmurs of celebration broke the subsequent silence. "Hold your place!"

He could see them in the trees, moonlight glinting on weapons and helms as they came on at a steady walk. Felnir would have preferred that they charge, but this unhurried approach told of warriors who knew their business. *The dogs didn't work so they're saving their strength for the fight,* he mused, eyes flitting from one foe to another. As far as he could tell in the gloom, their gear was non-uniform but well kept, with no signs of raggedness. They also held their arms with the surety of veterans, the gaps between them closing as they emerged from the trees.

Mercenaries, Felnir decided, hissing through clenched teeth when he saw that this band outnumbered his own by a half-dozen or more. Watching them form up, their line extending so that they would assault most of the circular cordon at once, he was surprised at the absence of archers. It was always prudent to try to weaken an enemy's strength before a charge, yet no shafts came whistling out of the trees. Sygna, untroubled by competing bows, tried her luck before these hired blades resumed their plodding advance, though her shafts rebounded from raised shields to no effect. Hearing her call his name, he glanced back to see her pointing urgently with her bow at the warrior she had targeted. He was a little taller than his comrades, his prominence emphasised by a horsehair plume atop his helm.

Their captain, Felnir decided. Sygna, ever keen of eye, had marked out the leader of this band of cautious veterans, men and women who fought for pay. With numbers on their side, the outcome was grimly inevitable. They would wear away at the shield wall, exhausting their overmatched enemy to the point that they were unable to contest the final rush. It was a tactic that demanded stamina, skill and discipline. But most of all, it required the one with the purse still being alive to pay you when it was over.

"Guthnyr!" he called to his brother, stepping forward. "To me! The rest of you form wedge!"

He didn't need to check to know his *menda's* response would be immediate, the shield wall shifting into an arrowhead in a matter of seconds. Waiting until Guthnyr hurried to his side, he pointed his sword at the large man in the plumed helm. "That bastard there," he said before raising his shield, levelling his blade and charging forward, eyes dark with the familiar red haze of battle lust.

CHAPTER TWENTY

Ruhlin

Ruhlin noticed Tuhlan's change in demeanour the moment he returned from practice in the circle. The Caerith kept his gaze mostly averted as the guards returned him to his cage. Before he sat on his bunk, he cast a short, guarded glance in Ruhlin's direction. The expression mixed fear with what Ruhlin could only term as awe. Tuhlan turned away quickly, keeping his back to Ruhlin and refusing to respond despite repeated entreaties.

"Will you not talk to me, my friend?" Ruhlin implored, reaching through the bars to make the open-handed gesture.

The Caerith hunched lower, the honed muscles of his back tensing. After a short pause, he consented to afford Ruhlin another wary glance, eyes flicking over his body with the same uncomfortable awe. "*Cohla slein ihs Eithlisch ilsen,*" he said before turning away. "*Aleha, uhli irihm.*"

Ruhlin's further attempts to elicit conversation achieved nothing. Turning away in exasperation, he drew up short at the sight of the naked woman in the cage opposite. The guards had just departed after locking the gate to her prison and she stood with her arms raised to rest on the bars, head cocked at a curious angle as she studied him. This, it seemed, was his unresponsive neighbour revealed in fulsome manner.

Ruhlin tried, at first without much success, to prevent his eyes roving her unclad form, though she displayed no sign of offence.

Like Tuhlan, she was well muscled and tall. Her light brown hair was cropped short and her right arm was decorated in a dense mass of tattoos. The absence of facial markings and the variation in colour and style made it clear she was not Ascarlian, so it came as a surprise when she opened her mouth to address him in his own language.

"Seems you've given him something to think about," she said. The words were heavily accented, but easily understood. "*Irihm* means 'think', if I recall correctly. Though what he said first is a good deal more interesting."

"You speak Caerith?" Ruhlin asked her.

The angle of her head increased, eyes narrowing. Ruhlin gained the impression of a cautious soul gauging the wisdom of imparting trust in a stranger. "A little," she said. "One of my shipmates was Caerith. Wasn't one for talking, but he did love dice, as do I." Her lips formed a faint grin. "Cheating sod still owes me thirty sheks. Pity he chucked himself over the side when these bastards caught us. Curious folk, the Caerith. Never really know what they're going to do one minute to the next."

"Ship?" Ruhlin asked. "You were a sailor?"

"I've been many things, dear boy." Her face hardened as she took hold of the bars of her cage. He tried not to stare at the sway of her breasts as she attempted to shake the metal barrier. "What matters most, just now, is that I'm a prisoner, and a slave. Neither of which are one of my chosen professions."

Her accent thickened as she spoke. This, and her earlier mention of sheks enabling him to identify her origins. "You are from Albermaine," he said.

"I am. The duchy of Dulsian to be exact, whence many a sailor hails. And you are Ascarlian." Her brow furrowed in appraisal. "From the Outer Isles, I'd guess."

"Ayl-Ah-Lyhsswahl," he said, which provoked a laugh.

"A lad from the arse end of nowhere," she mused, shaking her head as she looked him over. "But with a curious ability that seems to have upset our friend."

Looking again at Tuhlan, Ruhlin found the Caerith's back still turned, though the slight shift of his neck indicated he was at least listening to their conversation.

Returning his attention to the woman, Ruhlin asked, "You said his first words were more interesting. You know what they mean?"

"Just one: *Eithlisch*."

"What is that?"

"Not a 'that', dear boy. A who. A Caerith holy man of immense power, so the tale is told." She frowned at him in surprise. "You've never heard it before?" She sighed when he shook his head. "What about the Battle of Castle Ambris, where the Blackheart fell?"

"The Blackheart," Ruhlin repeated. Her story he knew, at least in part. The brief reign of the Tyrant Queen of Albermaine had come to an end in a mighty battle beneath the walls of Castle Ambris, the victory won by an alliance of rebels . . . and Caerith.

"Some say it was the *Eithlisch* that killed her," the woman went on. "Though I've heard far more fanciful stories regarding her end. He was certainly there, though. A man grown to monstrous size and strength by arcane means. He rampaged through the Blackheart's army, leaving bloody ruin in his wake, and neither arrow, steel, nor fire could harm him. I think our friend is confused by the show you put on yesterday. There's only supposed to be one *Eithlisch*, y'see."

Monstrous . . . The word echoed in Ruhlin's mind. *Neither arrow, steel, nor fire* . . .

He shook the intruding thoughts away, keen to explore the opportunities this woman represented. "Ruhlin," he said. "My name is Ruhlin."

Pursing her lips, she inclined her head in greeting. "Julette Ahlpert. Pleased to meet you."

Moving closer to the bars, he pressed his face into a gap, speaking just loud enough for her to hear. "Hear me well, Julette Ahlpert. I am determined to escape this place, wherever it might be, regardless of any risk. Do you wish to do the same?"

Her lips quirked in a smile. "Do dolphins shit in the sea? Of course I do."

"Well and good then." He turned, nodding at Tuhlan's cage. "To do that, we'll need him, and any other poor soul imprisoned here willing to risk their lives for a chance at freedom."

The smile slowly faded from Julette's lips. "You may have noticed, but they don't care if we talk to each other. They must know we'll plot to escape, but do nothing to prevent it. Doesn't that tell you something?"

"Yes. It tells me their arrogance makes them foolish. For now, I need you to teach me every word of Caerith that you know."

He spent the next few nights conversing with Julette, attempting to acquire as much Caerith speech as he could. She, Tuhlan, and the other captives were released from their cages for daily torment in the circle whilst he was left alone and ignored, save for the unspeaking guard who shoved bowls of porridge and water through the bars once a day. Ruhlin hoped Aleida might reappear during the practice sessions when the guards' attention was elsewhere. But she remained stubbornly absent, and he worried if his allusion to her Morvek heritage had offended her so much as to end her interest.

"She'll be back," Julette assured him. "I know a smitten wench when I see one."

"Smitten?" Ruhlin asked.

The sailor laughed. "With you, you idiot. Just make sure you speak nice when she does turn up again. She's likely to prove useful if we're ever to get out of here."

It was during their fourth night of lessons, when Julette corrected Ruhlin's pronunciation of the Caerith word for "guard", that Tuhlan chose to make an important interruption.

"*Taolisch*," he said, causing them both to fall silent and stare at him through the overlapping bars. The hour had grown late and the sunlit circle lay dark. Tuhlan's impressive form was difficult to make out, but Ruhlin could tell his back was no longer turned. "*Taolisch*," he repeated with careful emphasis. Ruhlin's pleasure at finding Tuhlan had overcome his reluctance to communicate swelled when the Caerith spoke on, this time in laboured Alberic.

"Well, that's a turn of the wind," Julette grunted when Tuhlan fell silent. "He says his people have no word for 'guard'. *Taolisch* means 'warrior.'" She grinned, affording Ruhlin a wink. "I believe our scheme just got a good deal less complicated, dear boy."

Ruhlin's command of Alberic was limited, but it dwarfed his nascent grasp of Caerith. He asked Julette to speak to him in her own tongue from now on, switching to Ascarlian only to clarify phrases beyond his ken. Over the course of the next two nights, he pieced together the tale of how she had come to find herself caged. Three months ago she had been second mate aboard a freighter plying the copper route between the southern seas and the Outer Isles. When the ever capricious winds of the Styrnspeld blew the ship far off course to the west, the vessel had been set upon by a trio of red-sailed warships. All her crew mates had been slain by warriors with tattooed faces, but she had been spared.

"I think because I fought so well," she said, slipping back into Ascarlian. "Cut down four of the bastards before they roped me up. Long days and nights in a stinking hold eating food spiced with drugs, then one day I woke up here."

She ran a hand over her brow and through her cropped hair, features taking on a reflective sorrow. Ruhlin found it hard to guess her age. Her body possessed a youthful strength and athleticism, but, watching grief overtake her, he saw lines around her eyes and mouth that bespoke a woman closer to forty years than thirty.

"Getting tired, dear boy," she said, rising to move to her bunk. "We'll do more of this tomorrow, should that big bastard with the whip spare us. I'd lay odds he, or one of his dogs, has heard every word we've spoken these last few nights."

The clatter of Radylf's whip handle on the bars roused him from a sleep blessedly free of drug-born nightmares. "On your feet, laddie," he instructed. He betrayed no pain at all as his bandaged hand worked the key in the lock. His sliced ear had been stitched back together, leaving it red and swollen, but the giant exhibited only the usual brisk cheeriness as he swung the cage door open. Ruhlin was surprised to find the whip-man accompanied by Eldryk and one other figure. Apparently, they felt no need of guards this morning. The Aerling's bearing was one of hard-faced purpose, which should have been more concerning than the person standing at his side, yet Ruhlin found she commanded most of his notice.

She stood barely an inch over five feet in height, clad in a plain brown dress with her hair, black streaked with grey, arranged into tightly woven braids. Her skin was the same hue as Radylf's, perhaps even a shade lighter. But it was her eyes that gripped Ruhlin's attention. She stared at him with unblinking concentration, dark pupils catching only the barest gleam from the torches, as if they had the power to swallow light.

Another Morvek who knows their place? Ruhlin wondered. If so, he couldn't fathom what use so diminutive a person could be here.

"This is Achela," Eldryk said, gesturing to the woman. "I'm afraid you'll be seeing rather a lot of her, thanks to your . . ." The Aerling paused for consideration of the appropriate word. "Intransigence."

He stepped closer, forcing Ruhlin to break his preoccupation with the woman. Other than their first meeting, Ruhlin couldn't recall Eldryk coming so close before, not without the protection of chains and bars. "Understand this, boy, the next time I set you to a killing you will not hesitate. Death is the price your blood demands. In refusing it, you insult both myself and the Altvar. I will not have that."

His breath, hot and unpleasant, wafted across Ruhlin's skin, stinging his nostrils and provoking a familiar lurch in his core. *Kill him now?* he wondered as his hands began to itch. His eyes flicked to the shadows, searching for guards poised with blowpipes but seeing none. Still, he assumed they must be there, else Eldryk wouldn't risk his anger so. But even if that were true, the Aerling was easily within his grasp. Ruhlin knew by now just how rapid the change could be; it was fully within his abilities to snap Eldryk's neck before the first dart could reach him.

Don't! he warned himself, dragging in a deep draught of air and ignoring the stain of the Aerling's breath. *Killing this one is too great a crime. If you die now, there will be no escape for anyone.*

Curiously, his restraint seemed to anger Eldryk. Curling his lip in annoyance, the Aerling stepped back, delivering a curt nod to Radylf. The whip strike came without pause or warning, Ruhlin shouting with the searing pain, muscles spasming from the lash's touch. Anger inevitably followed pain, and the change arrived soon after.

The red curtain descended and his hands began to swell, far quicker than before. He dimly perceived Eldryk's anger shift into near panicked alarm. The Aerling back-pedalled to avoid Ruhlin's swift monster's paw, but much too slow. Yet, as his fingers opened to fix a crushing grip upon Eldryk's neck, the Morvek woman stepped into view and everything changed.

Ruhlin knew instantly that the sensation flooding through him came from the ring encircling his collarbone. It was as if it unleashed some form of invisible liquid. Like all Islanders, he knew well the deep cold of winter, but this was far beyond any chill he had ever experienced. It flooded him from shoulders to feet, invading every muscle and sinew, forcing its way into his core and crushing the fire it found. Breath stalled in his throat, his chest now as unmoving as a stone. When he fell, he barely felt the bruising contact with the flagstones. Only his head remained free of the cold, allowing him a brief agonised choke that would have blossomed into a fulsome scream had there been air in his lungs to form it.

It ended as quickly as it began. Ruhlin's unfrozen limbs spasmed whilst the return of life to his innards made him convulse with nausea. He retched and shuddered for a time, fouling himself and the surrounding flagstones until his pains finally abated and he heard Eldryk's grimly satisfied voice.

"So, now you understand the *stagna*. I trust it will also lead to an understanding of your importance."

Through eyes swimming with tears, Ruhlin saw the Aerling crouched to peer at his face and body with sharp, cautious scrutiny. Letting out a soft grunt of approval, he gestured again at the Morvek woman. "As I'm sure you've realised, Achela has command of the *stagna*. She will be your shadow from here on. She will observe every word and deed and should you summon your blood again without my approval . . . Well, you have already experienced the consequences. Therefore, I suggest you learn to master your anger, boy. The *stagna* can kill as well as punish."

Straightening, Eldryk sniffed and turned to Radylf. "We may as well have him train with the others. Won't do to let him grow fat in his cage. Audiences tend to jeer at fighters who don't look the part."

"He'll be as lean as any thoroughbred soon enough, Aerling," the whip-man assured Eldryk with a respectful nod. After a pause, he inclined his head at Julette's cage. "He talks to this one a lot, mostly in that Teilvik gibberish, but I'd guess they're plotting something."

"Aren't they always?" Eldryk laughed and looked down at Ruhlin, still shuddering on the floor. "When you catch your first glimpse beyond these walls, boy, you'll understand why escape is just a childish dream." Turning to walk away, he waved a hand at Radylf. "Let them talk. They can fuck too, if they want. Might even get us a Vyrn Skyra whelp in time, eh?"

It was another four days before Aleida fulfilled Julette's prediction, and when she reappeared, it was to ask a question: "Aren't you going to?"

Interrupted in the act of poking at the blisters that had appeared around the *stagna*, Ruhlin looked up to find her standing on the far side of the cage. He was surprised to see how she made no effort to conceal herself from Achela, who sat on a stool at the edge of the torch's glow. True to Eldryk's word, the Morvek woman had remained in sight of Ruhlin since that first meeting. She said and did nothing apart from watch him. He swung wooden swords at Tuhlan, Julette, and the other captives, while she watched. He ate and she watched. He pissed and shat in the hole, and she watched. She watched when he strove to improve his Alberic in nightly conversations with Julette. He assumed Achela must see to her meals and ablutions when he slept, but wasn't even sure of this having woken in the night a few times to discover her still perched on her stool, watching. She continued to do so now, a small sideways flicker of her eyes the only indication that she had noticed Aleida's presence.

"Going to what?" he asked.

"Her." Aleida shot a scowling glance towards Julette's cage. "He said you could fuck her. Why haven't you?"

Julette had remained prone on her bunk until now, but Ruhlin saw her tense at this, face tightening in anger. Catching her eye as she began to rise, he gave an incremental shake of his head. Frowning, she settled back and turned onto her side.

"We are not animals," he told Aleida. "Even if we are in cages."

He watched her fidget at the shadow's edge, noting that she held something behind her back. *A weapon? Has she come to kill me?* Despite what Julette had said about the girl's interest in him, he thought it doubtful that any jealousy she felt could have blossomed to such a violent pitch.

"Aren't you angry with me?" she asked, coming closer.

"For what?"

"I didn't warn you about the *stagna*." Her feline features formed a grimace as she spared Achela a short look. "About *her*."

"I'm not sure I would have believed you if you had."

Her scowl softened into a frown, Ruhlin seeing a flicker of confusion in her face before she stepped closer still. Darting a glance to either side, she quickly thrust something through the bars, holding it out with evident impatience until he consented to take it. "For the blisters," she said. "Now our debt is settled."

Her gift consisted of a small clay pot about the size of an apple. Removing the lid, he found it filled with a grey substance resembling congealed cream. Dabbing a finger to it, he felt a slight tingle as he rubbed the stuff against his thumb. *Some kind of salve*, he decided. Looking up, he saw Aleida had retreated a step, though she still remained within arm's reach of the bars. Her face was downcast and guarded, as if expecting a taunt, or even a blow. It made him wonder about the reactions she had received when attempting previous acts of kindness in this place.

"My thanks," he said. "And worry not over any debt."

Taking a larger pinch of the pot's contents, he applied it to a portion of his afflicted skin. The effect was instantaneous, the itchy discomfort

"Slaves? Some are. Others are bound by less obvious chains." Aleida's expression grew sombre. Casting another cautious glance at the shadows, she leaned towards the bars, gesturing for him to come closer, and dropped her voice to a whisper. "My father has friends in the upper reaches of the Tuhlvyr."

"Tuhlvyr?"

"Those born to the highest status and the greatest wealth. My father is useful to them, though not as useful as Angomar was. With her death, and you within his grasp, he sees a chance to ascend, to be counted amongst their ranks so that he might too, one day, grovel in the Vortigurn's shadow. They come here from time to time to discuss business and arrange the spectacles for the next Meidvang. I hear what they say . . ." She trailed off and Ruhlin was surprised by the flicker of compassion in her eyes, a reluctance to impart unwelcome knowledge.

"You," she went on before jerking her head at Tuhlan, then Julette. "Them. Just the first of many. All your lands are slated to fall, and when they do, those found weak of blood shall count themselves fortunate to be granted the mercy of slavery."

The echo of footfalls somewhere in the gloom caused her to retreat from the bars. "I've lingered too long," she said, backing towards the shadow's edge and forestalling the welter of questions he wanted to ask. He saw her hesitate before turning and fleeing into the dark, swift and silent as any cat.

CHAPTER TWENTY-ONE

Thera

She had Annuk confined to a shearing shed a decent walk from the settlement. Her questioning was likely to result in sounds that even the hardened souls of three *menda* would find disturbing. Of all the vexatious duties to fall upon the shoulders of a Vellihr of Justice, this was the one she detested most. *The burden of your task is equal to its importance,* Sister Iron had said back when she wore the Vellihr's brooch and Thera had been her apprentice. She always found some comfort in it whenever this dire obligation presented itself.

She set Eshilde and Ragnalt to guard the prisoner and left him be throughout the following day. Depriving a captive of food and water whilst allowing them to stew on their fate was often an effective tactic in loosening a stubborn tongue. As she and Lynnea followed the trail to the shed, Thera distracted herself from the impending and unavoidable unpleasantness to come by inspecting the only piece of jewellery found on Annuk's person. It wasn't particularly surprising that a denizen of the Kast Geld would possess little in the way of personal trinkets, but there was a familiarity to this one that piqued her interest.

A silver knot, she thought, working the thing between forefinger and thumb. Its design differed from her great-grandfather's gift, featuring two looping strands of engraved metal instead of one. Also, it appeared less finely crafted to her admittedly inexpert eye. *Coincidence,* she decided, putting her other hand to her chest to feel the trinket beneath. Despite spending much of her adult life ignoring or avoiding Margnus Gruinskard, she had, either through sentiment for her fallen mother or lingering childhood habit, followed his instruction. His gift hung on a thin leather strap about her neck, the silver knot always next to her skin. Her conclusion regarding the significance of Annuk's paltry treasure felt hollow, however, for hadn't Sister Iron once said: *There are no coincidences. Just threads not yet revealed as part of the same web.*

Upon opening the door to the shed, one look at Annuk made it clear that a day of fearful isolation had done nothing to loosen his tongue. He had been bound upright to a beam with ropes encircling his legs, torso and neck, a horribly uncomfortable position that robbed a prisoner of sleep and birthed a plethora of aches, soon to blossom into full agony. Thera had seen the strong of body reduced to piteous weeping after just a few hours of such confinement. Not so Annuk. He blinked fearless eyes at her as she entered, his gaze narrowing only slightly at the sight of Lynnea. In addition to the ever faithful Snaryk, she had also taken Mohlnir along. The cat perched on her shoulders, lowering itself to hiss at the bound man whilst the huge dog greeted him with a growl of patent dislike. Thera saw Annuk fail to contain a small shudder, but his face remained free of expression. This would be no easy day.

"Wait outside," Thera told Ragnalt and Eshilde. "And close the door."

As Eshilde departed the shed, Thera caught her poorly concealed resentful glare in Lynnea's direction. *Keen to learn the lessons of torment,* Thera thought, whilst Lynnea guided Snaryk to a corner of the structure, her eyes averted from its bound occupant. *A sentiment not shared by all.*

She resisted the urge to voice a reminder that Lynnea had chosen the Vellihr's path willingly, and that not all its steps were easily taken. But it wouldn't do to display any sign of discord in the captive's presence.

"It was foolish," Thera told him. Planting the stool she had carried from the settlement in the centre of the hay-strewn floor, she sat, offering Annuk a bland smile before speaking on. "Not bothering to learn the Uhlwald's name, I mean. Or did you simply forget it?"

No answer, just a barely perceptible shift of his head towards Lynnea. "Ah," Thera said. "You caught her warning. How very astute of you. However, I'd wager my apprentice is even more perceptive. Lynnea." She put a hard edge of command in her tone as she beckoned the maiden closer. "Look upon this man's face as we continue our chat. Shake your head when he lies. Nod when he doesn't."

Thera unhitched the canvas satchel from her shoulder, opened it out and set it on the floor, revealing the many small implements it held. Most were sharp, some were blunt. "And know this, good man," she went on, settling a steady, purposeful gaze on Annuk, "every shake of the head earns you another hour's torment before I send you to the cold void that awaits those denied the Halls."

Still no reaction, his eyes sliding over the array of implements with no more interest than if he were regarding spilled refuse. His lack of fear stirred an urge to reach for the most wicked tools, forgo the usual preliminaries for an immediate demonstration of the consequences of silence. *Anger is your enemy when questioning a miscreant.* More of Sister Iron's advice, and she would heed it, for she had seen her mentor elicit copious information from even the most recalcitrant souls, often without recourse to the satchel's contents.

"I assume," Thera went on, "the plan was for me to sail my ships to Ayl-Ah-Vahrim, there to confront Veilwald Ossgrym with your vile accusations. Outrage and discord would follow, perhaps even conflict." She watched his face as she spoke, seeing only unyielding refusal to betray any emotion. "It wouldn't have worked. The Ironbones is many things, but a liar isn't one of them. My first glimpse of his face would have revealed the truth and you would be in exactly the same position as you are now. Whoever set you to this sent you to die. If I were you, I would consider any oath to them betrayed."

A slight hardening of Annuk's mouth told of continued defiance, even a measure of contempt. Apparently, his oath was not for breaking.

"As you wish." Leaning towards the satchel, Thera chose a knife with a narrow blade barely a quarter-inch long. Sister Iron always said it was better to start small. "My *Johten Apt* finally remembered the Uhlwald's name, by the way," she said, rising to approach Annuk.

Slicing open the thin woollen shirt he wore, she revealed the bony, emaciated chest beneath. She would have preferred he possess a more substantial frame as it gave her more to work with, but needs must. "It was Dagvyn. I think you would benefit from a permanent reminder of it." She pressed the tip of the knife into the sinews of his upper chest, drawing a trickle of blood. Annuk tensed and clamped his jaw tight, nostrils flared to snort hot breaths. But still he didn't speak.

"Sadly, I'm no scholar," Thera said, shifting the blade to begin the first rune. "So I don't have the neatest hand . . ."

The knife halted as Lynnea's hand grasped her wrist. Thera's outrage faded at the certainty she saw in her apprentice's unblinking blue eyes: *This is pointless. Cut him all you want. He will tell you nothing.*

Looking again at Annuk, she saw a curious mix of pain and anticipation on his reddened features. *What manner of man relishes his own torment?* she wondered, plucking the knife from his flesh. "He has answers," she told Lynnea. "We need them."

She nodded and made a polite gesture for Thera to step back. When she had done so, Lynnea plucked a stub of charcoal from the small purse on her belt and used her feet to clear hay from the floor. Crouching, she scrawled a name upon the flagstones. Her facility for runes was still poor and the characters were clumsily formed, yet Thera found she could read the completed word easily enough: IMROLF.

Thera could think of only one bearer of that name and grasped the significance immediately. Apparently, so did Annuk, for he cast a wide-eyed stare towards the cat and the dog still sitting placidly in the far corner of the shed.

"Imrolf Uhralvyr," Thera said, reaching out to clamp a hand to his jaw and force his gaze to meet hers. "The False-tongue. Do you know the story?" From the rapid blink of Annuk's eye and sudden sheen of sweat beading his skin, she could tell he did. Nevertheless, she felt it necessary to recite the tale. "Imrolf had broken so many oaths in his life the Altvar themselves cursed him. They sent Ihryka, a goddess of the Lower Hall, with dominion over games and tricks, to lure Imrolf into the darkest woods where dwelt the most vicious beasts. And there, bound by Ihryka's treacherous hands to an ancient oak, was the flesh of Imrolf feasted upon by bear, wolf, fox and crow. Long was his suffering, for he was not permitted to die until the last vestige of his agonies had dwindled. Even then, his torment didn't end, for he was condemned to linger at the door to the Halls of Aevnir. For it is the fate of those who fall victim to beasts to beg leave from the gods to open the doors, and many an age must they wait. Some say Imrolf is still waiting, even though his passing was centuries before even the Age of Kings."

She paused, looking down to see Mohlnir sniffing at the captive's bare feet. A few drops of Annuk's blood had dripped onto his toes and the cat angled his head to lick at them. The captive's whimper at the feel of Mohlnir's tongue became a sob when Snaryk stalked to the rear of the beam, his growl loud in the confines of the shed.

"How long do you think you'll have to wait?" Thera asked. "Perhaps Imrolf himself will be kind enough to hazard a guess when you meet him."

Annuk closed his eyes, Thera feeling him shudder with the effort of trying to contain his terror. His struggle proved fruitless when Mohlnir delivered a sharp nip to his ankle and Snaryk began to nuzzle his bound hands, the dog's growl now deepened to resemble rolling thunder. The captive sagged in Thera's grasp, tears leaking from the corners of his eyes as he grated out a single word: "Please . . ."

Releasing him, Thera stepped back and nodded to Lynnea. A single glance from her was enough to draw the animals back, the rumble of Snaryk's anger fading, but not completely.

Thera allowed Annuk a moment of weeping before delivering a hard slap to his face. "Open your eyes," she instructed. "And answer promptly when asked, or I'll leave you here and my apprentice's friends will do their work."

He shuddered and forced his eyes open, swallowing hard.

"The man in the well," Thera demanded. "Who was he?"

Annuk swallowed again before grating out a hoarse reply. "Nihlvar."

"His name was Nihlvar?"

The prisoner shook his head. "His people. That's what they call themselves. Their kingdom."

Thera shot a glance at Lynnea, who replied with a baffled frown. *Never heard of it either.*

"Where is it?" Thera said, turning back to Annuk. "This kingdom of Nihlvar."

"Across the Styrnspeld . . ." He squirmed, worried eyes straying to the beasts now standing to either side Lynnea. "Beyond the Fire Isles."

Thera let out a harsh, pitying laugh. "I told you not to lie."

"I speak true! Ask the witch!" Annuk jerked his head at Lynnea. "Ask her!"

Looking to Lynnea, Thera frowned when she saw her nod. The maiden's face was as serious as Thera had seen it, grave with reluctance and a small measure of anger. *Didn't like being called a witch,* Thera decided, though, given her apprentice's undeniable gifts, she found it hard to argue the term.

"Let's say I believe you," Thera said, resting a hand on the beam above Annuk's head and leaning closer. "How did he end up in that well?"

"I didn't see it. The other Nihlvarians talked of an islander with impossible strength. They seemed to think him possessed of some kind of Altvar blessing, something they called Vyrn Skyra: Fire Blood."

More nonsense, Thera thought, but another glance at Lynnea confirmed the man's truthful tongue. "Where is he? This unfeasibly strong islander."

"Captured, I think. They didn't like me asking about it. Told me to hold to our mission."

"And what is that mission? Why have they come here to do slaughter?"

"Not slaughter. Purification. They have built the true kingdom of the Ascarls, raised in the glorious sight of the Altvar." Annuk's face twisted into disgust. "Not this perverted remnant that mocks the Worldsmith's creation with its every deed. The queens you serve are naught but venal whores—"

His words ended in a guttural choke as Thera clamped a hand to his throat, squeezing hard. Seeing a glimmer of satisfaction in his otherwise terrorised eyes, she stopped. *Weakness,* she admonished herself, removing her hand. "You think if I kill you, your place in the

Halls is secure," she said. "No, wretch, those doors will never open for one such as you . . ."

She trailed off in irritation at the sound of pounding on the shed door, accompanied by Eshilde's shout, "Sails, Thera! Gelmyr sends word: sails sighted to the north!"

The horizon was bare by the time Thera joined Gelmyr atop the bluffs to peer at the sea beyond the northern shore. The always busy swell of the Styrnspeld made spotting passing ships difficult and she resisted the temptation to ask the *Johten Apt* if he was sure of the sighting. If Gelmyr said he saw sails, then sails there were.

"How many?" she asked instead, still squinting into the wind.

"Three," Gelmyr replied. "But close together, which means one ship. Heading north-east, I reckon."

Three masts, Thera mused. *So not Ascarlian.* "Warship?"

He shrugged in apology. "She was too far off to make out much, but I'd swear the canvas was red. Not a common sight, a red sail."

"She'll have many a mile lead on us," Ragnalt warned. "Catching her would be no easy thing. And we'll need to wait for the tide to shift before weighing anchor."

"They may well not have seen us," Thera said. "If they were the ones that did this, as far as they know, this island is occupied by nothing but corpses." Seeing Eshilde come to Ragnalt's side, Thera glanced back at the shearing shed. Since Lynnea and Ragnalt had also followed her here, Annuk had been left unattended. "I thought I told you to guard him."

"He's well bound . . ."

Her instinct for trouble flaring, Thera shouldered Eshilde aside and set off towards the shed at a run. "Ready the *Great Wolf* to depart!" she called to Gelmyr over her shoulder. "And send word to Alvyr and Gynheld to do the same. We sail with the tide."

Annuk's head lolled as low as the rope about his neck allowed, the beam behind stained red and flecked with bone. Grasping his hair, Thera dragged his blood-streaked features level with her own, seeing only emptiness in his rolled-up eyes.

"Must've taken him a few attempts before he cracked his skull," Ragnalt said, peering at the besmirched timber with a mix of awe and disdain. "What drives a man to this?"

"You should have been here!" Thera snapped. As he shrank from her anger, she turned her glare upon Eshilde. "Both of you. Whatever secrets this bastard had are now lost forever."

Ragnalt, always the more dutiful of the two, was the first to show contrition. Straightening, he composed his face into a rigid mask, saying, "I offer no excuse for my failure, Vellihr. Punishment is clearly warranted and accepted."

Eshilde followed suit a moment later, though with a more sour twist to her mouth as she voiced the expected words. Seeing her inability to conceal her truculence, Thera's doubts that Eshilde would ever make a Vellihr solidified into regretful certainty. *I'll tell her when this is over*, she decided, knowing the confrontation would most likely sever any vestige of a bond between them. The decision also made her settle upon a less arduous punishment than she might otherwise have imposed for so serious a lapse.

She had hung Annuk's trinket about her neck alongside her own. Putting a hand to both, she berated herself for not making it the subject of her first question. *No coincidences.*

"Cut him down, then strip and search his body," she said. "Every orifice, and make sure you're thorough. This one was a spy, and spies have a tendency to hide things in places most folk fear to look. When you're done, toss him off a cliff. I'll not have his carcass stain the soil of this island."

Whilst they awaited the tide, Thera called Alvyr, Gynheld, and Gelmyr to counsel at the harbour. Experience had taught her that a hasty pursuit often resulted in lost quarry, and it was always wise to seek the opinion of veterans.

"Iselda's Nail." Gelmyr's blunt finger nudged at a spot on the map so small that Thera might have taken it for a speck of spilled ink. "Just a rock, in truth, but with a deep pool of fresh water in its centre. Given the red sails' heading, it's her most likely destination. That's if we're assuming they've been sailing these waters a while now without use of a friendly port."

"This is a roll of the dice, old friend," Alvyr said. "Set out for Iselda's Nail and we may catch them at anchor. But if not, we lose them, possibly for good."

"I'm with Gelmyr," Gynheld said. "Even the *Swift Spear* couldn't catch a three-master with a day's start on her. The Nail's the only place to look."

Thera considered the map, dismayed by their options. Heading out into the Styrnspeld entailed risks aplenty, but their only other course would be to head for Ayl-Ah-Vahrim and seek counsel with Ossgrym Styrntorc. The Veilwald of the Kast Geld may well have intelligence to share, but there was no guarantee of that, and Gelmyr's sighting had presented her with a chance at securing both justice and much needed information.

"Then we roll the dice," she said. "The Nail it is." Furling the map, she hesitated before adding, "Have any of you heard the term 'Nihlvar' before?"

As expected, all they could offer were blank looks. "Something that lying fucker said, was it?" Gynheld asked.

"Yes." Thera contained a grimace at the need to elaborate, knowing it risked the appearance of foolishness, but she saw no alternative. "He said it's the name of a kingdom, one unknown to us. A true kingdom of the Ascarls that lies on the far side of the Fire Isles. The body we fished from the well was from that realm, so the spy said."

"Mad as well as deceitful," Gynheld snorted. "There's naught beyond the Fire Isles but endless, empty ocean."

"So the tale is told," Alvyr said. "But the tellers of the tale have never seen such an ocean. Nor has anyone for centuries."

"You actually give credence to this?" Gynheld shook her head, her laugh fading as she turned to Thera and noted her lack of amusement. "Ulfmaer's arse, Thera, surely you can't have bought this barrel of bilge."

"He wasn't lying," Thera said. "That much I know. But the mad will believe their own lies."

"Was he from there too?" Alvyr asked. "This great and hidden kingdom."

"He bashed his head in before I could get any more out of him. But I don't think so. His accent and ink were of the Outer Isles, though I doubt he hailed from Ayl-Ah-Lyhsswahl. It's more likely those who wrought murder here left him behind to sow discord when a Vellihr inevitably came to investigate."

"One of our own, then," Gynheld concluded with a sneer. "Turned traitor. I hope they paid him well."

Recalling the contempt on Annuk's face, Thera shook her head. "I doubt he did it for silver. I think he was of the Volkrath."

This brought silence and a mutual exchange of guarded glances. So far, Thera had said little of her suspicions regarding the supposedly extinct ancient cult. However, she had now arrived at the crux of this mission, and continuing to conceal information from her subordinates would be unwise.

"Sister Iron warned me before we set out," she said. "The Volkrath have returned and this—" she gestured to the surrounding devastation "—is partly their doing. What was unknown before now is that they appear to have acquired an ally. It falls to us to find them, and I'll sail all the way to the Fire Isles to do it if I must. If another enemy has come against this realm, we must discover all we can about them. The crew of this red-sailed three-master will receive justice, but their captain will be spared so I can place them, chained and humbled, at the Queens' feet."

Five days of difficult sailing were required before the triangular spike of Iselda's Nail broke the horizon. Gelmyr advised that the only sound anchorage lay on the northern flank of the islet, so Thera ordered a southerly approach. Apparently, the Nail's peak was too perilous a climb for even the most agile soul, meaning there was little likelihood their arrival would be witnessed by a lookout.

Lynnea joined Thera at the prow as they drew closer to the rocky spire, Thera reading the question on her face with customary ease: *Why is it called Iselda's Nail?*

"Iselda was an Uhltvar princess who fell in love with Ulfmaer," Thera explained. "And he with her. Theirs was the first union of god and mortal, destined to produce a son, Torkyl, a god of the Lower Hall and Master of Doors. But, although Iselda's Uhltvar blood gave her long life, in time she withered and died, as all mortals must. In his grief, Ulfmaer raised up a great slab of rock from beneath the sea and fashioned it into Iselda's likeness. Tallest of all statues, it stood for centuries, until, like the woman in whose honour it had been crafted, it fell to the depredations of time. It's said this small spike of rock is the nail of her mighty stone hand, forever reaching for the god she loved and lost."

The angle of Lynnea's brow altered, conveying a sense of puzzlement, and Thera knew she was posing a question she had once asked herself: *Why could a god not make Iselda mortal? Then they would have been together forever.*

"Some things are denied even the gods," Thera told her. "Or so Sister Iron said when she told me this story years ago."

Lynnea's expression darkened as her eyes drifted from the Nail to the dreadaxe, propped against the rail close to Thera's hand. *There will be battle today.*

"If we find that ship, yes."

Her apprentice took a firmer hold of her staff, standing straighter. *I will fight too.*

"No. Not unless there's no choice. You will remain aboard the *Great Wolf* with those two." Thera nodded to Snaryk and Mohlnir, the dog panting in contentment whilst the cat perched itself on his shoulders to lick at his ears. "Guard the ship. That is your charge this day."

A measure of grievance showed in the crease of Lynnea's brow and she stamped her staff to the deck boards. *I am not afraid.*

"Then—" Thera put a hand on her shoulder, drawing her close to whisper in her ear "—you would be far more of a fool than I took you for."

Lynnea let out a soft sigh of frustration, Thera finding the feel of her breath unwelcome in the sudden and distracting thoughts it conjured. The maiden shifted a little so that their faces were barely separated, eyes meeting in such a way as to bring a prickle to Thera's skin.

"Nail's less than three miles off, Thera!" Gelmyr called from the tiller, his voice sufficing to banish all other notions.

Thera squeezed Lynnea's shoulder and stepped away. Taking up the Dreadaxe, she strode the length of the ship, voice raised to a commanding pitch. "To oars! Pull hard and keep your weapons close!" Pausing at the mid-deck, she lifted the axe above her head. "There's fighting to be done and justice to deliver!"

CHAPTER TWENTY-TWO

Elvine

"Is he leaving us?" Crouched behind the stump of the statue's base, Elvine gaped at the sight of Felnir leading his entire *menda* into the forest. Watching their steadfast defence against the monstrous hounds, she had managed to quell her panic, at least to a certain degree. But now, it appeared the Redtooth may have decided she wasn't worth the trouble of further combat.

"No," Colvyn said. Putting a gentle but insistent hand on her shoulder, easing her deeper into shadow, something he had done several times now. "He's saving us."

Permitted only the most meagre view of proceedings, she caught flashes of moonlight on metal as Felnir and his warriors disappeared into the dark wall of trees. The subsequent uproar, however, told of a ferocious contest. The clatter of colliding steel and wood underscored a chorus of enraged yelling, itself interspersed by an increasing number of screams. Elvine felt herself to be back in the shed in Olversahl, clutching the edge of the marble base with frozen hands as new horrors vied with memories of the Supplicant's death and Uhttar's lifeless face. The tumult wore on for what seemed an age, Elvine finding herself unable to move whilst Colvyn remained crouched at her side. He had reversed the grip on his falchion, keeping the blade concealed within his cloak, and peered into the gloom with steady concentration.

Elvine jerked when Sygna's bowstring thrummed once more. She was still perched atop the base, methodically making her way through the arrows in her quiver. Whether she hit anything, Elvine couldn't tell, but she fancied each loosed shaft was accompanied by a loud yell somewhere in the dark. She started again when she felt Colvyn tense and shift at her side.

"There!" he called to Sygna, pointing at two figures detaching themselves from the gloom off to the right. The glow of the campfire flickered over the pair as they charged, Elvine's breath catching in her throat at the sight of the axe borne by one and the spear the other.

Sygna's bow thrummed and the spear bearer tumbled to the ground whilst the axe wielder came on undaunted. Elvine stared at him as he closed upon them, a large man in a leather helm and armour letting out a surprisingly shrill battle cry. Elvine's eyes snapped to Colvyn and widened at the sight of him still half-crouched, falchion not yet bared. *He's terrified too,* Elvine decided, heart thudding and hands twitching on the marble edge. *I should run . . .* But she didn't, or rather couldn't. Despite the fear racing through every part of her being, she remained huddled and frozen as the axe man pelted closer.

She didn't actually see Colvyn move. One second he was barely inches from her, apparently immobile, the next he was standing a yard away. She watched him twirl the falchion, seeing droplets flying from the blade, then saw the axe wielder slump to the ground. He let out a soft whimper as he twitched, Elvine's nostrils filled with the stench of fresh shit. Nausea raging in her gut, she watched him convulse and lie still.

"'Ware your back, boy!" Sygna warned, loosing off two swift arrows as more figures came charging out of the gloom.

Elvine saw Colvyn pause to retrieve the axe from the man he had slain, then he was gone, whirling into the oncoming attackers, blades flickering. More screams and falling bodies, silhouetted warriors reeling back from the foreigner's onslaught. One made it past him, a squat man with a sword and a large round shield who advanced upon Elvine with predatory care. She could see nothing of his face, but heard a pitch of triumphant excitement in his voice as he called over his shoulder. "Here! She's here! I found her—"

Sygna's bow thrummed and the squat man appeared to have grown an arrow from his right eye. He slumped to his knees, swaying as if drunk, a sluggish stream of gibberish coming from his lips.

"Stay put, Scholar," Sygna instructed, casting her bow aside. Drawing two broad-bladed daggers from her belt, she leaped from the base, slashing open the kneeling man's throat before rushing to join the fight raging only yards away.

Run! The thought sang in Elvine's mind with the utmost clarity, an implacable, irrefutable rejection of Sygna's command. Yet still, she couldn't move. *RUN!* she told herself again, staring at her hands clutching at stone with white knuckled insistence. Sheer effort of will dislodged one then the other and she turned, eyes scanning the trees for some likely avenue of escape, instead finding only more peril.

The dog kept close to the ground as it approached, Elvine catching the wet glisten of the wounds it had suffered to its flanks and face. Sadly, the blood leaking from its body didn't appear to weaken it, or dim the hungry growl emerging from its bared teeth. Panic flaring enough to banish the icy grip of her fear, Elvine lunged to the side, hoping to find a way past the beast. She came to a sudden halt when the dog matched her movement, crouching lower in preparation, snapping its jaws as if to savour the moment.

Elvine braced herself, ready to leap aside the instant the beast launched itself at her, then started in fresh alarm when a shadow stepped into view. Until now, Wohtin had remained still in the lee of the statue's base, Elvine realising with welling shame that she hadn't spared him a thought throughout this unfolding nightmare. "Don't," she began, reaching for his arm as he placed himself between her and the dog. It snapped its jaws again, issuing an angry snarl of warning that, to Elvine's astonishment, abruptly became a cowed whine. The madman stared at the hound for the space of a few seconds, silent and still, whereupon the beast whipped about and fled into the trees, its flight marked by a continual yelp of distress.

As she clasped his hand, Wohtin turned to her and for a second she saw the same fully aware, completely sane visage that had appeared on the hidden dock in Skar Magnol. Yet, this time she noticed something more, a sorrowful, almost apologetic cast to his brow. As before, it was gone in an instant and she once again found herself beholding the vacant stare and creased visage of a man with scant understanding of who and where he was.

"Stay low!" Colvyn's hand closed upon her arm, tugging her back to cover. Blood spattered his face, but he moved without sign of injury, the falchion he held dark and wet from blade to hilt. "You too, my friend," he said once Elvine had resumed her shadowed crouch, hurrying to usher Wohtin to her side.

The night seemed shockingly quiet now, the cacophony of violence and injury replaced by muted voices and the keening of the injured. "Spare those that'll live!" Felnir called out as he strode into the fire-light, his brother at his side. "I've questions to ask."

Elvine saw that Guthnyr had claimed a trophy, an iron helm with a long horsehair plume. As he came to a halt, the helm swayed, raising a hiss as it scattered liquid into the fire. She shuddered when the helm spun to reveal a flaccid, gape-mouthed face.

"Reckon we killed most of the bastards before they started running," Guthnyr said, hefting the helm to peer at the head inside. "Should've taken more care over your hirelings, eh?"

The torrent of gore spilling from the base of the helm was enough to cause Elvine to turn away, doubling over to heave her guts out. *And battle shall be our glory*, she thought, trying and failing to fight the sobs rising to her throat. It was a quote from the opening page of the Altvar Rendi, supposedly the words of Ulthnir the Worldsmith himself. As a fresh spasm of revulsion unleashed another gush of vomit onto the grass, she reflected that if she had ever perceived a mite of truth in the tales of the Ascarlian gods, she certainly didn't now.

"I'd wager most of you have heard the name folk call me," Felnir said, pacing behind the line of captives with the helmed head in hand. "So, I trust you understand the importance of honesty."

There were five prisoners in all, two women and three men. All bore some form of injury, from broken bones to deep, unstitched cuts to faces and limbs. They knelt in a row along the clifftop a short walk from the statue's base, all that was left of the band that had attacked them, save the few that had managed to escape. Felnir had the captives placed here long before dawn, Elvine assumed, so they could contemplate the long drop to the crashing waves as the sun rose.

"You don't have to see this," Colvyn said. They stood at the forest's edge, Elvine shivering despite her fox fur cloak. The wind coming off the sea was stiff, but she knew her unabated trembling had little to do with the chill.

"Yes," she said. "I do."

"Speak and you'll be spared," Felnir continued, pausing to dangle the head in front of the captive at the end of the line. "You can start by telling me this fucker's name." The prisoner was sturdy of frame, with a brutish aspect worsened by the diagonal slash across his nose and cheeks. He afforded the dead face a grim glance before looking away, muttering something.

"Speak up!" Felnir snapped, resting his boot against the man's back to lean him towards the cliff edge.

"Tahlvik!" the captive snapped. "His name was Tahlvik Fohlmend, the Longarm."

"Never heard of him." Felnir raised an eyebrow at Kodryn, the veteran warrior responding with a shrug.

"I know the name," Guthnyr said. "An exiled raider. He made a reputation for himself when you were in Ishtakar. Sister Iron pronounced death on him for one slaughter too many. Last I heard, he took himself off to the southern seas."

"Is that where he hired you?" Felnir asked the prisoner. "The southern seas?"

The scarred man nodded. "Only hired Ascarls, y'see. Couldn't abide foreigners, could Tahlvik, which was strange on account of him living amongst them for so long."

"Who hired him for this job of work?"

"No idea. He wasn't one for sharing talk of clients, or much of anything else. And, so long as we got our due, it wasn't for us to ask."

"What were your orders last night?"

Elvine's shudders increased as the prisoner craned his neck to turn his damaged face towards her. "Take the scholar alive," he said.

When he said no more, Felnir delivered a solid kick to his back. "And?"

The captive let out a loud groan, baring his teeth as he grunted a reply. "And kill all others."

Felnir questioned them further, subjecting each to a round of intimidation that had them all gabbling out confirmation of the scarred man's words, but little in the way of additional information. When finally satisfied, he tossed the severed head of Tahlvik Fohlmend off the cliff and into the sea, provoking a peevish gripe from Guthnyr.

"I wanted the helm."

"Your hoard takes up enough room as it is." Felnir jerked his thumb at the captives. "Take the little finger from each, and their boots, then cut them loose. Elvine." He inclined his head at her and gestured to the forest. "I think it's time we discussed your discovery."

"Was that necessary?" she asked as they made their way back to the marble stump. A series of short but agonised screams followed them, making her hunch each time they echoed through the trees.

"Those that live by violence tend to have dim wits and short memories," Felnir said. "In future, every time one of them reaches for a drinking horn, they'll remember the folly of crossing blades with me and mine."

Not for the first time, she noted how he avoided using his earned name. When those mercenaries looked at their maimed hands, it would surely be the name Redtooth that came to mind. Although, she wasn't convinced all would cower from the memory, recalling another line from the *Aphorismus: Punish a man with a fine and he'll hate you. Punish him with lash or blade and he's often tempted to do his best to kill you.*

"I take it you're content with your protection?" Felnir asked, glancing back at Colvyn, following at a respectful distance. "The lad's a fairer hand with a blade than I suspected."

She pondered the wisdom of describing Wohtin's mysterious intervention, unsure of Felnir's reaction. If the tattooed man was fully sane

288 · Anthony Ryan

and playing them all for fools, the Redtooth's anger might well be considerable. Yet, if it was just an act, Wohtin's performance was remarkable. Ultimately, she thought it best to leave the matter alone, at least until she could elicit some more signs of rationality from her subject of study.

"He saved my life," Elvine said, looking over her shoulder to favour Colvyn with a smile. "For which I'm grateful."

"No," Felnir corrected. "He saved you from being captured. It seems our competition, whoever they may be, is fully aware of your value."

"How could they be? We set out from Skar Magnol only a day after you brought Wohtin to the dock."

"In Ishtakar, the wiser courtiers have a saying: Nothing flies so swiftly as a secret. The fact that they were able to orchestrate such an elaborate ambush so quickly means we must move faster to avoid the next one. And so—" he came to a halt at the marble base, folding his arms expectantly "—I'm forced to enjoin you to more strenuous efforts. Last night you spoke of Trieya's Quill. What does it mean?"

Elvine crouched at the patch of earth she had scraped away to reveal more of the etched runes. Like the other inscriptions decorating this stone, it had been carved in a form of ancient Ascarlian common to the Inner Isles. The addition of unfamiliar symbols, presumably local modifications to the script, had complicated her initial attempts at a full translation. Perhaps the terrors of the previous night had served to clarify her mind, for she found she could read it without difficulty.

"'By the point of Trieya's Quill did he set his course,'" she recited aloud. "Trieya's Quill is an archaic name for the constellation known today as Fearnyl's Scythe."

"I know of it," Felnir said. "Rises in the west in late summer. Though, I can't recall any *Johten Apt* I've ever sailed with making use of it for navigation."

"That's because these days few see any reason to sail across the lower Styrnspeld. In ages past, when the Ascarls possessed more of a passion for exploration, those that sailed those treacherous waters noted that the tip of Trieya's Quill rises above a region into which even the most fearless captain wouldn't venture."

banished as if by a cool breeze. He gave a groan of pleasurable relief and began to apply more.

"Don't use too much," Aleida warned. "Not sure when I can get you any more."

He resisted the temptation to point out that, if their debt was settled, she needn't bother. Instead, he asked, "Won't you be in trouble for this?" He accompanied the question with a meaningful glance at Achela, who had continued to sit, watchful and silent, throughout this exchange.

"Don't worry about her," Aleida said with a sour note of dismissal. "She's only here for one thing, and it's costing my father a fortune. Besides, she's my aunt. The Morvek don't make trouble for their own kin."

"Your aunt?" Looking again at Achela, he discerned a faint resemblance of Aleida's cat-like features in the curve of her cheeks.

"Yes," Aleida said. "My mother's elder sister. Half-sister, in fact. Famed *kess-tuhk* to the Snow River Clan. And—" she raised her voice "—a vicious old, gold-grubbing bitch most of the time."

Achela betrayed no offence at the barb. In fact, Ruhlin thought he saw her lips curve a little in amusement. Her gaze, however, was as unwavering as ever.

"She commands this," Ruhlin said, tapping a finger to the *stagna*. "How is it done?"

Of all his questions, this one seemed to mystify Aleida the most. As she squinted at him, he felt like a child learning an obvious aspect of the adult world for the first time. "How do you turn into that . . . *thing*?" she asked. "How do the stars drift in the sky?"

"She is," he ventured, "Vyrn Skyra, then? Like me." He worried this might earn further disparagement, but instead it brought a frown to her brow.

"Morvek blood is different," she said. "Comparing it to those favoured by the Altvar is to compare liquid gold to pig slurry." He detected an echo of the dogmatic tone she had used before, but this time coloured by a bitter edge.

"Your father's people disdain the Morvek," Ruhlin realised. "They are servants here? Slaves even?"

Felnir's face darkened as he absorbed her meaning. "You expect me to take my ship *there*, of all places?"

"It corresponds to many of the legends. Velgard was said to be so favoured by the Altvar that they ensured safe passage wherever he went." She grimaced in apology. "I'm sorry, but as for where to look next, this is all I can offer. If we are to fulfil the mission Sister Lore set for us, we must make for the Fire Isles."

Chapter Twenty-Three

Ruhlin

As he trained in the circle over the course of the next few weeks, Ruhlin learned that there were a total of fifteen others incarcerated in this mysterious prison. Besides himself, all were either captive sailors or Morvek, with one notable exception.

"Have another, y'fecken dullard!" Sygurn said, slapping the flat of his wooden blade against Ruhlin's arse cheek as he sprawled on the sand. It was Sygurn's habit to salt the wound of injured pride whenever he succeeded in putting an opponent down. The matrix of scarlet-hued ink crinkled as he grinned at Ruhlin's scowl. It stirred a faint echo of dangerous rage, but the feel of the *stagna* upon his chest was enough to quell it.

Shooting a wary glance at Radylf's expectant face, Ruhlin got quickly to his feet to resume his position opposite Sygurn. His grin became a laugh as he crouched lower, stave held level with his chest. Ruhlin constantly attempted to match this stance, having learned its efficacy in fending off attacks. However, Sygurn always found a way past his flailing stave to administer painful jabs and swipes with his own. His appetite for taunts, of course, only made Ruhlin's sense of humiliation worse, engendering a deepening dislike of the man, albeit tinged with grudging admiration for his skill. Of all the prisoners, only Tuhlan could best Sygurn, though Julette at least managed to hold her own against him.

"May as well have matched me to a donkey," Sygurn said. His accent was so thick, and peppered with unfamiliar obscenities, it had taken

Ruhlin time to realise he spoke the same form of Ascarlian as Eldryk and the guards. However, the mass of scars on Sygurn's back, some old, many new, made it plain that this man was as much a slave as the rest of them. Apparently, the cruelty of these people was not confined to foreigners, or those they had conquered.

Without warning, Sygurn lunged, stave extended in a thrust at Ruhlin's midriff. He was accustomed by now to this man's fondness for surprise assaults, managing to raise his own weapon in time to deflect the blow. The staves barely connected, however, because Sygurn spun at the last instant, angling his stave down to slash at Ruhlin's leg. One lesson he had learned after tedious hours of practice was the value of nimble feet. A clumsy leap spared him the worst of the strike, though he suffered a numbing thud to his right foot.

"Huh," Sygurn grunted, his tattoos tightened by a frown of annoyance. Like many for whom violence is an amusement, he took it ill when his torments went awry. "Look who's all spry now. Have to watch myself from here on, won't I?" He spun again before the last word was out of his mouth, the stave whirling towards Ruhlin's head, enough strength behind it to crack his skull. Knowing he hadn't time to duck, Ruhlin stepped inside the weapon's arc, launching himself at Sygurn. He jerked to the side, but not sufficiently fast to avoid Ruhlin's enfolding arms.

"Get off me, y'fecker!" Sygurn raged, Ruhlin suffering a hard butt to the nose. He held on, however, their clumsy dance bearing them both to the sand. Sygurn had a good deal more bulk than Ruhlin and soon wrestled himself on top. Clamping a meaty hand to Ruhlin's head, he pushed him into the powdery surface.

"Not gonna change for me?" he hissed into Ruhlin's ear. "Go on, change. The witch can't see the *stagna* now. Do it!" Hearing the unexpected note of desperation in the man's voice, Ruhlin strained his eyes so their gazes met. The bully from seconds before was gone, his face riven by the stark entreaty of a truly wretched soul.

He wants to die, Ruhlin decided. *That's what this has all been for.*

Jerking his body, Ruhlin managed to free a hand. Slapping it to Sygurn's neck, he dragged him closer. Ruhlin moulded his features

292 · ANTHONY RYAN

into a hateful glare, voicing his question through clenched teeth so
Radylf would take it for an insult, but keeping the volume barely
above a whisper: "Do you want to get out of here?"

Snarling, Sygurn swiped Ruhlin's hand away and exerted more
pressure. His head now pushed deeper into the sand, Ruhlin felt
Sygurn's lips upon his ear. "How?" he demanded in a grating sigh.
"When?"

"Just wait," Ruhlin muttered back, spitting grains. "And watch. The
time will come."

Sygurn's breath brushed his skin for a second before he huffed a
disgusted laugh. "Don't you know where we are? There's no way clear
of here. And if you're not going to kill me, what use are you?"

The pressure disappeared, Ruhlin raising himself from the sand to
see Sygurn retrieving his stave and stomping back to his allotted
position. For the rest of the session, he plodded listlessly through the
sparring with a marked lack of aggression, earning himself a warning
cut courtesy of Radylf's whip.

"Even a disgraced cur such as you still needs to bite," the whip-
man said.

Sygurn thumbed the blood from his cheek with scant sign of
concern. When he turned to face him, Ruhlin saw the same anguished
appeal in his eyes: *Change! Kill me!*

Replying with a fractional shake of his head, Ruhlin let out a
challenging yell and hurled himself at Sygurn. His intent was to
arouse the man's warrior-born instincts, resulting in a display of
sufficient skill and aggression to satisfy Radylf. He wasn't disappointed, though when he woke in his cage hours later, sporting a
pulsing bruise on his temple and plethora of aches in his ribs, he
had cause to regret his charitable instincts.

It was another ten days before Ruhlin learned the reason for Sygurn's
certainty regarding the hopelessness of escape. Radylf arrived in the
morning, as was routine. But this time when he swung the gate open
instead of gesturing politely for Ruhlin to make his way to the circle,
he pointed his whip handle at the shadows to the rear of the cages.

"Best cover up well, laddie," he said, tossing a wolf pelt to Ruhlin. "The Aerling's likely to get peeved if you freeze your balls off today." The whip-man himself wore a cloak of dark fur Ruhlin assumed to be from a bear. He augmented his gift with a pair of boots, tapping the whip impatiently to the bars whilst Ruhlin pulled them on and donned the pelt.

No guards accompanied them as Ruhlin followed Radylf into the gloom. Their only escort came in the form of Achela, positioned directly to Ruhlin's rear, her ever-watchful eyes no doubt fixed upon the *stagna*. They moved through an unlit void before emerging into a torchlit expanse of stone abutting a curving wall. It ascended in a smooth arc to disappear into darkness some twenty feet above. Following the line of the curve, Ruhlin realised it swept all the way to the opening above the circle.

"A dome," Ruhlin murmured, pausing to run a hand over the buttress jutting from the wall. It was rough and hard to the touch, but lacked any seams. Peering closer, he saw what appeared to be grey stone impregnated with many smaller rocks. *Some form of mortar?* he wondered before his fascinated inspection was interrupted by a pointed cough from Radylf.

"What do they call this stuff?" Ruhlin asked the whip-man. He knew he risked punishment, but had noticed how Radylf tended to unfurl his whip only for physical displays of defiance or outright disrespect.

He squinted in faint irritation but consented to reply with a shrug: "*Kehlgruin.*"

The word was unfamiliar, but after some quick pondering, Ruhlin recognised it as a confluence of old Ascarlian. "Mud-stone?"

"It flows like mud before it sets," Radylf explained. "Then it's harder than any rock. Come." He flicked his whip-handle at an opening in the wall a dozen paces off. "The Aerling and his guests are waiting."

Upon entering the stairwell, Ruhlin was immediately struck by the sudden chill, misting his breath and making him grateful for his covering of wolf fur. "Bracing, isn't it?" Radylf commented, noting his shiver, voice echoing as they ascended the grey steps. Like the walls of the great dome, they were also fashioned from *kehlgruin*.

"So it goes when you venture from the heart of the mountain," the whip-man went on as they climbed. "Stray too far and no amount of fur will prevent your blood freezing in your veins. In case you were wondering."

His voice held a knowing, near mocking note that reminded Ruhlin of Juliette's certainty that their plotting was being overheard. As the chill deepened with every upward step, he had to concede that the air beyond the great chamber added further doubt to the prospect of escape. It was hard to gauge how high they had climbed by the time they reached the top, but Ruhlin estimated at close to a hundred feet.

Radylf led Ruhlin through a rectangular opening, whereupon he found himself blinking at the sight of an unobstructed sky. After so long with only glimpses through the opening above the circle, the vast sweep of white and blue was both marvellous and dizzying. So too was the mountain range that greeted him when he lowered his gaze. Tall, snow-capped peaks stretched away on all sides, the valleys and passes between partly obscured by a drifting mist.

"Behold the Vyrnkral Mountains," Radylf said, sweeping his arm wide to encompass the view. "Tallest range in all Nihlvar."

They stood on a long, narrow balcony. Like the dome and the steps, it was also constructed from *kehlgruin*, the rough surface sparkling with frost. Behind them, a steep granite cliff rose towards an unseen summit far above. *The heart of the mountain*, Ruhlin thought, recalling Radylf's words. *The dome sits inside a mountain.*

"Nihlvar?" he asked, provoking an amused squint from the whip-man.

"The name of this realm," he said. "I thought Aleida would have mentioned it before now. You have the honour of finding yourself a guest of the great Kingdom of Nihlvar, Realm of the Eternal Vortigurn, most favoured of the Altvar's children." He spoke with the quirked mouth and a half-raised eyebrow of the cynic. Radylf was surely Eldryk's faithful servant, but seeing this side of him, Ruhlin doubted he shared his master's fervent belief.

Lowering his arm, the whip-man pointed at something far below. "See there, laddie?"

Leaning forward, Ruhlin peered past the edge of the balustrade at the ground below. At first he saw only an anonymous maze of peak and channel, but then discerned a winding pale line tracing away from the base of the mountain.

"One road in, one road out," Radylf said. "It's a ten-day trek with sheer cliffs on both sides and at the end of it you'll find a holdfast manned by fifty warriors, that's if you don't freeze or starve long before you get there. So you see—" he nudged his whip handle to Ruhlin's shoulder, urging him along the balcony "—all your scheming with that pirate bitch will avail you nothing."

"She's a sailor," Ruhlin muttered, unable to keep the bitter disappointment from his voice. Radylf spared him an amused glance but confined his response to a short, disparaging laugh.

After twenty paces, the balcony opened out into a broad platform where Eldryk stood alongside two unfamiliar figures. Ruhlin found the change in Eldryk's posture significant. Instead of the customary straight-backed, flint-eyed superiority, he had a slight hunch to his shoulders, his head angled lower. He also stood apart from his two companions by several yards. Their stance was very different, both exuding a peerless authority as they regarded Ruhlin with expressions of intense appraisal.

The taller of the two commanded Ruhlin's immediate notice, for he almost matched Radylf in height, though his girth far exceeded the whip-man's. He was clad in silver grey furs that matched the shade of his copious but well-kept beard. More striking than his size, was his face. The skin not covered by his beard was decorated in the most extensive mass of red-inked tattoos Ruhlin had yet seen. They covered his forehead, brows, nose and cheeks so extensively it would have been easy to mistake them for some form of disfiguring disease. Ruhlin also noted the handle of a sword jutting from the furs about his waist.

The woman at his side was also tattooed, but with a good deal more restraint and elegance. Scarlet spirals traced back from her eyes and into the tight braids of her near white hair. Her features possessed a smooth, sculpted handsomeness that wouldn't have been out of place on a statue of Silfaer the Battle Maiden. The white wolf fur about her shoulders complemented her colouring perfectly, adding to Ruhlin's growing impression of wealth and status.

Both she and her towering male companion continued to look Ruhlin over when Radylf brought him to a halt, each of them shifting to inspect him from different angles. "Tell him to take that off," the woman said, flicking a hand at Eldryk.

"He speaks our tongue, Tuhlvyr," the Aerling said before nodding at Ruhlin to comply.

The icy grip of the mountain air brought a gasp as Ruhlin shrugged the wolf pelt from his shoulders, leaving him shivering and naked before their gaze. *Tuhlvyr*, he thought through the ache of rapidly numbed limbs. These then were of the highest order in this strange realm, which explained Eldryk's unusual subservience.

"Scrawny bugger," the large man grunted, angling his head to peer at Ruhlin's legs. "Would've thought a bearer of the fire blood would stand taller and broader, eh, Tuhlvyr Deyna?"

"You would, Tuhlvyr Feydrik," the woman mused in agreement. She circled Ruhlin as he shivered, reappearing on his left, her gaze lingering on the iron ring fixed into his flesh. "Scrawny or not, he had enough heart to cause you some trouble, I see, Eldryk."

"His training progresses well, Tuhlvyr," Eldryk replied. "But his breed of outlander often requires more correction than usual."

"Yes, I've heard that the Teilvik do not appreciate the mighty gift we bring."

Teilvik. By now, Ruhlin had come to understand this word as equating to "savage". These people looked upon him as a lesser order of human. Perhaps not even that.

"But there's no doubt?" the large man, Feydrik, enquired. "He is Vyrn Skyra?"

"I have seen it myself, Tuhlvyr," Eldryk assured him, head bobbing lower. "I shall be glad to arrange a demonstration, if you require. It may cost me a slave or two, but I shall willingly bear the cost."

Feydrik didn't turn from his inspection, so Ruhlin saw the contemptuous sneer beneath the large man's beard. "No need," he said.

"The truth of it will become plain soon enough." Coming closer, he peered down at Ruhlin's features, shaking his head as the curl of his lips faded. "Such defiance," he murmured. "So it was with the last one I saw, though I was just a boy then and he a Morvek, so his blood couldn't be counted as pure and his use confined to spectacle. The Vortigurn set a hundred of his most vicious hounds upon him at the Great Meidvang that year. He tore them all apart, sparing one, then allowed the fire to fade from his blood and just stood there whilst the beast tore his throat out."

"Does he have a name?" the woman, Deyna, asked. Ruhlin's shudders increased as he felt her fingers trace across his back. Her touch was light but her nails sharp enough to leave scratches. "Not whatever his fellow savages grunted at him," she added. "Something suitably impressive, a name that will inflame the crowd's passions."

"In truth, I hadn't yet given thought to it, Tuhlvyr," Eldryk said. Clearly not a man to miss a chance at ingratiation, he went on quickly, "I should consider it an honour if you would name him."

"Mmm." She pursed her lips as she came to Feydrik's side, her nails scratching their way from Ruhlin's shoulder to his neck. "What do you think, dear cousin?" she asked her fellow Tuhlvyr. "Naturally, it has to be something plucked from the Altvar Rendi."

"Sytrac?" the big man suggested. "The Rager who slew an entire horde of Elborians with but his bare hands."

"Too obvious." Deyna flicked her fingers in dismissal. "We need a name with more drama, a sense of . . . revelation, you might say. Ah." She extended a finger, a single nail ascending to Ruhlin's chin where it drew forth a bead of blood. "I have it. I give you Amundyr, the whelp born of Ihryka's forbidden tryst with a mortal of lesser Uhltvar blood. Despised and shunned all his life, Amundyr still honoured the Altvar and, for his devotion, was rewarded with the strength of ten men. He it was who unmasked the traitor Kuhlvyk, slaying his *menda* and burning him alive in his own hall. Henceforth, all honoured the name Amundyr and from his seed would flow a line of kings."

"Didn't Amundyr die an ugly death?" Feydrik said. "Captured by Kuhlvyk's vengeful kin and chained to a rock to be fed upon by Urhnsleyr, the dread beast of the deep."

"It's the Altvar Rendi," Deyna replied with a note of irritation. "Every mortal in it dies an ugly death." Removing her nail from Ruhlin's chin, she turned to Eldryk. "Amundyr it is. Have the necessary runes inscribed upon him, although—" she glanced back at Ruhlin "—not upon his face. I find I like it as it is."

Eldryk's head sank to its lowest angle yet. "As you wish, Tuhlvyr."

"The first Meidvang is but a month away," Feydrik said. "I trust he, and any lesser amusements you have for us, will be fully prepared by then?"

"Of course, Tuhlvyr."

"Good." Feydrik moved to clap a meaty hand to Eldryk's shoulder. "If all goes well, mayhap we'll be calling you Tuhlvyr by the year's end, eh?"

Until now, Ruhlin had thought Eldryk a guileful, even cunning soul. Strange then, that the Aerling should fail to notice the big man's patent insincerity. Eldryk flushed with all the pride of a son receiving praise from a usually indifferent father. *These people have no use for you*, Ruhlin concluded. *Just me.* Clearly, they saw him as some form of prize to be exhibited at this Meidvang of theirs, an event to take place a month from now. He didn't think it too much to hope that it would be held far away from this mountain with its single road.

"I saw that."

Ruhlin's eyes snapped to the woman, finding her studying him with a yet deeper pitch of interest. Smiling, she came closer. "Angomar wasn't exactly a friend," she said, voice lowered to a whisper. "In fact, had she risen any higher, I would probably have had to kill her. But it would have been a worthy end, something that befit her station and achievements. Instead, I'm told she died carting your savage carcass across the sea. Was it the result of some scheme of yours? I wonder. The kind I just saw kindling behind those eyes?"

Unsure if failing to answer her question would invite punishment, but fearing what his voice might betray, Ruhlin said nothing. Deyna failed to exhibit any offence, instead shifting to place her lips close to his ear. "Know this, *Teilvik*, you are being given the greatest of gifts. If you are all that groveller claims you to be, before long you will stand before the Vortigurn himself. Few are ever so honoured as to earn even a crumb of notice of the King of Nihlvar. You should rejoice." Ruhlin heard only marginal inflection in her words. There was none of the awe or reverence that possessed Eldryk when he alluded to the customs of this strange kingdom. He did, however, detect the smallest note of resentment when she spoke the word "Vortigurn".

This one does not love her king, he decided as she moved back. Apparently, his calculation showed on his face once again, for the scarlet wings framing her eyes arced in a frown. "Sees so much," she mused in a murmur too soft for the others to hear. "A scholar's mind confined to a body destined to be consumed by the fire of its own blood." She sighed, reaching out a long-nailed hand to scratch shallow cuts from his chest to his groin. Ruhlin trembled with both pain and rage as the blood trickled over his skin, the cold abruptly banished by a worrying flare of heat in his gut. The knowledge that Achela stood only yards away, her gaze locked on the *stagna*, sent a fearful wave through him, one thankfully strong enough to quench the fire before it spread.

"Such a terrible waste," Deyna added. She seemed to be unaware of how close she had come to witnessing the effects of his affliction first-hand. "Oh well." Shrugging, she turned away. "Eldryk, I find myself in need of diversion. I trust you still keep a stable of appropriately skilled, and expendable slaves. Have them brought to my chamber. Care to join me, cousin?"

Eldryk dutifully bobbed his head whilst the pair walked away, making for a door at the far end of the platform. When they had disappeared from sight, Ruhlin noted how the Aerling's subservience disappeared, his shoulders straightening and the old surety returning to his features. Although, just for an instant, Ruhlin caught a spasm of expression that he could only describe as deep, painful self-disgust. It made him wonder just how sincere the Aerling's previous fawning had been.

He averted his head before Eldryk turned his gaze upon him, the Aerling snapping out instructions to Radylf. "Get him back to the dome and see to the inking. Make sure it's done by the finest hand."

"Aerling," the giant said, inclining his head, then hesitating, a reluctant grimace on his sculpted face.

"What?" Eldryk asked.

"Aleida is our finest hand with a needle, Aerling."

"Oh." The Aerling winced in annoyance. "Very well. Set her to it. But, mark this well, boy," he added, fixing a glare upon Ruhlin, "if your hand, or anything else, strays even an inch towards my daughter, Achela will unleash the *stagna* for a full turn of the glass." Before stalking off, he paused to cast an aggrieved gaze over the bloody scratches on Ruhlin's torso. "And make sure those don't fester," he told Radylf. "He's no use if he sickens."

CHAPTER TWENTY-FOUR

Thera

The three-master was still at anchor when the *Great Wolf* rounded the eastern shore of Iselda's Nail, the *Wind Sword* knifing through the swell alongside. Outwardly, she maintained the expected fierce and resolute visage of a captain approaching battle, yet Thera was disconcerted by the sheer size of the opposing vessel. Her hull was a third again the length of the *Great Wolf* and her broad-beamed bulk probably exceeded the weight of both Ascarlian ships. Even so, she appeared to be sparsely crewed for so large a vessel. Thera counted only a score of sailors upon her deck with a half-dozen more in the rigging. This disparity in numbers, or basic cowardice, may have been the reason for the three-master's captain to raise anchor and unfurl sails. The huge ship wallowed as her crew scrambled, red canvas blossoming and dozens of oars appearing along the middle line of the hull, confirming that the bulk of her crew were below decks. With wind and oars to aid her, the three-master pointed her prow towards the north, leaving a broad white wake as she struck out for open sea.

Cowardice then, Thera decided. With so many hands aboard, the wiser course would have been to fight it out. Perhaps these Nihlvarians were only fearsome when faced with a defenceless foe. "Fast stroke!" she called out to her *menda*. When resorting to oars, the crew of an Ascarlian longship rowed at one of four strokes: slow, steady, fast and ramming. Until now, the *Great Wolf* and the *Wind Sword* had adopted the steady stroke, something experienced sailors could sustain for an hour or more. Fast was reserved for pursuit and ramming, only employed to cover that last few yards before the clash of hulls and all that followed.

The three-master had about a quarter-mile lead and, although heavier than her pursuers, her richness in oars made for a decent turn of speed. Thera could tell her crew were well drilled, the oars sweeping the sea with efficient regularity, whilst the helmsman rode the swell with barely a change to her course. If this chase continued, it would become a test of stamina, the outcome decided by which crew tired first. Given the disparity in oars, the red-sailed vessel might well have made good her escape, if not for the appearance of the *Swift Spear*.

Gynheld's ship rounded the western headland of Iselda's Nail with her oars at fast stroke. Thanks to her comparative lightness and the skill of her captain, she cut through the waves and closed the distance to the three-master in mere moments. The larger ship attempted to evade the *Swift Spear* with a lurching turn to starboard, sails sagging with the abrupt loss of wind and the impressive rhythm of her oars descending into clattering disorder. Gynheld had clearly anticipated the manoeuvre, ordering her crew to ramming speed and steering directly for the three-master's port side. Grapples flew when the distance dwindled to mere yards, whereupon the two vessels began a clumsy dance across the sea, revolving together in a broadening white spiral.

Thera resisted the urge to order an immediate acceleration to ramming stroke. Too long working an oar at full pelt would sap her *menda*'s strength for the inevitable fight to come. She was momentarily distracted by the sight of the three-master's largest sail as it caught a gust, revealing a black sigil emblazoned on the red canvas. Thera initially took it for the crossed hammer and sword of Ulthnir. But further inspection revealed the design to be inverted and therefore a corruption of the Worldsmith's sacred crest. Annuk had intimated that these Nihlvarians also held to the Altvar. If so, their form of worship amounted to sacrilege, yet another crime to add to their list.

Turning from the prow, she cupped her hands around her mouth, calling out to Gelmyr at the tiller: "Make for the stern!" Moving to the starboard rail, she waved to Alvyr on the deck of the *Wind Sword*, making a wide sweeping gesture with her right arm. Communication between ships at sea depended on such gestures and was often a haphazard affair, with signals easily being misinterpreted thanks to heaving decks or poor weather. Fortunately, Alvyr was quick to divine Thera's instruction and the *Wind Sword* altered course, angling herself to assault the three-master's starboard flank.

As the two struggling ships drew nearer, Thera heard the thrum of bowstrings and chorus of shouted challenges that always marked such moments. Using their grapples, the *Swift Spear*'s crew had dragged her into a close embrace with the larger ship. Before the waves caused the vessels to swirl again, Thera caught sight of Gynheld and several of her warriors launching themselves at the hull opposite, clambering up to the rail, heedless of the hail of arrows launched by the defenders above.

"Ramming stroke!" Thera cried, her *menda* responding immediately. The *Great Wolf*'s prow slammed hard against the three-master's stern, probably dislodging a few of Gynheld's crew from her hull, but Thera felt that preferable to allowing them to suffer the attentions of enemy archers.

"Grapples!" she called out, but the three-headed hooks were already flying, arcing high before descending to latch themselves onto the three-master's timbers. A few enemy sailors came running to hack at the tightened ropes with axes but quickly fell to Thera's own archers. The rest of the crew hauled the lines until the gap between the hulls was less than a foot wide.

"To arms!" Thera shouted, raising the Dreadaxe above her head. As the chorus of eager affirmation sounded, she paused to cast a glance at the mast, ensuring Lynnea had followed instructions and stationed herself there with her beasts. Her apprentice's face contrasted with the snarling animus of the crew, her expression the wide-eyed, pale mask of a woman who regarded the impending violence with no such zeal.

Worry not for her, Thera admonished herself, turning away. *There's a battle to be won.*

The *Great Wolf*'s size served them well, for her prow was only a few inches lower than the three-master's rail. Thera was able to vault it at the first attempt, landing with axe in hand in the midst of several prone bodies. A few lay twitching or inert with arrows jutting from chest and neck. But others were fully alive and, it transpired, not so filled with cowardice as Thera had hoped.

The uninjured man closest to her, a stocky figure in leathers, sprang to his feet and launched himself at her, red-inked features livid with bloodlust. Thera waited until he came within reach of the Dreadaxe's sweep, then crouched, whirling the double-bladed weapon to hack through his lower leg. He fell screaming, blood jetting from the stump of his ankle, his own axe clattering to the deck. Thera reversed her grip on the Dreadaxe as she rose, stabbing the sharp apex of the twin blades into the writhing man's chest before striding on, her *menda* now scrambling over the stern to fill the air with a hungry roar. The atrocities at Ayl-Ah-Veyn and Buhl Hardta had kindled a dark fire in their hearts that could only be quenched with blood. The nearby enemies were quickly cut down, Ragnalt dispatching one with a stunning jab of his shield boss into the man's face before cleaving his shoulder open with a downward stroke of his sword.

Thera led them on towards the mid-deck, finding most of their foes clustered at the port rail as they attempted to contest Gynheld's boarders. More red-faced warriors were issuing from hatches with weapons in hand; the rowers from the lower deck summoned to fight. "Gelmyr!" Thera called to the *Johten Apt*, pointing to the nearest hatch. He responded with a wordless shout, splitting off with a five-strong party to hack down the sailors already on the deck before staunching the flow of reinforcements, swords and axes raising a red mist as they assailed those attempting to scale the ladder.

Thera led the rest of her *menda* towards the port rail, determined to clear the way for Gynheld's crew. Some foes saw the danger and turned to face them, managing to form a ragged line of sorts, but too few to hold the charge. Two sweeps of the Dreadaxe sufficed to see

Thera through, allowing her to hack away at the dense throng beyond with vicious abandon. It wasn't often that she lost herself in the fury of combat, but rage at the crimes committed by this scum, combined with battle lust, temporarily robbed her of full awareness. Red-faced men and women reared up before her to be bludgeoned away or hacked into ruin before they could strike a blow. The Dreadaxe felt light in her hands, wreaking bloody havoc with every crimson stroke. When the red fog dissipated, it revealed the smashed skull of a woman being pounded into mush beneath Thera's boot.

"Think she might be dead enough, my friend."

Thera looked up to find Gynheld nearby, breath steaming in the chilly air. She had earned a fresh scar to her brow, and her shield and sword were covered in gore. Behind her, the Vellihr's *menda* spread across the deck, finishing the wounded twitching or screaming among the copious dead. A glance to the starboard rail showed Alvyr leading his warriors in a sweep towards the prow, the few enemies that had opposed their assault lying dead.

"The captain!" Thera called out to him. "Find the captain!"

Receiving a confirmatory wave in response, she turned back to Gynheld. "Tell your lot to stop their slaughter. I need at least one who can still talk."

Leaving Gynheld to harangue restraint into her *menda*, Thera went in search of Gelmyr. The *Johten Apt* was crouched at the hatch, now empty of enemies, the surrounding timbers stained dark. She was gratified to see all the warriors Gelmyr had led nearby, save one.

"Told her to wait," he told Thera. "But her blood was raging."

Looking at the hatch, Thera heard the sounds of combat echoing from below, the thud and clash of weapons interspersed with the profanity-laden shout of a familiar voice. *Eshilde.* Thera stifled a curse. With her recent list of errors weighing upon her mind, the would-be apprentice had evidently seized on the chance of glory. Venturing into the bowels of a recently stormed ship was always the most hazardous moment and best done with organised caution. Dark, cargo-filled holds made perfect hiding places from which desperate or courageous defenders might spring. More worrying than the tumult of fighting, however, was the thickening scent of smoke emerging from the hatch. As she watched, a yellow glow lit the gloom. Hearing a whoosh from the direction of the prow, Thera turned to see a column of flame erupt from one of the forward hatches. It was too bright and too tall to be anything but the product of a large stock of lamp oil set to flame.

"Get everyone back to the *Great Wolf*," she ordered Gelmyr before calling out to Gynheld. Fortunately, sound judgement had compelled the Vellihr to anticipate the command, Thera watching her hector her *menda* to the port rail. Only a fool would linger aboard a ship deliberately set to the torch. After checking to ensure both her own and Alvyr's crew had begun their escape, Thera lingered at the hatch, watching the burgeoning flicker of the inferno raging below decks, hoping Eshilde would reappear.

"Thera!" Gelmyr called from the stern. He was crouched, ready to leap onto the *Great Wolf* as the last few warriors slipped by on either side.

"Go!" she called back, drawing in as deep a breath as her lungs allowed before plunging into the hatch. The base of the ladder was thick with the bodies of those who had died attempting to scale it, allowing her a soft landing. She plunged on through the hold, nostrils filled with the increasingly potent pall of smoke seeping through the duckboards. The roar of flames rendered any attempt to call Eshilde's name pointless, forcing Thera to peer into every corner with stinging eyes.

A dozen paces on, she came to a row of cages, four in all. Two were empty, but the third held the slumped form of a young man, his wrists and ankles bound in chains. The door to the cage lay open. Thera entered to turn him over, finding a pale face with brows inked in blue. His throat had been recently slashed with a single, well-placed cut. Moving to the next cage, she discovered another body, an older man, also Ascarlian and slain in the same manner. *Two more souls who'll tell us nothing*, she thought in frustration.

She looked up as a new sound reached her through the cacophony of flame and cracking timbers. It took her only a second to recognise it as the hard, angry screech of Eshilde venting her anger. Thera found her a few yards on from the cages, repeatedly thrusting her dagger into the chest of a large, bearded man with scarlet tattoos covering his forehead. From the empty cast to his eyes and copious blood streaming from his mouth, he was beyond feeling the wounds Eshilde inflicted on him.

"Twisted bastard!" Eshilde raged, dagger blurring as she stabbed at the dead man's eyes.

"Enough!" Thera caught her wrist, dragging her to her feet.

"He killed them," Eshilde said, spitting at the corpse. "Slit their throats before I could free them, the sick fuck!"

Thera wasn't sure if Eshilde's anger arose from cold-blooded murder or the fact that her chance at glory had been stolen. Looking at the bearded man's clothing, she saw he lacked armour, his garb fashioned from fine, well-tailored fabric with collar and cuffs trimmed in fur. He also wore an expensive-looking gold chain about his neck. *The captain?* she wondered, stooping to claim the treasure with a swift jerk of her wrist.

"Here," she said, tossing the necklace to Eshilde. "One of us might as well earn something from this." Her voice caught as a thick gust of smoke swept the hold, leaving them both coughing. Grabbing Eshilde's arm, she tugged her towards the ladder.

Emerging onto the upper deck, she found the three-master wreathed in flames from prow to mid-deck, the ship listing as fire ate away the forward hull. She and Eshilde sprinted for the stern as it began to rise. Fortunately, a few grapple lines remained in place, sparing them too high a leap when they launched themselves at the *Great Wolf*. Gelmyr called out an order to sever the ropes the instant Thera's boots impacted the deck. The oars began sweeping at fast stroke a heartbeat later. As the gap between ships widened, she watched the flames consume the three-master, devouring rigging and wreathing her in a thick grey pall. Before long, the timbers below the waterline gave out and she slipped beneath the waves.

"No prisoners?" Thera asked Gelmyr, scanning the ship in the hope of finding a bound captive or two.

"No time," he said, shaking his head. "At least we secured justice for the slain."

Justice, but no information. Thera gritted her teeth, her frustration piquing into anger when Snaryk began barking. The dog rarely emitted more than an appreciative whine at Lynnea's petting, but when it did raise its voice, the sound could pain the ears. Thera turned to the mast, intending to snap at Lynnea to shut the beast up, instead finding her apprentice absent. For a panicked moment, Thera thought Lynnea might have snuck aboard the three-master in the midst of the battle. Then she saw the dog had braced his forepaws against the mast, casting his barks up at Lynnea, who was now perched atop the sail's crossbeam.

"Get down!" Thera called to her, exasperated and relieved in equal measure. Lynnea failed to comply, instead jabbing her arm towards the west. Following the gesture, Thera could see only the grey haze and choppy waves of the Styrnspeld on a calm day. Still, Lynnea continued to point with insistent urgency. Setting the Dreadaxe aside, Thera went to the mast, skirting Snaryk to grasp the pegs set into the tall timber. Climbing to Lynnea's side, she found her face grim and more than a little peeved. *Look!* She stabbed her finger at the horizon again, and this time Thera saw it.

It was just one sail at first, red like their recently burned foe, also bearing the same inverted corruption of Ulthnir's sigil. The hull below the sail was smaller than the three-master, a warship built for speed and manoeuvre, but no match for three similarly constructed enemies. Thera's confidence dwindled as a second sail appeared alongside the first, then a third to her port side, quickly followed by a dozen more. Within moments, the westward sea became filled with sails, spread out in a crescent two miles long.

Turning to Lynnea, for the first time she found her face blank of expression, save for the question in her unblinking eyes. *What does this mean?*

Casting a glance at the fast approaching fleet, Thera sighed and reached for a rope. "It means Ascarlia is now at war," she said before swinging herself to the deck, bellowing a string of orders. "All hands to the oars! Gelmyr, set course due east and haul hard the sail!"

The *Johten Apt* surprised her by not responding immediately, instead spending a moment to stare at the array of ships in hard appraisal. Finally, he shook his head, brows heavy with reluctance. "We head east and they'll catch us," he warned. "We're tired and they're fresh, and upon the Styrnspeld, wind and current flow north at these climes. Better to ride the wind and hope to lose them come nightfall."

"That," she said, pointing to the ever-growing sprawl of ships to the west, "is not a mere band of raiders. That is a great *menda*. They come for conquest, not plunder. We must warn the Sister Queens."

"And we will," he assured her. "Come darkness, we'll douse all lights and turn east, slip through them. But if we attempt to outrun them now, be assured we'll all be dead or captive before dusk and the Queens will have no warning."

Thera's jaw ached with the effort of caging further argument. When it came to the sea, Gelmyr's word was iron. "Set course north," she said and stomped towards the nearest unattended oar. There were three in all, the warriors who worked them lost to the battle or too wounded for labour.

"All hands heave like your place in the Halls depends on it!" she called out to the crew. "For it surely does this day!"

CHAPTER TWENTY-FIVE

Felnir

During the third night of sailing the lower Styrnspeld, he dreamed of the oasis. It was something he rarely did these days, but had been a regular trial during his years of exile. Those who led trains of camels across the Takarian Desert called this place simply Eluhsa: the emerald. Felnir's first glimpse of it, a green island in a sea of yellow dunes, left him in little doubt the name was well chosen. As ever in dreams, his approach to the cluster of trees around a pool of blue, irresistible water was different to the stumbling, desperation of his actual arrival. Instead of crawling into the blessed shade, this time he walked, crouching at the pool's edge to play a hand through its wondrous waters rather than plunge his weeping face into it, gulping and spluttering. Also different was the fact that he wasn't alone. In reality, all his fellow escapees from the rebel prison had succumbed to exhaustion or thirst miles back. Yet, on this occasion, his mind had consented to conjure a companion.

"Strange," his great-grandfather mused, his one eye engaged in a squinting survey of their surroundings. "To find a place of plenty in a land so barren."

"The Takaris say it was a blessing from Alnu, the Mother Spirit," Felnir said. "When her most favoured tribe were driven across this desert, she wept for their plight and from her tears, Eluhsa grew. Their thirst slaked, the tribe continued their migration and went on to found a small settlement on the coast to the south, in time destined to blossom into Ishtakar, the greatest of cities."

The Tielwald grunted, casting his eye over the pool. "Seems a bit cloudy. Didn't it make you sick?"

"Yes. I spent near an hour spewing most of it back up. Still had enough strength for when my pursuers came, though."

"You kill them?"

Felnir nodded towards the far end of the pool. "There's a mudbank over there. I covered myself in it and waited for nightfall. There were only four and they didn't trouble to post a guard. Strangled one and used his knife to slit the throats of the others."

In fact, he had spared the fourth, a lad of barely fifteen summers who had awakened in time to draw his scimitar. The fight he put up had been brief and ineffective, but not lacking in courage. Felnir put him on his camel and sent him back to the rebels with a stern warning as to what would happen should any others come in search of their lost prisoner. It was an act his great-grandfather, even in dream form, would have judged as weakness.

"So, from here you journeyed to Ishtakar, I assume?" Margnus asked. "And there to find fame as one of the Saluhtan's favoured mercenary captains."

"I never met the man, so can't speak as to his favour. In truth, I know not whether he ever heard my name. Arriving in Ishtakar with a train of camels and the gear of slain rebels earned me Kodryn's notice and a place in his company."

"And you spent the next few years fighting another people's wars, for mere pay, no less." The Tielwald shook his head. "I sometimes give thanks to the Altvar that your mother no longer lives to witness how far you fell. Of all her children, she took the most pride in you."

For his part, Felnir regretted that his mind hadn't seen fit to equip him with weapons in this dream, else he would have done what he couldn't in the waking world. Accepting the desire to murder his own great-grandfather should have provoked some spasm of guilt or shame. Instead Felnir found it settled into his heart quite comfortably. A man shouldn't deny his own truth.

"What do you want?" he asked Margnus. The old man raised an eyebrow at his uncivil tone but voiced no rebuke. Instead, he moved to the pool's edge and sat, resting his mighty stone axe across his knees.

"When we were last alone," he said, "we spoke of change, if you recall."

"Yes. Your curious interest in stockfish. What of it?"

The old man leaned forward to scrape a handful of sand from the ground and cast it into the pool. "A thousand grains birth a thousand ripples," he mused, eye fixed on the intersecting matrix disturbing the water. "Discerning a pattern is nigh impossible, so I am forced to regard the whole picture. My spies speak of ill rumours and dark deeds, covert murder and sabotage. But they are scattered, seemingly without direction. Yet I've walked this earth long enough to catch the foul scent of change on the wind, and never has its stink been more potent. Change is upon us. We now stand at the edge of its ragged blade."

He raised his gaze from the pool and Felnir saw in the narrowing of his empty eye socket the qualms of one forced to impart trust in the untrustworthy. "I take it you haven't found them yet," the old man said. "The Vaults."

"No," Felnir replied, voice rendered flat by resentment. Even this version of his great-grandfather possessed an unrivalled facility for stoking his anger. "We sail for the Fire Isles where Sister Lore's scholar believes further traces may be found."

"You should trust her word. Heretic Covenanter she may be, but she has her mother's gift for insight and—" the Tielwald grunted in soft amusement "—if I'm not mistaken, a decent measure of her father's guile."

"Her father?"

The old man waved a hand. "Doesn't matter. What does is that when she leads you to the Vaults, whatever you find there cannot be brought back to Skar Magnol. Be it treasure or a pile of ancient scrolls or the hammer of the Worldsmith himself. Do not bring it home, Felnir. Find your sister. Like it or not, and I know you don't, you two will need each other before this is over."

A sudden, hard wind sent a spiral of sand through the oasis then, carrying with it the taint of camel. His pursuers were closing, making Felnir conclude the dream was not about to spare him the murders to come.

"I've been trying to warn your sister too," his great-grandfather said, his substantial form mostly lost to the whirling grit. "Though she is proving harder to reach. Head for the Kast Geld after you find the Vaults . . ."

Felnir opened his mouth to reply that, should he actually complete Sister Lore's mission, his only object would be to return to her as swiftly as possible to claim his promised Vellihr's brooch. However, the reply died on his tongue, halted by a previously unacknowledged awareness that it wasn't true. Furthermore, any parting words he might have cast at the old man were staunched by the choking stream of wind-driven sand invading his mouth.

He was woken by his own retching throat and heaving chest, fingers scraping at his tongue in an attempt to clear imaginary sand. Beside him, Sygna grunted in annoyance and jabbed a toe into his calf before turning onto her side. It was her usual reaction to his occasional night terrors and he felt a spasm of gratitude for the sense of normality it engendered. *No oasis*, he told himself as his heart began to calm. *No judgemental old bastard with a plethora of ominous riddles. Only another dream . . .*

He felt it as the slowing of his pulse allowed for fresh sensation, a small circle of heat upon his chest. His hand moved instinctively to the source, fingers closing on the silver knot the old man had given him in Skar Magnol. Felnir had put it on a chain and hung it about his neck, more in reverence to an heirloom of his lost parents than in deference to the Tielwald's instructions. The metal cooled under his touch so swiftly that he wondered if it had been another product of the dream. However, probing the flesh beneath the trinket revealed a patch of warm skin.

Sitting up, he looked at the silver knot resting in the palm of his hand, small and unremarkable save for its craftsmanship. *Just metal*, he told himself, clenching and unclenching a fist around the trinket as his mind returned to that day in Olversahl when the librarian, Elvine's mother, had cast a similar token at the old man's feet. *Never again.*

Throw it away, he thought, clenching his fist once again. *Just a dream*, he countered, but still doubt lingered like an ache. Finally, he released his hold on the knot and lay down beside Sygna, resolving to ask Elvine on the morrow if her mother had ever spoken of the Tielwald.

The first indication of their proximity to the Fire Isles came two days later, during which Felnir had concocted a series of excuses not to pose his question to the scholar. He knew his reluctance stemmed from a basic aversion to hearing uncomfortable truths; in particular the danger that she would confirm his great-grandfather's ability to invade dreams at will. Much better to think of the old man's warning as just a product of his own worries. Felnir told himself it was more necessary to allow Elvine to study the madman's tattoos in peace. Also, it would be best not to interrupt her seemingly endless conversations with Colvyn, for it was important she have at least one friend in this crew. The lad had clearly heeded Felnir's warnings regarding amorous interest in the scholar. He remained affable instead of charming in her presence, and their talk consisted of mostly historical discussion or language lessons as she sought to improve her Ishtan. However, from the tendency for the scholar's gaze to linger on the lad when he wasn't looking, Felnir wondered if an apparent lack of romantic sentiment on his part might not be mirrored in her.

"But the Blackheart was the worst tyrant in Albermaine-ish history," he heard Elvine insist that evening. She and Colvyn stood at the prow, as had become their habit throughout the voyage. With his labours done and more scribbled pages and drawings added to her collection, the two would gather close by whilst Felnir took his ritual survey of the sea.

"There we must disagree," Colvyn replied. "For even a cursory perusal of the history of a realm rich in terrible rulers would reveal Evadine Courlain as one of the milder examples of tyranny."

"She killed her own father," Elvine scoffed. "And many others besides. Her reign may have been brief, but she spilled more blood in the space of months than many a monarch managed over the course of decades."

"King Jardin the First, better known as Jardin the Mad, decreed all the menfolk of Dulsian gelded, and that was after he had murdered not only his mother, but all his siblings and their many children too. Fortunately, his youngest son contrived to poison him before his grand scheme of castration could be carried out. That murderous son went on to assassinate his elder brothers before taking the throne as Jardin the Second. Curiously, he then ruled as a wise and benevolent monarch for the next twenty-six years. Cruelty doesn't always lead to despotism."

"But the Blackheart wasn't always cruel," Felnir said, drawing a surprised gaze from both. Until now, he hadn't made any contribution to these discussions. "So the tale is told, at least as I heard it. She was fierce, to be sure, but also kind and generous with both wealth and succour. Her soldiers certainly loved her and showed no hesitation in dying at her command."

"You were at Olversahl, were you not?" Elvine asked. "Did you see her there?"

"Sadly no." Felnir huffed a small laugh. "My great-grandfather did, though it cost him an eye. Came damn near to ending her, too. If her captain hadn't saved her that night, history would have taken a very different course."

"Her captain had a hand in it," Colvyn said. "But it was her scribe who saved her."

"Ah, yes," Elvine said, face brightening. "The infamous scribe. I found some of his work in Sister Lore's archive recently. Vile intriguer he may have been, but he had an elegant turn of phrase, not to mention one of the finest hands I've encountered. Whatever became of him, do you know?"

Colvyn shrugged. "No one does for certain. Some say he was slain at Castle Ambris, though he is recorded as attending the wedding of the Cordwain duke and duchess weeks later. After that, he slips from the pages of history."

"I'll find him," Elvine stated. "Once this . . . diversion is over, I intend to make him my special subject of study."

Colvyn raised an eyebrow, slipping into his courtly Ishtan to quote a proverb commonly spoken amongst the Saluhtan's army: "Before you let fly an arrow, be sure of your target. For it can't be drawn back."

"What—" Elvine began, only to be interrupted by a sudden, thunderous roar from the western horizon.

Peering at the sky beyond the prow, Felnir saw a pale flare amidst the reddish evening hue. It faded quickly, the rumbling disturbance to the air dissipating a few seconds later. "The Fire Isles are never quiet," Felnir said, angling a meaningful glance at Elvine. "We'll reach them soon. I suggest you put all thought of tyrants and scribes from your head and find me a course to sail that won't see this ship scorched to cinders."

Under Elvine's direction, the next two nights were spent keeping the *Sea Hawk* aimed at the lowest point in the constellation once known as Trieya's Quill. During the day, the ship slowed to a crawl to ensure they didn't lose the heading. Inevitably, as more thunderous outbursts rose from the increasingly dark western sky, the mood of the crew turned sombre. Even Guthnyr, whose ability to instil good humour Felnir valued almost as much as his sword skill, became noticeably taciturn the closer they drew to their destination.

"Think of the treasure," Felnir told him, nodding to the sack containing his brother's accumulated loot. "It'll make this seem a paltry collection of worthless scrap."

Guthnyr forced a weak smile and returned to dabbing paint to the face of his shield. "For now," he muttered, "I think I'd settle for a breath of air that doesn't stink like privy on a hot day."

Befouled air was one of the lesser but well-known hazards of sailing this close to the Fire Isles. At present it was just a taint to the wind, but Felnir had heard many tales of sailors choking their last amidst a poisonous miasma even before they caught sight of the fiery sprawl of islets.

Although their trepidation became increasingly apparent, Felnir took satisfaction, even a little pride, in his *menda's* lack of overt grumbling. A mercenary's life had taught him the folly of dismissing the gripes of warriors compelled to a hard life. When routine complaints shifted into constancy, they could, if not addressed, blossom into bloody mutiny. For now, they confined their worries to frowning stares at the approaching swathe of darkened sky and kept any misgivings behind their teeth.

"This lot would follow you to the heart of Lohkvar's forge," Sygna said during their third night sailing towards the point of Trieya's Quill. "Fret not over their loyalty, my love. Worry more for the scholar's judgement."

As ever, her ability to read his thoughts brought a smile to his lips and he pulled her to him. "You doubt her?" he asked, eyes flicking to where Elvine sat in a pool of lantern light on the otherwise darkened deck. The scholar had one of her drawings spread out on her knees whilst busily scribbling notes on a piece of parchment. "Only in the Saluhtan's palace have I encountered a more learned soul."

"I don't doubt her knowledge," Sygna said. Shifting in Felnir's arms, she stared at the strip of flickering red above the horizon. "Nor her heart, for I see in it both truth and kindness. But she is little more than a child and we have never sailed such hazardous waters." Felnir felt her stiffen in hesitation before adding, "All to go in search of mere treasure."

"As commanded by Sister Lore. And you know it's not treasure I seek, but a Vellihr's brooch."

She looked up at him, brows arched in the manner that told him she was tired of being taken for a fool.

"All right." He sighed in surrender, drawing her closer and lowering his voice. "No, we haven't come in search of the Fireraiser's fabled hoard, as you've no doubt reckoned with that ever sharp mind of yours." He paused, unsure of her reaction to his next words, whispering on in response when she jabbed an elbow to his ribs. "The Vaults of the Altvar. That is our mission. That's why we dug a madman out of a Cordwain prison and that's why we're sailing for the Fire Isles."

She stayed silent for a time, but Felnir could read her darkened thoughts in the sag of her shoulders. "A feat sure to put all your sister's deeds to shame," she said. Felnir couldn't help but notice the judgement in her tone, the disappointment.

"This is not about her," he said.

"Isn't it? I see it, Fel, the envy that eats at you. Didn't we hurt her enough?"

"What lies between us has nothing to do with her, and never has. You know that."

"I do. But she doesn't. To her, I am something you stole out of spite. So, if either of us has the right to resent her, it's me. For I am not a prize to be won, but a woman who knows her own heart. Still, it's a hard thing to hurt someone you were raised with, someone you love, even if it's not how they want you to love them."

Felnir thought back to the day he first returned to Skar Magnol. Three years ago now, and the memory remained raw. He arrived with a ship, a *menda*, and a decent stack of treasure piled into an ornate chest he had paid no small sum to have crafted just for this occasion. When he placed it at his great-grandfather's feet, the old man kicked the lid shut and said, "It'll take more than that, boy."

Thera had been absent then. Recently ascended to the role of Vellihr of Justice and sent off on some mission or other by Sister Iron. But Sygna had stood at the Tielwald's side, the skinny girl Felnir recalled from many a childhood misadventure grown into a woman who captured him at the first glance. Their union was immediate and inevitable, though not in his sister's view when she returned some days later. Felnir had known to expect a frosty welcome. When the woman who would later ascend to the mantle of Sister Iron had pronounced sentence of exile upon him, his sister had been at her side, her glower just as full of righteous condemnation as the Vellihr she served. Her recognition of Sygna and Felnir's union turned an awkward moment into a snarling exchange of mutual grievance, one that might have escalated to drawn steel if both Guthnyr and Sygna hadn't intervened to pull them apart.

"I wanted to sail for the southern seas," Sygna reminded him, settling her head against his chest. "Or even further south, into the waters beyond the Cape of Storms. Barely charted lands where a man such as you could find the greatness that is his due, perhaps even a kingdom of his own. But no, you insisted on staying and throwing your lot in with the old man, all in the hope that one day folk will call you by a different name."

She paused, a bitter sigh hissing through her teeth. "When he first took me in after my parents died, I thought the Tielwald both great and good. Many years under his roof taught me differently. I was not given shelter out of kindness, but merely because he thought I might one day prove useful. I had hoped we could both prise our way out from under his shadow, but still you insist on shivering in its chill." Sygna turned in his arms, raising her face to his. "The southern seas, Fel. We still could."

He looked to the western sky, dimming red above the ugly smear of grey black cloud that covered the Fire Isles. The stars of Trieya's Quill were just starting to glimmer as the last light of day faded. It seemed to him that the glittering point forming the quill's tip shone brighter than before, beckoning him on.

"Would you have me break my word?" he asked. "Besides, what manner of Ascarl would I be if I shunned the chance to look upon the Vaults with my own eyes?"

The Fire Isles came fully into view shortly after nightfall. At first glance, it appeared as if eruptions raged constantly along its entire length from south to north. Yet, as the *Sea Hawk* drew closer, Felnir saw dark gaps of calm in the fiery procession. Also, the scale of the fire mountains' anger varied considerably. Some cast flaming gobbets of lava high into the air, their fury marked by thunderous rumblings. Others emitted a more sedate flow that veined their flanks in lambent rivulets, or merely gave forth a flickering glow from their shattered summits. Most, Felnir observed with satisfaction, were quiet. Such insight, however, was largely lost to his crew. He saw naked fear on some and wariness on most. Many were the dire tales of those unwise enough to risk these waters, all rich in lurid detail. Then, of course,

320 • ANTHONY RYAN

there was the foulness of the air. What had been an acrid taint was now a nose-stinging stink that brought tears to the eyes and a scratch to the throat.

"Think we may have found the Altvar's shithouse," Felnir joked. Some consented to grunt out an obligatory laugh, most didn't. Deciding he could test their courage only so far, he ordered the sail lowered and anchor dropped. They were close enough to land now for the iron hook to find purchase on the seabed and the winds were curiously light for the Styrnspeld.

"The isles act as a shield against the gales," Behsla explained. Of all his *menda*, she appeared the least concerned at their proximity to the raging peaks a scant mile off the prow. Still, he saw a good deal of professional caution in the way her eye tracked over the isles. "We should wrap our faces against the stink," she suggested. "Fill some buckets, just in case."

"Fine notions," Felnir told her. "See to it then tell them to get some rest, for tomorrow we sail the coast of the Fire Isles." He leaned closer, lowering his voice. "And make sure they understand the folly of questioning our course. The last chance to turn from this was in Skar Magnol, and I'll hold any warrior's life forfeit if they forsake their oath now."

CHAPTER TWENTY-SIX

Ruhlin

Aleida's needle was six inches long with a slightly splayed point resembling a spearhead. She wielded it with a deft touch, dabbing it into the pot of scarlet ink before applying it to his skin with swift efficiency. Even so, Ruhlin felt that such skill did little to quell the pain it caused. She had arrived at his cage shortly after he awoke, bearing a tray of needles, bowls and pots of pigment, her features carefully blank and tongue stilled. With the other prisoners training in the circle under Radylf's eye, Achela was the only witness to her labour. Despite this, Aleida remained silent throughout the hours it took her to inscribe the outlines onto his skin that would form the basis for a more fulsome and elaborate design.

He lay on his bunk as she did her work, making occasional and, so far, fruitless attempts at conversation to distract from the pain. "Is there a meaning to this?" Ruhlin asked. The shape described by the red lines throbbing across his chest and shoulders was difficult to discern.

At first it seemed she wouldn't respond, face set in concentration as her needle jabbed its painful way to the *stagna*. Then, reclining a little to wipe a cloth to the implement, she muttered, "It's Amundyr's saga rendered in sigil form. This—" she tapped a finger to the vaguely triangular shape on his upper arm "—is the sign of the goddess Ihryka, his mother, or it will be when I'm done." Aleida fell silent, darting a glance at the shadows beyond the cage, a crease appearing in her brow. "Keep quiet. This is best done in silence."

"Your father threatened punishment if you speak to me, didn't he?"

The line in Aleida's brow deepened and she lowered her head, replying in a barely audible whisper. "It wasn't me he threatened. Now lie still and be quiet. Please."

Straightening, she switched to a smaller needle, dipping it into a pot holding a darker shade of red. Quelling a shudder at the pinpoint flares of discomfort, Ruhlin's gaze strayed to Achela. The Morvek woman sat atop her stool outside the cage, still and watchful as always. However, this time Ruhlin detected an additional keenness in her usually inexpressive features, perhaps even a sense of anticipation. *It wasn't me he threatened.*

He recalled Eldryk's warning after the meeting with the Tuhlvyr, how Achela would unleash the *stagna* for a full turn of the glass should Ruhlin's hand stray towards Aleida. Some foreign sailors used glass devices for measuring time, but they could span a day or an hour. It occurred to him that he had no notion if the witch could maintain her control of the *stagna* for so long. Was her power limitless? If so, it seemed far from likely he would ever be free of this irksome ring of iron. But what if it wasn't? What if he could exhaust her strength in a matter of seconds? The prospect was too tantalising to ignore, but there was only one way to test it.

Taking a deep breath, he reached out to grasp Aleida's wrist, halting the needle and causing her to glare at him in fright. "I'm sorry," he said before leaning forward to plant a kiss on her lips.

The *stagna's* icy grip froze him in place instantly, the cold spreading from his neck to every extremity in the blink of an eye. Once again, his breath stalled in his lungs, his heart hammering then slowing as it was starved of blood. He lay on the bunk, rigid and unable to even shudder, his vision dimming into vague shadows. Then, just as he felt the cold begin to erode his consciousness, the *stagna's* grip lessened. It wasn't enough to free him, but it did allow him to breathe. He managed to drag a short gasp of air before the cold flared anew. This time the agony was localised, concentrated in his gut where it birthed a series of sharp, lacerating aches that made him wonder if Achela had conjured some creature to gnaw at his guts from the inside. Once again, the flooding chill receded, the pain in his belly dissipating to permit him a brief scream before the *stagna* flared once more, sending a jolt of pure ice through his brain.

The torment continued for what may have been a minute or an hour, Ruhlin's shudders so violent he found himself on the floor. In between bouts of agony, he would dribble and flail about, catching a glimpse of Achela beyond the bars. The Morvek woman was on her feet, face still mostly impassive save for a small curve to her lips and narrowing of the eyes. It was the most expression he had seen in her, telling of a woman who enjoyed her work. Or was it that she felt her niece had been outraged in some way? Ruhlin had no chance to ponder the question before the torture resumed. This time the pain in his head was so acute that he assumed the witch had allowed her cruelty to overcome obedience, for he was surely about to die.

"*Tek pahr!*"

The release from pain was so sudden Ruhlin convulsed, back arching and limbs spasming. He would have screamed had there been sufficient air in his lungs. Instead, he gasped before subsiding into a series of wracking coughs. Looking up, he found Aleida standing over him, her eyes locked on the *stagna*. He was unable to contain a fearful groan when he felt the metal grow chill again.

"*Tek pahr*," Aleida repeated with slow, ominous deliberation, turning her unblinking gaze upon the woman outside the cage. Achela's face twitched as the two of them stared at one another. Ruhlin couldn't tell if the witch's reaction was one of fear or anger. Finally, she blinked, cast a hard glare at Ruhlin, then returned to her stool to resume her watchful and blank-faced vigil.

"Get up," Aleida hissed, stooping to take hold of Ruhlin's arms. She shot anxious looks towards the circle as she helped him back to the bunk. Fortunately, Radylf had either failed to notice the disturbance or felt it unworthy of investigation.

"Here." Aleida put a cup of water to Ruhlin's lips, the feel of it in his mouth and throat a wondrous contrast to his fading pains.

Despite his failure to exhaust Achela's powers, he still felt a surge of triumph; valuable knowledge had been gained this day.

"You . . ." he breathed, catching hold of Aleida's wrist once again. "You can do . . . what she does. Can't you?"

She winced and gently pulled his hand away, setting the cup aside to reach once again for her needle. "I must get this done . . ."

"Can't you?" Ruhlin insisted in a fierce, demanding whisper. "You can control the *stagna* too."

Aleida didn't reply, but he saw the answer plainly in her guarded features and constricting throat. Ruhlin settled back, allowing the residual shudders to diminish before gesturing to his shoulder. She resumed her work with the same efficient fluency. Ruhlin was impressed that she didn't allow her hand to shake despite the fear he saw in her eyes, the sight of it leading him to an important realisation.

"Your father doesn't know," he murmured.

The needle paused, her head moving in a barely noticeable shake before she resumed her work.

"If he did, you would be a slave too. Would you not?"

She shifted, ostensibly to peer more closely at the needle's track whilst coming close enough to whisper a response. "I'm already as much a slave as you are, except I have been chained from birth."

"Do you want to break those chains?"

"How?"

"I have learned that your father intends to take me from this place soon, for the Meidvang. You know this?"

She gave a fractional nod.

"Will you be coming with us?"

"Sometimes he takes me along. Sometimes he does not."

"This time he must." He stared hard into her eyes. "Beg if you have to."

Aleida took a long, slow breath. "If we were to be caught . . ." She swallowed again, a tear appearing in the corner of her eye.

"I will not live as a dog to others," Ruhlin told her. "Nor should you. And, if you can get this thing off me, there is none strong enough to stand against me. I've no love for killing, but I'll rend my way through a thousand guards to break our chains."

A smile ghosted over her lips before she wiped at her eyes and returned to her task. "You may have to."

It required another two weeks for Aleida to complete her task, during which time she sternly refused to converse. Achela remained as impassively watchful as ever, though he noted a stiffening of her shoulders whenever Aleida appeared with her tray of implements. Ruhlin worried constantly that the witch would betray Aleida's secret to Eldryk, but the daily routine of discomfort passed without further incident. *The Morvek don't make trouble for their own kin*, he remembered, and could only hope the woman's attachment to familial custom overcame any desire for increased favour or reward.

It was on the day that Aleida jabbed the last drop of pigment into his skin that Radylf and a dozen strong contingent of guards appeared, manacles in hand, and began to empty the cages. "The Meidvang awaits!" the whip-man announced with cheerful volume. "Your chance to reflect well on my expert tutelage. If you don't—" he shrugged his massive shoulders "—well, at least you'll no longer be a drain on the Aerling's purse. Right," he snapped at the guards, "let's get them out. Nice and careful, one at a time."

Not all the prisoners were chosen for this dubious honour, though Ruhlin heaved a sigh of relief at seeing Tuhlan and Julette amongst the line of manacled captives. Sygurn was there too, his scarlet-inked features sagging in shameful misery. Each of them had been given clothing to wear, dun-coloured jerkins and trews and shoes of soft fur, useful in warding off cold, but not much else. After donning his own garb, Ruhlin was spared the chains upon release from his cage, Radylf apparently seeing the *stagna* as sufficient insurance against disobedience or escape.

"Aleida's done herself proud indeed," the whip-man commented, casting an appreciative eye over the tattoos covering Ruhlin's upper chest and shoulders. They were still raw and puckered in places, making Ruhlin flinch when Radylf poked his whip handle at the pictogram on his right shoulder. It was one of the few designs he could see in full, depicting a burning hall beneath a starlit sky, the climax to the legend of Amundyr.

"There are those," Radylf mused, "who claim Amundyr was simply a drunken arsonist with a grudge to settle. And that he possessed no more fire blood than a common goat, his fame and glory merely the outcome of finding himself on the victorious side in an ugly feud." Ruhlin saw a mischievous glint in the giant's eye as he stepped back, a grin on his lips. "But that is a dangerous calumny to speak, for the Vortigurn's agents are harsh in their punishments of heresy."

He turned away, commanding the prisoners' attention with a flick of his wrist, the uncoiling whip cracking the air. "Listen well," he said. "Aerling Eldryk has honoured you all with a place in the Meidvang. The journey to the first gathering will take seven days. During this time you will be clothed, fed and watered only as long as your behaviour warrants it. Trust me when I say that any starved or thirsty soul who enters the *wuhltra* will not last long."

They were led from the cages in single file, spear-bearing guards on both sides. Ruhlin walked at the rear, Achela following as he tried not to scour the surrounding shadows for any sign of Aleida. He was resolved to escape or die in the attempt whether she accompanied this excursion or not. But, in his heart, he knew the only real chance of success lay in her.

They trooped through the shadows into a large, arched tunnel. Like the rest of the dome it had been constructed from *kehlgruin*, Ruhlin marvelling at the absence of bricks in the broad curved roof above. He had heard tales of fabulous cities of wondrous construction beyond the southern seas, where vast palaces and temples rose as high as mountains. Yet they had all been built of marble, at least according to Irhkyn and the braggarts in the mead hall. How tall could a tower stand if it were fashioned from stuff such as this?

After a hundred paces or so the tunnel ended at a huge steel-buttressed gate of thick timbers. It swung open as the party approached, Ruhlin expecting to see the sprawl of mountains once again. Instead, he was greeted with the dreary sight of a partially fog-covered yard.

Four wagons awaited them, teams of oxen snorting and lowing in the tethers. One of the wagons consisted of an ornately decorated roofed box, the swirling designs carved into its sides gilded in gold. The ostentatiously carved door remained sealed as Radylf led them into the yard, although Ruhlin had little difficulty in guessing the occupant. The other three wagons were starkly different in appearance, each one a wheeled cage open to the elements.

Watching Radylf allocate prisoners to each wagon, Ruhlin was dispirited but not surprised to see Julette and Tuhlan placed in separate cages. When Ruhlin's turn came, he was led to the third cage, finding it easy to read the thought behind the giant's knowing smile: *No more plotting for you, laddie.* Yet Ruhlin found a crumb of comfort at seeing Sygurn chained at his side. He assumed Radylf found it amusing to place them together given their obvious animosity, yet Ruhlin saw only opportunity. *Fear has no purchase on the soul of a man eager for his own death.*

They were joined in the wagon by three Morvek – two men and a woman Ruhlin had faced in training but never conversed with. They exhibited no inclination to do so now, huddling with their eyes averted and faces stony with studied indifference. Whether they were simply cowed, or detested those not of their kind, Ruhlin had no way of knowing.

When the wagons jerked into motion, he settled his attention on the ornate carriage at the head of the caravan. *Is she in there?* he wondered, trying not to let the hope show on his face. *Or has her father proven deaf to her pleading?*

The clomp of hooves drew his notice to the rear of the wagon, seeing Radylf and Achela mounted on horses with a score of guards riding behind. Achela was clearly an experienced horsewoman, staying firmly in the saddle despite the fact that her gaze remained fixed upon the *stagna*.

"Still dreaming of escape, then?"

He turned to find Sygurn regarding him with a mocking grin.

"Whilst you dream only of your own demise," Ruhlin returned. "Was your disgrace so terrible?"

328 · ANTHONY RYAN

The Nihlvarian's grin turned to a scowl. "Have no concern for me, boy. Worry more over your own torment when this scheme of yours fails. Even if it didn't, where would you go? Nihlvar is vast and all doors will be closed to you, all hands raised against you."

"Perhaps not if I had a guide."

"You're a persistent fecker, I'll give you that." Sygurn shook his head, pulling a fox fur blanket over his shoulders and shifting into a more comfortable position. "You know they won't kill you when this all goes to dung, right? Your precious blood preserves you. It's your savage friends who'll suffer and die. And be sure they'll make you watch."

Ruhlin hunched lower in the wagon, casting a cautious eye at the three Morvek and seeing only the same rigid indifference.

"They couldn't give a weasel's arse for your schemes," Sygurn said. "Wild Morvek to the core, these three. Sullies their spirit to even talk with us." He leaned towards the silent trio, voice raised. "Doesn't it, y'feckers? No place in the clan for you now, is there?"

Ruhlin saw the Morvek woman's mouth tighten in response, but otherwise she and her companions gave no indication they had heard the Nihlvarian's words.

"So, don't worry over them betraying you," Sygurn added, reclining into his furs. "But don't expect any help either. Nor from me."

Ruhlin remained silent for a time, knowing Radylf would be watching. He spent an hour or more peering at the befogged landscape beyond the cage. What little he could see of it confirmed the fact that they travelled along a narrow, steep-walled track. He waited until the fog dimmed with the onset of evening, then leaned closer to Sygurn, not looking at him and speaking in a low murmur.

"What if I told you I had a way?" he said. "That when the time comes, the *stagna* won't be a problem."

Sygurn emitted a tiny huff of air, his reply a weary sigh. "Then I'd curse you as the worst of liars."

"I speak no lie."

The Nihlvarian shifted, Ruhlin risking a glance to see him casting a wary eye in Achela's direction. "As long as that witch draws breath, that thing is never coming off." He pushed his manacled wrists forward, tapping a finger to a livid mark on the back of his left hand. "Raised to the forge, I was. This is what happens when a boy ventures too close to those glowing bars of steel. My father was the finest metal worker in northern Nihlvar. But even he could tell you nothing of how the Morvek can twist it to their will, and believe me, he tried to learn. Unless you know how, boy, forget all your nonsense dreams and seek a quick death, as I intend to."

Ruhlin hesitated, reluctant to admit that he had no clear plan for exactly how he would compel Aleida to contest her aunt's control of the *stagna*. There was clearly little closeness between them, but how far would the Aerling's daughter go when the time came? And would Achela's reaction to her niece's defiance be so meek next time?

"We must await our chance," he told Sygurn. "But know that I speak truth. When the time comes, the witch will be no obstacle."

Sygurn regarded him in silence for a time, face unreadable. Finally, he turned onto his side, pulling his furs over his head and muttering, "You're full of shit, Teilvik. Leave me be."

Life in the wagons soon took on a grim monotony of uneventful travel interspersed with daily interludes when they were ordered from their cages for food, exercise and voiding of bowels and bladder. The fog cleared after the first day, allowing Ruhlin a clearer view of their surroundings. It proved an unwelcome sight. The cliffs rising on both sides of the road dipped in places, but still presented an unassailable barrier even if he and the others could find a way to break their chains.

It was during the first break that he saw the door to the ornate box wagon open and, with a rush of relief, watched Aleida emerge at her father's back. She afforded him no notice at all, standing apart with her head lowered whilst Eldryk conversed with Radylf. Ruhlin chose to interpret this as an attempt not to arouse the Aerling's suspicions, but still her reticence during those last few days in the cage troubled him. After all, she had never actually agreed to aid him.

"Eyes down, y'fecking idiot," Sygurn instructed in a whisper. "Gawp at her too much and they'll know something's amiss."

Ruhlin duly lowered his head. They crouched with their fellow prisoners along the side of the road, eating the bowls of meat and turnip stew handed out by the guards. "I thought I was full of shit," he murmured back, drawing a scowl from the Nihlvarian, but not so fierce as before.

"She's your key, isn't she?" he asked, flicking his eyes at Aleida. "That's how you're going to do it."

Ruhlin said nothing. Until now, he had little alternative but to trust this one. But, unlike himself, Tuhlan and Julette, Sygurn was born of this realm. Disgraced and enslaved he may be, but what was to stop him buying his freedom with betrayal?

"*Now* you're worried?" Sygurn scoffed, reading the doubt on Ruhlin's face. "Too late for that, boy. You already told me too much. Besides, if I was going to sell you, I'd've done it before now. Not that it would've earned any release for one such as me. The best I could bargain for is a quick death. My people do not forgive."

"Trust buys trust," Ruhlin said, facing him. "You want truth from me, I'll have it from you first. Why are you here? What deed put those chains on your wrists?"

Sygurn dropped his gaze, the red lines on his face tightening and jaw clenching. For a time Ruhlin wondered if he was going to provide any answer, even a harsh, obscenity-laden refusal. However, when he finally spoke, it was with a grim tone, but free of anger. "In a land where there are few laws save the word of the Vortigurn, I committed the worst of sins."

"And what is that?"

A distance crept into Sygurn's eyes, his reply a terse mutter: "Weakness, boy." His tone made it plain no more information would be forthcoming on this subject. "Trust me or don't. Your choice." He returned to his meal, content to let the silence stretch until Ruhlin broke it.

"I need to know more about where we're going," he said. "About the Meidvang."

Sygurn didn't reply until he had wolfed down the remainder of his stew. "Lyhs Skarta is the largest town south of the Vyrnkrals," he said. "With an ancient *wuhltra* dating back to the Founding Age. Seems likely that's where we're headed."

"*Wuhltra?*"

"The circle where those chosen for the Meidvang fight in the Altvar's honour. And it's everything you imagine it to be, and more." He jerked his chin in Eldryk's direction. "Those who practise the same trade as him will bring their own slaves to fight us. There's a lot of beseeching the Altvar with offerings and such before things get started. Apparently that's how it all began, the bravest warriors called to do combat in honour of the gods. After a while, the Vortigurn decided that having your best fighters kill each other on the regular was a bad notion. Better to use captives, since the Altvar are supposedly satisfied by blood spilled in battle and they don't much care about the worth of those that spill it. But it's the wagering that matters, boy. That's the real value of the Meidvang. You can be sure the Aerling over there will have a big chest of gold in that wagon ready to be wagered on our success, and an empty one for his winnings. Some towns live off nothing but the coin brought in by four Meidvang a year, one for each season."

"Lyhs Skarta is a large town?"

The Nihlvarian shook his head. "Around here it is, but it's a tiddler compared to the ports to the south. Not a place a clutch of escaped slaves could lose themselves in, if that's what you're thinking."

In fact, Ruhlin had been more interested in Sygurn's mention of ports. Ports meant ships. "The south," he said. "We'll be taken there too?"

"In time." Sygurn let out a wry laugh. "Those of us that live long enough." His humour evaporated quickly and he leaned a little closer, fixing Ruhlin with an intent gaze. "All right, boy, here's our bargain. I'll aid you and those other two to break these chains, and you do the same for me. But mark this well, our chance won't come for a long time. As you've already reckoned, I'm sure, there's no point even trying until we get to a port and there'll be Vysestra knows how many

332 · ANTHONY RYAN

Meidvang ahead of us before that day comes. To seize that chance, you'll have to be alive, which means you'll have to kill. That precious blood of yours will have to burn. If you can't let it, we're already done." He leaned closer still, eyes locked on Ruhlin's, and hissed through clenched teeth, "Let it burn!"

Chapter Twenty-Seven

Thera

For all the dangers they had shared over the years, and the victories won together, Thera found it curious that she had never experienced more pride in her *menda* than during the *Great Wolf*'s flight from Iselda's Nail. They heaved their oars at fast stroke for nigh an hour, and this despite the strain of recent battle. Though they grimaced and cursed at the unending toil, not a face showed the smallest tic of fear or despair. Repeated glances to port and starboard afforded her the reassuring sight of the *Swift Spear* and *Wind Sword* keeping pace to either side. Less gratifying were Gelmyr's reports from the stern.

"They split their fleet," he said, crouching beside Thera as she worked her oar. "There's a dozen ships on our tail, the rest keep to an eastward course. Those chasing us are all one-masted and narrow of hull, most likely their fastest."

"They're closing?" Thera grunted, dragging her oar through the sea. The ceaseless chop of the Styrnspeld made an already arduous task truly exhausting.

Gelmyr replied with a grave nod. "Slowly. But if we keep at it, we should still have a good lead on them by nightfall. With the weather this poor, we can lose them in the dark if we turn west rather than east."

Thera squinted at him. "West?"

"They will expect us to head for home. A westward heading offers the best chance to slip the snare. We'll circle around to the south, head for the Aiken Geld."

Thera's heart lurched with a fresh wave of frustration, but once again she found she couldn't argue with Gelmyr's judgement. She spent the better part of the next hour calling out exhortations to the crew as they continued to fight the increasingly irksome swell. A small measure of good fortune came in the burgeoning wind. The sail bloomed full and the *Great Wolf*'s speed increased, although of course the wind also aided their pursuers. Eventually, with the first darkening of the sky, the waves became so tall as to render rowing a pointless task. Thera ordered the oars shipped, the groan of relief from the surrounding warriors audible even above the stiff gale.

Forcing a steady, unhurried gait into her aching legs, she made her way aft to view the pursuing ships. Through curtains of rain, she picked out only five red sails, but knew there were more. Like her, their captains had forsaken their oars and Thera took a mote of comfort from the fact that the *Great Wolf* possessed a larger sail. Not for the first time in her career, all now depended on the skill of her *Johten Apt*.

Pairs of warriors were given charge of each of the sail's four principal ropes, tightening or loosening the lines in accordance with the instructions Gelmyr called out from the tiller. His keen eye for the best angle to meet a wave and instinctive feel for the wind ensured steady progress through ever steeper seas. Thera could do little but shout encouragement to those working the ropes, in between casting worried glances at their pursuers. Due to the rain, they were reduced to just faint smudges of red that stubbornly refused to fade from view. As the storm worsened, she began to berate herself for not turning to face their foe. A headlong charge by the *Great Wolf* and *Wind Sword* might have confused their formation sufficiently for the *Swift Spear* to make it through. A worthy and necessary sacrifice to ensure warning reached the Sister Queens, though the risks would have been great. In any case, it was now a hopeless prospect amidst such a tempest.

A shout drew her attention to the prow, seeing the lookout waving his arms. His ongoing cries were stolen by the wind, but the reason for his alarm became dreadfully clear when Thera shifted her gaze to the sea. The wave was over twenty feet high, broader than ten ships set end to end. Water ascended into a white flecked cliff as it swept towards the three struggling vessels in its path. Thera lost her footing as Gelmyr hauled hard on the tiller. She watched several warriors tumble towards the port rail, seeing Ragnalt catch hold of Eshilde's arm before the pitching deck could cast her over the side.

Stumbling forward, she was relieved to find Lynnea huddled into a nook between two barrels. "Hold fast!" Thera said, leaping to the apprentice's side, clamping one hand to her forearm and the other to an iron stanchion in a deck beam. Lynnea offered her a weak, wavering smile, rain-lashed features paler than ever. Mohlnir's head poked out from the folds of her shawl to voice a peeved mewl. Snaryk was more vocal. The great hound had wedged his bulk under the deck boards, head raised to howl his objection to the storm.

Feeling the deck tilt, Thera risked a final glance at the prow. She had seen impressive waves before, but nothing to compare to this monster. Timbers groaned and ropes flailed as the ship met the wall of water, Thera sending silent thanks to Gelmyr. It was surely his hand on the tiller that kept the *Great Wolf*'s bows pointed into the wave else she would have keeled over. Thera shook brine from her eyes as she felt the ship settle, her deck momentarily levelling as she crested the great mass of water. Just for a heartbeat, the view beyond the prow showed only a sky of darkened clouds above a misted ocean. Then the *Great Wolf* dipped her bow to descend the far side of the wave in a rush, meeting the sea in an explosion of spume that threatened to flood the deck.

Thera met Lynnea's gaze, offering her a grin of reassurance before unclasping her hand. "Buckets!" she called out, clambering back onto the deck boards. "Get baling before Ulfmaer claims this ship for his own!"

Whilst the crew got to work heaving water over the side, she went to the stern, searching the storm's fury for the *Swift Spear* and *Wind Sword*. She found the larger ship first, heaving high and low to starboard. Her sail was partly detached from her mast, but she seemed otherwise undamaged. Finding the *Swift Spear* took longer, and when she did it was with a plummeting heart.

Gynheld's ship wallowed in the swell a hundred paces directly astern of the *Great Wolf*. Her mast dipped at a shallow angle to the sea, her deck partially swamped and slipping ever lower in the water. Thera thought she saw figures scrambling over her hull as she began to roll over, but couldn't be sure. In any case, they were too far off and the storm too fierce to offer any help. She refused to look away as the *Swift Spear*, perhaps the most fleet vessel ever to be born from an Ascarlian yard, turned fully over, exposing her keel. Thera was spared the sight of her final moments, the tempest carrying her off in a chaos of rain-thick gusts and heaving waves.

As was the nature of the Styrnspeld, the storm calmed with jarring swiftness. By nightfall, the *Great Wolf* and *Wind Sword* sailed placid waters beneath a mostly cloudless sky. A vast array of stars and full moon made for a glorious view that would normally have provoked murmured thanks to the Altvar, but not so now. The loss of the *Swift Spear* darkened the mood of all, but the sight of wakes below the southern horizon turned it black.

"Bastards," Ragnalt growled, gripping the aft rail with white-knuckled fists. "Witchcraft, it has to be. How else could they track us in a storm?"

In Thera's experience, blind chance always had more of a hand in events at sea than any arcane design. However, she had to admit their failure to shake these Nihlvarians was both irksome and suspicious.

"I reckon they lost a few of their own," Gelmyr offered by way of consolation. After squinting at the procession of wakes, he added, "Down to eight, maybe nine."

Odds still too long, Thera decided. Losing the *Swift Spear* made her nascent plan to turn and face their enemies redundant in any case. Neither the *Great Wolf* nor the *Wind Sword* had the speed to slip through this cordon, nor did they possess the strength to contest them in battle. Also, Gelmyr's hopes of tacking west before turning south were no longer viable since their foes would surely spot the course change on a becalmed and moonlit sea.

"If you have any other heading besides north to offer," she said to the *Johten Apt*, "I would hear it now."

His fingers teased his beard as he subsided into contemplation, brow furrowed and eyes hooded with reluctance. "I do not," he said finally. "We're perhaps two days from the most southerly reach of the ice. Not waters I'd ever willingly sail, but the deeper we go, the more of a maze it becomes. With luck, they won't be able to track us for long."

"Bergs that can rip a hull to splinters," Ragnalt warned with a grimace. "Not to mention it's home waters for white whales, and they don't like visitors."

Thera couldn't gainsay his words, although, in this moment, the prospect of placing themselves at even greater remove from an Ascarlian port worried her more than even the bergs or whales.

"Fight," Eshilde said. "We took one of their ships and lost few hands doing it. I'd match one of ours to six of theirs."

"Even at such odds, we're still far outnumbered," Thera replied. "It would be a glorious end, worthy of many a tale, if any lived to tell it. But they wouldn't. And glory avails the Sister Queens nothing. Our duty is to live and carry warning to Skar Magnol. Nothing else concerns us from here on." She straightened and turned to Gelmyr. "Into the ice it is."

The lack of wind compelled them to take up the oars again. So as not to exhaust an already weary crew, Thera maintained a steady stroke through the night and into the day. The sea remained calm, allowing her to judge the distance to their pursuers with dispiriting ease. Clearly, they were gaining.

One benefit of the placid waters was that they allowed the *Great Wolf* and *Wind Sword* to draw close enough for Thera to exchange shouts with Alvyr. She had Gelmyr steer them to within a dozen yards of the other ship's sweeping oars, waving to get her captain's attention. He came to the rail with a striker in hand.

"For Gynheld!" the Vellihr called to her, casting sparks into the sea.

"For Gynheld!" Thera called back, repeating the ritual with her own striker. More elaborate words would normally have been spoken to mark the passing of a fellow Vellihr, but such things were a luxury now.

"So, it's the ice, is it?" Alvyr went on, his words easily heard thanks to the absence of wind.

338 • ANTHONY RYAN

"There's no other course," Thera replied. "We'll lose them in the bergs."

Even at this distance, she could see the doubt on Alvyr's face as he cast a glance astern. "My *Johten Apt* says they've closed a quarter-mile in less than a day."

"We'll make it. We must."

This brought a frown of agreement to her fellow Vellihr's brow and a grave nod. "One of us must carry the warning," he called, turning his sombre gaze to the south.

"We both will," Thera insisted, a knot of unease forming in her gut. "We'll be at the ice soon."

His reply was spoken rather than shouted, but she still caught it: "Not soon enough, old friend."

He turned back to her, his familiar, affable grin upon his lips as he raised his striker. "Spare a spark or two for me, won't you, Thera?"

"Alvyr!"

But he was already moving, shouting orders to his *menda*. The warriors on the port side raised oars whilst the helmsman hauled the tiller. The *Wind Sword* turned swiftly on the untroubled sea, the rowers on the starboard side bringing her fully about whereupon all oars were lowered and she hauled away at the fast stroke.

"Alvyr!" Thera called again, hurrying aft to watch the *Wind Sword* speed directly towards the line of Nihlvarian ships. The intent of her captain was dreadfully clear, prompting Thera to turn to Gelmyr, the order to change course rising to her lips.

"He's buying us time with his life," the *Johten Apt* said before she could speak. His eyes were hard with the only sign of reproach he had ever shown her. "And the lives of his *menda*. Do not dishonour them."

An angry urge to snarl a reminder of his status died on her tongue, stilled by a sudden welling of shame. *One of us must carry the warning.* Heart hammering, Thera returned to the stern, forcing herself to stand in witness to the last act of Alvyr Kahlsten and his valiant *menda*.

The *Wind Sword* sped for the enemy line, closing the distance in what seemed mere moments. The Nihlvarian vessels were equally quick to respond, bespeaking disciplined and experienced crews. The ships on the edges of the formation veered inwards whilst those in the centre accelerated to meet the attack head on. The distance was too great to make out the full details of what came next. Thera assumed Alvyr ordered ramming speed as the *Wind Sword* closed on the ship in the centre of the line, for the thud and crack of colliding hulls were audible even at this remove. She fancied she heard the shouts of combat too, but that may have been her imagining. More timbers cracked as the Nihlvarian vessels closed in around Alvyr's ship. Thera caught sight of a mast tumbling like a felled tree, but whether it belonged to the *Wind Sword* or an enemy, she couldn't tell. Despite the unevenness of the struggle, it wore on for far longer than Thera expected. She imagined Alvyr in the thick of the fight, exhibiting the terrifying battle rage that had earned him fame.

Great will be the slaughter, she thought as the knot of struggling ships continued to recede into the haze. *Glorious will be the stand of the Silverlock.* Moments later, she saw an orange yellow flare in the centre of the struggle, followed soon after by a blossoming of black smoke. Either the Nihlvarians had set the *Wind Sword* alight or Alvyr had brought flame to his enemies. She would always prefer to think the latter. Soon, the scene dwindled into a thin, twisting black line above the horizon, then disappeared from view. Eshilde sighted the first iceberg an hour later.

"For Alvyr." The iron rod struck a brief scattering of sparks from the striker into the dark waters beyond the prow. Thera had chosen Nerlfeya's sigil to mark Alvyr's passing, acknowledgement of the fiery havoc he had wrought upon their foes. Thanks to the respite his sacrifice had bought, she had the leisure now to voice a fitting plea to the goddess of fire, beseech her to see the Silverlock and his *menda* safely to the Halls of Aevnir. But the words wouldn't come.

Feeling a touch to her arm, she looked up to find Lynnea at her side. Thera had become so accustomed to reading her apprentice's expression that she felt scant surprise when the words slipped into her mind: *He was a good man. And Gynheld was a fierce soul.*

Her hand moved to clasp Thera's, squeezing tight. *They were proud to sail at your side.*

Feeling a tear well in her eye, something that hadn't happened for many a year, Thera turned her gaze to the sea ahead. Bergs rose from the swirling current, silent, blue-white monoliths that seemed to grow taller with each passing mile. The early evening sky had taken on a faint green glow that Thera knew would brighten the further north they sailed. She had seen Nerlfeya's Lantern many times, often taking solace in this most spectral and beauteous of the Altvar's creations. Now, it stirred only sorrow. There would be no more wonders to see for Gynheld and Alvyr, or the warriors who died at their side. Thera reached for the comforting knowledge that such brave souls would surely find easy entry to the Halls, but couldn't grasp it. The sense that her friends were simply gone, vanished from her sight for all her days, brought more shameful wetness to her eyes. *All because they followed me . . .*

A new sound came to her then: a low, distant rumble that shifted into a prolonged, forlorn keening. Thera was quick to recognise it as whale song, but of a different, more ominous pitch than she had heard before. She detected a note of warning in it, a feeling that intensified as it doubled in volume. "More than one," she murmured, eyes busily scanning the sea for any betraying spout or cresting hump. The sense of being observed became acutely potent, banishing her grief with the urgency of required action.

"Everyone up!" Her shout reverberated the length of the ship, though she was obliged to repeat it several times to rouse warriors who had succumbed to much needed sleep. "Ready the oars," Thera went on, striding to the mid-deck. "I want all eyes on the water."

"Stands to reason they'd find us," Gelmyr said when she joined him at the tiller. Not a man given to overt expressions of concern, and never fear, Thera was struck by his widened eyes and the jerky glances he cast to port and starboard. Still, his hands remained steady as he continued to steer a northerly course.

"Doesn't sound much like a greeting," Thera observed when the whale song came again. Sound carried strangely amidst the bergs, echoing from ice cliffs to frustrate easy identification of the source. However, she was certain the unseen singers were closer now.

"You can be sure it's not," Gelmyr said.

"Should we wet the oars?" Thera asked. "Try to get clear."

"We can't outrun them. And, for all we know, they could be ahead of us."

"Thera!" Ragnalt kept his call muted to an urgent hiss, waving to her from the stern. Moving to his side, she followed his pointed finger to see a cluster of five sails rounding a berg to the south. White water flared on the flanks of each ship, indicating oars sweeping at a fast stroke.

"They must have rowed without rest for hours to draw this close," Ragnalt said, shaking his head.

"Only five now," Thera said, sending silent gratitude to Alvyr. "That's something."

Surveying her *menda*, she saw men and women standing with oars in hand, resolve and expectation on each face. Their pursuers were surely tired after such remarkable exertions, but for how long could they expect to keep ahead of them? Gelmyr had advised that they required another day at least before the ice provided the dense cover needed to make an escape. With the cold sapping already weary limbs, she was forced to accept the impossibility of the task.

Moving to her shelter, she retrieved the Dreadaxe, twirling it briefly before addressing the crew. "I'm tired of running. How about you?"

The subsequent mix of roaring approval and growling anticipation was all she could wish for, and would have brought more tears to her eyes if all sound hadn't been abruptly swamped by another chorus of whale song. It was far louder than before, a tide of rumbling anger that seemed to assail the *Great Wolf* from all sides. It thrummed the planking below her feet and stilled the hungry cries of her warriors before fading into a sustained keening.

A spout of vapour, taller than three men, appeared fifty yards from the stern. Thera glimpsed a shape beneath the water, pale as ivory and flecked in grey, before the beast dived from view. Another spout off the left, this time followed shortly after by the sight of a tail breaking the surface. Broader than the *Great Wolf*'s sail, it rose high as her mast before descending, propelling the huge creature below into a charge. The sea bulged about the hill-sized hump of its back as it sped through the water, not towards the *Great Wolf*, but the five ships to the south.

Other spouts appeared, a dozen or more jetting steam into the air as huge tails rose and fell. The whale song merged into a single note that resembled a human shriek, so piercing it forced Thera and her *menda* to clamp their hands to their ears. It ended when the first crunch of sundered timbers sounded from the Nihlvarian ships. Having recognised the danger, they had begun to cluster together for protection. It served them nothing.

Hulls splintered and masts tumbled in a churning froth of slamming tails and huge white bodies heaving from the water to crash down onto the hapless craft. Through the tumult of destruction, Thera could hear screams, cutting the mostly still air in a brief, discordant chorus of terror. Within moments, it was over, the Nihlvarian ships rendered into bobbing wreckage.

Silence reigned aboard the *Great Wolf*, every soul so shocked by the swift totality of the attack that none could even voice a plea to the Altvar. Thera had no doubts as to what would happen next. The famed antipathy of the white whale towards humans was surely all encompassing. Seething with mounting fury at the stark unfairness of facing inevitable destruction at the moment of deliverance, Thera watched another huge tail once again rise and fall. It propelled the creature below towards the *Great Wolf* too fast to have any hope of evasion. As the bulging wake closed, the whale song rose anew and in it Thera recognised the purest note of sheer loathing she had ever heard.

Chapter Twenty-Eight

Elvine

As they drew ever near to the Fire Islands, Elvine noted Wohtin's increasing silence. His Covenant invective and quotations from the Altvar Rendi had been mostly quiescent throughout the voyage, though he had been prone to the occasional outburst. Now, he simply sat and stared wordlessly at the approaching smoke-shrouded peaks whilst she studied the symbols inked onto his back. Like the rest of the crew, he had taken to wearing a strip of cloth over his nose and mouth to guard against the tainted air, concealing his expression. But she discerned a lessening of confusion in the angle of his frown, his gaze even betraying a glimmer or two of true understanding. She hoped for another moment of rationality, or perhaps a full return to sanity, but it didn't come.

"Such stories you could tell me," she sighed as she sketched one of the scenes tattooed across his upper spine. It consisted of an overlapping cluster of weapons: a spear, a sword and a bow. She assumed it to be an allusion to legend. Ascarlian lore was rife with all manner of deadly instruments, supposedly infused with some arcane power or other. However, she couldn't recall any single tale that gave prominence to all three objects.

"Where do you come from, Wohtin?" she continued, knowing there would be no answer. "What is your true name? Who set this down upon your skin? Did you ask for it or was it done against your will?

And, most of all, what for?" She leaned forward, whispering into his ear. "What does it all mean?"

She detected a twitch to his eye that might indicate irritation or discomfort. Either way, she took it as a sign that he could at least understand her intent. "You're in there somewhere," she said, putting a gentle hand to his shoulder and leaning back. "I know it. I just wish you would come out and talk to me more often."

As usual, there was no response beyond a shudder and Elvine returned to her sketch. As she pondered the combined sigils, she searched her copious memory for mention of weaponry. One of the later sections of the Altvar Rendi spoke of an Uhltvar warrior maiden who wielded a bow. Unusually for a text so rich in appellation, the great saga failed to record her name. Wielders of sword and spear abounded in the Rendi, and many a tale besides, leading her to the reluctant conclusion that the meaning of this particular tattoo may well lie outside her knowledge.

"Elvine!" Felnir's strident summons from the prow had her setting her parchment aside and hurrying forward. "What do your studies make of that?" he asked, voice muffled by the scarf covering his face. He pointed at the shore of the islet ahead. It was partly obscured by a drift of yellow-grey smoke, requiring her to blink several times before she picked out the object of interest.

"A tree," she murmured in surprise. This was the first glimpse of any vegetation since they began their survey of the isles, save for the kelp-covered rocks and stunted bushes that proliferated where the shore was free of lava flows. Elvine's optimism that Trieya's Quill would lead them directly to some previously undiscovered passage had been dashed upon her initial up close view of the islands. Every potential channel to the innards of the chain was shrouded in smoke thicker than any fog. Not even the most foolish captain would risk their ship in such waters. They had spent two days ploughing a slow course south, keeping close to the shoreline in the hope of finding a path that would allow further exploration. So far, this tree offered the only point of interest.

It was a solitary thing, rising from a patch of green to reach its leafless branches towards the sky. Elvine's puzzlement at how it could have grown in so harsh a place faded when a gust of wind thinned the smoke to reveal the narrow stream of water cascading down the cliff face beyond. "The silver spring," she whispered.

"What?" Felnir asked, but she was already rushing back to her nook. A few moments rummaging amongst her notes produced the required sheaf of parchment, whereupon she rejoined Felnir at the prow.

"'Beneath a silver spring did Velgard bathe,'" she said, reciting from a translation of runes tattooed near Wohtin's right shoulder, a dense, spiralling knot of words that had taken her hours to decipher. "'And, thus cleansed, rejoiced at the Altvar's revealed wisdom.'"

"Velgard went ashore to have himself a bath," Guthnyr said. "Fascinating." His mask hid his features, but the gruff derision in his tone was unmistakable. Elvine had noticed how the mood of their captain's brother had darkened as this voyage wore on. She assumed he would much rather be hacking people to death somewhere than enduring this stink and tedious searching. It was no mystery to her why Felnir had risen to command his own *menda* and Guthnyr had not.

"The key phrase is 'revealed wisdom,'" she told Felnir, ignoring Guthnyr. "Wisdom had many meanings in ancient Ascarlian. In some instances it relates to knowledge or insight, but in older texts it's sometimes synonymous with direction; a wisely chosen course. I've even seen it used to refer to a sacred pathway."

Felnir's brows tightened as he peered at the shore. To Elvine it seemed unassailable, a jumble of dark, glassy rock pounded continually by white-topped waves. The captain, of course, had a much better eye for such things. "Prepare the boat," he told Guthnyr before turning back to Elvine. "I'd prefer to spare you the trip, but I'll need your skills if we actually find anything."

Elvine was proud of her swift reply, though less so of the thin, bird-like chirp that emerged from her mask. "Of course."

Felnir chose not to overfill the boat, given the viciousness of the waves. Elvine found herself wedged between Guthnyr and Colvyn as they worked the forward oars. Wohtin sat to her rear, flanked by

Kodryn and Falk. Elvine took a morsel of reassurance from the sight of Sygna taking the tiller. She seemed the most sensible soul aboard the *Sea Hawk* and her skill at the helm was obvious even to Elvine's inexperienced eye. Still, as they cast off, her nascent confidence took a blow from Felnir's parting words to Behsla.

"Linger for two days, no more," he told the *Johten Apt*. "And don't send anyone after us."

As they made their way towards shore, Elvine attempted, without success, to quell her alarm at the tendency of the heaving swell to repeatedly slosh seawater into the boat. Curiously, her companions barely seemed to notice. Colvyn and Falk worked the oars whilst Felnir perched himself on the bobbing prow, calmly calling out directions to Sygna.

"There." He pointed at a spot on shore which, to Elvine's eyes, seemed just another patch of surf-assailed stone. Yet, as they drew closer, she saw that the wall of jagged rock was formed into a miniature inlet. It was barely wide enough to accommodate the boat's width and she tensed in expectation of a crunching collision. Fortunately, Sygna's touch proved as deft and skilful as ever, guiding the craft into the notch without even a scrape.

Felnir leaped from the prow when it heaved within a yard of the shore, bow rope in hand. The instant his boots met stone, he drew hard on the rope, hauling the boat closer before the seething sea could bear it away. Guthnyr and the other oarsmen were quick to join him, scrambling ashore to lend their strength to the endeavour. Once the prow had been hauled into contact with the rock, Sygna nudged Elvine into motion, urging her to jump. She did so with a slippery clumsiness that sent her sprawling face down atop a mass of kelp. Any embarrassment was swamped by her overwhelming sense of relief at the feel of firm ground for the first time in weeks. Once Sygna and Wohtin had disembarked, both with considerably more grace than Elvine, the boat was dragged fully from the water. Felnir had them drag it a good distance from the shore to prevent the tide carrying it off.

"Such elegance, esteemed lady," Colvyn said in Ishtan. Grinning, he stooped to offer Elvine a helping hand as she attempted to regain her footing on the bed of seaweed. "Clearly, you must have attended the finest dance schools."

Her reply consisted of two words in coarsely spoken Ascarlian, although she did consent to accept his hand. "I was made for libraries, not boats and ships," she grumbled before checking her satchel to ensure none of the contents had spilled or suffered a soaking during this escapade.

"Let's get on," Felnir said. "The day wanes and it would be best not to linger here come nightfall."

The smoke sweeping down the steep flanks of the mountain that dominated this island had thickened since their first sighting of the tree. Consequently, finding it proved a more prolonged business than expected. Sygna's keen eyes finally picked it out amongst the drifting, acrid haze. Up close, Elvine found the tree's height impressive, though its trunk was covered in greyish, flaking bark. She assumed it must have sprouted leaves at some point, otherwise it would never have grown so tall, but couldn't fathom how in such conditions.

"There must be seasons," Colvyn said, once again displaying his uncanny facility for tracking her thoughts. "Even here. Periods when the smoke thins and the sun shines, just often enough to keep this old fellow going."

"How do you know it's old?" Guthnyr asked.

"The thickness of the trunk and number of branches. I'd wager he's near fifty, or older." Colvyn reached out to run a hand over the tree's skin, then stopped when the bark turned to powder at his first touch. "Fragile though."

A quick inspection of the tree revealed nothing of interest, save the wonder of its survival. At Felnir's insistence, they moved on to the narrow waterfall. Unlike the tree, it was easily found thanks to the continual splash of its cascade into a pool at the base of the cliff. Peering upwards at the source of the stream, Elvine saw that it emerged not from the crest of the stone edifice, but from a fissure in its surface some thirty feet above.

"The Silver Spring, indeed," she said. "It's well named."

"Well named or not," Felnir said, "does it tell us anything?"

Elvine was about to voice a waspish reminder that their investigations had barely begun, but Falk interrupted her. "Might this be something, my lord?" He stood on the inner side of the waterfall's arc, partly concealed beneath a shadowed overhang. Coming to his side, Elvine found him playing a hand over a flat expanse of stone. It was weathered and scarred by many years' worth of trickled moisture, but its clear rectangular shape and relative smoothness made it plain this had been crafted by human hands. Scouring its surface, Elvine could find no markings save for a circular indentation in its centre.

"Do your researches make any mention of this?" Felnir asked.

Elvine responded with a vague shake of her head, still intent on her examination. Her fingers played over every inch of the rectangle, hoping to detect some runic inscription worn by the ages into near invisibility. But she found nothing.

"Whoever carved this," she said, stepping back, "didn't feel obliged to let others know what it is." Looking to Wohtin, her surety of this thing's significance was buttressed by the sudden focus of his gaze. He stared at the shape in the stone with unblinking and tense fascination. She wondered if he was about to exhibit another moment of sanity, but his stare was too intense to be rational and the fresh tremble of his limbs told of distress rather than comprehension.

"What is this thing?" she asked him, voice gentle as she clasped his hand. "Can you tell us?"

His eyes flicked towards her, then back to the stone, no answer coming from his lips. She felt his shudders intensify; it seemed their discovery was as frightening to him as it was captivating.

"Isn't it obvious?" Guthnyr said. Striding forward, he drew a dagger from his belt and jabbed the point into the seam between the rectangle and the surrounding rock. Elvine had judged it too narrow to allow passage of a tool, but the warrior's blade sank in all the way to the hilt with only slight resistance. "It's a door," he grunted, drawing the dagger free to flick away a covering of mingled moss and dirt. Sparing Elvine a wink, he applied the weapon again. "Bit of work and we'll have this free in no time."

A good deal of scraping was required before the door consented to yield to the combined shoves delivered by Guthnyr and Falk. Several more succeeded in creating a recess a few inches deep, whereupon it refused to budge further.

"Shift, you stubborn fucker!" Guthnyr growled, delivering a hefty kick to the door.

"Leave it, brother," Felnir told him. Stepping clear of the overhang, he cast a wary eye towards the sky. It was still obscured by the smoke, but the dimming light made it plain that dusk was fast approaching. "This is a good find. We'll return to the *Sea Hawk*, come back with hammers and chisels in the morning."

"Awful cautious fellow, the Fireraiser," Guthnyr said, leaning a hand to the door. "Going to such lengths to hide his treasure. You'd think it'd be easier to just dig a hole somewhere." The narrow, knowing gaze he turned on his brother made Elvine conclude she had underestimated this one's insight by a considerable margin.

"Tomorrow, Guth," Felnir said, starting towards the shore. "When we've fetched the hammers."

Guthnyr shifted his gaze to Elvine, brows raised in enquiry. She looked away, swallowing a cough. "He's right. We need daylight, and better tools . . ."

Her words trailed off when a soft grinding noise came from the door. The marginal weight of Guthnyr's hand had apparently succeeded in overcoming its last crumb of resistance. He let out a surprised curse as the slab collapsed inwards, toppling from view to disappear into a black void. The thud and scrape of stone on stone sounded briefly, followed by an echoing boom that slowly faded into silence.

They all stared at the revealed opening in speechless surprise, save for Wohtin, who let out a short, painful sob. Pulling his hand from Elvine's grip, he started forward on unsteady legs, intent on stumbling headlong into the black portal.

"Wohtin!" Colvyn said, stepping into his path. The madman regarded his former cellmate with a stark lack of recognition before casting an equally baffled glare at the rest of the party. To Elvine, he looked very much like a soul woken from an unpleasant dream.

She saw a flurry of questions behind his darting eyes, but then an abrupt, sorrowful frown of understanding before he lowered his face.

"Let's light some torches first, eh?" Colvyn said, patting Wohtin's shoulders and receiving a jerky nod in response.

"I get the impression," Guthnyr said, moving to peer closely at Wohtin's downcast face, "this mad bugger's been here before."

"Leave him be," Colvyn stated in a tone that had Guthnyr straightening, eyes narrowing in pleasant anticipation.

"Enough," Felnir said, jerking his head at his brother to step back. "Whatever he knows, it's clear he's not telling. Falk, fetch the torches from the boat."

Felnir was first through the door, something none of the others felt compelled to argue over. Elvine concluded that it was customary for the leader of a *menda* to accept the greatest risks, or at least it was in this one. The torch he held illuminated a narrow, descending passage, the wavering light playing over an arched ceiling of stone blocks. It was wide enough for only one of them to enter at a time. Guthnyr and Falk followed Felnir into the gloom, footfalls echoing long and loud. Sygna waited until the three of them had safely descended several steps before gesturing for Elvine to follow. Colvyn insisted on going ahead of her whilst she once again took Wohtin's hand and led him into the shadow. A backward glance revealed Sygna and Kodryn bringing up the rear.

"This is fine masonry," Elvine commented, running a hand over the wall. Each stone appeared to be of the same dimensions and had been set together without benefit of mortar. The surface became dry to the touch as they descended the stone steps, her fingers tracing through a thin covering of dust. "Old too."

The tunnel was steep but mercifully brief. The dislodged door was wedged into the base of an opening, obliging Felnir to step over it, his torch disappearing from view. Elvine heard his footsteps come to an abrupt halt followed by a soft exclamation: "Ulthnir's beard, it's all true."

Upon following his brother, Guthnyr was more vocal, his wonder tinged with a note of reproach. "Fuck me if the Fireraiser built this, Fel."

Elvine's excitement mounted at Felnir's faint chuckle. "That he did not, Guth."

Hurrying down the last few steps, she followed Falk and Colvyn onto a walkway that at first glance seemed to stretch away into a black void. As her eyes detected the light catching on the shapes in the gloom, the reason for the brothers' awe became clear. Straight lines were everywhere, resolving into tall structures and pillars when she allowed her gaze to linger. The pillars supported more walkways and stairwells, their endpoints lost to the shadows. Rising amongst them she discerned narrow, angular constructions, their sides interrupted by dark slots she soon recognised as windows.

"What is this place?" Colvyn asked, Elvine turning when she realised he had addressed the question to her.

Glancing at Felnir, she received a nod of permission. Continued secrecy was pointless now. "Unless I'm mistaken," she said, "I believe we stand at the threshold of the Vaults of the Altvar."

PART III

"Fight for gain, if you must. Fight for renown, if it pleases you. But the greatest glory is only to be found in fighting for your people."

Ulthnir Horuhnklehr – the Worldsmith

– from the Altvar Rendi

CHAPTER TWENTY-NINE

Ruhlin

Ruhlin's curiosity about what could be constructed with *kehl-gruin* was partially answered by his first sight of Lyhs Skarta. The rectangular tower ascending from the centre of the town stood at least fifty feet tall. A beacon fire blazed at its summit, casting a long trail of smoke into the clear sky. Sygurn told him it was a signal to settlements in the region that the Meidvang was at hand. The town itself was far less impressive than its tower, fashioned almost entirely of wood, its soot-stained hovels sprawled across a low hill rising from the rolling fields south of the Vyrnkral mountains.

As the caravan drew closer, Ruhlin realised the outer precincts were clustered around an inner defensive wall. Upon navigating narrow streets redolent with a melange of cooking stoves and dung, the procession halted before a large gate. The door to Eldryk's gilded carriage opened and the Aerling stepped down to converse with a brawny man in leather armour, presumably the one who oversaw entry to the town. Peering through his bars at the wall, Ruhlin saw it was also fashioned from *kehlgruin* but seemed to be in a poor state of repair. Long, deep cracks marred its surface, revealing a twisted matrix of iron within.

"Metal and stone combined," he murmured, drawing Sygurn's notice.

"It has to be," the Nihlvarian said. "For anything larger than a cowshed, that is. Even *kehlgruin* will crumble under the weight of wind and rain if it's not veined in iron." He glanced at the wall, squinting

356 · ANTHONY RYAN

in disapproval. "They've let it go to shit, like a lot of town walls these days. Time was every settlement in Nihlvar needed a wall lest these feckers—" he inclined his head at their Morvek companions "—would appear out of the night to slit your throat and burn it all down."

As usual, the Morvek ignored him, though Ruhlin caught a short but fierce glimmer of resentment in the woman's eye. *She knows a little of our tongue, at least,* he decided, storing the knowledge for later.

Eldryk concluded his business with the armoured man in short order whereupon the caravan proceeded through the gate. The streets beyond were less cramped and foul smelling than those on the other side of the wall, but Ruhlin's overall impression of this place and its people was one of befouled misery. Drably attired townsfolk walked with shoulders stooped but straightened as the wagons passed by, unwashed faces lit with near manic interest. Many called out in accents so thick Ruhlin had difficulty discerning any meaning, though Sygurn's disgusted grimace made it clear these were not words of welcome.

"They're keen to watch us die," he explained in response to Ruhlin's questioning glance. "It's likely the only amusement these feckers get."

A few minutes trundling through muddy thoroughfares brought them to a broad, circular structure sitting alongside the base of the tower. Unlike its far taller neighbour, it was constructed of quarried granite. Its walls rose no higher than twenty feet and were topped with an array of carved stone faces. These were clearly very old, having been weathered so much that the features of these gods or heroes could barely be made out. Even so, Ruhlin didn't need Sygurn's explanation to identify the nature of this building.

"The *wuhltra* is usually the oldest pile of stone in any settlement," the Nihlvarian said, scowling at the statue above the building's entrance. "Long have the Altvar demanded their due."

"They don't where I'm from," Ruhlin said.

"Probably explains why you're such a bunch of weakling savages."

Ruhlin ignored the taunt and watched Eldryk disembark his carriage once again, this time to exchange far less curt greetings with a well-dressed man in a bear-hide cloak. He hadn't seen the Aerling exhibit any warmth towards another soul before, but saw it now in the way the two embraced. He couldn't hear the words they spoke as they exchanged smiles, but their familiarity was obvious.

"He has a friend," he murmured aloud.

"Probably a fellow survivor of the *wuhltra*," Sygurn said. "See those scars?"

Squinting, Ruhlin made out the deep, overlapping marks on the well-dressed man's brow and cheeks. "He was a fighter in the Meidvang?" he asked in surprise.

"I'd guess they both were. Win enough victories and a slave can become a master in time. Our beloved owner is a bit unusual, though. It's rare for one who once suffered the lash to rise so high."

"Eldryk was a slave?"

"He was, and one of the most famed fighters to ever bestride the *wuhltra*'s sands. No scars for him, you notice."

"I assumed he had been born to wealth."

"He was. But his father pissed it all away and young Eldryk found himself saddled with debts he couldn't pay. To save his family from utter penury, he sold himself to a slave master. A rare thing, but not unheard of. Years of triumph in the Meidvang saw him freed, made wealthy, his family's name restored. But they say the stain of bloody sands never really fades."

Radylf exhibited considerable caution in emptying the wagons, having the prisoners led inside one at a time under close guard. Ruhlin was the last, his wrists and ankles manacled again, the chains far heavier than those worn by his fellow slaves. "Can't be too careful with you, laddie," the whip-man said, prodding him towards the entrance to the *wuhltra*. The reason for this additional weight of iron became clear when Ruhlin noticed that Achela wasn't anywhere in sight.

"Don't worry," Radylf said, whip handle nudging Ruhlin's shoulder again. "She's never far away. And be sure she'll be watching when it's your time on the sands. Until then—" he reached forward to dangle a blowpipe in front of Ruhlin's eyes "—I've got this to deal with any foolishness, and rest assured I'm very skilled with it."

As he shuffled towards the broad doorway ahead, it occurred to Ruhlin that this was, in fact, his first real chance at escape. Feeding his anger with hatred of Radylf should suffice to summon the beast within, and he doubted even these chains could contain him then. But what came next? He knew Radylf's mastery of the blowpipe was surely no boast. Had he sufficient command of himself when the monster emerged, Ruhlin could simply have closed his mouth, but that seemed an impossibility. When the rage took him, all control fled, leaving him a snarling, mindless creature. And should he somehow evade the whip-man's dart, what of Tuhlan, Julette, even Sygurn? What of Aleida?

Abide by the plan, he told himself as the gloomy interior of the *wuhltra* closed in around him. The smell of the place, a concordance of sweat and the effluent of fearful souls, served as a stark reminder of what that meant. To win freedom, he would have to kill today. *Let it burn.* He clenched his fists as he repeated Sygurn's instruction, hoping repetition would banish the increasing roil of terror and doubt in his gut. *Let it burn.*

"Sit there," Radylf instructed, pointing his whip handle at a bench where Ruhlin's fellow prisoners had been arrayed. Unlike him, they had all been clad in some form of armour, though it was incomplete. Leather vambraces worn on only one arm and a single shoulder guard instead of two. A line of iron rings was set into the floor along the length of the bench, the captive's chains looped through and drawn tight. They had been placed in a dimly lit corridor leading to a sturdy wooden door. Ruhlin could hear the murmur of voices from beyond. As time wore on, the sound steadily grew in volume, indicating a gathering crowd.

They sat in silence for what must have been an hour or more, dire expectation thickening the air. More than one of his companions let loose prolonged streams of piss and another vomited. Ruhlin didn't turn his head to see who had surrendered to fear. He expected a caustic comment from Sygurn, but it seemed even the disgraced Nihlvarian had no stomach for cruelty now. When the crowd's collective voice had grown to continual tumult, Eldryk strode from the shadows. He wore a long cloak trimmed in white fur, a thick gold chain about his neck. Ruhlin assumed the occasion demanded such finery.

"Today you fight in my name," the Aerling told them, his tone brisk and cold. "I neither ask for nor expect you to take pride in this. None of you have faced the Meidvang before, so I will educate you in its finer points. In short, there are none. The task set before you today is a simple one: fight well and you live. Survive today and you will face another Meidvang in a few days. And another after that. By the time this season ends, I fully expect most of you to die. For those still drawing breath at the end of this journey, I offer the most generous of gifts: freedom. The freedom I once won for myself. The freedom I granted to Radylf when he won victory after victory, did I not, my friend?"

The whip-man lowered his head in respect. "That you did, Aerling."

"So you see," Eldryk continued. "I offer not doom, but deliverance. All you need do is claim it." He tracked his gaze across them, his expression stern and commanding, until he came to Ruhlin. Just for a moment, something flickered across the Aerling's face. It was more than just uncertainty, a definite twitch of fear that betrayed a sense of much being risked this day. *How much has he wagered on me?* Ruhlin wondered, his mind returning to the meeting with the two Tuhlvyr. *And was it all just gold, or something more?*

A pealing of discordant horns sounded from beyond the door, wailing on for long enough to herald a potent silence amongst the crowd. It was broken by a portentous voice speaking easily understood Ascarlian, albeit part muffled by the wooden barrier.

"In Ulthnir's name art we gathered," the voice declared. "Under Aerldun's ever-watchful eye doth we offer our reverent attention. To Silfaer's twin faces doth we plead for her beneficence: Oh goddess of battle, bless this day with courage undaunted. Steel the hearts of the wretches brought to fight in thy honour. May their blood be our gift unto ye."

Although Ruhlin had no idea what the speaker might look like, his voice conjured the image of a man he found it very easy to dislike.

A luminary of this town, dressed well and adorned in gold, given the honour of celebrating base slaughter in the gods' name. A familiar heat kindled in Ruhlin's core as he began to savour the notion of getting his transformed hands on such a man. He made no attempt to fight it, allowing it to simmer, for today his rage was worth more than treasure. *Let it burn.*

More blaring of horns, a roar of appreciation from the crowd, then the door was flung open. Eldryk disappeared back into the shadows whilst the guards went about unlocking the chains of the captive at the furthest end of the bench. As she was hauled into the light, Ruhlin recognised the Morvek woman from his wagon.

"You drew a lucky lot," Radylf told her as she was led to the doorway. "Some barely trained cattle thief. Finish him quickly so we can get on to more fruitful wagers." He unlocked the manacles about her wrists and handed her a sword, jerking his head at the opening. With his eyes still adjusting from the gloom, Ruhlin could barely make out what lay beyond. He glimpsed an expanse of white sand and the dim silhouette of a thin man standing some yards off, but then Radylf shoved the woman into the circle and slammed the door shut.

There was no preamble to what came next, the crowd's fervour surging loud enough to smother all but the faintest ring of steel on steel. As Radylf had demanded, the contest was done in bare moments. Its conclusion was signalled by a triumphant cheer which soon subsided into distracted murmuring punctuated by a few derisory jeers. Apparently, some of the audience hadn't thought much of the contest. The door swung open and the Morvek woman came through, shoulders slumped and face like stone. The guards quickly relieved her of her bloodied sword and returned the manacles to her wrists. As she was led away, Ruhlin caught her expression in a patch of torchlight, finding it one of deep, heartfelt shame.

Another Morvek he recognised from the wagon went next. His contest was more prolonged, and ultimately fatal. "Kept telling him to raise his guard," Radylf sighed as a pair of guards carried the limp corpse along the corridor. "All right, Teilvik," the giant said, gesturing for Tuhlan to rise. "Time to earn your gruel."

The Caerith managed to spare a glance in Ruhlin's direction before he was shoved towards the door. Ruhlin saw no fear in Tuhlan's face, only the hard surety of a man determined to survive the impending trial. After the Caerith's manacles were removed, Radylf armed him with a short spear. When the door swung open once more, Ruhlin was alarmed to see not one figure awaiting his friend upon the sands, but two. Furthermore, both appeared to be far better armoured than their opponent. Despite this, Tuhlan stepped on to the sand without hesitation, Ruhlin seeing him crouch in preparation before the door slammed shut.

Prior to this contest, the noise produced by the crowd had been a mostly unvaried expression of collective bloodlust, continuing for as long as it took the battling slaves to conclude their contests. This time, it was different. It began as before, but soon the ongoing cheers shifted into gasps and momentary quietude before surging to a roar a heart-beat later.

"Putting on a decent show, at least," Radylf commented. He peered through a small slit at the contest raging beyond, broad lips pursed in approval. "Now that's a fighter," he added when the crowd let loose a yet more voluminous howl of acclaim. "If the rest of you can do half as well, I'll consider this a good season."

A final, near deafening outburst of acclaim signalled the end of Tuhlan's contest. Ruhlin stared at the door in breathless expectation, not knowing whether it would be his friend or a corpse that came through. The sight of the Caerith's bloodied but apparently uninjured form would have provoked a relieved exclamation from Ruhlin, but for the grimness of Tuhlan's expression. Their gazes met again as the Caerith was led away, Ruhlin seeing the same surety as before, but also a new depth of anger in the set of Tuhlan's jaw.

He hates what they made him do, Ruhlin thought. His eyes strayed to the door before it closed, glimpsing the two bodies being dragged from the sand. The sight sickened him, heralding more despair than anger. *I can't do this.* His fists bunched again as he tried to summon the rage he knew he would need. Instead, all he felt was a mounting sense of dread and disgust. Disgust for his captors, but also himself.

He had never actually chosen to fight before. The monster first unleashed at Buhl Hardta had chosen for him, banishing his cowardice with its all-encompassing fury. He hadn't killed anyone. The beast that lurked within was the true killer. At heart, Ruhlin ehs Kestryg was a just a cowardly fisherman.

"Bear up, y'fecker." The harsh, angry whisper speckled him with spit. Ruhlin looked up to find Sygurn leaning closer to him, voice raised as high as he dared. "You have to," he grated, then flinched at the dry slither of Radylf's unfurled whip upon the floor.

"Tongues still now," the giant warned. "Think on your own fights, not others."

Moments later, all six of the remaining Morvek were pushed through the door together, armed only with a dagger apiece. Julette, Sygurn and Ruhlin endured the subsequent contest in silence. Unlike Tuhlan's turn on the sands, it was impossible to gauge the course of this struggle for the crowd bayed continually throughout. Ruhlin detected an increased frenzy to the sound, an ugly hunger for gruesome spectacle stoked to its highest pitch.

When it finally abated, only two Morvek were able to walk through the door, Ruhlin picking out the slashes leaking blood onto their exposed flesh. A third still lived, but had to be carried by the guards, groaning as the slice to his belly left a red spatter the length of the corridor.

Ruhlin expected one or both of his remaining companions to be next, but instead a lull descended. The crowd's murmur was once again stilled by the cry of horns, whereupon the unseen but detestable local luminary held forth. "Be it known," he began with melodramatic gravity, "that today shall stand long in thy memory. Today shall ye witness a sight to tell thy children and grandchildren. For today, one of the Vyrn Skyra shall bestride this *wuhltra* and do bloody honour to the gods that blessed him. To none other than Aerling Eldryk do we owe this honour. Hail him well and stand ready to behold what will be the greatest spectacle ever to grace these holy sands."

Guards moved quickly from the shadows then, three of them hauling Ruhlin to his feet whilst others removed the chains from Julette and

Sygurn. All three of them were pushed to the door, which now appeared to shake with the clamour of the crowd. When it opened, Ruhlin was confronted with the sight of no less than ten armed fighters. All were well armoured and carried either sword or axe.

"You two first," Radylf instructed, pointing his whip at Julette and Sygurn.

"Weapons," Julette said. Ruhlin was impressed that her voice lacked any note of a plea, just an irate demand.

"If your friend plays his part as he should," the whip-man said, reaching out to clamp his spade-sized hand to Julette's neck, "you won't need them." He cast her through the door with enough force to send her sprawling, followed soon after by Sygurn.

"Aerling Eldryk felt you required some additional encouragement," Radylf explained as he took hold of Ruhlin's manacles, dragging him forward. "And it creates a nice air of drama. The mob always appreciates that."

"Take these off," Ruhlin said, jangling his chains.

"No," Radylf replied simply. He grinned as he swung Ruhlin round before letting go. Ruhlin spun face down into the sand, sputtering grains. "Where's the drama in that?" He caught the whip-man's grin before the door slammed shut.

Rising to his knees, Ruhlin saw the ten fighters opposite, exchanging uncertain glances. He assumed they had been primed to expect a monster, and the sight of three captives, two unarmed and one still chained, gave them pause. But not for long.

Seeing their opponents tense in readiness for a charge, Ruhlin struggled to his feet. "Get behind me," he told Julette and Sygurn. With scant alternative, they hurried to comply, both crouching at his back as he faced the onrushing opponents.

Strangely, time slowed in that moment. The assailants appeared to charge through thickened air, mouths open in challenging snarls and sand describing lazy arcs as it flew from their feet. Ruhlin even had the leisure to raise his eyes to the crowd. They sat in rows of tiered seats arranged in a bowl-like structure around the circle of sands. His gaze tracked over a mass of screaming faces, the sight of them raising both contempt and repugnance, but still no blossoming rage. Then he found Aleida.

She stood alongside her father on the lowest tier in a partitioned section, flanked by a cluster of people clad in far finer garb than the rest of the audience. The Aerling's face was stone-like in its rigidity, either through a desire to portray some form of peerless dignity, or unwillingness to reveal his need for this moment to work in his favour. Unlike Eldryk, Aleida either chose not to conceal her emotions or was unable to keep the stark desperation from her features, or prevent the tears streaming from her eyes. But it was not the sight of the Aerling and his daughter that roused the beast within, but the animalistic animation of those around them. Despite their finery, Ruhlin saw no difference between them and the leering, blood-hungry mob. Gold jewellery glittered and jangled. Drink flew from their goblets as they lost themselves in a frenzy of anticipation. The sheer nonsensical hypocrisy of pretending that this spectacle of sadism had some ritual significance to the Altvar sent a jolt of anger through Ruhlin's gut, and the rage followed soon after.

His skin had already hardened by the time the first blade attempted to pierce it. The man who jabbed the point of his short spear at Ruhlin's neck froze in surprise at the sight of the leaf-shaped steel head bending. He was Nihlvarian, features so densely tattooed in scarlet runes and sigils that he appeared to be wearing a mask. So it was his eyes that most occupied Ruhlin's attention, narrowed in mystification, then widened in outright terror.

He attempted to flee as Ruhlin's chains shattered. The links parted like brittle clay, the iron cuffs encasing his wrists splitting at the seams and falling away. A huge, veined hand lashed out to engulf the fleeing Nihlvarian's head, halting his flight and smothering the panicked shriek. A brief increase in pressure followed by a feeling of gritty wetness upon his palm and fingers, then the corpse was flung aside. It cast out a chaotic spiral of blood as it flew through the air, emitting a loud thud as it collided with the wall enclosing the sands. Had he more command of his thoughts, Ruhlin might have reflected on the fact of hearing that thud, for it meant the crowd was now utterly silent. But his rage was fully roused and the beast he had become had no interest in such distractions.

As before, the resultant slaughter would only ever be a dim collection of horrors in his memory. He recalled kicking off the remnants of the chains that had encased his now enlarged ankles whilst the remaining opponents turned as one and pelted for the door at the far end of the circle. Foolishly, they clustered into a desperate, clamouring knot, hammering at the wooden barrier for entry. It made them easy prey. A few moments of crimson, rending fury and Ruhlin found himself regarding a spectacular smear of gore covering the door and surrounding wall.

Still un-sated, Ruhlin whirled about in search of fresh victims, finding one had escaped him. A thin man in sparse armour, he scurried away on his hands and knees, trailing blood from a mangled leg. Ruhlin covered the distance to him in a single leap, his foot slamming down on the maimed man's head with the force of a sledgehammer. Snarling, he cast about for more.

He later recalled how his rage had decreased marginally at the sight of the two figures backing away from him. A man and woman with their hands raised. They gabbled out sounds that made little sense, but did birth a glimmer of puzzlement. For some reason, the woman's voice commanded most of his attention, for she kept repeating a word that found purchase on his raging mind.

"Ruhlin!" she called out, still backing away. "It's me! It's Julette!" The man at her side was shouting too, but his words were just noise delivered with a mix of anger and fear. Their voices stilled when their backs met the wall, both of them shrinking low as he loomed over them.

"It's me," the woman said again, her voice now diminished to a terrorised whisper. "Julette. Don't you remember?"

Julette. He knew that word. It was a name. He also had a name, but what was it? Grunting, he turned from the two cowering figures, mind churning. The heat that filled every part of his being began to dissipate then, the rage seeping away until true thoughts returned. "Ruhlin," he murmured. "My name is Ruhlin."

A wave of exhaustion swept through him, his enlarged muscles twitching as they resumed their former state. Groaning in weariness, Ruhlin slumped to his knees, whereupon the crowd found its voice again. It started as an awed murmuring, hundreds whispering the names of the gods, but soon built into a wordless, worshipful roar. The sound descended like a wave, rekindling his disgust but, fortunately for those now screaming their adulation for him, not his anger. He lay down upon the sands, putting his hands over his ears and letting himself fall into the void of sleep.

CHAPTER THIRTY

Thera

Thera tightened her grip on the Dreadaxe and strode towards the stern, determined at least to die with a weapon in hand. She might even leave a cut or two in the hide of the monster before it tore her ship to shreds. A fine end, though not the one she would have chosen, especially since no soul would live to tell of it. However, before she could climb the rail, a swift, lithe figure got there first.

Her heart lurched at the sight of Lynnea standing tall on the stern to face the onrushing whale. Lunging for her, Thera tried to drag the apprentice down, but came to a shuddering halt as a wave of confusion swept through her. Ship and crew wavered into liquid obscurity and Thera felt the hard deck upon her palms and knees. A throb filled her mind, the feeling made all the stranger by its familiarity. It was akin to the sensation she felt when discerning Lynnea's thoughts in the cast of her features, but greatly magnified. This time, she was unable to comprehend any words, but still found meaning in it, a combination of reassurance and warmth. Despite the confusion, it was blissful, like the purest, most beautiful dream. When it ended, the groan escaping Thera's lips held more regret than relief.

Blinking, she scrambled upright upon seeing Lynnea topple backwards from the stern. Thera caught her, the maiden's body limp in her arms but her face, more pale than ever before, forming a wan smile. *They'll leave us be.* The thought slipped into Thera's mind,

weak and fluttering like the wings of an injured bird. *For now . . .*
Don't linger.

Tearing her gaze from the apprentice's face, Thera looked up to see
the bulging wake was now absent from the water. The whale song
came again, even though the surrounding sea remained calm and
unbroken by fluke or spout. This time the sound lacked any ominous
rumbling, possessing a prolonged, wavering note that Thera felt
sounded almost like pity.

Sighing, Lynnea sagged in her arms, eyes closing. Thera pulled her
close, relieved and distressed at the feel of her slow, shallow breaths.

"To oars," she told her *menda*, the words catching in her throat.
Coughing, she repeated them and added, "Let's be gone from here."

The wreckage from the Nihlvarian ships had been carried by the busy
channels between the bergs to spread far and wide. The *Great Wolf*
rowed through patches of tangled rope, shattered timber and bobbing
barrels. Thera ordered the ship slowed to gather some of the casks
aboard, for additional supplies were always welcome. They were filled
with either a coarse, brandy-like liquor or pickled herring. Another
mile south, however, they happened upon more interesting salvage.

"Man in the water! Fifty yards to port!" Ragnalt's shout cut through
the frigid air, summoning Thera to the prow. "Finally, a prisoner," the
warrior commented when she came to his side. She had ordered the
oars shipped and course altered to bring them to the sprawl of debris
bobbing in the swell, feeling a grim anticipation at the prospect of
wringing answers from a captive foe. The man clinging to the shattered
section of hull was perhaps the palest human being Thera had ever
seen, including Lynnea. He also lacked any tattoos, red or blue. As
they drew nearer, she made out the chains attaching his ankles to the
timbers he clung to.

"I'd guess he was already a prisoner," Thera said. "Fetch tools."

The pale man watched in shivering but stern-faced silence as they
threw grapples to drag the wreckage close to the *Great Wolf*'s hull.
His chains were looped through an iron ring bolted into the planking
and removing it required some tricky manoeuvring. Eshilde dangled

over the side, a rope tied about her waist as she delivered a series of precise blows with a hammer and chisel. As the chains came free, Ragnalt and Thera hauled the pale man aboard. Given the sparseness of his clothing, bare feet and thin wool covering a lean frame, it seemed incredible that he had survived the cold. Yet, although he shivered, she saw no frostbite on his skin. She also found herself impressed by the way he forced himself to stand upon the deck, shuddering but refusing to be cowed. Nor did he shrink from returning their collective stares with a fierce glower.

"Here," Thera said, offering him a horn of mixed brandy and water. He regarded it with evident suspicion, but the demands of his chilled body left him unable to refuse. She watched him gulp down the full contents and gestured for Ragnalt to pour him some more.

"Nihlvarian?" she asked when he had drained another horn and his shudders quelled a little. Although emaciated and haggard by his hours adrift upon the sea, she noticed how young he was. His marble-hued skin had the smoothness of a man barely in his twenties.

Her question brought a deepening of his glower and an emphatic shake of his head. "Morvek," he said.

"And what's that?"

From his baffled squint, she deduced they may have reached the limits of linguistic understanding. "Thera," she said, patting her chest before gesturing to the surrounding deck and rigging. "This is my ship."

"Ship," he repeated, prolonging the word, features softening with a glimmer of comprehension. "You," he began, forming words with careful deliberation, "are not . . . Nihlvarian." His speech was thick with an unfamiliar accent that recalled the incoherent war cries and exhortations of those they had fought at the Nail. But his manner of speaking made it plain that this form of Ascarlian was not his native tongue.

"We are not," Thera assured him. Nodding to the chains on his ankles, she went on, "You were their prisoner?"

He replied with another shake of his head, Thera discerning a considerable depth of shame in his downcast eyes. "Not . . . prisoner. I was . . . slave. Many of us . . ." He grimaced in consternation and pointed at an oar propped against the rail nearby. "We used those."

"They have slaves doing their rowing for them," Gelmyr said. "Explains how they were able to catch up so quickly."

"Your name?" Thera asked the pale man. His reply came in a fluent stream of language so alien she hadn't even an inkling of what it meant. Noting her mystification, he gave a faint grin and spoke a single word. "Achier. Call me Achier."

"You're not a slave now, Achier," she told him before turning to Ragnalt. "Get those chains off. Then feed him and find him some dry clothes."

"Sure about this?" Gelmyr asked when Ragnalt led Achier away. "He seems honest enough, but there's no way to know for sure if he spoke true. One thing we've learned about our enemy is their facility for deceit."

"True," Thera admitted. "But chaining yourself to a shattered hull in the hope someone comes along to rescue you seems unlikely. But still, we'll watch him closely. Besides, we need more hands at the oars."

"Why does she not wake?" Achier asked, head angled in curiosity as he peered at Lynnea's slumbering features.

Since departing the domain of the white whales, Thera had spent most of her time at the maiden's side. They had wrapped her in a thick covering of blankets to ward against the chill. Snaryk and Mohlnir added their own warmth, the hound partly enclosing Lynnea in his huge, furred form whilst the cat nestled into her chest. As yet, the apprentice hadn't shown any sign of waking, though her breathing remained regular and her pulse steady, if not particularly strong. Thera's concern for her was deepened by the wariness of the crew. Despite the fact that this young woman had undoubtedly saved them from certain destruction, the glances they darted at Lynnea now showed both fear and suspicion. The word ringing in their minds was plain, though as yet unspoken: *witch*.

Thera teased the dark tresses from Lynnea's forehead, wishing she had an answer to Achier's question. The hour was late, but they were through most of the ice, though some white mountains still drifted into their path. Gelmyr had set a course that he hoped would skirt the worst of the northern Styrnspeld's fractiousness. Nevertheless, she took note of the worried glances he cast continually at the southern horizon. It appeared the Iron Dark Sea may not yet be done visiting its cruelty upon them.

"She ... exerted herself," Thera said, elaborating when it became plain the Morvek didn't understand. "Made herself tired."

"How? Did she fight?"

Even if this man hadn't lacked full comprehension of Ascarlian, Thera doubted she had the words to properly explain Lynnea's recent actions. Not least because she didn't understand them herself. "In a way, I suppose she did," she said.

She had summoned him when the day's rowing was done, hoping to glean some insight into her enemy. It had become plain after a few moments conversation that useful communication would only come with a good deal of time and effort. Still, she was a Vellihr and such was her lot in life.

"Morvek," she said. "They are enemies of the Nihlvarians?"

Achier nodded. "For long time. They came ..." His brow furrowed in calculation. "In the time of the grandmothers' grandfathers, they came. In ships. With weapons of steel. We had weapons of stone and wood. The old ones call it Ocha Slatka, the Red Time. Nihlvarians take land, forest, mountain. They drove the Morvek away. But still we fight."

"Where ..." Thera began, only to stop when it occurred to her that this man would likely have scant understanding of his current whereabouts. Also, any place names he might utter would be meaningless to her. "How far away is their land?" she asked instead, gesturing to the west.

"Far," Achier said. From the tension of his face, it was clear his frustration in conveying meaning matched hers. "Many, many ... miles," he continued, brightening a little as a thought occurred. "From beyond the mountains that burn. You know this place?"

The mountains that burn. Their land lies beyond the Fire Isles. How could that be? "I do," she said, opting for a different tack. "Have you heard the word Uhltvar?"

"Sometimes. Nihlvarians speak it when . . ." His annoyed frown returned as he struggled for the words. "When they talk of . . ." Achier paused and made a vague gesture towards the sky.

"The gods," Thera finished. "The Altvar."

"Altvar. Yes. Evil spirits who demand much blood."

Thera decided it would be best if she didn't yet enlighten him to the fact that Ascarlians and Nihlvarians appeared to share the same gods. "Do you know what they want here?" she asked. "Why have they come against us?"

This brought a quizzical frown to his brow, as if the answer were obvious. "To take. They took from us. Now they take from you."

"Do you know how many ships they have?"

Achier replied with a short, bitter mutter in his own language before offering Thera a regretful shrug. "Many. What has come is . . ." He paused to summon the appropriate words. "Small," he said finally. "What comes after, much bigger."

"That fleet is just a vanguard," Thera murmured in realisation. Her mind raced with dread possibilities. If all the *menda* and all the warships of Ascarlia were gathered, it could possibly match the fleet she had seen at Iselda's Nail. But if that was merely a fraction of their strength . . .

A sudden, stiff gust snapped the sail above their heads with distracting violence. Thera flinched as the wind drove a brief horizontal spatter of rain over the starboard rail. Rising, she saw an ugly roil of dark cloud obscuring the southern horizon, its appearance made yet more ominous by flashes of lightning. Turning to Gelmyr, the grave cast of his features made it plain that this storm would be far worse than the one that had chased them north.

"I have a task for you, if you're willing," she said to Achier.

"I . . . owe you much," he said with a cautious nod.

"Keep her safe." Thera crouched to tighten the furs around Lynnea. "A storm comes. A bad storm. Whatever happens, she must live. You understand?"

Achier nodded again. "She is . . . important?"

"Oh, yes." Thera cupped Lynnea's cheek, wishing she felt more warmth to her skin, willing her eyes to open. But they didn't. "More than even I realised."

She straightened, striding away to cast out her commands. "Storm to the south! Secure all cargo and draw tight all lines!"

Even before the full fury of the tempest was upon them, the gale had driven them back into the bergs. Thera had hoped the ice giants might offer some protection, but instead, they soon proved to be an additional hazard. Ever rising seas pitched the *Great Wolf* towards one, then another as Gelmyr wrestled the tiller. Thera had been forced to forsake shouting encouragement to the crew, unable to be heard above the wind. Instead, she clambered from one warrior to another, leaning close to speak what reassurance she could. Most bore the trial with the fortitude she expected, but in some she saw the wild cast to the eye that told of folk pushed near their limit. This *menda* had been through much, only to have apparent deliverance snatched away. In less fraught times, she might have railed at these fearful souls, even called them cowards. Now she merely clapped a hand to their shoulders and left them to their muttered pleas for Ulfmaer's mercy.

She began to make her way back to Lynnea when a flash of lightning revealed the sheer flanks of a mountainous berg looming directly ahead. "I see it!" Gelmyr sputtered as she struggled towards him. He had the tiller pushed as far towards port as it would allow, though the fractious sea kept threatening to tear it from his grasp. "Help me!"

Thera joined her weight to his, both of them managing to swing the *Great Wolf*'s prow away from the oncoming monolith. Even so, it was a close thing. She could make out the fissures in the berg's sides as it swept past, and shuddered in relief as the hull bobbed clear of its path. The ship heaved as a large wave rebounded from the berg, causing her to pitch to starboard at a sharp angle. Thera saw a figure, barely recognisable through the sheeting rain, tumble loose from the deck and disappear over the side. Yet the storm allowed no time for anguish.

As the *Great Wolf* settled, a deafening roar split the sky, accompanied by a blinding flash as a fork of purest light lashed down to strike the berg. The resulting explosion sent a cascade of white boulders into the sea, water rising high all around the ship. Thera watched in fascinated horror as a shard of ice the size of a house teetered then fell from the berg's summit. It described a perversely elegant arc as it descended, striking the *Great Wolf* just as another wave slammed into the port hull. The shard struck the tilting mast barely a yard from its base, shearing it away before slamming into the starboard rail then crashing into the swell. When the white fury of its impact faded, Thera looked upon what appeared to be a bite in the *Great Wolf*'s timber flesh, a chaos of splinters speckled with the remains of two of her crew.

A wordless cry came from Gelmyr, Thera turning to see him sagging against the tiller. "Up!" she raged. Lunging towards him, she hauled him to his feet. For a second, their eyes met, and she beheld the despair of a soul stretched near to breaking. *If the Styrnspeld can defeat a man such as this, what hope is there?* Snarling with rage, Thera crushed the treacherous thought with ruthless determination. "Hold to your task, *Johten Apt* of mine!" she shouted, shaking Gelmyr until he blinked and she saw his true self return, along with a shameful frown.

"The sea is clear of bergs now," she said, looking away to spare him further ignominy. "All you need do is keep us afloat. Can you do that?"

He didn't voice a reply, instead taking firm hold of the tiller and straightening his back. It was all the answer she needed.

Stumbling her way across a deck littered with debris, she came to Lynnea's side. Achier was crouched close to her, body braced between two beams to keep her in place. Thera pressed a hand to her apprentice's skin and was surprised to find it warm. Despite the wind and chilled rain, she also detected a new pinkness to Lynnea's cheeks. It made her wonder about the depth of the maiden's powers if she possessed the ability to restore her strength in the midst of all this.

"My thanks," she told Achier before casting a fearful eye over the stump of the vanished mast and the storm still raging all around. "Now it's up to Ulfmaer to preserve us all until morning."

* * *

Dawn broke upon a placid, windless sea. A head count revealed the loss of four warriors, all veterans who had sailed at Thera's side for years. She struck sparks from Trieya's bronze sigil, spoke their names, and implored the goddess to guide them safely to the Halls. As with Gynheld and Alvyr, it pained her to deny them proper ceremony, but their plight allowed for no indulgence of sentiment. They made what repairs they could to the *Great Wolf*. All wise captains carried a stock of additional timber and iron nails, so restoring much of the damage to the starboard rail required only a day's work. When it came to the vanished mast, however, they could do nothing.

"We have to make for the Kast Geld," Gelmyr said. He avoided her gaze as he spoke, Thera assumed to prevent her seeing the shame that lingered there. She quelled the urge to voice reassurance, knowing it would only deepen his guilt. Better to concentrate all efforts on their current tribulations and allow the memory of his momentary weakness to fade. "Rowing all the way back to Skar Magnol would take months," he went on. "To sail home, we need a mast."

"Then let's hope the Ironbones is in a generous mood," Thera said. Turning, she raised her voice to address her *menda*. They were tired after the sleepless trial of the storm and recent labour, but the luxury of rest was well behind them now. "We row until nightfall," she said. "And then we row more. Steady stroke. And anyone who wants to moan about it is welcome to swim."

She allowed a break an hour after dusk, trusting to Gelmyr's judgement to maintain a decent heading amidst the southward flowing currents. Settling down next to Lynnea, she reached out to check the warmth of her skin, then started when the maiden's eyes fluttered open. For an instant, Thera saw confusion reign in Lynnea's gaze. She sat up, looking around with an expression that failed to bring words to Thera's mind, but still conveyed a stark sense of surprise. Thera worried she might have lost her memory, perhaps her reason, but then Lynnea calmed. Blinking at Thera, a faint smile curved her lips, which promptly faded when she turned to regard Achier. *Who's he?* her frown asked.

"This is Achier," Thera told her. "A friend and former captive of our enemy. He's been taking good care of you these past days."

376 • ANTHONY RYAN

Watching the two of them, Thera saw a weight in their shared scrutiny that went far beyond the mutual suspicion of strangers meeting in perilous circumstances. Furthermore, she gained the impression of unspoken but formal acknowledgement between them, almost a sense of recognition. Or was it attraction? The thought stirred a familiar pang of jealousy, one Thera smothered with a potent flare of self-disgust. *War comes upon Ascarlia and this is what concerns the Vellihr of Justice?*

"We'll start rowing in shifts come the morning," she said, getting to her feet and addressing her words to Achier. "I'll need you to take your turn along with everyone else. And you, my apprentice—" she turned to Lynnea "—when fully recovered, will acquaint me with your knowledge of whales. I feel I've indulged your secrets long enough."

I don't know how. Thera saw a rare crease of annoyance in Lynnea's brow, but also honesty in the shrug that followed. *It has always been there.* The maiden extended a hand to Mohlnir, the cat purring loudly as he quickly scaled the limb to rest upon her shoulders. *They respond to me and I to them.* She looked at Thera with an expression that combined pride and defiance. *And I consider myself blessed.*

"A blessing that saved us all," Thera said. "For which you will always have my gratitude."

But not theirs. Lynnea's mouth formed a sour curve as she glanced at the crew, then softened. *I don't hate them for it. Such is the way of folk when they witness what they don't understand.*

It was far too complex a statement for Thera's understanding to result merely from an unusually nuanced reading of expression. The memory of the sensation that had gripped her when Lynnea confronted the white whale loomed large, bringing a curious mix of confusion and certainty. It was time to confront what she had known for some time, but not yet fully acknowledged. "The understanding between us," she ventured, unsure of how to phrase the question. "Do you know how it's done, or is it another mystery?"

Partly. Lynnea rested her arms on the rail, the receding green glow of Nerlfeya's Lantern reflected in her eyes. *Throughout my life, it has happened only with three souls. The first was my mother. The second my father, though it faded away as he surrendered his grieving soul to the ways of the Volkrath. The third is you. I don't know why. Mother always said not to question such things, for the blessings of the gods are not for us to comprehend. All we must do is use them in their service. It was her wish that I walk the Vellihr's path, and so here I am.*

"The white whales," Thera said. "What you did hurt you in some way."

Lynnea's face tightened and she lowered her gaze, then brightened as Mohlnir nuzzled her cheek until she consented to pet him. *They feel what I feel*, her thoughts explained. *I feel what they feel. The whales . . .* She closed her eyes. *So much rage, and justified too. They have suffered greatly at human hands. Countless of their kind slaughtered for meat and oil. Until one day, they learned the song of rage, a song that has never dimmed in their hearts.*

"Except for you."

Lynnea blinked, smiling as Mohlnir licked her finger. *I think they just found me . . . too unusual to kill. Should we meet them again, I doubt they will be so forgiving.*

"Our new crewmate." Thera nodded to Achier's slumbering form nearby. "Do you sense any deceit in him?"

Lynnea shook her head. *He is what he claims to be: a slave grateful for the breaking of his chains.*

Seeing hesitation in the maiden's face before she looked away from the Morvek, Thera asked, "Something more?"

A line of consternation creased Lynnea's forehead, her lips thinning in a faint grimace. *I'm not sure yet.*

"Sure of what?"

All souls have secrets, and a human is far better at guarding them than a beast. But you can trust him. I'm sure of that, at least. Lynnea's eyes narrowed a little, the corner of her mouth curving. *Especially since his regard for his rescuer runs* very *deep.* She laughed at Thera's scowl. *He is handsome, though. Don't you think?*

"Get some rest," Thera said, moving away. "Come the morning, I want you taking a turn on the oars too. Time we put some muscle on those bones."

Six days of hard rowing were needed to reach the northern most isle of the Kast Geld, a small, grassy mound barely a mile long. As the *Great Wolf* rounded the islet's western promontory, they were afforded the grimly predictable sight of burned and ruined crofters' dwellings along its southern shore. The Nihlvarian fleet had evidently been busy. At Thera's instruction, Gelmyr followed a course towards Ayl-Ah-Vahrim least likely to bring them into contact with any patrolling foes. It required much tricky navigation of narrow channels and violent currents, rowing by night and harbouring in secluded anchorages during the day. Night-time voyaging spared them the sight of the destruction ashore, but the prevailing silence and absence of lights told the tale with dire clarity. War of the worst kind had come to the Outer Isles, and they had been unable to stop it.

"I'd guess they wreaked what havoc they could and have moved on already," Gelmyr said as they tracked along several miles of unlit coastline. "With luck, they'll be many miles away by now."

"Not if their object goes beyond spreading terror and slaughter," Thera said. "We know this war was long planned, with the help of traitors. Which means they'll know that leadership in this geld lies in Ayl-Ah-Vahrim. The smartest thing would be to send the bulk of their forces there and deal with the Ironbones before he can organise a defence."

"Another two days and we'll find out." Gelmyr's beard bunched and she sensed a reluctance in voicing his next words.

"Out with it," she told him.

"If you're right, we'll be heading into battle," he said. "When we're in no shape to fight one. Might be better to head south. Ayl-Ah-Skorvelt lies not two nights rowing away. It's richer in trees than any isle in this geld. We can cut a mast and make for open sea. With luck, we'll have a clear run back to the Fjord Lands."

"There's no certainty our enemy won't be waiting for us at the forested isle. Or that they won't turn up when we're in the midst of crafting our new mast. It's good odds they'll need timber too."

"I think we're long past time when certainty had any meaning."

This was something she couldn't argue, nor did her *Johten Apt's* reasoning seem at fault. Yet, heading for the home island of Ossgrym Ironbones offered the prospect of fresh intelligence, a clear picture of the Nihlvarians' strategy. *If the miserable old swine's still alive to tell the tale*, she mused inwardly. Her few encounters with the Veilwald of the Kast Geld hadn't endeared him to her, or her to him. But his prowess as warrior and battle leader couldn't be doubted. If Ayl-Ah-Vahrim could be defended, he would have found a way.

"We keep to our course," she told Gelmyr. "But approach with caution. If the enemy is there in strength, we head south."

Gelmyr insisted on a daylight approach to the south-western coast of Ayl-Ah-Vahrim. He needed precise judgement to place the *Great Wolf* in the south-flowing current that would take them close to the island's shore without benefit of rowing. Even so, Thera had every oar greased and wrapped in fleeces to limit noise. When night fell and the ship began her eastward drift, she cautioned the crew against speaking a word without leave.

Even in darkness, Ayl-Ah-Vahrim proved an impressive sight. The bulk of its mass was formed of three mountains, two broad and one tall with a pointed summit. At certain angles it appeared twisted, as if a giant hand had descended from the sky to render it into a towering spiral, hence its name: Ulthnir's Reach. The one fortunate consequence of the *Great Wolf* losing her mast was that she presented a far less visible outline in the gloom. Even vigilant eyes would have difficulty spotting her at a distance. She had drawn to within perhaps a mile of the shore when Thera spotted the lights, a scattering of yellow flecks in the dark mass. They grew in number as the ship neared the shore, sprawling along a ridge line above the beach that Gelmyr said offered the most secluded anchorage. It was clear these were campfires, the number indicating a sizeable force.

"Could be friends," Gelmyr suggested as they both squinted at the coast. "The Ironbones may have sent part of his *menda* to guard the beach."

Thera moved the length of the ship, murmuring instructions to shift to the slow stroke. She paused upon coming to Achier's side, the Morvek meeting her eye with an urgent glare.

"We should go," he said. Nodding his head to the island, he added, "Listen."

"Halt oars," Thera hissed to the crew, straining to hear through the subsequent silence. At first there was nothing but the slap of waves against the hull, but then she heard the distant drone of voices raised in song. It was too faint for her to make out any words, but not for Achier.

"Nihlvarians," he said. "Song of . . ." He sighed, searching for the right word, eventually settling upon, "Winning."

"You mean victory," Thera said. Straightening, she watched the campfires flicker atop the ridge, hearing the song more clearly now, and its clear note of triumph. Moving aft, she voiced a soft but bitter instruction to Gelmyr. "Change course. Head south. The Ironbones has been vanquished. We'll find no allies here."

Chapter Thirty-One

Felnir

Go back or go on? The question prodded Felnir with ever more insistence as he surveyed this subterranean realm. They had ventured as far as the end of the walkway, pausing at the top of a series of descending stairwells leading into a vast cavern. The torchlight failed to reveal more than a few details, but these were maddeningly enticing. *The Vaults*, he thought. *The actual, real Vaults of the Altvar.* Wonder and triumph vied with each other as his hungry eyes drank in every impossibly tall pillar and empty window. However, both suffered an unwelcome blow upon Elvine's next pronouncement.

"A cross lintel," she said. "Far too recent."

Turning, Felnir found her running a hand over the stonework of the walkway's balustrade. The air here lacked the sulphurous taint of the world above, so they had all removed their masks, allowing him a clear view of the scholar's thoughtful face.

"What?" he asked.

"A cross lintel," she repeated, pointing to the topmost stone. Like many that crowned a wall, it featured a square protrusion on its underside, enabling it to be slotted easily into the stones below.

"So?"

"So, the cross lintel was not widely adopted by Ascarlian masons until the Age of Discord. The result of Albermaine-ish masons hired to construct holdfasts for feuding chieftains. Centuries after the supposed creation of the Vaults."

382 • ANTHONY RYAN

"You're saying this is not the Vaults?" Guthnyr asked, laughing in doubt as he cast a hand at the cavern ahead.

"I'm saying this couldn't have been constructed in concert with the Vaults," Elvine explained. "But many years later. However, in truth it's a good sign, for it fits with Velgard's legend. He didn't create the Vaults, but merely rediscovered them." Her voice took on the formal tone she adopted when slipping into quotation. "'And there didst he build a new kingdom amidst the glory of his forebears.'"

"Then the true Vaults lie deeper," Felnir said, returning his gaze to the cavern. *Go back or go on?*

"Proper exploration will require days," Elvine said. "Sister Lore will expect precise charts and tabulations . . ."

"Sod that," Guthnyr scoffed. "She'll expect treasure. As do we. Do we not, brother?"

Felnir looked at his torch. The flame guttering from the oil-soaked rag burned well, but wouldn't do so forever, and where would they find fresh fuel in this place? *Go back to the ship*, he told himself. *Return with more hands and more torches. The cautious course is almost always the right one. Almost . . .*

"We go on for one hour," he said, starting down the steps. "Not one second longer. Sygna, keep the count."

The time required to descend the series of stairwells to the cavern floor chafed on him, as did Sygna's obvious, if thankfully unspoken, disapproval. Entering the vast chamber, Felnir let out a soft grunt, irked by the unpleasant sensation of insignificance. The pillars rising to the roof seemed unfeasibly tall, the buildings between them dwarfing anything in Ascarlia. He and the others were like ants traversing a world built to a different scale.

"Just dust and a few bits of rubble, my lord," Falk reported upon casting the light of his torch into the entrance of one of the buildings. Inspection of the other structures revealed the same picture of destruction, also no sign of runes for Elvine to decipher and certainly no treasure.

"Interior ruined but exterior left intact," Colvyn mused. "The work of a strangely discerning enemy?"

"I'd guess the innards of the buildings were mostly constructed from wood," Elvine said. "Over time, it rotted."

As they proceeded, the main thoroughfare they traversed narrowed and the height of the pillars lessened. Eventually, they passed no more buildings and found themselves walking across bare stone. The torches failed to illuminate anything until they caught a jagged edge a dozen yards ahead. The shape was a stark contrast to everything Felnir had glimpsed in this place. The torchlight crafted abstract and irregular shadows from a mass formed of something his experienced eye had little difficulty recognising.

"That's a lot of bones, brother," Guthnyr said. They had all come to an unbidden halt, eyes wary as they peered into the surrounding gloom. Felnir knew their unease was misplaced, for these bones were ancient. Stepping closer, his torch revealed skulls lying amidst shattered spines and ribs, all long denuded of flesh and dark with age. Many of the skulls featured jagged holes and shattered jaws. He also picked out the telltale cuts to many a ribcage and arm bone.

"I've often seen the aftermath of battle," Kodryn said. "And this is it. Strange how they're all piled together like this, though. Usually, the bodies trail away when the rout takes hold and the slaughter begins. Looks like this lot hacked away at each other until their last breath."

"Some weapons underneath it all," Guthnyr added, squinting into the mass. "Swords and an axe or two. Rusted near to nothing."

A sharp, shuddering intake of breath snapped Felnir's gaze to Wohtin. The madman had his arms folded about his chest, clutching himself tight, eyes bright and unblinking as they stared at the bones.

"Something to tell us?" Guthnyr asked, shifting his torch to illuminate Wohtin's bereft expression. "Or just more drooling?"

"You're scaring him," Elvine said, moving protectively in front Wohtin.

"I'm getting tired of his silence. And I'm not all that sure his brain's as addled as he pretends. How about it?" Guthnyr's torch loomed closer to Wohtin. "Got any insights to share?"

Felnir resisted the impulse to restrain his brother. It was plain that

Wohtin possessed knowledge of this place and the time for indulging his frailty of mind, real or not, was over. However, seeing the dangerous narrowing of Colvyn's gaze as he shifted a hand to the hilt of his falchion, Felnir began to voice a command for Guthnyr to back down. Yet Wohtin forestalled them all by speaking.

"This is my doing."

The words, uttered with both clarity and clear-eyed certainty, heralded a thick silence. Wohtin didn't appear to notice their collective stares as he approached the mound of bones with a faltering step. His features showed no vestige of their customary frowning confusion. This was a man fully in command of his senses, and also stricken by a frightening depth of guilt. He peered into the overlapping tangle of bones as if searching for something he might recognise, but also fearing what he would find.

Predictably, it was Guthnyr who broke the silence. "How could he have anything to do with this?" he said, gesturing to the remains. "This was done centuries ago."

Felnir had to admit it was a pertinent question, but not one Wohtin seemed willing to answer. Catching Elvine's eye, Felnir inclined his head at her charge. However, before she could solicit any more words from him, Wohtin abruptly straightened. Moving around the piled bones, he strode off, features set in a purposeful grimace.

"Don't," Felnir told his brother as Guthnyr reached out to grab at Wohtin's arm. "Let's see where he leads us."

He found the speed of the man's steps significant, striding away into the shadows without benefit of torchlight. Any doubt that Wohtin had been here before faded as Felnir hurried in his wake. "It's been nigh an hour," Sygna said, but Felnir paid her scant heed. Providence, or perhaps destiny, had seen fit to gift him a guide to the Vaults of the Altvar. With such a prize at hand, caution was foolish.

The cavern narrowed as they followed Wohtin into the dark, shrinking into a short tunnel at the end of which stood an open gateway. It was formed of two pillars and a lintel that had been shaped from the surrounding rock, whatever lay beyond lost to darkness. Wohtin stood framed in the entrance, rigid with trepidation.

"Ancient runic," Elvine murmured, Felnir seeing her crouch to play her torch over the inscriptions set into the gateway.

"Can you read it?" he asked her.

"In part." The scholar ran tentative fingers over the carvings. "It's so very old. The phrasing is strange." From the fascination on her face, Felnir knew that whilst others present might hunger for more shiny forms of treasure, Elvine at least had found a portion of hers. Looking up in response to his pointed cough, she said, "'As legend spake, so ye shall find.'" She rose, translating more script as it was revealed by the torch. "'In honour of the Altvar didst we come. To their glory we build.'" Standing back, she paused, Felnir seeing a mix of delight and fear as she read the inscription upon the lintel. "'None shall enter without leave of King Velgard. Step beyond these gates and surrender thy soul for all the ages.'"

"A warning," Colvyn said. Meeting Felnir's eye, he added, "Perhaps one we should heed."

"Hadn't pegged you as a coward, foreigner," Guthnyr laughed. "Don't worry. I'll happily take your share if you're too craven to walk through a door on account of some old scratchings."

"He seems to have reason not to do so," Colvyn observed, nodding to Wohtin. Moving to rest a hand on his former cellmate's shoulder, he spoke on in gentle solicitation, "Just because we've come so far doesn't mean we have to keep going, my friend. You can still turn away from this . . ."

His words ended when Wohtin, letting out a pained sob, stepped through the gate and into the gloom beyond.

Felnir followed quickly, keen not to let their guide slip from view. Once through, the echo of their footfalls made it clear they were in another vast chamber. At first the only thing he could see was Wohtin's striding form, but then Felnir's eyes began to discern a lessening in the gloom. The darkness abated the further they ventured from the gateway, Felnir looking up to see a soft blue glow emanating from the distant ceiling of this space.

"The light of the Altvar," Kodryn breathed, but Elvine was quick to provide a mundane correction.

"Glow stone," she said. "Often found in the deepest caves. I've read of it but never seen it . . ." She trailed off as the glow silhouetted a collection of huge forms directly ahead. They might have come to a halt if not for Wohtin's unfaltering stride. He paid little notice to what at first appeared to be a massive but fathomless structure, skirting its edge as if it were just a minor obstacle. As they drew nearer, Felnir realised the nearest shape was in fact a pillar. It was far broader than those they had seen before, the blocks that formed it cylindrical rather than the hard-edged rectangular forms that characterised the structures in the cavern. A dozen paces on they passed another of identical dimensions, but positioned at an angle to the first, with more beyond, also offset.

"A circle," he realised, gazing up to see the summits of the pillars following the line of a curve where they met the ceiling.

"No," Elvine said. "A temple."

Felnir saw it then, a massive silhouette within the circle of pillars. The statue was so lifelike, his mind initially entertained the fantastical notion that it was in fact a giant woman, frozen in time by some arcane art. Looking closer, he made out the sheen of smooth, carved stone. The figure stood over twenty feet high, her regal features moulded into grave regard of the scroll she held in both hands.

"Vysestra," Elvine whispered. For one so apparently wedded to her Covenant faith, Felnir found it odd that her tone should be one of such abject reverence. "Never have I seen such a finely worked depiction. Ancient sculptures of the Altvar are usually crude, or so worn as to be barely identifiable—"

"Stop, you worm-headed loon!" Guthnyr's voice cut through her words. Turning, Felnir saw his brother shouting after Wohtin's rapidly receding form.

"Come." Felnir touched a hand to Elvine's shoulder. "We can't lose sight of him. There'll be plenty of time for study later."

Hurrying to catch up to their guide, they passed other circled pillars, each with a statue at their centre. "Aerldun, Trieya, Karnic," Elvine said, identifying each finely wrought god. She let out a particularly delighted gasp at the sight of Karnic. Instead of the thoughtful repose of the other Altvar, the God of the Hunt was locked in combat with a great bear, one of the more celebrated feats of his legend. "They're all here," Elvine continued, letting out a shrill laugh that told Felnir she had never fully expected their search to succeed. "This is truly the Vaults of the Altvar."

"Just statues," Guthnyr grunted. "Too much to hope they'd be clad in silver."

"Guard your tongue!" Kodryn snapped. "Remember where you walk, boy."

In all the years Felnir had known him, his veteran comrade had avowed only marginal observance of the Altvar. But now he beheld the face of a man possessed by fervent belief. Kodryn's wide eyes swung from one statue to another, his face stricken by awe. It made Felnir wonder at the absence of his own sense of wonder. The enormity of their discovery should have sent his heart soaring, for the Queens could never now deny him a Vellihr's brooch. Yet, although he strove to keep it from his features, he found himself partly in sympathy with his brother. *No treasure crafted by the gods' own hands*, he thought, squinting at the sight of Ulfmaer's temple. The god of sea and storm stood atop a mound of rock, poised to throw the lightning bolt clutched in his fist. *Just very old stone.*

Finally, Wohtin came to a halt. The temples were all behind them now, save one. It was the largest yet, the circle of pillars broader and the statue at its centre massive even in comparison to the others. The glow stone also shone brighter here, clearly illuminating the god's monument, although Felnir had already guessed its identity.

Ulthnir Horuhnklehr, the Worldsmith, stood tall with one hand resting on the haft of his famed hammer and the other the pommel of his sword. His face was lowered and features carved into an expression of stern regard. Felnir imagined those who had once come to pay obeisance to the Father of All Things cowering under the weight of his stare. It certainly had an effect on Kodryn, the veteran stumbling to his knees and bowing his head, lips moving in barely heard entreaties for the Altvar's favour.

For a time, the only sound came from Kodryn's murmured worship whilst Felnir and the others looked upon Wohtin in tense expectation.

Felnir saw that his face remained that of a man at least partially returned to sanity, although the purposeful tension had been replaced by the twitch of a reluctant and uncertain soul. Following the line of his gaze, Felnir saw another shape within the circle of pillars. It was small in comparison to Ulthnir, but still substantial. *Another statue?* he wondered, looking again at Wohtin only to find him returning the scrutiny.

"And so," Wohtin said, his brow creased in grim resignation, "hath we come to it at last, my king."

"King . . . ?" Felnir began, but Wohtin had resumed his rapid stride, heading directly for the temple.

Following him through the pillars, Felnir saw that the shape he had taken for a statue bore no resemblance to any god he could name. For that matter, it bore no resemblance to a mortal human either. It towered over them by several feet, Felnir at first taking it for some abstract, malformed stone. Perhaps something dug out of this cavern and left at the Worldsmith's feet as an offering, a curio for his amusement. Also, the thing's essential strangeness was enhanced by the fact that it appeared to have grown from the temple floor. Crouching, Felnir saw how it was fused to the flagstones, putting him in mind of the buboes that grew on the faces of plague victims he had seen in the east. Straightening, he discerned a semblance of recognisable form, a twisted, multi-limbed parody of humanity, albeit lacking anything that could be called a head. The impression was enhanced when he saw that each of its three elongated limbs were entwined about a different object: a sword, a spear and a bow. Both the sword and spear were free of rust, light gleaming on sharp edges, whilst the wooden stave of the bow showed no cracks or tarnishing.

"What is this?" he said, addressing the question to Wohtin. He didn't reply, continuing to stand in grave-faced contemplation of the misshapen stone. Felnir switched his gaze to Elvine, brows raised in the hope that she might have an answer.

"I have never read or heard of anything like this," she said, shaking her head.

"What of the weapons?" Sygna asked. "Surely there must be some tale of them. The legends speak of treasures crafted by the Altvar's hand. Arms can be treasure, can they not?" She stepped closer to the thing, reaching out a tentative hand towards the bow, then stopping at Wohtin's curt command.

"Don't!" He blinked and turned a fierce gaze upon Felnir. "Accepting these gifts is not to be done lightly, my king. This—" he pointed a wavering finger at the stone "—stands as testament to my greatest crime and worst folly. Once taken up, the Sword of the Altvar cannot be put down."

Looking again at the sword, Felnir's mind summoned the memory of his recent dream, and his great-grandfather's warning: *Whatever you find there cannot be brought back to Skar Magnol . . . Do not bring it home, Felnir. Find your sister.*

Just a dream, he insisted to himself. He wasn't aware of choosing to reach for the sword, yet he had done so. He had to lean into the twisted mass to bring his hand close enough to touch the pommel. As he pressed his body to the stone, a surge of repugnance coursed through him, even though it was odourless. *Do not bring it home.* The words repeated as his fingers grasped the sword's handle. He pushed them away with visions of his return to Skar Magnol with this blade in hand. The Sword of the Altvar. A gift from Ulthnir himself. And who then would dare to think of ever again naming him the Redtooth? He would be Felnir Altvar Kelven, the God Blessed. How high he would rise . . .

Felnir blinked, the sense of repugnance surging with increased vigour. It wasn't just proximity to the stone, but a surge of nausea provoked by his own ambition. He had never denied or shied away from his desire for restitution in the eyes of his people, or the riches and fame that would result. But the hunger that had gripped him upon reaching for the sword was something different, something not born of his soul.

Releasing the sword, he stepped back, heart hammering and a sheen of fresh sweat upon his brow. Turning again to Wohtin, he drew a ragged breath before demanding, "You will tell me exactly what this thing is and how it came to be here."

A yet deeper well of regret lit Wohtin's gaze. His shoulders sagged and he replied in a soft mutter, "I once pretended to the mantle of wisdom. But the greatest lie is the one you tell yourself. I thought I knew the nature of this thing when I opened the door to invite it in. Now I know only the vastness of my own folly."

"Invited it in?" Elvine asked. The question seemed to break something in Wohtin. Shuddering, he collapsed to his knees, a spasm of his previous madness on his grief-stricken features. He began to babble as he had before, Felnir recognising the cadence of Covenant doggerel: "'Knowest only that what lieth between worlds is forever to be a mystery. Seek ye wisdom only amongst the living and the Martyrs' example . . .'"

He continued in similar vein, his words descending into spittle-flecked incoherence that tempted Felnir to beat him back to rationality. Exchanging a helpless glance with Elvine, he sighed and looked again at the sword nestled within the malformed stone. *Do not bring it home.*

"Why all this dithering?" Guthnyr said, striding forward. "We didn't come here to just stand and gawp when there's priceless bounty to be claimed."

Felnir would always wonder what stilled his hand then. Why did he stand and watch his brother reach into the ugly swirl of frozen stone and grasp the spear? Why did he not bark an order to stop, or push him away? Perhaps it had been curiosity, a basic desire to know what would happen next. In his darker, and more honest moments, however, he would be forced to acknowledge that his inaction arose from cowardice. Let Guthnyr take the risk where he would not, then at least he would have someone else to blame.

Although the spear seemed firmly embedded in the stone, it came free at the first tug. The twisted limb enclosing it crumbled like dry plaster and Guthnyr laughed as he stood back to raise his prize. Felnir watched his brother's face closely, but saw no reflection of his own revulsion when reaching for the sword. Perhaps the spear possessed different qualities. Or, perhaps it and the sword were just pieces of crafted metal and his reaction the product of a fevered mind.

"Feels lighter than it should," Guthnyr said, giving the spear an experimental twirl. "Plain though." He paused to peer at the weapon's unadorned, leaf-shaped point. "Would've thought a weapon of the gods would have at least a small inscription . . ."

He trailed off when a fresh sound came to their ears, a soft, sibilant patter that emanated from the stone. Turning back to it, Felnir saw the limb that had held the spear was rapidly dissolving, sending a cascade of pale flakes onto the temple floor. A loud crack sounded from deep within the stone and it collapsed into two pieces, which also began to crumble. Within moments, the entirety of the thing had sublimed into a pile of grit, the sword and the bow jutting from it, apparently undamaged.

"Desecration!" Kodryn's gasp drew Felnir's gaze to the veteran, finding him backing away, his face set in a horrified gape. "We have despoiled this place . . ."

"Calm yourself, old friend," Felnir said, but Kodryn's distress was not so easily allayed.

"We invite their anger," he said, retreating through the pillars, shaking his head. Felnir had seen him worried before, even fearful, but never terrified. "We prove ourselves unworthy . . ."

His words were drowned by a deep rumbling vibration beneath their feet. The subsequent tremor was violent, tipping them all onto the ground. A series of loud, echoing cracks filled the air as the entire chamber shuddered. Felnir scrambled upright when he saw the pillars begin to sway around them.

"Up!" he shouted to the others. "We have to get out of here."

"Fel!" Sygna said, gesturing urgently to the sword and the bow still jutting from the pile of shattered stone. "We came a long way just to leave them behind."

"More desecration!" Kodryn called out, staggering to his feet. "Leave them be, Felnir! We have cursed ourselves enough . . ."

Whatever additional warning he intended to impart would be forever lost, for at that moment a block of stone detached itself from the summit of the pillar to his right, plummeted in a blur, and crushed him into a bloody pulp.

CHAPTER THIRTY-TWO

Ruhlin

He awoke in the cage wagon, jostled from a dream he instantly forgot, but was certain had been distinctly unpleasant in nature. Next to him, Sygurn offered a small grin of relief, but Ruhlin also saw the wariness in his eyes. It reminded Ruhlin that he had come very close to killing this man in the *wuhltra*, Julette too. Craning his neck to survey the other wagons, he was relieved to find the seafarer alive. Only he, Sygurn, and the Morvek woman remained in their own cage. She huddled in her furs, head lowered to conceal her features.

"They rioted, you know," Sygurn said.

"What?" Ruhlin asked, casting a bleary-eyed gaze at the passing scenery. It was all low, snow-speckled hills beneath grey skies.

"The crowd in Lyhs Skarta," the Nihlvarian elaborated. "After your ... performance. It was like every fecker in the place went mad at once. All screaming out to the Altvar, swarming the sands to get at you. Not sure if they just wanted to lay hands upon your divine flesh or tear you to pieces, though some of the women clearly had other notions. Reckon the guards had to kill a dozen or more before they got us out." Sygurn paused, Ruhlin gaining the impression of a man who took exception to experiencing awe. "Seeing something impossible will do that to folk, I s'pose."

Ruhlin sat up, groaning at the aches in his back and shoulders. A glance at the rear of the wagon revealed the familiar sight of Radylf and Achela astride their horses. The whip-man's expression was as cheerfully malevolent as ever, but Ruhlin perceived a new wariness in the witch's bearing. He recalled that she hadn't seen his monster in full before and concluded she found it unsettling. An increased pitch of fear might work to their advantage when the time came, but could also make her more vigilant.

Sighing, he pushed the quandary away for later consideration, turning his attention to the Morvek woman opposite. "What's your name?" he asked her. "I know you can understand us, so speak."

Slowly, she raised her head, revealing a face set in as much grief as it was disdain. "Leave me be," she told him in thickly accented Ascarlian, adding another word in her own tongue for good measure, "*Telchak.*"

"What does that mean?" Ruhlin asked, ignoring her injunction.

"It's one of their more choice insults," Sygurn explained when the woman continued to glower in silence. "Means 'cursed one'. Looks like she caught a glimpse of your other self yesterday."

"Yes, I am cursed," Ruhlin said. Keeping his eyes on hers, he leaned forward as much as his chains would allow. "Cursed to fight like an animal for the amusement of wretches. And so are you. But you don't have to be."

"Careful," Sygurn warned, casting a sideways glance in Radylf's direction. "He's ever watchful. And we don't know if we can trust her."

"We need allies," Ruhlin returned, still staring at the Morvek woman. "And I'll gladly break the chains of anyone willing to escape this disgusting spectacle."

"How?" the woman asked, the question voiced in a hoarse, reluctant mutter.

Ruhlin sat back, slumping at an angle that would conceal his face from Radylf. "We'll get to that. But first, let us introduce ourselves. He's Sygurn and I'm Ruhlin. Though you can keep calling me *Telchak* if you like. I don't care."

Her face twitched and eyes darted towards the whip-man before she grunted a reply. "Iyaka."

"It is good to meet you, Iyaka. Do you wish to break those chains?"

Another twitch, then a nod.

"That is good. It will take time, but the day will come. You need only be ready." Ruhlin paused, inclining his head at the wagons ahead of them in the caravan. "Will you speak to the other Morvek, ask them to join with us?"

"Trust is not easily forged between your kind and ours," she said.

"Seems you trusted one of us well enough to learn our tongue," Sygurn observed.

Iyaka afforded him a sneer before shifting her attention back to Ruhlin. "I will talk to them. But promise nothing."

Ruhlin gave her a tight smile and looked again at their surroundings. "Any notion of where we're going?" he asked Sygurn.

"Not to a port, if that's what you're hoping." Sygurn settled into his furs, clearly intending to sleep. "It'll be Ossvek next, I'd bet. The only true city in the north. If I recall rightly, the *wuhltra* there can accommodate nigh ten thousand people. When they riot, it's sure to be quite a show."

The sand was already stained with the blood of a dozen or more fallen fighters when Radylf pushed him through the door. Once again, Ruhlin's chains had been left in place, but at least he had no friends to worry over for today he stood alone. The four men awaiting him were all impressively tall and well muscled. Each one stood considerably taller than Ruhlin and were thickly armed and armoured with a fearsome array of weapons, their faces hidden behind leather masks. Two held broad-bladed axes with four foot long iron hafts. A third hefted some kind of club, a gnarled branch studded with brass bolts. The fourth bore a sword of such improbable size, Ruhlin wondered how such a thing could be wielded. The answer came when its bearer began to whirl the seven-foot-long blade in a disconcerting display of accustomed skill.

"Put down your weapons and stand still," Ruhlin called out to them, feeling an obligation to at least make an attempt at avoiding the horror to come. "Do that, and nothing will happen."

He saw a brief exchange of glances between them, hearing a muffled laugh from the man with the absurdly long sword. He didn't speak, but increased the speed of his whirling. Starting forward, shoulders hunched low, his laugh became a snarl, the blade flickering as it spun.

"Then I can't save you," Ruhlin said, not bothering to raise his voice as the huge man closed upon him. "For which I'm sorry."

It was different this time, for when the red fog dissipated, he found he could remember more of the preceding carnage. He recalled the sword wielder's startled curse when Ruhlin's massive hand had caught it mid-whirl, and the sight of the raw bleeding mess of his face when the blade swiped across it, tearing away the mask and much of the flesh and bone beneath. Other moments were vague, such as the fate of the two axe wielders. But he could easily bring to mind the final gurgling shriek of the man with the studded club in the moment before Ruhlin tore his head from his shoulders. It sat in his hands now, the mask still intact and the eyes visible through the slits showing a last flicker of life as blood seeped in a thick torrent from the ragged stump of his neck.

Most notable of all was his failure to faint. As his body resumed its normal dimensions, he stood slicked in gore, chest heaving from recent exertion but feeling none of the exhaustion that had claimed him at Lyhs Skarta. He did feel a pain in his ears, but quickly realised it to result from the roar of the crowd. The *wuhltra* at Ossvek was a taller structure than its northern counterpart, the rows of seating ascending above a high wall surrounding the sand circle. The over-seers of today's amusement had evidently heeded a warning from Eldryk. A cordon of guards had been stationed around the lowest tier to prevent the crowd spilling onto the sands to threaten the Aerling's most valuable asset. They had a difficult task, for Ruhlin found the frenzied adulation of these people equal parts repellent and jarring. Men and women screamed incoherent praise as they strained against the cordon, arms reaching out to him in desperate need. Some ripped their clothes to bare breasts and genitals like some form of offering.

"They're mad," he muttered to himself, an observation that summoned his whispering inner coward. *But also useful*, its seductive hiss suggested. *Throw that trophy into their midst. See what chaos it births. Mayhap it'll be enough to fight your way clear of this place.*

A glance at Achela, standing ever watchful at Eldryk's side on the lowest tier, disabused of him of the notion that he could act before she triggered the *stagna*. Besides, to fight his way out of here, he would need to surrender himself to the beast again, robbing him of the awareness needed to free Aleida and his friends. She also stood at her father's side, features set in the same tearful sympathy as before. Unlike this arena full of screaming creatures, she saw nothing to celebrate in his transformation. She, at least, was not in love with the beast.

Opening his hands, Ruhlin let the masked head fall and walked from the sands, Radylf flinging the door open to welcome him back into the dark.

The caravan moved on from Ossvek the following day, less one fighter who had failed to survive his contest. Through whispers exchanged at night, Iyaka confirmed the willingness of her fellow Morvek to join in the escape, but with an important condition.

"It must happen soon," she told him. Come nightfall, the wagons were corralled at the side of the road and fires lit close by for warmth. However, Radylf permitted no release from their chains, making unheard conversation difficult. Sygurn provided a solution by feigning sleep and snoring at a sufficient volume to smother their murmured discussion.

"We must wait," Ruhlin whispered back. "We'll need a ship—"

"Your kind needs a ship," she cut in. "Mine do not. Our lands lie west, not east across the big water. And, of us all, only you are certain to draw breath when this caravan reaches a port. We will lose at least one life at every *wuhltra*. He knows this," she added, nodding to Sygurn. The Nihlvarian's snores paused for a second, eyelids fluttering, before he resumed his grating drone.

"It will be difficult," Ruhlin said. "Much depends on choosing the right moment."

She shook her head, voice dropping further. "No. All depends on killing her." She flicked her eyes at Achela. As had been her habit in the Aerling's mountain holdfast, she spent her evenings sitting outside his cage. Although he was confident she couldn't overhear their words, her unending vigilance was a constant worry.

"I dislike killing my own people," Iyaka went on. "Even those who sell themselves to your kind. So many of us have been lost. Our blood is more precious than the gold you lust for. But she is *uhltcha*, a false heart, so hers I'll gladly spill. All I'll need is free hands and a blade. You can do that, *Telchak*."

"It's not so simple. When it happens . . ." He trailed off, struggling to explain something he himself barely understood. "This thing inside me is mindless, filled with bloodlust. I set it free and I know not who it will kill. Nor can I command it to break your chains."

"It didn't kill him." She jerked her chin at Sygurn. "Or the tall one. I saw it stay its hand. I saw *you* stay its hand."

Ruhlin thought back to the bloody slaughter in the *wuhltra* at Lyhs Skarta, how Julette's plea had found some small purchase on his disordered mind. Also, there had been his increased awareness during the combat in Ossvek. Could it be that when the beast was upon him, it wasn't so mindless after all? The notion troubled him, raising the uncomfortable thought that the distinction between himself and the monster within was not as marked as he preferred to imagine.

"Even so," he said. "The difficulty remains. She can summon the *stagna* within the blink of an eye . . ." He fell silent. *But there is another who can stop her.* Aleida's affection for him was obvious, but would she be willing to abet in her aunt's murder? *You can trust the Aerling's daughter.*

"When we come to the next *wuhltra*," Iyaka said, interrupting his thoughts. "It must happen then, or it will not happen at all. You ask for trust, *Telchak*. I and my kind have given it. Now return the gift."

Reaching the next city required six full days on the road. It was an extensive collection of mostly *kehlgruin* buildings sprawled across both banks of the wide river that flowed south from the mountains. Sygurn named it as Turihmvek, capital of the Vyrnkral Veld. A mile short of the city's edge, the caravan was met by a fifty-strong contingent of armoured warriors on horseback led by a figure Ruhlin had seen before. The wagon was close enough to Eldryk's carriage for him to hear what followed when the Aerling hurried to offer Tuhlvyr Feydrik a suitably obsequious greeting.

"Yes, yes," the hulking luminary said, waving an impatient hand. "It seems the streets of my city are thronged by a mass of maddened mud grubbers. The swine have been gathering for days, ever since word spread about your blessed fighter. Best to wait here for nightfall before making for the *wuhltra*, and even then it would be better to keep him out of sight. They're an excitable lot. No telling what they'll do if they catch a glimpse of him."

Eldryk bobbed his head. "I'll see to it, Tuhlvyr."

Feydrik grunted and cast his gaze over the wagons until he found Ruhlin. "Now that's the face of a fearless man," he observed to Eldryk, studying Ruhlin in narrow appraisal. "Got a taste for it now, has he? I've often noted that fighters in the *Meidvang* come to revel in the slaughter."

"He exceeds expectations at each contest, Tuhlvyr," Eldryk said. "Though the quality of opposition has been wanting thus far."

"Worried over the odds you'll get here, eh?" Feydrik barked a laugh. "Don't fret. I've got something that'll test even him." He tugged on his reins, turning his horse about. "My guards will escort you come nightfall. Be sure to keep him concealed."

"I will, Tuhlvyr," Eldryk assured him, but Feydrik was already cantering back to the city.

Ruhlin was denied the sight of the city's inner precincts, having been consigned to the Aerling's carriage for the journey to the *wuhltra*. Naturally, it featured a good deal more comforts than the cage wagon, featuring cushioned couches and a large bed. The Aerling perched himself upon one of the couches, sipping some form of red-hued liquor from a clay cup as he observed Ruhlin, silence reigning as the carriage swayed and jerked its way through the streets. Ruhlin's chains remained in place and he had been positioned on the floor beside the door. The Aerling's unspeaking scrutiny was discomfiting, but the atmosphere was thickened further by the presence of Aleida and her aunt. They sat next to each other on a separate, smaller couch. Achela maintained her inexpressive watchfulness whilst he could tell Aleida was engaged in a continual struggle to keep her features free of emotion. For the most part, she averted her gaze from him, staring at nothing with her jaw tensed and brows drawn. It was only when her eyes darted towards him that he saw the tightening of her lips and rapid blinking that told of considerable inner distress.

"Was he right?" Eldryk asked finally, the sudden break in the silence provoking Ruhlin into a small start of surprise.

"Aerling?" he asked, puzzled.

"Tuhlvyr Feydrik," Eldryk said. "Was he right in thinking you've acquired a taste for blood? That apparently common trait of those who fight in the Meidvang."

Ruhlin detected a bitterness in the Aerling's tone that said much for what he thought of the Tuhlvyr's judgement. "No, Aerling," Ruhlin said. "I have not."

"Of course you haven't. Only a fool would think so." Eldryk raised his cup to his lips, then, sighing, set it aside and leaned closer to Ruhlin. "I know you lot gossip. So I assume you've heard my tale by now."

"I heard you were also a fighter once. That you won your freedom after a season of victories."

"All true. But did you learn how I became a fighter in the first place?"

Ruhlin saw little reason to lie. "Your father left your family with debts when he died. You sold yourself to a slave owner to clear them."

Eldryk raised an eyebrow, pursing his lips. "Not exactly. You see, I was even younger than you are now when the chains were first clamped upon my wrists. Little more than a child, in fact. And the choice was made for me, by my mother, very much at my sister's urging. It's a curious thing to hate one's family, but that is how it was in our house. My father hated my mother, she hated him, I hated them both and Angomar hated us all. And yet, when given the maternal instruction to sell myself, I did so with little argument. For duty required it. Duty to family and, in a wider sense, duty to the very essence of what it means to be Nihlvarian. I know you Teilvik have long since lost the will required to match the ideal of humanity the Altvar ordained for us. But we have not. *I* have not. Surrendering to ignoble poverty was not the act of a true descendant of the Uhltvar. Far better to risk an ugly death in the *wuhltra* than suffer that most terrible fate: the acceptance of weakness. Strength brings reward, boy. It did for me, and it will for you. And not just the removal of those chains."

He leaned back, turning his gaze upon his daughter. "You think I don't see what grows between you two?" He let out a faint laugh. "Of course I do. For I orchestrated it. I know my daughter's heart. She is every bit the rebellious, stubborn bitch her mother was. Forbidding her from your presence guaranteed that she would seek it out. Bonds forged in secret are always the strongest, sealed as they are in shared trust. She can be yours. When the Meidvang ends and the last blood is spilled, I will give her to you. Is it not the most fitting reward? A union that will form the foundation of all that comes next. Your blood joined with mine, boy. Think of it. Consider what we might achieve. But . . ." He settled a stern, unblinking stare upon Ruhlin, speaking on with a tone devoid of all humour. "To give you both freedom and my daughter, I must know you are worthy. I must be sure that the heart that beats in your breast is as devoted to the Altvar's ideal as mine. I can tell this is not yet so. But, in time, once you have accepted the truth of what you are and been forged anew in the flame of the Meidvang, perhaps it will."

Aleida let out a small, choked gasp then. Putting her hand to her mouth, she turned away, eyes closed tight.

"Quiet!" Eldryk snapped, rounding on her. The impending violence in his bearing stirred a dangerous flare of heat in Ruhlin's core, bringing an unbidden growl to his throat. Achela sat fractionally straighter, though Ruhlin saw that her eyes flicked between him and her niece. A line appeared in her normally placid brow that might indicate concern. Fortunately, Ruhlin had recaptured the Aerling's attention.

"Too much Morvek blood in her," Eldryk said, relaxing back into the couch and reaching again for his cup. "Her mother was only a half-savage, you see. I hoped the worst of their weakness had been bred out, but, as ever, she disappoints me in most things."

The heat in Ruhlin's gut diminished, but not fully. He had never truly wished to take another life, but did so now. "I will never be as you are," he said. He knew he risked Radylf's whip when this carriage reached its destination, but found he didn't care. "You talk of the Altvar's ideal, but it is a twisted nonsense of their tale. Strength was not the entirety of their gifts. There was wisdom and compassion, too. Your people have lost these, as mine have not."

Eldryk regarded him in silence for a time, sipping his red drink with brow furrowed, as if he had heard an unamusing and baffling joke. "Your people will mostly be dead or in chains soon enough," he said. "Then we'll see who the Altvar favour most. Think on what I said, and best gird yourself well for what awaits you in the *wuhltra* tomorrow. I doubt the Tuhlvyr was making an idle boast."

CHAPTER THIRTY-THREE

Thera

That night she dreamed of Olversahl, a rare and unwelcome occurrence. Despite the glory heaped upon her shoulders in the aftermath of the city's fall, she preferred not to dwell on the event. As was ever the case with much celebrated tales of heroism, the reality had been far from glorious.

"Back, you foreign filth!" Kaeric yelled, sweeping his axe in a broad arc to keep the Blackheart's soldiers at bay. A giant of a man moving with the speed and aggression of one far younger than his sixty summers, he succeeded in hacking through the leg of one soldier and the chest of another before the rest swarmed him. From her hiding place beneath the mid-deck, Thera watched their frenzied daggers raise a fountain of blood. The ranks of the Blackheart's host were filled with the dregs of Albermaine, villainous scum well versed in knife work. Yet, despite their skill and ferocity, Kaeric kept his feet and continued to fight. Roaring, he dislodged the wiry man on his back with a heave, bared teeth to bite the face of the one repeatedly driving a blade into his shoulder, freeing his arm to swing the axe into the neck of a third who had just stabbed him in the lower gut.

Thera watched it all in frozen fascination. She didn't remember being scared in this moment, her immobility resulting from the shock of experiencing battle for the first time. No amount of practice under her parents' eye, or the less kindly tutelage of her great-grandfather, could have prepared her for this first encounter with such unrestrained violence. It was true that Kaeric had shoved her into this nook with stern instructions not to move, regardless of what happened. Still, she would always feel the shame of bearing mute witness to an old man's final act of valour.

"Ah," a familiar, gravelly voice sounded behind her. "There you are. Finally."

Margnus Gruinskard stood upon the deck, hands resting atop his stone axe, head cocked at a critical angle as he looked her over. "Were you really this thin back then?" he went on, heavy brows creasing in doubt. "I don't recall you being so scrawny."

The realisation that she currently resided in a dream brought a relieved groan to Thera's lips. "Whereas," she said, clambering from her hiding place, "you remain the same ugly old fuck I remember."

Instead of the expected growling rebuke, a smile played over the old man's lips and she even saw a glimmer of affection in his single eye. "Strange to say," he sighed, "but I find I've rather missed you, great-granddaughter."

"Then I regret I can't join you in the sentiment."

A scream drew her attention back to the struggle. Kaeric was on his knees now, the maimed or slain bodies of his foes all around. More were clambering over the stern, soon to finish him in vicious fashion. That had been her moment. By sheer happenstance, the nook Kaeric had consigned her to had been filled with casks of lamp oil. Now she would begin sloshing the contents about the under-deck whilst the last agonised seconds of Kaeric's life played out above. She had paused in the act of striking her flint, mesmerised by the sight of the old warrior's blood seeping through the boards.

"He had a good death," Gruinskard commented as Kaeric continued to die before their eyes. "And would have been proud that you witnessed it. He was always quite fond of you."

"And less so of you." Turning to face him, she found the Tielwald once again disappointing her expectations to offer her a countenance filled with grim import rather than criticism. This dream was growing stranger by the second. "Why have I summoned you here?" she wondered, shaking her head.

"You haven't," he told her. "I summoned myself, and a great deal of effort it required too." He reached into his furs, his hand emerging with a small trinket. "You recall my gift?"

"I do." Her hand went to the cord about her neck, finding the silver knot. She thought it strange that her mind should contrive to adorn her younger self with it. "I've seen similar baubles since, about the necks of our enemies."

"Ah." Gruinskard's brows arched. "They have their own *hahren krayma*. Only to be expected. It explains a great deal, in fact."

Hahren krayma. Thera frowned as she parsed the unfamiliar phrase. "Dream walker?"

"An ability I have borne all my life, though often thought it a curse. These—" he held up the silver knot "—enable me to walk in the dreams of any who wear them, though they can be fickle depending on the character of the wearer. Given the difficulty I had reaching you and your brother, you must both despise me a great deal."

Thera could only stare at him, wondering at the depth of her own somnolent imagination. She would have dismissed this as distracting nonsense and set about clawing her way back to wakefulness, if not for the trinket she had found on Annuk. *There are no coincidences.*

"You're saying you are truly Margnus Gruinskard," she said. "Not just an unpleasant phantom inflicted upon me by my own memories. And that you possess the ability to place yourself in the dreams of others."

"Yes," he replied with a small shrug. "I would relate the full story of how I came to understand my blessing, but time moves against us, even in dreams where it can often be stretched. I have guidance for you, Thera, and I beg you to set aside all doubt, and your hatred of me, and heed it well. For if you don't, Ascarlia will fall to our enemies and great will be the suffering of our people."

A series of sharp, scraping sounds drew her gaze back to Kaeric. A knot of soldiers surrounded him, daggers flashing. Soon the flames would blossom and they would die screaming whilst she swam to shore, there to learn come the morn that her parents were slain. The succeeding days had been a confusion of acclaim and grief, made even harder to bear by the absence of her kin. Her brothers shunned her in their shame, and her great-grandfather was too embroiled in the politics of a recently conquered city to offer her a word of consolation.

"I told Sister Iron the truth," she said, watching Kaeric bleed his last. "When they took me to Skar Magnol to receive the Queens' favour. The old Sister Iron was a kindlier and less guarded soul than she who now wears the mantle. I told her all of it. How I had hidden whilst Kaeric fought. How I was undeserving of the renown heaped upon me. She said, 'More wars are won with deceit than courage, girl. The cost of taking Olversahl was far higher than your great-grandfather promised. You mourn for your parents whilst many more mourn for lost kin. To make a bitter victory sweeter, we must have heroes.' Then she told me it was clear the Altvar had ordained me to take the Vellihr's path, and many would be the chances to win true glory in the years to come." She turned to face the old man. "You promised them an easy victory here. You lied. And your lie cost me dear."

He didn't flinch from the accusation in her gaze, his craggy features stern with a refusal to be diverted from his purpose. "We have not the leisure to indulge old grievances, Thera. I come to you with guidance. To preserve this realm, you must heed it."

She closed her eyes, listening to the Blackheart's soldiers banter in their foreign tongue, recalling her grim enjoyment when their laughter turned to shrieks. This, the most terrible night of her life, had been the consequence of this man's guidance to the Sister Queens. *Why should I heed him now?* The answer was inescapable, if unpalatable. *Because, despite the cost, he brought victory.*

"What guidance, Great-grandfather?" she asked with a sigh.

"First, I must know where you're currently sailing."

"Don't you know?"

"I can walk in dreams. It doesn't convey knowledge of all things. Now, where do you sail?"

"The Kast Geld. In a mast-less ship as we scurry from place to place to avoid our enemies."

"Enemies. You mean the red-faced horde from beyond the Fire Isles?"

"They're called Nihlvarians. You haven't heard the name before?"

"I knew a new enemy had come against us, aided by the Volkrath agents in our midst. But their name had so far eluded me."

"If you knew, why not warn the Sister Queens before now?"

"The scale of the danger that comes against us was not revealed to me. As for the Sister Queens, I have voiced warnings for years. Until now, my suspicions were too vague, too lacking in real peril for them to heed except with platitudes. Long have they looked upon me as just an irritant, a bothersome relic. At least now, with war upon us, they'll have no choice but to listen." He paused, grimacing. "Time runs too short for fulsome explanations. Are you able to reach the Veilwald of the Kast Geld?"

"We sail a day to the south of Ayl-Ah-Vahrim. A great *menda* of the enemy is already ashore. It can only mean Ossgrym Ironbones has been vanquished."

Gruinskard shook his head. "No. The Ironbones has been blooded, but not defeated. And with your aid, he won't be."

"My duty is clear. The Nihlvarian fleet is great, and I'm told by one I trust that more ships will follow. I must bring warning to the Sister Queens . . ."

"No. Do not return to Skar Magnol. I will relate all the warning they need. You must do what you can to stave off this invasion until our full strength can be gathered." Gruinskard lowered his head, brows furrowed in thought. "Make for the eastern shore of Ayl-Ah-Vahrim. A place called Endyr's Cut. That *Johten Apt* of yours should be able to find it. There will be one there to greet you, one who also wears the knot. You can trust him to guide you further."

Thera began to argue that her place was at Sister Iron's side, but her words were drowned by a cacophonous rumble from the port. Turning, she saw a wall of dust rise above the rooftops, obscuring the sight of the Ulthnir's great stone effigy collapsing into rubble. Thera was grateful to feel the tug of awareness drawing her back to the waking world, for it would spare her what came next.

"You ask me for trust, Great-grandfather," she said as the dream began to fragment around them. "It cannot be so easily given."

"Yet give it you must." He advanced towards her, his form beginning to dissipate into formless mist. "For the sake of your mother, who once wore this." Before slipping into nothingness, he brandished the silver knot, his parting words a fading echo: "She trusted me, Thera. So must you . . ."

She woke with a start, gaze flooding with morning light that had found a gap in the ragged roof of her shelter. Closing her eyes against the glare, she sat up, realising she had her silver knot clutched in her fist, the metal hot against her skin. She opened her hand, finding the trinket sitting atop a patch of reddened skin. The desire to dismiss the old man's visitation as just another ill-favoured dream fluttered and died in her breast. It had been too real. He had been too much himself. And this thing burned too hot.

"Gelmyr!" she called out, heaving aside the shelter's flap to emerge onto the deck. "Change of course!"

Come the evening, the mountainous bulk of Ayl-Ah-Vahrim once again rose ahead of the *Great Wolf*'s prow. The flicker of campfires was too far west to be seen from this vantage, but Thera was unwilling to risk being glimpsed by hostile eyes upon the shore. She ordered the ship to circle until full darkness before ceding to Gelmyr's guidance.

"Be thankful for a full moon," he said, casting a glance at the silver disc in the sky. "Endyr's Cut is hard enough to find in daylight."

"It's an anchorage?" Thera asked.

The *Johten Apt* shook his head. "A narrow channel in the cliffs on the eastern shore. It can only be navigated between tides, and even then it requires a deft touch on the tiller." Gelmyr's gaze narrowed a little. "Given that you commanded us to sail there, I assumed you must have heard of the cut before now."

No. The Tielwald told me about it in a dream. Thera bit down a bitter laugh at the absurdity of this entire enterprise. In truth, she had never heard mention of Endyr's Cut before her great-grandfather's night-time visitation. However, Gelmyr's confirmation that the Cut actually existed made it plain that the old man had been no figment.

He truly is a dream walker, she thought, the notion raising a plethora of uncomfortable questions. The Tielwald's mastery of secrets and facility for scheming was undoubted. Now she knew why. It occurred to her that a man who possessed such power could have made himself great, accrued vast riches, even challenged the Queens for supremacy in this realm. But Margnus Gruinskard never had.

"Something I remembered from my days as an apprentice," she told Gelmyr. "Sister Iron once spoke of a secluded berth in the northern Outer Isles. If the Ironbones needed a hiding place, it seemed likely he would seek it there."

It was thin. A poor lie she felt sure this wily old soul would see through in an instant. Yet he chose to sidestep the issue, confining his response to a soft mutter. "It's certainly a place the Ironbones would never want the Vellihr of Justice to see."

Hours of rowing brought them to a point a mile south of the tall cliffs dominating the east-facing shore of the island, waves scattering white along their base. "There," Gelmyr said, pointing to a barely noticeable interruption in the frothing line. Thera saw a mix of nostalgia and trepidation on his features as he took firmer hold of the tiller. "Haven't done this in a long while, and never in a ship so large."

Pondering his words, Thera could think of only one reason why a sailor would steer a small craft into a perilous channel on this coast. "Were you a smuggler, Gelmyr?" she asked.

His beard bunched in chagrin. "Not all who find themselves in service to the Sister Queens have so noble a past as you." He paused, shifting his grip on the tiller as the *Great Wolf* crested a swell. "For years I made a decent living running all manner of goods from Albermaine to nigh every port in Ascarlia until your predecessor caught up with me. The choice she gave me was simple: become her *Johten Apt* or suffer exile. It was easily made."

They approached the cliffs at a steady stroke, Thera's sense of danger welling as the sheer walls of granite loomed above. She didn't see the cut until the *Great Wolf*'s prow swung precariously towards the rocks crowding the shoreline. At first glance, it seemed too narrow to allow passage of so large a ship, appearing as just a sliver of shadow in an already darkened edifice. Then, as Gelmyr skilfully rode a wave to bring them closer, she saw that the tall fissure broadened at its base.

"Fast stroke!" the *Johten Apt* called, the resultant rapid sweep of oars successfully overcoming a swell that threatened to push the ship back. The subsequent shift in the current brought them into the cut, the moonlit sky vanishing to leave them in utter darkness.

"Torches!" Thera shouted, but the *Great Wolf* sped swift and untroubled through the gloom to emerge in a channel beneath an aperture in the rock above. For a time they wallowed in the rise and fall of a small lagoon whilst Gelmyr ordered the starboard oars stilled. The port rowers soon brought the prow around to point at another opening. This was broader than the seaward cut, but with a much lower ceiling. Looking up at the mass of rock passing above, Thera felt a perverse pang of gratitude for having lost the mast. This passage took several minutes to navigate, Thera noting how the water calmed the further they went.

"Waves get drained away into smaller channels," Gelmyr explained. "Makes for a gentle course, but only when the tides are kind. Try this at dusk or dawn and you'll find your hull dashed to splinters. Makes the dock unreachable for long stretches of the day."

"Dock?" Thera asked, but his response was forestalled by Ragnalt's shout from the foredeck.

"Lights ahead!"

Hurrying forward, she saw the familiar glow of ships' lights illuminating the hulls of three skiffs. She also made out the glint of helm and blade upon their decks. Thera opened her mouth to shout the command to draw arms, but stopped when a call echoed from the approaching craft.

"Thera Speldrenda!" The voice was male and unfamiliar, but also lacking the mangled accent of their enemies.

"Stop oars!" Thera instructed, then clambered up onto the prow. As the *Great Wolf* neared the three skiffs, she saw the warriors crowding their decks more clearly. All were girded for war with shields raised, swords drawn or axes held ready. Many were helmed, and she made out the ragged bandages on the heads of several who weren't; this lot had seen battle recently.

"Thera Speldrenda!" the call came again, delivered by a young man perched on the bow of the nearest skiff. He wore a sword at his belt but hadn't felt the need to draw it. Thera didn't know his face, but had little difficulty in identifying the small silver trinket he dangled from a cord as the two vessels approached to within yards of each other.

"That's my name," she told him, fishing in her shirt to extract her own silver knot. "I believe we're expected." The young man smiled in relief as she raised her trinket, Thera guessing his age at barely twenty summers. She found it odd that her great-grandfather would recruit one so youthful into his service, but the old man's ways were often curious.

"That you are, Vellihr," he told her. She watched his expression falter as he scanned the *Great Wolf*, taking in the damage she had suffered and the patent weariness of her crew. *He hoped for more impressive aid*, Thera deduced, finding she couldn't fault his disappointment. However, he brightened quickly to afford her a respectful nod. "I am Aldeyn. Come, let us escort you to my uncle."

"Your uncle?"

"Yes. Ossgrym, Veilwald of the Kast Geld. I believe you are already acquainted."

Ossgrym Ironbones could never have been called handsome, but Thera felt recent tribulations had rendered an already unwelcoming visage into something that would provoke fear in even the hardiest soul. Although not especially tall, his stocky frame was substantial, neck and arms thick with muscle that hadn't thinned with age. His stubby-fingered hands gripped the long-hafted hammer he favoured in battle with what Thera felt to be an undue tightness, as if greeting a potential foe rather than an ally come in time of dire need.

The *Great Wolf* had followed Aldeyn's skiff along a succession of narrow channels or water-crafted tunnels until they emerged into a vast space beneath overhanging rock. Two dozen vessels of varying sizes bobbed at anchor alongside a long timber pier. Thera quelled a dispirited sigh at finding most to be fishing craft, counting only three actual ships amongst them. To contest the Nihlvarian fleet, they would need one of their own, and this plainly wasn't it. Shifting her sight to the pier, she found Ossgrym standing there with a knot of warriors at his back.

"The dock you spoke of, I take it?" she asked Gelmyr, wondering just how much contraband must have been unloaded here over the years. Given Ossgrym's presence, she had little doubt it had all been done with his full contrivance. "Any reason you never felt obligated to disclose its existence to Sister Iron or myself?"

"You never asked," he replied with a sheepish grimace.

Upon walking the gangplank to tread upon the pier, Thera had to suppress the urge to pronounce immediate judgement on the Veilwald of the Kast Geld. The temptation was made worse by the man's patent hostility and lack of contrition.

"One ship?" he observed, voice curt and eyes hard. "That's all the Queens deign to send us?"

"Veilwald Ossgrym Styrntorc," she said, ignoring his comment to offer a respectful nod. She then stood in stern silence, matching his stare until he consented to grunt out a greeting.

"Vellihr Thera Speldrenda." His nostrils flared before he huffed out the rest. "I bid you welcome to Ayl-Ah-Vahrim. I would have been glad to convene a feast in your honour, but battle with unheralded foes has provided considerable distraction of late."

Thera's eyes strayed to the warriors at Ossgrym's back. Like those aboard Aldeyn's skiffs, they had the ragged, unwashed and bruised appearance that arose from recent combat. However, she took paradoxical comfort from the resentment she saw on their faces. Those cowed by defeat lacked the fortitude to indulge in animus.

"Clearly, Veilwald," she told Ossgrym, forcing a smile, "we have much to talk about."

CHAPTER THIRTY-FOUR

Elvine

S he couldn't hear herself screaming. Heeding Felnir's command, she had begun to sprint from the temple, meaning she was only a yard from Kodryn when the huge stone crushed him. Blood and bone grit splashed her full in the face, the iron sting of it invading her mouth. Rendered immobile by shock, she could only stand and scream out her distress, the sound swallowed by the cacophony of shattering rock that filled this vast cavern from end to end.

Arms enclosed her waist, lifting her off her feet and bearing her away. She twisted, catching sight of Colvyn's hard, intent features before a fresh tremor shook the ground and sent them both tumbling. She lay huddled upon the cavern floor, hands clamped to her ears as the tremors continued, punctuated by a series of stunning thuds she knew to be the sound of other pillars collapsing. As the certainty of death dawned, she was surprised to find her terror fading, replaced by a sharp, aching sense of regret.

"I'm sorry, Mother," she whispered, tasting Kodryn's blood upon her tongue. "How I would have loved to show you this . . ."

An interval followed in which she took advantage of her new-found calm to rehearse the events that had brought her here. She tried to suppress the memory of Uhttar's death, for she didn't wish it to be the image she carried to the Divine Portals. Also, she struggled to combat a palpable sense of unfairness. Berrine's grief would be dreadful, perhaps even fatal. Also, Elvine had risked death in pursuit of this place and now wouldn't live to tell another soul of it. *I would have been the most celebrated scholar of the age*, she mused. *Discoverer of the Vaults of the Altvar. Now just more bones littering a cave.* She began to calculate how long it might be before anyone discovered her smashed, presumably unidentifiable skeleton, when it occurred to her that she wasn't actually dead, at least not yet.

Sitting up, she dislodged a covering of dust and grit to find herself amidst a newly created sea of fallen stone. Panicked by the thought she could be the only soul still drawing breath in this place, she stood, letting out a fulsome sigh of relief at the sight of Colvyn staggering upright a few yards away.

"FELNIR!"

The shout came from Guthnyr. The warrior clawed at a mass of rubble, heaving boulders aside in what was plainly a hopeless endeavour. The temple to Ulthnir the Worldsmith was no more, just a mound of tumbled pillars. Elvine considered it possible that some portion of the mighty statue might have survived, but not Felnir, Sygna, Falk and, she concluded with a choked sob, Wohtin.

"Brother!" Guthnyr cried, dislodging another boulder from the pile. His hands were already bloodied by the task and his breath came is ragged heaves, but he showed no signs of tiring.

"He's . . ." Elvine began, but Colvyn held up a hand, bidding her to silence with a shake of his head. Turning away, Elvine surveyed the rest of the cavern, finding the other temples mostly destroyed. Ulfmaer's abode had suffered the least damage, although a falling pillar had sheared off the tip of his lightning bolt. The statue itself remained whole, however, provoking a small, shameful welling of gratification in Elvine's breast. *I'll have something to show Mother after all.*

She and Colvyn stood and watched Guthnyr exhaust himself trying to reach a man beyond saving. Finally, with hands stained crimson and body sapped of strength, he collapsed, breaths shifting into sobs. "Fucking spear," Elvine heard him gasp. She winced at the raw guilt in his voice, even as his words stirred her to action.

A brief search revealed the spear lying undamaged close by. Crouching, Elvine reached a hand to it, then hesitated. Hadn't Guthnyr's claiming of this thing summoned all this ruin? But had it? The malformed statue had collapsed after he wrested the spear from its grasp. She felt an inexplicable certainty that the tremors had been connected to the statue rather than the spear.

Swallowing hard, Elvine gripped the weapon and lifted it from the dust. She waited, ears alive for the crack of sundered rock or another rumble in the ground. When neither happened, she straightened with the weapon in hand, finding Guthnyr staring at her in stark amazement. Or was it suspicion? This was his prize, after all.

"It's . . . safe," she said, feeling a strange mix of shame and foolishness. She held the spear out to him. "Here."

He shook his head and looked away, remaining slumped and silent amidst the rubble.

"Leave the cursed thing here," Colvyn said, eyeing the spear as one might a venomous and angry snake.

"I can't," Elvine said. "Sister Lore would want us to bring this to her." *And when I do*, she concluded inwardly, *I can request any boon and she will surely grant it.* The spear was her key to freedom for herself and her mother. She couldn't abandon it.

"We can't stay here," Colvyn told Guthnyr, who responded with only a baleful glance before resuming his miserable slouch.

"Your brother wouldn't want . . ." Elvine began, trailing off when Guthnyr rasped out a hollow laugh.

"What would you know of my brother's wants?" he muttered.

"I know he found much to criticise in you," she returned. "And would so now. Sitting on your backside wallowing in grief avails this mission nothing."

"I could give a rat's turd for your mission, girl."

"Felnir did." This brought a sharpening to his gaze, reminding her this was a very dangerous man when the mood took him. She pushed her fear aside and stood straighter, planting the spear and speaking with stiff formality. "As appointed Scholar of Sister Lore, I remind you that we are here on her auspices. The *Sea Hawk* has lost its captain and will require another if we are to sail home. The task falls to you, whether you wish it or not." Seeing a mix of anger and grief put a quiver to his features, she softened her tone. "Do it for him, Guthnyr. Restore the honour he wanted so badly by finishing what he started."

Guthnyr closed his eyes, raising his face to drag in a long breath. "The Queens' judgement," he sighed. "My great-grandfather's schemes. That was all Felnir's worry. I never cared for any of it. All I ever wanted was to be at his side as he sailed this world and made it his own. Now what has it brought us . . . ?"

His words faded as a faint but detectable tremor thrummed the ground, followed by a series of ominous cracks from above.

"Let's go," Colvyn said, voice curt with a refusal to tolerate further argument. Taking hold of Elvine's arm, he began to pull her away. "Leave him."

"Guthnyr!" she called out, but he continued to sit and watch them flee. Snorting in exasperation, she turned and ran alongside Colvyn, feeling the ground shake with increasing violence as they pelted for the gateway. She heard the booming thud of dislodged stone impacting the cavern floor but didn't turn, keeping her gaze fixed on the portal ahead and resisting the panicked urge to cast the spear aside lest it slow her down.

They exited the Vaults of the Altvar in a thick cloud of dust. Blinking tears, Elvine turned to squint at the vague scene of destruction visible through the gateway, then gasped in alarm as a large silhouette loomed out of the haze. Guthnyr bore them both down in his rush, sparing them the hail of grit and shards that exploded from the portal. The three of them lay there, coughing in the settling dust and feeling the tremors fade from the floor.

The subsequent darkness was banished when Colvyn struck flint to his torch, illuminating the jagged wall of displaced stone now filling the gateway. *The Vaults of the Altvar*, Elvine thought. *Found then lost forever in a single day.* It occurred to her that Sister Lore might take a dim view of the outcome to this mission, although Elvine trusted the spear would ameliorate any royal anger.

"Take it," she said, once again offering the weapon to Guthnyr.

Pushing himself upright and shaking the grit from his hair, he afforded the spear no more than a cursory glance. "I'll never lay a hand on that thing again," he said. Lighting his own torch, he started along the passage back to the underground city, his voice a faint, weary echo in the gloom. "Come on then. I've a ship to claim. Let's hope I don't have to kill anyone to do it."

No voices were raised in objection to Guthnyr's claim to captaincy of the *Sea Hawk*, although Elvine felt the quiescence of the crew owed more to shock and grief than regard for their lost leader's brother. Behsla voiced the possibility of mounting a rescue, but her words were coloured by a note of forlorn desperation rather than fierce denial.

"Ten thousand couldn't dig them out," Guthnyr told her, raising his scraped hands. "And trust me, I tried." He surveyed his brother's *menda*, his face that of a man setting himself to an unavoidable but detested obligation. "Felnir died fulfilling a mission ordained by Sister Lore herself, and I'll see it done. All I ask is that you follow me as far as Skar Magnol. Once there, we settle our business with the queen and every soul aboard will be free to go their own way. If any would gainsay this course, speak now."

No one spoke, though Elvine saw a resentful scowl or two amongst the gathered crew. Guthnyr either failed to notice, or wisely opted to ignore them, instead continuing with a forced briskness. "Raise the anchor and let's be gone from here. Behsla, fastest course to the Fjord Lands, if you please."

It took the *Johten Apt* a moment to reply, her stricken gaze still preoccupied by the smoke-shrouded islet to Guthnyr's rear. Elvine could tell she still wanted to go ashore and see for herself, perhaps succeed where her new captain had failed. But Behsla was nothing if not a pragmatist. Mastering herself, she nodded to the north, where a grey haze had settled over the horizon. "There's a thick bank of fog rolling in. Common thing when you sail close to the Fire Isles. It'll quell the winds and slow us a good while until it clears."

"Make the best speed you can," Guthnyr told her. Eyeing the still unmoving crew at her back, he raised his voice to a shout. "Enough gawking! There's work at hand and miles to sail! Let's get this ship in order!"

The fog had closed in by midday, veiling the *Sea Hawk* in a dreary miasma that matched the mood of her crew. As Behsla predicted, the wind died to a faint breeze, obliging them to take to the oars. The misted air seemed unnaturally thick to Elvine's inexperienced eye. It was a common enough sight in Olversahl, especially when the seasons changed. Come the winter's thaw, a blanket of vapour would sweep along Aeric's Fjord in the mornings, banishing the sun and rendering the streets into a vague maze. But that had been merely a wisp compared to this.

"Mixes with the smoke from the Isles," Behsla explained. Her voice, already muted by the strip of cloth covering her nose and mouth, held the dull note of one struggling with loss. Elvine had hoped that quizzing her on the curiously dense fog might provide a distraction, but the *Johten Apt's* pain was far too raw.

"How do we find our way in it?" Elvine asked.

Behsla's mask fluttered with a snort. "We don't. I pointed her east before it closed in and kept the tiller true. Thanks to the currents, we'll still be miles off course when it fades, but that can't be helped. It's our good fortune that there's only empty sea ahead of us."

A brief flare of luminescence drew Elvine's attention to the prow where Guthnyr stood. He appeared to be holding something, but it was hard to tell in the haze.

"Striking sparks in honour of those lost," Behsla said. Her eyes narrowed above her mask, slipping to the spear sitting amongst Elvine's meagre pile of possessions. "I hope it was worth it, Scholar."

Elvine had no answer for her, save some asinine allusion to duty which would mean little to this woman. Felnir's *menda* were assuredly just as dangerous as Vellihr Ilvar's collection of fanatics, but there the similarity ended. This crew of former outlaws and mercenaries were partially bound together by a desire for profit, but much more by loyalty to a man who now lay crushed beneath a mountain.

"I don't know," Elvine said, settling upon base honesty as the best response.

Behsla continued to squint at the spear in stark suspicion. "Does it . . . do anything?"

"Not so far. It seems it's just a spear . . ."

She fell quiet when Behsla abruptly shifted her gaze to the port rail, a sudden tension in her bearing.

"What . . . ?" Elvine began, but the *Johten Apt* waved her to silence. Cocking her ear to the fog, Behsla hissed out a command to the rowers. "Still your stroke!"

At first, Elvine could discern nothing but the slosh of becalmed water. Then she heard the rhythmic sweep of oars. She was no expert in such things, but her weeks at sea enabled her to make out a rapid tempo.

"Wet oars!" Behsla called out, hurrying to take charge of the tiller. "Pull hard!"

"What is it?" Guthnyr demanded, rushing aft.

"Ship," Behsla grunted, hauling the tiller to send the *Sea Hawk* heaving to starboard. "Coming on at ramming speed."

"How could they find us in this?"

Although Behsla's face was mostly covered, Elvine read the thought behind the *Johten Apt*'s answering scowl. *Felnir wouldn't dither to ask questions.* Grimacing in unspoken acknowledgement of the rebuke, Guthnyr turned away, striding along the deck. "Heave!" he exhorted, drawing his sword. "And be ready to arm yourselves!"

Heart fluttering and unsure of what else to do, Elvine scanned the fog in search of the oncoming ship. She expended a few seconds peering into the swirling mist until it occurred to her that their foes may well have designs on whatever they had discovered in the Fire Isles. *Competition*, Felnir had said. It stood to reason that a clever foe would have waited for them to recover a treasure before attempting to seize it. She started towards her nook but covered only a yard before the deck tilted with unexpected violence, tipping her from her feet.

"Another sail to the south!" Behsla cried from the tiller, now shoved fully to port.

Rising, Elvine saw a large red square resolve out of the mist, the broad hull of a warship appearing below a heartbeat later. Water frothed white at its flanks as many oars drove it towards the *Sea Hawk*'s starboard flank. Guthnyr's roaring command rang out just before the two vessels collided in a crunch of splintering timbers, sending Elvine sprawling once again.

"TO ARMS!"

The spear! The thought banished all others. Elvine scrambled for her nook on hands and knees whilst the crew surged upright from their oars, reaching for shields and weapons. Battle cries and the clatter of colliding oars filled the air, soon joined by the clamour of combat she had first heard in the shadow of Velgard's statue. Elvine fixed her sight on the spear, now no more than a few paces away. Crawling towards it, she managed to get her fingertips to the weapon's wooden haft, then yelped in pain as a hand reached down to snare her hair. A voice grunted something in a language she didn't know, the hand jerking her head back as it attempted to haul her to her feet.

She caught a glimpse of a red face confined within the guards of an iron helm, eyes narrowed in scrutiny, then widened in shock as blood erupted from its mouth. She tumbled to the deck when the hand fell from her hair. A second later the face of the leather-helmed man slammed onto the planking before her eyes, his features now slackened in death.

"Get up!"

Colvyn stood over her with hand extended, his bloodied falchion gripped in the other. Elvine blinked gore from her eyes and turned back to her nook.

"The spear. . ."

"Leave it—" His command was cut short by a scrape and clang of multiple blades meeting at once. Elvine resisted the urge to turn, lunging towards the spear and grasping it firmly in both hands. She flinched from the hard stamp of boots close to her head, seeing Colvyn now backing away from two assailants. They had the same red features as the man he had just killed, though only one wore a helm. It didn't save him from the blinding slash of Colvyn's falchion. Staggering back, he clutched at a ruined eye, emitting a shrill, almost birdlike scream. The un-helmed one was evidently the more skilled of the two. A large man bearing an axe, he slammed his shoulder into the stumbling warrior's back, sending him into collision with Colvyn.

As the two flailed in untidy union, the axe wielder crouched and darted to Colvyn's flank, angling the weapon to hack at his legs.

There was no thought preceding Elvine's action and she would wonder later at the absence of anger or fear that accompanied it. In fact, there was a cold deliberation in the way she took firmer hold of the spear and thrust its point into the unprotected flesh below the axe man's leather breastplate. He reacted with instinctive swiftness, bringing his weapon down to hack at the spearpoint, tearing a jagged cut in his side in the process. Still, he managed to fix a murderous glare on Elvine and raise his axe before Colvyn's falchion descended to cleave a deep gash in his skull.

Elvine scrambled clear of the falling body, regaining her feet to take in the frenzied struggle raging along the *Sea Hawk*'s starboard rail. A web of ropes now connected the ship to the larger vessel, dozens of warriors using them to haul themselves across the gap. The ferocious resistance of Elvine's crewmates seemed to be holding their assailants at bay, for the most part. However, the cost had been grievous. She saw Druba lying a few paces away, multiple wounds marring his flesh and eyes half-closed in death. She counted four more comrades slain or wounded as her eyes tracked over the deck until they found Guthnyr.

He rose above the thrashing combat near the prow, sword rising and falling to wreak tireless havoc amongst his foes. For a brief moment, it appeared he might win victory single-handed. Elvine watched him hack down two red-faced warriors in quick succession, then hurl himself at a trio that swung across the gap to land upon the deck. Cleaving the face of one, Guthnyr ducked the sweep of a sword and spun, his own blade slicing through the legs of both enemies with a single stroke. Snarling, he dragged one of the fallen to the rail, blood pumping from the man's stump as he was thrown into the sea.

"'Ware to port!"

Behsla's shout drew Elvine's gaze to the other side of the ship, provoking a despairing groan at the sight of a second red sail looming out of the fog. The warship was barely two dozen yards off and coming on fast, her prow aimed for the *Sea Hawk*'s stern.

"I think, esteemed lady," Colvyn said in Ishtan, grasping hold of Elvine's hand, "it's time we bade farewell to this fine vessel."

"We can't just—" Elvine's protestations were cut off by the hard tug to her arm, Colvyn nearly pulling her off her feet as he dragged her towards the boat sitting in its tethers on the mid-deck.

"We stay, we die," he stated, this time in Ascarlian, delivered in a tone that brooked no argument. He shoved her against the boat's hull and began slicing through the securing ropes with his falchion. "Or, more precisely," he grunted as he started heaving the craft towards the rail, "I will. You, I suspect, these fellows are keen to take alive. And rest assured, they won't let you keep that if they do."

Elvine looked at the spear in her hands, both wet with blood. She hadn't come so far and risked so much to lose her prize now. However, the notion of abandoning the *Sea Hawk* and its crew provoked an unexpected lurch in her heart. Villains all they were, but she still owed them her life. Such concerns dissolved when the deck shuddered beneath her feet as the prow of the second ship smashed into the *Sea Hawk*'s stern.

"Help me!" Colvyn shouted, putting his shoulder to the boat. Gasping a shame-filled sob, Elvine turned away from the sight of Behsla taking up a hatchet to assail the fresh flood of warriors now boiling over the stern. Joining her marginal weight to Colvyn's, Elvine assisted in getting the boat's keel onto the starboard rail. Another hard shove and it went over. Hearing an upsurge of shouts behind her, she lost no time in hopping up onto the rail and tossing the spear into the boat, swiftly followed by herself. The impact propelled the craft away from the *Sea Hawk* by several yards, obliging Colvyn to leap into the water and swim for it. He reached the boat quickly, Elvine helping to haul him aboard whereupon they swiftly fixed oars into the rowlocks.

As they began to row, the disparity in their respective strength ensured the boat soon began to describe a broad arc across the water. Despite their wayward track, they rapidly put the trio of entangled ships behind them, the sounds of battle continuing to echo in the fog. After a few moments more of strenuous rowing, Colvyn avowed a worry that they would eventually circle back to the struggle they had just escaped. "Take command of the tiller," he told her. "I'll row."

"Which way?" she asked, placing an uncertain grip on the lever.

"Does it matter?"

As he resumed heaving the oars with undaunted vigour, Elvine concentrated on putting the tumult of combat behind them. She altered course whenever it seemed to be getting louder, although she fretted over the well-known tendency of fog to play tricks on the ears. Colvyn exhibited remarkable stamina as he continued to row with furious energy, though she saw the strain on his face. The tendons of his neck stood out in stark relief and he began to draw breath in deep, grating gasps. Still, he refused to stop until the last fading echo of conflict had faded. Dragging the oars through the locks, he slumped, shuddering with exhaustion.

"My satchel," Elvine said in a thin, choked voice, casting a desperate glance over her shoulder. "I left my books . . ." Her words dwindled into sobs as she clutched the spear to her, its point dripping chilled beads of blood down her neck. "My books . . ."

CHAPTER THIRTY-FIVE

Ruhlin

Upon arrival at the *wuhltra* of Turihmvek, Eldryk and Aleida departed the carriage to leave Ruhlin alone with Achela. As her father prodded a plainly reluctant Aleida through the door, her stooped posture and shuffling steps bespoke forlorn resignation. However, when she paused to cast a final glance at Ruhlin, he read both determination and farewell in the smile she forced upon her lips.

"What did that mean?" Ruhlin demanded of Achela when the door slammed shut. She stared back at him, inexpressive and unspeaking as ever. His mounting concern compelled him to try again. "She intends to do something. What is it?"

The Morvek woman maintained her stillness, slowly blinking her eyes. Ruhlin had concluded that he could assail her with questions for days and fail to elicit a single word from this woman. So, when she spoke, he jerked in surprise. "What do you think she will do?" she asked. Her voice lacked Iyaka's thick accent, the words flowing with the smoother Ascarlian of Eldryk or Tuhlvyr Deyna.

Hearing a sudden tumult from outside, Ruhlin's gaze shifted to the carriage's single, narrow window. By now he knew well the sound of a great many voices raised in excited acclaim. The Meidvang was about to start.

"It pains her to watch me . . . become what I become," he said. "She wishes to spare me that."

424 • ANTHONY RYAN

"Yes." Achela's eyes performed another slow blink. "She has a knife hidden upon her person. She intends to use it to kill me, her father, and the Tuhlvyr. She will fail and die shortly after. But she is beyond care for her own life. Such is the folly of love."

Ruhlin's chains drew taut as the fire began to kindle in his core, the veins of his arms standing out. He knew it was hopeless, that Achela was about to trigger the *stagna*, but he had to try.

"It is not yet time," Achela told him. The sheer incongruity of her fearless calm made him pause, the change receding from his limbs.

"What do you mean?"

For the first time, Ruhlin saw a fully realised emotion pass across Achela's features. It was a complex range of feelings, mixing a regretful frown with a small, rueful smile. But mostly, he beheld a woman accepting a long-awaited fate. "What must happen will happen," she said, resuming her serenity. "Always has it been so. Our roles in this story were written in ages long past, though to accept one's place in history is a hard burden to bear. I hope you, and my niece, are equal to the task that lies ahead."

"What task?"

"The same task I set myself to as a child. The task that required me to sell my abilities to a man who enslaved my sister and forced her to bear his seed. The task that demanded I bear the detestation of my own people for serving those who stole our lands and slaughtered us in the thousands. The task that will place us both in the *wuhltra* when the moment, at last, arrives."

"What moment?"

"You will know. As will I. You were told you could trust Aleida, were you not?"

Mehlga's whispered promise just before she sacrificed herself. It seemed so long ago now, and how could this woman know of it? He pushed his questions aside. Soon Radylf would come for him and he felt a growing certainty that all his plans now rested on the outcome of this conversation. "I was," he said.

"Then know also that you can trust me," Achela told him. "What must happen will happen. But it cannot happen anywhere but in the *wuhltra*."

"Why?"

"Because a moment of such import must be witnessed. A spark cannot birth a fire without kindling."

The sound of jangling keys sounded from beyond the door, forcing Ruhlin to voice his next question in a whisper. "What will you do?"

All animation seeped from the Morvek woman's features, though he would always wonder if her lips curled a little as she replied in a voice he barely heard. "Nothing."

Upon being ordered from the carriage, Ruhlin found himself in the gloomy vaults beneath the *wuhltra*. The numerous pillars and extensiveness of the ceiling made it clear this building was of a far greater scale than any he had seen before. The whip-man's typical cheeriness was nowhere to be seen as he led Ruhlin into one of the many tunnels, following it to a small cell. It featured two doors, an iron and oak barrier connected to the corridor and another worked by pulleys that he assumed would open out onto the sand circle. With Achela nowhere in sight, his captors took no chances, a trio of guards all poised with spearpoints an inch from Ruhlin's back whilst Radylf went about removing his chains.

"Tired of having to buy replacements?" Ruhlin asked him, rubbing at his wrists as the manacles came off.

The flash of anger on Radylf's pale features made Ruhlin wonder just how much of his prior affability had been mere mummery, a mask for the ugly malice that characterised the man's existence. But, as the whip-man spared a sour glance at the door to the circle, Ruhlin divined that his ire arose from another source.

"Something different waiting for me out there?" Ruhlin said. "Something you don't like."

Radylf grunted a muted response as he knelt to remove the chains from Ruhlin's ankles. "The Meidvang is sullied by the blood of beasts."

"Beasts?" Ruhlin repeated, but Radylf was already moving to the other door. He stepped into the tunnel before barking an order to the guards, who quickly drew back their spears and followed suit. The entrance to the tunnel slammed shut, though the whip-man continued to regard Ruhlin through the slat.

426 · Anthony Ryan

"If you can, make short work of it," he said. "Best not to allow this disgrace to continue one second longer than it has to."

Ruhlin turned away when the slat closed, hearing a now familiar blaring of horns to quiet the crowd. He was quick to recognise the voice that filled the subsequent silence, Tuhlvyr Feydrik holding forth with impressive volume whilst also conveying a sense of grave solemnity.

"Now we come to the crowning glory of this Meidvang!" he intoned. "For, as Tuhlvyr of the Vyrnkral Veld, I bear the sacred trust of ensuring only the greatest honour is shown the Altvar this day. Their ideals are given flesh in this most venerable place. The blood that has been spilled in their sight has surely pleased them greatly, but now we shall win their eternal favour."

Feydrik paused, allowing an anticipatory murmur to thrum through his audience before continuing, the solemnity of before now giving way to bombastic relish. "For now, I bring you one who possesses the blood of the Uhltvar themselves, first and most favoured amongst the races of men. Long have we laboured to match their divine achievements, to ascend to their heights. Now, with this contest, shall the Altvar bless us and raise us even higher in their esteem." Another, longer pause, Ruhlin hearing a mass of whispers as the crowd struggled to contain their excitement. Finally, Feydrik spoke again, presumably with a dramatic flourish. "Bring forth Amundyr, the Uhltvar reborn!"

As the pulleys raised the door, Ruhlin grimaced at the wall of sound invading the cell. He stayed put, letting it continue as he surveyed the white sand circle, seeing no enemies. He entertained the amusing notion of simply remaining here until the crowd's adulation dwindled into confused murmurs, but Achela's words rang loud in his mind: *What must happen will happen.*

Teeth gritted, he emerged into the light, moving with his back hunched and features still as stone. These people expected a figure from legend, instead he was happy to present them with a lean but not especially muscular youth clad in a leather cloth about his waist. Curiously, his absence of grandeur didn't appear to negate the audience's enthusiasm. Their acclaim continued as he cast a reluctant gaze upwards, surveying a mass of humanity that dwarfed those of previous contests. He searched the lower tiers of seating, fear rising as his eyes failed to pick out Aleida. Finally, there she was, standing alongside her father and Achela. They stood amongst the luminaries of Turihmvek in a box-like structure protruding from the wall surrounding the sand circle. Naturally, Tuhlvyr Feydrik stood tallest of all.

A fresh blaring of horns sounded, heralding a reduction in the crowd's cheers whilst Feydrik spoke again. "To truly honour the Altvar this day," he began, faltering in patent irritation when Ruhlin started to walk towards the box instead of obediently awaiting the commencement of whatever vile spectacle had been orchestrated this day. The Tuhlvyr ploughed on with creditable resolve, however, choosing to ignore the approaching figure in the circle below. "To honour the Altvar, we must provide Amundyr with a foe worthy of his blood. Why, it would have been an easy, if expensive, matter to simply pit him against fifty fighters." He paused again to laugh, apparently expecting the crowd to share his mirth, but the distraction of Ruhlin's steady approach ensured the Tuhlvyr received only a smattering of amusement.

"But that," Feydrik continued manfully, "would be both a waste and an insult to our divine witnesses. For today, Amundyr will face a foe born of legend." Ruhlin could see the Tuhlvyr clearly now, discerning the growing anger of a man unused to any form of disrespect. Teeth showing white and jaw working with stifled rage, he spoke on, "A foe harbouring the spirit of the mighty beast that once challenged Karnic himself."

Ruhlin came to a halt at the edge of the shadow cast by the box, looking up to see Aleida staring back. At such occasions, she was obliged to don a version of the finery worn by the local luminaries. Today it was a black satin gown embroidered in gold. The sleeves were long and wide, enabling her to conceal both her hands, and Ruhlin had no doubt what she held within the fabric.

Meeting her gaze, he pondered how best to dissuade her from her suicidal course. Any overt signal would surely alert her father, spelling disaster. He looked to Achela, hoping she might make some gesture to her niece, but the witch was as still and watchful as ever. Switching

428 • ANTHONY RYAN

his focus back to Aleida, Ruhlin had no option but to shake his head, keeping his unblinking eyes on hers to ensure she understood. He saw only fearful uncertainty in her face and had to hope it would be enough to stay her hand. However, Feydrik's final and most voluminous proclamation made it clear they were out of time.

"Behold Gruskhahl! Mightiest of beasts!"

The crushing weight of the crowd's cheers drowned all other sound, so Ruhlin didn't hear the clatter of a door being hauled open, or the roaring charge of what emerged onto the sands. By the time he turned to confront it, the thing was barely yards away, a mass of shaggy brown fur, flailing claws and a snarling, drool-flecked maw.

The change arrived with far more swiftness this time, a shout of pain and rage escaping Ruhlin's lips as his body swelled. Within a heartbeat, the emerging monster had assumed a form that felt even more powerful than its prior manifestations. His gaze was level with the beast's as it closed upon him, raising arms as broad as tree limbs to fend off its claws. He entwined the dagger-like barbs with his thick fingers, bracing against the animal's bulk to keep it at bay. Its head lunged at him, jaws snapping just short of his neck.

Ruhlin had heard of bears, but only ever seen them rendered upon parchment, for they were not found in the Outer Isles. He fancied this one was a particularly large example of its kind, also old, judging by the many healed scars he saw on its snout. The realisation that he could perceive such things caused Ruhlin to hesitate. The mindless fury from before was gone now, quelled to a harsh flame that put a tinge of red to his vision but still left him capable of reason.

He had no time to ponder the cause of this change, the bear redoubling its efforts to rip his throat out. Far stronger than any man, it succeeded in wrenching one of its massive paws free and slashed at Ruhlin's chest. The claws raked across skin and sinew without drawing blood or inflicting much in the way of pain. Still, the blow was sufficiently distracting to allow the creature to lunge forward and clamp its jaws upon Ruhlin's shoulder. The pressure was fierce at first, but slackened as his muscles swelled. Also, the redness in his vision deepened, a snarl coming from his lips.

Danger, Ruhlin decided, fighting to retain his reason as rage blossomed anew. *Threats. That's what feeds the monster.*

A curious, high-pitched grunt came from the bear. Ruhlin saw disconcertingly human-like bafflement in the cast of its brow as it drew back, puzzled by the absence of blood upon its tongue. Ruhlin didn't allow it the time to ponder further. Delivering a hard kick to the bear's belly, he sent it careening back across the sands. It writhed as it landed, churning dust, a mix of growls and confused whines issuing from its mouth. Moving closer, Ruhlin watched it try to regain its feet, slumping down and snorting blood with every attempt. His kick had done mortal damage.

Watching the bear's mighty frame succumb to weakness, Ruhlin noted the bare patches in its pelt. The revealed hide was rich in scars, some old, many new. He knew the sign of the whip well and understood that this animal had endured a great deal of suffering in recent days. *Hunted down, starved, and tormented*, he concluded, taking in the sight of the bear's starkly evident spine. *Just to face me so that these scum would have a more violent spectacle to gawp at.*

He became aware of the crowd's baying then, a mix of bloodlust and derision. Looking up, Ruhlin beheld a sea of screaming faces. Some were as wild in adulation as those in Ossvek, but others jeered or cupped their mouths to cast curses at him. It appeared that Tuhlvyr Feydrik's promised spectacle had been a disappointment for many.

Beholding such a multitude of maddened, vicious souls added yet more heat to Ruhlin's rage, also an additional, searing sensation he recognised as hate. His awareness wavered, red mist swimming in his eyes as he felt his form swell further. When the redness dissipated, he found he had turned his back on the dying bear and begun running towards the Tuhlvyr's box.

Reason vied with rage as he charged, Ruhlin fighting to calm the monster before the inevitable icy grasp of the *stagna* took hold. Yet, when he had covered half the distance to his quarry, he realised it hadn't. *What will you do?* he had asked Achela. He could see her now, standing still at Eldryk's side, seemingly deaf to the Aerling's shouted commands. Ruhlin knew that her answer was as loud in her own mind as it was in his, even as Eldryk drew a dagger from his belt and put it to her throat. *Nothing. She will do nothing.*

He saw Eldryk dither, his knife pressed into Achela's neck. Killing her left him with no defence against Ruhlin. But how to compel her to obey him? Ruhlin would always imagine the Aerling embroiled in this panicked quandary at the moment Aleida drew the knife from the sleeve of her gown and stabbed her father in the chest. Staggering back, Eldryk gaped at his daughter. His features were contorted into the perverse hurt of a man who had earned his fate yet contrived to feel betrayed. Shuddering, he coughed out a thick wad of blood and collapsed as uproar seized the surrounding luminaries.

The sight of Feydrik's guards rushing towards Aleida provoked a flare in Ruhlin's rage, the redness closing in again so that he was barely aware of leaping from the sands. He watched with a strange detachment as his monster self latched its massive hands onto the balustrade, then hauled itself into the box. Guards came against him, their blades rebounding from his hardened flesh before he swatted them aside and began his rampage through those they had sought vainly to protect. Bones cracked and bodies flew as he beat a bloody path to Aleida, pausing at the poke of something sharp to his stomach.

Looking down, Ruhlin beheld Tuhlvyr Feydrik. He stood tall and fearless, sword in hand and a stern command issuing from his lips. It was a courageous display and Ruhlin would sometimes regret his inability to grasp the man's words in that moment. They must surely have been noteworthy, even when cut short by the massive fist that turned his skull to pulp.

Ruhlin resumed his charge, casting nobles aside like chaff, his last vestige of control slipping away when he saw Aleida surrounded by guards. She spun in their midst, her knife flashing as she struggled to fend them off, but they were many. A roar escaping his throat, Ruhlin hurled himself towards them, the world disappearing behind a thick blanket of crimson fog.

CHAPTER THIRTY-SIX

Felnir

"Kodryn!" Felnir's cry was smothered by the roar of collapsing stone, his torch swallowed by a sudden, all-consuming darkness. The shuddering ground and overwhelming weight of the cacophony bore him down. Panicked thoughts made him call out for Sygna, but his words didn't reach his own ears. He tried to rise, entertaining the vain hope he might stumble free of this soon-to-be ruin, but the impact of something very large and very heavy directly in his path sent him reeling. From then on he could only huddle upon the ground, flinching from the unseen cascade crashing down all around. He expected death at any instant, finding it curious that, despite all the battles, storms and torments of his life, this should be the peak of his terror. Why was not a mystery. Battles could be won with skill and courage. Storms could be endured. Torture inflicted by sadistic hands could even be borne, especially when one held to the promise of vengeance. But here he was helpless, left to cower in the face of the gods' anger.

Seething at his own weakness, he sought to force a semblance of coherence onto his thoughts, fixing upon Kodryn's demise as something that demanded his full notice. It seemed doubtful he would get to honour his old friend with sparks struck from Silfaer's sigil, for the Battle Maiden was surely the most appropriate god to see a long-lived warrior to the Halls. The ugly suddenness of Kodryn's death also provided a welcome source of anger. For a man who had fought wars the length of the known world to meet his end in such a way felt like an outrage.

"Are you so cruel?" Felnir asked the Altvar, spitting dust. "He offered you reverence and this was his reward?" It was then that he realised he could now hear his own voice.

He lay still for a shamefully long time, flexing fingers and toes to convince himself of what seemed impossible: he was alive. The silence was broken by the hiss of cascading grit and, he realised with surging relief, the groans of others.

"Sygna." His voice was a dull croak as he pushed himself upright, dislodging a covering of stone shards. Regaining his feet, he grunted as his head collided with a jagged, unyielding ceiling. Ignoring the pain, and the resultant trickle of blood, he called out again. "Sygna!"

An answering groan not far off. The surrounding darkness was broken only by a few pinpoints of soft blue light, forcing him to navigate this constricted space with faltering, stoop-backed steps. He found her when his boot trod upon her hand, provoking a yelp and a hard punch to his thigh.

"It's me," he said, reaching for her.

"I know," she replied, adding a second punch, this time to his chest, but it was a weak blow. Tears were a rare thing for her, but she let them flow now as they held each other in the dark. When her shuddering abated, she retreated from him, her words emerging in a sputter of forced humour. "All things considered, Fel, I don't think we should've come here."

He replied with a laugh of his own, holding her close. Had he lost her too, he knew the burden of grief would most likely have killed him.

More groans drew his notice to the gloom-shrouded rubble nearby. His eyes had adjusted to the dark now, enabling him to make out a bulky, grit-covered form. "Falk?" Felnir prompted, moving to nudge the outlaw. The only response was another groan.

"His heartbeat's strong," Sygna said, having scraped away the shattered stone to press a hand to Falk's chest. Shifting her hands to his head, she felt for injuries. "Seems his head's un-cracked too. At least no more than it was before."

Falk jerked awake with a gasp, sitting up to cast a panicked gaze around until it found Felnir. "Is that you, my lord? Have you joined me at the Divine Portals?" He let out an aggrieved groan. "I confess, I hadn't expected them to be so dark."

"I'm not a lord, Falk," Felnir told him. "And this isn't the Portals."

"Fel," Sygna said, and he realised he could see her face clearly now, also the two points of soft blue light glimmering in her eyes. For a confused moment, as he discerned the source of the gleam emanating from a deeper recess beneath this pile of collapsed stone, Felnir wondered if he had it wrong. Had they, in fact, been conveyed to a realm beyond death? The notion faded when he saw a tall, hunched shape outlined in the glow. Wohtin shuffled towards them, Felnir making out the purposeful features of a man once again returned to sanity.

"We can't loiter," Wohtin said, beckoning. "The stones may shift at any moment."

"Wait." Felnir turned about, calling out for his brother. "Guthnyr!" No answer came and he began to rove the darkened space, eyes scouring the rubble. He was fearful of discovering a bloodied, limp hand poking from the ruins, or a sight yet more difficult to look upon, but found nothing.

"Come with me!" Wohtin hissed, but Felnir held up a hand as a very faint sound reached his ears. It was muffled by the stones to the point that he couldn't be sure if it was truly a voice. It could be just grinding rock, or something conjured by his own mind to spare him the unacceptable truth: Guthnyr, and the others, were dead, crushed to nothing like Kodryn.

His hopes dwindling, Felnir slumped against the enclosing stone. Feeling Sygna's hand cup his face, he found the weight of loss and guilt prevented him from raising his head. "This is not the time for grief, my love," she told him, voice soft but also laced with a note of command. She never liked it when he grew maudlin.

"I should have taken him to Thera," Felnir said. "Bound hand and foot and dumped on her deck so she'd have no choice."

"It wasn't what he wanted. He was a man grown and made his own choices."

434 · ANTHONY RYAN

Consenting to look up, he was alarmed to see that she held the bow that had been clutched in the grasp of the inhuman statue.

"You claimed it?" he asked, squinting at her.

"It just . . ." Sygna frowned, running her fingers over the bow stave ". . . seemed like I should. Like you should claim that."

Following her nod, he saw a glimmer of metal a few feet away. The sword appeared undamaged, the metal as untarnished as before. *Once taken up, the Sword of the Altvar cannot be put down,* Wohtin had cautioned. Yet Felnir reached for the weapon without pause, even though he fully expected a return of the repugnance from before. This time, however, the only sensation as his hand closed on the handle was the familiar chill of steel. Hefting it, he realised this sword had been constructed from but one piece of metal. In the eastern deserts, there were tribes who cast weapons entirely from bronze, but he had never seen such a technique applied to steel. The pommel, handle, guard and blade were all undeniably part of the same whole. *Remarkable crafts-manship?* he wondered, recalling the weapon's origins. *Or something else?*

Sygna grasped his wrist as he tilted the sword, gripping hard. "Guthnyr would have wanted you to take it, as he would want you to set aside your sorrow. We live on in the tales told of us. To tell his tale, you have to be alive. Now shift your arse, my love."

Yet a sorrowful lethargy still plagued him, also a growing knot of bitterness in his gut. He might have responded with an unfortunately chosen word or two, if a shudder hadn't thrummed the ground at that moment.

"We must go!" Wohtin said, beckoning with yet more urgency as he receded into the shadows.

"Go where?" Felnir demanded, but received no answer. Hearing an ominous clunk and clatter from the disturbed boulders above their heads, he quickly followed Sygna and Falk in pursuit of Wohtin. They found him at the base of what had been Ulthnir's statue. Felnir couldn't tell how much of the huge effigy remained, but the pieces of finely worked marble littering the ground indicated it had been at least partially destroyed. It also seemed highly improbable that anyone would one day dig out the shattered remnants.

Wohtin crouched at a rectangular opening in the statue's base, outlined in the light emanating from within. Felnir assumed it came from a concentrated seam of glow stone. He wanted to ask how the tattooed man had known of the opening's existence, but the ongoing tremors allowed no pause. After Wohtin disappeared into the portal, Sygna and Falk quickly followed. Before joining them, Felnir cast a final glance at the ruins. Grit spilled through the shuddering stones and it was clear the whole thing was about to collapse. If Guthnyr still drew breath somewhere amongst it all, he would surely be crushed.

"Fare you well to the Halls of Aevnir, brother," Felnir murmured, then lunged for the opening when a very large boulder thudded to the ground barely a foot away.

The tunnel beneath the statue possessed a roughly fashioned narrowness that set it apart from the Vaults or Velgard's subterranean kingdom. It had been hewn through the rock without regard to artistry, or the comfort of any who might one day make use of it. *Dug in a hurry?* Felnir wondered, running a hand over the uneven walls. Even so, it would have been the work of years rather than months. The tunnel continued in a long curving course for what felt like many a mile, though Felnir's growing set of aches may have had more to do with the constricting dimensions of the passage. The ceiling was too low to stand, forcing them all to shuffle along with back and knees bent.

Finally, the passage opened out into a far broader, but much gloomier space. The seam of glow stone was thinner here, robbing Felnir of a clear view of their surroundings. However, the echo of their laboured breaths, and the damp irregularity of what rock he could see, made it clear they were now in an expansive cave rather than a tunnel. Also, as their tired gasps abated, he detected the distant crash of waves upon shore.

"This way," Wohtin said, starting towards the sound. "It's not far."

"To where?" Felnir asked.

He saw Wohtin pause, hearing a faint huff of breath that might have been a laugh. "To the noble vessel that shall carry you home, my king," he said, disappearing into shadow before Felnir could ask more.

The gloom gradually abated and the hissing roar of surf grew louder as they proceeded through the cave. Felnir came to a halt at the sight of a bright half-circle ahead. At first it was just a blur, but, as his eyes accustomed themselves to the novelty of daylight, he recognised it as the mouth of this cave. Squinting, he made out the broad expanse of grey blue sea stretching away to meet a clouded sky. Realising he had lost sight of Wohtin, he hastened into the open, emerging onto the grassy crest of a bluff overlooking a rocky shore.

"By the Martyrs' many arses, that's a welcome sight, my lord," Falk said, stepping free of the cave, face lit with relief.

"That it is," Felnir agreed, although he was preoccupied with finding Wohtin. As he surveyed the shoreline to either side, he was struck by the richness of vegetation here. Grass clung to the clifftops whilst bushes and trees proliferated on the shallower slopes. It was a jarring contrast to the barrenness of the eastern Fire Isles. Turning, his gaze ascended the flanks of mountains rising to clouded summits, the billowing whiteness unblemished by fumes.

"The winds blow west to east here," Wohtin said, emerging from behind a tall granite boulder nearby. "This shore is a far richer land as a consequence. Crops can even be grown in places."

"So that's how Velgard fed his people," Felnir said. "How else to maintain a kingdom so deep underground?"

"Only a select few lived in Skar Altvar." Wohtin turned to point to a headland to the north. "That's where the true heart of Velgard's kingdom lay, the city of Oshtan Hardta, where we must go." He started off with his now familiar purposeful gait, deaf to the question Felnir shouted at his back.

"And how do you know this?"

"I think he made more sense when he was mad," Sygna commented when Wohtin failed to pause stride. She hefted her new bow, her free hand playing over the fletchings jutting from her quiver. "A nick to the ear might make him more forthcoming."

"We're short of guides at present," Felnir said, putting a hand to her shoulder. "He led us into the light. Let's see where he leads us next. Though, if he doesn't start making sense soon, feel at liberty to test that new toy of yours."

Reaching the headland required a walk of a mile or more, Wohtin leading them along a track Felnir judged to be ancient. It had been paved at some points, but the combination of age and weather had reduced it to little more than a vague line in the grass. Similarly, the stepped nature of the passing slopes indicated this land had once been cultivated, though all the tiers where crops once grew now lay under a blanket of wild vegetation. Yet more noteworthy were the goats he glimpsed dotting the higher flanks of the mountain.

"At least we know where to find meat," said Sygna.

"I doubt he intends for us to linger that long," Felnir replied, nodding to Wohtin. "He did speak of a vessel, remember?"

Sygna let out a doubtful snort. "No one has lived here for a very long time. Any ships left upon this shore will be rotted to nothing."

Evidence of human habitation grew more apparent as they neared the headland. Tumbled stones described lines that had once been walls and the track they followed became more solid underfoot. It traced a straight course through ever more dense ruins until, when they had reached the headland proper, they stood at the edge of what had once been a city. Wohtin slowed upon entering the maze of stunted walls, Felnir seeing the tension of suppressed emotion in the tall man's face. He looked on the remnants of houses or halls, some of impressive size, with a mostly unblinking gaze. Felnir knew well the sight of grief, but he saw something more in the cast of Wohtin's features: sombre recognition. As with the city under the mountain, Skar Altvar he called it, and the Vaults, he had undoubtedly been here before.

"Can't see no bones, my lord," Falk said, pausing to peer over the edge of a window. "There's a look to a city that's fallen to storm, and I don't see it here. Seems as if the folk that dwelt in this place all just decided to pack their chattels and make off one day."

"Age conceals truth," Sygna said. "Given enough years, bones will turn to dust." She ran a hand over a patch of weathered stone. "And this is all very old indeed."

Felnir watched Wohtin come to a halt up ahead. He stood before the broadest and tallest wall yet. The fact that it was still higher than a man's head in certain places told of a building that must have been mighty indeed.

"The king's hall, I assume?" he asked, moving to Wohtin's side.

The answer came in a subdued murmur. "Yes." Wohtin gazed into the gap in the wall where the door to this royal domicile had once stood, then raised his eyes to peer at the long vanished lintel. "His sigil was there. The Eye of Aerldun to signify wisdom, set above a lightning bolt to symbolise the swiftness of the king's justice. Those that looked upon it knew with certainty that any petition they voiced to the king would be heard, and his judgement rendered without favour or prejudice. Here, at the edge of the world, did Velgard craft his truest reign."

As was becoming aggravatingly familiar, he moved on before Felnir could ask anything further. He resisted voicing any angry demands, however, sensing that the tattooed man was now nearing his goal.

The innards of the king's hall were as worn and lacking in clues as to the fate of this city as the rest of it. Furnishings that surely adorned the broad rooms were nowhere to be found. Upon entering the largest chamber, Wohtin halted again before a circular stone dais in the centre of the room and bowed his head in grave reverence.

"Who's he bowing to?" Sygna wondered.

"A ghost, I suspect," Felnir said, nodding at the dais. "I'd guess this is where Velgard held court."

Her face tightened in baffled agitation. "That would have been centuries ago."

Felnir studied Wohtin's lowered features, noting his tightly closed eyes, his face twitching as he fought a great welling of emotion. "Not to him, it seems."

Wohtin let out a long, shuddering sigh and opened his eyes to regard the empty dais. Parting his lips, he spoke a soft stream of Ascarlian in an accent so thick and phrasing so archaic it almost sounded like a different language: "Unto thee I render all service, my king. Upon thee I bestow all wisdom. In thy name shalt I banish all mysteries." He bowed again, then strode on, skirting the dais to make for the tumbled walls at the seaward flank of the building. Following, Felnir's hunger for information dissipated, for he suddenly found himself fearful of the answers.

Emerging from the king's hall, Wohtin descended a stepped stone pathway towards what appeared to be a wharf of some kind. It had suffered like everything else here. Sections of the quay had tumbled into the sea long ago, but the central structure remained mostly intact. It consisted of a short pier jutting out into the water. It was roofed, not in stone, but bronze, the overlapping metal sheets green with age. It featured a stout door, also of bronze, the walls to either side of it decorated with small plaques.

Wohtin came to a halt at the door, his gaze entirely captured by the design it held. The bronze had been rendered into a man's face. Bearded and stern of expression, Felnir discerned an undeniable nobility to the verdigris-tinged features. He fancied he would have guessed the identity of this man, even if he hadn't noticed the sigil embossed above the face.

"Velgard," Felnir said. Moving to the structure's side, he judged its length at close to seventy paces, with a stone slipway descending into the water from its seaward wall. "This was where he kept his ship."

"Yes," Wohtin said, voice hoarse. "And fine she was. The finest ever crafted by the wrights of his kingdom, but intended never to feel the caress of the sea, for this was Velgard's barrow. The ship that rested here, filled with the things he treasured in life, would carry him to the Halls of Aevnir."

"Then why the slipway?"

A faint smile ghosted across Wohtin's lips. "A ship must have a means of launching, even into the realms of the dead."

His smile faded when he shifted his gaze to the plaque affixed to the left of the door. It also bore a face. Another bearded man, this one of less noble aspect, his features set in a frown that bespoke knowledge and wisdom. Felnir began to ponder its relationship to the long-dead king, an honoured advisor perhaps, or a revered scholar, when it struck him that there was something very familiar about those features.

Sygna saw it before he did, letting out a gasp as she came closer to peer at the plaque, her gaze switching between Wohtin and the bronze effigy. "Altvar preserve us . . ." she said, eyes wide and unblinking.

Falk had seen it too, retreating several paces, his face betraying mounting fear and confusion. "By the Martyrs," he breathed, casting a desperate glance at Felnir. "This cannot be, my lord."

"No," Felnir agreed, his voice rendered flat by the unfeasible but inescapable reality of what he saw. "And yet it is."

He was unable to restrain an involuntary backward step when Wohtin turned to him. The inescapable truth was made yet starker by the sight of his face and its bronze twin side by side. It was as if his reflection had been trapped in the metal.

"I don't suppose," Felnir began, finding it necessary to swallow before speaking on, "that you're about to tell me your great-great-grand-father was an honoured member of King Velgard's court."

"No," Wohtin said. "I am not."

A thousand questions roiled in Felnir's mind, but, as he continued to behold the impossible, only one succeeded in escaping his lips. "How?"

Wohtin gave a slow, weary blink of his eyes and turned away. "We both have tales to tell one another, my king. For now." He tapped a knuckle to the door. "We must get this off so we may launch your ship, which has awaited your coming for a very long time."

For such an ancient contrivance, removing the bronze door from Velgard's barrow proved to be a frustratingly prolonged task. The structure had been built by skilled hands intent on crafting something that would survive for many years upon a windswept shore. Such artistry couldn't be undone easily and they had accomplished little by the time the sun faded. Felnir's mood was not improved by their guide's continued refusal to answer questions.

"If this is your king's barrow," Sygna enquired, "are we not engaged in desecration of perhaps the most sacred grave known to the Ascarls?"

Wohtin merely blinked at her and returned to the labour of scraping mortar from between the stones securing the door in place. Felnir had lent him a dagger for the work, himself using the point of his sword. He decided to use the mundane blade he had carried for years rather than the Sword of the Altvar. Given the weapon's untarnished state after years underground, he suspected it would suffer little damage. Yet, despite his conflicted feelings towards the gods, employing it for such a task felt blasphemous.

They worked until full darkness set in, whereupon Felnir called a halt. Bushes cut from the overgrown verges flanking the stairs provided fuel for a fire. Sygna had brought along a wallet of hard tack, which served to stave off burgeoning hunger, but not for long. She avowed a firm intention to go hunting come the morning and, with his stomach voicing a persistent growl, Felnir was disinclined to stop her.

With night wearing on, the depredations of the day soon sent Sygna and Falk into an exhausted slumber. Felnir, however, remained awake, studying the Sword of the Altvar. He found a certain fascination in the flawlessness of the blade, the way steel captured the firelight like a mirror. The swirl of flame upon metal snared his tired eyes and he felt a curious sensation of being drawn in. Ascribing it to his fatigue, he began to look away, but found he couldn't. Feeling a flare of alarm, Felnir attempted to lower the sword, but his arm refused to move. The steel handle was hotter than it should be against his palm, provoking beads of sweat despite the chill breeze sweeping in from the sea.

What is this? he wanted to demand of Wohtin, standing at the quay's edge. But no words came from Felnir's lips. Nor would his gaze consent to shift from the blade. His heart became a persistent, rapid hammer when the blade appeared to grow in size, the flames within blossoming into an inferno that flooded his vision. For an instant, all was heat and light, then it cleared to reveal a forest clearing at night. Wohtin was there, seated close to a small fire. His garb was hardy but ragged in places, the clothes of a man well travelled. His features were much the same, perhaps younger by a few years, though the rapt, unblinking focus on his face made him appear younger still. The object of his interest sat on the opposite side of the fire, and Felnir found he couldn't fault Wohtin for staring.

The woman's garb was colourful in places, but couldn't be termed fine. Nor could the beaded necklace she wore. Yet Felnir doubted he had ever set eyes upon a personage with a better claim to the word 'beauty'. Her hair was the shade of pale gold, skin flawless but for a single red mark in the centre of her forehead that Felnir at first thought might be a ruby. She regarded Wohtin with a faint curve to her lips, speaking words in a tongue beyond Felnir's ken. Wohtin, however, appeared to fully comprehend her meaning, replying with a fervent nod and offering a halting reply in the same language. His words gave the woman pause. Angling her head, she arched a pale eyebrow and asked him a short question and, when Wohtin nodded again, near livid with eagerness, the woman's smile faded.

"Then," she said in Ascarlian, words coloured by regret, "I am sorry, my brother from the north." With that, she reached into the sack at her side and produced a leather-bound book. "I wouldst counsel that thee use it well," she said, holding the tome out to Wohtin, "but I know thee will not."

An abrupt hesitation seized Wohtin as he reached for the book, his hand stopping short, fingers trembling. "Then why dost thou giveth it to me?"

The woman's smile returned, but it was the resigned half-grin of one undertaking a necessary but unwelcome task. "Why dost thy assume I have any choice?" she asked before taking hold of his wrist and placing the book in his grasp. Saying no more, she rose to her feet, gathering up her sack before slipping into the darkened forest.

"Wait!" Wohtin called after her. As he began to follow, the campfire's flames erupted, once again flooding Felnir's sight. This time when they faded, he found himself regarding the sword, now returned to its prior size. Jerking to his feet, he cast his gaze around the wharf, finding it the same. Sygna and Falk lay huddled in their cloaks in slumber and Wohtin stood at the edge of the quay, arms crossed as he stared out to sea.

"Who was she?" he demanded, advancing upon Wohtin. "The woman in the forest. Who was she?"

Turning, Wohtin's expression barely changed from its sternly sombre frown, though his brows creased as his eyes flicked to the sword. "So, it finally decided to show you something," he said. "It is good to know my judgement hasn't been entirely wrong."

Felnir stepped closer to him, staring hard into his eyes. "My most valued friend and my brother died today," he stated. "I would have you tell me they were not lost in vain. And know this, old man, the time for silence is over and only one of us bears a sword this night. Now." He stepped closer still, voice lowering to a growl that promised the direst consequences for reticence. "Speak."

CHAPTER THIRTY-SEVEN

Thera

"**B**arely a week." Ossgrym Ironbones paused to let out a burp of impressive volume, then swigged another gulp of mead. "That's all it took to wrest my geld from me."

He and Thera conversed alone in a sizeable cavern that served as the Veilwald's Hall in the hidden refuge of Endyr's Cut. It featured a bed and a broad table bearing a pile of sundries that Ossgrym had clearly felt no restraint in reducing over the course of recent days. Empty flasks littered the floor and jars of preserves and sweetmeats lay opened and partially consumed. Evidently, the Ironbones was given to drowning his sorrows in indulgence.

Thera restrained the urge to voice her disgust, at least for now. Seated opposite Ossgrym, she rested one hand on the dreadaxe propped at her side, watching this famed warrior drink and eat in a welter of self-pity. As her disdain grew, a singular point of the Queens' law rose to mind with uncomfortable insistence. As Vellihr of Justice, she was invested with the power to remove this man from the Veilwald's seat and appoint herself, temporarily, in his place. From the repeated flicks of Ossgrym's eyes towards the dreadaxe, she divined he was also aware of this provision. His battle hammer lay on the table within easy reach.

He probably thinks that's why I'm here, Thera mused, reflecting on whether it would have been wise to have Lynnea attend this meeting. *Better to hear him out, for now,* she decided, managing to keep the curl from her lips as she watched the Veilwald dig his stubby fingers into a jar of pickled herring. In his current state, she doubted he would retain much facility for deceit.

"Want some?" he asked, proffering the jar before stuffing his fingers in his mouth.

"No." She allowed an impatient edge to colour her tone as she added, "You were telling me about the enemy's first attack."

Ossgrym let out a grunt and tossed the jar aside, eyes shifting from Thera as he swallowed a morsel of fish. When he finally consented to speak, it was with gruff reluctance. "Weeks back, folk from the smaller islands started turning up at my hall, bleating about red-faced monsters from the sea who'd come in the night to wreak slaughter, sparing none save a few they carried off in chains, and those fleet enough to take to their heels. Thought it was pirates, at first. Some mob of villains from Albermaine or beyond come far to the north to try their luck. I sent word to the Queens, of course, but decided it couldn't wait for one of you lot to turn up. So I gathered my *menda* and we sailed forth." He paused, brows arched as he sighed a humour-less laugh. "I was looking forward to finding them, if truth be told. Been years since I had a decent scrap, and more since I was in a proper battle. Olversahl, eh?" He afforded her a grin rich in patently false comradeship. "What a night it was."

"I take it you found them," Thera said, as always, disinclined to talk about Olversahl. "These pirates."

"That we did, and barely fifteen miles south of Ayl-Ah-Vahrim. Seems they were coming for us when we were coming for them. Far more of the bastards than I was expecting. They had twice our number in ships, and theirs were bigger. Knew their business too, sending half straight at us whilst the rest swung out to come at our flanks. It was a fine old fracas for a while, blooded my young 'uns good and proper, which is always to be welcomed, since few had seen real battle before."

Ossgrym fell silent, reaching for his horn to down more mead. When he spoke again, his voice had grown in volume, hardened by a defensive edge. "I want it fully recognised that we turned the waves red that day. Not one of my *menda* lacked for courage, and plenty are now resting in Ulfmaer's embrace as testament to that courage.

My own kin among them." He paused and drank again, fixing Thera with a defiant glare. "Also, the order to cut our way clear came from my lips and no other. If there's shame and the Queens' judgement to suffer for it, I'll bear it alone."

Thera thought about voicing a consoling comment regarding the wisdom of a prudent withdrawal in the face of overwhelming odds, but knew it would mean little to Ossgrym. If anything, he would take it as an insult. "I'm here to render aid," she said. "Not pass judgement."

"Unusually considerate of you. Weren't so discerning last time we met, were you?"

"A man stood before me and confessed his guilt to kidnap and murder of a girl not yet in her fifteenth summer. Exile was too lenient. If anything, his death was overly swift."

"Swift or not, he was my kin. Son to my cousin orphaned when his parents were lost at sea. I raised the ungrateful little bastard, which made him mine to punish."

"Then perhaps you should be grateful I spared you the anguish. As I said, Veilwald, I am here to render aid. I have neither time nor inclination to discuss matters settled years ago under the Queens' law."

He lapsed into silence again, eyes baleful above his horn as he drank. Thera also said nothing, returning his stare until he consented to continue his tale.

"We made it back to Ayl-Ah-Vahrim with about a third of the ships I sailed with," he said, voice little more than a mutter. "Turns out a bunch of the *Skyrnlohk* had gotten here ahead of us."

"*Skyrnlohk*?"

"Red faces. It's what my folk have taken to calling them. Don't suppose you know their true name? Or what gods-cursed land they hail from."

"They call themselves Nihlvarians and they hail from beyond the Fire Isles. They also speak a version of our tongue and worship the Altvar, if you can believe such things."

Ossgrym's brows knitted in doubt. "Not sure I can. Even if it's true, what do they want?"

"As far as I've been able to establish, they want everything. All we have, and more." She nodded, indicating he should complete his account.

"They've built themselves a port at Danith's Bay on the south-west coast of the island," he said. "Piers surrounded by a tall stockade. The whole thing went up seemingly overnight. Hard to credit they could build it so quickly."

"They carry slaves upon their ships. Go on."

"As soon as they saw us hove into view, they sallied out. Too many to fight after all the losses we'd suffered." Ossgrym's face twitched in shame. "I ordered my lot to scatter, took my own ships to Endyr's Cut to await the arrival of our Queens' great *menda*. Instead, I got you and your mast-less wreck. About as much use as a bull with no knackers."

Thera's hand tightened on the dreadaxe, teeth aching with the effort of caging a retort. Studying the defiant challenge writ large in Ossgrym's features, her anger cooled. *Hungry for judgement*, she decided. *And release from the knowledge of failure.*

"Who did you lose?" she asked. "Son or daughter?"

The Ironbones worked his jaw, maintaining his glare for a heartbeat before slipping into miserable contemplation of his drinking horn. "Both," he murmured. "And a grandson into the bargain."

"Then you have a weight of blood to balance. Attend yourself to that and cease this pointless wallowing, unless you would rather surrender the Veilwald's seat to me here and now."

The reddish hue that crept across his brows indicated Ossgrym retained at least a vestige of pride. "Never," he grated, fingers inching towards the haft of his hammer. "You'll have to take my head first."

Thera grunted. "It's so pickled in liquor I don't think I want it."

The Ironbones stared at her in frozen silence, his hand halting its progress to the hammer, then let out a loud, rasping laugh. His mirth continued for a while, Thera offering only a bland smile in return as she waited for him to calm. "I forget, sometimes," Ossgrym said, his laughter subsiding, "just who your great-grandfather is. You've certainly got his tongue."

Thera found herself more offended by this than anything the Veilwald had said before. Still, duty demanded she attend to the issue at hand. "I need to know more about the enemy's dispositions," she said. "How substantial is this stockade they've built?"

"The walls are twelve feet high and mostly fashioned from stripped timber, so I'd guess they brought a lot of it with them. Although, they've been busy sending parties out to fell trees and visit their cruelties on my folk. Villages that have stood for centuries burned to the ground, their people cut down or sent scurrying to the hills. And these *Skyrnlohk* are greedy bastards, too. Gathered up all the livestock they could and killed what they couldn't. My scouts tell me they've corralled a mighty herd of cattle alongside their stockade. So starving them out isn't an option, if that's your plan."

"It's not. What of numbers? How many have they, and how many have you?"

"Their ships come and go all the time, so the number changes, but I'd put it at near three thousand at any given time. As for my *menda*." Ossgrym's expression shifted into a bleak grimace. "I've little over three hundred warriors here, but could probably count on five hundred more drawn from other hiding places nearby. There's surely more to be had upon the island entire, but gathering them all would take weeks."

"We can't wait that long. Allowing them to entrench will only make it harder to drive them out later."

"If you've a trick to pull here like your great-grandfather did at Olversahl, I'd be pleased to hear it. The simple truth is we lack the strength to storm that stockade, from land or sea, even if we had the ships, which we do not."

Olversahl. Thera concealed an annoyed sigh. *Always with these ageing brutes, it comes back to Olversahl.* Despite her dire misgivings about the supposedly great victory, she had to concede its singular importance in demonstrating the value of a diversion. Mounting a seaward assault on the Nihlvarian fleet would be doomed to failure, but their enemy didn't know that. Any substantial cluster of ships would be bound to draw their eye from land to sea. Which left the prospect of attacking a fortified position on foot when substantially outnumbered. Ascarlian history was replete with examples of victories won against longer odds, but usually only with the intervention of the Altvar. *Or*, she added to herself, *some other form of arcane providence.*

"You said they had stolen a great herd of cattle," she said. "Just how great is it?"

She saw Gelmyr off the following day, finding him upon the pier in the hidden harbour overseeing the loading of additional torches to the *Great Wolf*. Not having him at her side for what lay ahead was a hard choice, but one she couldn't shirk. There were none amongst Ossgrym's *menda* who possessed even half his skill at sea, making him the only real choice to lead their makeshift fleet.

"The Ironbones says much of the north-east shore is still untouched," she told the *Johten Apt*. "Gather what additional craft you can there. Also tell any willing to fight to make for the forest at the base of Ulthnir's Reach. Don't attempt to force any to hand over their boats, or to take up arms. Just speak the truth and trust it'll be enough."

"It would help if I could tell them what you're planning. Calling them to battle only to bob about offshore with torches lit when there's fighting to be done will sit ill with many. As it sits ill with her." He jerked his head at Eshilde, stern faced with resentment as she stowed bundled torches on the foredeck. She had reacted with predictable anger upon being told she would sail with Gelmyr rather than march with the *menda*. Despite her voluble, and near-insubordinate protestations, Thera had refused to shift on the issue. She needed at least one of her more capable fighters to accompany Gelmyr and see him to safety if this scheme went awry.

"Whether it sits ill or not, it must be done," she told him. "As for fighting, this is but the first of many battles. If it's glory they want, they'll have a gutful before this war is over. Tell them that."

The *Johten Apt* nodded before turning a sombre glance upon his fleet. Altogether, they had near twenty craft of varying sizes. Of Ossgrym's two surviving warships, one had suffered too much burning to be of use. However, her mast remained intact and was swiftly dislodged and carried over to the *Great Wolf*. The rest of the force comprised skiffs, fishing craft and a few sea-going rowboats. All were crewed as sparsely as possible. The *Great Wolf*'s complement now consisted of Gelmyr, Eshilde and only five others. The oars would therefore be near useless, but she trusted his gift for harnessing the wind.

"As a lad," he said, "I dreamed one day of leading a fleet into battle. Must say, I imagined something a bit grander."

"We have what we have," Thera said. "Besides, at night, when all torches are lit, they'll make a fine sight indeed. In any case, I'd take any fleet commanded by Gelmyr Johtenvek over all others." It was thin gruel, but all she had to offer. Still, he seemed to take heart from it.

"Six days then," he said, affording her a formal nod.

"Six days," she repeated, grasping his hand. "If it goes badly . . ."

"It won't." His hand tightened upon hers before he let go and mounted the *Great Wolf*'s gangplank. Watching him board, Thera discerned a stiffness in his bearing, as if he was resisting the urge to cast her a parting glance for fear it might be the last he ever caught of her.

Traversing Ayl-Ah-Vahrim over the course of the next few days proved to be a tortuous business. Advised by Ossgrym that their foes possessed horses and would send mounted scouts ranging across the island, Thera decreed they move only at night. Marching at a punishing pace without pause for rest, they proceeded from one secluded spot to another. As befit a man who had garnered much from the smuggling trade over the years, Ossgrym knew many a cave and hidden gully. Often, these refuges were already occupied by people who had fled the Nihlvarian onslaught. They bore their misery with a stoic fortitude that gave Thera heart, as did the willingness of all those of fighting age to join with the Veilwald's *menda*. By the time they reached the thick forest blanketing the flanks of Ulthnir's Reach, they had acquired close to another two hundred warriors. Armour was scarce, but all bore at least one decent weapon, for no Ascarlian household was complete without a sword, axe or spear hanging upon the wall.

"Always found that hate breeds the most courage in battle," the Ironbones commented during their first day in the forest. He had guided the *menda* to a tall, overgrown outcrop of rock on the lower slopes of the great mountain. It provided both shelter and vantage points to spot approaching enemies. So far, their march hadn't encountered any Nihlvarian scouts, but Thera knew continued evasion would prove difficult when they closed upon the stockade.

They couldn't risk the betraying smoke of a fire, so clustered in small groups to eat hard tack and salted fish, blanketed and cloaked against the morning chill. Thera saw how Ossgrym felt the cold more than his warriors. His bones might be iron, but they were also old. He bore it with determined stubbornness, however, striving to keep the shudder from his hands and face, though it did little to improve his temper.

"More so than loyalty," he went on, turning a hard glare upon Aldeyn. "Though, even that has been in short supply lately."

The Veilwald's nephew appeared incapable of meeting his uncle's eye. Thera had spoken little to Aldeyn since their initial meeting, but was keen to discover more of his connection to her great-grandfather. It was clear Ossgrym had learned of the youth's association to the Tielwald only recently, and hadn't welcomed the news. The Veilwald's silent, accusing regard of his younger kinsman continued until Aldeyn rose and walked off.

"The Tielwald has ways of twisting his fingers around the hearts of even unwilling servants," Thera said. "I wouldn't judge the lad too harshly."

"Once again, you seek to take the right of judgement from me, Vellihr," Ossgrym growled back. "The boy was a spy in my hall for years, and that's all there is to it."

"A spy who brought me to your door. A spy in service to the Queens' interests."

"The Queens' interests, is it? Or the Tielwald's?"

"For all his faults, Margnus Gruinskard's efforts have always been directed towards preserving this realm. And given it was he who orchestrated the great victory you take so much pride in, perhaps you should trust his servant more." Matching stares with Ossgrym, Thera found herself puzzled by this urge to defend her great-grandfather. Perhaps decades of resentment were no shield when it came to fending off jibes against family. Though, she thought it doubtful she would have been so vociferous if the Veilwald had directed his ire at her elder brother.

The Ironbones' lip curled, ready to sneer out some more choice words. However, they were forestalled by a call from one of the lookouts atop the outcrop. "Warriors to the north, Veilwald!"

"How many?" Ossgrym called back, getting to his feet with hammer in hand.

"Dozens so far. With more behind."

"*Skyrnlohk?*"

The lookout raised his hands in a helpless gesture. "I can't tell, Veilwald."

Ossgrym muttered a curse, then cast out a shouted command to his *menda*. "Ready shields and form the wall! Face to the south! Those without shields form up behind!"

The battle line drew up on the relatively clear ground in the lee of the rocks. The lack of shields made it short but thick and therefore vulnerable on the flanks. To negate the danger, Thera gathered her own warriors to the right of the line, set back a little and crouched amidst the fern-covered forest floor. At her instruction, Lynnea and Achier kept close to her side. The former slave had armed himself with a hatchet and taken to his allotted role of protecting Lynnea with diligent care. For her part, Lynnea crouched with the stiffness common to those with scant experience of battle. Her knuckles were bone white as she clutched her staff, scanning the trees with wide eyes. Snaryk, always attuned to her moods, shuffled his bulk closer to Lynnea, resting his massive head on her shoulder and letting out a soft huff of reassurance. Thera resisted the impulse to add an encouraging gesture of her own. If battle were to rage this morning, she couldn't allow herself the distraction of Lynnea's safety. Henceforth, she would have to trust her apprentice to rely on her own resources.

Turning her attention to the forest, Thera watched for the twitch of branch and shift of shadow that would betray the arrival of their foes. It seemed the turn of events had served to frustrate her plans. If the Nihlvarians had brought their full strength against them, then there was no option but to seek victory here and now. It would be a chaotic slaughter amidst the trees, but war was rarely a neat and tidy business. She smoothed a hand along the haft of the dreadaxe, keeping the blade in the shade of the ferns to conceal the gleam.

Yet when the first warrior stepped clear of the treeline, he was greeted not with the battle cry of Ossgrym Ironbones, but his laughter. "Kahlvik, you ugly bastard!" the Veilwald said, striding forward to greet the newcomer. "You're late, but I'll forgive you."

Thera thought Ossgrym's choice of words curious, for the man he hailed was far from ugly. Standing several inches taller than the Veilwald, but almost as broad, his handsome, angular features were part concealed by a short black beard. A sword hung from his belt, but his shield was slung across his back, as were those of the other warriors who stepped from the forest to either side.

"I had pig pens in need of mucking out, cousin," the black-beard said with a rueful grin as he clasped hands with the Ironbones. "Always best to see to one's chores before visiting family."

Ossgrym laughed again and beckoned to Thera. "Come, Vellihr, meet Kahlvik Vahrimdorr, Uhlwald of the Northern Shore, and the only relative I'm ever actually pleased to see."

So this is the Grey-eye, Thera thought, approaching the pair to afford Ossgrym's kinsman a nod of appropriate respect. She had heard of this man, one of the few warriors to have earned renown without having fought at Olversahl. Instead, his reputation had been won thanks to a famed voyage across and beyond the southern seas, undertaken when he was barely in his manhood. After years of absence, during which his kinfolk had assumed him dead, Kahlvik's ship had appeared at Ayl-Ah-Vahrim laden with all manner of fine goods and treasures. He told tales of many fights with pirates and sundry exotic foes. Although, Thera also recalled that his voyage had cost the lives of fully two-thirds of his crew. Such losses might explain why so celebrated a figure had lived a quiet life in the years since.

"Vellihr Speldrenda," Kahlvik greeted her with a formal nod of his own. Thera saw that he was well named, possessed of eyes the colour of the sea on the eve of a storm. "Heartening to see one of the Queens' servants at my cousin's side."

"It'd be more heartening if she'd brought a great *menda* with her," Ossgrym said. He paused to cast his eye over the men and women now thronging the trees to Kahlvik's rear. "Seems you've outdone her in that regard by a decent amount, cousin."

"Gelmyr Johtenvek came by some days ago, bearing grim tidings," Kahlvik said. "I'd heard dire rumours for weeks and the scouts I sent south failed to return." He offered Ossgrym a grimace of apology. "If I had known the full measure of our plight sooner . . ."

"You're here now." The Ironbones jostled his cousin's shoulder. "That's what matters. How many swords do you bring me?"

"Six hundred and forty marched with me from the northern shore. All that could be gathered in a short time."

Ossgrym laughed again, raising his voice to ensure all present could hear. "Joined with us, that's enough to defeat any mob of red-faced bastards."

Despite the Veilwald's bluster, Thera detected a forced undercurrent to it. A thousand-strong *menda* was a decent force at most times, but she recalled the sheer size of the fleet she had glimpsed off Iselda's Nail. Even should her plan succeed, one victory here did not win the war, especially should it prove costly.

"Were you seen on your march?" she asked Kahlvik.

"Not so far as I could tell, Vellihr," he replied. "We were cautious and saw no scouts."

"Even so, the greater our strength, the greater the threat we're noticed before we can strike. From here on we move in daylight, trust the forest to cover our approach."

"Our enemy is not foolish," Ossgrym warned. "They will surely have patrols ranging across the southern flank of the mountain."

"A risk we'll have to run. We must be within sight of their stockade in three days. Gelmyr will be waiting and I'll not leave him dangling on the end of a hook."

Fortunately, there were a number of hunters amongst Kahlvik's band with intimate knowledge of the forest. Skilled archers all, they proceeded ahead of the *menda* to ensure their path was free of enemies. On the second day after their union with Kahlvik, Ossgrym's prediction was borne out when the hunters encountered a trio of mounted

Nihlvarian scouts. All were brought down by well-placed arrows before they could ride off. Thera chafed over the necessity of killing them, since their failure to return would provide some measure of warning to the stockade, but it couldn't be helped. However, the slain scouts also offered a boon in the horses they left behind. As was to be expected, they had fled when their riders tumbled from their saddles. But, after Thera bemoaned the loss that evening, Lynnea and Achier had disappeared into the forest, returning an hour later with all three mounts in tow.

"You've a way with horses, I see," Kahlvik observed, affording Lynnea a smile as he smoothed a hand over the flanks of the animal she led. Seeing more in the Grey-eye's smile than just a compliment, Thera fought down a flare of jealousy, the nauseous roil made worse by a familiar sting of self-recrimination. However, Lynnea's answering smile was as bland as ever when responding to such interest. Inclining her head, she offered the horse's reins to Kahlvik.

"My apprentice makes you a gift, Uhlwald," Thera said.

Kahlvik's brow's knitted in slight puzzlement at Lynnea's silence, but Thera found herself liking him when he accepted the reins with grace. "Most gratefully received."

She's for you. Lynnea held out another set of reins to Thera before nodding to the horse led by Achier. *And one for me, too. I suspect we'll need them soon.*

Thera had learned to ride as a child, a skill both her parents and great-grandfather insisted upon imparting to their children. Whilst it was rare for Ascarlians to fight on horseback, her lessons had included instruction on mounted combat, though her career had so far provided no opportunity to put it to use. The mare gifted to her by Lynnea was evidently bred for speed and endurance rather than battle, lacking the bulk of muscle common to warhorses. She proved a tractable beast, allowing Thera to mount her with little more than a snort. Thera didn't puzzle over the mare's placidity, noting that her eyes rarely strayed from Lynnea.

"I think I'll name you Elkor," Thera said, patting the animal's neck. "For I've a sense you'll run as swift as any arrow."

She likes you. Lynnea smiled and ran a hand over the nose of her own mount, a russet-coloured stallion a hand shorter than Elkor. *Though this one likes me more.*

"I hope he likes you enough to charge a thicket of spears," Thera told her. "For that's what we're likely to face soon enough."

The stallion nickered, shuddering a little as it detected Lynnea's abrupt shift in mood. Thera quelled a pang of regret at that shadow that crept over her apprentice's face. *Sparing her fears avails her nothing,* Thera told herself. Climbing down from Elkor's back, she saw how Kahlvik's gaze lingered on Lynnea, and not with any lustful intent. Seeing the shrewd narrowing of his eye, Thera concluded he had discerned the unspoken communication betwixt Vellihr and apprentice. *Now he knows there's more to this beauteous maiden than a way with horses.*

Her estimation of the Uhlwald's intelligence increased further when he commented, "I'll confess to doubts when Ossgrym told me you had some clever trick to bring down the walls of that stockade, not that he seems to know what it is. Now, I find myself less doubtful."

Thera offered him a restrained smile before setting about unhitching Elkor's saddle. "Come dusk tomorrow, I trust all doubts will be dispelled fully."

"Shitting bastard fuck shit . . ." The profanity issuing from Ossgrym's mouth faltered when he apparently exhausted his repertoire of obscenities. "Shit!" he repeated after some wordless growling, his face livid with rage and frustration as he gazed upon the stockade raised on the shore of Danith's Bay. "How could they have known?"

The *menda* had reached a vantage point on the lower slopes of Ulthnir's Reach in late afternoon, settling down to await twilight and, hopefully, the appearance of Gelmyr's torchlit fleet offshore. It duly arrived when the sun had half dipped below the horizon, the many lights creating the impression of a force twice its size. Less welcome was the sight of many more torches lighting the stockade and its inner precincts, the glow revealing the warriors thronging the parapet, all armed in expectation of an attack.

"Our enemy is wealthy in spies," Thera said. "But it's more likely they were forewarned when their scouts didn't return. Or another patrol spotted us and we failed to spot them."

"Then what now?" Ossgrym demanded. "Will this plan of yours still work when they're fully alerted?"

Thera had used the last hours of daylight to fix the layout of the stockade in her mind. It was clear the Nihlvarians, or rather, their slaves, had been busy. In addition to the wall of stripped timbers, they had constructed several buildings within its confines, and expanded the piers jutting into the bay. She felt the Ironbones' estimate of the occupants' numbers had been overly optimistic, putting them at closer to four thousand than three. However, her principal interest lay in the large herd of cattle crowded into the fenced half-acre that sat outside the wall. To augment the torches blazing along the parapet, the defenders had posted more around the corral. Anyone approaching within a few yards of the fence would be an easy target for even a poor archer.

She turned to Lynnea, finding her standing with arms clutched tight about her chest. Her face, paler even than usual, was downcast, although she darted glances at the stockade. This time, Thera couldn't fault her apprentice's fears. Nor would she ask her to commit suicide.

"We'll need to pause for a night," Thera said. "Reconsider—"

"Thera," Ragnalt cut in, voice hard with urgency. Turning, Thera saw him pointing to the shadowed trees to their rear. She also saw that Lynnea was no longer at her side. A short, excited whinny came from the gloom, followed by the drum of hooves when horse and apprentice sped from the cover of the trees, galloping straight towards the stockade.

"Form your *menda*!" Thera told Ossgrym, rushing towards where she had tethered Elkor. "Attack when ready!"

"Where?" he asked, staring in bewilderment as she hauled herself onto Elkor's back. "The wall still stands."

"You'll see a gap soon enough," Thera assured him. "Don't linger for a second longer than necessary."

With that, she gripped the dreadaxe in one hand, Elkor's reins in the other, and drove her heels hard into her flanks, sending them hurtling in Lynnea's wake.

Chapter Thirty-Eight

Elvine

For a time, they drifted in silence. With the danger at least temporarily abated, the fear that had been so mysteriously absent finally arrived. *I stabbed a man,* Elvine thought, heart thumping and limbs shaking. Her eyes inevitably found the spear. It rested across her knees, the blood staining it mostly congealed and she watched a sluggish drop detach itself from the metal to besmirch the wool of her shawl.

Suddenly, she hated it. This is what she had risked her life for? This was what so many had died for? An old, unadorned weapon that might command a single clip of silver if she bargained hard enough. There weren't even any markings on the haft or metal to speak to its origin. She could have found it anywhere. Would Sister Lore really look upon this meagre offering and bestow the gift of freedom?

Hands trembling with a mix of fear and despairing resentment, she took hold of the spear with the full intention of casting it overboard . . .

He is lying to you.

She stopped, staring at the weapon in her grasp. The voice hadn't been spoken, but she had heard it. Also, it had been accompanied by a small tickle of warmth to her palms.

I have gone mad, she decided, lowering the spear. The need to throw it into the sea had vanished as quickly as it had arrived. The disaster of the Vaults and the horrors of battle had evidently combined to unseat her reason, at least temporarily. Settling the spear across her knees once again, she turned her attention to Colvyn, watching him massage his wrists in preparation for taking up the oars once more.

"Where are we to go?" Elvine asked. "For that matter, how are we to get there? I see no provisions aboard this boat."

"Rain will provide drinking water," he said, his encouraging smile plainly forced. His next words rang equally hollow. "I recall Behsla saying the winds of the lower Styrnspeld run west to east. They'll carry us to the Outer Isles. We're sure to find a friendly berth there."

She might have been grateful for the kindness of his lies if not for the imaginary warning from the spear. *He is lying to you.* An obvious truth at this juncture, but she doubted that was the real meaning behind the statement. Sighing in annoyance, she tightened her grip on the spear's haft, as if punishing it. *There was no true meaning*, she admonished herself. *This thing cannot talk . . .*

He is not what he pretends to be.

The same voice and the same flush of warmth to her hands. There was a calm surety to its tone, a note of certainty mixed with compassion that reminded her where this thing had been found. It was a gift of the Altvar, after all. Elvine closed her eyes, steeling herself against the notion with an internal recitation of Covenant scripture. *Gods are the falsities of the weak and the venal. Embodiments of abstract nature wrapped in legend . . .*

Ask him.

Elvine started, her eyes snapping open to find Colvyn regarding her with a concerned frown. It occurred to her that she knew relatively little about this young man. He was well read, skilled in several languages, and, at least according to Felnir, possessed of outlaw inclinations that saw him confined to a Cordwain prison. Beyond that, her knowledge was scant indeed. During their shared voyaging he had made allusions to far-flung travels in the southern seas, allusions she now recognised as deliberately vague. He had made no mention of family, or of his birthplace. She recalled that Felnir had offered to pay him off with a decent purse in Skar Magnol, which he declined. And only rarely had he strayed from her side in all the weeks since.

The actions of a protector, certainly, but could they not also be that of a spy, or a competitor?

Ask him, the voice in the spear said again. Elvine detected no warning in it, perceiving instead a kindly note as it spoke on. *He will tell you.*

"What is it?" Colvyn said. His frown deepened and he leaned closer, reaching for her hand, then drawing back when she snatched it away.

"Who are you?" Elvine demanded.

"What?"

"I know you've been lying." She shifted back from him as far as the confines of the boat would allow, clutching the spear against her chest. "This . . ." She paused, feeling both foolish and defiant. "This told me."

Colvyn raised an eyebrow, lips quirking. "A spear told you I was lying . . . ?"

"I hear it!" Her shout echoed across the fogbound water, loud with anger.

"All right." Colvyn raised his hands. "I believe you. Given where we found it, I suppose it stands to reason."

Elvine detected no subterfuge in his bearing. He was not humouring a madwoman he found himself alone with on a small boat in a very large sea. Instead of mollifying her, the speed of his acceptance deepened her suspicion. She could scarcely believe it, so why should he?

"I've seen many strange things," he went on, reading the doubt in her face. "You might not credit it, but a talking spear is not the strangest. What did it tell you?"

"That you're a liar," she said. "That you're pretending to be what you're not."

Colvyn sat back, resting his forearms on his knees and regarding her in inexpressive silence. Elvine found the weight of his stare increasingly uncomfortable. Although she had stabbed a man today, she had scant illusions regarding the outcome of any struggle with this one. *He can take if he wants,* she knew. *Perhaps that was his design all along. Who knows what Wohtin told him in that cell?*

"Who are you?" she demanded again, forcing the words past a catch in her throat. "What do you want?"

A soft sigh escaped Colvyn's lips as he shook his head. "How can you not know?" he asked in a puzzled murmur. "I knew the moment I saw you."

"Knew what?"

He didn't answer immediately, lowering his gaze and clasping his hands together. She hadn't seen him fumble for words before and found it perhaps the most disconcerting thing yet. Finally, he raised his gaze to meet hers and said, "Your mother's name is Berrine Jurest, formerly employed at the Library of King Aeric in Olversahl." It wasn't a question, just a statement of information easily obtained. Although, as her mind raced, Elvine couldn't recall telling him either her mother's name or much detail of her previous life.

"What of it?" she demanded.

"For a librarian, your mother led a remarkably eventful life in her youth. Possessed of deep convictions regarding her Ascarlian heritage, she chafed at Algathinet rule over her city, and joined with a group working in secret to undo it. They called themselves the *Skard-ryken*. The Priestly Axes, unless my translation plays me false."

"The Sacred Axe," Elvine corrected. "A minor fanatical sect, extinct for years, and my mother never had any truck with them."

"And who's lying now?" He arched an eyebrow before speaking on, sparing her further denials. "When she was about your age Berrine Jurest sailed with the *Skard-ryken* to join forces with the Pretender to the throne of Albermaine, Magnis Lochlain. He had promised them freedom for the Fjord Geld should they lend aid to his cause, but their only reward was defeat in their first battle, which obliged them to flee into the Shavine Forest. And it was there that Berrine Jurest first met a young outlaw with a liking for words, even though he hadn't yet learned how to read or write."

Elvine's arms ached as she hugged the spear ever closer to her chest. She recalled her mother's tale of the unwise youthful expedition to Albermaine. *I'm afraid I didn't make much of a warrior, but I did meet some interesting people.*

She pressed her cheek against the flat of the spearpoint, wanting very badly for Colvyn to stop talking but nevertheless listening with rapt attention as he continued.

"A mutual regard blossomed between scholar and outlaw that night, yet in the morning they went their separate ways. She back to Olversahl, her determination to free her city undimmed but now intent on doing so by more subtle means. He to follow a path that would lead him to the Pit Mines, where he learned his letters skilfully enough to be called a scribe. A perilous escape led him to service in the ranks of a company captained by noble woman of deep Covenant beliefs. Her name was Evadine Courlain, but your people know her by another."

"The Blackheart," Elvine whispered.

"Yes." A shadow passed over Colvyn's features before he resumed his tale. "Much of what transpired next you already know. After playing a crucial role in securing victory over the Pretender at the Battle of the Traitor's Field, Evadine and her company were sent by a jealous and suspicious King Tomas to garrison Olversahl. And so were outlaw and librarian reunited, and this time their regard for one another was far more heartfelt."

He fell silent, lowering his eyes as if to afford her a moment of privacy. He didn't elaborate, but then he didn't need to. Elvine had been born near nine months to the day after Olversahl was taken for the Sister Queens. "My father," she grated, "was an Albermaine-ish sea captain with a liking for books. He sailed away the night the city burned—"

"No," Colvyn interrupted, gentle but firm. "He was not. He was Alwyn Scribe, later to become Sir Alwyn Scribe. And I'm sure you know what happened at Olversahl was merely the start of Evadine Courlain's crusade, one that would eventually end in her death outside the walls of Castle Ambris."

"Brought down by the Scribe's treachery, so some say." The words emerged from Elvine's lips in a whisper as her mind churned. Anger and denial swirled in fiery union, her body shaking with it. But, cutting through the confusion and rage was something more powerful: icy, implacable certainty that every word spoken in the last few minutes had been no lie. It all made too much sense. Absurd, messy sense, to be sure. But still, even as she railed against it, she knew he had told her only the truth.

"Those still so deluded as to follow the word of the Risen Martyr name him traitor even now," Colvyn said with a shrug. "But, in reality, his principal aim that day was to secure the life of his son. That part of the story is true, despite the Risen-ites' claims to the contrary. Alwyn Scribe fathered a child with Evadine Courlain. She named him Stevan, in honour of the first Martyr. He named him Colvyn, a plain and common name for a child he hoped would grow up to lead an unremarkable life. I'm afraid I've managed to disappoint him in that regard many times."

His smile broadened, but faded when he saw the numb immobility of her features. "My father never lied to me, Elvine," he said. "As I won't lie to you. It's an ill thing to harbour secrets between family."

She had no answer to that, her rage from seconds before subsiding into a curious, sorrowful fatigue. The depredations of recently survived battle, flight, and now this tumult of revelations combined to bear down upon her. Her grip loosened on the spear and she sagged, a low groan escaping her lips.

"You asked what I wanted," Colvyn said, reaching out to her. "I wanted to find my sister . . ."

"Just stop!" she snapped, incapable of absorbing any more of his truth. She huddled into herself, turning away from him. "Leave me be. Let me rest."

His face registered a spasm of suppressed hurt before shifting into an apologetic grimace. "It would be best if we tried to keep a steady course," he said, pointing to the tiller.

Letting out a wordless snarl of annoyance, she rose, gesturing for him to move aside. After a few seconds of awkward manoeuvring, Elvine slumped down at the boat's prow whilst Colvyn took up the tiller. She closed her eyes, hoping her exhaustion would bring the welcome release of sleep. Yet, as she lay there, her mind couldn't help but work over all he had told her. Also, her shawl offered scant protection from the chilly caress of the foggy air, birthing a distracting shiver.

"Here," Colvyn said. She didn't open her eyes as he covered her with his cloak, but neither did she protest. With the cold at bay, weariness exerted its inevitable grip. Although, before she fell into slumber, the diminishing babble in her mind summoned an accusation, emerging from her lips in an mutter: "You should have told me sooner."

His answer was a vague distant thing, but she managed to take it with her into the dark. "Yes. And taken you home."

She was jerked awake by the hard thump of the boat's rail against her cheek. Blinking bleary eyes, she beheld a sea that was thankfully free of fog, but no longer calm. The boat swayed upon choppy waters stretching away to a horizon lost behind a curtain of rain. Elvine had no knowledge of how long she had slept, but the encroaching gloom made it clear that night was fast approaching.

"You'll have to take over," Colvyn said from the tiller. "I need to row us through this."

Once again, she endured an uncomfortable instant of mutual proximity before taking position at the stern. She had hoped to find her thoughts more ordered upon waking, but instead they were much the same jumble of insistent questions. Her anger had cooled, however, partially because she wasn't entirely sure it was justified. This man, her brother, had saved her life more than once. His revealed secrets still left her raw, but she couldn't deny the absence of malice in his actions.

She waited until he had taken up the oars and begun to row before asking what she knew would be the first of many questions. "You said you came to find me," she said. "Did your father send you?"

He laughed, Elvine discerning a relieved cast to his face as he hauled them through the busy swell. "My father never sends me anywhere if he can help it. I'm fairly certain he has not the slightest inkling of your existence, and neither did I before we met. It was only when I set eyes upon you for the first time that it all became clear."

"What became clear?"

"My goal. The object of this lengthy and intrepid quest. I knew I had to find someone, or something, but hadn't been told what or who it was."

"Told? By who?"

He didn't reply at once, continuing to row whilst his features took on a contemplative frown. Coming to a decision, he shrugged and said, "If you've studied the tale of Evadine Courlain, you'll know that she claimed to experience visions."

"Prophecies gifted to her by the Seraphile," Elvine said. "So her adherents claim. All heretical nonsense."

"Whether they came from the Seraphile or not, I can't say. My father certainly thinks otherwise. However, he left me in no doubt that they were real, and often disturbingly accurate. It also transpires that such abilities appear to be hereditary."

Elvine surprised herself by laughing, a short and ugly sound that was more a bark. "You experience visions?" She laughed again. "In which case, I'm compelled to wonder why you didn't warn us about the calamitous outcome of this mission."

"It's never so precise. They come to me in dreams, mostly. Whispered riddles and glimpses of places I've never seen. It was small things at first. The arrival of ships bearing interesting news from across the seas. Lies told by some of my father's less trustworthy associates. Then, one night, I was woken by the most terrible nightmare of men in masks invading our home intent on bloody murder. In need of comfort, I rose from my bed and went to my father's room. And there, standing in the hallway, were three men in masks with daggers in hand. I was only small at the time but had a very loud scream, loud enough to wake my father and the rest of the household. Curiously, they were all far more skilled with weapons than the men who had come to kill us."

"Who were they?"

"Hired blades, so far as could be told. Two died in the fight and the third took poison to still his own tongue. We never discovered who paid them, but my father suspected the Risen-ites. The next day, we began packing for a long journey to the east and, for most of my childhood, didn't remain in one place for more than a few months. It made for an interesting but lonely life. Although, it did enable me to add some languages to my repertoire. Eventually, we settled in the port city of Leynkora under the protection of the Saluhtan of Ishtakar himself. I'm still unclear how my father arranged it, but he has his ways of being useful to those in power. There I remained, save for a few unsanctioned sojourns that irked him greatly, until the night I dreamed my most potent vision yet."

He angled his head, studying Elvine's features. "Strange to think that the dream didn't show me your face," he mused. "Your form was vague, as if I viewed you through distorted glass. 'Find her,' the whispered voice told me and from the moment I woke, it was all I could think of. Once I had successfully slipped free of my father's home, other dreams came to guide me throughout what was a long and oft dangerous journey. Fortunately, my expensive education included expert tuition in how to defend myself. Eventually, the dreams set me on the path to Castle Granoire, the famed prison of the Cordwain. Gaining access was relatively simple. All I needed to do was present myself to Duchess Ayin, since she and father are old friends. She found my request somewhat odd, of course, but agreed after some persuasion." Colvyn paused to smile. "'You have your father's tongue,' she told me. 'I just hope you have more sense than he did at your age.'

"Upon being consigned to Castle Granoire, I found myself in a cell with a madman who spoke a mix of archaic Ascarlian and Covenant scripture. It made for some interesting conversation, though I had no idea he would be the means of my escape when Felnir came calling. The rest, you know."

Elvine's eyes strayed to the spear, now lying in the boat's hull. Reaching for it, she felt a tingle of warm reassurance, though the voice within didn't consent to speak again.

"What did it tell you?" Colvyn asked, stilling the oars.

"That you're not lying," she said. "I think." Looking up at him, she found herself exasperated by her sudden absence of questions. Her confused hunger for information had calmed into a numb acceptance, something Colvyn was astute enough to notice. When he reached for her hand again, she didn't pull away.

"This much I know," he said. "When I return home with you at my side, our father will be, perhaps for the first time in his life, truly overwhelmed with joy. Leynkora is a beautiful city, Elvine. And it's been untroubled by war for many years. And the libraries." He squeezed her hand. "So many books . . ."

Elvine didn't hear his next words, her attention abruptly snared by the flicker of something beyond his shoulder. Seeing her alarm, Colvyn turned to scan the waves. "What?"

"A sail . . . Maybe."

"Was it red?"

"I couldn't tell. I don't think so."

They both peered towards the rain-lashed horizon. After a tense interval, a small grey rectangle resolved out of the haze. "Steer to starboard," Colvyn instructed, hauling hard on the oars. "It should put us in their path."

"Just because it's not red doesn't mean they're friendly," Elvine said, the word "competition" ringing loud in her mind.

"We're in the middle of the Styrnspeld with no supplies," Colvyn grunted, continuing to row hard. "Even an unfriendly ship is welcome at this point."

In fact, the ship turned out to be a fishing boat crewed by three Outer Islanders, all squinting at their unexpected visitors with brows creased in unalloyed suspicion. When Colvyn tossed a rope across, the fishermen allowed it to slip uncaught into the water.

"Our ship was taken by pirates!" Elvine called to them. "I demand rescue in the name of the Sister Queens!"

From the pained glance Colvyn shot at her, she divined this may not have been the best tack to take.

"Demand all you want, girl," the taller of the three called back. "Don't know you. Don't know him, and there's all manner of foul rumours flying across the sea these days. Talk of war in the north, and spies abroad. The kind who'll claim the Queens' favour then cut your throat as thanks for your kindness."

"My name is Elvine Jurest," she returned, trying to force a measure of authority into her tone. "Appointed Scholar to Sister Lore herself. This man is in my service. You will take us aboard and convey us to the nearest port."

The fishermen exchanged glances before clustering to engage in murmured conversation. Elvine couldn't be sure, but she fancied she heard the words "just kill them" arise from the muttered debate.

"A moment, if you please," Colvyn called out, stalling their discussion. Crouching, he removed his left boot and reached inside. "Here," he said, holding up a silver coin Elvine recognised as an Albermaine-ish sovereign. "For safe passage." The coin described a flickering arc through the air as he tossed it towards the other boat, the taller fisherman catching it with ease. Elvine's alarmed notion that they may just sail away with their prize was allayed when Colvyn added, "You get another when you deliver us to a port."

The fisherman turned the coin over, Elvine experiencing a jolt of dismay at seeing more suspicion on his face than greed. "Toss the rope over," he grunted. "We'll take you to Skyrn Hardta. There you can explain yourselves to Veilwald Hakkyn. And don't expect silver to sway his judgement."

"Where did you get that sovereign?" Elvine murmured to Colvyn as he tugged his boot back on.

"Poor old Guthnyr was very bad at guarding his loot." He began to coil the rope for another throw. "We'll need to be especially nice to these three, since I only had the one."

It transpired that the fishermen, all brothers, were themselves recent victims of misfortune. "Storm blew up a week back," Ahlgrun, the tallest and eldest of the trio explained in gruff, guarded tones. "One of the worst I've ever seen. Cast us many miles out into the Styrnspeld. Lucky we'd already hauled our catch aboard or likely have starved."

The brothers' distrust of their passengers diminished as the voyage wore on, but didn't fade completely, something Elvine ascribed to good sense rather than ignorance. The rumours Ahlgrun shared of war in the Kast Geld and sightings of unfamiliar ships encroaching on the southern reaches of the Outer Isles made such caution fully justified.

"Red-sailed pirates with faces to match, so they say," the fisherman elaborated. "The Veilwald's been gathering his *menda*, and well he might. Most likely find ourselves called to it when we get back."

"Where do they hail from, these red-sailed ships?" Elvine asked.

"Some say the southern seas. Some the west, though that's hard to credit. Wherever they're from, they've chosen a poor land to scour for spoils." Ahlgrun nodded to her spear. "Seems you've already taught a few that lesson."

The blood staining the spear had mostly flaked away from the iron but dried into a dark brown smear upon the upper haft. It occurred to Elvine that she should probably clean it. "Just one," she said. "Do you perhaps have a rag spare?"

"This'll work better." He tossed her a horsehair brush. "And use the rain barrel to wash it. Saltwater births rust."

"Thank you."

The last few dregs of gore came away from the iron point after a few swipes of the brush, but the discolouration of the wooden haft proved more stubborn. As she scrubbed at it, she wondered why an artefact that had remained in pristine condition for so long would now stain so easily.

"Has it spoken again?" Colvyn ventured, voice low.

"No." Sighing in exasperation, Elvine set the brush aside and began running a cloth over the spear. She supposed Sister Lore wouldn't mind a few marks. The mere fact of the spear's existence was what mattered, especially when Elvine told her about the voice that lurked within it.

"I was hoping it might have advised a change of course," Colvyn said.

"Our rescuers seem disinclined towards sailing anywhere but home," Elvine pointed out. "Besides, where would we go?"

"Leynkora." There was an insistence to his tone that made her pause in her task, turning to find him regarding her with serious intent. "From what I can gather, there are plenty of ships from the southern seas in Skyrn Hardta. Finding a berth shouldn't be difficult, especially when I mention a few choice names. Come home with me and meet your father, Elvine. I'm very keen to see his expression when I tell him who you are."

Your father. It sounded so strange to her ears. All her life, her curiosity about a singularly important figure in her life had been muted.

As a girl she had occasionally pestered Berrine for information, but it had always been a passing fancy, never something that took root and blossomed into a need. As she grew older, the reasons for her indifference became clear: he had sailed away and left his lover in peril. It was hard to care about such a man. Also, never at any point in her childhood had she felt the want of another parent. Berrine had been everything she needed, and more. Still, faced with all Colvyn had told her, the pull upon her ever potent inquisitiveness was strong. To be presented with a father possessing a singular place in history seemed like a gift, despite the discomfort of contemplating her mother's deceit. Yet, however deceitful she had been, thoughts of Berrine led Elvine to but one answer.

"I can't," she said. "Not whilst my mother remains Sister Lore's prisoner, honoured though she may be. With war in the offing, I can't just leave her there." She gave the spear's leaf-shaped point a final wipe. "In Skyrn Hardta I will appeal to the Veilwald for passage to Skar Magnol, there to present the Queens with this mighty gift. You . . ." she paused to afford him a kindly smile so her next words didn't sting ". . . may go where you wish . . . brother. Mayhap one day I'll make my way to Leynkora. Who can say?"

Colvyn turned to regard the sea beyond the boat's stern, grimacing in resignation. "As you can't leave her behind, I can't leave you. But then, I think you know that. To Skar Magnol, it is. But then, dear sister of mine, we are done with this realm. This mad voyage has cost me a friend. I won't lose a sister too."

Chapter Thirty-Nine

Ruhlin

"Wake up!"

Ruhlin felt his head sway upon his shoulders as he was jostled by a series of hard, insistent shoves. Opening his eyes, he found Aleida staring down at him. Her paleness was accentuated by the dark spray of blood across her features, raising the panicked notion that he might have injured her. However, as she sagged against him, shuddering in relief, he saw no wounds upon her. The blood was not hers. Nor, he realised as he scanned his body, was it his. Although slicked with gore from head to toe and now returned to its normal dimensions, so far as he could tell, he lacked a single cut or scrape. Although unharmed, he shuddered from the familiar, sickly chill.

"S-*stagna*," he stammered, attempting to rise.

"I had to." Aleida took hold of his arm, helping to drag him to a sitting position. "You might have slaughtered the whole *wuhltra* otherwise."

"You . . . ?"

She pointed towards the circle, Ruhlin turning to see a small figure kneeling alongside the bear he had maimed. Achela's head was bowed, her hands pressed into the creature's fur.

"What is she doing?" he asked Aleida.

"I don't know." She winced as a flurry of screams filled the air nearby. Ruhlin fought down a wave of nausea to see a cluster of blood-spattered people huddled together at the furthest edge of the box. They gaped at him in collective terror. Bodies in various states of disordered mortality littered the floor. Noting the besmirched finery of the cowering bunch, Ruhlin understood these to be the local luminaries he had failed to kill when fighting his way to Aleida's side. Curiously, they seemed to find his true form just as terrifying as the monster.

"Spare me, Amundyr!" a matronly woman cried out, words garbled by fear as she lowered herself, arms spread wide. "Always have I honoured the Altvar!"

"We need to be gone from here," Aleida said, jerking her head at the tiered rows of seating. "Not all of them fled."

Looking up, Ruhlin found the crowd that had thronged the tiers had thinned considerably. Dense knots of people clustered at the exits, fighting each other in a frenzied attempt at mass escape. Others were far less fearful, or perhaps so struck by the ugly spectacle Amundyr had wrought they were incapable of more than gawping immobility. Threading their way through the sparse crowd from different directions, however, were several dozen guards. Ruhlin detected a wariness in the warriors' bearing, but their pace and determination increased as they drew closer and the monster failed to reappear.

"Come," Aleida grunted, placing Ruhlin's arm over her shoulder and attempting to lever him upright. His first attempt to stand failed when his legs, seeming sapped of strength, folded beneath him. The monster and the *stagna* had taken a toll. He tried to fix his mind on the fast-approaching guards, hoping it would stir the rage once more, but nothing came.

"Go," he told Aleida.

Meeting his gaze with an annoyed scowl, she stated her reply in flat and unambiguous tones: "No."

Perhaps it was her stubbornness, or the prospect of impending death, or worse, recapture, that finally kindled a morsel of anger in his gut. Either way, it enabled him to summon the strength to stand, albeit upon legs that now seemed to be fashioned from a mix of wool and ice. Gazing around the *wuhltra*, he could see no avenue of escape until his gaze alighted on the raised door to his cell. "There," he said. "Though I'm not sure I can force our way into the tunnel."

"Don't worry about that," Aleida said, tugging him to the edge of the box. The drop to the circle was cushioned by the sand, though once again it required considerable effort for Ruhlin to regain his feet. When he did, he saw Aleida standing uncertainly at Achela's side.

"Aunt . . ." he heard her venture in a tremulous voice, extending a tentative hand to Achela's shoulder. "We must go."

Stumbling closer, Ruhlin saw Achela raise a much transformed face to regard her niece. In the space of moments, it seemed she had aged many years, her cheeks hollowed and the lines about her eyes deepened like scars. She had her hands buried in the fur of the stricken bear. Ruhlin was astounded to see that the animal still drew breath and, although it may have been a figment of his fatigue-addled mind, he was sure the dark, glowering eyes it turned on him gleamed with life rather than the dullness of impending death.

Achela said something to Aleida in Morvek, a short, croaking statement that caused her to stiffen and retreat a step. Turning to Ruhlin, Achela's sagging features formed a smile, and she said, "What must happen has happened. I can do . . . no more."

She gave a slow blink of her eyes and collapsed onto the bear's flank, all life seeping out of her with her final breath. "Aunt?" Aleida said, crouching to jostle Achela's unmoving form. She didn't respond, but the bear let out a sudden, and angry, growl. Stooping, Ruhlin grasped her arm to pull her away, then flinched as something fast buzzed the air above his head.

"He's not worth anything dead, you feck-wit!"

Looking back at the box, Ruhlin saw a Nihlvarian guard bearing a strongbow recoil from a blow delivered by one of his comrades. Several dozen now crowded the tiers surrounding the box, with more hurrying to join them. The sight of several warriors bearing chains provoked another flare of anger at Ruhlin's core, but still not enough to summon the monster.

"I'm sorry," he said, hauling Aleida away from her aunt's corpse. "We have no time."

She gave a short plaintive sob but, after a few stumbling steps, grasped his hand with firm resolve as they ran for the open cell. Once inside, Ruhlin threw his shoulder against the iron and wood barrier sealing the tunnel. He knew it was a hopeless prospect, but hoped the pain would serve to summon the monster. It didn't. Grunting in frustration, he drew back in preparation for another try, stopping when he felt Aleida's hand on his arm.

"Move aside."

He did as she bid, his gaze snapping to the sand circle at the mounting babble of apprehensive but increasingly determined voices. "What are . . . ?" he began, turning back to Aleida. Her face was hard with concentration, her hands pressed flat to the metal bracket sealing the door's lock. She winced and Ruhlin heard the clatter of a shifting mechanism, whereupon the door swung open at her first shove.

A way with metal, Ruhlin thought, recalling her intervention back at the dome. It seemed her ability extended to more than just the *stagna*.

"There were many locks in my father's home," she said, stepping through the door. "How did you think I always found my way to your cage?"

Entering the tunnel, they came to a sudden halt at the sight of a guard. He stood with his spear levelled at Ruhlin, although the confusion on his face made it plain he had no inkling of what had occurred in the *wuhltra*. "Please help!" Aleida gasped, rushing towards the guard. "The bear got loose! It killed dozens!"

"Got loose?" the guard asked, baffled by the presence of his Aerling's gore-spattered daughter. Still, his fear of Ruhlin compelled him not to alter the angle of his spear as she approached to clutch at his arm. It was a fatal mistake. Aleida's knife slammed into the guard's neck up to the hilt, unleashing a thick red torrent as she twisted it before drawing it free. She stepped away from the falling body and, beckoning for Ruhlin to follow, disappeared into the tunnel's gloom.

"Wait," he grunted, slumping next to the guard's twitching corpse to drag his sword free of its scabbard. With his monster still refusing to emerge, it stood to reason he would need a weapon before long.

He caught up with Aleida at the tunnel exit, finding her crouched in a shadow with a finger pressed to her lips. The reason became clear when he glanced at the chamber beyond. It was a circular space formed of caged cells, dimly lit by guttering torches. Through the bars, Ruhlin made out several of his companions, all standing in tense wariness, their eyes fixed on Radylf. The giant prowled back and forth in the centre of the chamber, face lacking all vestige of anything that could be called cheerful. His heavy, pale brows were set in a predatory frown, anvil-sized jaw grinding. Ruhlin counted six more guards besides the whip-man. Too many to fight, not that Radylf would allow him the opportunity once he stepped into view.

An echoing shout from the depths of the tunnel, strangely discordant even for fearful warriors, convinced Ruhlin that any further delay would be fatal. "Get to the cages," he murmured to Aleida. Taking a breath, he emerged into the light.

"He's dead," Ruhlin announced, immediately capturing Radylf's attention. "The Aerling," he continued, stepping to the left to ensure the whip-man's gaze tracked away from the tunnel entrance. "I killed him." Ruhlin summoned a grin to his lips. Slathered in sand-speckled gore as he was, he must resemble something from a nightmare. "Like the worthless dog he was."

A lie, but that didn't matter. All that mattered was that whip-man and guards failed to notice Aleida's lithe form slipping from the shadows. "You did say I should finish it quickly." Ruhlin let out a laugh, taking another sideways step. "And I did, far more quickly than I would have liked. He begged me, Radylf." He laughed again, twirling the sword in his hand to ensure the giant's eyes didn't stray. "Just before I tore him open, he shat himself."

Radylf snarled, shoulders hunching low in preparation for a charge. Yet, a measure of caution must have cut through his fury. Pausing, the giant's eyes flicked to the tunnel and saw Aleida creeping towards the cages. Before he could open his mouth to bark an order at the guards, Ruhlin hurled himself at the whip-man. Letting out a scream filled with all the accumulated humiliation and pain he had suffered at this man's hand, Ruhlin gripped the sword in both hands as he closed. He brought it down in a swift overhead swing, hoping to split the bald head of his enemy from crown to neck. Radylf's arms blurred, catching Ruhlin's wrists before the sword came within an inch of his skull.

"Where is it?" Radylf asked, shaking Ruhlin like a doll, the sword tumbling from his grip. Hissing through gritted teeth, the whip-man lifted him up until their faces were level. "Where is your fire blood now, you weakling wretch?"

Ruhlin thrashed in his grip, jerking his body to slam both feet into Radylf's chest, a blow he barely seemed to feel. However, it added yet more fuel to his rage. Releasing Ruhlin's wrists, the giant enfolded his massive limbs about his captive's arms and waist, and began to squeeze.

"Where is the witch?" he demanded, Ruhlin letting out a short, agonised groan before the increasing pressure forced the air from his lungs. "Did you kill her too?"

Ruhlin could feel his bones grinding, the imminence of death serving to stir the rage at his core. It wasn't enough for the monster to fully emerge, but it did send a pulse of thickened muscle through him, staving off the whip-man's crushing strength for an instant.

"No," he grunted back, staring defiant hate into Radylf's eyes. "She stood and watched me. Your master should have been more discerning in his choice of servants."

The whip-man's features became a mask of dire purpose, the muscles of his arms bulging as he increased the pressure. Ruhlin struggled as much as he could, but it was a feeble effort against such strength. As his vision began to dim, he entertained the faintly amusing notion that now he actually wanted the monster to emerge it failed to do so.

The clang of a cage swinging open heralded a lessening in Radylf's grip. The giant's head snapped towards the sight of Tuhlan and a pair of Morvek prisoners charging from their cell to hurl themselves at the guards. Distracted by the unequal contest between the whip-man and Ruhlin, the guards were quickly borne down. Tuhlan snapped the neck of one and snatched up his spear to neatly skewer the neck of another who rushed to his comrade's aid. Surging to his feet, the Caerith hurled himself at the other guards, spear whirling. Beyond the struggle, Ruhlin saw Aleida rush to the next cage and press her hand to the lock.

Snarling, Radylf cast Ruhlin aside, sending him into hard collision with the chamber wall. He lay upon the tiled floor, too stunned to do more than drag air into his lungs. Hearing more cages open, he raised his shuddering head to see Radylf encircled by freed prisoners,

A TIDE OF BLACK STEEL • 477

the guards all slain. As they assailed him with spears and swords claimed from the guards, the giant lashed at them with his whip.

"To arms!" he shouted continually, casting his voice at the tunnels leading away from the chamber in a desperate attempt to summon aid. "They're loose! To arms!"

"Shut the fecker up!" Sygurn yelled, darting forward to jab his spear at Radylf's throat, instantly reeling back with a whip cut to his temple. However, his thrust had distracted the giant enough for Julette to deliver a sword slash to Radylf's thigh. He roared in rage and swung a punch at the pirate woman's head. She ducked it with ease, then sliced a second cut into the whip-man's forearm.

"Not smiling so much now, eh?" she asked, dodging clear of the whip.

Radylf let out a wordless howl and redoubled his efforts, the whip cracking so fast it created an echoing cacophony through the surrounding maze of tunnels. If the giant's cries didn't summon more guards to his aid, Ruhlin knew the sound of his whip surely would. Spying his stolen sword lying only a yard away, he crawled towards it, grasping the hilt and forcing himself to his knees.

Radylf backed towards a tunnel, his whip striking like an angry and tireless snake. Ruhlin fixed his gaze on the whip-man's legs and dragged himself closer. If he could get close enough without being noticed, he could at least create a diversion for the others to finish the task. Once again, Radylf frustrated him, retreating further into the tunnel before Ruhlin could close the distance. Hearing a thunder of boots from the other passages to this chamber, his heart plummeted at the knowledge they were out of time.

"Don't worry," Radylf panted, his old cheery countenance re-asserting itself. "I won't let them kill you—"

Whatever dire promises he had been about to make were abruptly curtailed when a large befouled maw loomed out of the shadows and clamped itself to his head. Radylf's statuesque features disappeared in an explosion of flensed tissue and shattered bone. His mostly headless body sank to its knees, tottered, then toppled forward to cast a broad crimson wave across the tiles.

"Ulthnir's arse, what the feck is that?" Sygurn breathed. He and the other freed prisoners retreated from the huge, shaggy form shambling from the tunnel. The bear shook its massive head, scattering gore, then dipped its muzzle to afford Radylf's corpse an inquisitive sniff. Seeing a long pink tongue lap over its lips, Ruhlin worried they were about to witness the beast gorge itself on its prey. Fortunately, the increasing tumult from the surrounding tunnels captured the bear's attention before it could sate its hunger. Growling, it charged into the nearest chamber. Within seconds, the pounding of boots was transformed into a chorus of screams.

"That," Ruhlin groaned, dragging himself to his feet, "is our way out."

He started to follow the bear's path, managing only a few faltering steps before collapsing.

"Is he wounded?" he heard Julette ask, feeling several hands hauling him upright.

"His blood no longer burns," Aleida replied. "I don't know why."

"Well he better start burning again soon," Sygurn said. "Else I doubt we're getting out of here, bear or not."

Ruhlin sagged between Tuhlan and Julette as they bore him along the tunnel, stepping over the remains of guards left in the bear's wake. Sygurn, Iyaka and the other Morvek led the way, occasionally pausing to jab a sword or spearpoint into any guard still groaning or struggling to rise. They soon entered another chamber, its walls lined with cages holding more slaves. Seeing none he recognised, Ruhlin realised these were the fighters brought here by other Aerlings to take part in the Meidvang.

"Stop," he told his helpers before turning to Aleida, jerking his head at the cages. "Free them."

"You sure?" Sygurn asked, casting a wary eye over the tense figures behind the bars. "They don't seem too friendly."

"We need allies," Ruhlin said, nodding to Aleida to hurry.

Once free, most of the slaves immediately fled into the tunnels, although a half-dozen stayed. All were Morvek, a rapid exchange with Iyaka sufficing to convince them to follow when the group resumed tracking the bear's bloody trail. A succession of slain or wounded guards led them to the outer vaults of the *wuhltra*. The bear was busily pounding its paws into the torso of a not-quite-dead guard. Sensing their arrival, it paused, licking a reddened maw as its gaze settled briefly on Ruhlin before moving on to Aleida, where it lingered.

Watching the two match stares, he recalled the Achela's final moments in the circle, her hands buried in this creature's fur. He couldn't know what arcane rite the witch had used her last breaths to conjure, but the unmistakable awareness he saw in the bear's gaze was anything but natural.

"Is that ... ?" he ventured to Aleida as she continued to regard the beast with a mix of trepidation and amazement.

"There were tales I heard as a child," she murmured back. "Tales of Morvek who could share minds with the creatures of the forest." She shook her head, the fearful wonder on her face darkening into anger. "The old bitch kept so much from me."

Any doubts Ruhlin harboured regarding the bear's intelligence vanished when it let out a growl of patent annoyance. Delivering a final, bone-snapping blow to the unfortunate guard, it turned and loped towards the massive gate sealing the entrance to the vaults. A few swipes of its paws sufficed to dislodge the beam from the brackets, whereupon it pressed its bulk to the barrier and began to push it open.

"Wait!" Ruhlin called out, the bear rounding on him with an inquisitive huff.

"We need to get out of here," Julette said.

"Looking like this?" Ruhlin returned. He flapped a wavering hand at himself and then at the door. From the excited clamour audible through the doors, it was clear that a large crowd of confused, panicked people were now milling around the precincts of the *wuhltra*. A group of barely dressed bloodstained slaves would be sure to stand out amongst such a multitude. "Word of what happened here will have spread," he added. "More warriors will be coming."

Fighting down a wave of fatigue, he swung his gaze around the vaults until it alighted on a familiar sight. Eldryk's carriage had been placed alongside several others, most far less opulent in style but all covered against the prying eyes of the non-privileged.

"Slaves fleeing the *wuhltra* will quickly find themselves chained again," he said. "But not a caravan of Aerlings. And—" he nodded to the guard's corpse "—we have disguises at hand."

Sygurn took on the role of captain, donning hastily wiped leather armour and positioning himself on the board of Eldryk's carriage. Tuhlan and Julette also garbed themselves in suitably martial attire, each taking charge of a carriage whilst the Morvek concealed themselves within the conveyances. There was clearly no possibility of accommodating the bear. The oxen lowed in fright when the beast came near, jerking in their tethers and liberally staining the ground with fear-born effluent. The creature appeared to understand the predicament and kept close to the doors.

"Can you . . . talk with it?" Ruhlin asked Aleida as she helped him into her father's carriage.

"How?" she asked. "I don't happen to speak bear. Do you? Besides, I've a sense it knows what needs to be done."

She and Iyaka settled him onto the cushioned couch and hauled the carriage door closed. The Morvek pounded her fist to the roof, answered by the snap of Sygurn's reins before they lurched into motion. The grinding squeal of the vault doors being pushed open was instantly smothered by the sound of many voices raised in surprised terror. It seemed the bear was intent on clearing a path for them.

Lying on the couch, an overwhelming tide of exhaustion descended upon Ruhlin. So fierce was its grip he jerked in fear that he might not wake from the slumber he was about to fall into. His shudders ceased at the feel of a cool hand on his brow, Aleida's face coming into view. He found it odd that he hadn't seen her smile before. Not a true, real smile. There was no artifice to the honest curve of her lips, the gratitude that shone in her eyes before she pressed a kiss to his forehead.

"You did it," he heard her say as shadows crowded his vision. "You set us free."

"No," he whispered back before the void claimed him. "*We* did it. I knew, you see . . . She told me I could trust you . . ."

CHAPTER FORTY

Felnir

Wohtin's head gave a fractional movement in the face of Felnir's implacable visage, though his expression barely changed. Nevertheless, Felnir sensed a man suppressing an unwise urge to laugh. "It's a lengthy, and very old story," Wohtin said, Felnir finding the mildness of his tone more irksome than if he had responded with an outright insult. "It's hard to know where best to start."

"With who you are," Felnir said, striving to keep his anger in check. "Your true name. And no more riddles, if you value keeping that head upon your shoulders."

"I've grown fond of the name Wohtin, so I think I would prefer if you continued to address me so. As for the name I was born with, and the name I earned . . ." The tall man paused to glance at the plaque bearing his image. "If dear, kind, clever Elvine had lived, I fancy she would have guessed it by now."

"But she didn't. So just tell me."

"Upon my birth, my mother named me Angmund. Later I would earn the name Eikralvyr, the Wise Tongue, a name I believe has become corrupted by centuries of legend."

Angmund, Felnir repeated inwardly. Although he didn't possess the knowledge of a scholar, there were few of Ascarlian blood without a passing knowledge of Velgard's legend. "Velgard had a Tielwald named Angmund," he said. "Better known to history as Angmund Sictalvyr, the Dire Tongue." He angled his head, studying the faint but resigned bitterness in Wohtin's frown. "A traitor who plotted the foul murder of his own king, so the tale is told," Felnir continued. "His scheme uncovered, the Altvar cursed him, denied him the mercy of death so that he might never escape his guilt."

Wohtin sighed, shaking his head. "I plotted no murder. The thought that I would ever raise a hand to . . . *him*." He let out a mirthless laugh that quickly faded. "But I was cursed. That cannot be denied. Whether it was the Altvar or something yet more unknowable, I cannot say, and I have had many years to ponder it."

"Why? Why were you cursed?"

"For the worst crime committed by those who claim wisdom: pride." Wohtin cast a glance towards Velgard's barrow. "It is hard for those who never met my king, never served him, to understand how much the desire to please him could consume a soul. He never demanded, never threatened, but just the merest suggestion of a want would have his servants scurrying to meet it. Like many a man subsumed in guilt, Velgard was a restless soul, possessed of an unquenchable need to never rest, never submit himself to the terror of indolence. For, it is my belief, that in times of quietude, the ghost of his brother, the man he killed to secure peace for the Ascarls, would appear to torment him. Whether a phantom born of a guilty mind, or truly his brother's unquiet shade, I never knew. But that was what drove him, first to unwanted kingship, then across the Iron Dark Sea to find the Vaults of the Altvar. Yet, having found them, still he feared the quiet, and so set me, his most learned counsellor, to the task of seeking more mysteries. No longer content with this world, he wished to know what lay beyond it. 'Find me a path to the Altvar, Angmund,' he told me. 'For I wish to beseech them for the tools I shall need to craft a world that will do them honour.' And, to my eternal and deserved shame, I strove to do as he bid."

Felnir's thoughts returned to the Vaults, the abject sorrow upon Wohtin's face as he beheld the misshapen stone at the feet of Ulthnir's statue. "That *thing*," he said. "The bow, the sword, the spear. That was your doing."

"It was. To secure the tools he wanted required reaching into a realm no mortal should touch. Gifts of the Altvar, so we thought. With them, he would sail to new lands, not as a conqueror, unless they were so foolish as to stand against him, but as the herald of the Altvar's beneficence."

Wohtin looked up at the sky, thinned of cloud to reveal a glittering sprawl of stars. "So many lands did this same sky guide me to. Departing this hidden kingdom, I scoured the realms beyond the Southern Seas for shamans. Sought ancient books in the Ishtan ports of the east. But it was only when I ventured into Caerith lands that my search bore fruit. They are a secretive people, not overly welcoming of strangers, and yet I was permitted to wander their dominion without fear. I pestered their elders for insight, but received little beyond cryptic allusions to a lost age of glory that existed before a great calamity they call the *Morkletha*, the Fall. After months without result, I resolved to depart for the Alberic-speaking kingdoms to the north, where at least there were libraries. And that was when *she* found me."

A distance crept into Wohtin's eyes then, and Felnir knew he was picturing himself in a forest clearing conversing with a woman of improbable beauty. "I thought of myself as wise," he said. "But meeting her, I knew myself to be little more than an ignorant fool. She gave me no name, but in time I learned that she was known amongst the Caerith as the *Doenlisch*, and their tales of her stretch into the uncharted depths of history. It was from her that I learned the secret of reaching between worlds."

"The book," Felnir said. "It was a book of spells?"

"Nothing so prosaic. Although half had been written in the Caerith script, the other half contained a translation in Ascarlian. The ink and pages were so ancient I doubt our tongue had even been conceived when the words were set down. One of many mysteries I was never to solve."

"But it told you how. It gave you the power to summon the gifts of the Altvar."

"No. The power it gave came in the form of knowledge. You see, to reach between the worlds requires an innate ability, something that flows in the blood and cannot be learned. To fulfil my king's mission, I needed someone with that blood. And, may the Altvar forgive me, I found him."

Wohtin's face clouded, Felnir seeing a flicker of hate in the twitch of his features as he sorted through presumably ugly memories. "For nigh a year I searched for the one I needed, eventually finding him in a back alley in the squalid collection of hovels that would later grow into the mighty city of Couravel. Half starved, clad in rags, cast out by a family that couldn't feed him when the harvest failed. A more pathetic a soul I never met, yet he had the power in his blood. The power I needed. He was barely aware of it, ascribing his continued survival through thievery to lucky chance. But I knew what he was. I saw it in the way he could make others forget him. A baker who reached for his rolling pin to administer a beating for a stolen loaf, only to blink in confusion and return to his toil. A market trader who would abruptly abandon her pursuit of an urchin with a purloined apple. When I enticed him to follow me with promise of silver, I congratulated myself on finding one with so meagre an understanding of their own gifts. Even now, so many ages later, I stand in awe of my own stupidity. I should have known that what lay behind those apparently uncomprehending eyes was a depth of deceit and cunning beyond imagining.

"I called him Moyirn, 'seagull', since he claimed to have no name and it seemed fitting for one so given to theft. He followed me willingly enough, after some initial, violently expressed suspicions. Our journey home was long, and I found him a surprisingly gifted pupil. It was necessary that he learn, not just our tongue, but the nature of his blood. The speed with which he absorbed knowledge should have been a warning, for it went beyond mere intellect. By the time I led him into Skar Altvar to present him to my king, Moyirn could speak fluent Ascarlian and write as well as most scribes. Velgard welcomed him, of course, as was his way, and Moyirn seemed to form an instant bond with the king. Velgard had no sons and was ever fond of taking orphans under his wing, but none were so favoured as this spindly foreigner.

"Over the course of years, as I sought to complete his education, Moyirn grew tall and broad, learned warrior skills at Velgard's side whilst learning lore at mine. When the time came for me to fully expl. in his role, he set himself to the task with fearsome dedication, poring endlessly over all the books I possessed, especially the one given to me by the *Doenlisch*. I had struggled with the text, finding it dense and opaque, yet to Moyirn it was like peering into unclouded waters. 'I have it, Angmund,' he told me one day. 'I have the key to unlock the door between worlds. The king shall have his tools.'"

Wohtin paused to let out a soft, bitter laugh. "It is in such moments that the world turns. The excitement of discovery, of securing a dream long sought, masks all doubt, quells the questions that should be asked. Still, sometimes I like to think I harboured a small kernel of suspicion, that the slight but still potent incidents of cruelty exhibited by my so apt pupil gave me pause. They were not especially remarkable at first. An excessively strong blow with the practice sword that left one of Velgard's other favoured orphans with a broken arm. The abrupt disappearance of a pet cherished by a maiden resistant to Moyirn's charms. Over time, such incidents became more frequent, as did Moyirn's willingness to use his particular ability, despite my stern injunction against doing so. 'Merely a prank,' he said when I berated him for having compelled one of Velgard's more honoured advisors to venture into the Vaults and piss upon the base of Silfaer's statue. The fact that the man in question was the most pompous, conceited fool I ever met served to negate my anger and minimise my punishment. In my way, I was as blind to Moyirn's nature as Velgard, a blindness that would cost us both dear.

"Come the day, we presented our findings to the king and, without pause to consider the consequences, he commanded that we proceed forthwith. Moyirn avowed that the task required a location of significance, a place where the air was thick with a concordance of belief, for this would fuel his work. Where better than the heart of the Vaults, the statue to the Worldsmith himself? Strange to think that I recall finding the act of reaching between worlds somewhat lacking in spectacle. There were no flashes of light. No mysterious gales blowing through the Vaults as we stood gathered beneath Ulthnir's statue. I understood later that Moyirn's explanation of the process had been deliberately vague, perhaps because he barely comprehended it himself. Though I suspect it was more due to his desire to hoard whatever power he could. He said it was a matter of will coupled with focus, concentrating the mind through inward repetition of mantras listed in the Caerith book. These words had no power in themselves, but were merely a means of focusing one's intent, allowing what lay in his blood to seek out the path to the hidden fissures in this plane.

"For near an hour he just stood there, more still than the stone god that gazed down upon us, his expression unchanged. Eventually, however, he began to shudder and blood trickled from his nose. It soon thickened into a torrent and his shudders wracked his entire body until, at last, he collapsed. I went to him, speaking comforting reassurance, for I was certain we had failed. My last clear memory of him was his smile, so wide it was more a snarl, baring teeth red with blood. Upon his face I beheld the expression of a man beset by both deep satisfaction and boundless malice. I've often pondered whether the act of reaching between worlds transformed him, or revealed him. Either way, the wrong he had crafted that day was so vast that I cannot believe there was ever any true kindness in his soul.

"The spectacle I had hoped for arrived then, and terrible it was. A great tremor shook the Vaults, the stone beneath us rippling as if transmuted into water. Then *it* rose. That twisted, sickened thing erupted from the altered ground and with it came terror. It was not just the sight of it, ugly as it was. It was the essence of its realm bleeding into ours, invading every mind it touched. Rending some into such madness they died there and then. Some turned on each other, transforming the city beneath the mountain into a scene of senseless battle that raged until every bloodthirsty soul lay dead. Others, like me, it left a gibbering, twitching wreck of a man. I learned later that the madness had not only assailed those gathered in the Vaults, but all of Skar Altvar too. It even reached out to afflict the denizens of this city, though its effect was not so marked.

"How long I lay there, writhing and screaming, I know not. The people here recovered quickly and when they did . . ." Wohtin turned again to regard the barrow of King Velgard ehs Trehka. "Our monarch was gone. They found no trace of him in the Vaults, nor of Moyirn. Of those that had drawn breath in Skar Altvar that day, only I remained alive. Those not fallen to the plague of madness had destroyed themselves in ravening violence. Yet *it* lingered. That foul, conjured thing bearing its three gifts. Those foolish enough to venture a hand to them suffered terrible visions and never did so again." His eyes went to the sword in Felnir's hand. "Yet, as I hoped, you, your brother, and your woman were unaffected."

"You hoped?" Felnir asked, finding his heart beating faster as grim understanding took hold. "This was all your design. All that has happened throughout this cursed journey has been your doing."

"Has it? I don't recall being asked for an opinion since you dragged me from that castle. Your queen hungered for the treasures of the Vaults and you hungered to give them to her, all to restore a status that is beneath you."

"Elvine," Felnir grated. "Kodryn, Guthnyr . . ."

"It is the nature of kingship to sacrifice those you cherish." A hard gleam of judgement shone in Wohtin's eye, his voice coloured by a flinty, uncompromising note. "Velgard understood that. As I hope you will too, in time."

"I told you. I am not a king."

"Not yet. But when we undo that barrow come the morning and sail forth from here, you will have a choice to make, Felnir of the Redtooth. Head south and attempt to find a passage through or around the Fire Isles, a voyage that's likely to have us starved or drowned soon enough. Or—" Wohtin gestured at the sky, indicating a familiar constellation above the western horizon "—continue to follow Trieya's Quill."

Felnir tracked his gaze along the arc of glittering stars. The celestial guide had led to so much grief, yet he still felt it beckoning him on. "Why?" he said. "What awaits me there?"

"Your kingdom," Wohtin said, the shortness of his tone indicating that he had no further explanation to offer, at least for now.

"You promise a kingdom yet unseen," Felnir told him, raising the sword. "When I have the greatest gift to offer Sister Lore."

"You imagine she will restore all honour to you." Wohtin shook his head. "Tell me, why did they name you the Redtooth?"

Felnir's fingers flexed on the sword's handle. He could simply ignore the question and demand more answers, but knew the balance between them had changed. The treasury of knowledge Wohtin possessed made him far too valuable to discard now. Furthermore, he knew it. It was there in the unyielding cast of his eyes and stern set of his features. This was the face of a man accustomed to authority, a man who had stood at the side of Ascarlia's greatest monarch. Although Felnir detested the prospect of confiding in him, he sensed no more information would issue from Wohtin's lips until he did so.

"For killing a man," Felnir said. "Why else?"

Wohtin said nothing, merely raising an eyebrow in expectation until Felnir consented to speak on.

"His name was Volund, son to the Uhlwald of Turon Hardta, a copper mining settlement far to the north of Skar Magnol. My brother and I had been sent there on an errand for my great-grandfather. He would occasionally send us off to different corners of the realm with some message or other. I thought it mainly a device to spare him our irritating company for a few weeks, but realised later it was his way of introducing us to the important folk of Ascarlia. I had barely eighteen summers and Guthnyr fourteen." Felnir paused to let a small grin pass over his face. "But even then he was fierce with pride, and overly sensitive to those unwise enough to make mention of our supposed disgrace in Olversahl, as was I. The youth of Skar Magnol had learned well to still their tongues in our presence. But the youth of Turon Hardta had not.

"Guthnyr always had a fascination for blacksmithing so I left him to gawp at the forge whilst I went to deliver the message to the Uhlwald. When I returned, I found Guthnyr surrounded by a mob of youths who seemed intent on kicking him to death. Apparently, one lad had been unwise enough to name him a coward and suffered a broken jaw for his pains. His kin hadn't taken it well. Taking an axe handle from the blacksmith's stock, I waded in, forcing them back and breaking several bones in the process. So many injured boys were bound to draw the notice of the adults, including the father of one.

"Volund Stolntalv, the Strongback, was well named. His strength was such it was said he could bend a horseshoe into a straight line. He was also no slouch with weapons, having won renown in battle several times. When he challenged me, I tried to demur, pointing out the unfairness of the massed attack on my brother, but he wouldn't hear it. Nor would his father, the Uhlwald, intervene. Family pride had been injured and they needed blood to heal the wound. So we fought."

Felnir stopped, his mind filling with the details of that dread day. Long had he sought to suppress it, and not just because it stood as the root of his disgrace. Across the span of a less than admirable life, his contest with Volund Stolntalv remained his darkest act.

"He was strong, as I said," Felnir continued. "And skilful with it. I was well trained thanks to years of tutelage, but Volund knew true combat with an intimacy that countered my every thrust and slash. With expert care, he wore me down, put cuts on my arms and legs to bleed my strength until finally he shattered my shield and left me at his mercy.

"There is a performance to many challenges. Not all are supposed to end in death. This, I'm sure, he intended as a lesson. Send the Tielwald's boy back to Skar Magnol to bear witness to the folly of insulting the miners of the north. So, when he levelled his sword at my kneeling form, I knew he was about to spare me. And yet, before he spoke, he laughed. If only he hadn't laughed.

"He was formidable, but I was swift and filled with the deadly fire of humiliation. I was on him before he could shift his blade, biting at his throat. I recall how foul his blood tasted, how the tendons of his neck stuck in my teeth. Rising from his body, I spat their kinsman's flesh at the people of Turon Hardta and avowed the intention to kill any who would ever again dare raise a hand or speak insult to me or my brother."

"A fair fight," Wohtin said. "If an ugly one. Unworthy of exile. At least that would have been Velgard's judgement."

"Perhaps. But the Sister Queens are not so forgiving, and the copper that flows from the northern mines too valuable to risk offending those that dig it out. Volund's kin claimed he had spoken the words to spare me before I killed him. A lie, but there were many voices to speak it. They wanted my head, but my great-grandfather's intervention won me exile instead. But he could do nothing about the name I earned. That has stuck ever since, a stain that won't wash. With this—" he twirled the Sword of the Altvar "—Sister Lore will finally cleanse me of it."

"Though my mind was clouded when I set eyes on your queen, I saw enough to know her kind have no rewards to offer any but themselves. To her, you would only ever be a useful servant, to be discarded or betrayed as her ambition dictates. As for the name you so detest, no queen's edict will ever scrub it from the minds of your people. Follow me, Felnir, and be no one's servant, earning a new name into the bargain."

Felnir lowered the sword, discomfited by the enticement of this ancient man's promises. "You ask for trust," he said. "Then earn it. No more secrets. If all you say is true, then you must have lived for the span of a dozen lifetimes. How is that possible?"

"Moyirn unleashed more than just madness when he reached between the worlds. We sought power, and we found it. But power is like a flame: it warms but it also burns. Upon me, it bestowed the curse of madness, but also the blessing of a life beyond the reach of age. My people carried me from the Vaults to this city, hoping I would tell them where our king had gone. But I had no answer beyond the ramblings of a crazed mind. I was barely aware of the passage of time. I recall events as small islands of calm in a sea of confusion. In time, the storms became less frequent, though they never faded. Some would last for years. Others mere days. But, in those times when my mind returned to me, I pursued my search."

"For what?"

"Velgard. As it was my folly that took him from us, it fell upon me to recover him. In between bouts of madness, I scoured all known corners of the world for him, finding nothing. Once I awoke to find myself cloistered in a Covenant seminary. Given that I could recite every word of every Martyr Scroll, it was clear I had been there for some time. How and why they took me in I never discovered, since the clerics who had first done so had long since gone to the Portals. Their successors took a dim view of a man they had regarded as some form of undying, divine messenger avowing a sudden detestation of their faith and adherence to the Ascarlian gods. I suppose I was lucky they chose to drive me out with pelted stones rather than hang me.

"However, my time amongst them had taught me the value of something I had hitherto overlooked in my search: prophecy, for the Martyrs' tales are rich in those who could discern the future. During my previous journey, I had encountered a few souls with the same ability, or at least a portion of it. They were all long since dead, of course, and finding another required years of patient enquiry.

"Perhaps two centuries ago, after more bouts of madness, I found myself standing at the door of a secluded hovel in the slums of Ishtakar. The woman who dwelt there appeared to be of middling years, with brusque manners and mercantile inclinations. The exterior of her home bespoke poverty, but the interior was all fine silks and treasures drawn from many lands, most of ancient origin. One look into her eyes told me I had at last encountered one who had walked this earth as long as I had. In fact, I suspect she was probably older than I, though she was too jealous of her secrets to tell me her true age. Fortunately, my lack of coin didn't matter, since she knew well the value of the wisdom accumulated in the mind of so aged a traveller as I. 'Write it down,' she told me. 'All of it. And I'll set you on the path to your king.'

"And write I did. For the better part of three years, I sat in her mean dwelling and scribbled out the contents of my head, all I knew of history and power, arcane and otherwise. When satisfied with my labours, she told me that my madness would soon return, this time lasting for the space of a lifetime. Velgard was now lost to me, she said, and I heard no lie in her voice. And, though that grieved me to the point of utter despair, she had another prophecy that offered hope. In time, my derangement would lead me not to Velgard, but to his heir. All I need do was inscribe the tale I had written upon my flesh in such a manner that a clever soul would one day appear with the knowledge to read it."

Wohtin crossed his arms again, Felnir reading raw grief in the man's tensed features. This, he knew, was not for his long vanished king, but for one far younger who deserved many more years than she had been given.

"Clever she was," Felnir said by way of grudging consolation for he, too, felt the loss. He had met many a remarkable personage in his travels, but few shone so bright of mind and spirit as Elvine Jurest. *Better that she stood here now than you*, he thought, watching Wohtin steel himself against his sorrow.

"If only I had returned to myself sooner," he said. "But it wasn't until I looked upon the Vaults again that my full measure of reason returned."

"For how long?"

"There is no way to know. It could be a day or a century. All I know is that our course is clear. Across this sea, Felnir—" Wohtin extended a hand to the horizon "—lies a kingdom that is yours to claim. I'll not promise an easy voyage, nor a peaceful path to kingship, for when was a crown ever won without blood? But it will be yours. That was her prophecy to me. Come with me, and make it real."

The morning broke bright and clear, Felnir waking to find Sygna had made good on her promise. "Wish I had more salt," she commented, turning the butchered goat upon the spit suspended over the fire. "Won't be able to preserve much for the voyage. Still—" she cast a glance towards the southern shore of the island "—stands to reason there'll be more game to be had before we find an eastward passage. And Falk's always been a deft hand with a fishing line."

His mind still busy with all he had learned the night before, Felnir avoided further discussion of their course by nodding to the Bow of the Altvar. "It shoots well, then?"

"Fine and true," she replied, grinning whilst tapping a knife to the roasted haunch. "Dropped this unlucky fellow at sixty paces."

"There was nothing else?" he ventured, recalling the vision he had seen in the sword's blade. "When you used it? You felt . . . nothing?"

Sygna squinted at him in puzzlement before her eyes slid to the sword at his side. "No. Should I have?"

"I don't know yet." A persistent scraping drew his notice to the barrow where Wohtin had resumed the toil of chipping away at the mortar around the bronze door.

"He was at it when I woke," Sygna said. "Didn't want any meat either."

Getting to his feet, Felnir pondered whether Wohtin needed to eat at all. He had seen him consume food and water on the *Sea Hawk*, but wondered now if that had been just a performance. The notion raised another question: *Was he always as mad as he appeared?* Felnir knew that there would never be complete trust between himself and Wohtin, but he also felt the compelling tug of the hooks the ancient man had sunk into his ambition.

Another hour's labour finally succeeded in loosening sufficient brickwork to allow Felnir and Falk to dislodge the bronze door. Still, it required three hard shoves of their shoulders to send it clattering from the portal. The interior of the barrow was mostly dark save for the light from the opened door, revealing the arc of a ship's hull. The air possessed a musty tinge but lacked the acrid dampness typical of old abandoned places, a testament to how well sealed this structure had been.

Lighting torches, they ventured inside. Felnir's regard for the lost denizens of this city swelled as he took in the vessel revealed by the torchlight. The smooth, elegant sweep of her hull and craftsmanship was evident in every nail and precisely cut timber. From the prow jutted the head of a hound. Apparently carved from a single block of oak, it was more a true statue than a motif. This was truly a ship fashioned for a king.

"Does she have a name?" he asked Wohtin.

"*Dehlgra*," he replied in a distracted grunt, preoccupied with something at the seaward end of the barrow.

"Faithful and beloved hound to the goddess Aerldun," Sygna noted with a sniff of approval. "A fitting name indeed."

"True enough," Felnir agreed. "Although, how we're going to launch her . . ."

His words were drowned by a loud clang from Wohtin's direction, followed shortly after by the growling rumble of many stones collapsing at once. Dust billowed as the barrow's seaward wall fell away, revealing the stone slipway descending into the risen waves of the morning tide.

"Lynchpin," Wohtin said, briefly brandishing an iron peg before tossing it away. "Installed at my insistence, since a king never knows when he might have need of a fine ship, even one slated to bear him into the next life. Velgard was always a practical soul at heart."

It transpired that Wohtin's foresight had extended to installing levers below the *Dehlgra*'s stern to enable her to be tilted onto the slipway. They were raised by a pair of windlasses attached to thick iron screws, Felnir marvelling at the ingenuity of the contrivance as he and Falk turned the handles to ready the ship for launch.

"I brought more than just lore back from my travels," Wohtin explained. "There are lands far to the east where such devices are commonplace. It was my hope that this kingdom would be made greater still by such ingenuity. Sadly, it wasn't to be." His expression narrowed as he turned to regard the sea, adding in a quieter tone, "At least not here."

Felnir wanted to ask what he meant, but the ship's sudden forward lurch forestalled the enquiry. "Here!" Sygna, having already climbed aboard to stow their gear, tossed ropes to the three men below. "Best haul y'selves up quick," she advised. "This old girl seems keen to feel brine on her timbers."

They managed to scramble onto the ship before *Dehlgra*'s descent accelerated, Felnir swinging his legs over the side just as she trundled onto the slipway. She birthed a broad fan of displaced water as her prow met the sea, the great hound head dipping amidst the spume.

"To the tiller, if you please, my love," Felnir told Sygna with a gracious bow. "Falk, let's get this sail raised."

He had worried that age had rotted the ancient canvas, but, though stiff, it proved whole and capable of catching the wind. Once filled, they beheld the crest of King Velgard, Exiled King of the Ascarls. In accordance with Wohtin's description it showed the eye of the goddess Aerldun above a jagged, vertical slash of lightning, both stark white against the dark grey of the sail. Within moments of securing the lines to set the cross mast in place, the great square blossomed with a hefty gust and began to draw them away from shore.

"Tacking south shouldn't be too hard," Sygna advised. "Get the right angle on the sail and I reckon we could be in sight of the southern reaches of the Fire Isles in a week."

"Steer south-west," Wohtin said. "You'll find a shift in the winds three days' sail from here. From there we follow Trieya's Quill."

"Keep heading west?" Sygna laughed, then sobered when Felnir failed to share her mirth. "What's he talking about?"

"You said I could be a king," Felnir told her. "To the west lies a kingdom to be claimed, or so he tells me."

"And you believe him?"

"I believe I've had my fill of being a dog to my great-grandfather's whims. With Guthnyr lost . . ." He trailed off, fighting down a spasm of grief before meeting Sygna's gaze. He saw doubt aplenty but also a kernel of hope that perhaps her oft-repeated desire to see him broaden his ambitions had finally borne fruit.

"We've sailed far together, my love," he told her. "What's one more voyage?"

"It's not just him, is it?" She nodded at the Sword of the Altvar. "It's that too."

"It showed me something," he admitted. "A . . . vision."

"Of the future? Of yourself as a king?"

"No. The past, but it was enough to make me believe what Wohtin told me. Most of it, at least. If it turns out to be a madman's folly, we cast him adrift and turn for home."

Sygna's eyes narrowed as they shifted from the sword to Wohtin's tall form, now standing at the prow. "If it is all a lie," she said with a note of dire promise, "I'll do more than just cast him adrift."

Felnir concealed his relief with a tight smile before turning to Falk. "How about it, old friend? Care to see what lies beyond the Fire Isles?"

The outlaw appeared perplexed by the question, merely shrugging his hefty shoulders. "You set the course and I follow, my lord," he said.

Felnir clapped him on the arm and went forward. "You haven't told me yet," he said, coming to Wohtin's side, "the name of my kingdom."

Wohtin hesitated before replying and Felnir was disturbed to read a measure of doubt in the cast of his brows. The night before, he had been a picture of composed certainty. Now, with their course set, it appeared this may have been another piece of mummery.

"It has a name," he said. "Though it's been so long since I set foot there it may have changed since. But, I doubt it. Those who named it did so with care and love, for it was to honour a man they revered above all others, even though he was destined never to see it. We sail to Vorunvahl, the King's Land. If the Altvar bless our course, then your throne will be secured without need of battle."

"And if they don't?"

Wohtin turned away from the sea, his eyes settling on the Sword of the Altvar tucked into Felnir's belt. "Then we'll see how keen this divine blade truly is."

CHAPTER FORTY-ONE

Thera

Arrows began to fly even before Elkor brought them within bowshot of the walls. Thera fought the instinct to track the arcing shafts across the darkening sky and kept her focus on Lynnea. She was still several lengths ahead despite the evident inexperience she displayed attempting to stay in a saddle affixed to a galloping horse. Thera's alarm flared when she saw her apprentice almost tumble free of her mount's back, only for her to cling on. The arrows grew thicker as they closed on the stockade, Lynnea heading straight for the corralled cattle with missiles whipping the air all around.

Deciding a distraction was in order, Thera raised the dreadaxe above her head and kicked her heels to encourage Elkor to greater efforts. Angling away from Lynnea's track, she whirled the axe, casting a challenging cry at the warriors lining the parapet. As she hoped, the archers amongst them altered their aim and soon she found herself ducking a hail of arrows. Feeling the rush of air from one passing within an inch of her neck, she was grateful for the gathering dark. Had it still been day, she was sure she would already be lying upon the grass, her body skewered several times over.

"Cowards!" she railed, tugging Elkor's reins so that he galloped at a shallow angle to the walls. "Send out your best to fight me!"

Judging by the laughter rising from the wall, and the undiminished hail of shafts, the Nihlvarians feared neither her insults nor the dishonour of an ignored challenge. Daring a glance at Lynnea, Thera grunted in relief: her apprentice was now only a dozen paces short of the corral. Thera expected some delay before Lynnea's power took hold, yet the change in behaviour amongst the cattle began immediately.

The air above the corral steamed as a low-pitched chorus rose from the herd, shaggy bodies and horned heads rising and falling. The first splintering crack from the stockade abutting the enclosure came a heartbeat later, followed by more. The tall timbers wavered, Thera hearing the shouts of warriors dislodged from the parapet. Then the cattle let out a simultaneous lowing that was more like a roar, surging in unison to throw their entire mass against the wooden barrier.

The shouts from within and crack of shattered timbers were drowned by the continuing tumult of the herd as it smashed its way inside. A gap some six feet wide appeared, then quickly doubled in size. The cattle thundered through, Thera catching sight of several bodies tossed into the air by flailing horns. Looking to the forest, she was gratified to see Ossgrym had lost no time in following her order. His *menda* came streaming from the trees in a tight wedge, a thousand warriors aimed squarely at the newly crafted rent in the wall.

Thera's ride towards Lynnea was untroubled by arrows, since the stockade's defenders were now scrambling from the parapet, presumably hurrying to seal the breach. Coming to the maiden's side, Thera found her sagging in the saddle. She raised hollowed cheeked features to greet Thera with a tired smile.

They didn't like . . . being taken from their fields. Lynnea's thoughts were a weak flutter in Thera's mind. *I let them know . . . they were allowed to vent their rage . . .*

Seeing a vacant cast seep into Lynnea's gaze, Thera reached out to steady her before she toppled from the saddle. As her mount shifted, Thera saw the arrow jutting from her apprentice's left thigh. *It hurts . . .* Lynnea let out a sound that mingled a whimper with a groan. *A lot more than . . . I thought it would . . .*

"Stay awake!" Thera instructed, delivering a hard shake to Lynnea's shoulder. She could see blood welling around the embedded shaft and worried it had found a vital vein. She began to climb down from Elkor's back, intending to bind the wound, but stopped when she felt Lynnea's hand grip hers.

You have to go. Lynnea's face was still drawn in pain, but her expression fierce. Releasing Thera's hand, she pointed at the breach in the stockade. *They won't stay angry . . . forever.*

Through the gap in the wall, Thera saw a picture of chaos. Bodies littered the ground, unmoving or twitching humans lying amongst the shaggy mounds of fallen cattle. Beyond them, buildings lay wrecked as the herd continued its rampage through the makeshift port. Their impassioned lowing was counterpointed by the shouts of the stockade's defenders. She heard a good deal of panic, but also the more clipped, repeated calls of steadier hearts. Someone was rapidly restoring discipline to the Nihlvarian garrison.

Go! Implacable command flashed in Lynnea's eyes. *You are the Vellihr of Justice!*

Feeling a hard fist form in her chest, Thera took hold of Elkor's reins and turned him about. "Find Achier!" she told Lynnea before spurring away, hating the curtness of her tone. "Get that wound seen to."

Once through the breach, Elkor leaped a succession of corpses, beast and human, to bear her into the stretch of open ground between the stockade and the shore. The herd had fragmented now and the shaggy animals ran rampant everywhere, goring cornered Nihlvarians with their horns and stamping the fallen. However, amongst the chaos, Thera spied increasing signs of order. Groups of warriors were forming, harangued into loose formation by their surviving captains. Others surrounded isolated cows with spears, bringing them down with frenzied stabbing. They were still disunited, but far more had survived the beasts' assault than Thera hoped, and it wouldn't be long before they cohered into a battle line.

Spying a growing knot of warriors nearby, she steered Elkor directly towards them, tearing through their loose ranks, axe whirling. She didn't linger to assess the damage done, instead spurring onwards to cut down a cluster of enemies a dozen paces away.

As in her first battle wielding the dreadaxe, it felt remarkably light in her hand, scything through armour and flesh to spatter her and Elkor in a red mist.

Hearing an enraged shout to her rear, she brought Elkor around in time to see a hatchet hurtling directly towards her face. She ducked in time but felt the fall of sliced hair upon her brow as the spinning blade grazed her crown. The man who had thrown it lost no time in making use of the distraction, sprinting forward to leap at her with his second hatchet held high. The dreadaxe caught him in mid-air, cleaving his midriff through to the spine. Thera attempted to tug it clear as the assailant fell, blood erupting from his mouth, but the blade had lodged too deep and his weight tugged it from her grasp.

With no time to dismount and work the weapon free, Thera pulled her black-bladed spear from the ties binding it to Elkor's flanks and spurred on. Galloping back towards the wall, she lanced the dark point through a succession of Nihlvarians, most taken unawares before they could dodge clear. Despite her efforts, and the continuing damage caused by a diminishing number of wrathful cows, she discerned a definite return of order to the enemy host. A line had begun to form near the breach with more rushing to join it.

Bringing Elkor to a halt, she prepared to charge at the nascent shield wall, but at that moment, Ossgrym's *menda* came streaming through the breach and spared her the task. She saw the Ironbones at the forefront of the charge, his battle hammer raised above his head. Uhlwald Kahlvik ran at his kinsman's side, his shield warding off a brief flurry of Nihlvarian arrows. The Ascarlians broke the Nihlvarian line at the first rush, it being too thinly held to withstand so concentrated and furious an onslaught. Within moments, all sense of order had been lost as the struggle became a chaotic melee.

Thera had seen warriors driven to battle rage before, but the islanders' naked ferocity that night was beyond her experience. They hurled themselves at their foes without regard to safety, some casting their shields away in their eagerness to hack at the enemy. Naked hate shone in every face as the folk of Ayl-Ah-Vahrim seized the chance to extract recompense for recent humiliation. Whilst the Nihlvarians retained a partial advantage in numbers, the sudden loss of cohesion and the fury of the Ascarlian assault soon began to tell. Whilst some fought on with impressive courage, others fled for their ships. A trickle of runners swiftly became a torrent and the struggle transformed from battle to rout.

Turning her gaze to the sea, Thera saw the three piers jutting into the bay crowding with warriors attempting to get aboard the ships moored alongside. The captains of some vessels had clearly read the tide of battle and already raised anchor. Oars sweeping, they pulled away from the piers and began to make for open water. However, their escape route was already being frustrated by the arrival of Gelmyr's ships. Apparently unwilling to forgo a part in impending victory, the Johtenvek had steered the *Great Wolf* into the bay. Behind her, the collection of skiffs and smaller fishing craft followed suit, sails full and torches blazing along their rails. As she watched, the *Great Wolf*'s prow smashed into the hull of a smaller Nihlvarian warship, forcing it back against one of the piers. Planking splintered and bodies spilled into the waves, birthing yet more panic amongst those attempting to hurl themselves onto the remaining Nihlvarian vessels.

"To the ships!" Thera called out, urging Elkor forward and waving her spear to gain Ossgrym's attention. "We have to stop them fleeing!"

The Ironbones was too preoccupied with pounding his hammer into the chest of a fallen adversary to heed her, but his cousin was not. Raising his sword to acknowledge her command, Kahlvik set about marshalling warriors for an advance to the shore. A glance at the *Great Wolf*, now surrounded by enemy vessels bobbing amidst the wreckage of the pier, convinced Thera she couldn't wait. Spurring Elkor to a gallop, she sped towards the bay, jabbing her spear at any unfortunate foe straying into her path. Reaching the pier, she leaped from the saddle and sprinted along its remnants, then launched herself across the gap to the nearest wallowing vessel.

Fortunately, the ship was sparsely crewed and her progress was contested by only two unarmoured sailors. Displaying more desperation than courage, one came at her with an axe and the other a sword, both dying for it after a left and right slash of her spear. As she stepped over the bodies, she noticed a shifting gleam beneath the duckboards. Crouching, she made out several pairs of terrified eyes peering at her from the gloom. Heaving aside the deck hatch, she found half a dozen people clad in threadbare garb. They all wore manacles upon their wrists and ankles, secured to the beams with the same chain. Rising, she spied a youth crouched near the mast, staring at her with terror shining bright in his widened eyes. She guessed his age at perhaps thirteen summers, his garb mean but less ragged than those in the hold, and he was unchained.

"Keys!" Thera demanded, advancing towards him. Shrinking back with a pool of piss staining the boards beneath him, he extended a wavering hand to one of the men she had killed. Moving to the larger of the two corpses, Thera kicked it over, finding a ring of keys fastened to its belt. Returning to the hatch, she tossed the keys to the slaves below. "Free yourselves and get ashore," she instructed, having no time for further delays. "And you'd best start swimming," she advised the cowering youth as she strode past him to the port rail.

Vaulting aboard the next ship, she found it richer in crew to the tune of half a dozen. Fortunately, they were all fully preoccupied in attempting to board the *Great Wolf*. The warship loomed above, Thera seeing no defenders on her rail which spoke ill for Gelmyr and the skeleton crew left aboard. Heart pounding, Thera lost no time in spearing down three sailors. The remainder displayed good judgement in promptly casting their weapons aside and leaping into the sea.

"Gelmyr!" Thera called, taking hold of a rope to scale the *Great Wolf*'s hull. Upon achieving the deck, she grimaced in consternation at finding it apparently deserted. However, her elevated view enabled her to take in the scope of the unfolding struggle in the bay. Lacking the numbers and bulk for close combat, the Ascarlians had adopted the wise tactic of assailing their foes with fire. She saw the crew of a skiff cast a flurry of oil casks at a Nihlvarian warship before tossing torches over to set a decent blaze along her port side. Within moments, the fire spread to her deck and main sail. Others were more fortunate, Thera counting five making for the sea with their oars working at the fastest stroke, although she took satisfaction from how high they sat in the water. *Prepared to abandon their own in a moment of crisis,* Thera concluded, a lesson she stored for future consideration. This, she knew, would not be the last battle she fought against these people.

Looking to land, she found a slaughter raging at the water's edge. Forced to forsake the piers by a wall of struggling ships, some now fully alight, many Nihlvarian warriors were attempting to wade ashore only to be met by Ossgrym's vengeful *menda*. The glow of flaming ships added a nightmarish aspect to the ugly spectacle of blades flashing amidst the smoke drifting over the surf. The triumphant laughter of the Ascarlians mingled with the screams of the hapless foemen they cut down. Thera knew the sands would still be red come morning.

A sob drew her attention back to the *Great Wolf*'s deck, eyes picking out a shift in the shadows near the stern. Hurrying closer, Thera came to a sudden halt at the sight of Gelmyr lying next to the tiller, one arm draped over the pole. A glance at his pale, slackened features told the tale with dreadful clarity. Eshilde knelt at his side, hands covering her face and slim form jerking as she vented her grief.

"I told him we should stand off," she gasped through tears. "But he wouldn't . . ."

Thera found her tongue robbed of speech. Stumbling wordlessly to slump at Gelmyr's feet, she stared at his empty eyes, noting the curious expression death had seen fit to freeze upon his brow. It was as if he had found the fact of his demise incomprehensible. It was a sentiment she shared in full measure.

"The others?" she asked Eshilde in a rasp.

"Lost." The warrior lowered her hands to regard Thera with features set in abject desolation. "We sailed close to a warship with very keen-eyed archers. I said we should stand off, Thera. I told him that's what you would want."

Thera nodded, unable for the moment to offer more in the way of comfort. Looking back to Gelmyr, she frowned at the absence of a shaft jutting from his body. "An arrow took him?" Leaning forward for a better look, she felt a flare of purest agony in her side.

At first she thought it an injury suffered during her ride through the stockade, the pain smothered by the fury and urgency of battle. So, when she lowered her gaze, she was puzzled to find Eshilde's fist pressed hard against the leather of her breastplate. Even stranger was the narrow blade revealed as Eshilde drew back her hand, six inches of reddened steel emerging from a small gap between the plates.

"Tell me, Thera," she said, her tone one of faint curiosity, "were you ever going to make me a Vellihr? Or did you just like fucking me?"

"What?" Thera asked, instantly recognising it as possibly the stupidest question ever to emerge from her lips. Why she didn't immediately reach for her spear was a mystery, as was her failure to do more than grunt in surprise when Eshilde stabbed her again. She sank the blade into the same gap, angling it to cause more damage. The pain blossoming from the wound finally compelled Thera to act, grabbing at Eshilde's knife, but she had already drawn it clear and stepped away.

"It's been a merry dance," she said, a fond smile on her lips as she gazed down at Thera. "But all revels must end."

She laughed again when Thera lunged at her, attempting to thrust a spear that now weighed more than a sackful of iron. The point fell short by a foot, Thera growling in frustrated rage as she staggered upright and tried again.

"I must say I wasn't expecting it to work," Eshilde said, ducking under the sweep of the spear. "This clever scheme of yours. I did warn them you'd be coming. It appears I should have also warned them about your new pet and her way with animals. Have you fucked her too, by the way?"

Snarling and tasting a metallic sting to her tongue, Thera attempted a feint at Eshilde's legs before aiming a slash at her neck. She evaded it all with ease and replied with a kick to Thera's chest, sending her stumbling into the rail.

"You found the trinket on that fool in Buhl Hardta," Eshilde told her, swaying clear of a flailing slash. "You really should have paid it more notice. Did you think your great-grandfather was the only one to walk in dreams?"

She attacked again before the last word was out of her mouth, darting closer to stab at Thera's neck. It was a killing blow, one she barely evaded by dropping the spear and snaring Eshilde's wrist in both hands. She responded by slamming a punch into Thera's jaw before shoving a shoulder into her chest. Grunting, Eshilde pressed with her full weight, the rail hard against Thera's back. She could feel blood running in rivulets down her hips and thighs, a sickly chill creeping through her straining muscles as she strove to prevent this traitor tipping her over the side.

"I slew Thera Speldrenda!" Eshilde hissed through clenched teeth, her face close enough for Thera to see her eyes shine with manic pride. "For the Volkrath! For the Altvar! For the Queen that will be . . ."

Eshilde's words came to an abrupt end at the sound of a short growl, followed by the hard snap of a closing jaw. The malicious triumph vanished from her face, replaced with a painful grimace before she was torn from Thera's sight. She watched Snaryk drag Eshilde across the deck, wanting to call out an order to prevent him tearing her throat out.

"She has more to tell . . ." But the words emerged as a meaningless groan and the hound was too lost in his rage. As Snaryk ravaged Eshilde's neck, Thera saw Achier clambering over the starboard rail. Eyes wide with alarm, he ran towards Thera with his arm outstretched, but to her fading vision it seemed as if he moved through thickened air. The chill had spread to every fibre of her body now, stealing away all strength.

Achier's mouth opened in a shout as she toppled over the side, barely feeling the cold embrace of the sea. She could still see him reaching for her, rendered into something ghostlike by the water's surface. As he receded into darkness, she found herself grasping the cord about her neck. A few seconds fumbling and she felt the hard metal of the old man's gift.

Will you find me? she wondered, watching the last flickering light fade from view as she sank ever deeper, her life's blood blossoming around her in a crimson mist. *Will you dream of me again, great-grandfather?*

Chapter Forty-Two

Elvine

"They must hear you!" Veilwald Hakkyn's grip was tight upon Elvine's wrist as he placed the scroll in her hands. Though he kept his voice low, the fierceness of his tone and the unblinking cast of his eyes bespoke a man beset by a terrible responsibility. Around them, the port of Skyrn Hardta bustled as warriors ported arms and supplies onto an impressive assemblage of ships. She guessed the vessels gathered here at the Veilwald's summons to number over three hundred, although only a few dozen could be classed as true warships. The rest were a collection of larger fishing boats and deeper draft freighters.

"I sent three messengers since the Vellihr of Justice sailed for the Kast Geld and received no word from the Queens," Hakkyn said, still grasping Elvine's wrist. She had already heard much of these tidings at her first meeting with the Veilwald the previous day, personally inscribing them on the scroll she held. However, he clearly felt the need to reiterate his message. She wondered if he worried over entrusting carriage of his missive to so youthful a courier, or was simply compelled to repetition by the burden of his woes.

"Whilst we receive naught but dire tidings from the north," he went on. "It's said Veilwald Ossgrym lies in Ulfmaer's care after a terrible defeat at sea, his geld now defenceless against the foreign menace. There can no longer be any doubt: these are no mere pirates we face, but a great *menda* come for conquest. I trust you, Scholar, to make sure the Queens hear this truth."

"I shall, Veilwald," Elvine said, putting as much assurance into her bearing as she could muster.

Apparently satisfied, Hakkyn released her and turned his grave visage towards his fleet. "My folk are brave," he said, "but our numbers small in comparison to what we face. When the evening tide rises, I shall lead them forth. How many I shall lead back . . ." He trailed off, Elvine watching him summon the fortitude to stiffen his back and strip the worry from his expression. "Fare you well, Scholar Elvine," he said with stiff formality. "I would prefer to send you on your way with more substantial protection, but cannot spare a single warship."

Elvine turned to regard the three sour-faced fishermen waiting aboard their boat. Ahlgrun and his brothers had reacted with gruff acquiescence to their Veilwald's command that they bear Elvine and Colvyn on to Skar Magnol. With battle in the offing, they resented the lost chance at renown. Still, none had voiced an objection, each retrieving their swords from their cottages in the hope that even so mundane a mission would yield some prospect of glory.

"I couldn't ask for more, Veilwald," she told Hakkyn, turning back to offer him a respectful nod. "Your diligence honours me, and the Queens."

"At present, I'll take a score of warships over any measure of honour." He pointed to Ahlgrun's boat. "Now be off, and may the Altvar speed your course."

The voyage to Skar Magnol required nine days and proved a more uncomfortable experience even than their journey to Skyrn Hardta across the lower Styrnspeld. The three brothers worked their sail with a tireless industry that ensured a swift passage but a great deal of heaving through tall waves. She had thought herself accustomed to sea travel, but the endless pitching of this small craft soon disabused her of the notion. By the end of the first day, she was battling a return of the nausea that had plagued her aboard Vellihr Ilvar's ship of fanatics.

"Put your fingers in your ears and blow out through your nose," Colvyn advised. "It also helps if you cross your eyes at the same time."

Elvine followed his advice but felt no better. "That didn't do anything," she moaned, hunching lower beneath the tarpaulin shelter.

"No," Colvyn agreed with a grin. "But it was funny to watch."

He ducked as she cast her untouched bowl of fish stew at him, managing to avoid most of it. At least it removed the grin from his lips.

"Is our father as given to stupidity?" she asked.

"He would say no," Colvyn replied, wiping a speck of broth from his cloak. "But, having read a portion of his testament, I'm bound to say yes, he most assuredly is."

"His testament?" Despite her malaise, this was something certain to arouse her interest. "He's already written a testament?"

"He writes many things. Histories mostly, but he's also fond of the occasional treatise on diplomacy or finance, which is strange given that he's so terrible with money. Juhlina handles all that."

"Juhlina?"

"His wife, and my . . . mother, in any way that matters. She it was that suffered most of the tribulation of raising me since father was always so lost in his books, when not off intriguing somewhere. He does that a lot, too."

"But his testament," Elvine persisted. "It is complete, and honest?"

"Complete? In so much as it relates the course of his life until recent years, I suppose so. As for honest?" Colvyn frowned. "My father has a tendency to both exaggerate and diminish his role in certain events, at least according to Juhlina. Still, I sensed an underlying truth to his account. I suspect a liar wouldn't confess to so many misjudgements."

The Testament of Alwyn Scribe, Elvine thought, her nausea momentarily banished by so tantalising a prospect. *A first-hand account of both the Pretender's War and the Blackheart's rise and fall.* Such a thing would be treasure to any library.

"Do you think," she said, "he would permit me to read it too?"

"I believe he would be very disappointed if you didn't." Crouching, Colvyn joined her under the tarpaulin, putting an arm around her shoulders. "For now, dear sister, allow me to regale you with the tale of Alwyn Scribe's defence of Walvern Castle . . ."

* * *

Approaching Skar Magnol, Colvyn took charge of guiding the boat to the private dock of the Sister Queens. Upon rounding the headland to bring the secluded anchorage into view, they were waved away by a group of stern-faced warriors standing guard on the wharf. Their demeanour changed swiftly when Elvine rose to announce herself.

"Scholar Elvine Jurest," she said, raising the Spear of the Altvar above her head. "Bearing treasure for Sister Lore and urgent tidings from Veilwald Hakkyn Rohnlank of the Aiken Geld."

She expected to be hastily conveyed to Sister Lore's presence, but instead she and Colvyn were obliged to wait upon the dock for nigh two hours. The sky had dimmed with the onset of evening by the time Vellihr Ilvar appeared with no less than a dozen of his *menda* in tow.

"Scholar Elvine," he said with a formal nod and a flat tone that indicated his disdain for her Covenanter self hadn't diminished since their last meeting. His stony features changed, however, when his eyes lit upon the spear in her grasp. His unblinking regard echoed the reverence she had seen during the voyage from Olversahl, but with a yet greater depth of awe. So enraptured was he by the spear that he continued to stare at it until Elvine broke the silence with a pointed cough.

"The Spear of the Altvar," she said, holding it out. "Would you like to hold it?" She had hoped whatever mind lived within the weapon might offer some insight into this man's unpleasant nature, but it failed to speak and the metal remained cool.

"I . . ." Ilvar raised a hand to reach for the relic, but stopped short of touching it, his fingers trembling until he swiftly drew it back. Clearing his throat, he recovered his curtness in addressing Colvyn. "You. Hand over your weapons."

"He can wait here . . ." Elvine began, drawing a reproachful glare from Colvyn and an interruption from Ilvar.

"I am instructed to escort you both to the Hall of Nerlfeya," the Vellihr stated. "There you will give your account to the Sister Queens. They may have questions for this one, too."

"All the Queens?" Elvine repeated. She had assumed he would take her directly to Sister Lore's tower. There she would hand over the spear and relate the various calamities that had beset her journey before, with due courtesy, they would turn to the subject of Berrine's release from service. The thought of facing all three queens summoned a resumption of nausea to her gut, and also a measure of self-reproach. *All you have witnessed,* she chided herself, *battle, the storms of the Iron Dark Sea, and the fall of the Vaults of the Altvar, and yet you squirm like a little girl at the prospect of speaking to three women.*

"Then let's be about it," she said, nodding to Colvyn to hand over his falchion and dagger. "My business being urgent. I assume you have heard that war assails the Outer Isles as we speak?"

Ilvar's answer was confined to a narrow glance as he relieved Colvyn of his arms. Nor did he speak throughout the length of their subsequent trek through the bowels of the Verungyr. They passed the stairwell that ascended to Sister Lore's tower and entered an unfamiliar and extensive maze of tunnels. As the journey wore on, Elvine became aware of an increasing warmth to the spear. At first she thought it simply the result of a change in air. But, by the time Ilvar halted before a large iron-braced door at the end of a particularly long tunnel, there was an undeniable heat to the steel head.

As the door swung open, Elvine hesitated at the number of people waiting in the vast chamber beyond. She had read many descriptions of this place, most commenting on its size and the mystery of Nerlfeya's undying and smokeless fire. However, all accounts had agreed that the Sister Queens held court in private, shunning the audience beloved of foreign monarchs. Today, it appeared tradition had been broken for Elvine estimated the size of the gathering at near two hundred people, arranged in a broad semicircle around the central firepit. Following Ilvar into the hall, she saw that these were the assembled servants of the Verungyr, the scribes, custodians, and artisans that maintained the great holdfast and administered the Queens' rule. Also present were the rest of Ilvar's *menda*, standing in another circle behind the servants.

Upon entering the Hall of Nerlfeya, Elvine heard a collective intake of breath from the gathering, all eyes fixed upon the spear she held. The weight of scrutiny was hard to bear as she strode towards the firepit where the Queens waited. She had endured a great deal, it was true, yet the experience of finding herself at the centre of so much attention threatened to put a stumble in her step. *Not a girl!* she rebuked herself, the flare of self-recrimination fuelling the resolve needed to scan the line of awed spectators, hoping to find her mother. Berrine, however, was nowhere in sight. As they came to a halt before the trio of monarchs, Elvine's gaze settled on Sister Lore. The smile she afforded Elvine was aglow with pride, even a measure of gratitude. But any succour she might have taken from such approval was muted by the knowledge that her mother's absence was no oversight.

She also saw that the Tielwald was another notable absentee. She found it strange given that he had co-sponsored the mission to find the Vaults. From what little Felnir had said of the man, it was evident they hadn't been close. But, at the very least, she felt the old scowler owed it to his great-grandson to bear witness to her tale of Felnir's demise.

Turning to Sisters Silver and Iron, Elvine greeted them both with a formal nod as, incredibly, she suffered a small spasm of humour at the absurdity of this spectacle. A Covenanter with no adherence to the Altvar come to present one of their gifts to those who ruled the Ascarlian people. Fighting down the dangerous temptation to laugh, she offered another nod to Sister Lore and waited, her features composed into a dutifully serious mask.

It was Sister Silver who spoke first, as was custom. Elvine knew her to be by far the oldest of the three, and saw a good deal of shrewd suspicion in the crinkled squint of her clouded eyes.

"Since my sister," the aged Queen said, the forefinger of the hand clutching her staff flicking in Sister Lore's direction, "insisted upon grand formality for this occasion, I'll ask you to state your name and business here."

"Elvine Jurest, my queen," Elvine responded, impressed by the steadiness of her voice and how well it carried in this chamber. "Scholar in Service to Sister Lore. I come before you to report the outcome of my mission to discover the Vaults of the Altvar. I also bear an important message from Veilwald Hakkyn—"

"A subject to be attended to shortly," Sister Lore cut in. Elvine saw that her smile didn't waver, but there was a clear instruction in the hardened cast of her eyes. "For now, please tell us of your mission and the treasure you bear."

Elvine resisted a sudden, terrible temptation to ignore her and proceed directly to reading out Hakkyn's missive. In this moment, with this spear in hand, her words carried a great deal of weight. Yet, the clear message conveyed by Berrine's absence gave her pause. Sister Lore clearly intended to remind her where power lay in this chamber, divine weapon or not.

"As you wish, my queen," Elvine said. "At your behest, I accompanied the warship *Sea Hawk*, under the command of Felnir Redtooth, to go in search of the Vaults of the Altvar. In time, our search led us to the Fire Isles. There, deep beneath the mountains, did we discover the long abandoned realm of King Velgard ehs Trehka, which had been built in proximity to our goal. I can report that the Vaults themselves were filled with tall statues of the Altvar and were truly wondrous to behold. The mightiest of which was that of Ulthnir Worldsmith, at the feet of which lay three weapons: a sword, a bow, and—" she raised the weapon in her hands "—a spear."

"Three?" Sister Iron asked. Meeting her blunt features, Elvine wondered why she found so renowned a warrior to be less intimidating than Sister Lore. "What became of the others?"

"I regret that when we attempted to claim the weapons, the Vaults were shaken by a great tremor. They are destroyed, my queens. I am sad to report that Felnir Redtooth perished in the calamity. I was able to secure the spear, but the bow and the sword were lost beyond recovery. Upon return to the *Sea Hawk*, the vessel was set upon by warships of unknown origin. I believe them to be the same enemies now attacking the Outer Isles. Myself and my companion escaped by boat, but I suspect all aboard the *Sea Hawk* were slain or taken. We were fortunate to be rescued by fishermen and taken to Skyrn Hardta, where Veilwald Hakkyn sent us to you with . . ."

"The Vaults are lost?" Sister Lore said. Her smile had disappeared and Elvine found her composure unsettled by the edge to the queen's voice. "How could this happen?"

"I know not, my queen," Elvine replied. "Only that it did happen."

"The Altvar's judgement," Sister Iron grunted. "It has to be. Seems they weren't as happy about your scholar stealing their treasures as you thought they'd be, Sister Lore."

"A gift cannot be stolen, Sister," Lore returned. "And I, for one, will not claim to know the minds of the gods, but merely show due gratitude for the blessings they choose to bestow." She extended a hand to Elvine. "Truly, you have performed feats beyond the call of all duty, my dear. Know that your reward will be great and you will forever bear the deepest gratitude for bringing us this mightiest of gifts."

The command in her bearing was unmistakable, yet when Elvine began to comply, she felt a sudden blossoming of heat from the spear. It was so intense that Elvine marvelled at the lack of a shimmer to the air surrounding the spearpoint. Furthermore, she heard the voice again, speaking no words but instead filling her mind with a formless hiss of alarm.

It doesn't want you, she thought, looking up at Sister Lore. *It wants me.*

She saw a flicker of uncertainty pass over the queen's face as Elvine remained still. *What right do you have to this?* she asked inwardly, the spear's warning hissing louder still in her mind. *What dangers did you suffer to claim it? What friends did you lose?*

"Elvine," Sister Lore prompted with a note of impatience. All affection had fled her gaze now, and Elvine needed no arcane insight to read the thought behind those eyes. *Remember your mother, girl.*

Thoughts of Berrine, perhaps confined in some dungeon, sufficed to quell the spear's voice. Yet the heat it exuded was undimmed, so much so that when Elvine stepped forward to place the weapon in Sister Lore's grasp, she was amazed that the Queen showed no sign of noticing. Taking it from Elvine, she held it up, face filled with a mingling of satisfaction and fascination as she smoothed her fingers over the haft and the iron point. Her awe, however, didn't appear to be shared by her fellow queens.

"Doesn't look like much," Sister Iron observed. "Seen many a finer weapon in my time. Are there no markings? Runes or symbols?"

"I see nothing," Lore said, peering closer at the leaf-shaped head.

"Not that I'd doubt your scholar's word, sister," Silver commented, "but it strikes me a weapon crafted by the hands of the Altvar would bear some form of decoration."

"Wait," Lore murmured, eyes narrowing as she brought the spear point closer. "There may something . . ."

As she continued to inspect the weapon, Elvine debated the wisdom of sharing what she knew of the spear. Blurting out "Actually, it can speak," would sound absurd in the extreme. But she felt Sister Lore would take a dim view if she were to withhold any pertinent knowledge. As she opened her mouth, she felt Colvyn's hand close on hers. It was a strong grip, causing enough discomfort for her to turn to him in annoyance. The muttered rebuke died on her lips when she saw the utterly serious cast of his face.

Colvyn's gaze was not focused on the Queens but on the assembled audience of servants, or rather, the warriors of Ilvar's *menda* arranged at their backs. The wavering shadows cast by Nerlfeya's fire made it hard to discern details, but Elvine was sure she saw an increased tension in their bearing.

"Do nothing." Colvyn's instruction was the faintest sigh emerging from lips that barely moved. Yet Elvine heard the dire warning in it, nonetheless.

"Here," Sister Lore said, a smile once again curving her lips as she tapped a finger to the spear's point. "A mark. I believe it only just revealed itself."

"Can you read it?" Iron asked.

"It's unfamiliar to me. I'm not sure it's even a rune. Here, sisters." Lore stepped closer to the other queens, extending the spear for their inspection. "Can you see?"

"Can't make out anything." Iron sniffed, moving to squint at the spearpoint. "Are you—"

Sister Iron's next word transformed into a guttural exclamation of shock as Sister Lore swiftly altered the angle of the spear and thrust it up through her fellow queen's chin. Blood exploded from Iron's lips as Lore forced the point through her mouth and into her brain. Without pause, Lore jerked the weapon free and thrust it through Sister Silver's chest, piercing her slight, aged form with ease.

Elvine's shocked shout was smothered by the upsurge of horrified screams from the assembly. Her involuntary forward step brought to a sharp halt when Colvyn gripped her arms, holding her tight, his whisper harsh in her ear: "Do nothing!"

Trapped in his embrace, Elvine could only gape in terror at the scene before her, then cast a sickened gaze around the hall as a dreadful spectacle of slaughter unfolded. Everywhere she looked, she saw the warriors of Ilvar's *menda* hacking down the servants of the Verungyr. Dozens of defenceless men and women suffered bloody murder in the space of a few heartbeats, the warriors wielding sword and dagger with grim efficiency. Most died before they realised their plight, frozen by the horrible reality of Sister Lore's act as blades slit their throats or cleaved their flesh. Others, either quicker of wit or more attuned to danger, managed to evade the first assault. Some tried to fight, most to flee. For a time, the Hall of Nerlfeya was a chaos of running, yelling figures and pursuing assassins. All the while, Elvine could only remain fixed in her brother's grasp. She closed her eyes to spare herself the last few murders, though the final despairing cries of the victims lashed at her like the strokes of a whip.

Finally, the screams ended and she opened her eyes to find Sister Lore walking towards her with the spear in hand. As she did so, Colvyn shifted his hold on Elvine, pulling her into a tight, protective embrace. Her face pressed into Colvyn's chest, Elvine watched Sister Lore come to a halt and heard the tramp of boots as Ilvar and his *menda* closed the circle around them.

"No," Sister Lore sighed, her blood-speckled features drawn in a frown as she cast another glance over the wet spearpoint, "I was mistaken. No markings at all. You didn't happen to notice any, did you, dear heart?"

Elvine's first attempt to answer ended in a retching cough. Swallowing, she tried again, forcing the words out in a series of small, dry grunts. "No . . . my queen. I did . . . not."

"Oh well." Sister Lore shrugged her slim shoulders, favouring Elvine with one of her brighter smiles, hard to look at because it seemed so utterly genuine in its fond regard. "It's the fact of the thing that matters in the end. For now, none can deny I bear the Altvar's blessing, and it's all thanks to you, my most excellent scholar."

Her smile broadened as she stood back, baring teeth flecked in red as she raised the spear above her head, declaring with a joyous laugh, "Rejoice, my wonderful child, for you are privileged to witness the dawn of the Volkrath Empire!"

The story continues in ...

BORN OF AN IRON STORM

Book Two of the Age of Wrath

ACKNOWLEDGEMENTS

Thanks once again to Paul Field for all the proofreading. Also heart-felt appreciation to my agent Paul Lucas, my UK and US editors, James Long and Bradley Englert, for their sterling efforts in bringing the tale of Alwyn Scribe to a conclusion.

extras

orbit

meet the author

Ellie Grace Photography

ANTHONY RYAN lives in London and is the *New York Times* best-selling author of the Raven's Shadow and Draconis Memoria series. He previously worked in a variety of roles for the UK government, but now writes full time. His interests include art, science and the unending quest for the perfect pint of real ale.

Find out more about Anthony Ryan and other Orbit authors by registering for the Orbit newsletter at orbitbooks.net.

if you enjoyed
A TIDE OF BLACK STEEL

look out for

THE PARIAH

Book One of
the Covenant of Steel

by

Anthony Ryan

Born into the troubled kingdom of Albermaine, Alwyn Scribe is raised as an outlaw. Quick of wit and deft with a blade, Alwyn is content with the freedom of the woods and the comradeship of his fellow thieves. But an act of betrayal sets him on a new path—one of blood and vengeance, which eventually leads him to a soldier's life in the king's army.

Fighting under the command of Lady Evadine Courlain, a noblewoman beset by visions of a demonic apocalypse, Alwyn must survive war and the deadly intrigues of the nobility if he hopes to claim his vengeance. But as dark forces, both human and arcane, gather to oppose Evadine's rise, Alwyn faces a choice: Can he be a warrior, or will he always be an outlaw?

Part I

"You say my claim to the throne was false, that I began a war that spilled the blood of thousands for nothing. I ask you, Scribe, what meaning is there in truth or lies in this world? As for blood, I have heard of you. I know your tale. History may judge me as monstrous, but you are a far bloodier man than I."

From *The Testament of the Pretender Magnis Lochlain*,
as recorded by Sir Alwyn Scribe

Chapter One

Before killing a man, I always found it calming to regard the trees. Lying on my back in the long grass fringing the King's Road and gazing at the green and brown matrix above, branches creaking and leaves whispering in the late-morning breeze, brought a welcome serenity. I had found this to be true ever since my first faltering steps into this forest as a boy ten years before. When the heart began to thud and sweat beaded my brow, the simple act of looking up at the trees brought a respite, one made sweeter by the knowledge that it would be short lived.

Hearing the clomp of iron-shod hooves upon earth, accompanied by the grinding squeal of a poorly greased axle, I closed my eyes to the trees and rolled onto my belly. Shorn of the soothing distraction, my heart's excited labour increased in pitch, but I was well schooled in not letting it show. Also, the sweat dampening my armpits and trickling down my back would only add to my stench, adding garnish for the particular guise I adopted that day. Lamed outcasts are rarely fragrant.

Raising my head just enough to glimpse the approaching party through the grass, I was obliged to take a deep breath at the sight of the two mounted men-at-arms riding at the head of the caravan. More concerning still were the two soldiers perched on the cart that followed, both armed with crossbows, eyes scanning the forest on either side of the road in a worrying display of hard-learned vigilance. Although not within the chartered bounds of the Shavine Forest, this stretch of the King's Road described a long arc through its northern fringes. Sparse in comparison to the deep forest, it was still a place of bountiful cover and not one to be travelled by the unwary in such troubled times.

As the company drew closer, I saw a tall lance bobbing above the small throng, the pennant affixed beneath its blade fluttering in the breeze with too much energy to make out the crest it bore. However, its gold and red hues told the tale clearly: royal colours. Deckin's intelligence had, as ever, been proven correct: this lot were the escort for a Crown messenger.

I waited until the full party had revealed itself, counting another four mounted men-at-arms in the rearguard. I took some comfort from the earthy brown and green of their livery. These were not kingsmen but ducal levies from Cordwain, taken far from home by the demands of war and not so well trained or steadfast as Crown soldiery. However, their justified caution and overall impression of martial orderliness was less reassuring. I judged them unlikely to run when the time came, which was unfortunate for all concerned.

I rose when the leading horsemen were a dozen paces off, reaching for the gnarled, rag-wrapped tree branch that served as my crutch and levering myself upright. I was careful to blink a good deal and furrow my brow in the manner of a soul just roused from slumber. As I hobbled towards the verge, keeping the blackened bulb of my bandaged foot clear of the ground, my features slipped easily into the gape-mouthed, emptied-eyed visage of a crippled dullard. Reaching the road, I allowed the foot to brush the churned mud at the edge. Letting out an agonised groan of appropriate volume, I stumbled forwards, collapsing onto all fours in the middle of the rutted fairway.

It should not be imagined that I fully expected the soldiers' horses to rear, for many a warhorse is trained to trample a prone man. Fortunately, these beasts had not been bred for knightly service and they both came to a gratifyingly untidy halt, much to the profane annoyance of their riders.

"Get out of the fucking road, churl!" the soldier on the right snarled, dragging on his reins as his mount wheeled in alarm. Beyond him, the cart and, more importantly, the bobbing lance of the Crown messenger also stopped. The crossbowmen sank lower on the mound of cargo affixed to the cart-bed, both reaching for the bolts in their quivers. Crossbowmen are always wary of leaving their weapons primed for long intervals, for it wears down the stave and the string. However, failing to do so this day would soon prove a fatal miscalculation.

I didn't allow my sight to linger on the cart, however, instead gaping up at the mounted soldier with wide, fearful eyes that betrayed little comprehension. It was an expression I had practised extensively, for it is not easy to mask one's intellect.

"Shift your arse!" his companion instructed, his voice marginally less angry and speaking as if addressing a dull-witted dog. When I continued to stare up at him from the ground he cursed and reached for the whip on his saddle.

"Please!" I whimpered, crutch raised protectively over my head. "Y-your pardon, good sirs!"

I had noticed on many occasions that such cringing will invariably stoke rather than quell the violent urges of the brutishly inclined, and so it proved now. The soldier's face darkened as he unhooked the whip, letting it unfurl so its barbed tip dangled onto the road a few inches from my cowering form. Looking up, I saw his hand tighten on the diamond-etched pattern of the handle. The leather was well worn, marking this as a man who greatly enjoyed opportunities to use this weapon.

However, as he raised the lash he paused, features bunching in disgust. "Martyrs' guts, but you're a stinker!"

"Sorry, sir!" I quailed. "Can't help it. Me foot, see? It's gone all rotten since me master's cart landed on it. I'm on the Trail of Shrines. Going to beseech Martyr Stevanos to put me right. Y'wouldn't hurt a faithful fellow, would you?"

In fact, my foot was a fine and healthy appendage to an equally healthy leg. The stench that so assailed the soldier's nose came from a pungent mix of wild garlic, bird shit and mulched-up leaves. For a guise to be convincing, one must never neglect the power of scent. It was important that these two see no threat in me. A lamed youth happened upon while traversing a notoriously treacherous road could well be faking. But one with a face lacking all wit and a foot exuding an odour carefully crafted to match the festering wounds this pair had surely encountered before was another matter.

Closer scrutiny would surely have undone me. Had this pair been more scrupulous in their appraisal they would have seen the mostly unmarked skin beneath the grime and the rangy but sturdy frame of a well-fed lad beneath the rags. Keener eyes and a fraction more time would also have discerned the small bulge of the knife beneath my threadbare jerkin. But these unfortunates lacked the required keenness of vision, and they were out of time. It had only been moments since I had stumbled into their path, but the distraction had been enough to bring their entire party to a halt. Over the course of an eventful and perilous life, I have found that it is in these small, confused interludes that death is most likely to arrive.

For the soldier on the right it arrived in the form of a crow-fletched arrow with a barbed steel head. The shaft came streaking from the trees to enter his neck just behind the ear before erupting from his mouth in a cloud of blood and shredded tongue. As he toppled from the saddle, his whip-bearing comrade proved his veteran status by immediately dropping the whip and reaching for his longsword. He was quick, but so was I. Snatching my knife from its sheath I put my bandaged foot beneath me and launched myself up, latching my free hand to his horse's bridle. The animal reared in instinctive alarm, raising me the additional foot I required to sink my knife into the soldier's throat before he could fully draw his sword. I was proud of the thrust, it being something I'd practised as much as my witless expression, the blade opening the required veins at the first slice.

I kept hold of the horse's reins as my feet met the ground, the beast threatening to tip me over with all its wheeling about. Watching the soldier tumble to the road and gurgle out his last few breaths, I felt a pang of regret for the briefness of his end. Surely this fellow with his well-worn whip had earned a more prolonged passing in his time. However, my regret was muted as one of many lessons in outlaw craft drummed into me over the years came to mind: *When the task is a killing, be quick and make sure of it. Torment is an indulgence. Save it for only the most deserving.*

It was mostly over by the time I calmed the horse. The first volley of arrows had felled all but two of the guards. Both crossbowmen lay dead on the cart, as did its drover. One man-at-arms had the good sense to turn his horse about and gallop off, not that it saved him from the thrown axe that came spinning out of the trees to take him in the back. The last was made of more admirable, if foolhardy stuff. The brief arrow storm had impaled his thigh and skewered his mount, but still he contrived to roll clear of the thrashing beast and rise, drawing his sword to face the two dozen outlaws running from the treeline.

I have heard versions of this tale that would have you believe that, when confronted by this brave and resolute soul, Deckin Scarl himself forbade his band from cutting him down. Instead he and the stalwart engaged in solitary combat. Having mortally wounded the soldier, the famed outlaw sat with him until nightfall as they shared tales of battles fought and ruminated on the capricious mysteries that determine the fates of all.

These days, similarly nonsensical songs and stories abound regarding Deckin Scarl, renowned Outlaw King of the Shavine Marches and, as some would have it, protector of churl and beggar alike. *With one hand he stole and the other he gave,* as one particularly execrable ballad would have it. *Brave Deckin of the woods, strong and kind he stood.*

If, dear reader, you find yourself minded to believe a word of this I have a six-legged donkey to sell you. The Deckin Scarl I knew was certainly strong, standing two inches above six feet with plenty of muscle to match his height, although his belly had begun to swell in recent years. And kind he could be, but it was a rare thing for a man does not rise to the summit of outlawry in the Shavine Forest by dint of kindness.

In fact, the only words I heard Deckin say in regard to that stout soldier was a grunted order to, "Kill that silly fucker and let's get on." Neither did Deckin bother to spare a glance for the fellow's end, sent off to the Martyrs' embrace by a dozen arrows. I watched the outlaw king come stomping from the shadowed woods with his axe in hand, an ugly weapon with a blackened and misshapen double blade that was rarely far from his reach. He paused to regard my handiwork, shrewd eyes bright beneath his heavy brows as they tracked from the soldier's corpse to the horse I had managed to capture. Horses were a prize worth claiming for they fetched a good price, especially in times of war. Even if they couldn't be sold, meat was always welcome in camp.

Grunting in apparent satisfaction, Deckin swiftly turned his attention to the sole survivor of the ambush, an outcome that had not been accidental. "One arrow comes within a yard of the messenger," he had growled at us all that morning, "and I'll have the skin off the hand that loosed it, fingers to wrist." It wasn't an idle threat, for we had all seen him make good on the promise before.

The royal messenger was a thin-faced man clad in finely tailored jerkin and trews with a long cloak dyed to mirror the royal livery. Seated upon a grey stallion, he maintained an expression of disdainful affront even as Deckin moved to grasp the bridle of his horse. For all his rigid dignity and evident outrage, he was wise enough not to lower the lance he held, the royal pennant continuing to stand tall and flutter above this scene of recent slaughter.

"Any violence or obstruction caused to a messenger in Crown service is considered treason," the thin-faced fellow stated, his voice betraying a creditably small quaver. He blinked and finally consented to afford Deckin the full force of his imperious gaze. "You should know that, whoever you are."

"Indeed I do, good sir," Deckin replied, inclining his head. "And I believe you know full well who I am, do you not?"

The messenger blinked again and shifted his eyes away once more, not deigning to answer. I had seen Deckin kill for less blatant insults, but now he just laughed. Raising his free hand, he gave a hard, expectant snap of his fingers.

The messenger's face grew yet more rigid, rage and humiliation flushing his skin red. I saw his nostrils flare and lips twitch, no doubt the result of biting down unwise words. The fact that he didn't need to be asked twice before reaching for the leather scroll tube on his belt made it plain that he certainly knew the name of the man before him.

"Lorine!" Deckin barked, taking the scroll from the messenger's reluctant hand and holding it out to the slim, copper-haired woman who strode forwards to take it.

The balladeers would have it that Lorine D'Ambrille was the famously fair daughter of a distant lordling who fled her father's castle rather than suffer an arranged marriage to a noble of ill repute and vile habits. Via many roads and adventures, she made her way to the dark woods of the Shavine Marches where she had the good fortune to be rescued from a pack of ravening wolves by none other than the kindly rogue Deckin Scarl himself. Love soon blossomed betwixt them, a love that, much to my annoyance, has echoed through the years acquiring ever more ridiculous legend in the process.

As far as I have been able to ascertain there was no more noble blood in Lorine's veins than mine, although the origin of her comparatively well-spoken tones and evident education are still something of a mystery. She remained a cypher despite the excessive time I would devote to thinking of her. As with all legends, however, a kernel of truth lingers: she was fair. Her features held a smooth handsomeness that had survived years of forest living and she somehow contrived to keep her lustrous copper hair free of grease and burrs. For one suffering the boundless lust of youth, I couldn't help but stare at her whenever the chance arose.

After removing the cap from the tube to extract the scroll within, Lorine's smooth, lightly freckled brow creased a little as she read its contents. Captured as always by her face, my fascination was dimmed somewhat by the short but obvious spasm of shock that flickered over her features. She hid it well, of course, for she was my tutor in the arts of disguise and even more practised than I in concealing potentially dangerous emotions.

"You have it all?" Deckin asked her.

"Word for word, my love," Lorine assured him, white teeth

revealed in a smile as she returned the scroll to the tube and replaced the cap. Although her origins would always remain in shadow, I had gleaned occasional mentions of treading stages and girlhood travels with troupes of players, leading me to conclude that Lorine had once been an actress. Perhaps as a consequence, she possessed the uncanny ability to memorise a large amount of text after only a few moments of reading.

"If I might impose upon your good nature, sir," Deckin told the messenger, taking the tube from Lorine. "I would consider it the greatest favour if you could carry an additional message to King Tomas. As one king to another, please inform him of my deepest and most sincere regrets regarding this unfortunate and unforeseen delay to the journey of his trusted agent, albeit brief."

The messenger stared at the proffered tube as one might a gifted turd, but took it nonetheless. "Such artifice will not save you," he said, the words clipped by his clenched teeth. "And you are not a king, Deckin Scarl."

"Really?" Deckin pursed his lips and raised an eyebrow in apparent surprise. "I am a man who commands armies, guards his borders, punishes transgressions and collects the taxes that are his due. If such a man is not a king, what is he?"

It was clear to me that the messenger had answers aplenty for this question but, being a fellow of wisdom as well as duty, opted to offer no reply.

"And so, I'll bid you good day and safe travels," Deckin said, stepping back to slap a brisk hand to the rump of the messenger's horse. "Keep to the road and don't stop until nightfall. I can't guarantee your safety after sunset."

The messenger's horse spurred into a trot at the slap, one its rider was quick to transform into a gallop. Soon he was a blur of churned mud, his trailing cloak a red and gold flicker among the trees until he rounded a bend and disappeared from view.

"Don't stand gawping!" Deckin barked, casting his glare around the band. "We've got loot to claim and miles to cover before dusk."

They all fell to the task with customary enthusiasm, the archers claiming the soldiers they had felled while the others swarmed the cart. Keen to join them, I looked around for a sapling where I could tether my stolen horse but drew up short as Deckin raised a hand to keep me in place.

"Just one cut," he said, coming closer and nodding his shaggy head at the slain soldier with the whip. "Not bad."

"Like you taught me, Deckin," I said, offering a smile. I felt it falter on my lips as he cast an appraising eye over the horse and gestured for me to pass him the reins.

"Think I'll spare him the stewpot," he said, smoothing a large hand over the animal's grey coat. "Still just a youngster. Plenty of use left in him. Like you, eh, Alwyn?"

He laughed one of his short, grating laughs, a sound I was quick to mimic. I noticed Lorine still stood a short way off, eschewing the frenzied looting to observe our conversation with arms crossed and head cocked. I found her expression strange; the slightly pinched mouth bespoke muted amusement while her narrowed gaze and drawn brows told of restrained concern. Deckin tended to speak to me more than the other youngsters in the band, something that aroused a good deal of envy, but not usually on Lorine's part. Today, however, she apparently saw some additional significance in his favour, making me wonder if it had something to do with the contents of the messenger's scroll.

"Let's play our game, eh?" Deckin said, instantly recapturing my attention. I turned back to see him jerk his chin at the bodies of the two soldiers. "What do you see?"

Stepping closer to the corpses, I spent a short interval surveying them before providing an answer. I tried not to speak too quickly, having learned to my cost how much he disliked it when I gabbled.

"Dried blood on their trews and cuffs," I said. "A day or two old, I'd say. This one—" I pointed at the soldier with the arrowhead jutting from his mouth "—has a fresh-stitched cut on his brow and that one." My finger shifted to the half-bared blade still clutched in the gloved fist of the one I had stabbed. "His sword has nicks and scratches that haven't yet been ground out."

"What's that tell you?" Deckin enquired.

"They've been in a fight, and recently."

"A fight?" He raised a bushy eyebrow, tone placid as he asked, "You sure it was just that?"

My mind immediately began to race. It was always a worrisome thing when Deckin's tone grew mild. "A battle more like," I said, knowing I was speaking too fast but not quite able to slow the words. "Something big enough or important enough for the king to be told of the outcome. Since they were still breathing, until this morn, I'd guess they'd won."

"What else?" Deckin's eyes narrowed further in the manner that told of potential disappointment; apparently, I had missed something obvious.

"They're Cordwainers," I said, managing not to blurt it out. "Riding with a royal messenger, so they were called to the Shavine Marches on Crown business."

"Yes," he said, voice coloured by a small sigh that told of restrained exasperation. "And what is the Crown's principal business in these troubled times?"

"The Pretender's War." I swallowed and smiled again in relieved insight. "The king's host has fought and won a battle with the Pretender's horde."

Deckin lowered his eyebrow and regarded me in silence for a second, keeping his unblinking gaze on me just long enough to make me sweat for the second time that morning. Then he blinked and turned to lead the horse away, muttering to Lorine as she moved to his side. The words were softly spoken but I heard them, as I'm sure he intended I would.

"The message?"

Lorine put a neutral tone to her reply, face carefully void of expression. "You were right, as usual, my love. The daft old bastard turned his coat."

if you enjoyed
A TIDE OF BLACK STEEL

look out for

THE SWORD DEFIANT

Lands of the Firstborn:
Book One

by

Gareth Hanrahan

Many years ago, Sir Aelfric and his nine companions saved the world, seizing the Dark Lord's cursed weapons along with his dread city of Necrad. That was the easy part.

Now when Aelfric—keeper of the cursed sword Spellbreaker—learns of a new and terrifying threat, he seeks the nine heroes once again. But they are wandering adventurers no longer. Yesterday's eager heroes are today's weary leaders—and some have turned to the darkness, becoming monsters themselves.

If there's one thing Aelfric knows, it's slaying monsters. Even if they used to be his friends.

Chapter One

His story had not begun in a tavern, but Alf had ended up in one anyway.

"An ogre," proclaimed the old man from the corner by the hearth, "a fearsome ogre! Iron-toothed, yellow-eyed, arms like oak branches!" He wobbled as he crossed the room towards the table of adventurers. "I saw it not three days ago, up on the High Moor. The beast must be slain, lest it find its way down to our fields and flocks!"

One of the young lads was beefy and broad-shouldered, Mulladale stock. He fancied himself a fighter, with that League-forged sword and patchwork armour. "I'll wager it's one of Lord Bone's minions, left over from the war," he declared loudly. "We'll hunt it down!"

"I can track it!" This was a woman in green, her face tattooed. A Wilder-woman of the northern woods – or dressed as one, anyway. "We just need to find its trail."

"There are places of power up on the High Moor," said a third, face shadowed by his hood. He spoke with the refined tones of a Crownland scholar. An apprentice mage, cloak marked with the sign of the Lord who'd sponsored him. He probably had a star-trap strung outside in the bushes. "Ancient temples, shrines to forgotten spirits. Such an eldritch beast might . . ."

He paused, portentously. Alf bloody hated it when wizards did that, leaving pauses like pit traps in the conversation. Just get on with it, for pity's sake.

Life was too short.

" . . . be drawn to such places. As might other . . . legacies of Lord Bone."

"We'll slay it," roared the Mulladale lad, "and deliver this village from peril!"

That won a round of applause from the locals, more for the boy's enthusiasm than any prospect of success. The adventurers huddled over the table, talking ogre-lore, talking about the dangers of the High Moor and the virtues of leaving at first light.

Alf scowled, irritated but unable to say why. He'd finish his drink, he decided, and then turn in. Maybe he'd be drunk enough to fall straight asleep. The loon had disturbed a rare evening of forgetfulness. He'd enjoyed sitting there, listening to village gossip and tall tales and the crackling of the fire. Now, the spell was broken and he had to think about monsters again.

He'd been thinking about monsters for a long time.

The old man sat down next to Alf. Apparently, he wasn't done. He wasn't that old, either – Alf realised he was about the same age. They'd both seen the wrong side of forty-five winters. "Ten feet tall it was," he exclaimed, sending spittle flying into Alf's tankard, "and big tusks, like a bull's horns, at the side of its mouth." He stuck his fingers out to illustrate. "It had the stink of Necrad about it. They have the right of it – it's one of Bone's creatures that escaped! The Nine should have put them all to the sword!"

"Bone's ogres," said Alf, "didn't have tusks." His voice was croaky from disuse. "They cut 'em off. Your ogre didn't come out of Necrad."

"You didn't see the beast! I did! Only the Pits of Necrad could spawn such—"

"You haven't seen the sodding Pits, either," said Alf. He felt the cold rush of anger, and stood up. He needed to be away from people. He stumbled across the room towards the stairs.

Another of the locals caught his arm. "Bit of luck for you, eh?" The fool was grinning and red-cheeked. *Twist, break the wrist. Grab his neck, slam his face into the table. Kick him into the two behind him. Then grab a weapon.* Alf fought against his honed instincts. The evening's drinking had not dulled his edge enough.

He dug up words. "What do you mean?"

"You said you were going off up the High Moor tomorrow. You'd run straight into that ogre's mouth. Best you stay here another few days, 'til it's safe."

"Safe," echoed Alf. He pulled his arm free. "I can't stay. I have to go and see an old friend."

The inn's only private room was upstairs. Sleeping in the common room was a copper a night, the private room an exorbitant six for a poky attic room and the pleasure of hearing the innkeeper snore next door.

Alf locked the door and took Spellbreaker from its hiding place under the bed. The sword slithered in his grasp, metal twisting beneath the dragonhide.

"I could hear them singing about you." Its voice was a leaden whisper. "About the siege of Necrad."

"Just a drinking song," said Alf, "nothing more. They didn't know it was me."

"They spoke the name of my true wielder, and woke me from dreams of slaughter."

"It rhymes with rat-arsed, that's all."

"No, it doesn't."

"It does the way they say it. *Acra-sed.*"

"It's pronounced with a hard 't'," said the sword. "Acrai-*st* the Wraith-Captain, Hand of Bone."

"Well," said Alf, "I killed him, so I get to say how it's said. And it's rat-arsed. And so am I."

He shoved the sword back under the bed, then threw himself down, hoping to fall into oblivion. But the same dream caught him again, as it had for a month, and it called him up onto the High Moor to see his friend.

The adventurers left at first light.

Alf left an hour later, after a leisurely breakfast. *Getting soft,* he muttered to himself, but he still caught up with them at the foot of a steep cliff, arguing over which of the goat paths would bring them up onto the windy plateau of the High Moor. Alf marched past them, shoulders hunched against the cold of autumn.

extras

"Hey! Old man!" called one of them. "There's a troll out there!"

Alf grunted as he studied the cliff ahead. It was steep, but not insurmountable. Berys and he had scaled the Wailing Tower in the middle of a howling necrostorm. This was nothing. He found a handhold and hauled himself up the rock face, ignoring the cries of the adventurers below. The Wilder girl followed him a little way, but gave up as Alf rapidly outdistanced her.

His shoulders, his knees ached as he climbed. *Old fool.* Showing off for what? To impress some village children? Why not wave Spellbreaker around? Or carry Lord Bone's skull around on a pole? *If you want glory, you're twenty years too late*, he thought to himself. He climbed on, stretching muscles grown stiff from disuse.

At the top, he sat down on a rock to catch his breath. He'd winded himself. The Wailing Tower, too, was nearly twenty years ago.

He pulled his cloak around himself to ward off the breeze, and lingered there for a few minutes. He watched the adventurers as they debated which path to take, and eventually decided on the wrong one, circling south-east along the cliffs until they vanished into the broken landscape below the moor. He looked out west, across the Mulladales, a patchwork of low hills and farmlands and wooded coppices. Little villages, little lives. All safe.

Twenty years ago? Twenty-one? Whenever it was, Lord Bone's armies came down those goat paths. Undead warriors scuttling down the cliffs head first like bony lizards. Wilder scouts with faces painted pale as death. Witch Elf knights mounted on winged dreadworms. Golems, furnaces blazing with balefire. Between all those horrors and the Mulladales stood just nine heroes.

"It was twenty-two years ago," said Spellbreaker. The damn sword was listening to his thoughts again – or had he spoken out loud? "Twenty-two years since I ate the soul of the Illuminated."

"We beat you bastards good," said Alf. "And chased you out of the temple. Peir nearly slew Acraist then, do you remember?"

"Vividly," replied the sword.

Peir, his hammer blazing with the fire of the Intercessors. Berys,

541

flinging vials of holy water she'd filched from the temple. Gundan, bellowing a war cry as he swung Chopper. Gods, they were so young then. Children, really, only a few years older than the idiot ogre-hunters. The battle of the temple was where they'd first proved themselves heroes. The start of a long, bitter war against Lord Bone. Oh, they'd got side-tracked – there'd been prophecies and quests and strife aplenty to lead them astray – but the path to Necrad began right here, on the edge of the High Moor.

He imagined his younger self struggling up those cliffs, that cheap pig-sticker of a sword clenched in his teeth. What would he have done, if that young warrior reached to the top and saw his future sitting there? Old, tired, tough as old boots. Still had all his limbs, but plenty of scars.

"We won," he whispered to the shade of the past, "and it's still bloody hard."

"You," said the sword, "are going crazy. You should get back to Necrad, where you belong."

"When I'm ready."

"I can call a dreadworm. Even here."

"No."

"Anything could be happening there. We've been away for more than two years, *moping*." There was an unusual edge to the sword's plea. Alf reached down and pulled Spellbreaker from its scabbard, so he could look the blade in the gemstone eye on its hilt and—

—Reflected in the polished black steel as it crept up behind him. Grey hide, hairy, iron-tusked maw drooling. Ogre.

Alf threw himself forward as the monster lunged at him and rolled to the edge of the cliff. Pebbles and dirt tumbled down the precipice, but he caught himself before he followed them over. He hoisted Spellbreaker, but the sword suddenly became impossibly heavy and threatened to tug him backwards over the cliff.

One of the bastard blade's infrequent bouts of treachery. Fine.

He flung the heavy sword at the onrushing ogre, and the monster stumbled over it. Its ropy arms reached for him, but Alf dodged along the cliff edge, seized the monster's wrist and pulled with all his might. The ogre, abruptly aware of the danger that they'd both fall to their deaths, scrambled away from the edge. It was off balance, and vulnerable. Alf leapt on the monster's back and drove one elbow into its ear. The ogre bellowed in pain and fell forward onto the rock he'd been sitting on. Blood gushed from its nose, and the sight sparked unexpected joy in Alf. For a moment, he felt young again, and full of purpose. This, this was what he was meant for!

The ogre tried to dislodge him, but Alf wrapped his legs around its chest, digging his knees into its armpits, his hands clutching shanks of the monster's hair. He bellowed into the ogre's ear in the creature's own language.

"Do you know who I am? I'm the man who killed the Chieftain of the Marrow-Eaters!"

The ogre clawed at him, ripping at his cloak. Its claws scrabbled against the dwarven mail Alf wore beneath his shirt. Alf got his arm locked across the ogre's throat and squeezed.

"I killed Acraist the Wraith-Captain!"

The ogre reared up and threw itself back, crushing Alf against the rock. The impact knocked the air from his lungs, and he felt one of his ribs crack, but he held firm – and sank his teeth into his foe's ear. He bit off a healthy chunk, spat it out and hissed:

"I killed Lord Bone."

It was probably the pain of losing an earlobe, and not his threat, that made the ogre yield, but yield it did. The monster fell to the ground, whimpering.

Alf released his grip on the ogre's neck and picked up Spellbreaker. Oh, *now* the magic sword was perfectly light and balanced in his hand. One swing, and the ogre's head would go rolling across the ground. One cut, and the monster would be slain.

He slapped the ogre with the flat of the blade.

"Look at me."

Yellow terror-filled eyes stared at him.

"There are adventurers hunting for you. They went south-east. You, run north. That way." He pointed with the blade, unsure if the ogre even spoke this dialect. It was the tongue he'd learned in Necrad, the language the Witch Elves used to order their war-beasts around. "Run north!" he added in common, and he shoved the ogre again. The brute got the message and ran, loping on all fours away from Alf. It glanced back in confusion, unsure of what had just happened.

Alf lifted Spellbreaker, glared into the sword's eye.

"I was testing you," said the sword. "You haven't had a proper fight in months. Tournies don't count – no opponent has the courage to truly test you, and it's all for show anyway. Your strength dwindles. My wielder must—"

"I'm not your bloody wielder. I'm your gaoler."

"I am *bored*, wielder. Two years of wandering the forests and backroads. Two years of hiding and lurking. And when you finally pluck up the courage to go anywhere, it's to an even duller village. I tell you, those people should have welcomed the slaughter my master brought, to relieve them of the tedium of their pathetic—"

"Try that again, and I'll throw you off a cliff."

"Do it. Someone will find me. Some*thing*. I'm a weapon of darkness, and I call to—"

"I'll drop you," said Alf wearily, "into a volcano."

orbit

Follow us:

f /orbitbooksUS

X /orbitbooks

▶ /orbitbooks

Join our mailing list
to receive alerts on our
latest releases and deals.

orbitbooks.net

Enter our monthly
giveaway for the chance
to win some epic prizes.

orbitloot.com

"Irhkyn?" Ruhlin stumbled to a halt, a wholly unfamiliar and uncomfortable chill coursing through him from head to toe as he watched Irhkyn convulse, then cough a red spatter onto the sand.

Ruhlin dithered for another few beats of his labouring heart, fascinated by the deep hue of Irhkyn's blood, then by the long, gull-fletched arrow that jutted from his back. He might have dithered longer if the *mahkla* hadn't reached out to snare his ankle in a large hand and drag him down. A rush of displaced air and a flicker of movement, then Ruhlin found himself staring at a second arrow embedded in the beach less than a yard away, shaft still shuddering.

"Go!" Fresh blood erupted from Irhkyn's mouth as he gasped out the command, Ruhlin looking into fierce, implacable blue-grey eyes. "Warn them…" The dying *mahkla* jerked, his grip loosening on Ruhlin's ankle and his head slowly subsiding into the damp grains. "Go…"

As Anthony Ryan

THE RAVEN'S SHADOW
Blood Song
Tower Lord
Queen of Fire

THE DRACONIS MEMORIA
The Waking Fire
The Legion of Flame
The Empire of Ashes

THE RAVEN'S BLADE
The Wolf's Call
The Black Song

THE COVENANT OF STEEL
The Pariah
The Martyr
The Traitor

AGE OF WRATH
A Tide of Black Steel

As A. J. Ryan

Red River Seven